LUKE SOMERTON;

OR,

THE ENGLISH RENEGADE.

A ROMANCE.

BY THE AUTHOR OF "TREACHERY," "TEMPTATION," "POVERTY," Etc.

There's a divinity which shapes our ends,
Rough hew them how we will.
SHAKSPERE.

Embellished with Superior Engravings.

LONDON:

PRINTED AND PUBLISHED BY EDWARD LLOYD,

AT THE OFFICE OF "LLOYD'S WEEKLY LONDON NEWSPAPER," 12, SALISBURY-SQUARE.

1845.

PREFACE.

ALTHOUGH it has been the pleasure of certain critics to declaim against cheap literature, the number of readers increases every day. This fact, of course, spurs on the writers of such compositions to greater vigour and animation in a cause that, to say the least of it, has popularity on its side. It would be as unnatural for an author to lay down his pen under flattering circumstances, as for a candidate to decline going to the poll when the majority of suffrages have been declared in his favour.

The advantages to be derived from works of fiction are manifold; for it is an acknowledged fact, that many will dwell with pleasure on grave reflections and moral admonitions in a novel, who would not peruse an essay full of dry arguments, containing the very same sentences. The writer of fiction, therefore, cannot be altogether an useless member of society; for, as such is the diversity of public opinion, it must undoubtedly be more beneficial to society that there should be writers who can induce their fellow-creatures to reading not wholly useless to their morals, than that there should be no writers who can tempt them to read at all.

The class of fictions which are at the present day most popular, are undoubtedly those which unite, with a considerable degree of the marvellous, some portion of history, and it is not the business of an author to inquire why such is the public taste, but to comply with it. In the opinion of some persons, he is, perhaps, so far accountable for such deviations as he makes from historical facts, as to be called upon to acknowledge them, for the benefit of his readers at large, that he may at least save them from gathering errors, if they cannot derive improvement from a perusal of his pages. In the present instance, however, the historical portion is rendered subservient to the rest of the narrative, so that little or no explanation is requisite in this place. Most of our readers are doubtless aware that the principal incidents of LUKE SOMERTON have been drawn from the very popular drama of the same name, written by GEORGE SOANE, ESQ., and produced a few years since at the Adelphi Theatre. To that gentleman, therefore, we cheerfully accord whatever merit the reader may discover in the work offered for his perusal.

LONDON, AUGUST, 1845.

LUKE SOMERTON;

OR,

THE ENGLISH RENEGADE.

BY THE AUTHOR OF "TREACHERY; OR, THE MODERN IAGO;" "TEMPTATION," &c. &c.

CHAPTER I.

Ships are but board, sailors but men ;
There be land rats, and water rats ; water thieves,
And land thieves—I mean pirates.

SHAKSPERE.

IT was towards the close of an autumn day, in he year 1706, that Sir Charles Radcliffe, the overnor of the Isle of Man, was enjoying himself n the society of a few friends, when the mirth was uddenly interrupted by the loud discharge of can- on ; and the quickness with which each shot suc- eeded the other left but little doubt, in the mind f any of the company, that an engagement had aken place at sea between the British and some of heir enemies. This incident was sufficient to raise he enthusiasm of every one present to the highest itch, and, rising from the table, they hastened to

the window from whence it was expected a view of the engagement might be obtained. In this, how- ever, they were disappointed, for a heavy fog over- hung the sea, and all that could be discerned was the awful flashing of fire as it belched forth from the cannons, carrying death and destruction amongst those who were engaged in the terrible scene of bloodshed.

"How provoking in this fog, that veils the battle from our sight," exclaimed Sir Charles Radcliffe, as he left the window, from which he had been vainly endeavouring to penetrate the gloom. "This is no child's play that is going on yonder, and yet, though the action is going on within reach of our battery, we cannot fire a gun, lest the shot should happen to injure our own ship more than the enemy's."

"The best way is to let them fight it out like brave fellows, as they are," returned Mr. Mayhew, who was one of the guests on the present occasion. "They seem to contest the affair gallantly enough ; and, for my own part, I have sufficient confidence in the spirit of our British sailors to feel assured that victory will be declared on our side."

"Under more favourable circumstances I should have little fear as to the result," observed another of the guests ; "but, in a fog like this, a brave man can do little more than sacrifice his life recklessly."

"True," exclaimed Sir Charles Radcliffe ; "and the very circumstance of the enemy venturing to fight so near our shores proves that they have bravery and spirit at least equal to our own tars. Queen Anne has noble fellows ready to sacrifice their lives in the defence of her throne and person ;

but, in a fog like this, no man can say whether a chance shot from the enemy may not prove more than a match for the well-known courage of our sailors."

"Then all we can do is to await the result with patience," interposed Mr. Mayhew. "Already the firing is less rapid than it was, and my life for it this engagement will end, as most others have lately done, in the honour of Old England. But how now, Sir Charles!—whither are you going in such a hurry?"

"To the sea shore," replied the governor; "my presence may be required there, and this is no time to be wasted in idle parley, when the lives of many of our countrymen may depend upon the promptitude with which we tender them our assistance."

He was leaving the room as these words were uttered, but ere he could do so, Catherine Radcliffe, pale and trembling with emotion, hurriedly presented herself before him.

"In the name of mercy, dearest father, do not leave me!" she frantically cried. "Your life will be in peril should you venture to the sea shore; and if aught happens to you, who will then be left to protect your orphan daughter from the danger with which she will be surrounded?"

"There are no dangers to apprehend, my child," he replied; "and even if there were, it is my duty to run all personal risks when the lives of our fellow-creatures are in peril."

"But you can give no aid," answered Catherine, "for the faithful Caleb has just returned from the beach, and he has assured me that the fog is so thick as to prevent all hope of ascertaining the condition of the combatants. Some, however, have been wounded while standing on the shore, and it was to prevail on you to remain at home that I came hither, dreading lest my influence should not be sufficient to guard you against the evils I can but too plainly foresee."

"Why, Kate, my girl, would you make a coward of your father?" he exclaimed, good-humouredly. "Have I not been placed here by my sovereign for the performance of certain duties, and shall I neglect them because a foolish wench has taken it into her head that a stray ball might happen to carry me off a little sooner than was expected? No, no; as a younger man I never turned my back upon my enemies, and my old age shall not be disgraced by an act of cowardice."

"Then ask Caleb if I have magnified the dangers to which you will be exposed," cried Catherine. "He has just left the beach, and speaks of the perils to be encountered there, though I have heard you say a braver fellow than he never entered into the service of his country. He is here, sir, and will tell you the madness of risking a life which, if preserved, may yet prove of the highest service to our country."

"Perhaps his honour wouldn't like me to speak my mind?" exclaimed Caleb, a weather-beaten tar, who, having devoted the best part of his days to the service of his country, was now living with the governor, more in the capacity of an esteemed friend than as an humble dependant.

Sir Charles paused a moment, and then, addressing himself to the old man, inquired if he knew the ships that were engaged at a little distance from the coast.

"Why, I can't say I know what they are, sir,"

replied Caleb; "but whatever country the ships may belong to, they seem to have set to work in real earnest, and, by the smart firing that's been going on, I've a notion that one of them must be under the English flag."

"Humph! Does the fog seem likely to clear away before long?"

"I hardly think it will, your honour," answered the old sailor; "but there's no saying what the wind may do presently. I've seen the fog lifted up like a curtain sometimes, and perhaps by and by this one will be kind enough to disperse, that we may look about, and see what's being done out yonder."

"Have none of the fishermen ventured out in their boats to see what ships they are?" asked Mr. Mayhew.

"Lord bless you, no, sir," exclaimed Caleb, in reply. "There's been no saving of cannon balls, as you may have heard with your own ears, and men don't like to risk their lives for mere curiosity, when they may keep out of range by staying at home. Give a man something handsome, in the shape of a reward, and he'll run the chance of a stray shot for the sake of those he may happen to leave behind him."

"And yet," observed Sir Charles Radcliffe, "you have been down to the shore, though, from your own account, there was no little danger in it."

"Ay, ay, sir, that's very true," replied the other; "but then I'm an old man, and this is not the first time I've been in danger, when my arm could be raised to give a drubbing to the enemy. I used to be happiest when in the midst of battle, and we can't forget old times, you know, sir, even though duty don't happen to call upon us to serve our country any longer."

"But duty does call upon me," exclaimed the governor, "and I am, therefore, wasting time that ought to be very differently employed. My friends will, I trust, remain here till my return; and, if I should be the bearer of news that our country has gained another naval battle, we will spend the remainder of the night in drinking the health of her majesty, and success to her arms all over the world."

"Nay, we will go down with you to the sea shore," returned Mr. Mayhew, "for we should be but sorry friends were we to remain behind whilst you run all the danger."

"But my daughter will need company to cheer her spirits during our absence."

"Then let Caleb remain with her," said the other, "for he has already seen enough service, and it is now time that he should be excused from attending at posts of danger."

"But Caleb would rather not be excused from anything of the sort," exclaimed the old sailor warmly. "He has always been happiest when a little bit of a scrimmage was going on, and he'd be a miserable fellow if you left him behind, with no better duty to perform than to look after the petticoats."

"Nay," cried Sir Charles, "it is my most earnest request that you stay here to appease the terrors of Catherine. She is unnecessarily alarmed by the rattling of a few cannon balls, and the company of an old sailor, like yourself, can alone assure her that the chances of peril have been magnified.

So stay where you are, Caleb, and after ascertaining what all this roar of artillery means I will return with my friends, and you will then be discharged from a duty that I dare say you will be ungallant enough to believe anything but a pleasant one."

Sir Charles Radcliffe and his friends took their departure directly afterwards, and Catherine, dreading lest any accident should befal her father, seated herself near the window, to watch him in his progress towards the beach. The thick haze, however, soon obscured the party from her view, and she was about to retire to her own chamber, in order to indulge her grief in loneliness, when Caleb, plucking her by the sleeve, said,—

"I hope you won't be offended with me, miss, but it's foolish to give way to fears, when there mayn't be any occasion for 'em. The firing out yonder ain't quite so sharp as it was, and I dare say in a short time it will be all over."

"Still," she cried, "I cannot overcome the terror inspired by his danger."

"Psha! there ain't half so much danger as you may think, miss," retorted the old man. "I was a foolish fellow to say anything about it to the governor, when you were by; but it slipped out unawares, and now I'd be glad if you'd only take my word for it that there's nothing to be afraid of on your father's account."

"Of that neither you nor I can be assured at present," sighed Catherine. "The ships I know are engaged at a very short distance from the shore, and there must consequently be danger to those who trust themselves too near the spot."

"Well, there's no denying that, to be sure," replied Caleb; "but then your father's governor of the Isle of Man, and if he didn't do his duty, her majesty—God bless her!—would send somebody here in his place, and he and you might all of a sudden find yourselves sent to the right about with a flea in your ear. Besides, he knows the duty of a brave man, and would rather die at his post than have a word whispered against his honour."

"He would indeed," cried Catherine, "and I was perhaps to blame for showing my womanly fears when duty called him from his home. I will, however, be firm, and convince him on his return that I am not unworthy to be the daughter of a soldier. And now, Caleb, tell me what they say about the enemy;—to what country is the ship supposed to belong?"

"That's more than anybody can tell at present," replied the old sailor; "but folks do say she's a French privateer, and if that's the case our English bull dogs will not let her sheer off without writing their names at full length on her hull."

"Is it known why she was hovering so near upon our coast?"

"People can only guess that, miss," answered Caleb. "I dare say it was thought our little island was not over well guarded, and the mounseers fancied they were going to do great things with very little trouble to themselves. But I'm thinking they will find out their mistake before long; and all I wish is that I had been on board our own little ship, that I might have had one more turn with the frog-catching varmint before my turn comes to go to Davy Jones's locker."

"You are better where you are, Caleb."

"And why so, ma'am?"

"Because you have already served your country long and faithfully," she replied, "and it is now time you should enjoy the reward that has been so fairly earned. My father has often spoken to me of your gallantry, and it is but fair that a brave man who escapes the perils he risks, should pass the last few years of his life in ease and comfort."

"Very true, young lady," exclaimed Caleb; "that's all quite right enough; but you know how the sound of a battle sets an old soldier or sailor longing to be in the thick of it. I didn't half like coming away from the beach just now, only I thought Sir Charles ought to know how matters were going on, and so I hastened my way here just to give him the signal for sailing. But hark, miss! the guns are beginning to talk louder than ever, so, with your leave, I'll just run down to the rocks, lest our folks should happen to want a hand by-and-bye."

Without further ceremony the old sailor ran off, and Catherine was left to all the agonies of doubt and dread that were conjured up by the thunder of artillery that rang upon her ears. It was in vain that she endeavoured to calm the agitation of her spirits, and at length tottering from the room, she sought her own chamber, where the bellowing cannon were less distinctly heard.

CHAPTER II.

'Twas his the vast and trackless deep to rove.
Alternate change of climates has he known,
And felt the fierce extremes of either zone
Where polar skies congeal th' eternal snow,
Or equinoctial sun's for ever glow. FALCONER.

UPON approaching the beach Caleb found the governor and a large assemblage of the inhabitants intently occupied in endeavouring to obtain information by which they might be enabled to shape their course. The fog still hung over the sea like a thick mantle, but a light breeze had just sprung up, and all eyes were now eagerly turned towards the scene of action, in anxious expectation that the haze would be so far dispersed as to allow the two ships to be seen. Sir Charles Radcliffe seemed to be more deeply interested than any one, and after maintaining a profound silence for some time, he turned towards Caleb, who stood near him, and said,—

"The firing begins to slacken, and I think one of them has by this time got nearly enough."

"So I think, your honour," was the old man's reply.

"Can you make them out yet?"

"No, Sir Charles," answered the other; "but I'm pretty certain they're close in with the shore. A fog like this deadens the sound of their great guns; but when it lifts—and I'm sure it won't be long first—we shall know something more about 'em."

"Have you heard who is supposed to be in command of the enemy's ship?"

"No," replied Caleb; "but by the question I suppose your honour has?"

"There is a rumour," answered Sir Charles, "that it's the French privateer we've seen so long about the coast. I hope the report is correct, and that our own ship will either send her to the bottom, or drive her far away from our seas."

"If it's the privateer you speak of," returned Caleb, "it easily accounts for the hard battle that's been fought."

"And why so?"

"Because it's commanded by old Somerton, who has so long been the terror of this island," replied the other.

"Hah!" exclaimed the governor; "then if fortune is propitious, we shall at length rid the seas of an enemy more deadly even than a foreigner."

"Somerton!" interposed Mr. Mayhew, who had hitherto been a silent listener to the conversation; "why the name is that of an Englishman."

"He is an Englishman," replied Caleb, "and in spite of his turning against his own country, I'll uphold him for as stout a one as ever stepped between stem and stern."

"And yet he fights against his own countrymen," exclaimed Mr. Mayhew.

"Lord love your honour," exclaimed the sailor, "you don't understand the geography of the thing nohow whatsumdever; but I'll make it all plain to you in the turning of a capstan, for it so happened that I sarved on board the Billy Ruffin at the very time when old Luke Somerton was first luff."

"First luff!" reiterated Mr. Mayhew; "and pray what may be the meaning of first luff?"

"Why, as your honour's a landsman, and can't be expected to know nothing," replied Caleb, "I'll try and make it all appear ship-shape. When I say Luke Somerton was first luff, I mean to tell you that he was what the land lubbers call a first lieutenant."

"I understand you, Caleb, so now proceed with what you were going to tell me."

"Well, you see, your honour, he and the skipper——"

"Hold," interrupted Mr. Mayhew, "for again I must confess my ignorance of your nautical terms. Pray what do you mean by a skipper?"

"Why a captain, to be sure," answered Caleb; "and so, sir, as I was going to tell you, Luke Somerton and the skipper were hand and glove together—who but they!—till one day, we were cruizing off Ushant at the time, the skipper invites the luff to dine with him in his own cabin; they got rather merry over their grog, I reckon, for the skipper said some ugly things of the luff's sister, whereby the luff told him he was a d—d liar, and a scoundrel too for his pains! These was sharp words, you know, and the upshot was the luff called him out, but the skipper, who had no mind for fighting, had him arrested for insulting a superior officer, and after a court martial had been held, Luke Somerton was dismissed from the service in disgrace."

"And upon that provocation, I suppose," observed Mr. Mayhew, "the lieutenant accepted naval promotion from the enemies of his country?"

"Yes, sir," replied the old sailor, "and more's the pity, for England lost by it a warm friend, and has gained a bitter enemy. He's a brave fellow, is this Luke Somerton, and the mounseers fight under his command like so many born devils."

"And how many years is it since this happened?"

"Oh, a great many," replied Caleb; "but I can't exactly tell you how long, though I know his daughter, Louisa Somerton, was a very little creature, when first he went away from us."

"Is she still in the island?"

"Yes, sir," answered Caleb; "but, of course, nobody is cruel enough to tell her about the disgrace that fell upon her father. She lives with a Mr. Walford, who has always been as a father to her, and neither she nor any one in the place would know Luke Somerton, if ever he should happen to return among them."

At this period Sir Charles Radcliffe, who had quitted the spot some little time before, approached them, and intimated that the fog was clearing off, and a boat was making its way towards the shore, that seemed to be filled with sailors. All eyes were instantly directed towards the spot that had been indicated, and presently afterwards, Luke Somerton, disguised in the habit of a Dutchman, with three or four sailors, leaped ashore. The governor, upon seeing them land, naturally believed them to be in the service of England, and advancing towards them with an air of cordial greeting, he exclaimed:—

"You are most welcome, gentlemen, for, by the heavy firing we just now heard, you must have had smart work with the enemy."

"Yaw!" replied Luke Somerton, in broken English; "you may say dat, sare, but den we have beaten our foes all into noting."

"And pray, sir," asked Sir Charles, "what may be the name of your vessel? You don't carry her majesty's colours, I perceive."

"We do not," replied Christopher Dalton, who acted as Somerton's mate. "We have no commission from your government, but fight like Harry Wynde, on our own account."

"Oh," exclaimed Sir Charles; "then I presume yonder vessel is a privateer?"

"Exactly so," answered the mate; "our vessel is the good ship Dragonfly, of Bristol, and if you happen to hold any power in this island, here are our letters of marque."

"They are quite right, sir," said Sir Charles, as he returned the papers, after having glanced over them; "and now, may I ask who was the enemy you were just now engaged with?"

"Certainly, sir," replied Dalton, somewhat confused at this unexpected question. "The truth is, we have been fighting with that devil's brother, Luke Somerton; and, thanks to the gallant fellows that man our ship, we have given him a drubbing that he'll not forget in a hurry, I'll warrant him."

"Have you destroyed his vessel?"

"Yaw," replied Somerton; "we hab sink him to de bottom of de sea."

"Poor fellows," exclaimed Caleb, feelingly.

"Himmel and Erde!" vociferated Somerton, with feigned anger; "was for you make de hone and de groan for de hundsfott? He was von big scoundrel."

"And who told you he was a scoundrel, Meinheer Sourkrout?" exclaimed Caleb. "I knew him well enough at one time, and can answer for it he was a better seaman than ever stepped in your shoes."

"Donner and Blitzen!" roared the supposed Dutchman; "was you know about him? He vos a rogue—ein big landlaufer."

"Say that again, meinheer," cried honest Caleb,

"and I'll split your sconce with this oar as if it was an old calabash."

"Come, come," interrupted Sir Charles Radcliffe, as he perceived that the seaman was preparing to carry his threat into execution; "I'll allow of no fighting; and you, captain—for I take it you are the captain—will do well to keep your men under better discipline."

"Very good advice," said Christopher Dalton, to whom these latter words had been addressed; "very good advice, indeed; but you must know my men are such devils that they will not submit to be commanded by any one except when they are in the vessel."

"Then the sooner you ship them on board again the better," returned Sir Charles; "and so good evening to you;" then addressing himself to those who had accompanied him to the beach, he added, —"It's getting late, my friends; and poor Catherine will be kept in a state of torturing suspense till we return home. Besides, by this time I should think my intended son-in-law must have arrived according to his promise, and it would be a cold welcome to give him were he to reach my house when the host is not there to receive him."

Upon this he left the place accompanied by Mr. Mayhew and his other friends, taking the direction which led towards that part of the island in which his house was situated. Caleb, however, remained behind, for his curiosity had been somewhat excited, and being occupied in examining their vessel, which was now plainly visible at no great distance from the shore, his presence was not observed, either by Luke Somerton or his companions, and the conversation that ensued was, therefore, carried on without the least restraint.

"As I live by bread, Captain Somerton, you are too bold in this matter," exclaimed Christopher Dalton, as soon as it was believed they were left quite to themselves.

"And why so?" demanded his superior, throwing aside his foreign accent, and speaking in his own natural tongue.

"Because I see plainly enough that we shall all get into a scrape about this business," replied the other. "What, in the devil's name, man, could tempt you to put in here, where we can gain nothing but a short shrift and a high gallows?"

"Tut, man; what have you to fear?" demanded Somerton. "Has not the English privateer, the Dragonfly, gone to the bottom with all her crew? And have we not her letters of marque to deceive people with in case they should be suspicious?"

"Very true, captain," replied Dalton; "but, for all that, I wish we had stood off on the other tack."

"And why do you wish it, Mr. Dalton?"

"Because you may chance to have the ill luck to meet with some of the people belonging to this place that will remember you in spite of the disguise you have assumed."

"Psha!" returned the other impatiently; "why, you see even honest Caleb, who served with me in the Bellerophon—the Billy Ruffin, as he calls it —can't make out the old ship now she's rigged in this Dutch fashion. Ha! ha! ha! how the old rogue raked me fore and aft when we were upon the point of quarrelling just now."

"Hang me, then, if I'd trust myself to such a chance," exclaimed Dalton, "for I have strange misgivings, Captain Somerton, and you may live to repent your rashness yet, if you scorn to take the advice of a man that is only anxious for your safety."

"Tush, Dalton," returned the other; "I verily believe you are beginning to grow a coward."

"A coward, Captain Somerton," cried Dalton, warmly; "did you call me a coward?"

"I certainly said something very like it," replied Luke, composedly. "However, it must be acknowledged, I was a fool for my pains; so you must look over it this time, for I believe I am as much too hasty as you are too cold and cautious. Nay, man, never look so glum upon me; I'm sorry for what I said, so give me your hand, and let nothing more be thought of a few hasty words."

"Are you really sorry, captain?"

"I have said so, Dalton," replied the other; "and I think I can flatter myself as far as to say that you have never had reason to call me a hypocrite. I spoke in haste just now, but in sober seriousness it must be admitted that I have ever found you true and faithful in your friendship to me."

"You do me no more than justice, Captain Somerton," exclaimed Dalton, "and what has just passed between us shall be forgotten as much as if it had never been uttered. So now tell me in cool blood, what made you land on this coast, where we count no more friends than those we brought with us."

"Why, to tell you the truth, Kit," replied Somerton, "I am little better than a fool for my pains. But thus it is :—when driven by my wrongs to turn my back on home and country, about twelve years since, I left my daughter, a child then six years old, to the care of my brother, who then lived in my native county of Devon."

"Well, captain," retorted the other, "if you left your daughter in Devonshire, why should you come to look for her in the far off Isle of Man?"

"That I have yet got to explain," answered Somerton. "About three months since a letter reached me from my brother. It seems that my name had become such a bugbear to his fellow-townsmen, that he was fain to leave his home and cast anchor here on the Isle of Man, under other colours."

"Ah, that is to say, I suppose, he has changed his name to something else?"

"Exactly so."

"And pray what name does he now pass under?"

"That of James Walford."

"Humph! and I suppose you are anxious to see your child once more?"

"I am indeed."

"Well, that's natural enough," returned Dalton; "and now that I know the motives which brought you here, I can no longer blame you for the risk you have run in landing upon the island."

"You are a kind friend, Kit, and a brave fellow to boot!" exclaimed Luke Somerton, warmly. "I have certainly taken rather a rash step in the business, and, to confess the truth, I know no more than yourself how to find out where my brother is living. But I see Caleb is watching us rather suspiciously yonder, and once more I must assume my Dutch character, lest mischief should chance to befal us." Then assuming his former slouching manner, he advanced towards the old sailor, and exclaimed in guttural accents,—" Ich say, mine freend, kannot you dell us where von Meinheer Walford lives in dis island ?"

" Maybe I can," replied Caleb, sullenly ; " and what if I can do so ?"

" Why, den," replied Somerton, " be kind enough to open dat mouth of yours, and give us our bearing, dat we may be off."

" Follow your cursed ugly Dutch nose," retorted Caleb tartly ; " it's long enough and broad enough to serve for a direction post, and you can't miss the road, if you happen to go right."

" Ha ! ha ! vell, it is no mattere, not in de least," answered Somerton. " I sall not trouble you, mine freend, and sall save de gelt I vos going to giff you for your pains." Then whispering to Dalton, he added, " I shall trust to finding some peasant on the road who will be tempted to guide me to the house of my brother for the sake of a reward. Do you look after the sloop, Kit, and when my errand is accomplished, I will return and sail away from the island with all despatch."

" That's just what I was going to do, captain," answered Christopher Dalton, " for, to tell you the truth, I've no great affection for the land, and the sooner we get to sea again the better I shall like it. Here we are in danger from our enemies, but once upon salt water again, and I don't care if we have to fight our foes every day we live."

" A very few hours will serve to complete all I have to do here," replied Somerton, " and then I shall gladly return to the good old ship that has borne us through so many victories. You can walk with me a little part of the way, Dalton, and I'll tell you further of the project that has tempted me to land where so many dangers beset us."

" I will go with you, captain," returned the other, " because yonder fellow seems to watch our motions with surprise. You can then proceed alone, and I will return here, lest he should try to pump Scipio of any of our secrets."

" Hark ye, Scipio," exclaimed Luke Somerton to the negro, who was standing near the boat ; " you are to keep a bright look out while we are away, and mind, if any questions are asked, you are not to know anything."

" Iss, massa," replied the nigger, distending his mouth from ear to ear as he grinned his assent.

" And if anybody should come from the ship," added the captain, " you may tell them I shall be back before the morning dawns."

He waited for no further reply, but, followed by Christopher Dalton, pursued a road that led from the sea coast towards the interior of the island. The curiosity of Caleb was by this time excited to the highest pitch, and having watched the retiring parties till they were lost in the turning of the road, he approached the nigger, and patting him on the shoulder, said,—

" I say, Mr. Blackee ——"

" Blackee !" retorted the other, shrinking back with offended dignity ; " what you mean by dat, sir ? do you mean 'front me, sir ?"

" Not I, messmate," replied the veteran ; " I never mean to affront any one, but how the devil am I to hail you ?"

" Why," answered the nigger, " when gentlemens accost me, dey call me Massa Scipio."

" Then, Massa Scip, I should be glad ——"

" Scipio, sir," returned the nigger, angrily.

" Curse on the name—what a fuss you make about it !" exclaimed Caleb, impatiently. " I thought fellows of your colour were not particular about names ; but it seems a fellow must break his jaws rather than offend your black highness."

" You 'front me, sir, wid dis talk," exclaimed Scipio. " I'm here to keep de guard, and don't wish to speak to fellows such as you are."

" Come, don't be angry with me, messmate," said Caleb, soothingly. " You and I ought to be the best of friends, you know ; and though I called your name wrong, I only meant to ask if you'd have any objection to take a glass of grog with me."

" Ah, dat am mor ecivil," exclaimed Scipio, softening as this proposition was made. " You are better fellows dan I took you for ; and now I can hear reason, if you hab got any ting to say to your friend Scipio. Did you say I was to hab one glass ob grog ?"

" Aye, a dozen, if you like to drink them, my fine fellow," replied Caleb.

" And where are we to hab 'em, Massa Inglisman ?"

" Oh, at a nice crib a little way from here," replied the other. " We shall meet some rare boys there ; and I'll shew you what it is, my fine fellow, to get into comfortable old English quarters."

" But I'm on de watch," exclaimed Scipio ; " and if dey was to catch me off my post, dere would be de debil to pay, and no pitch hot."

" I'll tell you what it is, old fellow," returned the sailor ; " this is the land of liberty, and every man does as he likes, without asking anybody's leave. We've no slaves here ; and if your captain should ask you why you didn't stay upon your guard, you've only just to tell him that you're your own master here, and don't care for any one."

" And what'll him say to dat ?"

" Why, nothing at all, to be sure."

" But den dere's de d—d cat and nine tail !"

" Oh, you needn't be afraid of that," replied Caleb. " Only let them flog you if they dare—that's all. You can give 'em pepper for it afterwards ; and if you don't happen to know how to go about it, just send word to me, and I'll let 'em see that a nigger ain't to be flogged only because a friend asks him civilly to drink a glass of grog with him."

" Den me go wid you, Massa John Bull, and taste de good stuff you talk of."

" Taste it, man !" exclaimed Caleb. " By Jove, you shall swill a pailful. So, come along, old fellow, and trust to me for getting you well over the business."

But Scipio still had his doubts as to the propriety of quitting his post ; and it was not till Caleb took his arm, and fairly dragged him from the place, that he moved towards the grog shop.

CHAPTER III.

Let us no more contend
Each other, blamed enough elsewhere, but strive,
In offices of love, how we may lighten
Each other's burden in our share of woe.   MILTON.

ON the same evening to which the events of the two last chapters belong, Louisa Somerton was involved in a labyrinth of perplexities as to the course she should pursue between duty and inclination. For some time past her hand had been sought by Lieutenant Granger, a young officer, of good family, and whose honour stood unimpeached. His love was returned with all the ardour of youthful passion, and nothing remained to complete their happiness but the approbation of Mr. Walford, who, we have before observed, was believed by Louisa to be her father, and whose kindness had well supplied the place of her absent parent. Knowing, however, the disgrace that was attached to the name of Somerton, her guardian had peremptorily refused his sanction to her union with Lieutenant Granger, and had even drawn from her a promise to discontinue the stolen meetings that had taken place between them.

Left alone in the house, Louisa gave way to the melancholy thoughts which this apparently harsh decision had given rise to, and, perhaps, the most perplexing part of her reflections was the method she should adopt for acquainting him with the final determination of Mr. Walford. While she was still musing on the painful alternative to which she was reduced, the door opened, and to her unutterable confusion Lieutenant Granger presented himself before her. She rose to greet him as in former times, but, overcome with agitation, she sank again into the chair, and burying her face in her hands, gave way to the tears that she in vain tried to suppress.

"Dearest Louisa," cried her lover, "why do I find you thus absorbed in grief? Am I no longer welcome here, that you chill my heart with a reception such as I never before experienced?"

For some few seconds she was unable to make any reply, but at length, with an effort to embolden her mind, she stammered forth,—

"Indeed, indeed, Lieutenant Granger, the task imposed upon me by stern necessity is one that I would have given worlds to have been spared. In a few moments, sir, I shall have gained more composure, and you shall know all, even though my heart breaks while I am telling it."

"Lieutenant Granger!" exclaimed her lover, with surprise; "these are cold words, Louisa, and give terrible presage of what is to follow! Why do you not call me Frederick? It has been so for many months till now."

"I have been wrong—very wrong," she replied; "yet is it you who ought to chide me for an error that I fear will mar our future happiness?"

"Chide you, my dear Louisa," exclaimed her lover, in still greater perplexity; "believe me, nothing can be further from my thoughts. But you are agitated, and dreading as I do the worst, I implore you to tell me what has occasioned this sudden change in your demeanour towards me."

"For Heaven's sake, leave me," she cried, "for, overwhelmed as my heart is with grief, I cannot utter the words I have been charged to deliver."

"I see it all, Louisa," exclaimed Frederick, in a voice almost choked with emotion. "My presence here is forbidden, and I am doomed to wear out the remainder of my days in vain regrets that chance ever threw us in each other's way."

"It is indeed too true," she sighed, "for this morning I solemnly promised my father never to encourage your visits here in future."

"And wherefore?" demanded Frederick; "why should he extort such a promise, when the happiness of both depends upon our union?"

"His motives I know not," she replied; "I cannot even guess them; but my word is pledged, and, once offended, his anger is terrible. But hush! I hear his footsteps coming this way! Leave me, I entreat, lest you should confront each other."

"It were all the better that we should do so," answered Frederick, "for I shall then have an opportunity of telling him my mind upon the matter."

"Oh, no, no, no," cried Louisa, imploringly; "indeed, indeed he must not find you here."

"Nay," answered her lover, "if I attempt to pass out of the house he must meet me."

"Then conceal yourself."

"Conceal myself, Louisa!"

"Yes," she replied; "in yonder closet you will be safe from observation. It is only for a few moments, for he never stays long in the room."

"If I must do so," returned Frederick, "I will no longer hesitate to obey your request. Yet, to confess the truth, Louisa, I like not these ambuscades, when fair fighting would better answer the purpose."

By this time Walford was heard near the door, and scarcely had the young soldier entered his place of concealment than the other strode into the apartment in which Louisa was sitting. With an effort she regained sufficient composure to avoid any particular observation; and, addressing herself to Walford, bade him good evening, remarking that he had been absent from home longer than usual.

"Not long enough," he replied, "to get an appetite for supper." Then, falling into his former train of thought, he muttered to himself, "Oh, Luke! Luke! what evil destiny was it that brought you to this part of our coast? And yet, why should I grieve? It is better that he should have fallen bravely than to meet his fate upon the gallows; and that, sooner or later, must have been the end of it."

"You seem ill, sir," said Louisa, who had watched his changing countenance with intense anxiety; "or has anything occurred during the day to vex you?"

"Shall I trust her?" muttered Walford to himself. "I may as well, for she must know it all one day or other."

Then addressing himself to her, he said,—

"Sit down, Louisa, and listen to what I have to communicate. You are a child no longer, and I have that to tell you which it is fitting you should know without further delay."

"What means this mystery?" she cried, anxiously.

"Can you keep a secret?" he demanded.

"You have known me long enough," answered Louisa, "to be assured that I never betray anything which has been communicated in confidence."

"True, my dear girl!" he exclaimed; "I must needs say for you, that you were prudent beyond your years; and therefore it is I now trust you with a secret dear to me as my own life."

"You alarm me, sir," cried Louisa, glancing anxiously towards the closet from which Frederick could hear all that passed. "If your secret is of such weight I would rather not be trusted with it—at least, not now;—let me entreat you to wait till some other opportunity offers."

"And why not now?" demanded Walford.

"Believe me, I have no reason for urging such a request," stammered Louisa;—"that is—no very particular reason."

"Well, then," he replied, "I *have* a reason for my confidence, and therefore prepare yourself to listen. The name of Walford, which I now bear, is one assumed for an especial purpose."

"Indeed!"

"Yes, girl," he replied; "the name is a feigned one, and henceforth you will know me as James Somerton."

"Somerton!" she cried, with amazement; "why that is name of the terrible pirate of whom every one speaks with so much alarm."

"True," answered the other; "that fearful man is my brother, and more, he is ——"

At that moment the door flew open, and Luke Somerton, still disguised as a Dutchman, strode into the apartment. Alarmed at so sudden an apparition, Louisa uttered a piercing scream, when the intruder, striding a pace or two nearer, exclaimed, in his assumed foreign accent,—

"Potz tanzend! why suld de maiden scream? Sapperment! I am no dievel."

"Who are you?" demanded Walford, "and what brings you here at such an hour as this?"

"Who am I?" asked the other, gaily. "Ha, ha! dat is vera goot! Are you alone, freend?"

"Not so much alone," answered Walford, "but I can get help in a minute if a rogue enters my house to rob me. I don't like your looks, sirrah, and command you to depart."

"James!" exclaimed Luke Somerton, in his natural tone, "have twelve years of rough weather so changed me, that you cannot recollect the form and features of your unhappy brother?"

"What, Luke! can it be possible?" cried the other, in amazement. "They told me your vessel had gone to the bottom in this day's engagement, and that all had perished with her."

"They told you false then."

"So it seems, indeed."

"Humph!" retorted Luke; "you don't seem to be over and above pleased to see me, though."

"Yes, I am," answered his brother; "but what, in the name of mischief, made you venture on this coast? Do you think hemp grows here no longer? or that we have not wood enough left in all the island to build a gallows with?"

Louisa could not forbear shuddering as she heard these words, and Luke Somerton, after a pause of a few moments' duration, exclaimed,—

"You speak like a land-lubber as you are, brother James. A brave man chooses his own death, and does not wait till other folks have reeved a Tyburn tippet for his throat, no leave asked."

"Yet, for all that, Luke," answered his brother, "I wish you were safe aboard your sloop, and she a hundred or two leagues from this coast."

"Psha, man!" exclaimed Luke; "if my reckoning be as nearly closed as you seem to say it is, this visit is all the better timed. In plain truth, I have ventured here because I wish to see my daughter once more before I die."

"True, true," returned the other, suddenly recol-

lecting himself; "in the surprise of seeing you so unexpectedly, I had forgotten all about that. Here, Luke, is your daughter, and I trust you will see no reason to regret having entrusted her all these years to my care."

"Is this my own little Louisa?" cried the astonished parent. "And yet I could have sworn as much, too. Egad, it makes my old heart feel warm again to see one that I can love and call my own. What a trim-built thing she is, and how like *her* that brought her into this world of vanity and trouble. But how is this, Louisa?—won't you greet your father, and welcome his return to you?"

"My father!" she faintly ejaculated.

"Yes, Louisa!" exclaimed Walford, "it is indeed your father, of whom I was about to speak to you when we were interrupted."

"She has forgotten me!" exclaimed Luke Somerton, in the bitterness of his disappointment.

"And that is scarcely to be wondered at," returned Walford, "for remember she was scarce six years old when she left England. Come, niece, bid your father welcome, after his long absence. Why do you tremble so, my child?"

"Because," answered Luke Somerton, "she has heard my name ere this, and has learnt to loathe the crimes with which I have been charged. I see how it is,—she hates me; so farewell, brother; I'll not curse her, nor will I shed a tear, though my heart is sorely hurt with the disappointment I endure. 'Sdeath! I would rather meet the great fiend himself from burning hell than have my own child look me in the face like that! Joy, joy be with ye both, and my blessings to the boot of that —the blessings of an apostate, and, some will tell you, you cannot have a curse to bite more deadly. Farewell for ever, and when next you hear of me it shall be that the earth is no longer cumbered with a wretch whom all conspire to despise!"

Having uttered these words he was frantically rushing from the room, when Louisa, rousing herself as from a torpor, rose from the chair upon which she had sunk, and with a cry of agony threw herself into his arms.

"Oh, my father!" she cried, "do not let us part thus—if you would not drive me to madness. I did wrong, very wrong; but let these tears witness for me how deep is my contrition."

"Are these tears real, girl?" exclaimed Luke, almost choked with emotion. "Do you indeed love the old renegade, in spite of all that has been said against him?"

"I do—I do!"

"Well, girl, I believe you," he replied, "and let this kiss seal my forgiveness. But tell me, Louisa, why did you regard me with such coldness when it was announced to you who I was?"

"Surprise rendered me incapable of utterance," she answered, "and the doubt I felt is little to be wondered at when it is remembered that for years past I have looked upon Mr. Walford as my father, and ——"

"And you were taken somewhat aback," interrupted Luke, "at finding a parent in a rough old fellow, who looks grim enough to frighten the very devil himself. That's natural enough, for it's as if I hailed a ship under merchant's colours, and found I had got under the guns of a king's cruizer. But stand up, girl, and let me look at thee:—thy

mother's eyes—thy mother's brows, too,—by St. Nicholas, but I have a mind to take her from thee, James. How say you, girl?—wouldst like to lay up in a French harbour? It's a gay land, I promise thee, and the gallants there have ten times more metal in their heels than the best of your foggy islanders."

"Hark!—what noise was that?" exclaimed Walford, as a low groan sounded through the room. "'Twas like some one in pain; and the person, whoever it may be, is not very far from us. By Heavens, it comes from yonder closet."

"Then, be who it may, he dies!" cried Luke Somerton, and drawing a pistol from his belt, he pointed it towards the door, and was in the act of pressing the trigger with his finger, when Louisa, uttering a cry of horror, rushed forward and threw herself between the weapon and the place where her lover was concealed.

"Hold! for mercy sake, hold!" she exclaimed, in an agony of terror; "or, if you will kill him, let the bullet reach him through my heart!"

At that moment the door of the closet was thrown open and Lieutenant Granger discovered himself, to the utter amazement and consternation of all present. Walford uttered the name of the intruder, and Luke Somerton, lowering the pistol which he grasped in his hand, addressed himself to his brother, exclaiming,—

"You know him, then? But no matter; he's a spy, and shall have a spy's portion."

"I am no spy," answered Frederick, indignantly; "and but that you are the father of this lady, I had given you the denial at my sword's point."

"If you are not a spy," exclaimed Luke Somerton, "what in the name of fortune made you hide yourself in yonder closet?"

"I believe," interrupted Walford, "I can answer that question."

"With your leave, sir, I will answer it myself," exclaimed Lieutenant Granger. "I loved your daughter, Captain Somerton, and would have married her, but your brother, for reasons best known to himself, thought proper to refuse me."

"And there was reason enough for my refusal," exclaimed Walford, "for I did not choose to betray my brother's secret, nor would I let you marry my niece under false impressions."

"And now," added Luke Somerton, "that you have overheard all, I suppose your mind is altered: you will not marry the daughter of an old privateer, who fights against his country."

"Resign my Louisa!" exclaimed Lieutenant Granger, indignantly; "not if her father were ——"

"Go on, young man," cried Luke Somerton, as the young man paused. "I like folks—and especially young folks—to speak their minds out plainly."

"Plainly then, I love your daughter," answered Frederick, "and with your consent would marry her in spite of all other obstacles."

"What says my daughter?" demanded Somerton.

"Oh, you need not ask there, I fancy," interposed Walford, with a significant smile.

"Nay, I would have the girl speak for herself," retorted her father.

"Then let me at once declare," cried Louisa, "that I have no other will but yours."

"Why, then, the matter is settled at once," he exclaimed, "and the marriage shall take place. I like the young fellow well enough, and being a sailor is quite enough to convince me that I might have looked further and fared worse, before I had met with a son-in-law that I could sooner have approved of."

At that juncture a shrill whistle was heard outside the house, and immediately afterwards a voice shouted a signal of danger. All were startled by so unexpected an interruption, but Luke Somerton appeared to understand what was meant, and throwing his cloak about him, he was about to leave the house when the notes of a distant bugle were heard.

"I have been betrayed!" he exclaimed; "but let my enemies beware, for I have arms about me, and will not perish till some of my pursuers have paid dearly for their temerity."

"Nay," cried Lieutenant Granger, "it is the bugle of our soldiers."

"What soldiers?" demanded Somerton, quickly.

"The troop to which I belong," answered Frederick, "and which has been stationed in this neighbourhood for some months past."

Here the signal was repeated by the person who was stationed outside the house to give warning, and Luke Somerton once more prepared to take his departure."

"I must away," he exclaimed, "or the huntsmen will soon entrap their prey."

"Nay, but brother," interposed Walford, "shall we not see you again?"

"Perhaps so," he replied, "I may return here at the hour of midnight."

"Let me caution you to take heed," exclaimed Lieutenant Granger, "for several detachments are out patrolling the shore for the smugglers."

"Never fear, sir, never fear," returned Luke Somerton; "I am prepared to encounter a few of my foes, and dearly will they pay for it if I am interrupted in my way towards the sea coast, where I have a boat in readiness to convey me to the ship. If any difficulty should rise in my path, I shall conceal myself in this neighbourhood, and in the silence of night will return here to let my friends know how matters have gone on. Should I depart without seeing you again, Lieutenant Grainger, you will understand that my consent has been given to your marriage with my daughter. So now farewell, and my parting prayer is, that all here may be happier than has been the fate of Luke Somerton."

He darted from the house as he uttered these last words, and at the same moment the bugle was again heard, but on the present occasion the sound was much nearer than before. Louisa threw herself into a chair overpowered with terror lest her father should fall into the hands of his enemies, and it was not till some time had elapsed that Frederick could restore her to composure.

CHAPTER IV.

- Hah!—so near?—
Then I may chance to meet him face to face,
And end this lengthened feud.—*The Duel.*

PURSUING his way with all speed, Luke Somerton directed his steps towards a wood at no great distance off, and scarcely had he entered the friendly shelter than a whistle was heard which he well knew was a signal from one of his own crew. This he immediately answered, upon which a noise was heard as of some one forcing a passage through the entangled underwood, and, within a few seconds, Scipio came running nearly breathless towards him.

"Hah, Scipio," exclaimed Somerton, "was it you that hailed me just now?"

"Iss, massa," replied the negro, "me called because dere was danger."

"Indeed! and from whom?"

"Oh, I hab seen de big debble! he come among us, and if he see you, massa, it is all over."

"How is this?" exclaimed Somerton; "why, you are drunk, you infernal black rascal."

"Ah! dat cause me drink a lily drop, massa," replied the negro; "but for all dat, captain, me hab seen de big debble just now."

"What mean you, scoundrel; will you speak out that I may know if any danger threatens me?"

"Iss, massa," replied Scipio, "me speak out, only you get in such terrible passion wid poor nigger. Scipio am frightened enough without massa flying into such furious rage."

"I shall be in a still greater rage in another minute if you go on in this tantalizing way," exclaimed Luke Somerton, impatiently. "If you have really seen anything, Scipio, to cause alarm, let me know what it is, that I may guard against it. Who is it, sirrah, that has crossed your path?"

"Captain Aylmer, massa."

"Aylmer! are you sure 'twas he?" demanded Luke, in a voice trembling with suppressed rage.

"Oh, iss, massa, me quite sure ob dat," replied the nigger, with a grin of self-satisfaction.

"I am glad to hear we are so near each other," muttered Somerton. "I have long sought him in vain, and now that he is within reach, I will have the satisfaction my vengeance has so long demanded. But where am I to find him, Scipio?"

"Him come to visit de great man at de big house," replied the negro. "Dey say him going to marry de gubbernor's pretty daughter."

"Humph! and what brought him here, so far out of the beaten road?"

"Don't know 'bout dat, captain," replied Scipio, "but him were terribly frightened when him see me."

"He has seen you, then, and of course recollects you as having been on board the Bellerophon?"

"Iss, massa."

"Did he speak to you?"

"Iss."

"And questioned you?"

"Iss; him ask a mort o' questions."

"And so," exclaimed Luke Somerton, "though aware of the risk of his following your footsteps, you were fool enough to come after me?"

"Poor niggger know not what to do," replied Scipio, "and so him run to tell massa all about it."

"Do you know whether he followed you?"

"Oh, iss, I spy him follow," replied the other, "and den I creep, creep, for all de world like our lily serpent."

"And, doubtless," exclaimed Somerton, "he is now lurking in ambush somewhere near?"

"I dare say he am, massa," answered the other, "for me see him just before you came here."

"Would that I knew where to find him!"

exclaimed Somerton, furiously. "But the coward knows the wrath he has excited in my breast, and will avoid a meeting, lest his own worthless life should be the sacrifice."

"Him berry great coward, captain," observed Scipio.

"Ay, and villain more than coward, if that be possible," muttered Luke. "I have received injuries from him, greater than can ever be repaired, and yet years have rolled by, and he lives to triumph in the wrongs his baseness has inflicted. But the hour of retribution is not far off, if he is indeed within the compass of this island, and were even my own daughter to shield him with her bosom, I would have his heart's blood, though hers were to mingle with the base, polluted stream."

"Will massa kill him, den?"

"Out, prating fool, and question me no further," exclaimed Somerton, furiously. "Away to the shore, where our boat lies, and see that everything is in readiness to put off at a moment's notice. Go, sirrah, and see that my orders are obeyed, or your own life will answer for the neglect."

Thus admonished, the negro hastily took his departure, and Luke Somerton, leaning against a tree, gave free scope to the feelings that had thus been awakened within his bosom. The desire for vengeance upon a hated foe was now even greater than it had ever been before; and though he himself would run no little hazard in attempting to accomplish his designs, he resolved to let no fear of personal danger interfere with a project that had long possessed his heart, and which had only been delayed thus far from the circumstance of his having lost sight of Captain Aylmer, who, he doubted not, kept aloof from him through feelings of the most abject fear. Now, however, he possessed a clue, and, come what might, he determined never to leave the island till he had poured upon his foe the full power of his wrath. Having wrought himself to this pitch of excitement, he was preparing to quit the wood, when approaching footsteps arrested his attention, and in another moment Christopher Dalton stood before him.

"Well met, captain," exclaimed the mate. "I have been searching for you in every direction, and should have missed my object at last, but for Scipio, whom I met just now, and who told me where I was most likely to fall in with you."

"What want you with me?" demanded Luke.

"To tell you," replied the other, "that there is some one near us at the present moment whom you have long been looking after."

"You mean Aylmer?"

"I do. Scipio, I suppose, has told you that he is now in this island."

"Aye."

"And do you mean to risk your life by staying here, for the mere purpose of executing a vow of vengeance?"

"My life is of little consequence," answered Somerton, "so that I can but have the heart's blood of that man. *Man* do I call him? Is he not rather a fiend, who first insults one that never wronged him, and then seeks to brand him with the name of villain?"

"It must be acknowledged that you have had nough of provocation from him," observed Dalton; "and yet I can't see the use of following him up so closely, when it can only tend to your own undoing. Remember, captain, you have few friends in this place; and should you chance to fall into the hands of justice, they will not spare the man whom the law calls a traitor to his country."

"Yet revenge is so sweet to me," exclaimed Luke Somerton, "that I would not forego it had I fifty lives depending upon the issue. Aylmer is my sworn foe. He is now within reach of my arm, and shall perish like a dog, as he is. And now, Dalton, since you know my determination, tell me if you have seen the man I seek."

"I have."

"And of course he recognized you?"

"I took care that he should not have the opportunity," replied Dalton; "for I avoided him, lest he should guess that you were somewhere near at hand."

"That was well done," exclaimed Somerton; "and of course you have made some inquiries, by which I may find him."

"I did," replied the other; "and, from all I have learned, he seems likely to remain long in this place."

"Aye," exclaimed Luke Somerton, fiercely; "but it will be as a tenant of the grave. Yet, say, Dalton, from whom did you gather your tidings?"

"From the old sailor, whom they call Caleb."

"What did he tell you?"

"That Captain Aylmer has arrived on a visit to the governor, Sir Charles Radcliffe, whose daughter he is about to marry."

"She will be a widowed bride, then," muttered Somerton, "if, indeed, the nuptials are ever solemnized between them."

"Well," exclaimed the other, "I should have been glad if you had let this matter drop; but I suppose it would be in vain to offer advice where there's a determination to go on, whatever may be the end of it. Twelve years have passed away since you received the injury from Captain Aylmer, and yet it seems to rankle in your mind just as much as if the occurrence had taken place only yesterday."

"A whole lifetime would not obliterate it from my memory," answered Luke Somerton, bitterly. "Have I not seen all my fairest prospects blighted through the devilish arts of this vindictive man?— is not my name branded with dishonour, and can I know all this without nursing in my heart thoughts of deep and terrible revenge?"

"That may be all very true," replied Dalton; "but it mustn't be forgot that others must suffer if this man perishes by the hand of violence."

"Who else would suffer, because a villain falls?"

"As one instance, I may mention the young lady he is about to be married to. People speak of her as an amiable and generous-minded girl; yet to what a depth of misery are you about to plunge her, for the mere gratification of a feeling that you might conquer without much effort."

"The girl is nothing to me," muttered the other, sullenly; "and, more, if she were my own sister, I would not forego the pleasure of revenge to save her a single pang. Besides, the innocent must sometimes suffer with the guilty; and though she may spend a few tears at the death of one lover, they will soon be dried up when another offers to supply his place."

"That's settling the matter very coolly, at any rate," observed Christopher Dalton.

"The truth is," answered the other, "I am so bent on having the heart's blood of this man, that I will suffer nothing to step in between me and the objects I have sworn to accomplish. I have waited years in the hope of one day meeting with my rival; and now that he is within reach of my arm, I will not let him escape me, though my own destruction should follow the instant after."

"You won't take my advice, then, and return to the ship, that is ready to spread her sails and carry us from a place where every moment threatens you with danger?"

"No," replied Luke; "I am no coward, and have faced death too often to run from it now."

"Well," returned Dalton, "I have perhaps as little fear of it as yourself; but we have messmates, you know, that ought to be cared about, and if it should happen to be known that you are on the island, our ship will be taken, and every poor devil on board will swing on the gibbet for having enlisted themselves under the command of Luke Somerton."

"Then do you return to them and take the place I have so long held," exclaimed Somerton. "Make all sail till you reach some friendly port, where you may chance to hear how I have fared, after fulfilling the design that detains me here. If I fall, the command of the ship will devolve upon you, but should I escape, I will cross over to the Continent, and join you again with as little delay as possible."

"There's little chance of that, I believe, captain," answered the other, "for if Aylmer falls by your hands, the whole place will be raised against you, and a strict watch will be set all round the island to prevent all chance of your escape."

"In that case," exclaimed Luke, "I shall know what to do. A death of shame shall never be my doom, and if matters come to the worst, it will yet be in my power to save myself from falling into the hangman's hands."

"Or, in other words, you would blow out our own brains rather than surrender yourself a prisoner?"

"Ay, that would I," replied Somerton; "death has no terrors for me, and I would cheerfully yield up my existence did I but know that my vow of retribution had been accomplished."

"And yet," exclaimed Dalton, "it is still easy to escape from this place, and to pass many a happy year among your old comrades. Forget the wrongs you have endured from Aylmer; leave him to the tortures of his own troubled conscience, and I'll answer for it he'll suffer more than need be desired by his most remorseless enemy."

A slight rustling in the bushes was now heard, and Luke Somerton, grasping a pistol in his hand, stood ready to discharge its contents at any person who might be found lying in ambush. For a moment or two he stood with his eyes fixed upon the spot from whence the sound had proceeded, and then, seeing a figure dart from it in an opposite direction, he exclaimed,—

"By all my hopes, Dalton, it is he! Vengeance, thou art now sure, and the villain dies!"

With this he madly rushed forward, and aided by the moonlight, soon came in view of his retreating enemy.

CHAPTER V.

Why dost thou plead for mercy?
Dost thou not know me for thy mortal foe,
And seeker of thy life?

The Serf's Revenge.

PURSUED by an inveterate enemy, Captain Aylmer ran with so much speed that his strength soon became nearly exhausted, and in his despair he saw but little chance of escaping from a fate which he had brought upon himself. Being unarmed, it would have been in vain to turn round and face the danger from which he was fleeing, and as no other alternative presented itself, he was compelled to exert all the energy that remained to him in order to reach the house which he was to occupy during his sojourn in the Isle of Man. But with all the efforts he made, it became too apparent that Somerton was slowly and surely gaining upon him, and as every prospect of escape disappeared, his spirits sank, till he became a prey to the most absolute despair, and death, with all its attendant horrors, was presented to his view.

Had any weapon been in his hand, he would have ceased his almost hopeless flight, and trusting to the result of chance, have met his opponent, and contested with him the palm of victory. But to do this under present circumstances, would have been the height of madness, and he was therefore compelled to exert his utmost speed in order that he might reach the house towards which his flight was directed, and when once there, defend himself as well as he could against the furious assaults of his terrible antagonist. In his onward progress he leaped hedges and ditches, which at any other time he would have thought it impossible to clear; but even these feats of desperation availed him not, for Somerton was no less powerful and active than himself, and still did he continue to pursue his flying foe, gaining upon him by slow yet perceptible degrees, that promised ere long to bring them into closer quarters than they had yet been.

Finding himself thus reduced to almost the last extremity, Aylmer, in the height of his despair, began to reflect within his own mind whether it would not be better to yield at once, and throw himself upon the mercy of his pursuer. This for a moment seemed to be the only chance that remained of escaping the death with which he was threatened; yet even this he was obliged to abandon, when he reflected on the unrelenting disposition of Luke Somerton, and the resolution which seemed to actuate him in the pursuit in which he was then engaged.

Under these circumstances he had no resource but to continue his flight, in the faint expectation that Somerton would at length grow wearied from his exertion, and abandon the revenge he contemplated till some other opportunity offered itself. But he little knew the fearful extremities to which a thirst for blood will urge a man, and still less did he know the nature of Luke Somerton, whose hatred was as unquenchable as the eternal fires of Vesuvius. Still, however, he collected all his energies for securing this last remaining chance, bounding forward with lengthened and rapid strides, and seeming to be inspired with fresh vigour to outstrip the speed of him who was rushing forward on his errand of blood.

By this time was heard the voice of Luke Somerton, as he shouted aloud in the madness of his rage. Curses, deep and terrible, followed the fugitive as he continued his headlong career, and occasionally a wild, demoniac laugh burst from the pursuer, as if deriding the efforts that were made to escape from him, and exulting in the certainty that a very little longer must place him within arm's length of the wretched man he was about to sacrifice. These discordant yells carried dismay into the heart of Aylmer, who felt as if already in the grasp of his unrelenting enemy; and, almost yielding to his despair, he was at one time on the point of casting himself upon the earth, and thus surrendering himself to the man from whom he had no hope of mercy. At that moment, however, he obtained a distant view of the house towards which he was making his way, and feeling as if inspired with fresh courage, he once more resolved upon a further effort, and rushing across a bridge that was interposed between him and the place he was in quest of, he felt so certain of effecting his escape, that he laughed derisively at the efforts Somerton was still making to overtake the object of his pursuit; indeed, so desperate had his situation become, that he was urged into far greater speed than he had thought it was possible for him to attain, and by the time he had reached the house, he saw that Luke had lost a considerable distance during the last few minutes. Some little time, however, was occupied in getting the door open, and scarcely had he succeeded in effecting this than the report of a pistol was heard, and at the same moment a bullet struck the house a few inches only above his head.

This afforded sufficient proof that no time was to be lost, and hurrying into the house, he bolted and barred the door and windows to keep out his exasperated pursuer, and then threw himself into a chair to recover from the violent exertion which he had undergone.

"The murderous villain!" he muttered to himself; "I was sure, when I spied the rascally black, that Somerton could not be far off. Here, however, I am safe for a while, and I may defy the ruffian and all his arts to reach me whilst I remain beneath the protection of this friendly roof."

He paused, for footsteps could be plainly heard near the house, and scarcely had Aylmer ran to the door and windows to see that they were all secure, when a loud knocking was made, as if the person without was making a peremptory demand for admittance.

"Ay, ay," cried Aylmer, "knock away, my lad, and wait till I am fool enough to give you admittance. Surely the door will not give way, though. Hold fast, good oak—hold fast, or I am lost beyond redemption. By Heavens, he is trying the shutters!—they seem to yield, too. Oh, fool—fool! why did I trust myself within sight of that man, when I knew him to be actuated with the feelings of a fiend? Ha! all is quiet again—ha! ha! ha! What, I have foiled you, villain—have I? Fore George! I don't know that anything could have happened more fortunately for me than knowing that I have a good stout wall between me and the ruffian who is longing to cut my throat."

Again a pause ensued, and from the utter silence that reigned without, Aylmer more than once began to suspect that his foe had seen the impossibi-lity of getting into the house, and had abandoned the task in despair.

In that case, he had no doubt Luke Somerton would be glad to escape from the island before the morning, and then he would himself be safe from all further dread on his account.

From these comforting reflections, however, he was presently roused by the heavy tread of footsteps without, and directly afterwards a huge piece of timber was struck with such violence against the door that it burst open after the application of a few blows, and Luke Somerton strode into the house.

"It is long," he exclaimed, "since we have greeted, Captain Aylmer, and yet I should have known you had we met on a single plank in the broad Atlantic."

"Luke Somerton," cried the other, trembling with alarm, "what is the motive of this visit?"

"You can guess that, I should imagine, Captain Aylmer," he replied, coldly.

"Is it to murder me?"

"Humph! What makes you think I came on such an errand as that?"

"The suddenness of your visit, and the wildness of your looks, assure me that your purpose is a bloody one. Besides, have you not pursued me to-night as if I was a wild beast? and was not a pistol fired by your hand as I was about to enter this house? These circumstances, and your well-known hatred towards me, all serve to confirm the suspicion that you have come here to take my life."

"And what better can you expect from such as I?" demanded Somerton. "Folks call me the pirate, the traitor, the outcast, and for that matter I know not that they are very wrong in their reckoning. In honest truth, I am all that the world has thought proper to say of me."

"Do you acknowledge your own infamy?"

"I do, Captain Aylmer," he replied; "but who was it that made me all this? Answer me that, messmate, and then let me know how your heart feels when you think of what I once was, and what you have since made me. Do you feel no contrition for the wrongs that have been heaped upon me, or does your black soul still exult in the ruin and degradation produced by yourself?"

"The past," replied Aylmer, "cannot be recalled; but deeply have I repented the rashness that prompted me to the step I took; and I would give worlds, were it in my power, to replace you in the situation you once held in society."

"Aye, but repentance comes too late, now," exclaimed Luke Somerton, "and your words do but recal to my mind that which lashes my soul to madness. What I now am you made me; and can it be wondered at, then, that I have cherished my thoughts of vengeance all these years?"

"Let all be now forgotten," answered Aylmer, "and reparation may yet be made for the past. I may still have it in my power to save you, for my interest with the government—"

"I ask no such favour of you," interrupted Somerton, haughtily; "nor would I accept any, even though it might be to save my life from the hangman's hands. Briefly, then, answer me a plain question, honestly, if you can, and don't stand nipping your words as if you were the purser weighing out a short allowance of mouldy cheese to a poor sailor. Have you not been my foe? and is it not natural that I should seek to make matters even between us both?"

"I confess, Luke, I have been much to blame," replied Captain Aylmer; "but we were both younger men at that time, and did things which our present experience makes us ashamed of. In one word, I have done you a grievous wrong, and do not attempt to deny it."

"These are fine words, Aylmer, to the man whom you have ruined," exclaimed Somerton, in a tone of bitter contempt. "You see before you the wreck of him who was once happy in the world's esteem, but who is now loathed and despised for those acts which he was driven to commit. These thoughts have rankled in my heart like poison, and many a time, in the dark hour of night, have I reflected, with satisfaction, that the day would yet come when a heavy retribution might be demanded. The day *has* come, Captain Aylmer, and I am here to announce you have taken your last look of this world."

He stepped back a couple of paces, and, cocking the pistol which he held in his hand, presented it at the head of Aylmer, who, stepping aside to avoid the fire of his antagonist, exclaimed with trembling alarm,—

"Hold, Luke Somerton, I charge you, and reflect a moment, ere you take this mean, cut-throat advantage of an unarmed man. If you fancy yourself wronged, give me one of those weapons, and let us decide our difference like seamen and brother officers."

"That would be too much honour for a poor lieutenant," answered Somerton, ironically. "So at least you said twelve years ago, when you refused a challenge from the very man you now ask to meet upon equal terms. But perhaps you think the renegade captain a nobler personage than Lieutenant Somerton of the Royal Navy?"

"Why should not the past be forgotten," cried Aylmer, "since I have offered to make all the recompense in my power for the injuries complained of? I may perish by your hand, it is true, but, by the commission of such a deed, you will bring upon yourself the retribution of the laws, and perish with ignominy and shame."

"For myself I am reckless of any fate that may fall upon me," answered Somerton.

"But you have a daughter who would experience the world's coldness, were her father to meet the doom of a felon."

"I have a daughter," replied Luke Somerton; "but through your villany I have not seen her for twelve years till this very day."

"For her sake, then, spare me," cried Aylmer; "nay, as you hope that Heaven may prosper you here and hereafter, I implore you, do not tear me from the world with all my sins unatoned."

"Hah!" exclaimed Somerton, exultingly, "this is indeed the beginning of my vengeance, when I see the haughty Captain Aylmer sueing to a humble person, like myself, for his worthless life. I have waited long for this hour, and, at one time had almost despaired of its ever arriving; but, by Heaven, it has come at last, and brought with it a glorious recompense."

"You triumph, Luke, in my abject fears, and I can freely pardon the bitter words you pour

forth to wound my pride. All that is nothing more than I might have expected; but there let your advantage end, and I swear to exert whatever influence I possess to obtain a pardon from government for the course you have adopted, and, after that has been accomplished, it shall be my task to render your future days happy and serene."

"I will accept no favour from you," exclaimed Luke Somerton, doggedly.

"And why not?"

"Because I know you to be a villain."

"A villain!"

"Aye, there's no denying it," replied Somerton.

"I may have erred, certainly," returned the other, "but the fault shall be acknowledged, and I have already said that every exertion in my power shall be made to satisfy the injuries you have unhappily received at my hands."

"And I have already said that I will receive no favour from you," replied Somerton. "The years that have intervened since you and I last met, have been chiefly passed in brooding upon my wrongs, and anticipating the pleasure I should experience whenever the day arrived that should bring us within arm's length of each other. Now, Captain Aylmer, we stand face to face, and I accuse you of deeds that have made me an outcast from the world; and I ask you if it is at all likely I can forego the satisfaction I have so long promised myself?"

"What satisfaction can it afford you to take away the life of a fellow-creature?" demanded Aylmer, who now saw that there was little chance of exciting compassion in the heart of his mortal enemy. "My blood will be but a poor recompense for any wrongs you may have endured; and even should you escape punishment for the crime of murder, it will be to pass a life of agony and remorse for having deprived me of existence in a moment of ungovernable passion."

"With that you have nothing to do," answered Somerton, "nor shall I stop now to reflect upon what may be the future consequences of the act I have come here to perform. One only passion now fills my heart, and that is revenge for the cruel injuries inflicted by your contrivance."

"Are you, then, resolved to take my life?" cried Captain Aylmer, despondingly.

"What better fate do you deserve of me than to die the death of a dog?" demanded the other. "Have I not, through your means, been made the despised outcast you now behold me? Think you I can ever forget the happiness it was your pleasure to deprive me of, for no other reason than that I resented an insult, and demanded satisfaction? Like a coward, you refused to meet me, and I was degraded and driven from a honourable profession because you have thought proper to bring me before a court martial for challenging a superior officer."

"It was done in the heat of the moment, Luke," answered the other, "and I have never ceased to regret the course I took on the occasion."

"Aye, you would now fawn upon me in order to save your own worthless existence."

"Nay, I am not so abject a wretch as you take me for," replied Aylmer, "and, if need be, am willing to meet you fairly, and upon equal terms. If I fall, the crime of deliberate murder will not be at your door ; and, should we both survive, it shall be my care to make every recompense in my power to make amends for the past."

"All this is very fine talking," exclaimed Somerton ; "but, whenever a man's mind is made up, it's not easy to turn him from it. However, I don't want to commit a cold-blooded murder, so I don't care much if I give you one chance for your life. You shall have one of these pistols, and the matter shall be fairly settled on both sides."

"That is all I ask."

"But the chance is a poor one, though," added Luke Somerton ; "for, if I missed you, it will be the first time I ever missed my man within rifle distance. Here is your weapon, and now I take my stand at the further end of the room."

Luke Somerton then turned to take his station at the spot he had named ; and, whilst his back was still towards Alymer, the latter discharged his pistol at him, but in the hurry or agitation of the moment the ball with which it was loaded missed the object. With the speed of lightning, Somerton rushed upon Alymer, who, falling upon his knees, implored mercy in the most abject and piteous terms.

"Mercy !" vociferated the other, furiously ; "how can you have the face to ask it of the man who gave you a fair chance of life, by risking his own, when all power was in his hands ?"

"I will give you wealth," cried Aylmer ; "you know I have the means—a thousand pounds—the sum twice doubled—trebled—but do not—do not murder me, I implore you !"

"Ha ! ha ! ha !" shouted Somerton, with a wild and fiend-like laugh ; "why, hang me if I am not half ashamed to strike such a puling miscreant as he who kneels before me. Hast thou not even the heart to die like a man ?—for die you must, and that before the night is many minutes older."

"I meant you not unfairly," cried Aylmer ; "the pistol went off unawares, on my honour, on my soul it was an accident."

"Avast ! messmate, avast !" exclaimed Luke Somerton, pointing upwards ; "there's one above hears you, who does not like liars ; don't swear away your precious soul, as you are so near dying."

"Grant me but an hour."

"Not half an hour," vociferated Somerton ; "not the fourth part of one—on the stroke of ten, by yonder clock, you perish."

"Save me, oh, save me !" cried Aylmer, with clasped hands ; "I meant not to take your life, yet would you sacrifice mine, under an impression that I treacherously sought to kill you."

"It is vain to plead for your miserable existence," answered Somerton, "for at the moment I have mentioned you shall die. So make up your account with Heaven, for you have not many minutes to live. See, the hand is drawing close upon the hour which is to be your last in this world."

"Oh, do not become my murderer !" exclaimed Aylmer, in despairing accents. "Let me live, I entreat you, and the remainder of my days shall be passed in proving my gratitude for your forbearance. My fortune shall be all at your disposal, and I will live in poverty as a just punishment for the wrongs I have inflicted upon you."

"Whining hypocrite," returned Luke ; "how can you ask a favour of the man who spurns you as he would a dog? Ask mercy of Heaven ! thou base slave, but do not supplicate it from me, for I am deaf to all your entreaties."

"Alas ! will nothing move your heart to have compassion on me ?"

"Nothing that you can urge will prolong your wretched existence a moment beyond the time I have given you," replied Luke Somerton. "You might have had an equal chance with me just now, yet, like a coward as you are, you took advantage of my back being turned, and would have killed me treacherously, and without the slightest warning."

"Indeed, Luke, you wrong me," cried the other, trembling at the near approach of death. "The pistol was discharged by an accident, yet am I condemned to die as if I had intended to become your assassin."

"And that's just what you did mean," replied Somerton ; "so don't think to deceive me by telling any more lies about it. But see, the dial's hand has almost reached the hour, and no prayers, no entreaties shall prolong your life one single instant beyond the allotted time. So to your prayers man,—to your prayers, and I'll stand aside the while."

"Is there no hope—no chance for me ?" muttered the wretched man, as Luke turned away from him. "The seconds fly like lightning, and a thousand bells are ringing in my ears as if Satan himself were pealing me a welcome into hell. Ah ! pray did he say ?—yes, I will—I'll try—what was it the good pastor taught me when I was a child ?—gone—all gone and forgotten ! I can think of nothing—speak of nothing but death—death—I hear it in the roaring flames ! I see the ghastly forms in the shadows on the walls !—Is there no hope ?"

"I tell you there is none," answered Luke Somerton, hoarsely. "Have I not vowed to revenge the many wrongs I have endured at your hands, and shall I withhold myself at the voice of a puling slave who fears to meet the death he merits through his own infamy ? I tell you, Aylmer, there is no power in the world that shall save you beyond the moment I have allotted as the termination of your existence."

"Will you not give me a chance of defending myself with equal weapons ?"

"You have had such a chance and abused it," replied Somerton. "I gave you an opportunity to save yourself, even though I had little reason to exhibit so much forbearance, and what was the use you would have made of my misplaced confidence ? My own blood had nearly been shed when I was not prepared for your cowardly attack ; and it is in vain, therefore, that you plead to a man whose hatred grows more intense with each passing moment."

"Then Heaven help me !" groaned Aylmer, shuddering, as the last hope of life vanished utterly from his sight.

"Have you no other prayer to offer up when the grave yawns to receive its victim ?"

"Had my life been spared, I could have sacrificed all to make amends for the wrongs I have heedlessly done you," answered Aylmer. "I would have beggared myself to enrich you ; but my prayers are unheeded, and I must perish with all my sins unrepented."

At that moment the voices of many persons were heard near the house, and Aylmer made a sudden bound toward the door, and would have flown for protection to those whose arrival had inspired him with fresh hope. Somerton, however, instantly interposed himself, and ere the wretched man could effect his purpose, he fell beneath the fatal fire of his antagonist.

This done, Luke made towards a window at the rear of the premises, and having quitted the house, he dashed across the country almost heedless of whither he went.

CHAPTER VI.

Oh, heinous crime!
And yet the assass'n, trembling for his doom,
Hides f om th' avenging foe.   DESMOND.

WHEN Caleb and his companions entered the house after Luke Somerton had quitted it, they were horror-struck at the dismal spectacle that presented itself. The discharge of fire-arms had indeed somewhat prepared them for some such scene, but when the murdered man proved to be Captain Aylmer, their alarm was excited to the highest pitch, and various were the conjectures offered as to who could be the person guilty of so heinous an offence. In order to discover who the assassin was, the dying man was questioned and pressed to disclose the events which had led to this dreadful tragedy, but death was already at his heart, and after a few unavailing efforts to articulate, he expired in the arms of Caleb.

"This is a foul job, my masters," exclaimed the old sailor, as the unfortunate man breathed his last; "and it shall be through no fault of mine if the murderers escape their deserts. At any rate, they can't be very far off, and if a bright look out is kept, there's little chance of their getting away from the island without being overhauled."

"I wonder who could have done it?" said Peter Titmouse, the constable, whose fears had so far kept him at a respectful distance. "There must have been more than one person engaged in it, I should think, or the captain would have been able to save his life.'"

"Psha! what signifies talking about how many fellows it took to do a thing like this," returned Caleb. "Perhaps there was only one villain engaged in it, and all we've got to do is to find out whether Captain Aylmer had an enemy so that we may fit the saddle on the right horse."

"Aye," interposed another of the men; "and Jack Ketch will have the pleasure of fitting him with a new cravat, that won't sit very easy, I'm thinking. Talk about enemies, indeed! I don't think the captain reckoned many such among his acquaintances."

"Humph!" retorted Caleb; "but what should you say if I happened to tell you that the poor fellow lying at your feet had any enemy that is likely to have done just such a deed as this rather than be disappointed of his revenge."

"Who is it?" demanded Peter Titmouse.

"Why, the very man, to be sure, that we were in search of to-night."

"What! Luke Somerton?"

"Aye! that's the name of the man I mean," replied Caleb; "and, take my word for it, my lad, it will turn out that I'm not very wide of the mark when I say that Luke Somerton had a hand in this business. I've often heard Captain Aylmer say that something bad would happen to him if ever he should meet with Luke, and it seems he was a pretty true prophet if it should turn out that my notion of the thing is correct."

"But perhaps it won't turn out so," observed Peter Titmouse.

"Why, then, you may set me down as a know-nothing fellow for ever afterwards," returned the old sailor. "However, there's very little chance of that, I believe, for Luke don't bear the best of characters, as all of you must allow; and, as we know he bore the captain no good will, there's reason enough for believing, that he either murdered him with his own hands, or got some one to do the job for him."

"And I'm partly of your way of thinking, Master Caleb," exclaimed Titmouse, "for people haven't given him the best of characters lately, and I don't know anybody else in the whole island that would have committed such a deed as this. However, something must be done, and that quickly too, so one of us had better go and tell the governor what has taken place, and then he'll take care to bring the murderers to punishment."

"You needn't trouble yourself about that," said one of the bystanders; "for Gideon Dawson bolted away as soon as he saw that murder had been committed, and I dare say by this time his excellency has ordered out the troops to arrest the assassin."

"In that case," observed Titmouse, "we must remove the body, and then wait the further orders of Sir Charles Radcliffe."

"You're a pretty fellow for a constable, if you don't know better than that," exclaimed Caleb. "Remove the body, eh! when every one knows that it ought to remain where it is till after the crowner's 'quest has sat upon it. Or, if it must be taken away, let's wait for orders from the governor, and then if anything's wrong about it we shall not be called over the coals for it."

"Well, do as you like, Caleb," answered the constable; "only recollect, if there's any blame, you must take it all upon your own shoulders."

"Ay, ay, they're broad enough to bear it," exclaimed the seaman; "so make yourself quite easy about that, old boy, and I'll answer for it his excellency won't find fault with me. Besides, it's most likely he'll be here soon, as Gideon Dawson has gone to tell him of what has taken place; and then we shall have orders from him that we may follow without any fear of of doing wrong."

"And, by all that's lucky, here is his excellency," said Peter Titmouse, as the door opened, and Sir Charles Radcliffe, accompanied by a guard of soldiers, entered the house.

"Alas!" he cried, as the melancholy sight presented itself before his eyes, "the evil tidings are but too true, and my friend has fallen by the hands of a ruthless assassin."

"Yes, your honour," answered Caleb, "the poor gentleman is dead enough; and the worst part of it is that he expired without being able to tell us who it was that committed the deed."

"Then the villain has escaped?"

"For the present he has," replied Caleb ; "but it's not likely he'll have his liberty long, for he can't be out of the island yet, and, as I can pretty well guess who's work this is, we'll have him safe in our clutches before he's many hours older."

"Who do you suspect?" demanded the governor.

"The right man, as I fancy," answered Caleb ; "and perhaps your honour will agree with me when I name Luke Somerton as the villain that has committed this bloody deed."

"Luke Somerton !" exclaimed Sir Charles ; "why, have we not heard that he and his crew went to the bottom in the late storm?"

"To be sure we did," returned the other ; "and yet, for all that, we must not put too much faith in reports till they have been confirmed. For my own part, I have good reasons for knowing that Luke has been on the island since the battle was fought, and, as he hadn't any very great liking for Captain Aylmer, there's no doubt but he's done this crime out of revenge."

"I have heard my friend speak of a quarrel with Somerton," returned the governor, "yet, it would be unjust to accuse him of this crime upon no better foundation than we have at present."

"Then look at this dagger, Sir Charles," exclaimed the sailor, as he stooped to pick up the weapon he named, and which had hitherto been nearly concealed beneath the body of the murdered man ; "it has the name of Somerton cut upon the handle, and if that don't convince you as to who is the murderer, I don't know what will."

"This is indeed a suspicious circumstance," returned the governor, as he gazed upon the weapon, " and affords circumstantial evidence that will warrant me in giving orders for his arrest. On the other hand, however, it must be admitted that we have no proof against Somerton, and the more particularly as the wound which occasioned death seems to have been inflicted with a pistol-shot, and not with a poniard."

"That's very true, your excellency," replied Caleb, "but how came this weapon here, unless Luke Somerton has been at the house?"

"A dozen reasons may be given to account for it," answered Sir Charles. "For instance, the poniard may have been given to one of his companions, and that man may be the very person who committed this cruel outrage."

"Then you believe Somerton to be innocent?"

"Every man should be deemed so till we have proved him guilty," returned the governor. "Luke, it must be admitted, has borne but an indifferent character of late, and I am rather inclined to be of your way of thinking with respect to the perpetrator of this crime ; yet, on the other hand, we must conquer our prejudices against him till we have further proof to corroborate the opinions we may have formed."

"Well, your honour knows best what ought to be done, I dare say," observed Caleb ; "but, for all that, I think Luke Somerton ought to be laid by the heels, or he'll get clear away from the island, and afterwards laugh at us for our pains."

"Nay, there is very little fear of that, I believe," returned the governor ; "for I have given orders to have the whole coast strictly watched, and all suspicious persons to be arrested and placed in custody till I have had an opportunity to examine them as to what they have been doing in the island, and the motive that induces them to leave it. Thus we may hope to find out the guilty party, and avenge the blood of my unfortunate friend Aylmer."

"And I suppose," observed Caleb, "there'll be no objection to my making myself a little bit busy about looking after this Luke Somerton?"

"I am pleased to observe that you are so zealous in the cause," answered Sir Charles, "and shall not fail to reward you for it in the event of your suspicions proving well founded. We have sufficient grounds for detaining Somerton in custody, and perhaps if he should be remanded for a few days, we may be able to gather concurring testimony in support of the opinion you have formed."

"It shall be no fault of mine if we don't," answered Caleb; "for I've a keen nose when game like this is to be hunted out, and will never give up the chase till the murderer of Captain Aylmer has been brought to the gibbet."

"That is," Peter Titmouse ventured to interpose, "if the poor gentleman really has been murdered."

"If he really has been murdered!" cried the sailor, with surprise; "and can you be such an errant fool as to doubt it, when he is lying before your eyes, weltering in his own blood?"

"But it don't follow," returned Titmouse, "that he has been assassinated. Haven't people before now put a pistol to their own heads, and mayn't Captain Aylmer have done the same thing for anything we know to the contrary?"

"Humph!" growled Caleb; "pigs may fly, Peter, but it ain't very likely that Captain Aylmer should have blowed out his own brains, when we all know he came over to the island on purpose to marry the governor's daughter. Besides, this dagger shows that somebody besides himself must have been here; and, whether it was Luke Somerton, or any one else, I'll find out the truth of it, unless the devil assists the murderer to escape the fate he deserves."

"The mystery, Caleb," exclaimed Sir Charles, "may not be so easily cleared up as you imagine, or, at all events, it is likely to take more time and trouble than you at present believe. Murder is seldom committed in the presence of witnesses, and is therefore a crime more difficult of discovery than any other."

"But the cunning man frequently overreaches himself," replied the sailor; "and a guilty conscience will sometimes sit so uneasily as to lead to detection. We will therefore get this Luke Somerton into our custody, and it will then be seen whether he can carry out his bravado for any length of time. At first, perhaps, he may vaunt his innocence, and talk of the injustice he endures, but only let him get a near view of the gallows, and he'll begin to think it better to make a clear conscience by confession."

"By your leave, friend Caleb," suggested Peter Titmouse, "I would beg permission to observe, that few men are brought to confession when a free tongue can only serve to bring their necks within a halter."

"You are an ass, Peter, and know nothing of what you are talking about," exclaimed Caleb. "'Tis your vocation, man, to take rogues into custody, and to keep them safely till your betters have done with them; but who ever heard of a constable that had wit enough to give an opinion upon a matter of importance like this?"

"But, Master Caleb ——"

"Don't presume to bandy words in presence of his honourable excellency," interrupted the sailor. "You have your duty to do; and when Sir Charles gives his orders, it will be your place to see that all the commands he gives are properly executed. A foul and bloody murder has been committed, Mr. Peter Titmouse, and yet you would stand arguing over the corpse as if the governor had nothing better to do than to listen to the foolish advice of a half-witted constable."

"Peace!" exclaimed Sir Charles, "and let me know under what circumstances the murder of my unfortunate friend was discovered."

"Why the truth is, your excellency," replied Caleb, "I got a notion that Luke Somerton, instead of being sunk to the bottom of the sea, was prowling about the island, and keeping out of people's sight as much as he could. So, thinking he was after no good, I called upon Peter Titmouse for his assistance, and having got four or five more to follow us, we began to search about for the man we wanted."

"And did you get upon the track of Luke Somerton?"

"Why, we fancied we did," replied Caleb; "and so we kept walking on, keeping a bright lookout, till we came within sight of this house, and then the report of a pistol was heard, which I suppose was the one that brought poor Captain Aylmer to the end of his days."

"And upon hearing the report of fire-arms, you, of course, made all speed to ascertain what had caused it?" asked the governor.

"We did, Sir Charles."

"And did you gain immediate admission?"

"Not so soon as we wished," replied Caleb; "but it was not long before we broke the door open, and the first thing we saw upon coming into the house was the body of Captain Aylmer, just where you see it."

"He was not quite dead, I suppose?"

"Not quite, your honour," replied Caleb; "but so near it that we could not get a word out of him. He tried all he could to speak, poor fellow, but it was of no use, for the blood was gurgling from his mouth; and in a minute or two after we came in he cast anchor in the waters of eternity."

"You saw no one in the place, I suppose, when you came in?" exclaimed the governor.

"Not a soul, your excellency," answered the other; "but as the shutters of yonder window had been broken, it's likely the murderer had got out that way, when he heard us coming."

"Had some of your men been stationed there," said Sir Charles, "the villain would now have been in safe custody, and the ends of justice would not have been defeated, as they now seem likely to be."

"I hope your honour don't blame me for it," exclaimed Caleb. "I took good care that nobody should pass through the door; and if the assassin got out at the window, it was Peter's fault, for he wouldn't leave the place where I was, for fear anything should happen to him."

"You want to make me out a coward,'" retorted

the constable ; "but for all that I did my duty as manfully as any of the rest of you. Besides, who was to know that he would get out of the window? or, indeed, how could I tell that there was anybody in the place wanting to make his escape?"

Caleb was about to make a sneering reply, but luckily for the peace of all parties the controversy was broken off by the arrival of Mr. Mayhew, to whom the murder which had been committed, and the circumstances connected with it, were related. He had, however, been previously informed of the catastrophe that had befallen Captain Aylmer, and addressing himself to the governor, he said,—

"Knowing the orders you would wish to give for the purpose of securing the assassin, I have been down to the guard-house and informed the officers on duty of what has taken place. It seems they were aware of the tragical occurrence ; and as a party of the military has been ordered out, I next inquired where it was likely you might be found. One of the officers happened to know that you had come to the scene of this fearful crime, and hither I followed, to offer any services that may be most useful towards discovering the villain who has ruthlessly robbed a fellow-creature of his life."

"This is, indeed, an act of friendship, my dear Mayhew," exclaimed the governor; "but I believe, with the measures that have been adopted, we are almost certain of securing the assassin before many hours have passed away. At any rate, no one can leave the island, except under the observation of our guards, and all persons against whom suspicions may be formed will be detained till they give a satisfactory account of themselves."

"And I'm thinking," observed Caleb, "that a good many suspicious persons will find themselves in limbo before this time to-morrow."

"At all events, the innocent will not have to complain of a very long detention," replied Sir Charles ; "for I shall be ready to give each case a hearing as soon as the prisoner is taken into custody. The guilty alone will have reason to tremble; for I have resolved to bring him to punishment, if a lucky chance should throw him into my power."

"Which is by no means certain," observed Mr. Mayhew ; "for doubtless the miscreant had previously arranged means for his escape, and perhaps, by this time, he is making all sail for some distant part of the world."

"In that case," said Peter Titmouse, "we shall be spared all further trouble, and my own precious life will not be risked in hunting after a fellow that would no more mind murdering me than he did killing the poor gentleman that's lying here before us."

"You are a coward, Titmouse," exclaimed Caleb—"a white-livered coward, that it would be a charity to the world to rid it of."

"Ah, so you may think, Caleb," retorted the other ; "but what would become of my poor wife and blessed babies if the head of the family was to be cut off by a sudden death?"

"Much better without than with you," was the gruff reply of the plain-spoken sailor.

"But what's to support 'em, if anything should happen to me?"

"Why, I'd give 'em half my own pay rather than they should starve," replied Caleb, "and I'm

thinking that would be a much better living than they've ever had since you have written yourself down a married man."

"A truce to this idle controversy," interposed the governor, "and let us now see what had better be done in order to secure the culprit. Let the body of my unfortunate friend be conveyed from this place, and when that has been done, I will give further instructions as to the course you are to adopt for discovering the retreat of the assassin."

"But where are we to take the body, Sir Charles?" inquired Caleb.

"To the vault that adjoins the chapel dungeon beneath the castle," replied the governor. "Let that be its resting-place for the present, and when your task is accomplished, I will see you again to give further instructions."

Leaving them to fulfil their melancholy task, Sir Charles Radcliffe, accompanied by Mr. Mayhew, left the cottage and hastened away to ascertain if any clue to the murder had yet been found.

CHAPTER VII.

This night, methinks, is but the daylight sick,
It looks a little paler; 'tis a day
Such as the day is when the sun is hid.
Merchant of Venice.

UPON leaving the cottage where his vengeance had been so fearfully accomplished, Luke Somerton ran forward at his utmost speed, fancying that in every stunted tree he beheld an officer, and feeling for the first time in his life a sensation of dread, that it seemed nothing could remove from his heart. The image of the murdered man was still presented before his eyes with frightful reality, and even the slightest rustling of the leaves seemed to warn him of coming danger, and added to the speed he had exerted to avoid the pursuit he so much dreaded.

It was not, however, that he feared to die, for his course had long been a perilous one, and almost every hour of his existence was fraught with danger ; but, to meet an ignominious fate was a result to be avoided, whatever the consequences might be, and should no other alternative remain, he determined to perish by his own hand rather than meet the fate of a malefactor. Yet, in spite of this resolution, he was anxious to prolong his existence while a hope remained to him, and with this view it was that he continued his flight, under an impression that he should find a boat upon the shore to convey him out to sea, or, in the event of that failing him, that he might meet with some place where he could remain in concealment till after the ardour of pursuit had began to slacken.

Having reached the middle of the wood he paused to rest, and seating himself upon the trunk of a fallen tree, he planned a thousand schemes by which he might elude the vigilance of those who he had no doubt were by this time in pursuit of him. But a quarter of an hour had scarcely elapsed when the rustling of branches near him gave signal of some one's approach, and starting up, he would have resumed his flight had not Scipio presented himself at the moment before him.

"Oh, massa!" exclaimed the African; "him berry glad to meet you, for de fellows are running arter you, and poor Scip was 'fraid capt'n got nabbed."

"The cursed fools," cried Somerton ; " and for what are they looking after me ?"

"On'y for de murder of ——"

"Psha !" interrupted Luke ; " what murder are you speaking of, prating idiot ?"

"What ! ain't you heared den, of de 'sassination of Capt'n Aylmer ?"

"Captain Aylmer murdered !" exclaimed the fugitive, with affected surprise.

"Iss, massa, him berry dead, indeed," answered the African ; " and folks say you know more about it dan anybody else. Dey hunt over de island for you, and so Scipio ran off to put you on your guard."

"'Twas well done of you, my good fellow," answered Somerton ; " but they must have more proof to support this charge before they can hope to destroy me."

"Ah, massa," returned the other, " dey say dare am proof enough. Folks will hab it you am de 'sassin, and if dey swear you kill Capt'n Aylmer, de hangman will have a job in spite ob all you can say."

"Humph ! they must first catch me, Scipio."

"And dat won't gib 'em much trouble," he replied ; " for dis island am but a small place, and a guard has been placed all round to prevent anybody from getting away widout giving a good account ob himself."

"I have enemies," replied Luke Somerton ; " and 'tis thus they seek to ensure my destruction."

"Dey say you owed de capt'n a grudge."

"So I did," answered the other ; " but it don't follow that I must be his murderer."

"Berry true," returned Scipio ; " and I 'spose you can deny dat he fell by your hands."

"That is a question that I can answer when the proper time arrives," replied Luke Somerton ; " I can freely acknowledge that there was enmity between me and Captain Aylmer ; but who shall dare stand forward and accuse me of having slain him ?"

"A good many, I believe, Massa Somerton, wouldn't mind saying so," replied Scipio. " Dey swear you are de murderer, and I set out to gib you warning to hide yourself till you can get away from dis cursed island."

"And where am I to seek concealment ?" demanded the fugitive.

"Not far from the spot where you are now standing," exclaimed Christopher Dalton, who at that instant made his way through the thick underwood with which the speaker were surrounded.

"You have overheard us, Kit," answered Somerton, " and well it is for me that a foe instead of a friend had not intruded himself so near us. But tell me, what news do you bring that I have not already heard from the lips of this faithful negro ?'"

"I have to tell you," replied Dalton, " that matters are growing more desperate every minute, and if you don't quickly get out of the way of these land lubbers, your hours won't be long in this world."

"Are they so mad-headed as to believe that the crime was committed by me ?"

"There ain't two opinions about it, captain," answered the other ; " and, between ourselves, I rather think they found something in the house to prove that you must have been there about the time of the murder."

"What have they found ?" demanded Somerton, in a tone of alarm.

"What it is I can't exactly tell you," replied the mate, " but they seem to be quite satisfied of your guilt, and as everybody happens to be of the same opinion, I fancy that the verdict of a jury may be pretty well guessed at."

"A trial shall be risked at all events."

"Why surely, captain, you wouldn't trust yourself to a chance like that !"

"How can it be avoided ?" asked Luke, impatiently. " My escape from this island seems to be a matter of utter impossibility, and the only chance which remains, is boldly to face my foes, and dare them to the proof. That will look like a consciousness of innocence, and would go further towards changing men's opinions of me than any other course I could pursue."

"And yet," observed Dalton, " there are few who would trust themselves in the tiger's den whilst a place of refuge was to be found elsewhere."

"I know not of any place of refuge," answered Luke ; " and even if I did, it is likely I might not avail myself of it, since it would only be to prolong my existence at the expense of liberty. I should not dare to venture forth from my lurking-place, and even if I did so, it would be by stealth, and at the risk of falling into the hands of those you counsel me to avoid."

"Which would only be for a short time," replied Dalton. " I should still be at liberty to concert means for your escape from the island, and Scipio would lend a hand, I know, to get his captain out of trouble."

"Iss, dat him would," cried the negro. " Scip am a berry cunning chap, and loves Massa Somerton so well, dat him risk him own life for captain wid all de pleasure in de world."

"There, I told you he was to be depended on," exclaimed Dalton, " and if you refuse our services, it will be your own fault if any mischief comes of it. You have looked danger in the face before now, Captain Somerton, and though affairs may wear rather a blackish look at present, it don't follow that the game's up, while a couple of staunch friends remain, that don't mind going through thick and thin when their commander requires their services."

"You are an honest fellow, Dalton," cried Luke, with emotion, " and your words have almost prevailed on me to change my resolution. Scipio, too, I can fully rely on ; and with such friends I believe the difficulties that surround me may be overcome."

"Then I suppose you will no longer refuse to act by my counsel ?"

"In other words, I am to conceal myself till you can make arrangements for my escape ?"

"Exactly so."

"And where is there a place in which I may hope to elude the vigilance of my pursuers ?"

"There is a cave close by," replied Dalton, " where you may be safe."

"Will they not seek me there ?"

"No."

"Why not?"

"Because these islanders are a superstitious race," answered Dalton, "and the cave is reported to be haunted by the spirit of a hermit, who dwelt there some three centuries since, and fell by the hands of assassins."

"Hah!" cried Luke, wildly, "would you have me seek shelter in a place where murder has been committed?"

"And why not there as well as anywhere else?" demanded Dalton. "The place is more secure than any other that I can think of; and if your conscience is free about the murder of Captain Aylmer, I can see no reason why you should object to seek safety there, merely because it happened to have been the scene of an old man's death in days long gone by."

"You are right, Dalton," exclaimed Somerton, with an effort to regain his composure. "A momentary weakness seized me, but that has now passed away, and I could almost laugh at a superstition that had nearly unmanned me. Lead me then to the place you speak of, and I will patiently wait till the efforts of my friends have provided the means of escape."

"The cave is close at hand," replied Dalton; "and when once you are safely there, Scipio and I will lose no time in making preparations for your speedy departure. So follow me as stealthily as you can, lest foes should be lurking near this spot, and I promise you a temporary abode, where none of these timid islanders will venture to seek after you."

They now moved cautiously from the beaten track, and making their way through an unfrequented part of the wood, reached a spot overgrown by trees of stupendous height, in the midst of which rose a small mound, towards which Dalton led the way. At the foot of this was a small space, covered with underwood, through which they crept on hands and knees, till they reached a narrow opening, communicating with the subterranean abode in which the fugitive was to conceal himself. On the inner side of this was a roughly hewn flight of steps, which Dalton was the first to descend, and being followed by his two companions, they soon reached the cave which was the scene of so much superstitious dread among the inhabitants. The gloom which surrounded them, however, prevented any accurate notion being formed of its dimensions, but the echoes that accompanied their footsteps proved that the place was not only of considerable extent, but that it was formed of various chambers, branching from it in all directions. The scene was one indeed that might well have inspired dread in a heart less capable of fear than that of Luke Somerton, and he was about to express his determination to remain there in solitude, when the sharp click of a flint and steel was heard, and in a few seconds the cavern was illuminated by means of a lantern which Dalton had brought with him. He then led the fugitive round to show him the interior of the cavern, and having completed the survey, inquired whether he approved of the lodgings which had been rendered necessary by his present emergency.

"It must be confessed," replied Somerton, "that a worse hiding-place might have been found, yet the recollection of what has taken place within it, must render my stay here anything but pleasant."

"Then don't think anything about it," returned Dalton; "and that part of the difficulty will be overcome. All you want at present is to find a hole to shelter you in, and if we had searched the whole island over, we should not have met with another place where you would have had as good a chance of keeping out of sight."

"Oh, massa Somerton," exclaimed Scipio, "you are all right here. De dam rogues won't come to dark place like dis; and if it am a little lonely like, Scipio can stay behind to keep you company."

"You are a good, faithful fellow, Scip," returned Luke; "and if I only get clear off this cursed island, your fidelity to an unfortunate master shall not be forgotten. At present, however, I believe we must separate, for Mr. Dalton has much to do before my safety can be secured, and he may require your assistance in getting a boat to take us away from hence."

"That I certainly shall," answered Dalton; "and I should be sorry to think so meanly of Captain Somerton, as to imagine that he needs a companion for the short time he is to remain here."

"There is no occasion for it," returned Luke; "for though I felt some little reluctance to take up my abode in a place where murder has been committed, the weakness has now fled, and I feel half ashamed that it should have been witnessed by men who have fought bravely under me upon so many occasions."

"As for that, Captain Somerton," exclaimed his mate, "a man can't always command his feelings, and it must be confessed that the scene of a murder is not the most pleasant place for ——"

"For what?" demanded Somerton, as the other stammered and hesitated in his speech.

"Why, I was going to say," resumed Dalton, "for a man that is suspected to have taken away the life of a fellow-creature. I don't mean to say that you are really guilty of the crime, and as it's no business of mine, I shall believe you know nothing about it, and that people have accused you of it for no other reason than that they don't know anybody else that they can so well lay it to."

"Ay," replied Somerton, "the enmity that existed between Captain Aylmer and me is well known, and my presence in the island serves to give some colour to the accusation they have made. But they still lack proof, and as I can safely defy them to produce any, their charge must fall to the ground, even though I may always be suspected as the murderer."

"And the dagger found in the house immediately after the crime was discovered goes far towards confirming the suspicions that were formed."

"True, Dalton," answered the other; "yet another may have been in possession of that weapon, and who shall say that it was not left there purposely to throw suspicion upon me?"

"Why, that certainly may appear to be likely enough," replied the mate; "but when once people have made up their minds to anything, it's not very easy to change their opinions; besides, the people hereabouts have taken it into their heads to form a very indifferent notion of you, so that I am afraid anything you may say in contradiction of the charge will be scarcely heeded."

"Then you think my case a hopeless one in the event of their getting me into their infernal clutches?"

"Why, as a plain spoken fellow, I can't say but what you have just guessed my thoughts about it," replied Dalton; "you would have but a poor chance among them, I believe, but here you may safely defy them for some days to come, and, in the meanwhile, I shall lose no time in making preparations for your escape with as little delay as need be."

"And mustn't Scipio stay along wid massa capt'n?" asked the negro.

"I have already said your services are required elsewhere," answered Dalton. "Here you can be of no use, and Captain Somerton can hardly require such companionship as yours, when he knows the consequence of every exertion being made to effect his escape without delay."

"Mr. Dalton is right, Scipio," exclaimed Somerton, after a brief pause; "and you will therefore obey his orders with the same alacrity that you would mine. With two such zealous friends acting in my behalf, I can hardly despair; and should fortune favour my escape, I promise myself such a revenge upon these islanders as shall be remembered for many a long day afterwards."

"Let your revenge slumber awhile," said Dalton, "for there is much to be done before you will be able to accomplish your designs, and even if we should succeed in getting you on board the sloop, it will be dangerous to show yourself here while the people hold this murder in their remembrance."

"Well," replied Somerton, "for the present I shall place myself under your guidance, and will follow any course you may think proper to recommend."

"In that case all will go well," exclaimed Dalton; "and I have no doubt a few hours will serve to place you beyond the reach of danger. At any rate, Scipio and I will prove ourselves worthy of your confidence, and should we unfortunately fail in our efforts to accomplish your release, it shall not be from any lack of zeal on our part."

Shaking hands with Somerton, the mate then left the cavern with Scipio, and once more Somerton was left alone to ruminate upon the dark destiny that threatened him.

CHAPTER VIII.

Where is he? Has the deep earth swallowed him?
Or hath he melted like some airy phantom,
That shuns the approach of morn and the young sun?
Or hath he wrapped himself in Cimmerian darkness,
And passed beyond the circuit of the sight,
With things of the night's shadows.
ANON.

THE reflections that crowded upon the mind of Luke Somerton, now that he was thus left in solitude, were of the most gloomy description, and all the efforts he made to change the current of his thoughts were vain and ineffectual. The stillness that reigned within the cavern added to the heavy oppression which hung upon his soul; and, yielding to a feeling of fear that at any other time he would have laughed at, he half wished that the faithful negro had remained behind as a companion through the long, weary hours of darkness that were to succeed.

And reflection brought with it repentance for the act which the impetuosity of his revenge had hurried him into, for though his hatred towards the unfortunate victim remained undiminished, he saw the danger in which it had involved him, and the probable consequences that might follow an act which had aroused the whole island against him.

That Dalton would prove faithful to his word he had no reason to doubt, and there was even some slight chance that he might succeed in the object he had promised to accomplish; but there were many difficulties in the way, which he could not avoid seeing, and in the event of this one hope failing, it was but too certain that he must fall into the hands of his pursuers.

These thoughts, added to the legend connected with the place in which he sought refuge, oppressed his heart with a sensation of dread that no effort of his own could remove. Occasionally, too, he was startled by sounds which terror magnified into warnings of impending danger; but when he at length discovered that these were caused by the bats which had been disturbed by his intrusion upon their haunts, he tried to dissipate his alarm by pacing up and down the gloomy cavern in which he had become a voluntary prisoner.

Finding, however, that his thoughts still turned towards one point, in spite of all his efforts to banish them, he at length took the lantern which had been brought by Dalton, and commenced a search over the cave which superstition had long rendered an object of terror to the credulous. Upon examination he discovered that several other chambers were connected with the principal one on three sides, some of which retained half-perished fragments of antique furniture indicative of the uses to which the several apartments had been adapted. One had been a sleeping chamber; and another, from the rude altar that yet remained, had evidently been used as a chapel by its former unfortunate tenant. A statue of the Virgin had fallen to the ground through the decay of the pedestal upon which it had stood; paintings of various saints which had once decorated the walls were hanging in tatters from the places they had formerly been intended to adorn, and the floor was covered with huge fragments of loose stone that had fallen from the roof since the cave had ceased to become a human habitation.

As he contemplated the ruin that time had made, the thoughts of Luke Somerton recurred to the past, and the murderous deed that had there been perpetrated within that place seemed to present itself to his mind with startling reality. This brought to his recollection the crime which had lately been committed by his own hand, and uttering a groan which no effort could suppress, he was startled by hearing it repeated three or four times in accents as appalling as his own. For a moment he paused under the influence of terror, and trembling with apprehension, gazed round, expecting every moment to see some gaunt form gliding from its darksome retreat. At length reflection served to restore him to confidence, for he became convinced that the sounds were only the echoes of his own voice, and shaking off the fear, of which he was now ashamed, he quitted the ruined chapel to continue his examination of the other parts of the cavern.

Angry with himself for the superstitious dread

which at any other time he would have laughed to scorn, Luke Somerton scarcely heeded the other objects that met his view; but from all he observed there could be little doubt that the place had at one time or other been occupied by tenants far different to him whose untimely fate had rendered the spot an object of terror through four or five generations. In all probability it had been the resort of robbers, and within it might have been committed crimes that even the lapse of ages had not yet brought to light.

These reflections were at length broken in upon by a loud noise that seemed to proceed from the cavern which formed the principal part of the subterranean abode, and the sound, which appeared to be occasioned by the falling of some one down the broken steps that gave entrance to the cavern, was accompanied by what appeared to be a groan from the person who had been precipitated to the earth. Luke's first thought was, that his pursuers had traced him to his lurking-place, and his next was to seek some corner in which to hide himself till the danger had passed away. In this respect, however, his search proved unavailing, and feeling half ashamed of the terror which had taken possession of his soul, he resolved to face the danger, whatever it might be, and to die, if he needs must do so, in defending himself from those who sought to drag him before the seat of justice. Thus armed with renewed courage he looked at his weapons to see that they were all ready for immediate use, and having satisfied himself in this particular, he strode boldly forward to ascertain how far he was endangered, and take such measures as might be necessary for his own safety.

Carrying in one hand the light with which he had been supplied by the forethought of Dalton, and in the other a pistol, he hastened towards the entrance, where, sitting upon the lowest step, he saw the black form of Scipio, who was still rubbing his limbs and uttering a low wailing sound as if suffering from the bruises that had been occasioned by his abrupt descent into the cave. Upon seeing his master, however, the poor fellow's moans were changed into a cry of joy, and throwing himself at his feet he implored pardon for any alarm that he might have occasioned, and declared that anxiety for his captain's safety had alone prompted him to return, in order that he might be close at hand in case there might be need for his services. Angry at the unnecessary alarm which had been occasioned, Somerton had nearly spurned him with his foot; but remembering that the faithful fellow had been prompted by a generous zeal in his behalf, he suppressed the feeling which had well nigh urged him into the commission of an ungrateful return; he bade the negro arise, and inquired of him where he had left his companion.

"About de middle ob de wood," replied the other, still trembling with alarm. "Scipio know berry well massa left all to himself and come back to stay wid him till de morning."

"Did Mr. Dalton know of your coming, sirrah?"

"No, Scipio slip away and leave him friend to get out ob de wood himself."

"Humph!" retorted Somerton, "and I suppose you have not reflected upon the consequences of this act when you happen to meet him again?"

"Oh, yes, I have thought of all dat," answered the negro; "but Scipio don't mind anything if he o'ny stop here all night wid him old massa."

"Well, at any rate," answered Luke, "your faithful zeal disarms me of anger, and on the present occasion I will forgive your disobedience of orders in consideration of the motives that prompted you. Mr. Dalton, however, will not be so easily satisfied, and I would have you keep out of his way till he has forgotten the trick you have been foolish enough to play him."

"If he love him captain as well as Scipio does, he'll not be berry angry wid poor nigger," was the reply.

"But he had a particular service for you to perform," answered Luke Somerton, "and your desertion of him may be the means of destroying the hopes he had formed of effecting my speedy deliverance."

"Den Scipio hab done wrong arter all!"

"You have," replied Somerton; "but as it was not wilfully done, I can overlook the act in consideration of the intention that occasioned it. Mr. Dalton may not be so easily reconciled, it is true; yet I will endeavour to make peace between you as some recompense for the kindness that urged you to make this effort in my behalf."

"Dat am all I ask for," exclaimed Scipio, "and if Massa Dalton won't hear reason, I can take his kicks and cuffs widout grumbling, so long as I know dat dey am given only because de nigger know how to be grateful to de capt'n him hab served so long."

"Did he miss you soon after being left in the lurch?" inquired Luke Somerton.

"Oh, iss, berry soon."

"And returned, I suppose, to ascertain whether you were loitering on the way?"

"Iss, him did."

"But of course you contrived to keep out of his way?"

"Oh, iss, I hid behind some bushes, and heard him swearing because him couldn't find me."

"It was well for you that he was unable to do so," answered Somerton, "for he is not very particular when excited to passion; and had he seen that you intended to desert him, the chances are that he would have had his revenge by sending a brace of bullets through your head."

"So him might," replied Scipio undauntedly, "and den I should hab had de satisfaction ob knowing dat I died in trying to do my duty to Massa Somerton."

"Well," exclaimed Luke, "at all events this circumstance has served to assure me that I have one other faithful friend left, upon whom I may rely in case of any emergency that may require his services."

"Hasn't Scipio always been faithful den?" inquired the negro, earnestly.

"It must be confessed you have," replied Somerton, "but a man never really knows who are his friends till he has occasion to test them in the hour of need. You once saved my life in battle at the hazard of your own, and I now take shame to myself for not having shown my gratitude by granting the freedom you have so justly merited."

"Him want no oder freedom den dat he already hab," answered Scipio quickly. "To be near Massa Somerton am all him require, and if him die in saving de life ob him best friend he will——"

"There is no need for you to make so great a sacrifice," interrupted Somerton, "and now my desire is that you will return to the sea-coast, where Dalton may be found without much difficulty. He will doubtless find employment for you, and the surest way to secure his pardon for what has passed, will be to execute his commands with alacrity and despatch. Do this, my good fellow, and I can promise you that Mr. Dalton and you will never quarrel upon a subject that has served to prove how faithful you have been to me in the hour of my greatest need."

"Ah!" replied Scipio, "but if him passion ain't got cool he'll maybe put a pistol to my head, and den what become ob me?"

"He'll not dare do so," exclaimed Somerton, "lest he should draw down upon himself the anger of one who he knows is terrible in his wrath."

"But I heard him swear to kill me if ever we met again," replied the negro.

"Then tell him from me," answered Somerton, "that it is my desire no further notice is taken of the step you have this night taken. If you have erred, it was through your attachment to a comrade in his trouble, and any act of violence perpetrated by Mr. Dalton will not be forgotten, should I again find myself in a position to call him to an account for it."

"All dat am berry good, massa," returned the negro, "but what if him leave you to your fate when him hears de message you send?"

"Mr. Dalton is not so dishonest as to forsake me when I need his assistance," replied Somerton. "Hot words have occasionally passed between us, it is true, yet reflection brings him to his senses again, and I have always found him more ready to do a good action than a bad one to the man he has so long called his friend."

"You are right," exclaimed Scipio after a short pause. "Massa Dalton am a right sort ob chap enough, ony he dam passionate sometimes, and den Scip take care to get out ob him way till de fit work off, and he knows what him about."

"Silence, on your life, Scipio!" whispered Luke, as he grasped the negro's arm with the strength of a giant.

"What am de the matter?" demanded the other, in a voice scarcely above his breath.

"Matter enough, unless I am much mistaken," replied Somerton. "I hear footsteps round the entrance of the cave, and people are talking there, as if in consultation, before they descend in search of me."

"I hear 'em," answered Scipio, his teeth chattering, and his whole frame shaken with alarm at this new danger with which they were beset. "Dey are come to look arter poor massa; but if 'em venture down here, dey may look out for 'emselves, for Scip don't mind dying if he can ony sabe him capt'n from being taken by 'em."

"There is no occasion for you to run any risk," replied Luke Somerton. "Indeed, the best service you can do me will be to make your way out of the cavern, and seek after Mr. Dalton, who will lose no time in taking measures for my release."

"Must him leabe you den?" returned the other, in a tone of chagrin.

"If you would really save me from those men, there is no other alternative," answered Somerton.

"I shall presently be surrounded by numbers, and though one or two of the knaves may bite the dust before I have done with them, there is no doubt I shall fall into their clutches; and in that case my next lodging will be in a prison, unless my friends find means to extricate me from their hands."

"It shall be done," exclaimed Scipio; "and if I hab de good luck to find Massa Dalton, we'll show dese rascal people what it am to come and disturb gennelmans when dey ——"

"Hush!" interrupted Somerton. "I hear them beginning to descend the steps, and in a few moments they will be here. Stand out of sight, and when all have come down, slip out of the place, and make the best of your way towards the beach, where I have no doubt you will find Mr. Dalton, and, perhaps, three or four more of our crew. Be speedy, good fellow, and all may yet be well."

Scipio made no reply, for the intruders were now making their way down the entrance; and, standing on one side, he suffered the whole party to assemble in the cave, without making any attempt to get out of it himself. At last, seeing that the man who bore a torch was approaching the spot to which Somerton retired, the faithful negro sprung forward, and having knocked the light out of the fellow's hand, sprang up the steps, and was on his way through the wood before any one had time to pursue him. Great was the consternation at finding themselves thus involved in darkness; and as they tried to grope their way from a place of such evil repute, one of them, with an oath, demanded why the torch had been extinguished at such a moment as that.

"How could it be helped, Dick?" returned the man to whom these words had been addressed, "when the devil, or some of his imps, came and knocked the light out of my hand before I was aware that any one was here beside ourselves and the fellow we are looking after?"

"What makes you think it was the devil, Hal?" asked the first speaker.

"Because he was black," returned the other.

"And I can answer for it," added a third party, "that he had a pair of horns upon his head, half as long as my arm."

"Then let's get out of this infernal place as soon as we can," squeaked out another of the pursuers, "for I was all along against coming here; and we shall smart severely for coming to a place that the old gentleman has made his home."

"Aye," exclaimed Dick, "let's leave this infernal cavern, and make the best of our way home again."

"And get laughed at for our pains," cried Hal, with a contemptuous sneer.

"People may laugh at us as much as they please," returned Dick; "but if they want to catch Luke Somerton, they may come and do it themselves. I never had a fancy for groping about in these dark, under-ground places; and hang me if I'll stop in a cave where two out of our party are ready to swear that they've had a sight of Beelzebub."

"They are only cowards that say so," answered Hal; "and, for my own part, I'm not inclined to believe that his infernal majesty has had anything at all to do with it. We were too much frightened at the moment to notice who it was that

knocked the light out of my hand ; but for my own part, I have no doubt it was Luke Somerton himself, who found he had no other way to escape from us."

"Then no doubt he is still lurking near us," squeaked the before-mentioned personage, "and if so he is ready to pounce upon us, and put every soul to death."

"We'll soon know all about that," replied Hal ; "for, luckily, I didn't come unprovided with a tinder-box and matches, so that we may soon have a light to assist us in searching for the fellow we have come after."

Whilst thus speaking he occupied himself in striking a light with his flint and steel, and having once more kindled the torch, he raised it high above his head, in order to see whether the fugitive was anywhere near them.

"I'll be bound we soon have him fast enough," he exclaimed, with a chuckle ; "and then the reward that tempted us to come on this errand will be ours. So now follow me, all those who are not afraid, and in a few moments Luke Somerton will be in our hands."

"Luke Somerton now stands before you," vociferated the fugitive, in a voice of thunder, as he stepped forth from his place of concealment. "You start back with amazement, gentlemen, as if my very appearance brought terror with it, yet surely one man is not much to fear, when so many have taken the trouble to come and capture him."

"In the name of her majesty, Queen Anne, I command you to surrender yourself our prisoner," exclaimed Hal, in dismay, as he perceived that all his companions had shrunk back in terror.

"I will surrender myself to no man whilst strength remains to me, or I have arms to use in my own defence," answered Somerton, resolutely. "You have hunted me here like a beast of prey, but it now remains to be seen whether there is one here who will madly risk his life in attempting to capture a man against whom no crime has been proved."

"But you are charged with having committed a murder," returned Hal, "and, if innocent of the foul deed, there can be no fear but you will be speedily set at liberty again."

"What ! when I have foes that are ready to swear anything to get my neck into a halter ?"

"I know nothing about enemies, Luke Somerton," answered the other ; "but if you are guiltless of this crime there can be no doubt that you will be set at liberty after an examination or two. The magistrates will at any rate act fairly, since they are sworn to do justice between all parties."

"I shall not place my trust in them," replied Somerton ; "and the man that steps forward to lay hands upon me will die for his temerity."

"Are you then determined to commit another murder ?" exclaimed Dick.

"Who is there that dares say I have committed one already ?" demanded Luke, furiously. "A man, it seems, has been slain, and, for lack of some other person to throw the blame upon, you must needs fix upon me as the only person that could have been guilty of so heinous an offence."

"And if we have done so," replied Hal, "it is because we all know that you had a long standing quarrel with Captain Aylmer, and as both happened to be in the island at the time there is good reason to believe that he fell by your hands."

"So," returned Somerton, "upon no better proof

than that you expect me to surrender myself your prisoner, though with every chance that I should be made a sacrifice to your sanguinary laws!"

"We have been sent here to do our duty," exclaimed Hal, "and if my comrades here will only stand by me I will run the risk of being made the victim of your fury."

"You had better let him alone," squeaked the cowardly loon who had spoken before. "Don't you see, Hal, that he's armed to the very teeth, and though it may all be very fine to talk about doing one's duty, I, for one, don't feel inclined to lose my life in an affair that I have nothing at all to do with."

"What would you do then?" inquired Hal.

"Why," replied the other, "I would advise you to make the best of your way from this place, and if that proposition don't happen to come up to your own notions, I shall take myself off, and leave you to settle this matter between you in the best way you can."

"Then mark me, Simon Stitchley," exclaimed Hal, in a tone of resolution, "and remember that I was never more earnest in my life than in what I am now saying. We all came here together in search of Luke Somerton who now stands before us, and I for one am determined either to take him or lose my life in the attempt. There shall be no one suffered to sneak off because a little danger happens to stare us in the face, and if any man dares to leave this cave before we all go together I'll send a bullet through his body, and run the risk of any consequences that may afterwards follow."

This speech had a powerful effect upon Simon, who now took care to ensconce himself behind three or four of his companions, and having thus made himself tolerably safe, he exclaimed :—

"You think me a coward, Hal; but I'd have you to know that I'm as brave as those that vapour about their own courage. Remember, I'm kept here against my own will, and if there's law in the land, I'll make all those smart for it that have taken any part in preventing my getting out of danger."

"He's quite right in what he says," interposed Peter Titmouse, the constable, "and I join with him in opinion that every man ought to be allowed to go away whenever he thinks proper."

"You're a very pretty sort of fellow for a constable," exclaimed Dick, "and for aught that I can see we had better be without you and Simon than be troubled any longer with your company."

"They shall remain where they are, if it's only to punish them," replied Hal; "and as I happen to know what the duty of a constable is, I call upon Peter Titmouse to seize upon Luke Somerton and convey him to a place of safety, where he may remain till the magistrates have appointed a time for the examination."

"And I say," exclaimed Luke, "that if the trembling caitiff approaches me nearer but by another foot, it will be with a certainty of perishing as a punishment for his own folly."

"You hear him, my friends," cried Peter; "and now I ask you if it would not be the act of a madman to seize upon a villain that we all believe to have been guilty of one murder, and who, no doubt, is quite ready to commit another."

"Fool!" exclaimed Somerton, "another such speech as that will provoke me to take even such a worthless life as your own. I have told you I know nothing of the crime laid to my charge, and for that reason I have refused to surrender myself up to those who have been employed to pursue me."

"But if you are really innocent," said Hal, "why did you seek shelter in this place, which few people in the island have ventured to enter in consequence of certain reports, that it is the haunt of some unearthly visitant?"

"I am not bound to answer your questions," replied Somerton; "but to satisfy you upon that point I will at once frankly admit that I heard the rumours that had been raised to my prejudice, and knowing the hatred in which my name is held, I intended to have escaped from the island as the only means of avoiding the danger I was threatened with. Some friends told me that a pursuit had already commenced, and as no time was to be lost, I sought a shelter in this cavern till they could make arrangements for my speedy departure."

"Which we have arrived just in time to prevent," observed Hal, with a sneer.

"I don't know that," replied Luke; "for you have heard my determination, and self-preservation will often drive a man to extremities sorely against his will. Fortunately, I am well provided with arms, and sooner would I perish among you in open strife, than yield myself a prisoner till every hope of overcoming my foes has failed."

"You will feel no remorse then," observed Dick, "in shedding the blood of those who have been sent against you by the commands of those that they dare not disobey?"

"It is in vain to reason with a desperate man," replied Luke Somerton; "for any fate is preferable to that of the gibbet; and rather than yield myself up to such a doom, I will meet death from those who have been sent to capture me."

"And rather than return like cowards," exclaimed Hal, "I will myself arrest you in spite of the threats that have been held out."

"Let me caution you to do no such thing," replied Somerton," lest your rashness should drive me to an act that I would fain avoid. I wish to spare myself the crime of shedding blood; but if once you drive me to desperation the consequences must be upon yourself, and those who are mad enough to follow your example."

"It shall be tried, at all events," exclaimed Hal, and springing suddenly forward he seized upon Luke Somerton before he could throw himself upon his guard, and, exerting all his strength, endeavoured to throw him upon the ground in order that he might be the more easily bound. This, however, was no easy matter, for Luke was possessed of almost a giant's power, and recovering from the surprise into which he had been thrown a fearful struggle ensued, during which the weapon he grasped in his hand was discharged, though fortunately without injuring any of those who were watching the same. One source of their alarm being thus removed, three or four of the men, headed by Dick, now rushed to the assistance of their comrade, and, being provided with cords, they soon bound his limbs so firmly, that there was no longer any danger to be apprehended from his violence. The next care was to remove from him all the weapons with which he had armed himself, and this having been done he was assisted to rise from the ground preparatory to being removed from the cave, near the entrance of which a vehicle had been left to convey him from the place in the event of his being found there. Yet, even bound as he was, the strength of Luke Somerton enabled him to resist all the efforts of those who captured him, and throwing himself with his back against the wall, he exclaimed:—

"Cowards! had my arms but been free, I would yet hurl upon you such terrible revenge for this, that the remembrance should not die away for many generations to come. You have made me your prisoner, it is true, but stronger bonds than these have I broken ere now, and should fortune again favour me, you may look for just as much mercy as I have myself to expect from the bloodhounds that are hunting me to death."

"You forget," returned Hal, "that your weapons are now in our possession, and should I see any reason to believe that you are likely to release yourself I should not hesitate to lay you dead at my feet with the contents of one of your weapons."

"Do it at once then," exclaimed Luke Somerton, "and thus release me from a life that is now a burthen to me. Pour forth my blood, I charge you, and my latest breath shall be uttered in blessings upon you for the deed."

"I have nothing to do with shedding your blood unless my own safety depended upon it," replied Hal, "and having succeeded in making you our prisoner we have only got to take you to a place where you will be kept in secure custody. It will then be for the magistrates to inquire into the evidence your accusers have to bring against you, and if that ain't strong enough, why, of course, they will set you at liberty, and there will be an end of the matter."

"I'm afraid the matter would not rest there," cried Simon Stitchley, "for Luke ain't a chap to forget such matters as these, and if he should happen to get his liberty again it would be a bad day for all who have had any share in making him a prisoner."

"You are both a fool and a coward, Simon," exclaimed one of the men, "for if he should be lucky enough to escape the gibbet he'll be glad to get away from this place without waiting to revenge himself upon any of us."

"Release me now," cried Somerton, "and I promise you all safety on condition that you will not interfere to prevent my reaching the sea coast."

"If you were to offer me five hundred pounds I would not listen to such a proposal," replied Hal. "The truth would soon be known, and then a very pretty example would be made of us as a warning to all other people not to forget their duty. So resign yourself to your fate, Master Somerton, and if you go quietly with us we will try and finish this affair with as little annoyance to yourself as possible."

"It's easy to talk to a man that's bound as I am about resigning himself to his fate," answered Luke Somerton, "but, if I had only one arm free to strike a blow for my deliverance, there's not a man among you but should repent the hour that brought him into my presence. However, it's my own fault for not defending myself just now when I had my liberty, and since I have brought it all upon myself, you may do with me as you please without any fear of my offering any resistance."

With that he quietly resigned himself into their hands, and having been led up the steps which gave egress from the cave, he was conducted to the spot where a vehicle stood in readiness, and having been placed in this the cavalcade set forward towards the nearest town.

CHAPTER IX.

WHEN Scipio left the cave in which Luke Somerton had sought for refuge, he took an obscure path which it seemed likely would assist in aiding the secrecy of his errand, and following this for a distance of rather more than half a mile, he at last came to a bye road, which he rightly conjectured would bring him to the sea coast on that side of the island that it was his present object to visit. On reaching the shore, however, nothing was to be seen of Dalton or the crew, and as it was necessary to find some of them without delay, he was returning with all possible haste, when the mate and three or four of the sailors made their appearance at no great distance off, and in a brief space of time he was surrounded by his companions and questioned as to what news he had to tell of their captain.

"Speak quickly, dog, and that, too, without equivocation," exclaimed Dalton, furiously, "or I shall presently find means to punish you for the scurvy trick you played when I was left alone to finish this business by myself as I best could."

"What scurvy trick do Massa Dalton mean?" cried the negro, with affected surprise.

"Rascal!" exclaimed the mate, "didn't you run away from me when your services were most needed?—and yet you now have the impudence to feign ignorance of having given me any cause for anger."

"Him only go back to poor capt'n," answered Scipio. "De cave am d—d dark and dismal place, so him run back to Massa Somerton to see if he was in want of any one to keep him company."

"And I was to be left to get through my own task as well as I could."

"Don't be angry wid poor nigger, and him promise nebber to do so any more," supplicated the other.

"Well," replied Dalton, "for the present I shall let you off better than you deserve, but let this be a warning to you never to serve me such a trick again unless you would have every bone in your body broken. For this once you will escape; so tell me, sirrah, where you have left the captain."

"In de cavern, ob course."

"And was he safe there when you came away?"

"Iss, him quite safe."

"Have you met with no obstruction in your passage to this place?"

"Obstruction! What am dat?"

"I mean, have you seen any persons during your progress who might have been in pursuit of our friend?"

"No."

"And round the neighbourhood of the cave all seems to be as I left it about an hour ago?"

"Exactly."

"Did you come direct from there?" asked Dalton, "or come a further way round in order to avoid meeting with any persons that might be out that way in pursuit of him ?"

" I came a bye-path," replied Scipio, "but was not berry long on my journey."

" Nor fell in with any one, I suppose ?"

" Dat him certain'y didn't."

" That is strange, too," said Dalton, thoughtfully, "for a great many parties have distributed themselves over every part of the island, and I myself saw about a dozen fellows who were making their way towards the wood, under an idea that they would be sure to fall in with him there."

" Are you sure, sir," asked Harry Hawser, one of the sailors, " that they were looking after the captain ?"

" Of course I am," replied Dalton, "for they stopped near the place where I had hid myself behind some bushes, and I could distinctly hear every word they uttered upon the subject of their errand."

" They spoke of the skipper, then ?"

" Ay, and were determined to find him if he had not already made his escape from the Isle of Man. This rascally fellow, Scipio, has only just come from the cave, and yet he declares that no one had arrived there when he came away."

" Ah !" exclaimed the negro, " dat was because him afraid Massa Dalton shoot him for running away as dey were going to de sea-shore."

" Dog !" cried Dalton, furiously, " if you trifle with me, it will be at the hazard of your own life ; but a few moments since you declared that you had not seen anybody in search of our commander, and yet now you have as good as confessed that there is some danger we are not yet acquainted with."

" Forgive me, Massa Dalton," exclaimed Scipio, falling upon his knees in terror, " and you shall know all about what dey hab been doing since you left de cave."

" Then speak quickly," returned the mate, fiercely, " for if you delay but another half minute it will be at the cost of your worthless life ! Out with it, villain, and say if Luke Somerton has had the misfortune to fall into the hands of his persecutors ?"

" He has, indeed," answered the trembling negro.

" Hah ! and you have been all this time without telling me of it."

" Dat was because poor Scipio thought Massa Dalton would kill him in his passion."

" And if I had done so," replied the mate, " it would have been no more than you richly merit. Your captain has fallen into the toils of the enemy, and I suppose no effort of ours will save him from the doom these people will pass upon him."

" Shall I shoot him, your honour ?" demanded Harry Hawser. " The snivelling lubber deserves nothing better, and when he's been sarved out for what he's done, we can go and see if something mayn't be tried for getting the captain out of limbo."

" No, no, Harry, we'll not shed his blood just yet," answered Dalton, " for we have enough trouble on our hands already, without bringing more upon ourselves by the murder of that black rascal. He shall go back with us to the cave, and if nothing can be done to save our captain's life,

we'll hold a court martial on Scipio, and if the majority should happen to decide against him, we'll take him on board the sloop, and hang him up at the yardarm, as a punishment for what he has done."

" Poor Scipio warn't nebber born to be hanged," cried the trembling negro.

" We shall see that if matters don't turn out better than they seem likely to do at present," answered Dalton, gloomily.

" There's more ways of killing a dog besides hanging him," interposed Harry Hawser. " A brace of bullets would do the job well enough, or, if that should be objected to, we carry knives about with us, so that we can accommodate the black rascal in any way he likes best."

" Scipio don't want to be 'commodated any how," replied the poor fellow ; " and if it am all de same to de gentlemans, he would rather not die till he can't help it."

" I can take your word for that, blackee," exclaimed Harry ; " but when people do wrong, they must take the consequences without grumbling."

" But I habn't done wrong, as I know of."

" Ah !" growled the sailor, " that's just where the difference of opinion between us lies. Now I mean to say that the man that deserts his captain when his services are wanted deserves death ; and if Mr. Dalton only gives the word, he shall see that I can obey his commands better than you did."

" I didn't desert de capt'n," replied Scipio.

" How come you to leave him, then, when them rascally land lubbers went to take him away ?"

" He told me to come," answered the negro, " or I shouldn't hab left him. De capt'n thought I should be in time to bring Massa Dalton and some o' de crew, and den we might hab rescued him widout much trouble."

" Well," said the mate, " I begin to think the fellow is not so very much to blame after all, if he followed the commands of our captain. So far there may be some little excuse for him ; but I shall have something else to say to him after a bit, when we come to talk about his slipping away from me, when I thought he was following close at my heels, like a dog as he is."

" I only did it," replied Scipio, " 'cause I wanted to get back to Massa Somerton, and keep him comp'ny in de dark cave. I'd ha' fought for him only he wouldn't let me ; and when de people had all got down into de place, I crept out ob it, and came here to tell you what had happened."

" We shall know the truth about that by-and-bye, when we see Captain Somerton," observed the mate ; " and if matters turn out as you say, I may perhaps be your friend, and save you from the punishment you have been threatened with. Of course you were bound to obey the commands of your leader, and if he only clears you in that respect, you may yet live to make older bones than I thought for a little while ago."

" You'll find I hab spoken nothing but de truth," answered Scipio, a little revived at hearing these words of consolation.

" That remains to be proved," exclaimed Mr. Dalton ; " so now tell me, Scipio, how many men there were that went to take him ?"

" Can't say 'xactly," replied the negro, " because

I knock'd de light out when dey got down into de cavern; but I 'spose dere might be somewhere about a dozen on 'em in all."

"You think there were no more than a dozen?"

"Dereabouts, Massa Dalton."

"We could easily have overcome them if we had happened to have been there at the time," observed the mate to his comrades. "We should have mustered seven to their twelve, at any rate, and we have fought against greater odds than that before now."

"And perhaps it ain't too late to do it as it is," exclaimed Harry Hawser. "The captain, I dare say, will keep 'em in parley for a little while to give us a chance of going to his assistance, and, if we only have the good luck to fall in with the land-lubbers, we'll teach 'em what it is to make prisoners of men only because they chance to have set foot upon shore for a little while."

"I'm afraid there's not much likelihood of falling in with them," returned Dalton; "but, as the captain's life and liberty may depend upon it, we'll go and see whether there's any good to be done. At any rate, in such a cause as this, I can rely upon every man here present doing his best, and let it be remembered, that if we should get into close quarters with the enemy, we must not spare any of them, or we know what will be the consequence."

"Oh, never fear but we'll serve 'em out for what they've done to our leader," replied Harry Hawser. "A dozen cowardly loons such as them won't give us much trouble, I should think, and if we only set the captain at liberty, and give him an opportunity of fighting on our side, it's a very poor chance that the others will have of returning home to tell what has happened."

"Are all willing to follow me?" demanded Dalton; "and to lose their own lives rather than leave their gallant captain to his fate?"

"Ay, ay, sir," replied every voice.

"You now see, Mr. Dalton, what you've got to depend upon," exclaimed Hawser; "and as they've given their words to go with us, you may depend on it they'll stand by you to the very last."

"Then let us lose no more time in parleying upon the matter," returned the mate, "for even a moment may be of the greatest consequence, and delay at a time like this might prove fatal to the cause we have engaged in. So now let the strictest silence be kept amongst you, lest spies should be watching us; and do you, Scipio, act the part of our guide, and see that you conduct us to the cavern with as much despatch as possible."

All being now in readiness, the negro commenced retracing his steps, and having conducted them to the skirts of the wood he sought out the path he had taken not long before, and which would lead them, without much fear of discovery, to the place they were in quest of. Fortunately, this was done with very little difficulty, but the progress they made was necessarily slow, and several times during their passage through the intricacies of the way, they were obliged to pause and examine the paths where they diverged in various directions, lest they should happen to take one that might lead them far from the place it was their present object to visit. Eventually, however, they succeeded in reaching a spot that was well remembered by both Dalton and Scipio, and as no further doubt re-mained to perplex them, they were enabled to pursue their way with increased speed, and a few minutes served to bring them to the entrance of the cave, where they paused to listen if any sound might give them notice of what was doing within.

"All seems as silent as the grave," whispered Dalton to his companions; "and I begin to fear our captain has fallen into the hands of those that will keep him safely in spite of any efforts we may make to get him out of their infernal clutches."

"I'm afraid it's all over with him indeed," muttered Harry Hawser; "but we musn't let him perish either while there's a chance of cheating the gallows of a victim. There are some stout hearts among us, I believe, and, with weapons in our hands, we may force the prison doors, and carry him off in triumph, if we only set about it quickly."

"Before we do that," returned Dalton, "I think we had better search the cavern to see whether he has really been taken away."

"Massa Somerton can't be here," Scipio ventured to observe, "or we should have heard something ob him before this time."

"Who asked you for an opinion, you rascally black nigger?" demanded Hawser, peremptorily. "Mayn't he have routed the fellows that came to take him, and have been wounded in the skirmish, so that he can't raise a signal of distress?"

"It will be worth while satisfying ourselves upon the point, at any rate," said Dalton; "and so I and Scipio will go down and see if the place is clear or not."

"See!" exclaimed Harry, contemptuously; "why, the place is as dark as pitch, and there ain't one among us that's got the means of striking a light."

"But Scipio and I happen to have been down there before," replied the mate; "and if we can't see much, we can grope our way about sufficiently well to convince ourselves whether anybody is in the cavern. If Captain Somerton is there, we'll save him yet, and if they have taken him away—and I fear they have—we must think of some other plan for his rescue, and act upon it with promptitude. So here goes to be the first to enter, and do you, Scipio, keep close beside me, in case of a surprise, that we may give the fellows a warmer reception than they expect."

Upon this he began to descend the steps, followed by the negro, and having reached the bottom, they paused for a few seconds in order to convince themselves whether any one remained behind. All, however, was silent, and as the impenetrable darkness which surrounded them rendered it impossible to examine the dreary vault, they were obliged to content themselves by groping through a portion of it to ascertain if Somerton had fallen in the fray, and then, ascending the steps, they once more joined their anxiously expectant comrades.

"Well, sir, what news do you bring us?" demanded Hawser. "No one there, I suppose; and of course our only plan now is to go and release him from prison by force of arms."

"Dark as the place is, it is impossible to make any satisfactory report," answered Dalton. "The captain may have lost his life against the numbers that were opposed to him, and in that case I should suppose they have left his body behind in the cavern, to be removed at some other opportunity."

"Only let it turn out that they've killed him,"

exclaimed Harry Hawser, "and I'll be revenged upon 'em, if I have to do it single handed."

"It shall be bitterly revenged," answered Dalton ; "but we must first learn if our surmises are correct, and, when that is done, we will ascertain the names of those that were sent against him, that our vengeance may light upon the guilty parties."

"The governor is the man we have most to look to," replied Harry, "and I propose that we make an attack upon his house, and burn it to the ground."

"Let us wait, at least, till we know what has become of our captain," answered Dalton. "He may have fallen into their hands as a prisoner, and, if so, any act of violence committed by us would only serve to make his enemies the more inveterate against him."

"Would you have us leave him to his fate, then ?"

"By no means, Harry," replied the mate. "Something must, doubtless, be done to rescue him ; but we should first learn what they have done with their prisoner, and then take measures accordingly. For my own part, I am ready to die in any attempt to serve him, but we must not act rashly, lest our over zeal in his behalf should happen to throw him still more under the fury of his enemies."

"Well, your advice is generally pretty good, sir," returned the sailor, "and so we'll obey your commands, whatever they may be ; yet, for all that, I can't help thinking that we ought to surprise the foe, and not give 'em a chance of making preparations to defeat the plans we may form for the captain's release."

"I would rather see his daughter, Louisa Somerton, before we do anything else," replied the mate ; "they say she is a girl of spirit, and, as woman's wit is very often the best, we'll hear what she has to say about it, and then shape our course accordingly."

"Where does she live ?" asked Hawser.

"At her uncle's, James Somerton, who, for years past, has been regarded by the whole neighbourhood as her father," replied Dalton.

"And you will see her alone, I suppose ?"

"Yes," answered the other, "for it would only alarm her if we were all to go there together. But see, the daylight is now coming on fast, which will enable us to explore the cavern more carefully ; and, when we have satisfied ourselves whether Somerton is there or not, we can shape our course accordingly."

In accordance with this suggestion, they waited till the dawn had advanced sufficiently for their purpose, and then proceeded to the subterraneous retreat, which they thoroughly searched ; but, as the reader may have anticipated, without making any discovery to clear up their doubts respecting Luke Somerton. The next step, therefore, was to see Louisa, and consult her upon the subject, for which purpose Dalton quitted his companions, and betook himself to the house of her uncle.

CHAPTER X.

EVIL news flies apace, and never was the old saying more truly illustrated than in the instance of Luke Somerton's arrest ; for, no sooner was it known in the neighbourhood that he was in the clutches of the law, than some good-natured people hastened to the house of James Somerton to convey the intelligence of the capture to his relatives. Indeed, there seemed to be an anxious struggle among them for precedence in this respect, for several of them set out for his house as soon as the arrest was made known, and it was not without much unusual exertion that Peter Titmouse distanced all his competitors in the race, and reached the door, at which he knocked with a violence that startled the inmates, who, after long watching through a great part of the night, were about retiring to rest.

"Who's there ?" demanded James Somerton from within.

"'Tis I, Peter Titmouse," replied the constable, with some little difficulty, for he was almost exhausted with the speed he had made, and stood panting at the door, which was not opened so speedily as he wished.

"What want you here, at this late hour of the night ?" demanded the person from within.

"Give me admission, and you shall soon know."

"I will open to no man, unless he first answers my inquiries," replied James Somerton. "Tell me your message quickly, or leave the place, and return in the morning, when I may be more disposed to hear your idle prattle."

"Ah, Master Somerton," answered the constable, "it is no idle prattle this time, I can assure you. The devil has been busy to-night, and you'll be sorry for it afterwards, if I don't come in and tell you what has happened."

"What has happened," demanded the other, "that I can be at all interested in ?"

"Your brother, Luke Somerton ——"

"Hah ! what of him ?"

"Has been taken prisoner, and is now in gaol on a charge of murder."

In an instant the chain and bolts were removed by the trembling hands of the person within, and, the door being thrown open, Peter Titmouse entered the house.

"Now," exclaimed James, as he closed the door to prevent the admission of any other persons, "what wild news is this you come to tell me ? My brother, you say, is arrested on a charge of murder—tell me who has been slain, fellow, and keep me no longer in this terrible suspense."

"Why, you have heard, I suppose, that Captain Aylmer has been assassinated ?"

"I have," replied James ; "and you have now come to tell me that there are people who dare accuse my brother of having committed the foul deed ?"

"It is indeed said so," replied Titmouse ; "and, what's more, I'm afraid there's no doubt that the charge will be fully proved against him."

"He is innocent—he is innocent !" cried Louisa, rushing forward as these words were uttered. "This is a false accusation, brought against him by his worst enemies, and he will yet be enabled to hurl back the accursed charge upon those who have made it."

"I'm sorry to be the bearer of bad news," answered Peter Titmouse, with a hypocritical attempt to squeeze out a few tears ; "but all the people agree in saying that he committed the murder, and what everybody says, you know, must be true."

"In the present instance," replied James Somerton, "I have sufficient reason to believe that what everybody says is utterly false. My brother has many enemies in this island, and what so easy as to accuse him of this murder, since all he may say in vindication of himself will not be heeded."

"Yet his persecutors shall be foiled," cried Louisa; "for there are some persons in this island who are not to be imposed upon by the voice of slander, and he has a daughter who will never rest till she has saved him from the fate to which they would doom him."

"I'm afraid all your trouble will be thrown away," replied the constable; "for it is well known that he had an old grudge against Captain Aylmer, and his arrival only a few hours before this murder was committed must convince every one that it was perpetrated by no other person than him. Besides, Captain Aylmer was much respected by all else in the place, and I'm sure there's no one but would have laid down his life in his service, instead of committing violence against him."

"That is only your own opinion," exclaimed James Somerton; "and it may so happen that in a few hours I shall be able to prove that there were others who are more likely than my brother to have committed the atrocious act that malignity has brought against him."

"That I doubt," replied Titmouse, "for, as I said before, there is not another person in the place that would have been guilty of such a deed."

"Villain," cried James Somerton, furiously, "do you persist in accusing a person against whom, at present, no proof can be brought?"

"Nay, you are getting in a passion," returned the constable, with a provoking coolness, "and after all, you rather owe me thanks than reproaches for having taken the trouble to come and tell you what has happened."

"Aye," replied the other, bitterly; "and I have no doubt the errand was a very pleasing one, since it enabled you to gloat upon the misery it has thus been in your power to inflict upon the relations of the accused person. But your task is now accomplished, and I would now have you depart with as little delay as possible, or passion may so far overpower my reason as to impel me to inflict an exemplary punishment upon the paltry wretch who can thus exult in the pain his venom causes."

"Would you turn me out of the house?" demanded Titmouse violently.

"Aye," answered Somerton, "or it is likely I may proceed to extremities, which I have no wish to do if it can be avoided."

"Have a care how you commit any violence," replied the constable with a sneer; "for I hear people just outside your door, and if I raise an alarm, they will soon break in to my rescue."

"Who are they?" cried Louisa, whose ear by this time had distinctly caught the sounds to which he alluded.

"Only some friends of mine," he replied, "who have come to bring you the same intelligence that I did. But they have been disappointed, for you and Mr. Somerton have already heard all they can tell from me."

"And they, like yourself," exclaimed James Somerton, "were anxious to be the first to communicate news that they must have been aware would bring sorrow and wailing to this house."

"Why, the fact is," replied the constable, "you must have heard it from somebody, and I thought the pleasure of first breaking it might as well be mine as anybody else's."

"Then now," said the other, fiercely, "having gratified your malignity to your heart's content, you will please to quit my house without the delay of another minute. Leave me, wretch, or my hands will presently be defiled with your blood."

"What!" shouted Peter Titmouse, loud enough to be heard by those without, "would you be guilty of the same crime that is likely to bring your brother to the gallows? But I caution you to beware how you lay hands upon me, for there are friends near ready to save me from violence, and if you approach another step near me, I'll raise a cry of murder, and bring yonder people to my assistance."

"They will not be in time to save you," answered James Somerton; "and, therefore, do I once more warn you to leave me, for, by the Heaven that is above us, I will no longer endure the presence of a wretch who has dared to exult in the misery his cruel announcement has caused to me and this hapless girl."

"Oh, in mercy, do not involve yourself in trouble by an act of violence," cried Louisa, in accents of the greatest terror. "Without your aid, my father must perish by a death of shame, and his wretched child will be left to linger out a miserable existence, cursing the hour of her birth, and invoking death as the only means of escaping from thoughts that are too horrible even for anticipation."

"For your sake, Louisa," he replied, "I will endeavour to control the feelings which this man's conduct has given rise to." Then addressing himself to the constable, he added, "At the intercession of my niece, you will be permitted to retire from this house without the punishment I intended to inflict. Go, fellow, rejoin your companions, who are waiting without, and tell them I have already heard all that they are so anxious to communicate, and that, so far from being overcome by the misfortunes which have befallen my persecuted brother, I am resolved to use every effort in his behalf, and have every reason to hope that I shall succeed in finding means to save him from the fate to which his bloodthirsty foes would consign him."

"Ah!" exclaimed Peter, "I dare say you think it's easy enough to save him, but murder is a crime that's never pardoned, and as he's certain to be found guilty, I would advise you and this young woman to make up your minds for the worst?"

"Your advice is neither needed, nor will it be attended to by those to whom it has been proffered," answered James Somerton. "I have already warned you to quit our presence without delay, and unless you instantly obey my orders, your life may pay the forfeit of your temerity."

"Oh, if that's the case, I'm your very humble servant," replied Peter Titmouse, as he crept cautiously towards the door. "I came here to do what I thought was a good-natured act; but it seems my kindness is thrown away, and as I don't wish to be made the sacrifice of your fury, I shall take my leave, though it is likely I may have to pay you another visit on a very different errand to the present one."

While he spoke the door was opened by James Somerton, whose impatience was scarcely to be controlled ; and as the constable still lingered, with the evident intention of saying something more, a little force was applied to thrust him forth, and the door being instantly closed and secured, James hastened to the assistance of his niece, whose terror had, by this time, nearly overpowered her.

"My dear Louisa," he exclaimed, "I had expected more fortitude from you at a moment when firmness is so necessary for the furtherance of our plans in your father's behalf. I am, myself, prepared to make a bold effort to save him ; but if you yield yourself up to sorrow, any attempt must prove unavailing, and he will surely perish."

"The weakness is but momentary," replied Louisa, rousing herself from the torpor into which she had nearly fallen, "and I will yet prove myself worthy the favourable opinion you had formed of me. The daughter of Luke Somerton can be courageous when necessity requires her exertions, and from this moment she will, under your directions, devote herself to the task of saving her father from an ignominious death."

"Why, that is well said, my girl," exclaimed the other, "and having thus roused you to a sense of your duty, I believe we may almost reckon ourselves certain of ultimate success."

"Does my father's safety, then, so much depend upon me ?" she asked.

"All rests with you," answered James Somerton ; "but it yet remains to be seen whether you will have courage enough to perform the task I have projected."

"Oh, never fear it, dear uncle," she exclaimed earnestly, "I have never yet shrunk from my duty, and surely when a father's life is in the balance, I shall not weakly hesitate, even were his safety to be purchased at the hazard of my own existence."

"There is no such hazard in my proposition," replied her uncle, "nor, perhaps, is the difficulty so great as I imagined. In the morning we will ask permission to see the prisoner, and having thus let him see that he is not forgotten in his captivity, you must prepare yourself for a journey to seek an interview with one who alone can save my brother's life."

"Who is it I am to see ?" demanded Louisa.

"No less a personage than our gracious sovereign, Queen Anne."

"Oh! then my journey is to London."

"Nay, the distance you will have to travel is not so great as that," replied James Somerton. "I have ascertained that her majesty is now on a royal progress through England, and about this time she is expected to visit Whitehaven, which lies on the coast nearly opposite this island. Thither you must repair, and, at the feet of her majesty, implore that pardon which it is one of her best privileges to bestow."

"Your words, dear uncle, inspire me with hope," cried Louisa. "I feel that my father may, indeed, yet be saved ; but I would ask how a poor and unfriended girl, like myself, is to obtain an audience with the queen of England."

"More easily than you imagine, my child," re-

plied her uncle, "for her majesty is gracious and condescending to even the humblest of her subjects, and will not turn a deaf ear to one who comes upon such a mission as yours. She will enter the town in state, and if you throw yourself at her feet and implore mercy for an unfortunate parent, I feel assured your journey to Whitehaven will not have been made in vain."

"It shall be tried, were the task ten thousand times more difficult than you have proposed," answered Louisa. "The news of my father's arrest had filled my bosom with despair, but your words have inspired me with hope, and no efforts of mine shall be wanting to carry the design into effect. But delay may prove fatal to us, and I would not lose a single instant in repairing to the place where I am to seek this interview with her gracious majesty."

"There is no need for your immediate departure," replied James Somerton, "because the queen is not expected to arrive at Whiteheaven till tomorrow evening ; besides, it would be better to see your father previous to undertaking the mission, and as there will be no great difficulty in obtaining an interview, we will repair to his prison at an early hour, and cheer him with the assurance that every effort is being made to procure his deliverance from captivity."

"Yet, should my mission fail," cried Louisa, "how bitter will be the disappointment that follows !"

"I have no apprehension of failure," replied her uncle, "for a daughter's pleading will not pass unheeded by one who holds the sacred prerogative of mercy. The queen will hear you with pity, dear Louisa, and then imagine to yourself the rapture with which you will return hither, the bearer of your father's pardon."

"Aye," answered Louisa, with a shudder, "but mercy must ever be blended with justice, and the queen is bound to act with impartiality to all those who live under the laws that she has herself sworn to administer equally to all her subjects."

"You believe, then," returned James Somerton in a tone of reproach, "that your father is guilty of the heinous offence he is charged with ?"

"Heaven forbid that I should be guilty of such filial ingratitude," she replied. "I have every reason to believe my father is innocent of the crime he is accused of ; yet her majesty may not be so easily convinced of it ; and I fear, lest in her anxiety to punish the murderer of Captain Aylmer, she should lend too willing an ear to those who accuse my father of a crime that I tremble even to name."

"Yet if she condemned him without sufficient evidence," answered the other, "she would be guilty of a crime fully equal to that of murder."

"That may be very true," exclaimed Louisa, after a brief consideration, "but even princes are not infallible in their opinions, and her majesty might err in her extreme anxiety to hurl retribution upon the party supposed to be guilty of Captain Aylmer's death."

"Humph !" ejaculated James Somerton, "you are resolved, then, it appears, to believe that your father must perish, even though innocent of the crime that has been brought against him."

"As Heaven is my judge, I am fully persuaded that he is free from the crime you have named,"

exclaimed Louisa. "That he has enemies in this place I am but too well aware, and I also know they would leave no scheme untried that might serve to bring him to an ignominious fate. Yet if my single aid may serve to rescue him, you may count upon my utmost exertion, even though death itself should be the portion of her who makes the effort in his behalf."

"This is exactly the degree of spirit I wished to see you manifest," said the other in accents of admiration. "Timidity would ruin the project I have in view, for it would seem to betray a consciousness of your father's guilt, and thus foil the holy errand upon which you are going."

"But may not those by whom she will be surrounded prevent me from making my way to her presence?" asked Louisa.

"I think not," replied the other; "and even if they should do so, her majesty will give orders for you to be brought before her. The world speaks highly of her love of impartial justice, and it is said that even the humblest of her subjects can obtain the honour of an audience. if wrong has been done them, or they have injuries to be redressed."

"But may she not believe my father to be guilty, and leave him to whatever fate may be pronounced upon him by his judges?"

"That will depend upon the manner in which you represent the case," answered her uncle. The

statement you make should be as brief as possible, yet comprising all the points that bear most favourably in his case. This will procure for you the attention of her majesty, and no doubt she will grant the pardon you go to supplicate."

"And if she does," cried Louisa, "my next task shall be to prevail on my father to abandon the wild career he has lately followed, and become once more a faithful subject to the queen to whom he owes his life. I have a hope that he will spend the remainder of his days in England, and should that be realized, I will follow him thither and devote myself to the task of banishing from his mind the recollection of events that could not but fill him with sorrow and regret."

"Humph!" ejaculated James Somerton, "so it seems then that you have made up your mind to think no more of Lieutenant Granger, whose attentions I believed were not disapproved?"

"To say that I love him not would be to utter an untruth," replied Louisa. "My heart was indeed given to him; yet your commands have ever guided me, and in obedience to them I have so far prevailed over my own feelings as to abandon the prospect of happiness which lately dawned upon me."

"The sacrifice has doubtless been great," answered the other, "and most deeply do I feel for the grief it must have given rise to. Affairs, however, may yet change for the better, and perhaps a few days will effect a change that you at present do not anticipate. That, to be sure, will depend upon the success of your mission to Whitehaven, of which, in my own mind, I have scarcely a doubt. But you will require rest, Louisa, before commencing this journey, and I would therefore have you retire to your chamber, for we must be up betimes in order to see your father, who is, doubtless, in anxious suspense till he meets those from whom he has been so haplessly separated."

To this Louisa instantly acquiesced, and having bade her guardian good night she proceeded to her own chamber, and throwing herself, dressed as she was, upon the bed, vainly sought the oblivion of sleep to banish from her mind those reflections which harassed and perplexed her soul. But the thoughts of what had occurred, as well as of the journey she was about to undertake, prevented the slumber she sought, and when daylight had pretty well advanced, she rose and went to the sitting-room, where she found James Somerton busily occupied in writing, which he had indeed been employed at from the time when she had left him. She would again have retired, but he bade her remain, and having folded some papers together, he placed them in her hand, saying,—

"You will find in these, Louisa, a statement of all the facts which you will have to relate to the queen. On your passage across the waters you can peruse them, and thus store your mind with the various circumstances which it will be necessary to remember. Be of good heart, my girl, and I feel confident that the blessing of Heaven will crown with success your pious efforts to save the life of a father."

Louisa was about to reply, but was checked by a knocking at the door, which, upon being opened, gave admittance to Christopher Dalton, who, after having made a genuine sailor's salute, commenced the business which had occasioned his visit.

"I believe," he exclaimed, "that I have the honour of speaking to Mr. James Somerton?"

"That is my name, sir," replied the other, wondering what was coming next.

"You are the brother of my captain, I believe, whom these land-sharks have sent to the bilboes?"

"I am."

"And this young lady is his daughter, I suppose?" added Dalton, bowing to her.

"She is."

"Humph! and of course some good-natured friend or other has been here to tell you all about what has happened to Luke Somerton?"

"We have indeed received the fatal intelligence," answered the other; "but we know little more than that he has been arrested on a charge of murder."

"He has," replied Dalton; "and, what's more, I'm afraid they'll hang him for it, if we don't find some means to get him out of limbo."

"Nay," exclaimed James Somerton, "there must be no violence, if we would really save him from the fate with which he is threatened. The law must be respected, and those who wish to see Luke Somerton at liberty, will do well to remember that any outrage will but render his fate the more certain."

"That's just what I told our fellows when they proposed making an attack upon the prison as the only way to save their captain. Some were for setting fire to the governor's house, by way of striking terror into the hearts of these islanders; but I was afraid that would only make matters worse, so I came here to ask what steps you would advise us to take."

"You have done well," answered the other; "for such an act of violence as you speak of must have terminated in the destruction of him you would serve."

"Must he be left to his fate, then?"

"By no means," replied the other; "his daughter and I have concerted a scheme that I think will ensure the safety of my unfortunate brother,

and in a few hours, if I mistake not, he will be once more at liberty."

"Hurrah!" shouted Dalton. "This is good news, at any rate; but perhaps your honour will tell me how all this is to be done, for if I don't take back a good account to our chaps, I'm afraid they won't be easily persuaded to give up their own plan."

"Oh! entreat of them, for my sake, to forbear," cried Louisa, earnestly. "Say that my father's life depends upon their remaining peaceable, and assure them that I am about to make an effort which there is every reason to hope will prove successful."

"I'll tell them anything you like, young lady," answered Dalton; "but, between ourselves, I don't think they'll be satisfied unless I can explain what you are going to do for the captain."

"The truth is, my friend," said James Somerton, "she is going to seek an interview with the queen at Whitehaven. Her majesty is known to be merciful when she can exercise the royal prerogative with fairness, and I have no doubt she will grant a pardon to my brother, when it is explained to her that he has been charged with the crime of murder upon no better ground than that of mere suspicion."

"All this sounds very well, certainly," replied Dalton; "but, for my own part, I don't see how she is to get the ear of her majesty, and even if she should do so, and be inclined to grant a pardon, there may be some d—d evil-minded fellows about to persuade her that Luke Somerton don't deserve mercy."

"The queen suffers no one to interfere in matters of this kind," exclaimed the other; "and even if such counsel should be given, those who offer it would do so at their own peril. Besides, a daughter's pleading for the life of a father must be held sacred, and black indeed must be the heart of that man who could interfere to render her prayer of no effect."

"Why, that's very true, Mr. Somerton," returned the other; "yet it can't be denied that there are men who delight in doing mischief."

"Not when their own favour at court may be lost through it," answered James Somerton. "The queen is said to be prompt in her decisions, and has spirit enough to maintain them in spite of any evil counsel that might be offered by those who surround her throne. It, is therefore, with full reliance that I propose this alternative, and I am sure Louisa will perform her task with so much zeal that her father's liberation from prison may be looked forward to with certainty."

"I hope you may prove a good prophet," returned Dalton; "for if there's much delay about it, I'll not answer for keeping my men in order. They are a rough and ready set of fellows, I can tell you, and as they've made up their minds to set Captain Somerton free, it will require more persuasion than I can use to keep them in anything like order."

"Yet they must be prevailed on to abstain from acts of violence," exclaimed the other, "or the consequences will be fatal to the man they profess to regard. So far as I can at present see this case, there appears to be no evidence to prove the crime he is charged with; and as we well know that his enemies are at the bottom of all this mischief, there can be no great difficulty in prevailing on the queen to rescue him from the peril with which he is threatened. This, however, will depend upon the prudence manifested by your followers, and I must therefore entreat you to exert all your influence over them till the result of Louisa's mission is known."

"That's all very well," replied Dalton; "and I can promise to keep the chaps quiet, provided their patience is not taxed for too long a time. They long to have a brush with these islanders of yours, and if matters should come to that, I rather fancy there's a good many in this place that will rue it for some time to come."

"The delay shall be no longer than there is an absolute occasion for," returned James Somerton. "My neice will go on board the boat which is to convey her to Whitehaven as soon as she has had an interview with her father, and as Queen Anne is expected to reach the town at an early hour this evening, the object of her leaving us will be speedily brought about. At all events, a few hours will serve to inform us whether her application has been successful or not, and in the event of its proving a failure, I will not only give my assent to my brother's liberation by violent means, but it is even likely that I may myself assist in it."

"Upon that understanding, we part," exclaimed Dalton; "and if any aid of mine should be wanting to get the young lady over the water, you have only to send down to the shore, where I and a brace of comrades shall be ready to do your bidding. So farewell for the present, and Heaven speed Miss Louisa in the task she has taken upon herself."

He left the house, after having given utterance to these words, and, having partaken of a hasty breakfast, Louisa and her uncle set forth to visit the prison, and inspire the unfortunate captain with courage, by informing him of the steps that were about to be taken for his deliverance.

CHAPTER XI.

The cheerless aspect that surrounds me here
Doth fill my soul with such a melancholy,
That I could welcome even death itself,
Come in what guise it may.—RAMONI.

THE remainder of the night, short as it was, that succeeded the arrest of Luke Somerton, was passed by him with impatience that he found it impossible to control.

The place to which he had been conveyed for security was the chapel dungeon beneath the castle, and so gloomy was its aspect, that his soul recoiled with horror from the grim visions that seemed to float before his eyes, and he longed for the return of daylight to dispel the hideous forms that, in imagination, succeeded each other with frightful rapidity.

Left to solitude and his own reflections, his mind recurred to the deed which revenge had urged him to commit; and now that his furious passions had somewhat cooled, he would have given all he possessed in the world, had his hand been guiltless of the blood which stained it.

Captain Aylmer he still regarded as a villain, who had sought his ruin in furtherance of his own sinister views; yet the time that had elapsed ought to have softened the rancour which had taken possession of his heart, and produced oblivion, if not entire forgiveness of the past. But these reflections came too late, for Aylmer had perished by a miserable death, and most heartily did Luke wish that the grave would enclose him also, as it was only there that he could hope for that entire forgetfulness for which his soul groaned.

Thus drearily passed the few hours that intervened before the keepers of the prison rose from their beds, and inspired something like life in the melancholy abode of crime, as they bustled about from one part of the place to another. At length the morning's meal was brought to him by one of the keepers; but the man maintained a rigid taciturnity to all questions that were put to him; and when at length the prisoner inquired if any visitors had yet applied to see him, he merely answered by a solemn shake of the head, and immediately disappeared.

Another hour of doubt and anxiety passed away, and Luke began to think that all had forsaken him in the time of trouble; that even his brother and Louisa were ashamed to own the relationship that existed between them, and that, consequently, he would be left in solitude and the torture of his own maddening thoughts, to await the period when an ignominious fate should put an end to his earthly sufferings.

From this state of suspense, however, he was a length aroused by the opening of his door to give admittance to Scipio, who, throwing himself at his feet, manifested the most extravagant joy at being thus once more permitted to see his master, even though it was within the dreary walls of a prison.

"Ah, Massa Somerton," he exclaimed, "him berry glad to see you, but him been much better pleased if de meeting had taken place on ship-board, and far away from dis infernal island."

"It is in vain to grumble at fate, my good Scipio," replied Luke, "for they have got me fast enough in the bilboes, and I must e'en reconcile myself to whatever fate may be in store for me."

"Why, dey won't hang you, massa—will dey?" asked the negro, in a tone of commiseration.

"I am almost inclined to think they'll be glad of so good an excuse to get rid of me," replied Somerton, with a grim smile. "There are few in this place that hold me in much favour, and whether they believe me innocent or guilty, I rather suspect they'll send me to the gallows in payment of old scores. But there is another subject I would speak to you about, Scipio. I have looked in vain for the arrival of the only two persons who claim relationship to me, and I would now commission you to convey a message from me to say that I would fain speak to them, if only for a few moments."

"Oh, you mean your brother and de young lady dey call your daughter?"

"The same."

"Dey are on deir road here already," replied Scipio, rubbing his hands for joy; "I left dem just now wid Mr. Dalton, and dey will both be here before I could get out of de prison doors."

"Had they any business with Mr. Dalton?" inquired Luke, eagerly.

"Iss; him fancy so, at least."

" What is it ?"

" Dat him can't say," replied Scipio ; " but de gennelmans dat am your brodder, told Massa Dalton to get de boat ready widout delay, and den to come here and tell him when it was ready to put to sea."

" What project can have entered his head?" muttered Luke Somerton to himself. " Some notable scheme for my deliverance, I can answer for it ; but time and trouble will be thrown away, for nothing that he can now do will save me from the fate determined on by those harpies."

" Here dey am, I declare !" exclaimed Scipio, as the door opened, and James Somerton, accompanied by Louisa, and followed by a corporal and two soldiers, entered the dreary dungeon.

" James," cried the prisoner, grasping the hand of his brother, " I thought your visit somewhat long delayed ; but you are welcome, though I would have wished the meeting had taken place in a less gloomy abode this. And you, Louisa.—I had almost feared that you would not venture to come here, where vice groans forth its wretchedness, and, in most instances, pays the penalty of its evil deeds."

" Nay, my dear father ——"

" Hush !" interrupted Luke Somerton, " I must not suffer you, girl, to brand yourself with my name. No, no, Louisa, pass still for the child of James Walford, and I shall die all the happier for knowing that the world will not raise towards you the finger of scorn as the daughter of Luke Somerton."

" Oh, talk not of dying !" she cried, in accents of the bitterest grief ; " talk not of dying, for it sounds to me as the passing bell smites on the ear of a sick man, freezing the hope that the warm breath of day had called into existence."

" You are a fond, foolish girl, Louisa," exclaimed Luke, as he imprinted a kiss upon her pale, cold forehead. " By the mass, child, if aught could make my eyelids quiver, or my heart palpitate more quickly, it would be the thought of leaving thee with the foul stigma of my crimes clinging to thy name."

" You shall not leave me, dear father," cried Louisa, " for I have yet one project in view that, I trust, will save you from the doom you anticipate."

" A project, Louisa !" exclaimed her father ; " why what wild vision fills your brain, that you can believe there is a chance of saving me from the gibbet ?"

" My design is not so visionary as you imagine," answered Louisa, with a forced smile. " Our good Queen Anne is all gentleness and virtue ; she will not deny my prayers, nor pass unheeded the tears of a daughter pleading for the life of her father."

" Tears !" exclaimed Luke Somerton ; " she'll mind them as much as I mind the salt spray the sea dashes in my face when the winds howl a requiem over the poor wretches that are doomed to perish in the storm."

" But my prayers ——"

" Prayers !" he ejaculated ; " you may as well preach to the figure-head at the ship's bows, as to a head that happens to wear a crown."

" Then you doubt the goodness that all the world, besides yourself, attributes to our gracious sovereign ?"

" No, no," replied Luke, " I won't say a word against Queen Anne, either. She has her excellent qualities as well as a few indifferent ones, and I have always said that she was too good a mistress for the servants that throng about her."

" You will consent, then," interposed his brother, " to Louisa's trying her fortune with the queen ?"

" Humph ! the chances of failure make it scarcely worth the trouble."

" Nay, you will consent," cried our heroine, imploringly ; " I know you will, if it is only for the sake of your poor heart-broken Louisa."

" For your sake, girl !" exclaimed Luke ; " you know I would scarce refuse you anything ; but believe me, it would be better for yourself that the governor should hang me up at day-break as he has promised. Besides, I know what it is to ask mercy from sovereigns ; they don't like to be interrupted by their poorer subjects, and, take my word, Louisa, you'll make nothing of this wild project of yours."

" Oh, yes," she cried, " There is something whispering at my heart, that assures me I shall not fail."

" 'Tis a mere chance," answered Luke ; " and to tell you the truth, I am not inclined to expose you to all this risk, when, in my own mind, I feel assured that no entreaties of yours can save my life."

" Believe me, you are wrong," answered Louisa ; " for what but Providence has brought the queen so unexpectedly to Whitehaven ? And may we not hope that the same beneficent power will incline her heart to mercy ?"

" I'm sorry to interrupt your honour," said the corporal, " seeing as how you came down with the gold dust so handsomely ; but the time allowed for visitors is almost up, and I shall get into disgrace if your friends stay much longer."

" Where you larn politeness, I wonder ?" exclaimed Scipio, indignant at this interruption. " D—d rascal, to poke him long nose in de way when old massa palaver young missy !"

" It's all very well for you to talk," returned the corporal, " but I know my own business, and it won't do to get yourself into trouble merely to serve other people."

The reply of Scipio was interrupted by the opening of the cell door, and Dalton entered, exclaiming—

" Now, young lady, there's no time to be lost ; for all our preparations are completed, and we have got both wind and tide in our favour."

" The finger of Providence in our behalf is again manifest," cried Louisa, once more addressing her father. " You see that everything works admirably for our purpose, and again I ask if you will consent to my undertaking a task of filial duty upon which your safety depends."

" Why should he not consent, my girl ?" demanded Christopher Dalton. " Why should you make any doubt about the matter ?"

" My brother has interdicted her," answered James, " and she hesitates to disobey one whose commands she holds herself bound to yield to. But let me prevail on you, Luke, to offer no further opposition, and my life for it all will turn out better than you anticipate."

" Iss, massa," interposed the negro ; " little

missy go to sabe your life, and Scip stay here to keep you company."

"No you won't, though," exclaimed the corporal. "My orders are strict, and I can't allow anybody to stay with the prisoner."

"Ugh!" ejaculated the faithful black ;—"hold him dam tongue, infernal rascal."

"I sha'n't hold my tongue," growled the soldier, "and what's more, if you don't all leave the cell directly, my comrades and I will drive you away at the points of our bayonets."

"Den you cross old debil."

"No I ain't," replied the corporal ; "but I must do my duty, if I'd escape punishment."

"Come, come, friend, be civil for once," said Scipio, coaxingly, and at the same time holding a guinea between his finger, so that it should be seen by the person he was addressing. "Dis am de current coin ob de realm ;—you loyal subject and lub Queen Anne ?"

"I know it."

"Well, den, stow her pictur' away in him pocket, and hold him dam tongue."

During this brief conversation, Louisa, James, and Dalton, were occupied in trying to persuade Luke Somerton to consent to the plan they had proposed. Still, however, he remained obdurate in his refusal, and breaking away from them abruptly, he exclaimed,—

"It's in vain that you try to persuade me when I know well enough that Louisa would only be running a hazard without the chance of succeeding in her errand. My fate is already sealed, and if she leaves the island, it would be only to return and find that the law has already hurled its vengeance upon me."

"As I live by bread, you must be mad—raving-mad !" cried Dalton, impatiently. "Come, come, Captain Somerton ; e'en let the poor girl go her way, and my life on it, we shall yet drink many a glass together, and laugh over the remembrance of the time when you managed to slip your head out of the halter."

"At all events, Luke," added his brother, "I can see no harm in letting her go upon this mission, and there is no telling what good may result from it. For my own part, I feel almost certain of success, and it would be a wilful throwing away of your life to oppose the project that has been set on foot for your deliverance."

"Enough said, enough said," answered Luke Somerton, impatiently. "Steer your own course, James, and if you come back in ballast as you set out, don't say I was your pilot, that's all."

"A daughter's love for her dear father shall be my pilot," cried Louisa, overjoyed at this first symptom of her yielding to their entreaties. "Conscious of the rectitude of my purpose, I can be firm amidst the greatest difficulties, and though my supplication must be made at the feet of England's Queen, I can maintain my courage even though my own death should be the penalty of my presumption in trespassing upon the presence of royalty."

"Bravely said, my good girl," exclaimed Christopher Dalton ; "by my soul, but I would sooner have such a noble child of my own than a pocket full of silver,—though Heaven knows I have need enough of it, too."

"She is a brave lass," said Luke Somerton, thoughtfully ; "yet it wrings my heart to part from her, when, in my own mind, I feel certain that we shall never meet each other again in this world."

"Ah, but we shall," replied Louisa ; "and that too, under more happy circumstances than the present. For my own part, I am confident that my mission will prove successful, and you will yourself have to acknowledge that royalty is never deaf when mercy can be worthily bestowed."

"Who is to accompany you, girl ?"

"Your faithful friend and comrade, Christophe Dalton."

"'Tis a generous act, certainly," answered Luke, "and shall be well rewarded if all turns out to your expectation. Remember, Dalton, to your protection I commit my daughter ; shield her as you would have done me in the battle's hottest strife, and earn the blessings of a father for aiding his daughter in the sacred task she has imposed upon herself."

"Rely on me, and by my soul you shall not be deceived," returned Dalton. "We have been friends and companions together for years, and never shall you have cause to reproach me with forgetting my duty to one whom I regard as my own brother."

"Enough," exclaimed the captive ; "and you, James, what part do you take in this almost hopeless effort to save me from a death of shame ?"

"I will remain in the island to watch the motions of those who have got you in their grasp," replied the other. "Had it been necessary I would have accompanied Louisa on her journey, but my confidence in the honour of her protector releases me from that duty, so that I shall be able to serve you in the event of any emergency requiring my presence here."

"Well, then, do you, Louisa, depart with your companion without further delay. Every moment may be of the utmost consequence, and I shall be racked with suspense till you return with your tidings, be they for good or for evil. Heaven bless you, my child, and may this one act of yours prove a balm of consolation to your heart, even though it may fail of saving a father from the hands of the executioner."

With a heart swelling with the deepest emotion, Louisa embraced her hapless parent, and murmuring prayers for his safety till her return, she left the cell, followed by Christopher Dalton, whose anxiety to remain with his captain gave way to a desire to assist our heroine in the prosecution of her design. When they had left a few minutes, James Somerton was also about to retire from the abode of gloom, when he was called back by his brother.

"Stay," he exclaimed, hoarsely, "I would have a word with you, before parting ; to be brief, I have a commission for you, in case it should happen that I'm to be knocked off the hinges. Now, brother, can you have patience to stay and hear what I've got to say ?"

"Aye—proceed."

"Then, Scipio, stand out of ear-shot whilst I speak a few words to this gentleman."

"Why me no hear ?" demanded the negro. "Scipio am berry faithful, and lub massa better nor any broder in de world,"

"Who the devil doubts you ?" exclaimed Luke

Somerton, impatiently ; " I know you to be faithful, but for all that you must obey orders."

" Bey ! bey !" cried Scipio ; " poor nigger do noting but bey—him might as well marry a wife as be a sailor."

After this grumbling, he retired to the further extremity of the cell, and then Somerton, drawing nearer to his brother, said, in a wh sper,—

" James, my lad, you know I am no coward, but I have no mind to die like a dog, upon a scaffold."

" Alas !" cried the other ; " the only hope of escape from death is in the Queen's mercy—should she refuse ——"

" Why, then," interrupted Luke, " I know how to die as a seaman should do, and, as luck would have it, they missed this little friend when they overhauled me."

Saying this he took from his bosom a small pocket-pistol, which having shown to his brother, he returned it to its hiding-place, so that it should not be seen by any of the soldiers.

" Would you, then, perish by your own hands ?" cried James Somerton.

" Ay," answered the captive ; " anything to avoid such a death as they would doom me to. But no more of this—what I wanted to say to you you shall now hear. If the queen makes out my pardon, do you hoist a white flag at your mizen, that I may know which way to steer in time. If I am to blow my brains out, I should like to have it all over before Louisa sets her foot on land again."

" You would have me accompany them to Whitehaven, then ?"

" To be sure I would," replied Luke ; " here you can do me no service ; but before the queen your entreaties, added to those of Louisa, may help to get me out of a scrape that promises to end in death."

" I will do your bidding, certainly," replied James Somerton ; " but let me implore you not to raise your hand against your own life till you are quite certain that all hope is entirely at an end."

" Not I," answered Luke. " I'm in no hurry whatever to trip my anchor ; but I'll be d—d— Heaven forgive me for swearing, when I ought to be praying—but the hangman shall never lay his hand upon my throat. So now that you know my mind, leave me, or you will be too late to get on board."

" Beg your honour's pardon," exclaimed the corporal, " but if I stop here another five minutes, I shall stand a very fair chance of being tied up to the halberts."

" What is it you want, then ?"

" For this gentleman to go."

" Well, you'll not be troubled with him much longer," replied Luke, " for if he don't go at once he'll lose the tide, and then all his efforts in my behalf will be useless."

" Farewell, then, brother," exclaimed James Somerton ; " and if it should be for ever on this side of the grave ——"

" In that case, James," interrupted the captive, " the less that's said about the matter the better. I don't want to have my head filled with gloomy thoughts just now ; so away on your errand, and should it prove successful, you will find that I am not wanting in gratitude to those who have taken so warm an interest in that of a weather-beaten tar."

" Comrades," exclaimed the corporal, " you will see this gentleman to the castle gates, and when he is gone, repair to the guard-room, where I will meet you after having seen that all's right hereabouts."

Thus urged to depart, James Somerton took a farewell of his brother, and ascended the steps which led towards a door in the upper part of the vault. The soldiers immediately followed him, and Luke, sinking into a chair, laid his head upon the table, and groaned aloud, for his forced spirits now forsook him, and he felt as if abandoned to his melancholy fate.

———

CHAPTER XII.

These things are sure precursors, sir, of death.
Some call them old wives' fancies ; yet I've known
When they did augur truly, and I know
These sights are meant as warnings.—*Renald's Curse.*

UNACCUSTOMED as he was to abandon himself thus to grief, Luke Somerton at length started upon his feet, and glaring wildly round him, sought through every portion of the vault to see if any one was present to witness the weakness he had yielded to. At length his eyes fell on the corporal, who stood an amazed spectator at no great distance off, and clutching him by the arm with an iron grasp, he exclaimed,—

" Wretch ! why am I to be thus watched and gazed upon in the hour of my trouble ? You have seen me shed tears such as a woman might be ashamed of. Go and tell your governor what imprisonment has reduced me to, but at the same time tell him that I have subdued the weakness, and have now fortitude enough to endure the hardship of my fate without repining."

" I am not sent here to be a spy upon you," replied Corporal Matchlock, " nor is the governor so much of a foe as you seem to imagine."

" What !" exclaimed Luke Somerton, " does he not believe me to be the murderer of Captain Aylmer ?"

" He does," replied the soldier ; " but for all that, he exults not in the punishment of a criminal, however much he may deserve his doom."

" But he will be glad of the fate I am soon to meet," answered Luke ; " the tears of his daughter for her slain lover will wake feelings of vengeance in his heart, and he must curse me as the supposed author of the wailings that now fill his house."

" I don't know anything about that," replied the man ; " but Sir Charles Radcliffe is beloved by everybody in the island, and I'm sure he would do everything in his power to save your life if only one witness could be brought forward to say a word in your behalf."

" Psha ! who is there that would speak for me," exclaimed Somerton, " when all have conspired to accuse me of the crime for no other reason than that there was an old quarrel between us ? There are plenty ready to come forward and give testimony against me, but not one friend who would utter a word to deprive the gallows of its expected prey."

" There you are mistaken," replied Matchlock, " for I have no enmity towards you, and if a word from me would be of any service, I would be ready to go into the witness's-box, even though it might be the means of making half the people here my enemies."

"Well, then, you are the best fellow among them," exclaimed Luke Somerton, "so take this guinea for your honesty, and try if you can't think better of me than the greater part of your islanders do."

"What service do you expect from me for this?" demanded the soldier, with hesitation.

"None at all," answered Somerton. "I give it because you spoke with more kindness than I have heard from most people here, and, between ourselves, my friend, I rather think I shall have but little use for money in the course of a few hours."

"Humph!" ejaculated the corporal, "you don't give it, then, by the way of a bribe?"

"A bribe!—for what?"

"To assist you in escaping from this place."

"I have neither thought of escaping, nor have I any wish to do so," replied Luke Somerton. "Of what service would it be were I to find means to get on the outside of these stone walls? An alarm would immediately be raised, and I should be brought back again to endure a yet more rigorous imprisonment."

"That's just what I was thinking myself," returned Matchlock, "and I'm glad to find you dinn't give me the money to make me betray my trust. We soldiers are often called upon to perform very disagreeable duties, and if it was my own brother that I was set to keep guard over, I wouldn't lend him a hand to escape, even though the gallows stared him in the face."

"Humph!" muttered Luke Somerton, "that is carrying your sense of duty somewhat far, and, methinks, I should act differently myself if placed in such a situation. For my own part, I have no desire to quit this place, unless I can do so under the queen's free pardon; and if that should luckily be obtained, the rest of my life shall make some atonement for the last few years of it."

"I'm afraid if your only hope is in the queen's pardon, the case is rather a dangerous one."

"It must be confessed you are right there," answered Luke Somerton, "but as I am rather reckless about my fate, the disappointment will not be very great. I have lived to see myself despised, and can now leave the world with very little regret."

"But you have a daughter," observed the soldier, "and I should have thought for her sake you would have been glad of a pardon."

"For her alone, do I wish it," replied the captive. "She has been long separated from me, and it is hard to be thus parted immediately on my return here to clasp her once more in my arms."

"Well, things may turn out better than we expect," said Matchlock, "so, for the present, I'll leave you, and if anything can be done to soften the rigour of your confinement, I'll see what I can do towards it."

He left the dungeon with these words, and scarcely was he gone when Luke Somerton saw that, by some means or other, Scipio had found means to be left behind.

"How now, sirrah!" he exclaimed; "why did you not leave when the others went away?"

"Because him want to stay wid old massa," re-plied the negro; "so him hide himself down yonder, and when de corp'ral go away, him creep out to see if anyting was wanted."

"What were you doing when I first saw you?" demanded Luke Somerton.

"Me ony count de thirteen pillars yonder," answered Scipio. "Who ebber come in dis dam, tarnation dungeon, and count de pillars, him short time be prisoner himself. Eberybody say so—ax anybody in dis castle if I habn't told you de truth."

"You are a fool, Scipio," exclaimed Luke Somerton, throwing himself into a seat. "Against you, at least, they have no charge, and sorry, indeed, should I be to see an old comrade like you placed in a situation similar to my own."

"Oh," replied the negro, snappishly, "of course Scip's a fool if massa pleases to say so."

"Psha! are you offended with me for using the freedom of a comrade?"

"No," he replied, "if massa not angry, Scipio don't care what him called."

"Psha!"

"Chaw?" exclaimed the negro, "him noting to chaw but baccy;—will you take a quid, massa? No! ah! den you a drop too low; but neber be afeered dey hang you."

"I see but little prospect of any other fate," replied Luke Somerton.

"Ah!" he replied, "but lilly missy go on her knees, cry, ax de queen to pardon her father;—de queen, she, good young creter, cry too,—say yes, Luke Somerton sha'n't be hanged, because him nice chap—den, we all cry for joy and hab a jolly carouse togeder."

"Yours is a flattering picture, Scip," answered the prisoner, "yet I cannot but see that the chances are all against me, and that my fate is sealed."

"Ah, massa, what for you look so glum?" inquired the other. "He! he! he! I know what you want—smoke pipe—he! he! he! nothing like baccy when a man feels a cup too low."

Upon this he produced a pipe from his pocket, filled the bowl with tobacco, and, having lighted the weed, offered the tube to his captain.

"Dere now," he exclaimed,—"dere, a pipe ob raal Varginny—him do good, massa—pull up him old heart. Eh! you berry cold!—take Scip's boat-cloak, and wrap it round your shoulders for warmth."

"Scip!" cried Luke Somerton, abstractedly, as he suffered the good-natured offices of the black to proceed.

"Iss, massa."

"Scipio, I say."

"Well, massa, me at your elbow;—what you want?"

"By heavens, 'tis a corpse candle! Twice before I have seen that flame, and each time it lighted a brave man to the grave, and it burns for me now. Well, be it so. What matters it when or how death meets us? In darkness or in daylight, on land or on water? I have looked on grim death in the face too often to be afraid of him now."

"Him no burn for you, massa," exclaimed Scipio. "See, him steal away above de steps where de door am."

"It does," answered Luke Somerton, "and lingers there, as if waiting for me to follow it."

"Capt'n," said the negro, trembling with apprehension, "you, surely, won't be mad enough to go arter dat dam wild-fire ting? It am omen o' bad luck, and will lead poor massa to ruin."

"What ruin have I to fear more than that which already stares me in the face?" demanded Luke Somerton. "Have I not death already before my eyes, and shall I turn coward merely because yonder meteor floats through this dreary vault?"

"Massa Somerton no coward," answered Scipio; "but for all dat, dere are no 'casion to run himself into danger."

"The danger you speak of shall not deter me from my purpose," exclaimed the prisoner. "I will know the mystery of yonder omen, be it for good or for evil; and if it should lead me to death, there will, at least, be the satisfaction of perishing without the aid of the executioner."

Upon this he ran up the steps, and finding that the corporal had accidentally left the door unfastened, he called upon Scipio to follow, and instantly disappeared.

The negro, however, was too much alarmed to obey him at the moment; but, at length, mustering all the courage he could, he slowly ascended the steps which gave egress from the cavern.

CHAPTER XII.

'Tis solemn then to find oneself within
The chamber of grim death; yet sadder still
To know that he who lies before us
Fell by our murderous hand.   *Don Raphael.*

FOLLOWING the mysterious light, which had thus become his beacon, Luke Somerton passed through a darksome passage of no great length, which brought him to a massive iron gate, that flew open at his touch, and gave him admittance to a place that proved to be the castle chapel. The meteor that now burned a little in advance of him, afforded sufficient light to enable him to see with tolerable distinctness the various objects around him; yet its lurid glare added a solemnity to the scene, which imparted a melancholy to the heart of the captive that he could not overcome.

Pausing, irresolute whether to advance or retire, his thoughts recurred to the events of the last few hours; but cowardice formed no part of Luke Somerton's nature, and, gazing around upon the richly adorned walls of the sacred edifice, he muttered to himself, almost unconsciously,—

"So, this is the chapel, is it? and truly a proper shore for yon corpse-light to pilot a man to! And yonder it is, burning and quivering like a beacon-fire, as if it would say, 'Here's the port you are bound for, messmate.' St. Nicholas! what's that yonder, I see before me, black as the night itself, and curdling my blood, as if some new horror was coming over me? By heavens! 'tis a funeral bier, covering some cold remains, abiding here for interment. Yet I might have guessed as much, for what says the old rhyme, that I have often heard and laughed at, for its superstitious absurdity;—

'Where the corpse-light
   Dances bright,
Be it by day, or be it by night,
Be it by light, or be it by dark,
There shall a corpse be, stiff and stark.'"

He paused on concluding these lines, and stood absorbed in the reflections which had thus been conjured up. His blood seemed to stagnate in his veins; and, appalled by the terrors that crowded upon his brain, he was about to retreat, when a low, wailing sound rushed past him, that seemed like the dying accents of some expiring mortal.

"Who spoke?" he exclaimed, with startling vehemence. "Surely the dead have no voice for the living; and yet no one else is near, except he who lies, dead and cold, beneath yonder funeral pall. Yet, if ever I heard mortal man hail, a voice called 'Aylmer!' 'Tis his body, I'll be sworn, lies beneath that bit of sombre velvet. I know it—feel it—see him as plainly as if he sat bold upright on his bier. Well, suppose it is; I have looked on dead men enough in my time, not to flinch from a blue lip and a white face. At all events, I will gaze once more upon his face, and see how my victim looks, now that he has no longer the power to exult over the wrongs he has done me."

Having formed this resolution, he hastily approached the tressels, and tearing off the pall, discovered the pale face of Aylmer lying in the rigidity of death. At any time the scene would have been one to excite feelings of horror, but, lighted as the body was by the pale gleam of the meteor which remained stationary above it, the sight was rendered doubly hideous, and, unable to gaze for more than an instant upon the corpse, Luke turned from it with a shudder.

"'Tis he, by heavens!" he exclaimed; "I was sure of it, yet had not the power to repress my curiosity to gaze once more upon him whom I fear more in death than I did when he was living! How he glares at me, and the blood oozes out afresh from the wound as if denouncing me as the murderer. Poor Aylmer! I shouldn't be the worse for a spell of prayer, if I could but think of any, but they're all gone, and many a good thought with them. If there's truth in sight, the hand beckons me with its red stark finger!'"

At this instant, a terrific peal of thunder shook the building to its foundation, and ere the sound had died away the meteor vanished, leaving the place in almost total darkness.

"Aye," muttered Luke, "you are gone; yet can I read this bloody book without the aid of light."

Gazing upon the almost indistinct form before him, he remained for some little time unconscious of all wordly sensations. At length, however, he was startled by approaching footsteps, and almost at the same moment, the well-known voice of Scipio was heard close behind him.

"Now, massa," he exclaimed, "ain't you almost tired ob being in dis dam melancholy place, all alone by your own self?"

"Nearly so," replied Luke, "and am not sorry that you have come to break the melancholy that this scene has conjured up in my mind."

"You glad I come den?"

"I am," answered the other; "so cover up that body, will you, lad? for I can't bear any longer to look at the blue, ghastly face, that reminds me of a deed that cannot be recalled."

"Why, as I live," exclaimed Scipio, "if it ain't de corpse ob Capt'n Aylmer!"

"It is."

"Ah, you dere, are you, massa capt'n?" chuckled the negro. "You quiet enough now, and nebber flog poor Scip any more."

And, as he threw the pall over the ghastly fea-

tures of his former benefactor, he burst forth into one of the negro songs which had so often set his shipmates in a roar of laughter.

"Scoundrel !" exclaimed Luke Somerton, seizing him by the arm, " would you give way to mirth when death thus grimly lies before you ?"

"Eh !" ejaculated Scipio, with surprise ; " am massa angry wid poor nigger chap ?"

"How dare you yell out your devil's matins, and *he* so near you !" exclaimed Luke Somerton. "Howl again, dog, and by the rood, I'll tear the tongue out of your misbelieving jaws !"

"Do, massa," exclaimed the other ; " kill poor Scip at once ; you sorry arter, more nor you sorry for him dat lies dere."

"And why, in the fiend's name," demanded Somerton, "should I care a straw about the matter ?"

"For de same reason why you lub de spaniel," replied Scipio ; " 'cause him honest, faithful dog ; more massa beat, more spaniel fond ; eber ready to die for him massa, and lick him hand dat hab taken away de life from him."

"Well, well," replied Luke Somerton, somewhat moved by the logic of his faithful comrade, " I'll not deny but I might sleep the worse for having harmed you. But cover up the face, Scip, do you hear ? The sight of it puts wild dreams into my head, and I can no longer bear to look upon one

whose injuries to me while living have brought him to this fearful state."

"Me take care you not see him nebber no more," exclaimed Scipio, as he threw the pall completely over the body, so as to hide it from view. " Him lay snug enough now, and nebber trouble massa again."

"All is not right here," muttered Luke, pressing his burning forehead with his hand ; " there is a rushing through my brain, and a noise like the flapping of the topsail in a squall, when it has broken from the boltropes. Louisa—the hangman—Aylmer—and I know not what beside—one drives out the other as fast as my brain pictures them."

"Den don't think of 'em at all, massa," replied Scipio. " Talk to me about something else, and den you'll soon forget 'em."

"St. Nicholas !" continued Luke Somerton, wildly, " but it blows a downright hurricane in my brain, and the wind veers about from every point of the compass before a man can cry ' luff.' And this it is to have a bad conscience, for had I been innocent, I could have stood in the presence of fifty corses without feeling what I do while standing near this one."

"Come away from de place, den," exclaimed Scipio, " and it'll soon be all right agen."

"Presently," replied Luke ; " speak to me not just now, and I shall shortly recover myself."

In obedience to this command, Scipio remained silent for some few minutes, and then suddenly breaking forth, he exclaimed,—

"Oh, massa, massa, sich bright tought jist popped into him head."

"Humph ! what is it ?" demanded the other.

"What for you no escape now dat you am out ob de dam dungeon."

"By the mass, you have just hit it," exclaimed Luke, recovering from his stupor ; " if I hadn't been a fool and a coward to boot, I should have thought of this half an hour ago."

"It am not too late, now, I should tink," observed the negro.

"Perhaps not," answered the other ; " or, at any rate, it may be worth while to try what may be done. Here I am certain to meet my doom, so come what may of it, we'll make a bold effort to get out of the castle, and if we can only succeed in reaching the sloop, we'll show these islanders that our ship can sail more gallantly than any they may send out in pursuit of us."

"Ah! we shall be sure to 'scape, capt'n."

"At any rate, we'll have a try for it," replied Somerton ; "and if we fail I shall be in no worse a predicament than at present. So follow me cautiously, Scip, and we'll see if a way can't be found to get on the outside of these infernal walls."

"Hist, massa!" whispered Scipio, in alarm ; "for Goramity's sake, don't stir a foot just yet!"

"What ails the fool now?" muttered Luke.

"Stop a lilly, massa," again whispered the negro ; "me hear pat-pat-pat, trip-trip-trip, along de passage out yonder. Some one comes dis way, so step behind dis pillar, along wid me, and den dey won't see us if dey come into de chapel."

By this time Luke Somerton heard the sounds alluded to by his companion, and, as no other alternative presented itself, he gently crept to the place pointed out by the negro, and scarcely had they ensconced themselves there, when Lieutenant Granger entered the chapel, apparently in no very good humour.

"Fools! cowards!" he exclaimed aloud ; "the whole island is mad with superstition, and, faith, I begin to feel a touch of it myself, in this solemn-looking edifice. There is no light burning here, after all : yet I could have sworn I saw a lamp moving to and fro. It must have been the moon-beams reflected on the walls, or—hah!" he added, startled by some sound near him, "who goes there? Speak! or, whether it be friend or foe, I fire!"

"Aye, but two can play at that game," answered Luke Somerton, advancing from his place of concealment, and presenting the pistol, which he had concealed in his bosom, at the person who had threatened him.

"Captain Somerton!" exclaimed Granger, in accents of astonishment.

"Ah!" cried Scipio, "it am Massa Granger ; so it am all right now."

"It is," replied the lieutenant, advancing a few steps nearer to them ; "but how, in the name of wonder, have you found your way hither, Captain Somerton!"

"I can scarce tell you," answered Luke ; "nor, indeed, does it much matter, for the next thing to consider is, how we are to get off from this lee shore."

"It will indeed be a difficult matter," returned Lieutenant Granger ; "for every precaution has been taken to prevent your escape, and, as bad luck will have it, a double guard has been placed about the chapel."

"Then we shall have to fight for it, I suppose," observed Luke Somerton, with indifference, "though I can pretty well guess what the upshot will be."

"That would be sheer madness," replied Granger, "for what can you hope to do against a dozen men, and they armed to the very teeth?"

"Do!" retorted the other ; "why, surely, it's better dying in the free air, like a man, than waiting quietly in yonder kennel, to be slaughtered like a beast at the shambles."

"So it am, massa capt'n," interposed Scipio ; "and dere will be one close at hand ready to take part wid him massa, if dere should be need of it."

"I can trust to you, Scip, for that," replied Somerton ; "but I've been in as shrewd a pinch as this ere to-night, and fought my way out of it without getting so much even as a scratch."

"Ah! to be sure him hab," answered the negro.

"A moment—give me a moment only," exclaimed Lieutenant Granger, "that I may think how I ought to act in this case. Your case is a desperate one, Captain Somerton, and as I am the officer of the guard ——"

"The devil you are!" interrupted Luke ; "that's a bad piece of business for me, certainly."

"Would to Heaven," cried the young soldier, "that any one but myself had been appointed to this accursed station."

"We are on the rocks again," exclaimed Luke ; "but there shall be no favour or affection shown in the business : so do your duty like a man, and call your soldiers here to seize upon the prisoner that was plotting to make his escape."

"And thus be the cause," cried Lieutenant Granger, "of your perishing by the hands of the executioner, when, but for me, you might escape from a doom that I tremble to think of."

"I'll tell you what it is, my good lad," answered Luke Somerton, "it's either you or I that must be the worse for this encounter, and both of us may plainly see without the help of a glass. Now, it's clear to me that Louisa loves you ; and as I've no mind to break the poor girl's heart, for the chance of keeping this old shattered hulk afloat a few years longer, I shall remain where I am, and if they choose to hang me up for my pains, it can't be helped."

"Den you die on de gibbet," exclaimed Scipio, "and dat, for sartain, will break poor young missy's heart, and she go to kingdom-come also."

"He speaks truly," said Lieutenant Granger, "and I trust you will now think better of it than to surrender yourself whilst a hope of escape remains."

"It's all moonshine in the water," returned Somerton, gloomily. "Besides, I have yet one chance left me ; the girl has gone across the water, to seek an interview with the queen at Whitehaven, and who knows but her errand may prove successful?"

"I fear there is but little chance of that," answered the young officer.

"Be there little or much," returned Luke, "I shall abide it, at any rate."

"And what massa say, him sure do," interposed Scipio. "Him so dam obstinate, when once him take anyting into him head."

"Ha! ha! ha!" laughed Somerton ; "you hear how freely the rogue lets his tongue run? He speaks downright Dunstable."

"I marvel how you can laugh," exclaimed Granger, "and your life in such imminent peril."

"Why, what you have me do?" demanded Somerton. "Would you see me cry like a maudlin drunkard, or a young miss over the last new novel?

I can't do it, lad, I can't indeed ; so, if it offends your ears, I'm sorry for it."

"You are much changed, methinks, from what you were," said the other.

"That can't be denied," answered Luke Somerton, "for I feel that in nothing am I the same man that I was only a short time since."

"And what has brought about this change ?"

"Oh! there are many reasons for it," replied Luke ; "one of which is, that I can't help thinking of him that lies yonder, beneath the pall. My limbs shake as if I had been stricken with palsy, and, even while I talk to you, I am listening to his voice!"

"Then do not think of such things," returned Lieutenant Granger, "but look steadily forward, or your fate will surely overtake you. I will remove the guard, to facilitate your escape."

"And what would be the consequence of my selfishness?" demanded Somerton, "Why, man, they would shoot you with as little remorse as I should bring down an enemy if I saw him attempting to board my ship."

"For myself I care not," answered Granger, "if I can only save the life of my Louisa's father."

"Aye, aye," returned Luke, "your intention is a very good one, my young friend ; but my own mind is made up, and all the persuasion in the world won't make me budge an inch."

At this moment, Scipio uttered a cry of terror, and, running towards them, he announced that the governor was in the chapel, listening to all that had passed between them.

"Sir Charles Radcliffe !" exclaimed the lieutenant, as his eyes encountered those of his superior officer.

"Even so," replied the governor, sternly.

"Then we are all under arrest ?"

"I have not yet made up my mind how to act in the business," replied Sir Charles, who then, addressing himself to the guards, desired them to let Scipio pass, as there was no charge against him, since fidelity alone had prompted him to remain in the castle with his master.

"I am grateful to you, Sir Charles," exclaimed Somerton, "and if I could only hear you pardon Lieutenant Granger, I could suffer death with indifference."

"You are a brave man, though a guilty one," answered the governor. "I respect your manly spirit, and most sincerely do I wish it were in my power to save you from an ignominious death."

"And Lieutenant Granger ——"

"Has been guilty of forgetting the duty of a soldier," replied Sir Charles, "and therefore has little to expect from the clemency of one who has been placed here to keep discipline and order among those who have been placed under him."

"I own my offence, and——"

"Not a word, sir !" interrupted Sir Charles Radcliffe, sternly. "Your father was my friend— my best and earliest friend. I—I—I will talk with you in private, when my feelings are less acute than they are at present." Then addressing himself to the soldiers that had accompanied him, he desired them to raise the bier which contained the body of Captain Aylmer, and convey it to the chamber where it was destined to remain till the day of the funeral. This order was promptly obeyed, and, as the governor was about to follow them, Luke Somerton stepped forward, exclaiming,—

"A word with you, Sir Charles Radcliffe. I, too, have old recollections clinging about me, that I would fain speak of. That man ——"

"Of whom do you speak ?"

"He that lies there in his bloody shroud !" replied Luke, shuddering as he uttered the words. "He was once my near and dear friend——"

"Yet you murdered him !"

"Aye," replied Luke, "and, what's more, never thought to be sorry for the matter. But, somehow, there's a change wrought in my heart since I looked at him on his bier, and reflected whose hand it was that had made him the pale and inanimate object I beheld. Aye, sir, the change is as great as there is in the features of the man I once called my friend."

"Well, Luke Somerton," returned the governor, "I respect your honest courage, that refused to take advantage of this youth's weakness. Name your wish at once, if you have one to make, and, saving always my duty to my king and country, it shall be granted."

"Why, then," replied Luke, "you must know we are a strange race of fellows, we sailors, and pick up wild notions in our night watches on the lonely deep. I should like well to be friends with him again—Captain Aylmer, I mean—aye, you may laugh at me, if you will ; but, since I can't shake hands with the living man, I'd fain follow the dead one to his last earthly home. It is a friend's part, and with the last spadeful on his head, I shall know that all grudge between us is forgiven and forgotten."

"It is a singular request, indeed," observed Sir Charles, "and, taken, as I am, unawares, I scarcely know whether I shall be able to grant it."

"Surely there can be no reason to refuse me," exclaimed Luke Somerton. "The dead man cannot be injured by it, though the survivor may feel some gratification in being permitted to follow him to the grave."

"But there may be more in this than I understand," observed the governor.

"I know what you mean," exclaimed Luke : "you fancy I should take an opportunity to make my escape, if a chance should happen to be offered me. But you judge me wrongly, Sir Charles, for, as Heaven is my witness, I would not take advantage of the kindness."

"Are you, then, so anxious to pay this mark of respect to the man whom your revengeful hand has deprived of existence ?"

"It is now time that all thoughts of vengeance should cease," replied the captive. "There were reasons, that you know not of, for the hatred I bore him, and though years passed away after the offence was given, I never could pardon him, though I tried to prevail on myself to do so. Well, chance at length brought us together ; we quarrelled, and agreed to decide the difference by a fair duel. I turned round to take my place, and whilst my back was towards him, he treacherously discharged his pistol at me. That, you will own, was enough to excite my utmost fury, and the fatal consequences you are already aware of. I gave him a few minutes to make his peace with Heaven, and, when the allotted time had expired, I shot him through the head, as I would a dog!"

"Yet, this is the man," exclaimed Sir Charles, "that you would now follow to the grave!"

"And if such is my desire, surely it is not a very unworthy one," replied Luke. "When he fell, my animosity ceased, and since it is probable my own life is now drawing to a close, it would afford me a last consolation to see him laid in the grave."

"Unhappy man!" cried the governor; "had your thoughts ever been thus guiltless, I should not now have had to mourn the death of a friend, nor my daughter to weep for the loss of a lover."

"It's no use talking about that now," exclaimed Luke, "for that which is passed cannot be undone, and the remembrance only serves to fill my mind with thoughts that it would be better to banish. I would fain be at peace with the man of whose injuries I complain, and, though you may smile at my superstition, I know not of any other way of being so, than by following him to the grave to which his own conduct has driven him."

"And, in the event of my doing so," asked Sir Charles, "what security have I that you will not attempt to make your escape?"

"The security of my word, that never yet was forfeited," answered Luke Somerton, proudly.

"But should that be broken," returned the governor, "the whole blame would rest upon myself, and I should lose the confidence and regard of those who placed me in the office of trust."

"I can only give my solemn promise," replied Luke, "and, if that is not sufficient, I must endure a disappointment that I would gladly have escaped."

"Upon consideration, I am half inclined to place reliance in you," answered Sir Charles, after a pause. "You see, however, my responsibility, and in the event of my complying with your request, it will be in the most perfect reliance that you will not abuse the obligation."

"If my word is doubted," replied Luke Somerton, "let a guard surround me, to prevent the possibility of my escape."

"I will rely upon your own word," answered Sir Charles Radcliffe, and then motioning for the procession to move on, Luke was taken under the charge of a guard of soldiers, and conveyed back to the dungeon he had previously occupied.

CHAPTER XIII.

I grant her good, and worthy of thy love;
But there's a blemish resting on her 'scutcheon
That may not mate with thine.
The Feud.

WHEN Sir Charles Radcliffe had seen the body of his friend deposited in the chamber where it was to lie till the funeral took place, he retired to his usual sitting-room, with a mind still intent upon the tragical event that had cast a gloom over his house. His first feelings towards Luke Somerton, as the perpetrator of the deed, had been those of unmitigated vengeance; but the recent interview had greatly softened the hatred he bore towards him, and, had any excuse presented itself for doing so, he would have thrown open the doors of his prison, and set him at liberty. That, however, was a course that he dared not adopt, and his thoughts were next turned to the means by which he might preserve him from a death that appeared to be inevitable.

The more he considered this matter, however, the less probable did his chance of success appear to be, for murder admits of no claim for mercy, and the confession made by Luke placed his guilt beyond a doubt, so that no alternative remained but to yield him up to the fate which is awarded to all those who are guilty of shedding human blood. In himself, too, was reposed the power of adjudging all criminals belonging to the island, and thus his must be the voice that adjudged Somerton to meet the death of a malefactor. Yet the duty was an imperative one, and much as his soul shrank from the task, he resolved to utter the fatal words, and thus give him up to those laws which, in a moment of madness, he had so foully outraged.

Turning gladly from this sickening reflection, his thoughts next recurred to Lieutenant Granger, who had been placed under temporary restraint for the part he had been so willing to take in aiding the escape of a prisoner placed under his charge. Whatever anger he had felt at first was now dispelled; but as it was necessary to admonish him upon the conduct he had been guilty of, he ordered him to be summoned before him, that he might hear what excuse he had to offer before he received a reprimand. Deeply mortified at the disgrace into which he had fallen, the young officer appeared before him, and so plainly was his contrition manifested, that the heart of Sir Charles relented towards him, and, speaking in a voice of greater kindness than he had intended, he inquired how it was that he had so far forgotten his duty as to offer his assistance for setting at liberty a prisoner that had been placed under his own especial custody.

"Indeed, Sir Charles," replied the young man, "I feel deeply the degraded situation in which I have placed myself. Pity for the sufferings of a fellow-creature is the only excuse I have to plead, and that, I fear, will go but little way towards extenuating the conduct I have been guilty of."

"Pity is a feeling that does honour to the human heart," replied Sir Charles, "but there are too many instances to be found in which it is our duty to repress it. Luke Somerton has been guilty of the worst deed to be found in the whole catalogue of crimes, and it is but just that he should pay the forfeit of his own evil deeds."

"Granted, sir," answered Granger; "yet I had a motive in serving him, that, perhaps, weighed heavier with me than any other."

"A motive, young man!" exclaimed the governor; "and pray what excuse can you offer for having proposed the escape of a culprit?"

"One that will scarcely be received as an apology for my indiscretion," answered the other. "In brief, Sir Charles, he is the father of one whom I regard with the fondest affection."

"Ho, ho! love for the daughter, then, prompted you to the commission of an offence that might have been followed by the severest punishment."

"As it is one of the strongest passions," answered Lieutenant Granger, "I may, perhaps, be pardoned the thought, though the offence is one that I must needs confess admits of little palliation."

"That is manfully spoken, at any rate," exclaimed Sir Charles Radcliffe, "and goes far towards restoring my favour, which you had nearly lost. Now, I have heard that Luke Somerton has a daughter, and, of course, if I ask you respecting her, I may expect to hear such a flattering description of her as a lover only could imagine."

"I must draw largely upon my fancy, sir," replied Granger, "before I could give you a notion of half the excellencies she possesses."

"Is she young?"

"Scarcely twenty, I believe."

"Handsome?"

"As Venus herself."

"But more virtuous, of course?"

"A vestal could not be more pure, both in mind and body."

"An admirable description, truly," observed the governor. "Has she any more virtues than those you have already mentioned?"

"To sum up all in a few words," replied the lover, "she is perfection itself."

"A very model for all the ladies of our island," exclaimed Sir Charles. "'Tis strange I have never seen the young lady, though; but perhaps that is in consequence of the very secluded life she leads."

"She is seldom abroad," replied Granger, "and never, I believe, unless compelled by absolute necessity."

"With whom does she live?"

"With her uncle, Mr. James Somerton, who, ever since he came to this island, has passed under the assumed name of Walford."

"And why should he have been ashamed of his own, if guiltless of crime?"

"I believe it was on account of the odium that was attached to his brother, Luke Somerton," replied the young man. "Be that as it may, however, he has been a worthy guardian to Louisa, and though a resident in this place for many years, I never heard a word of slander whispered to his prejudice."

"Nor have I," answered Sir Charles Radcliffe; "and it is, therefore, the more to be regretted that there is an insuperable bar to your union with the object of your affections."

"Who shall dare oppose it?" demanded Lieutenant Granger, boldly.

"Nay," answered the other, "this is a matter that must be argued fairly and coolly by both of us. Your father, as I have said before, was my earliest and best beloved friend; at his death, he placed you under my care, and I should be wanting in duty to my dead companion in arms were I to suffer his son to become the husband of the daughter of a murderer."

"I believe him innocent," replied the young man, "and it will be no easy task to convince me of the contrary."

"Glad should I be were it in my power to confirm your impression," answered Sir Charles Radcliffe; "but facts are stubborn things, and perhaps you will begin to agree with me in opinion, when I tell you that, within this last hour, Luke Somerton acknowledged himself the murderer of my friend, Captain Aylmer."

"Is it possible that he can be guilty?" cried the young officer, in despair.

"The fact is as I have stated it to you," answered the governor, "and you may, therefore, judge whether I have acted over harshly in forbidding a marriage between the son of my friend and the offspring of one who must shortly pay the penalty of his crimes by the hand of the common executioner."

"Alas!" groaned the other, "is there no way of saving him from an ignominious doom?"

"None whatever," answered Sir Charles; "all laws, human and divine, have declared that the shedder of human blood shall die, and such must be the fate of Luke Somerton, though, it must be confessed, I would gladly have availed myself of any opportunity to save him from such a doom."

"Then why not have suffered me to favour his escape when I had the means of doing it?"

"Because I should have been forgetting my own duty, in permitting you to break yours," replied the governor. "Here I am an administrator of justice, and am bound by my oath to measure it out fairly between the queen and her subjects."

"Is there no chance of saving him?"

"None whatever.

"Then I fear the daughter will not long survive the ignominious fate of the father."

"I am deeply grieved for the sufferings that must be inflicted on his innocent offspring," answered Sir Charles, "but duty allows me no alternative, and I must, therefore, do violence against my own feelings, when I would, in reality, gladly restore Luke Somerton to life and liberty."

"You can, at least, postpone the day of execution?"

"Neither can I do that," replied the governor, "for the law has stated the exact time that shall intervene between the trial and the hour of execution. To act otherwise, without special cause being shown, would be to bring upon myself a charge of having favoured the convict."

"But," cried Lieutenant Granger, "the trial has not yet taken place."

"It will have been gone through ere many hours have passed," replied Sir Charles. "Here justice is administered differently to other parts of the kingdom, for the chief officers are assembled together, the depositions of the various witnesses are read over, and, if a verdict of guilty is pronounced, execution follows ere twelve hours have elapsed."

"Yet the fatal verdict of guilty may not be pronounced against him."

"How can it be otherwise, when he has himself voluntarily acknowledged the crime?" demanded Sir Charles. "He is self-convicted, and, therefore, must inevitably meet the doom awarded in all such cases."

"This is, indeed, dreadful news," exclaimed Granger, "for though I doubt not Luke Somerton will meet his death firmly, yet I fear the effects upon his daughter, whose love for him almost amounts to devotion."

"If she inherits any share of her father's firmness," returned Sir Charles, "she will endure this terrible infliction better than you anticipate. At any rate, I have now opened your eyes to the dreadful truth, and it is my earnest entreaty that you will no longer think of a union that must bring dishonour upon a name that has hitherto been without reproach."

"It is a hard task to impose upon me, sir," exclaimed Granger, "and I must be pardoned for not giving a decided answer till I have reflected on the course it will be my duty to pursue. And now, as I have a desire to be admitted into the presence of Luke Somerton, I ask your permission to have a private interview with him."

"When?"

"Immediately, if it meets your approbation."

"Well, I see no objection to it, certainly," replied Sir Charles Radcliffe. "Remember, however, there must be no more plotting to escape, for I have ordered a strict watch to be kept upon the prisoner, and should you again attempt to favour his release, it will be at the hazard of my future friendship, and must terminate in a punishment that I should be sorry to inflict on you."

"I give you my word that nothing of the kind shall be attempted," replied Lieutenant Granger, "for I should hold it unworthy of myself were I to abuse the confidence I have asked you to repose in me."

The governor then wrote out a pass for him to the dungeon of Luke Somerton, and the young man instantly taking his departure, Sir Charles was once more left to the anxious reflections that solitude again brought to his mind. Fortunately, however, he was not long permitted to remain alone, for, shortly afterwards, a servant entered to announce that a person wished to speak to him, and, permission being given, Peter Titmouse came into the room, with a countenance that betokened him the bearer of some important communication.

"Your business, friend?" said the governor, not a little amused at observing the fidgetty motions of his newly-arrived visitor.

"My business, Sir Charles," replied the little man, "is private and confidential. A plot has been discovered—a horrid plot!—being no less than a plan to assassinate the queen and all the great officers of state!"

"Psha! what are you talking about, man? What plot is there, and where has it been concocted?"

"In this very island, most noble governor," replied the constable.

"And who is the principal, most sapient officer?"

"A woman."

"A woman!"

"Aye, Sir Charles," replied Titmouse; "never, since the days of Eve, was there any piece of mischief that hadn't a woman in it. My wife has heard me say so many a time, and there's no denying the truth of it."

"Humph!" returned the governor; "proceed with your rigmarole story, I beg. Who, pray, is this woman, whose treason has filled you with so much alarm?"

"Louisa Somerton, your excellency."

"Louisa Somerton!" cried Sir Charles; "what, the daughter of the unfortunate man who is charged with the murder of Captain Aylmer?"

"The same."

"And how know you that she has formed the traitorous plot you speak of?"

"Because she has set off for Whitehaven," replied Titmouse; "and, as all the world knows the queen is expected there on a visit, it's reasonable to suppose that the girl has gone there to assassinate her."

"Are these the only grounds upon which you make the preposterous report?"

"Preposterous report!" exclaimed the constable. "Haven't I done my duty like a loyal subject? and wouldn't it have been treason, after smelling out this plot, to have kept this horrid secret to myself?"

"My life for it, there is no plot at all, except what is contained in that muddy brain of yours, Master Titmouse," exclaimed Sir Charles. "The girl may have left the island, as you say, but I can answer for it she has no such purpose in view."

"Why did she go away upon the sly, then?"

"I don't know that she did so," replied the governor; "and, even if she did, I suppose she wished to avoid the inquisitive questions of such persons as yourself and a few others in the island."

"There you wrong me, your excellency," returned Peter Titmouse, "for I flatter myself there's few persons with so little impertinent curiosity as myself. In this instance, however, duty required me to set a few inquiries on foot, and now, if any traitorous attempt should be made against the life of her most gracious majesty, I shall have the consolation of knowing that I, Peter Titmouse, did my duty like a loyal and affectionate subject of her majesty."

"I am not inclined to doubt your zeal and loyalty," answered Sir Charles; "but, in the present instance, I believe your discretion has rather exceeded itself."

"You think, then, there's no plot, after all."

"Nay, I am sure there is none."

"In that case, why has Louisa Somerton chosen this time for going over to Whitehaven?"

"Perhaps to satisfy a very natural curiosity," answered Sir Charles, "or, which is more probable still, to seek an interview with the queen in behalf of her unfortunate father."

"Humph! I never thought of that before, your excellency."

"So it seems," he replied; "but it shows the necessity of considering these matters carefully, instead of coming to a hasty judgment. This girl, I'll dare be sworn, has not an evil thought in her head, and yet you come here, post-haste, to charge her with one of the greatest crimes in the statute-book."

"But it ain't proved yet that I'm wrong, most illustrious excellency."

"Nor will it ever be proved that you are right," answered Sir Charles. "I can understand the motives that have induced her to take this journey at a time when nothing else would have prevailed on her to quit her father, and most sincerely do I hope her mission will prove successful."

"If that's all she's gone for," exclaimed Titmouse, with a dolorous expression of countenance, "I'm afraid you'll set me down for a fool."

"Perhaps I may rather be inclined charitably to attribute it to over zeal," replied the governor, good-humouredly. "You have always proved yourself an active officer, Master Titmouse, though somewhat too hasty in jumping at conclusions."

"Then hang me if ever I'll jump any more, Sir Charles," exclaimed the constable.

"If you do, let it be with discretion," returned

the other, " or you will find yourself in hot water once too often. Now this goor girl, I have no doubt, has gone upon an errand of mercy, yet her motives have been misconstrued, and, I dare say, by this time it is whispered half over the island that she has crossed over to Whitehaven with the treasonable design of assassinating the queen and all the nobles who attend her. Why, man, you will have raised a laugh against yourself that will last for the remainder of your life."

" I don't know that, your excellency," answered Peter Titmouse, " for it's not quite clear to me yet that there isn't treason in it, for her uncle, James Walford, and an old comrade of her father's, named Christopher Dalton, have gone with her."

" And very proper that they should," replied Sir Charles Radcliffe, " for she needs some protection, and who could she so well take with her as the brother and former shipmate of her father ? Upon my word, my friend, instead of mending the matter, you make it all the worse the further you proceed with it."

" Then perhaps I'd better not say any more about it."

" I really think it would be the wisest course," replied the governor, " for there appears to be no foundation whatever for the suspicions you have formed, and you may take my word for it, she has no other purpose in view than the preservation of her father from a death of shame."

" Then I don't much think she'll succeed in it," exclaimed Peter.

" How that may be, I know not," returned Sir Charles ; " but it is my most earnest wish that she may prosper to the utmost of her wishes. The queen is said to be a great lover of mercy, where it interferes not too much with the fair administration of justice. Louisa Somerton will, no doubt, plead her cause well, and, notwithstanding certain faults in the character of her father, I do most sincerely hope her generous efforts in his behalf will not prove unavailing."

" But there's no doubt he murdered poor Captain Aylmer."

" We must not judge too harshly of others," answered the governor, " lest, being weighed in the balance, we are ourselves found wanting. So now, good master Titmouse, we will part ; and should you ever have any real plot to inform me of, you will always find me ready to listen with all the attention it deserves."

Peter Titmouse felt his dignity terribly lowered by this cut direct, and, having made his bow to the governor, he left the room; but his muttering could be distinctly heard as he descended the stairs, and till he was fairly out of the house.

CHAPTER XIV.

Inquisitive! I'll hold him 'gainst a thousand
For prying into things of trifling import,—
For worming out the secrets of his friends,
And making mischief of them.
The Village Doctor.

NOTWITHSTANDING the violent storm that had risen, and which was heard by Luke Somerton in his subterranean prison, the voyagers succeeded in reaching the shore at Whitehaven, where they landed, and proceeded to an inn to refresh them-

selves and await the expected arrival of the queen. As the time approached, however, the spirit of Louisa seemed to shrink from the task she had imposed upon herself, for the act of intruding upon royalty was one which might excite the highest displeasure, and thus mar the very object which it was her chief aim to accomplish. So entirely had this notion taken possession of her mind, that it required the greatest exertion of Mr. James Somerton and Dalton to persuade her that fortitude alone was required to bring the affair to a successful termination. Eventually, however, she promised to nerve all her energies for the trying occasion ; but as she was anxious to know how long it was expected to be before her majesty arrived, Dalton was dispatched to make inquiries upon the subject, though with a strict injunction to keep secret the motives he had for asking the question.

Being left to themselves, James Somerton tried, by every argument he could think of, to revive the failing courage of his niece. He reminded her that the life of her father depended entirely upon the manner in which she executed her task, and once more alluding to the reputed beneficence of the queen, assured her that there could be no fear of exciting her anger, but that, on the contrary, her admiration and compassion would be aroused by hearing a young and almost broken-hearted girl pleading at her feet for the life of a parent. While he was still urging this, the conversation was broken off by the entrance of a stranger, who, nodding familiarly, as if he had been an old acquaintance, seated himself near them, and, after grinning and grimacing like a mountebank, commenced a conversation in the true old English style, by observing that it had been " a very fine day."

" Very," was the laconic reply of James Somerton.

" You were caught in an awkward storm, though," resumed the stranger, not in the slightest degree abashed by the evident desire to cut the question short. " Storms are disagreeable things at sea, sir, especially when people happen to be in a small boat."

" How do you know, sir, that we were in a small boat ?" demanded the other impatiently. " In short, how came you to be aware that we have been to sea at all ?"

" Oh, in the easiest manner possible," replied the little man. " I make it my business to be on the look-out for news, and happened to be upon the beach when you and this young lady landed. By the bye, there was a third party that I don't see here at present."

" Humph ! if you must know, sir, he has just stepped out on a little business that concerns no one, I believe, but ourselves."

" Very good, very good," answered the stranger. " If there's any secret in it, I can assure you I'm not at all inquisitive. By the bye, there is one question I was going to ask of you, Mr.— Mr.—, let's see, what name shall I have the honour of calling you by, sir ?"

" Buggins," exclaimed the other, in accents of displeasure.

" Buggins! queer name, very—respectable family, though, I dare say. Upon my life I begin to take uite a fancy to you ;—always liked open-hearted, free sort of people, and, since you have been so obliging, you shall know my name in return. I, sir, am called Gregory Guager, holding the office of exciseman in this town, and owing nothing to any man."

"Then, perhaps, Mr. Gauger," said James Somerton, "you will allow this young lady and me to continue the private conversation in which we were engaged when you entered the room."

"Certainly, my dear sir," replied the exciseman, "proceed with whatever you have got to say; and I can assure you that whatever passes between you will be perfectly safe in my keeping."

"But, sir, we do not wish what we have to say to be overheard."

"Sorry for that, sir," replied Gauger, "because where there's secrecy there's danger."

"You are insolent, sirrah."

"Don't fly in a passion, my dear friend, but take things coolly, as I do," exclaimed the exciseman. "I dare say now you think me a very inquisitive, impertinent fellow?"

"I do, indeed."

"Ah, that shows how much people may be deceived," answered Guager. "But I take my money from the queen, sir, and am a loyal man, and if I see a chance of her gracious majesty being assassinated, it's time for me to step forward and prevent the deed."

"Why, you prying, mischief-making villain," exclaimed Somerton, furiously, "do you think I am come here on so cold-blooded an errand as to attempt the life of my sovereign."

"You have called me hard names, sir, but I can forgive you that," replied the exciseman. "I may be thought a prying, impertinent villain; but when I see strangers come into the town on the day of her gracious majesty's expected arrival, and they refuse to answer my questions, I must say it does look very much as if there was a treasonable plot on foot."

"Will you leave me, sirrah, or must I thrust you from the room like a dog?"

"Mr. Buggins, Mr. Buggins, you are growing warm!" exclaimed the exciseman, with provoking indifference to the anger he had excited. "Now, I, as you may observe, take these things with the most perfect composure; for I have often met with passionate people like yourself, and though threatened with kicks and cuffs, I have always shown an example of good nature. It brings 'em round, sir, and so it will you, Mr. Buggins, in a very little time."

"For Heaven's sake, sir!" interposed the terrified Louisa, "do not further excite the anger of my uncle."

"Uncle! O-ho! He's your uncle—is he?"

"He is."

"And a very passionate one, too, I can answer for it."

"Now, sir, if you have any further questions to ask, I request that you will do so at once," exclaimed James Somerton. "I may refuse to answer them, perhaps; but at any rate you will have no excuse for thrusting your company upon us any longer."

"In the first place, then," commenced Gauger, "I suppose you will not deny that your business here is to see the queen?"

"Undoubtedly it is."

"What is your object, may I ask?"

"Perhaps merely the gratification of an idle curiosity," replied Somerton.

"Oh, a loyal wish to see your sovereign! That's very good, as far as it goes; but how am I to be convinced that you have no evil design against her?"

"Upon my life," exclaimed the other, "your impertinence is enough to draw down a storm of indignation. So far I have been tolerably patient, but I warn you to desist from further inquisitorial questions, or you will rue it before many minutes have passed over your head."

"Why, there you are flying in a passion about nothing," returned the exciseman, quite unmoved by the fury that was manifested during the delivery of the words. "I merely ask you a civil question, and you reply to it as if I had committed an offence."

"You *have* committed an offence," replied Somerton, "and since this meeting was not sought by myself, you will do well to bring it to a speedy close."

"Let me again entreat you to leave us," cried Louisa, whose fears were now excited to the highest degree.

"Oh, certainly—certainly, young lady," replied Guager, "I've no wish to force my company upon any one when it's not wanted; but when I have reason to fancy there's a dangerous plot brewing against the head of the nation, it's my duty to inquire into it, and, if necessary, to bring the guilty parties to justice."

"And suppose," exclaimed James Somerton, "it don't happen to jump with my humour to make you my confidant in the present instance?"

"Why then I shall form my own notions about it," replied the exciseman; "and you may, perhaps, very shortly, find yourself in a dilemma that won't easily be got out of."

"In other words, you will go and lay an information against me, upon no better warrant than your own evil imagination?"

"How can a loyal man act otherwise, I should like to know?" demanded the other. "You choose to be very close and short with me, and if that ain't a sign of something being wrong, I don't know what is."

"Fool!"

"Ay, you may call me a fool if you like," replied Gregory Guager, "but that won't hinder me from doing my duty, when I know myself to be in the right. So explain yourself, Mr. Buggins, or I shall raise such a clatter about your head, that you'll soon be sorry for the disrespect you have shown to an officer in the service of her most gracious majesty."

"Louisa," exclaimed James Somerton, "I can no longer endure the insolence of this Jack-in-office. Follow me, girl, and we'll find some other place wherein we may be secure from his annoying presence."

"Stop, stop," cried the exciseman, placing himself between them and the door; "you will please to remain where you are for some little time to come, or I shall call those to my assistance who will take you both before his worship, the mayor."

"Indeed! and upon what charge, pray, will you dare execute that threat?"

"One that will give you a little trouble to get over," answered Guager. "I have strong suspicions that you are here with treasonable intentions, and that, I take it, will be quite sufficient to occasion your confinement in the town gaol till after her majesty is far beyond the reach of mischief."

This argument produced considerable effect in mind of James Somerton, for the mischief threatened by the impertinent fellow who had thus thrust himself upon them, was but too evident, and were he to fulfil his threat, the expected interview with the queen would be foiled, and thus all hopes of saving his brother would be at an end. He could see, too, by the piteous glance directed towards him by Louisa, that her thoughts were also turned in the same direction, and, yielding at once to the exigency of the moment, he subdued the passion which had been kindled in his soul, and assuming an appearance of calmness, demanded of his tormentor what reason he had for suspecting him of any evil design against the person of his sovereign.

"Why, the truth is," replied Gregory Guager, "I never like people to make a secret of their intentions when I put a few harmless questions to them. It looks bad; and, between ourselves, there's quite enough ground for believing that a desperate attack is about to be made upon the life of our royal visitor.".

"Psha! I would rather hazard my existence in her behalf than do aught against one whom I reverence as the monarch of this country."

"Of course, I couldn't expect you to say otherwise," answered the other; "but, for my own part, I shall not be satisfied till you have told me the object that has brought you to Whitehaven."

"It was to see the queen," replied Louisa.

"Very likely; and will you swear, young woman, that it was nothing but mere curiosity that made you take all this trouble to come and see her?"

"It must be confessed," replied Louisa, with hesitation, "that we had a motive far more urgent than the indulgence of an idle curiosity."

"Ah! now we shall come at it," exclaimed Guager, rubbing his hands with extasy. "You had another motive, it seems; pray may I inquire what it was?"

"To plead for her mercy."

"Plead for mercy, eh? then I see what it is, young woman; you have been guilty of something very bad, and expect to get off by the gracious condescension of her majesty."

"You judge me too harshly," replied Louisa; "for I have been guilty of no act that requires the mission I have thus imposed upon myself."

"Humph! you would plead for some one else, then?"

"That is it," exclaimed James Somerton; "and now, as your questions have been fairly answered, I trust you will not subject us to any further annoyance."

"But I have not yet heard who it is that she comes to plead for."

"That is a matter which cannot possibly concern you," replied Somerton. "The motive that brought us here has now been sufficiently explained to convince you that we have no evil designs, and I therefore command my niece to say nothing more for the gratification of mere idle curiosity."

"Mine is not idle curiosity," answered Guager; "for there may be something yet that has not been explained, and it's my duty to know everything before we part company. For instance, how can I be certain that you are not both armed with deadly weapons, to be used against the queen's life?"

"Wretch!" exclaimed James, fiercely, "your insolence can no longer be borne. Too much has already been endured, and, unless you leave the room instantly, your life will pay the forfeit of your temerity!"

"Halloo! what breeze is blowing now?" cried Christopher Dalton, as he suddenly entered the room. "I heard high words as I came into the house, and, thinking a little bit of a spree might be going on, I just ran in to see if my services were required."

"For Heaven's sake do not interfere," exclaimed Louisa, in an agony of alarm. "This man has thrust himself upon us, to our great annoyance; but we are somewhat in his power, and any act of violence will rather serve to injure than benefit us."

"Oh! I won't be very violent with him, because, you see, it ain't in my nature to hurt such poor contemptible vermin as this," replied Dalton. "But I'll tell you what I'll do, Miss Louisa; I'll just give him a gentle squeeze of the throat, by way of a remembrancer, and then drop him quietly out of the window, to save him the trouble of going down stairs. That's what I call a moderate way of doing business, and can't do much harm to any one."

"Except me," exclaimed Guager, trembling and quaking with apprehension.

"Then cut your cable, and set all sail before a fair wind," returned Dalton. "I don't want to lay hands on such a loblolly-boy as you, but I've now spoken my mind fairly and truly, and if you don't mizzle, why, anything that may happen afterwards will be your fault, and not mine."

"Nay, but, my good friend ——"

"Come, come, none of your fine-weather words, for they won't do with me," exclaimed Dalton; "sheer off, will you, and save that miserable carcass while there's a chance given you."

"If I do go, Mister Sailor," returned the exciseman, "it shall be to get a warrant against you all, and then we shall see which gets the best of it."

"Ho, ho! the wind sets in that quarter, does it?" cried Christopher Dalton. "You'd first turn spy and then informer, would you? but never mind, we understand each other a little better than we did, so just hear a warning of what's to follow in case any tricks are played upon us. I'm an awkward customer to deal with, as I dare say you've found out by this time; and, if you say or do anything to put us into quod, I'd advise you to keep a bright look-out afterwards, for your life won't be worth an ounce of old junk."

"Why, you wouldn't murder me?"

"No, but I'd shoot you through the head like a dog, though," replied Dalton; "and that, I take it, would be doing the world a service, since there would be one rascal the less left in it to plague and annoy honest folks."

"Leave us, I entreat of you," cried Louisa, "and thus terminate a quarrel that has already proceeded too far. Our object in visiting this town has no evil in it, and I therefore earnestly entreat that you will not do anything to prevent our interview with the queen, whose royal pardon we seek in behalf of one whose life is far more precious to me than my own."

"Well," exclaimed Guager, "as I don't wish to offend the gentleman that threatened me, you may depend upon it I shall not go to lay any information before the magistrates. But I shall keep a sharp eye upon you, for all that, and, if any attempt should be made to assassinate the queen, shall be at hand to save her from the evil design of her enemies."

Mr. Gregory Guager then hastily decamped from the room, wisely thinking that discretion was the better part of valour when the odds were so much against him as in the present instance. Dalton laughed heartily at the precipitancy of his flight; but, observing that Mr. Somerton still looked gloomy and thoughtful, he inquired what the exciseman had alluded to when he spoke of an attempt being in contemplation to assassinate the queen.

"Why, the truth is," replied the other, "he has taken it into his head that our visit to Whitehaven must have been prompted by a treasonable design against her majesty. It is in vain to argue him out of it, and should he go and whisper his idle notion abroad, I fear the total overthrow of the plans we had formed in favour of my unfortunate brother."

"Oh, there's very little fear of his saying anything about it just at present, I think," answered Dalton, "for he seems to be a rank coward, and will not forget the hint I threw out as to what he might expect in the event of his babbling anything that might do us harm. Besides, the queen is expected to arrive at Whitehaven within half an hour, and he will hardly have an opportunity of doing mischief before that time."

"Is she expected here so soon?" cried Louisa, in a tone of deep anxiety.

"Aye," replied Dalton; "the streets are crowded with people anxious to view the pageant as it passes through the town on its way towards the mansion of Lord Derwent, where her majesty is to be sumptuously feasted, and afterwards to pass the night."

"How long is the queen expected to remain here?" asked Louisa.

"That I have not been able to learn with any certainty," answered Christopher Dalton; "but some people, that I have spoken to about it, say she is expected to leave in the course of tomorrow."

"Then would it not be better," she inquired of her uncle, "to seek an interview with her at the mansion of his lordship, where I may chance to obtain the favour of a private interview? I should thus avoid the gaze of the curious throng, and, it is likely, might speak more eloquently in the cause him whose terrible fate has driven me to this alternative."

"There must not be an instant's delay, if you would save your father," exclaimed James Somerton. "Every moment that is lost teems with increasing danger, and were we to delay this interview till to-morrow, I fear we should not reach the Isle of Man in time enough to rescue him from the hands of the executioner."

"Then I will no longer suffer my woman's fear to delay a task that, it must needs be confessed, I ook forward to with trembling and alarm," replied Louisa. "It is the uncertainty of success that disarms me; for, were I assured that the queen would deign to hear me with compassion, I could endure all else for the sake of preserving the author of my being."

"Why, how is this, young lady?" demanded Dalton, with surprise. "A little while ago, you made no doubt that everything would be settled comfortably to your own mind, and now, it seems, you are afraid lest the queen should frown upon your petition, and order you to be arrested, for presuming to approach her royal presence without due permission."

"It is not for myself that I entertain the slightest fear," answered Louisa. "Death has no terrors for me, yet sure am I, that were her majesty to be obdurate, I should not leave this place alive, to bear the fatal news to my father that all hope of saving him is at an end."

"This is what I call meeting troubles half-way," exclaimed the mate; "and you are the last person, too, that I should have expected to give up when everything is in a fair way for success. As for Queen Anne, she is no more to speak to than any one else, except that she wears a crown, and I should be sorry to think so badly of her as to believe that her heart is harder than anybody else's in her dominions."

"I believe her to possess all the virtues attributed to her," returned our heroine; "yet duty must be performed, whatever station we may fill, and I am afraid lest her majesty should deem it too great an exercise of mercy to extend her royal pardon to a man who stands accused of having committed a cold-blooded and deliberate murder."

"But you believe him innocent," observed James Somerton, "and it will, therefore, be your chief aim to urge that point, and to describe the vindictive feelings which have urged the islanders to bring this charge against him."

"Yet there may be some present among her suite," observed Louisa, "to persuade her that, in this instance, mercy would be misapplied."

"Queen Anne has too high a spirit of her own to endure dictation from any one," replied her uncle. "Besides, who is there so base as to suggest the shedding of human blood, when, by the interposition of the royal will, it may be averted?"

"Oh! it will be all right enough, depend upon it," exclaimed Christopher. "For my own part, I can't see any doubt about it; and, if you still fancy that they'll hang the captain, in spite of everything, you may tell her majesty from me, that Luke Somerton will have myself and a few other dare-devil spirits behind him, that will play up such pranks in the Isle of Man, as shall make this time to be held in remembrance for many a day to come."

"Psha!" ejaculated Somerton, "would you have her threaten the queen?"

"Why, perhaps, it may be as well not to say anything about it," returned the other; "but, for all that, what I've said shall come to pass if they only dare to hurt a hair of the captain's head. He and I have been friends too long a time to desert each other when matters come to the worst; and, more than that, sir, we promised each other, some

years ago, that if either happened to die by the hands of the executioner, the other would avenge it, by destroying all that took any part against the one that falls."

"A very romantic notion, truly," returned James Somerton. "But, I suppose, you have calculated that a certain punishment would speedily await you?"

"Yes, but they must stop till they can catch me before they do that," replied Dalton. "I have been used to play the game of hide-and-seek, and I rather think they'd have a troublesome job to find me, if I'd only half an hour's grace before they commenced the pursuit."

"Well," exclaimed James Somerton, "it's to be hoped there'll be no occasion to put your boast to the test. The prayers of my niece, I have no doubt, will be graciously listened to by her majesty, and, in that case, we shall be the bearers of joyful intelligence to the island, instead of carrying war and devastation against its inhabitants."

"Then I must see the queen," cried Louisa, "even while crowds are standing round, and gazing upon me with wonder and surprise?"

"Aye, girl," answered her uncle, "there is no help for it, I believe, so all you have got to do, is to keep up your courage for the moment when it will be required. But hark! I hear a joyous shout, that announces the near approach of her majesty; she comes, Louisa, and now, let it be remembered, all will depend upon the firmness and resolution you maintain during the next half hour."

A violent tremour shook the frame of Louisa as this announcement was made, but, quickly recovering herself, she expressed her readiness to attend her uncle whenever he thought proper to leave the house.

CHAPTER XV.

I beseech you—
These tears beseech you, and these chaste hands woo you,
That never yet were heav'd but to things holy—
Things like yourself—you are a god above us;
Be as a god, then, full of saving mercy.
                                        Old Play.

IN expectation of the royal pageant, a vast concourse of people had assembled in the streets of Whitehaven; but their patience was doomed to be severely taxed, for a long while over the appointed hour passed away, and yet nothing was seen or heard of the procession, of which anticipation had formed such magnificent notions. Then some began to grumble at the waste of time, for all Englishmen claim the privilege of finding fault at trifles, and some even went so far as to declare that they would go home, as they'd be bound the sight would be only a paltry affair after all; yet there they stood, grumbling on, every now and then venting their ill-humour upon the unfortunate wights who happened to tread upon their toes, or give them a poke in the side with their elbows.

But then, in contradistinction to these, others were found that carried the thing off with surprising good humour, joking their neighbours upon the profitable day's work they had made, and keeping all around them in the most hilarious merriment, by a fire of raillery at which even a stoic must have smiled, if he had thought it worth his while to be present in the throng. In truth, like all large assemblages, it was made up of a diversity of characters, such as only meet together, by chance, on exciting occasions like the present.

At length, a buzz at some distance off, announced that the long-expected procession was in sight, and, as it advanced nearer and nearer, the applause became deafening, and never did enthusiasm grow to a greater height, than on the occasion of the royal visit to the good town of Whitehaven. Then marched the corporation to meet her majesty, who received the mayor and his brethren with a degree of condescension that drew forth fresh plaudits from the mob ; and, when these functionaries had fallen into the proper place in the procession, Lord Derwent, mounted on horseback, and attended by a large retinue of servants, ambled up to the carriage in which sat her majesty, and, in a speech of some length, intermixed with a great deal of flattery, welcomed her arrival at the neighbourhood of his mansion. Doubtless, the queen could not listen to all this without making a suitable reply, and, leaning forward, so as to be seen by all the people, she said,—

"My Lord Derwent, I am happy in having accepted your proffered hospitality ; the journey has made me acquainted with some, not the least loving and loyal, of my subjects."

"Hurrah ! hurrah !" shouted the mob, with stentorian lungs.

"I thank you, my good people," continued the queen, "for the manifestation you have this day made in my favour. If the way has proved somewhat longer than I expected, your love has prevented it from being tedious."

"Will it please your majesty to move on ?" asked Lord Derwent.

The queen nodded her assent, and the pageant was about to proceed, when a movement was seen in one portion of the crowd, and the voice of a female was heard, imploring of the people to make way.

"She must be mad !" exclaimed one of the crowd.

"Keep her back !" shouted another.

"How now ?" cried the queen, with surprise ; "what is the occasion of this sudden movement on my right hand ?"

"It is a crazy woman, as I think, my liege," said one of the attendants, " and we had better proceed, without giving her an opportunity of approaching your majesty's carriage."

But scarcely had these words been uttered, when Louisa Somerton, breaking a passage through the crowd, threw herself upon her knees between the wheels of the carriage, and, in a tone of touching agony, earnestly implored for mercy.

"Is it for yourself, maiden, that you ask it ?" demanded the queen, and then, checking herself, she added—"Yet, if looks speak truly, my poor girl, your youth can hardly have done aught that calls for pardon."

"Had I not better order the coachman to drive on ?" asked one of the lords in waiting. The queen, however, paid no attention to this, and, looking kindly upon the supplicant, she continued, in a voice of compassion—

"Why art thou silent, maiden ? Why dost thou not answer one whose mercy thou hast claimed, and

who is willing to hear thy wrongs, and, if possible, to give thee what thou asketh. What ! still silent ? stand back, good people, I pray you ;—gentlemen of my suite, it may be that maiden bashfulness seals the poor girl's lips in the presence of so many strangers."

All retired at this command, and her majesty, again addressing Louisa, said, with even more than her former kindness,—

"Now, then, my child, rise up, and think it is a mother who is listening to thee. What, or whose is the fault that brings thee thus to the feet of thy sovereign as a supplicant for pardon ?"

"'Tis for my father, gracious queen," exclaimed Louisa ; "his life is in peril, and nought can save him from a death of shame, but your royal command."

"But he may be guilty of the crime laid to his charge," replied the queen, "and in that case an act of mercy would be most unworthily bestowed. But proceed, maiden, and let me know in what he has offended ?"

"Alas !" cried our heroine, " the crime alleged against him is no less than that of murder."

"Hah ! and can you ask the life of one who has shed the blood of a human being ?"

"He is innocent, my queen," cried Louisa in accents of the most intense grief ; "indeed, indeed, he is guiltless of this foul deed, though evil men have accused him of it to secure his destruction."

"His name ?"

"Luke Somerton ——"

"Hah ! the pirate, the renegade !"

"He has erred, my liege," cried Louisa ; " but persecution has driven him to the commission of acts that his soul would otherwise have abhorred. Now, alas ! he has fallen into the power of those who seek his destruction, and his daughter throws herself at the feet of England's queen to sue for pardon."

"Know you not, maiden," answered her majesty with more sternness than she had yet exhibited, " that those who commit murder are never pardoned when the proof is clearly against them ?"

"I have heard that such is the fatal decree," replied Louisa ; "but I am here to assert that no proof can be brought to fix upon my unhappy parent the deed for which they have condemned him to die."

"In that case you have nothing to fear," returned the queen, " for his judge will not yield him to the hands of the executioner without the fullest proof that the charge is founded upon truth."

"But the fatal word has ere now been uttered," cried Louisa ; "and if you, royal lady, refuse the entreaties of your wretched suppliant her father will be unjustly given up to a doom of shame."

"Believe me, maiden, I grieve for you," answered the sovereign, " yet duty forbids me to interfere in behalf of one who has taken away the life of a fellow creature. I may, however, hear more of this, and should there be any doubt of his guilt, I will then interpose to save him from the fate you dread."

"It must be now," exclaimed our heroine, wildly, " or all will be too late."

"Nay, that may not be," replied the queen, firmly ; " for even mercy,—noble as the quality is, —cannot be overstrained without injustice, and it is the duty of a sovereign to hold the balance equally in favour of all parties. But it is time this interview should have an end, and if aught should be discovered in favour of the accused, I will then exercise the prerogative entrusted to me, and restore him once more to the world."

"My liege!" cried Louisa, frantically grasping the garments of the queen—"you must not—shall not stir till my father's pardon has been pronounced."

"How, girl!" exclaimed Anne, with indignant surprise—"Know you to whom you speak thus boldly?"

"Aye, to my great and good mistress," replied our heroine, meekly—"to the beneficent protectress of all those whom oppression and sorrow bring as supplicants into her presence."

"Thou art over bold, maiden."

"It is in the cause of a father, royal lady," cried Louisa, with increasing earnestness.

"True," answered the queen; "yet my decision has been given, and it would be more seemly to wait till further inquiries can be made into the subject that has led to this interview."

"Hear me, great queen," exclaimed our heroine; "hear me, I say, as you would yourself be heard at the last day, when kings and subjects shall be weighed in the same balance. Spare, spare my father! His minutes are numbered—but so, too, are your's, though not by an earthly judge. Nay, even now, while I implore your mercy, the hour may be at hand, which, sooner or later, must strike for all—peers as well as peasants, monarchs as well as their subjects. Death spares neither the young nor the old, the mighty nor the humble."

"True, maiden," answered the queen; "all of us must indeed die; but therein lies no argument why guilt should pass unpunished, or a monarch grant forgiveness to one, who, there is every reason to believe, has committed a deed that renders him unworthy the merciful consideration you claim in his behalf."

"Oh, my gracious liege," cried Louisa, with increasing earnestness, "leave, I implore you, the fearful office of the avenger to him who hath said 'vengeance is mine,' and who best knows how to temper punishment with mercy. Lady,—noble lady, it is not the anointing oil on the regal brow that can still one single throb of pain, when the body writhes with the last sickness, and the heart beats fearfully at the near approach of all-conquering death."

"Girl," exclaimed the queen, "why need you remind me of that which cannot fail to cast a shade of gloom over a heart that ought to be all gladness at such a period as this?"

"My queen," answered our heroine, "I would remind you that, come the hour of death when it may, the recollection of one deed of mercy will do more to smooth your pillow than the physician's drugs, or the fulsome flattery of your heartless courtiers—aye—even though it were as sincere as all knew it to be hollow."

"You plead your cause strongly, young maiden," returned Queen Anne, with emotion, "and if I trusted to the dictates of my own heart, I might extend mercy to your father, even though I believe him to be guilty of the heinous crime laid to his charge."

"Oh, trust to the generous feelings of your heart, noble lady," cried Louisa; "trust to it, my gracious mistress, and be assured that, in this instance, at least, it has not deceived you."

"Aye—but justice ——"

"If every fault," interrupted our heroine, "should be weighed too strictly by justice, who may hope to share the joys of heaven? The saint who has passed his days in fasting and his nights in prayer, will he yet dare to stand before the face of the Eternal and say, 'Judge me, O Lord, after my desert?' No, lady, no; we are all weak and erring beings—we must all be saved by mercy, or perish. Then spare—spare my father! kill not two wretched creatures with one blow, for when his grey head falls into the grave, this heart will surely break!"

"Poor creature!" sighed the queen; "I feel I am too much a woman—too little a queen, when urged thus to save the life of a subject. What will my council say should I weakly yield to the dictates prompted by my own heart?"

"Think not of them, lady," answered Louisa; "but rather think of your own peace of mind when reflecting upon this generous deed. And, oh! how sweetly will the recollection of a life saved mingle with your prayers this night—how light will throb your bosom—in the low whispers of contented conscience you shall think to hear the answer of some unseen angel murmuring a blessing on the prayers you offer up to Heaven."

"This," cried the queen, "is, indeed, the very eloquence of passion. Rise, girl, rise, for the interview has already lasted too long."

"Your gracious pardon first," exclaimed Louisa, with increasing earnestness, "your pardon, gracious lady, and then my blessings upon her who is not deaf to the prayers of the unfortunate."

"Nay, I must ——"

"Hold!" interrupted our heroine, "a moment, I beseech you, ere you pronounce the dreadful sentence—let me live another moment—for the word of doom will kill me where I kneel."

"Be calm, girl—be calm."

"I will, gracious princess," answered Louisa—"I will be as calm as this moment of agony will allow me—not a sigh shall escape my lips till you have again spoken."

"You have nothing to fear, maiden," exclaimed the queen, after a brief pause; "but compose yourself, and rise—rise, I say, for this lowly posture is unworthy of you."

"Ah!" cried Louisa, joyfully; "may I—may I, indeed, look again upon the pleasant face of heaven, and return the happy messenger of my dear father's pardon?"

"Have I not said it?" replied the queen. "Rise, girl, and all shall yet be well."

"Oh," exclaimed Louisa, "the joy—the agony of this moment!"

"I must not trust my council," added her majesty, "lest they should argue me out of my better feelings. My Lord of Sussex, draw out a full and unconditional pardon, leaving the name of the offender blank. And now, my poor child," she said in a whisper to the supplicant, "be happy, for your father shall not die. But be calm, or those about us will guess all that has taken place."

"I will—I will be calm," answered our heroine —"I will not breathe a word, but I cannot—cannot help my tears of joy and gratitude."

"And well do they become you," exclaimed her majesty, "though I would fain prevail upon you to suppress those feelings till your return with the pardon that has been won by your eloquence. You must be firm, maiden, and years of happiness, I trust, are yet in store for you."

During a pause that now succeeded, Lord Sussex approached and handed to her majesty the paper on which he had drawn out the pardon. This was carefully perused by the queen, in order that no fatal error might be suffered to creep in, and, having satisfied herself that it was correct, she inserted the name of Luke Somerton in the blank space which had been left, and then adding the royal sign manuel, handed it to Louisa with a smile of joyous beneficence.

"There, my good girl," she exclaimed, "there is your father's pardon; if I have erred in granting it, it is a fault, I hope, that will not, henceforward, sit too heavily on my bosom."

"My kind, my honoured mistress," cried Louisa, "how can I express the gratitude with which this generous act has filled my heart?"

"By saying no more about it," replied the queen. "Your entreaties were urged with such irresistible force that I could not control my own inclinations for mercy, and in giving happiness to a fond and affectionate girl, I have afforded to myself a satisfaction that will not soon be forgotten."

"Happy, happy Louisa," cried our heroine, "what have you done to merit the gracious approbation of your sovereign? But deign, gracious lady, to receive my thanks ——"

"Nay, I need not words to thank me," interrupted the queen, "for I am already more than repaid in witnessing the joy it has thus been in my power to bestow. And now, maiden, wear this necklace in memory of your interview with Queen Anne; it will remind you of the good deed you have this day done, and may the thought bring with it the peace of mind that is ever the reward of those who possess virtue and innocence. Now, my lords," she added, turning towards her noble retinue, "time wears on apace, and we must now proceed to partake of the festivities prepared in honour of our visit by our good and loyal Lord of Derwent."

The procession now began to move onwards, and the queen, after glancing affectionately at our heroine as she departed, entered into conversation with the ladies of her suite, as if to drive from her memory a scene which had not passed without feelings of deep emotion. Louisa remained gazing in speechless wonder upon the splendid procession as it moved towards the further part of the town, and so completely was she absorbed in the bewildering thoughts which occupied her mind, that she was unconscious of the presence of Christopher Dalton, till he had addressed himself to her three or four times.

"It was bravely done, my good girl, bravely done, indeed," he exclaimed; "but why, in the name of fortune, do you stand here, staring like a silly wench as you are?"

"I know not where I am, or what I do," she replied, "for joy has so completely taken possession of me, that my brain spins round, and my thoughts can find no subject upon which to fix themselves."

"Then you must place yourself under my guidance for a little time," exclaimed Dalton, "or after all you have been doing, matters will not turn out so well as they might."

"In what respect?"

"Why, there's not much time to lose, you may be quite assured," he replied, "and if we don't make all the haste we can, we shall be too late to save the old man from his fate."

"True, true," answered Louisa, rousing herself from the abstraction into which she had fallen; "there is not a moment to be lost, or we shall be too late on our errand of mercy."

"And that would be sad work after all the trouble you have had to obtain his pardon from the queen," observed Christopher. "So let's get back to the inn where we left your uncle, who, by this time, I suppose, has returned from the errand he went on."

"Of what errand do you speak?" inquired our heroine, anxiously.

"I'll tell you all about that as we go along," replied the other, taking her arm and proceeding in the direction of the inn. "You must know, Louisa, that he has a friend in this town who possesses a good deal of court influence, and fearing lest your supplications to her majesty should fail, he has gone to his house to entreat him to supplicate for the life of an unfortunate fellow-creature. For my own part, I thought it a wild-goose chase, but a man is not to be convinced against his will, so I e'en said very little against his project, and by this time, no doubt, he has discovered that friends have not the power to serve, though they may have every inclination to do so."

"Yet it was worth trying," observed Louisa, "and his intercession might have proved of the highest importance had my efforts proved unavailing."

"Why, of course, I don't blame him for trying to save his brother's life," answered Dalton, "though I could not see much use in his trusting such an important business as this to the good-nature of another party. Friendship sounds mighty pretty to the ears of young folks like yourself, but when you come to test it, 'tis a thousand to one but they leave you to get out of a dilemma in the best way you can."

"But it fortunately happens," replied Louisa, "that in the present instance it matters very little whether my uncle succeeds in his mission or not. The pardon I sought for has been granted, and I trust the mercy which has been bestowed upon my father, will induce him to return once more to the loyalty which the beneficence of his royal mistress so richly deserves. For years past a dark shade has rested upon his name, but his arm may yet be raised in behalf of his queen and country, and should he fall in deadly strife with the enemies of England, I would bless the hour that enabled me to preserve him that he might prove himself worthy the mercy that was vouchsafed to him."

"You think, then, he will quit the companionship of his old associates?"

"I do, indeed."

"In that case I should follow his example," replied Dalton, "for, to tell you the truth, I begin to be ashamed of the sort of life we have been leading for some years past. But here we are at the

where we left your uncle, and if we are lucky
enough to find that he has returned, we'll lose no
time in getting back for the boat, and then, hey
once more to the little Isle of Man."

CHAPTER XVI.

Her air, her manners, all who saw admired;
Courteous though coy, gentle though retired;
The joy of youth and health her eyes displayed,
And ease of heart her every look conveyed!

CRABBE.

Upon entering the room which they had before
occupied, they found James Somerton pacing uneasily up and down, and impatiently awaiting their
return with news as to the success of their application for the royal mercy. His own countenance
was gloomy and disturbed; but no sooner did he
glance upon that of Louisa, than a brighter gleam
lit up his face, and in hurried accents he demanded
the result of their interview.

"All, all is as our fondest hopes could have
wished," she replied. "The queen was not deaf to
the entreaties of a heart-broken girl, and she who
went forth sorrowing has returned with the joyful
tidings that her father has been rescued from the
hands of his implacable enemies."

"He is pardoned, then?"

"He is."

"And is it unconditional, or must he pass the
remainder of his days as an exile from the land of
his birth?"

"Oh," answered Christopher Dalton, "the pardon
is full a one as you could have desired; but I
must tell you it was not granted without a good deal
of trouble, for her majesty seemed to think he was
guilty of the murder, and it was not till Louisa had
urged her entreaties a long while that the pardon
could be obtained."

"It was scarcely to be expected," observed
James Somerton, "for the queen is bound by her
oath to administer strict and impartial justice, and
the shedder of human blood rarely finds mercy,
however strong may have been the provocation that
led to the act of violence."

"Alas!" cried Louisa, "you, then, believe him
to be guilty of this fearful crime?"

"Trust me, dear girl, I do not," answered her
uncle, "yet circumstances, it must be acknowledged, are against him, and it but too frequently
occurs that the judgment is biassed by prejudice
when the party accused does not stand high in the
world's esteem."

"And such, I suppose, was the case with your
friend," observed Dalton; "at all events, we have
as yet heard how you succeeded with him; so, of
course, he was not willing to grant a favour when
the person you interceded for was not likely to find
grace in the eyes of her majesty of England."

"It must be confessed my application was listened to with coldness," answered James Somerton; "yet, now that the pardon has been granted,
I am not without hopes that something may be
done for my brother in the way of patronage. I
hope to see my friend again in the course of half
an hour, and, through his influence, it may be easy
to obtain for Luke a commission in the navy, that
may enable him to retrieve the character he has
unfortunately lost."

"Between ourselves, sir, I rather think that is
more easily said than done," replied Dalton. "He
may be appointed to the command of a ship, I
have no doubt; but how would he be regarded by
the officers and men placed under him? This
murder would be always uppermost in their minds,
and, instead of having the respect of his inferiors,
he would be regarded with suspicion and dislike;
and the end of it would be, to find himself placed
in a situation anything but agreeable."

"At first, perhaps, it might be so," returned the
other; "but a brave man soon works himself into
the esteem of his fellow-creatures, and, my life for
it, we should quickly see him regarded for his gallant qualities, in spite of everything that former
transactions might bring to the mind."

"All that may be true enough, to be sure," replied Dalton; "but Luke Somerton has not yet
been consulted upon the subject, and we don't
know that he would accept of a commission in her
majesty's service, after having once left it to engage
himself in the free trade traffic."

"He is sick of it," returned the other, "and
would gladly avail himself of an opportunity to retrieve his lost character. He is not so far lost to
honour as to reject an opportunity of raising himself once more in the world's esteem; and, though
I speak it in his absence, I am not the less assured
that he will accept of any terms that may serve to
remove the stigma which at present attaches itself
to his name. Indeed, had I believed him capable
of continuing his former evil course, I would have
suffered the law to claim its victim, rather than
assist to preserve him for the continuance of such
a life as he has led during the last four years."

"Oh, do not believe it of him," cried Louisa,
"for I feel certain that he will gladly avail himself
of any chance that presents itself to regain the
honour he has unfortunately lost. That he has
erred in leaguing himself with men of wild and
reckless life, I cannot deny, but persecution drove
him to it, and he will now awaken, as from a dream,
to be all that the most ardent of his friends can
desire."

"Ay, ay," interposed Dalton, "if he has been a
wildish chap of late years, it was not all his own
fault, I can tell you. Captain Aylmer has got all
that to answer for in another world, for if it had
not been for his evil doings, Luke Somerton would
have been high in her majesty's service, and his
daughter would not this day have had to ask his
life from the queen of England."

"Yet having succeeded in my mission," exclaimed Louisa, "we will speak no longer against
one whom the grave has by this time covered. Let
his faults be forgiven and forgotten in the satisfaction we feel at having rescued my father from a
doom which, in my own mind, I believe to be
unjust."

"Be it so," returned James Somerton; "for my
own part, I bear no malice against Captain Aylmer,
though I would wish he had adopted a more
generous course towards my unfortunate brother.
The quarrel that was known to exist between them
might well give rise to suspicions prejudicial to my
brother, and there is every reason to believe he
would have fallen a sacrifice to the laws of his
country, had not his daughter nobly stepped forward to rescue him from an ignominious fate.

"And well has she been rewarded," cried Louisa, "since it is now her joyous task to return home the messenger of pardon. Yet not to me, but to the queen, be all honour for this deed, for had her majesty hesitated to perform an act of mercy, my father must have met the doom of a murderer."

"And his daughter," observed Christopher Dalton, "must have lingered on a life of hopeless misery."

"Nay," she replied, "my sufferings would not have been of long duration, since a broken heart would have laid me in the grave with him. I could not have lived to return home with the fatal news, or even if I had survived so long, it would have been to die at his feet, ere the words of his doom could have escaped my lips."

"And a very pretty tragedy that would have made of it," observed Dalton, "for of course Lieutenant Granger could not have outlived you any great time, so there would have been an end of a whole family, to the great wonderment of all lovers of the marvellous residing in the Isle of Man."

"Nor will the marvel be much less," said James Somerton, "now that my niece returns with a pardon, which she herself has succeeded in obtaining from the Queen of England. Why, they will never cease to persecute you with inquiries as to how you set to work, and whether her majesty was pleased to give you a gracious reception."

"Then I will tell them she was pleased to listen to me like a beneficent mother, who hears the supplications of her daughter," answered Louisa, ardently. "They shall know that Queen Anne is endowed no less with grace than with virtue, and that even to the humblest of her subjects she can be as affable as to the highest lord or lady that throng around her throne."

"But," exclaimed Dalton, "I am thinking that there's not many people in the Isle of Man that will thank her for pardoning Luke Somerton, whom they all agree in believing guilty of this murder. They have been anticipating the pleasure of witnessing his execution, and great will be their disappointment when they find that a free pardon has been granted him; indeed I should not be surprised if a riot was to take place in consequence, and in that case it would not be very easy to get him out of the island with a whole skin."

"Ah!" said Louisa, "would they murder one whom the queen has set at liberty?"

"I rather expect such would be the case, if they could only get at him," answered Dalton. "However, Luke Somerton is not without friends, while any of his shipmates are within hail, and as we can make a pretty strong body-guard among us, there's not much to fear for his safety."

"There will be no occasion for your interference," exclaimed James Somerton, "since the governor will be answerable for my brother's life as soon as he has received the queen's commands upon the subject. A few soldiers will be sufficient to guard him till he arrives on board ship, and I know enough of him to feel assured that he will never have a desire to visit, at any future period, a place where he has met with such rough treatment. But I will now once more see my friend, and in half an hour meet you on the beach, near where our little vessel lies at anchor."

He immediately hurried away upon uttering these words, and Dalton was about to go and make preparations for their departure, when a servant entered to announce the arrival of a visiter, who presented himself before them almost as soon as the words were uttered.

"I believe," he said, "I have the honour of addressing myself to Louisa Somerton, who not long since had an interview with the queen?"

"Such is indeed my name," she replied, "though I must needs confess myself at a loss to guess the errand upon which you have come."

"I am the bearer of a message from her majesty," answered the other, "and crave to speak with you a few minutes without the presence of a third party."

"Humph!" exclaimed Christopher Dalton, "may I ask the name of the person who makes so singular a request of a young lady?"

"Sir Edmund Hardress," replied the other, with a grave and formal bow.

"Oh, in that case, I'm your most obedient servant," exclaimed Dalton, in an altered tone. "Great folks ought to be above suspicion, even when a lady is in the case, and so, Sir Edmund Hardress, I shall take my leave till it pleases you to give me permission to return."

With a rough, sailor-like bow, he quitted the room, and the baronet, advancing his chair nearer to that occupied by Louisa, said,—

"The queen has been graciously pleased to speak of your conduct with admiration, and, upon further consideration, has expressed a desire to mark her favourable impressions by a gift of greater value than the one she bestowed upon you just previous to taking her departure."

"The gift was a costly one," answered Louisa, producing the necklace, "and far greater than was deserved by one so humble as myself. As a token of her gracious favour, I shall ever retain it in my possession; and changed, indeed, must be my heart if ever I forget the gracious act which, this day, saved my father's life."

"It was a bold game," observed Sir Edmund, "though, as luck would have it, you played it successfully. Orders were given some time back, not to admit persons, on any pretence, to intrude unbidden upon her presence; yet you contrived to elude the vigilance of her guards, and to avoid the anger which, at another period, or by any other person, might have been called forth."

"When a father's life was depending upon the issue," replied Louisa, "I thought little of the royal anger, even though my own death had been the consequence. One object alone occupied my mind; and I was resolved to go on with it, death himself had stood before me, to bar my progress."

"Perhaps," observed Sir Edmund, "it was the boldness of your manner, and the fearlessness with which you advanced, that disarmed the queen's anger. At any rate, you succeeded to admiration, and her majesty is so well pleased with the firmness exhibited by you on the occasion, that a situation awaits your immediate acceptance, and which will keep you almost constantly about her person."

"I thank her majesty for her royal condescension," replied Louisa; "but there are reasons which must prevent my acceptance of her gracious offer."

"How! Do you decline an honour that would be gladly accepted by half the ladies in England?"

"There is no help for it, Sir Edmund."

"Humph! What reason can you give the queen for so singular a refusal?"

"In the first place," replied Louisa, "I have vowed never again to separate from my father till death parts us for ever. It is but lately I have known him as my parent; and having, by the kindness of my queen, rescued him from death, I would become his companion, lest temptation shoul lead him again to follow the reckless life that had but too nearly proved fatal to him."

"That is one reason," observed Sir Edmund Hardress; "now, let me hear what other you have to allege."

"The other is," replied Louisa, "that I would not willingly associate myself with those exalted persons who can scarcely fail to regard me as far beneath them in rank, and unworthy to mix in the society to which they belong."

"Nay, that can hardly be," answered Sir Ed_

mund, "since the queen wills it; and they are bound to yield implicit obedience to her pleasure. Anne is a kind and excellent mistress; but those about her know that she is not to be thwarted by the cabals of those who flutter in the sunshine of the court."

"Still," exclaimed our heroine, "her majesty must pardon me, if I refuse an offer that I feel assured has been made from the kindest motives. I am poor, and have been brought up in an humble station, that unfits me for the atmosphere of a palace; and even had I been weak enough to indulge my vanity by an acceptance of her generous offer, it would have been to render my future life less happy than it might otherwise have been in the station to which my lowly birth had fitted me."

"But use would soon wear off the rust," answered Sir Edmund; "and I can take it upon myself to pledge my word that in less than three months you will be among the gayest of those who help to make up the glare and tinsel of our court."

"It is that very glare and tinsel which I would most avoid, Sir Edmund," she replied. "Such things have no charms for me, and I should afterwards despise myself, were I to yield so far to vanity as to take my station in a place for which I am totally unfitted. My father has been long known as a smuggler—his name has lost the honour that once attached to it, and his daughter, of course, shares in the degradation into which he has fallen. All this the queen's favour may, in some degree, remove, yet people will not fail to remember all that is most to my prejudice, and thus I should find myself scorned and neglected, when it might be least in my power to escape from the misery that my own act had produced."

"You are resolute, then, in the course you have thought proper to adopt, though, it seems to me, without sufficient consideration having been given to the subject?"

"It requires but little consideration," she replied, "when we believe ourselves to be following a prudent course, and that, it seems to me, I am doing in the present instance. To the queen, Heaven bless her! I owe a debt of gratitude that nothing can ever repay; and I feel assured she will pardon my refusal to accept of a kindness that, however graciously meant, will be better declined—at least till I have an opportunity of consulting my father upon the subject."

"Suppose you consult the friend who left the room when I entered?" suggested Sir Edmund. "He appears to be worthy of your fullest confidence, and, no doubt, will give such advice as you may fearlessly venture to follow."

"With all my heart," she replied; "though, to confess the truth, I should be likely to follow my own inclination, should he happen to propose my acceptance of the queen's gracious offer."

"We will see that, at all events," said the baronet; and, opening the door, he summoned Christopher Dalton, to whom he at once explained his message from the court, and then demanded how he would counsel the young lady to act when so brilliant a prospect had began to dawn upon her fortunes.

"How would I counsel her?" demanded Christopher, with surprise; "why, I should think she hardly needs advice from me, when it's as plain as the nose on her face what she ought to do."

"In other words, you think she ought not to refuse a proposal that holds out so flattering a view of future grandeur?"

"That's exactly my notion about it."

"But it is not mine," exclaimed Louisa; "and, as a proof it, I have already declined an offer which, at present, I deem it imprudent to accept."

"And why do you think it imprudent to accept that which any other girl would jump at as one of the luckiest chances that could occur?"

"That I will explain to you another time, Mr. Dalton," she replied. "At present, let it suffice that I have seen sufficient reason to adopt this course; but I will not say that, upon further consideration, my answer is a final one."

"Well, I should hope it is not."

"Why?"

"Simply because I think you will afterwards repent having declined the gracious offer of her majesty," replied Christopher. "These lucky chances don't occur every day in our lives, and it strikes me that, before long, you will see reason to be sorry for giving an answer without first of all turning it well over in your mind."

"I have already done so," she replied; "and the reasons that impel me to adopt this course seem to be quite sufficient."

"Then my advice has been asked," returned Dalton, "though, it appears, you had previously made up your mind not to follow it, unless it happened to agree exactly with your own notions upon the subject."

"It must be admitted I deserve your rebuke," answered our heroine. "My resolution was, indeed, formed, and it was only at the suggestion of this gentleman that I heard your opinion upon a subject that I had already decided upon."

"You are resolute in your refusal, it seems," exclaimed Sir Edmund Hardress, "and I will no longer endeavour to prevail over your objections. I have, however, another commission to execute, which, I trust, will meet with more favour than my previous one. Her majesty anticipated your refusal to her first proposition, and gave me this pocket-book, containing five hundred pounds, which she desires you to accept as a mark of her admiration at the heroism you displayed when

pleading before her the cause of an unfortunate parent."

"Indeed, indeed, I cannot take it."

"The girl's mad, for certain!" muttered Dalton.

"Nay," exclaimed the baronet, "this is a command from her majesty that I dare not disobey. She charged me to deliver it into your hands, and on no account to bring it back with me."

"Foolish girl!" whispered Dalton; "don't you hear what the queen has said, and would you be crazy enough to send it back again, as if you were too proud to accept a favour even from royalty?"

"If I accept the generous gift of my royal mistress," exclaimed Louisa, "it will only be to prove that I am not insensible to the kindness she has been pleased to show me. I will take it, Sir Edmund, and, in return, you will be pleased to convey my humble gratitude for the goodness that has been vouchsafed me by her whom all hearts reverence for her kindness and condescension."

"Why, that's more sensibly said," exclaimed Christopher Dalton, "though, egad, I began to be afraid you were going to be as foolish in this instance as you were in the last."

"I should certainly have refused it," answered our heroine, "had it not been for fear of offending one who has shown so kindly a feeling in my behalf."

"Then you have, luckily, avoided a great act of folly," returned the other; "for, if money is of no use to yourself, I know one that will be glad enough to find you are so rich all on a sudden."

"You mean my father?"

"No, I mean Lieutenant Granger, who, I suppose, will soon be your husband, now that this disagreeable business has been brought to a satisfactory conclusion. Nay, never blush, girl, at his name, for he has the character of being a gallant officer, and will bring no discredit upon the girl he makes his wife."

"He is, indeed, deserving the high estimation in which the world holds him," replied Louisa, "yet I believe there is little chance of my ever meeting with him again."

"And why, may I ask?"

"Because he can no longer wish to ally himself with one whose father has been doomed to meet the death of a felon."

"Psha! but the queen has pardoned him, hasn't she, and oughtn't that to be enough?"

"I believe it will not be deemed sufficient, when all things are taken into consideration," replied our heroine. "Besides," she added, "he has been desired to discontinue his visits to me by my uncle, and it can hardly be expected that he will again subject himself to a similar repulse."

"There I must differ with you, young lady," interposed Sir Edmund, "for it so happens that love increases in proportion to the obstacles that are raised against it, and, I dare say, it will prove to be so in the present instance. But a truce to this; time urges your immediate departure, for, according to the laws of the island, execution speedily follows the pronouncing of sentence, and you have but little time to accomplish the voyage that lies before you."

"I do but wait for my uncle," replied Louisa, "who promised to meet us on the sea-shore in half an hour from the time he left us."

"Then proceed thither immediately," exclaimed Sir Edmund, "and, if he is not already waiting here, embark on board your vessel, and make what speed you can across the water."

"And leave him behind?"

"Why, what matters it, when he can follow shortly afterwards?" demanded the baronet. "You have not an instant to lose; so hasten down to the beach, and leave him to make the best of his way after you."

Urged by the importance of her errand, Louisa at once yielded to this suggestion, and, bidding farewell to Sir Edmund, she left the house, accompanied by her faithful friend, Christopher Dalton.

CHAPTER XVII.

Wilt thou go on with me?
The moon is bright, the sea is calm,
And I know well the ocean paths,
Thou wilt go on with me?

THALABA.

HURRYING through the streets of Whitehaven, our heroine and her companion made their way towards the beach, where, however, they vainly sought in every direction for James Somerton, who had not yet reached the place of appointment. By this time night had set in, and, as it was absolutely necessary to reach the Isle of Man before noon on the following day, they made towards the spot where the vessel lay, intending to take their departure without losing any further time in waiting for James Somerton. To their bitter disappointment, however, they found that neither of the men who had been left in charge of the boat were then in attendance, and bitterly were they deploring this untoward circumstance, when a party of sailors approached, and inquired if they were going to risk the perils of the ocean just when the darkness of night was beginning to set in.

"We are indeed, messmate," replied Christopher Dalton; "but our crew seem to have deserted, and, between ourselves, I hardly know how we shall get across the Channel, without sufficient hands on board to work the boat."

"If you take the advice of Jack Splicebrace," exclaimed the first speaker, "you'll stay in comfortable quarters ashore, and weigh anchor the first thing in the morning."

"We have not a moment to lose," cried Louisa, "and, the night being fair and favourable, we must risk the voyage, let the consequences be what they may."

"Aye, aye, young madam," retorted the sailor, "the night looks fair enough at present, but you don't foresee what clouds will be rising up yonder before you get into mid-channel. I've seen many a fairer sunset than the one just now, and yet, in less than half a dozen hours afterwards, the shore was covered with wreck, and many a brave fellow had found a resting-place at the bottom of the ocean."

"Let us hope such will not be the case on the present occasion," said Louisa, glancing fearfully round to see if there were any visible indications of the coming storm.

"You don't see it, perhaps, ma'am," exclaimed Splicebrace; "and yet, for all that, I've a notion that we shall have a smart gale before long. Your companion seems to know something about such matters, and I just ask him if he don't think I'm in the right of it?"

"It must be confessed I don't like the appearances above," answered Christopher Dalton; "and yet, for all that, if our fellows were where they ought to be, neither I nor this young lady would hesitate to trust ourselves in our little bark."

"I suppose your chaps didn't think you'd be back quite so soon," observed the sailor; "and so, as there was a sight to be seen ashore, they've taken French leave, and gone into the town to have a look at good Queen Nance."

"By which," cried Louisa with a shudder, "they may sacrifice the life of a fellow-creature."

"Perhaps more might have been sacrificed if you had set sail to-night," returned the rough son of Neptune; "so, if I was you, I should make my mind up to the disappointment, and to-morrow morning you may weigh anchor with something like a chance of reaching the island in safety."

"Alas! we have no choice left," cried Louisa, in despair, "for a father's life depends upon the utmost haste being made, and the loss even of a moment may prove fatal to him."

"That's a hard case to be sure, miss," replied Jack Splicebrace, "but, if there's no help for it, the ship's parson tells us we ought to be resigned. Besides, I should think four or five hours can't make much difference, and by that time, I should think, your fellows will have returned."

"An hour would ruin all my hopes," she cried; "nay, even a moment might render vain the errand upon which we are returning home."

"Why, mercy on us, what can be the matter, that you are in such a hurry?"

"She has spoken but too truly," answered Dalton; "for her father has been condemned to die, and unless we can see the governor before noon to-morrow, the execution will have taken place ere our arrival. You see the urgency of our case, my friend, and will, therefore, cease to wonder at the distraction of this poor trembling girl."

"Come, come, ma'am," exclaimed the sailor, "matters ain't so bad as you fancy; for, with a fair wind, there's plenty of time to get across the water; and, as it will be fairer sailing in daylight, I should advise you to make your mind easy till those tippling dogs of yours find their way back to the vessel."

"They will not return till too late," she cried; "and all must be lost, though I carry with me the pardon of our gracious queen."

"What!" exclaimed Splicebrace, "has the queen—God bless her!—been merciful to him, and must he die a dog's death, after all?"

"It must indeed be so," replied Dalton, "unless we can meet with friends who will assist us in crossing over to the Isle of Man."

"Do you hear that, messmates?" exclaimed the sailor, addressing his comrades, "and is there a man among you that will refuse to give a little assistance to people in distress like this? No, no, I'm sure there's at least one that will follow my example, and if so, we'll be aboard in the turning of a handspike, and then hey for the port they want to go to."

"If you go, Jack, I don't mind bearing you company," replied one of the men, "for I never could bear to see a woman in trouble, and, hang me, if I was certain of going to the bottom in a squall, I'd lend a hand with all my heart to put her safe on t'other side the water."

" That's spoken like a brave fellow," exclaimed Christopher Dalton, " and your reward on reaching the other side shall be something more than bare promises, I can give you my word."

" Fifty pounds a-piece—nay, a hundred," cried our heroine, " shall be gladly bestowed upon those who are willing to assist us in this our moment of greatest need."

" That's a good deal to offer, ma'am," returned Jack Splicebrace, " but I don't think either I or my comrade will be much inclined to take so much for such a trifling job."

" Aye, but there may be danger."

" A British tar should never think of danger, young miss," answered the other ; " because, you see, it comes natural to him like, and he never goes through his work half so well as when he's got his enemies about him. For my own part, death and I have been pretty near each other a great many times, but my cheek never grew pale, because I thought it would be an honour to die in defence of the country I love, and that pays me for what I do."

" We are to understand, then," observed Dalton, " that you and your comrade undertake to assist me in getting the vessel across the water ?"

" Aye, aye, sir," he replied, " we'll not be worse than our word, though, for the young lady's sake, I wish you could have put it off till daylight."

" It is impossible !" exclaimed Louisa, " for, should the wind prove adverse for us, we shall barely have time to reach our place of destination in time to save my father from the doom to which he has been sentenced."

" Why, then, bear a hand, my lad," cried Splice-brace to his companion, " and let's see how soon we can get the little craft under weigh. It's beginning to get darker out there I see to the windward already, and if we don't get off at once, we shall be hugging the shore too closely if a bit of a gale should happen to spring up."

Upon this, instant preparations were made for getting on board the vessel, and with such hearty good will was this managed, than in less than half an hour the whole party was on board, and the anchor being weighed and the sails set, they dashed forward before a favourable wind towards their place of destination. But the prognostications of Jack Splicebrace were soon afterwards to be realised, for thick masses of clouds began to spread themselves over the sky, and the moon, which at first had been clear and bright, was now frequently hidden from the view, casting a gloom upon all around, that added in no inconsiderable degree to excite the alarm of our heroine, lest they should lose their course, and thus reach the Isle of Man when it would be too late to rescue her father from his much-dreaded doom. She, however, contrived to conceal the terror that had taken possession of her heart ; and concealing her own feelings, she endea-voured to inspire courage in her companions, by affecting not to be aware of the dangers with which they were threatened.

Leaving them, however, for the present, we must now return to James Somerton, who reached the sea shore just after they had set sail, and when it was too late to entertain a hope of being able to over-take them. The sailors were still standing on the beach when he arrived there, and from them it was that he learnt the departure of his friends on an errand that he feared would be in vain, unless he was with them to give the signal according to the directions imparted to him by Luke Somerton, a short time previous to leaving him. At this intel-ligence he stood transfixed for some few moments, and then, muttering half aloud, " Lost ! lost !" he paced to and fro with the frantic gestures of a madman.

" Begging your honour's pardon," said one of the sailors, stepping up to him, " it's not quite so much *lost* as you seem to fancy, for there's a couple of as good seamen on board as ever had berth in a fore-castle, and, for all there seems to be a bit of a storm rising, I can answer for it they'll reach land without the vessel being a bit worse than when she left this place about a quarter of an hour ago."

" I know the sailors that man her," replied James Somerton, " but I fear all will not turn out so well as you would fain induce me to believe."

" I don't much think you do know the chaps, though," said the other, " for the men you came over with have thought proper to make a holiday for themselves ; and about this time I should say they are comfortably enjoying themselves, and drinking the health of her most gracious majesty."

" How !" exclaimed Somerton, " have the scoundrels dared to desert us in the very moment when their services were most needed ?"

" I don't know whether they have deserted or not," replied the other, " but I suppose they thought they had as much right as anybody else to see the queen, so they left the vessel, and if it hadn't been for a couple of our comrades, your friends must have stayed ashore all night, and that, I suppose, would have been anything but what they wanted."

" And are the men who went with them to be depended on ?" asked Somerton.

" Why to be sure they are !—a couple of stauncher fellows ain't to be found in her majesty's service ; and if they don't do their duty while one plank of the craft holds to another, why then say there's no faith to be placed in man. They've both fought for their queen and country—aye, and that bravely, too, as their officers are ready to swear—and if that ain't character enough for a man, why I don't know what would be."

" I have no doubt they will do their duty faith-fully," answered Somerton, " yet in an urgent case like this, they may not use all the speed that is necessary to save the life of a fellow-creature."

" Oh ! yes, but they will though," replied the sailor, " for they know the errand your friends are going on, and I could wager my existence they'll not leave a chance untried but what they'll reach the island in time to save the executioner the trouble of going through his office. Besides, the young lady promised a large sum of money by way of re-ward, and I'm sure they wouldn't deceive her while there's a chance of doing a service."

" Aye, aye," replied Somerton, " if gold is in the way there is indeed some probability that the men will prove faithful to their word."

" It won't be for the sake of the reward though," exlaimed the man, " for I don't believe either of my shipmates would take a farthing of money for merely doing their duty. They liked the generosity of the offer, however, and would do as much for 'em without pay, as if there was a shipful of gold to be had for making good their bargain."

"And is there any way," demanded Somerton, "by which I may follow them, so as to land in the Isle of Man nearly at the same time they do?"

"Why, as far as that goes, master," replied the tar, "there's nothing too difficult for us sailors when once we've made up our minds about it."

"Will anybody take me over yonder if I pay a liberal sum for the trouble?"

"Humph! if it could be left till the morning, it would be all the better."

"Why should there be any delay?" asked James Somerton.

"Because we can only have an open boat to go in," replied the other, "and a storm seems to be coming on that will make our passage rather a dangerous one. See! the lightning already begins to flash, and a wind is rising that promises to increase into a stiff gale before we can get clear away from the shore."

"Yet all must be risked," exclaimed Somerton, "even if I undertake alone to row myself through a tempestuous sea. Life and death depend upon my immediate departure, and rather would I perish than sacrifice a brother through any cowardice of my own."

"But suppose you happen to be lost in the storm that's coming on," demanded the sailor, "wouldn't he be just as badly off as if you stayed here till the passage can be made safely?"

"You madden me with these obstacles," exclaimed the other, "for I know the exigency of the case, and my resolution is formed to hazard my own life for the preservation of my brother. In short, I promised to hoist a signal at the mast-head on approaching the island, and as those who have just gone before me know nothing of the arrangement, their omission in not showing the flag will be taken as a proof that our application to the queen has failed, and my brother will perish by his own hand, rather than die by the executioner."

"Well, this seems to be a bad job," observed the sailor to his companion; "a poor fellow has got into a confounded scrape, and if we don't lend a helping hand to get him out of it, there's nothing left but for him to swing upon the gallows like a dog. Now I, for one, don't mind running a little risk; so if there's another among you of my way of thinking, we'll take the gentleman over, even if we should get nothing for our pains."

The men retired together a few paces to consult each other about the proposition that had been made, but it was evident, from their manner, that none of them were willing to venture upon the ocean that night, and presently afterwards one of them, who acted as spokesman for the rest, advanced towards Somerton, and announced that as a storm was brewing above, they had all come to the determination not to venture their lives where the chances were so much against them.

"Then you're a set of cowardly rascals," exclaimed the sailor, "and hang me if ever I own you again as comrades as long as I live."

"Can't help it, Sam," answered the other; "you've no family and home to look to, so that

makes all the difference. Ain't it beginning already to blow great guns, and shouldn't we be fools to risk our lives for a stranger that none of us can care anything about?"

"I will reward you amply for the service," cried James Somerton.

"I dare say you would if we chanced to get safely to land," answered the other. "It's all very fine to talk about what you would do if we happened to escape the dangers of this night's storm, but what would be the use of your money, I should like to know, if you and the whole boat's crew were to go to the bottom?"

"It's no use in the world, sir, talking to a parcel of fellows that haven't got the spirit of a mouse among 'em," exclaimed the sailor to James Somerton. "They've made up their mind not to pull an oar to-night, so all we've got to do is to think of some other plan for getting across."

"How is it to be done without their assistance?" demanded the person he had addressed.

"Why, it won't be a very easy matter, I must allow," replied the other; "but where there's a will there's a way, and if you can give me a little help, I think it might be worth trying, as it seems there's no time to be lost."

"With heart and soul I'll do my best," exclaimed Somerton, eagerly catching at the proposition, "and if we succeed in landing safely, all I possess in the world shall be freely yours."

"As for that, I don't want to make anything out of it, sir," replied the sailor, "for the truth is, I don't like to see a man sink for the want of a hand to be put out to save him. These skulking fellows don't care what happens, so that they don't come to any harm, so let the swabs go home to bed, and leave us to battle with the waves as well as we can."

"And do you think there's any probability of our reaching the Isle of Man in safety?"

"That'll depend upon the winds and waves, your honour," replied the other. "They're both of them roughish customers to meet with in these seas, I can tell you; but I've had the luck to weather many a storm before, and I fancy we may reach port in safety, if you can handle an oar, and will only place yourself under my command during the trip."

"You may depend upon me in both instances," replied Somerton, "for the occasion is an extremely urgent one, and your honest zeal convinces me that all hope has not yet disappeared, though the cowardice of these men a few minutes since filled me with alarm."

"Oh, never mind them, your honour," exclaimed the sailor; "for if they didn't go willingly with us, I'd rather have their room than their company. Let 'em stay where they are, and if anything should happen to us, their conscience—if they're got any about 'em—won't sit very easy, when they remember that we might have been saved if they'd had any spirit. But it's no use talking, sir, when there's so much to do, so bear a hand, and let's get on board the boat, for we must make the shore before the surf begins to run any higher."

With this he made his way towards the place where his boat was lying moored, and with the assistance of James Somerton the little vessel was, with some difficulty, pushed off, and they found themselves riding upon a tempestuous ocean, that threatened every moment to swallow them, in spite of all their efforts to avert so terrible a fate. But the skill of the seaman proved equal to the difficulties they had to encounter, for under his management the boat was at length got fairly out to sea, where, though still tossed about at the mercy of both wind and waves, they had less danger to apprehend than when floating among concealed rocks, that threatened them every moment with destruction. The darkness of the night, too, added to the peril of their situation, and it was only by the frequent flashes of lightning that they were able to keep in their right course.

CHAPTER XVIII.

Death I have long defied—
But thus to perish is a thought so horrible,
That frenzy fires my brain, and urges me
To deeds I else should shudder at.—*Old Play.*

THE reader will now accompany us to the Isle of Man, where, during the absence of Louisa, the trial of her father had taken place, with a result that has, no doubt, been already anticipated. But five witnesses were brought forward, one of whom proved the finding of the prisoner's dagger in the house where the murder had been committed, while the others were only required to give testimony as to the enmity which had existed between Luke Somerton and Captain Aylmer, and to swear that the former had been heard on several occasions to vow the death of his antagonist, whenever chance should happen to throw them in each other's way. This was sufficient for men whose minds were deeply prejudiced against Luke, and as he neither called witnesses in his behalf, nor offered any defence, a verdict of guilty was pronounced without hesitation, and a sentence passed condemning him to die at noon on the following day.

In the solitude of his dungeon the prisoner gave way to the dark thoughts that crowded upon his mind, and the dreadful fate to which he was adjudged filled him with sensations of horror that he had been a stranger to till the present moment. It was not, however, that he feared to die, but the shame which it would bring upon his daughter agonised his soul to madness, and as he paced up and down his gloomy cell, he bitterly reproached himself for having suffered her to depart for Whitehaven on an errand that he felt assured would end in her utter disappointment. As a murderer, he could hope for no mercy, and all that remained for him was to fall by his own hands rather than suffer a death which, to his child, would be a reproach that would cling to her through the remainder of her days. Resolved as he was upon this course, he yet wished to see her once more ere he perished, and as a few hours intervened, he determined to await her return, and defer the deed he meditated till the moment when the last terrors of the law were to be accomplished. The pistol he had secreted about him was still in his possession, and that at least would save him from the ignominy to which the governor had doomed him.

He was still reflecting upon this subject, when the gaoler entered to announce a visitor, and immediately afterwards Lieutenant Granger presented himself, and having requested the turnkey to withdraw, he inquired in a whisper if the prisoner would make one last effort to escape. Luke heard him with surprise, and, as a frown gathered upon his brow, he exclaimed, in accents of displeasure,—

"I know not, sir, whether you have been sent hither to mock me in this hour of woe, but if such is indeed your errand, return to Sir Charles Radcliffe, and tell him that I never yet feared death, and when the appointed hour arrives, he shall see that I can perish with as much fortitude as I have lived."

"You wrong me, sir, by the suspicion," answered Granger, "for, by my honour, which has never yet been sullied, I swear to you that Sir Charles Radcliffe knows nothing of my visit to you."

"The act, then, was a voluntary one on your part, Lieutenant Granger?"

"It was."

"Do you know the consequences that would fall upon yourself were I to accept the offer you have just now made me?"

"I care not what the consequences may be," replied the young officer, "since it is the father of my Louisa that I would save from the doom that awaits him."

"Ha!" exclaimed Luke Somerton, "you love my daughter, and would hazard your own life to preserve that of her unfortunate parent?"

"Willingly," answered Granger; "yet, believe me, I think your escape may be contrived without my incurring so much peril as you imagine."

"Indeed! then you believe the governor would not punish the man who aided in the escape of one whom he has sentenced to die?"

"Sir Charles Radcliffe pities you from his heart," replied the young man, "and would rejoice in your escape, since he has no power to pardon you, or even to grant a respite for an hour beyond the time appointed for the execution to take place."

"I owe him but little gratitude for his pity," returned the prisoner, "since his were the lips that pronounced my doom, though he might have interposed to save my life, had he been so inclined."

"Believe me, you wrong him," exclaimed Lieutenant Granger, "for, painful as the duty was, he had no alternative after the verdict of the jury had been given. To have hesitated then would have implied favour towards yourself, and your enemies here are sufficiently powerful to procure his disgrace from government had he omitted to proceed to the utmost extremity."

"It may be as you have said," answered the prisoner, "yet your argument does not prove that he would be pleased at my escape from the gloomy dungeon to which he has consigned me."

"But I know his mind upon the subject," replied Granger, "and nothing would afford him greater satisfaction than to hear that you had succeeded in leaving the island."

"Aye," exclaimed the other, "but would he like to know that you, in whom he has placed so much confidence, was the person who aided my flight?"

"I think his anger would not be of very long duration," replied Granger. "At first it might be necessary for him to appear displeased, but, after the people's excitement had worn off, he would take me again into favour."

"At least you would fain persuade me so," exclaimed Luke Somerton, "in order to induce me to make an attempt that, in my own mind, I feel convinced would fail. Why, every outlet is strictly guarded by the soldiers, and how would it be possible to elude them when it is their business to prevent it?"

"My plan," answered the other, "would render success almost certain."

"And pray what is your plan?"

"That you should exchange clothes with me," replied Granger, "and then, favoured by the darkness of night, you may pass from the castle and reach the sea shore, where the means of flight will be easily found."

"And do you believe the guards will be so remiss in their duty as to let me leave the place without challenge or inquiry?"

"They will do that without doubt," replied Lieutenant Granger, "but, as I can supply you with the pass word, the chief difficulty will be removed."

"So you would persuade me to seek my own safety, though at the same time I know your life may be endangered by the act?"

"There is no fear of it," replied the other, " and, even if there was, I would cheerfully run the risk to save the father of Louisa from the fate that hangs over him."

"And, think you not, young man," demanded Luke Somerton, "that the grief of my daughter would be as great for her lover as for her father?"

"I believe not," he answered, with a sigh, " for she has forbidden my future addresses, and there is but too much reason to believe that she is lost to me for ever."

"She is," exclaimed Luke; "for the shame that has fallen upon her father will, of course, prevent your union with the daughter."

"Not if she will consent to be mine," returned the other, with animation. "I have loved her long and faithfully, and no false pride shall ever make me look with coldness upon one whose sorrows have made her yet dearer to my heart."

"You are a kind, noble fellow," exclaimed Somerton, "and deeply do I regret the disappointment your hopes are doomed to encounter. Louisa is indeed worthy of you, but her own sense of honour will prevent her ever becoming your wife."

"At present, it must be admitted, my prospects are overclouded," answered Granger, "yet a happier turn may take place, when she will no longer hesitate to unite her destiny with mine."

"Nay, it is a vain thought," replied the other, " and, for your own sake, Lieutenant Granger, I trust you will no longer encourage it. Louisa knows her duty, and let the sacrifice be what it may, she will rather endure it than bring disgrace upon one whom she sincerely loves."

"Disgrace!"

"Aye! Who, think you, would hold fellowship with the man that married the daughter of Luke Somerton?"

"Is the child, then, to suffer shame for the supposed crime of the father?"

"Such is the custom of the world," answered Luke; "and the only thing that gives bitterness to these, my last few remaining hours, is the thought of the unmerited disgrace that will fall on her."

"It shall be my care," exclaimed Granger, "to guard her from the shafts of malice, and to render harmless the evil deeds of a heartless world. Give out your consent to our union, and there will be no fear but her own will follow, when she sees that my love is not to be quenched by the misfortunes which it was not in her power to prevent."

"Your generosity unmans me," cried Luke Somerton, with deep emotion. "I had believed that not one pitying friend remained to us; but even in the midst of adversity, when the finger of scorn is pointed towards me, you have proved yourself to be above the mean prejudices of a selfish world. The consent, therefore, that you have asked for, is yours—but do not let that too much elate you, for I know the disposition of my daughter, and feel convinced she will be firm in the decision she has already given."

"Louisa will not refuse me when she knows that it is the wish of her father," replied Lieutenant Granger. "That she loves me I am thoroughly convinced, and whatever scruples she may at present entertain will vanish, when she sees that my happiness depends entirely upon our union."

"Yet, will she not afterwards reproach herself, if the marriage should bring upon you the scorn of your fellow men?" demanded the other.

"Not if she sees that I care nothing about it," replied Granger; "besides, I am not without hope that her application for mercy to the queen will prove successful, and in that case the stigma will be removed, and with it all ground for apprehension."

"The queen," returned Luke Somerton, "bears the character of being a merciful sovereign; but have I not been an outlaw? and can I, then, expect favour from her whom I have grievously offended?"

"But she may yet be inclined to mercy," answered the other, "in consideration of your gallantry in her services ere you left it, through the baseness of Captain Aylmer. I have heard your name mentioned in the highest terms of respect, and it was only when you leagued yourself with men of reckless character, that people began to regard you as one who had forfeited all claim to the esteem of his fellow creatures."

"Wasn't I driven to it even against my inclination?" cried Luke Somerton, bitterly. "Disgraced and calumniated by the man I had called my friend, what resource remained for me but to seek new associates, even though they might not stand quite so high as those amongst whom I had formerly been used to mix? I became a smuggler—fought sometimes—and successfully, too—against those who were sent either to destroy or drive me from the seas, and became at length so notorious, that proclamations were issued, declaring me to be an outlaw, and offering a reward to any person who would take me dead or alive. But I laughed at all their puny efforts, and should have continued to do so but for my unfortunate visit to this island, and the meeting that afterwards took place between Captain Aylmer and myself."

"Let me hear no more, I entreat you," exclaimed Granger, "for I would fain believe you innocent of the crime, and another word from your lips upon the subject might serve to alter my favourable opinion."

"You are right, young man," answered Somerton; "the secret may indeed die with me, for the sake of her from whom I am about to part so soon. Men may deem me guilty, and blacken my name when I am no longer present to answer them ; but they will speak only according to their own prejudices, since to one person only have I spoken plainly on this unfortunate subject."

"Who have you made your confidant ?" demanded Lieutenant Granger.

"The governor of this island."

"Then your secret is in safe keeping," answered the other ; "for Sir Charles Radcliffe is an honourable man, and nothing will ever induce him to betray the trust, unless, indeed, he sees an opportunity to rescue your name from the foul blot that rests upon it."

"You also can assist in that good work," exclaimed Luke, earnestly. "Louisa may believe me, in her own mind, to be guilty of the crime they have condemned me for, but you will, I hope, often see her when I am no more, and it may be in your power to remove any impression that she may have formed against me. I do not say that my hand is free from blood, Lieutenant Granger, but a daughter need not know the crime of her father, and her peace of mind can only be secured by inducing her to believe that Aylmer did not owe his death to me."

"I understand you," replied the other ; "but let us now change the subject for that which brought me hither. Escape from this place is less difficult than you seem to imagine ; every arrangement has been made to ensure perfect success, and it only remains for you to exchange clothes with me to secure yourself from the fate of a criminal."

"What !" exclaimed Luke Somerton, "would you have me basely leave you, in my place, and thus sacrifice a friend for the sake of a life that I have almost ceased to care about preserving."

"Nay," replied Granger, "if it is valueless to yourself, you should at least consider that there is one who holds it more precious than her own existence."

"You mean my daughter ?"

"I do."

"She has fortitude to endure greater trials than this," answered the prisoner, "and upon her firmness under affliction do I place my entire reliance. You possess no little influence over her mind, Lieutenant Granger, and your words of consolation will not be uttered in vain. Tell her that I entertained no fear of death, and that I rather sought than shunned it as the only means that offered to escape from the fangs of a crushed and broken spirit."

"Ay," answered the young officer ; "but you seem to forget the heavy grief your death will inflict upon Louisa. Her anxiety in your behalf is manifested in the journey she has taken to see the queen, and her only chance of happiness rests upon obtaining the pardon for which she has ere this supplicated."

"I know it," replied Luke Somerton ; "but what chance is there of her succeeding, when the crime laid to my charge is one that is never pardoned ?"

"But the queen is said to be merciful, and who can say that she will not be moved by the prayers and entreaties of a heart-broken girl ?"

"Sovereigns are made of sterner stuff than you think for," replied Luke ; "and even if her majesty were disposed to be lenient, there are those

about her who would take care to prevent it. Let them only remind her that I have lived by setting the laws at defiance, and she will refuse the application of my daughter, even though the poor suppliant chanced to perish at her feet."

"I am inclined to think otherwise," returned Granger, "for Anne has a spirit of her own that will not endure contradiction when once she has made up her mind upon a subject. There are few persons that can withstand the tears of suffering innocence ; and, pleaded as your cause will be by Louisa, I feel assured the journey to Whitehaven will not have been tried in vain. Nay, at this moment she is most likely on her return with the cheering intelligence of your pardon."

"Heaven forbid !" exclaimed Luke Somerton, as a vivid flash of lightning shot across the dungeon. "If in this storm she is upon the water, I fear there will be little chance of her reaching the island in safety."

"She may already have returned to the island," answered Granger, "for her errand would not take very long to accomplish, and whether the mission were successful or not, she would hasten back to relieve the deep anxiety we all feel upon this painful subject."

"She will be lost !" cried Somerton, in an agony of alarm, as flash after flash succeeded each other in rapid succession. "Affection has induced her to go upon this perilous errand, and nothing can save her from the fierce elements she will have to contend against."

"This despair unmans you when even more than your usual fortitude is demanded," exclaimed Granger.

"Talk not of fortitude to a father when he feels but too well assured that his daughter is about to perish through her devotion to him," madly exclaimed Luke Somerton. "Hear you not how the winds howl as if exulting over the prey they are about to seize upon, and think you my heart is stone that I can listen to this wild music without feeling for her who, perhaps, ere now, is lost to me for ever ?"

"Nay, I would but prevail on you to be more calm."

"Do not mock me, sirrah," fiercely exclaimed the captive, "lest in my madness I dash your head against yonder wall ! As well might you bid the hoarsely roaring waves be calm, as to preach patience to a man whose mortal sufferings are as great as those I endure at this moment."

"Oh, pardon me, if I have heedlessly offended you," said Lieutenant Granger, soothingly. "I would see you maintain the firmness so necessary at a moment like this, and await with what composure you can till news reaches us of your daughter. Perhaps, ere now, she has landed, and a few minutes more will serve to bring you the joyful news of her safety."

"Aye," groaned Luke Somerton ; "but minutes are as long as hours to a man that's tortured with suspense. See how the storm increases in fury, and the winds raise their voice as if to drown the peals of thunder that shake even this castle to its very foundation !"

"It is, indeed, a fearful night," answered Granger ; "yet the violence of the storm may soon pass away, and granting that Louisa is still at sea, she

accompanied by those who are well accustomed to encounter tempests full as violent as this."

"But man cannot always contend against the elements when they rise against him," replied Luke, "and this is a storm that will bring desolation to the heart of many a distracted widow and orphan. Each blast is enough to send a goodly ship to the bottom, and how then can I hope that the frail bark in which she has ventured will escape destruction."

"Let us at least hope for the best," exclaimed Granger, "and the morning may bring with it more comfort than you anticipate. Louisa, I trust, will reach the island in safety, and bring with her the pardon, for the sake of which she undertook this mission."

"Let her but once more present herself to my longing gaze," exclaimed Somerton, "and I care not though she come back with news that no entreaty could move the heart of Queen Anne to mercy. I have no fear of death, and can meet it cheerfully if I do but know that she who has risked thus much for me is safe."

"You forget," returned the young officer, "that should her errand prove a fruitless one she will soon follow you to the grave, a sorrowing and broken-hearted girl."

"I fear you have spoken too truly," answered Luke, "yet what avails it to speak of that which I would fain forget? Why remind me of horrors that wring my soul with torture?"

"It is that I may prevail on you to accept the terms I come here to offer," replied the other. "Escape from this place whilst there is an opportunity to do so, and you may hasten down to the beach where tidings of your daughter's fate will soon be known."

"Aye," answered Somerton, with a heavy groan, "and perhaps the first sight that greets me there will be the pale, cold form of all I love dearest in the world! No, no, Lieutenant Granger, this is the fittest place for me to indulge my griefs, and nothing shall induce me to quit it till they came to lead me forth to execution."

"Is this your final answer?"

"It is."

"Then I will myself repair to the beach and make inquiries respecting the vessel in which she sailed," exclaimed Granger. "In a short time I hope to return, and may the news I bring restore you to that happiness which recent events have destroyed."

As he uttered these words he pressed the hand of Luke Somerton, and having summoned the gaoler, he quitted the dungeon to hurry off upon the errand he had thus taken upon himself. Ere he could leave the castle, however, he was met by Sir Charles Radcliffe, who, beckoning for him to follow, led him into the nearest apartment, and having closed the door against any listeners that might be near, he demanded with more sternness than it was usual for him to exhibit, if Granger had been to pay another visit to the dungeon of the prisoner.

"I have, sir," was the reply.

"I thought so," exclaimed the governor, "and my next question should, perhaps, be whether you have again proposed his escape. I will, however, refrain from doing so because I know honour would not permit you to utter an untruth, and I should be unwilling to hear a confession that would compel me to punish such an act with the greatest severity. I will, therefore, only ask you if the prisoner is resigned to a doom that I begin to fear is inevitable?"

"He is ready to meet death firmly," answered Granger; "but I trust ere the appointed time arrives a pardon will have been received from the queen."

"It is in vain to expect it," exclaimed Sir Charles, "though to no one would such a result have been more gratifying than to myself. Queen Anne has the power to restore him to life and liberty, but I much doubt whether it will be held expedient to extend the royal mercy to a convicted murderer."

"But he may have been convicted upon insufficient evidence," replied the other, "and in that case the earnest supplications of a heart-broken daughter may not prove without effect."

"Poor girl!" cried the governor, "I much fear there is but little chance of her escaping the violent tempest that has been raging for the last hour. At all events it must have driven the vessel considerably out of its direct course, and any delay will prove fatal, as it is not in my power to postpone the execution a moment beyond the appointed time."

"Not in such a case as this?" demanded Granger, with a faltering tongue; "can you not respite him till it is known whether the mission of Louisa Somerton has proved successful?"

"If it could be done, I should have been but too happy to grant the delay," answered Sir Charles. "I am, however, responsible for the due administration of the law, and if I fail in any respect, the whole burden would be thrown upon myself."

"And what would be your feelings," asked the other, "if a free pardon should arrive after the sentence had been executed?"

"That is a question which I scarcely dare ask myself," replied the governor. "Such an event is indeed possible, and my only hope is, that the girl will reach the island in time to let us know the will of my gracious sovereign. Yet even should the worst occur, I shall have the consolation of knowing that Luke Somerton will not have died innocent of the crime for which he suffered."

"Ah!" exclaimed Granger, "then he has confessed as much to you?"

"Nay, I will not go so far as to say that," replied Sir Charles Radcliffe, checking himself; "he certainly has spoken to me on the subject, but what passed during that interview was in the strictest confidence, and it shall not be abused. I may have other reasons, young man, for coming to the conclusion I have rather thoughtlessly expressed, and you will therefore take no further heed of words that escaped my lips most unguardedly."

"From this moment they shall be forgotten," replied Lieutenant Granger. "My own impression is certainly in favour of the unfortunate prisoner, and most sincerely do I hope his daughter will return the messenger of glad tidings for him."

"I hope so too, young man," returned the governor, "but at my time of life we are less apt to be sanguine than at yours. There is, too, another reason, if I mistake not, why you are so anxious for Luke Somerton's pardon; — you love his daughter, and of course could not marry her should the parent perish ignominiously."

"My love would be unworthy the name," answered the young man, "were I to abandon a virtuous girl under no better plea than the transgressions of her father."

"But the world, my dear sir, would scarcely be so charitable," exclaimed Sir Charles; "and there are few, I believe, who would hold companionship with the offspring of a man that has paid the penalty of his crimes by an ignominious death."

"Which circumstance," replied Granger, "would prove the stronger incentive for the husband to throw around her the protection of his love. Louisa Somerton is in every respect worthy of admiration, and should the world look coldly upon her, it would reflect but little credit upon itself."

"The notion is a chivalrous one," observed Sir Charles, "and is perhaps natural enough to one so young and ardent as yourself. I would, however, advise you to be cautious how you bring upon yourself the sneers of mankind, for your profession is an honourable one, and an officer in her majesty's service is not permitted to bring discredit upon himself with impunity."

"I can at least resign my commission," answered Lieutenant Granger, proudly, "and that would occasion me but little regret since the world is wide enough to afford me an honourable means of living in some other profession."

"Well, I see it's no use arguing with you in your present temper," said Sir Charles Radcliffe, "and we will therefore speak further upon the subject some other time. A pardon may arrive in sufficient time for Luke Somerton, and that would certainly remove some of the difficulties that I at present foresee."

"Then here let our present conference end," exclaimed Lieutenant Granger; "for the perils that involve Louisa Somerton engross all my thoughts, and my heart is upon the rack till I have ascertained whether she has escaped the fearful tempest that has been so long raging."

"Aye, aye, hasten down to the sea-shore, my young friend," answered Sir Charles; "and let me hear the news as soon as tidings of the girl reach you. That her errand may prove a prosperous one is my earnest prayer, though I cannot conceal from you my fears that the queen will hesitate to grant her royal pardon to one who has been convicted of so heinous a crime as murder."

Lieutenant Granger scarcely heard the concluding words, for he hurried impatiently from the room, and leaving the castle at his utmost speed, took his way towards the sea-beach, which was by this time crowded with people.

CHAPTER XIX.

Hast thou heard aught that may inspire hope,
Or does the star of evil destiny
Still reign predominant?

Don Raymond.

LEFT once more in the solitude of his dungeon, Luke Somerton gave way to the thoughts that he found it impossible to banish from his mind. That his daughter would perish in the storm that was yet raging with fearful violence seemed to him certain, and bitterly did he now reproach himself for suffering her to depart upon an errand that he felt convinced in his own mind would prove a fruitless one. It was to save him that she had gone forth to tempt the perils of the deep, and should aught happen to her in this luckless mission he took all blame to himself, since her death could be attributed to no other cause than her intense anxiety to rescue him from the fate which had been brought by his own fatal hankering after revenge.

And even when the storm began to lull, the dismal moaning of the wind filled him with a thousand fears, that at any other time would have appeared childish. Now, however, it sounded to him like the voice of his murdered victim exulting in the punishment that was speedily to follow, and with a sinking heart he abandoned himself to the terrors which he found it impossible to banish from his mind. Till that moment he had never really known what fear was, and vain were all the efforts he made to shake off a feeling that in former days he had been used to laugh at as childish. At times, too, he half regretted that he had not accepted the offer of Granger to escape; but when at length daylight broke in upon the last morning that the law permitted him to live, he resumed some of his former recklessness of spirit, and laughed—though the laugh was a wild and fearful one—at the terrors which had so unnerved him during the night.

Then again occurred to him those thoughts which connected his daughter with the perils of the storm that had raged with such fury during the past night, and in imagination he beheld her at the mercy of the warring elements, shrieking aloud for help, yet abandoned to a fate from which there was no hope of rescue. No effort that he made could remove these harrowing impressions from his mind, for still her image seemed to be before him, and in the madness of despair he dashed himself against the wall with such violence that he fell upon the ground stunned and stupified by the violence he had thus committed upon himself.

How long he had remained in this condition he knew not, but upon recovering the partial use of his senses he found himself supported in the arms of a stranger, while around him stood three or four others, in one of whom he recognised the chaplain of the gaol, who on the preceding day he had dismissed from his presence, declaring that he had no need of his assistance; as he was ready to meet death with the same fortitude that he had lived. Now, however, a change had come over him, and beckoning for the clergyman to approach, he inquired faintly if there was any hope of his life being spared beyond that day.

"I fear not," was the reply.

"Has aught been heard of my daughter?"

"At present," answered the chaplain, "we have heard no tidings of her, and there is a painful feeling of doubt that the vessel she was in has gone to the bottom."

"Ah!" exclaimed Luke, furiously, "come you to inflict tortures upon me before I die? Is it nothing, think you, that I must meet the fate of a dog, but you must lacerate my heart with tidings that are worse to me than ten thousand deaths?"

"I speak only of the reports that are current through the island," replied the chaplain. "News has arrived of several ships that have foundered in the last night's storm, and there is but too much reason to fear that the vessel in which your daughter sailed has shared a similar fate. Under Providence, however, she may have escaped, and if so, her preservation will afford the greatest joy to all those who admire that heroism that urged her to make so noble an effort to save the life of her father."

"She may have escaped," cried Luke Somerton, "and should I but ascertain that, I can yield up my own life without a single regret."

"Your time is now but short, Luke Somerton," exclaimed the clergyman, "and it is my duty to prevail upon you to give your last few moments to repentance. Accompany me, I beseech you, in prayer to heaven for that mercy which you showed not to the unfortunate victim, for whose death you are about to suffer the last dreadful penalty of the laws."

"What prayers I have to offer can be uttered in silence and without assistance," replied Luke. "When it is time to leave this dungeon for the place of execution I shall be ready to attend you; but do not hurry on the moment, for my daughter's probable fate hangs heavily on my soul, and I would be spared till the latest period, that every chance may be given me to ascertain whether she lives, and how she has fared in her interview with the queen."

"I would not have you place too much reliance either in the one thing or the other," exclaimed the clergyman. "The case for which your daughter goes to plead for mercy, possesses no features that can make an impression on the mind of our sovereign, who is expected to do equal justice between all her people. The murder of Captain Aylmer was committed under peculiarly aggravating circumstances, and nothing can be brought forward why the assassin should not suffer for his grievous offence."

"There's not much Christian charity in you, I see," exclaimed Luke Somerton; "but as I care very little about the death you would so mercilessly consign me to, there's not much harm to be done by a few harsh words. All I desire is to live out the full time allotted by the law, and I suppose, sir, *you* will not wish to send a man out of the world sooner than need be?"

"Heaven forbid!" exclaimed the chaplain, "for I would rather add to your life than diminish it even by a single hour. You have need of repentance, Luke Somerton, and the time is brief that you have to make your peace with an offended maker."

"Why, aye, time's short enough with us all," replied the prisoner; but who shall say that my life draws nearer to a close than anybody else's that's standing here about me? Has the queen never pardoned a criminal before that it should seem impossible she can do so now, when a young and broken-hearted girl kneels at her feet to implore the same mercy from the queen, that one day or other she will herself ask from a Judge who knows all hearts, and grants pardon only to those who have yielded it to others."

"Her majesty," answered the clergyman, "will, I have no doubt, give your daughter an interview when she knows the urgency that demands it. The name of Luke Somerton, however, cannot but be familiar to her ears, and it will be no easy task to induce her to give liberty to a man who has long set her laws at open defiance."

"But if she knows my faults," returned Somerton, "she is as likely as not to know the cause that drove me to them. I have been a smuggler, you would say, and I care not about denying it; but surely the crime is not so great a one that a poor fellow should swing for it on the gallows?"

"Nay," answered the other, "it is for the murder of Captain Aylmer that you are to die."

"And suppose I am innocent?" demanded Luke. "Many a poor fellow has suffered for a crime that he had nothing to do with, and it is the merciful man's creed that it were better to allow a hundred guilty men escape than to punish one that is innocent. Not that I would myself ask mercy from the queen, but I have a daughter, whose fair fame I would preserve untarnished, and that can scarcely be if her father ends his life ignominiously upon a public scaffold."

Here the conversation was interrupted by some of the officers of the prison, who entered to announce that only a brief period remained ere the time arrived that was appointed for the execution of the sentence.

"I am ready," answered Luke Somerton, with an effort to retain all his firmness. "You will see that no coward fears will have the power to overcome me, and if I can but hear that my daughter has escaped the perils of last night's storm, I shall die with the same firmness of heart that has ever sustained me through a life of continual danger."

"The governor," added the man, "has desired me further to say, that if you have any reasonable request to make, he is ready to grant it on his own responsibility."

"A dying man can have but few favours to ask," returned the prisoner, moodily; "unless, indeed, it '- that he will be kind to my poor Louisa, when her father is no more. She will grieve sadly for me, I fear, yet a word or two of kindness from a friend may serve to reconcile her to that which is about to take place. Sir Charles Radcliffe bears the character of being a humane man; let him prove it to the world by his acts towards a defenceless girl whose heart is crushed with sorrow."

"I will myself undertake to promise that every attention shall be paid her," interposed the chaplain. "In me she shall find a watchful friend, though I doubt not there are many others who will be equally inclined to extend their kindness towards an innocent and heavily afflicted girl. Besides, there is Lieutenant Granger, who ——"

"Name him not," interrupted Luke, "for to him, least of all, would I entrust so precious a treasure."

"And yet the world has ever regarded him a young man of unblemished honour," said the chaplain.

"I myself believe him to be incapable of wrong action," answered Somerton; "but, for a that, I cannot rely upon him as a guardian for my child, when she has no longer a parent to whom she can look for protection. True, he has offered to make her his wife, but how can I hope for the fulfilment of such a pledge, when he reflects upon the disgrace that such an alliance must bring upon him? The world generally takes an uncharitable view of things, and, when the tragedy of this day is over, Louisa Somerton will be shunned and scorned as the daughter of a man whose life has been sacrificed to the offended laws of his country."

"Do you acknowledge the crime of which you have been found guilty and are condemned to die?" inquired the clergyman.

"I have before told you that to no priest will I make confession," answered Luke, sternly. "Let it suffice that twelve men have returned a verdict against me, upon circumstantial evidence, and the consequence is, that I now stand upon the very threshold of eternity. Spare me, therefore, a repetition of questions that I am resolved not to answer further than I have already done."

"It is my duty to urge it," exclaimed the chaplain; "for I would know that you are repentant in the last hours of your existence. You are accused of having taken the life of a fellow-creature, and it would afford some slight consolation to your judges to know that you fully acknowledge the justness of your sentence."

"They will know that when I am no more," replied the culprit. "There is one person in whom I have reposed my confidence, and it will remain with him either to divulge our conversation or keep it secret in his own bosom, as he may think proper."

"But it is a well-known fact that you have long borne a rancorous hatred towards Captain Aylmer."

"Granted; yet it follows not that I should take away the life of the man I hated," said Luke Somerton.

"Unhappy man! would that I could overcome this perversity," exclaimed the chaplain. "My duty has obliged me to persevere in putting these questions to you, and you may believe me when I declare that the mere gratification of idle curiosity has nothing whatever to do with it. If you are guilty, there can be no reason for any longer withholding a confession of the crime."

"Think you, then, that I have forgotten the future welfare of my daughter?" asked Luke Somerton. "The brand of shame has already been stamped upon her fair brow, but time may serve to erase the mark if I do not babble of things that are better left untold."

"In other words," observed the clergyman, "you tacitly admit your guilt, while trying to conceal it."

"If a trap has been laid for me, I will speak no further on the subject," exclaimed Luke. "I have no need of your services, sir; but a short time longer remains to me in this world, and that period, brief as it is, I would fain have to myself. It will be your duty, I suppose, to attend me to the scafold, but mark me, ask no further questions as to my guilt or innocence."

"This anger is unseemly, considering the situation in which you stand," answered the chaplain. "There is no man so faultless but he has something to atone for, and, if I have been urgent to obtain a confession, you may attribute it to my zeal in the fulfilment of an office that demands all my firmness."

"Once for all, understand me that I have no confession to make," exclaimed the prisoner, doggedly. "If the blood of Captain Aylmer stains my soul, I am soon to answer for it on the scaffold; but, if I am innocent, and there is no direct proof against me, then will my judges suffer their share of punishment in another world."

"But you dare not, Luke Somerton," cried the chaplain, "you dare not, at such a moment as this, deny the justice of your doom. True, there was no direct evidence to prove that the deed was committed by your hand, but murder is a crime that is seldom perpetrated in the presence of a witness, and, therefore, circumstantial testimony, when the chain is unbroken, is considered sufficient to procure the conviction of the culprit."

"And has an innocent man never suffered?" demanded Luke Somerton, glancing haughtily at the chaplain.

"I am afraid some few instances have occurred," returned the other; "but that circumstance has served to make both judges and juries more careful in sifting every particle of evidence brought forward before they come to a decided opinion. In your own case, for instance, the jury deliberated for a very long time before they came to a decision, and I believe there are few people who do not agree with the verdict they gave."

"Aye," muttered Luke, "that's because I happen to have got my full share of enemies in the world."

"And why have you more enemies than other people?" demanded the clergyman. "Ask your own heart, Luke Somerton, if there is any one else besides yourself to blame for it. For years past you have been the terror and detestation of your fellow-men; your deeds have been marked with violence and outrage; the laws of your country have been set at open defiance, and you have gone on from bad to worse, till this last horrible crime has been laid to your charge. A good resolution alone was wanted, yet you refused to see your errors, and now behold the fearful strait to which it has brought you!"

"I never knew till now," said Luke, sullenly, "that it was part of a parson's duty to rip up old grievances."

"That depends upon the condition of the person he is called upon to assist with his advice," answered the other. "There are some whose hearts are softened when the hour of affliction comes upon them, while others brave out their danger, wholly unmindful of the great peril into which they have fallen. I was in hopes to have found you penitent, Luke Somerton, but, to my sorrow, I see you utterly regardless of the death you are about to suffer."

"Would you have me go out of the world like a coward?"

"There is no cowardice in repentance," replied the chaplain. "I ask you, even at this twelfth hour, to make a full confession, and you reject my advice with scorn."

"That's because I've never been 'used to take advice from any one," answered Luke Somerton.

"But you have never before been so near death."

"Haven't I?" exclaimed the prisoner; "do you mean to tell me I've not been a pretty near neighbour of death's when the bullets have been whizzing about me like a shower of hail, and when a dozen boarding-pikes have been aimed at my heart at the same moment? The truth is, I've been so often in danger, that I've got used to it, and I can look to what's coming without much fear."

"Yet, for your daughter's sake, you might have shown some tokens of regret for your past misdeeds."

"Ha! you would have me go out of the world like a snivelling fool, I suppose. But I'll do nothing of the kind, Mr. Parson, so keep your advice for those that may want it more than I do. There's others in this prison, I dare say, that can listen to you with more patience than I happen to possess, and, if so, you had better go and preach to them, for I don't mean to stir from what I have already said."

"Do you wish to see any one before we leave this place for the spot which is appointed for your execution?"

"Yes, there is one."

"The name?"

"Louisa Somerton."

"Your daughter?"

"Aye, is it to be wondered at that I wish to see my child once more ere I take my departure for ever?"

"The wish is a natural one," replied the clergyman, "but you are aware of the impossibility of your desire being gratified. As you know, she has crossed over to Whitehaven to sue for a pardon, and the storm which raged last night will prevent her return for some hours."

"You know not my Louisa's love for me as I do," replied Luke Somerton, proudly, "or you would not think she is to be easily turned from her purpose when the object is a pure and holy one. Her own life she cares not for; but, to save mine, she would brave even a worse tempest than that which last night shook this old fortress even to its very lowest foundation stone."

"Well, then," replied the chaplain, "even granting that she was rash enough to venture out to sea, there is little chance that a small boat can have weathered the storm, when even our largest vessels were obliged to slip their cables during the night, and some of them, it is feared, are lost."

"You do not believe, then," said Luke, "that the Almighty would watch over a helpless girl, who has perilled herself to save the life of her father? Methinks, sir, your religion might have taught you that even the humblest of God's creatures are equal objects of his bounty and protection with the highest."

Ere the chaplain could make any reply to this, Frederick Granger, pale and dispirited, entered the cell. The prisoner immediately perceived the heaviness that oppressed his spirits, and, requesting to be left alone with the last arrived visitor, he eagerly inquired if any news had been heard of Louisa or his brother James.

"Alas! we can hear no tidings of either of them," answered Lieutenant Granger; "many reports are current here among the people; but as all of them take the gloomiest side of the picture, you will pardon me for not speaking of them to you under your present hapless condition."

"And why should I not hear all—ay, even the worst that you have to tell me?" demanded Luke Somerton, with a forced appearance of composure. "You will tell me now, perhaps, that she has perished in her noble effort to preserve me from the fate to which I have been doomed,—that she has fallen a sacrifice to the affection which prompted her to risk the perils of last night's storm?"

"Believe me, Luke Somerton," answered the young man, "nothing is yet known, or at least nothing upon which we can place any reliance. It is merely conjectured that the danger she was threatened with would not deter her from making an attempt to return to this island; and, if that should indeed have been the case, there is but too much reason to fear that she has perished in the tempest."

"And if she has," murmured Luke, in a tone of deep emotion, "there is at least the consolation of knowing that she will be spared the heavy affliction that was in store for her when I perish by a shameful and violent death. At any other time I should have grieved bitterly for the loss of one so loved as she was; but now, lieutenant, my heart has grown callous with the near approach of my own doom; and that which at one period would have bowed down my heart with grief seems now scarcely to afford me a single pang."

"Have you then made up your mind that her mission to Queen Anne has failed?" asked Lieutenant Granger.

"I have never placed any confidence in it, and therefore, am not disappointed," replied the prisoner. "The act was solely that of my daughter: she believed that the royal heart was not less tender than her own; and, urged by the promptings of her own goodness, she determined to run all risks for the accomplishment of her design. I would fain have persuaded her that there was no chance of success; but even my authority failed when she learned that I was condemned to die like a dog for a crime of which she believes me guiltless."

"But is there no way by which the execution may be postponed till it has been ascertained whether the queen has withheld or granted her royal pardon?"

"Sir Charles Radcliffe has given orders for it to take place at the hour appointed," replied Somerton. "Such is his will, and I have nothing to complain of, since there is little chance of the queen's mercy being extended to one who has been sentenced as a murderer. The task undertaken by Louisa was a hopeless one, and from the first I have made up my mind to the worst."

"It was better to do so, certainly," replied Frederick Granger, "and yet I cannot but confess that I entertained strong hopes in your favour. Queen Anne is said to possess a heart susceptible of every feeling of womanly kindness; and surely, when one of her own sex kneels before her a supplicant for mercy, it is not too much to hope that she would pause ere she rejects a prayer which it is in her power to grant."

"Had the crime been of less magnitude than murder, it is possible her majesty might have yielded," replied Luke Somerton. "I have heard high praise spoken of our queen, and should have been among the most devoted of her subjects, but for Captain Aylmer, whose harsh treatment made me what I afterwards became."

"Did he never give you any redress?"

"Not the slightest; on the contrary, I was even treated by him with the utmost contempt, till I left an honourable service to become the scorn of my fellow men."

"But surely," observed Lieutenant Granger, "the laws would have afforded you protection against an oppressor?"

"The laws!" exclaimed Somerton; "and of what use are they to the weak against the powerful? I belonged to a grade inferior to that of Captain Aylmer. I was poor, whilst he was rich. I had no friends, whilst he was surrounded with powerful ones, who would have have assisted him in trampling me still further into the dust. If I remonstrated he added insult to oppression; he made me the scorn of the whole ship's company; and I would ask where the man is to be found who could patiently endure the upstart arrogance of such a contemptible reptile?"

"I have heard something of his character before," replied Granger, "and must admit that he was a man whom few would esteem. You, however, appear to have taken a wrong course, though it is, perhaps, harsh to say so now, when the fearful penalty is about to be paid."

"Ay, ay, it's no use preaching, lieutenant," exclaimed the prisoner, "for what's done cannot be undone; so the best way is to keep a still tongue about it. Captain Aylmer is now in his grave, and a few short hours will serve to send me also to my last account."

"Not if I can prevent it," answered Granger, "I will seek one more interview with Sir Edward Radcliffe. He is ever lenient when an opportunity is afforded him of being so; and, as I shall but ask a brief respite of the execution, I doubt not he will yield to the only favour I have ever yet asked of him."

"And what think you I care for the few hours he may, at your intercession, add to my life?" demanded the prisoner. "I feel convinced there is no hope of a pardon being granted by her majesty; and the brief respite you would ask for the miserable criminal would, perhaps, enable him to live just long enough to learn the fatal truth that his daughter had perished in her generous effort to procure mercy from the queen."

"But it may so happen that her efforts will not prove so unavailing as you imagine," answered Frederick. "She has youth and beauty in her favour, and stern must be the heart that could feel no emotion at the earnest words of a child pleading in behalf of her unfortunate parent."

"All that sounds very well, lieutenant," exclaimed Luke, "but justice, we are told, is blind, and it may be that she is deaf also, when there is no inclination to hear what the petitioner has to say. Besides, kings and queens are not so easily to be got at as your common folks, and if it is known that Louisa has a favour to ask of her majesty, she would be driven away as if her presence brought contagion with it."

"I see you are determined to take the most unfavourable view of the matter," said Lieutenant Granger. "My object in coming hither was to afford you some hope that death is not so near as you imagine; but it seems my errand has been frustrated, and you are still resolved to look upon your fate as being irrevocably sealed."

"That is because I have ceased to care about living beyond the time fixed by the judge for my execution. Even were I spared, what is it that I have to look forward to? There is scarcely a friend left to me in the world, for all regard me as guilty, and I should pass through a wearisome pilgrimage, pointed at and execrated as a wretch who had escaped from a well-merited punishment. On the other hand, I have no fear of death, for my whole life has been passed amidst strife and peril, though it seems to have been my fate to escape from every danger to die at last upon a public scaffold."

"Does not the thought of that make you anxious to avert a doom so horrible?" asked Lieutenant Granger.

"No," replied Luke Somerton; "I can regard even the worst malice of my enemies with indifference, and am resolved that they shall not have it to say that I go out of the world like a coward. As a proof that I utter no boastful words, I could even now die by my own hands, and thus cheat the gallows of its intended victim."

"Have you then a weapon?"

"Ask me no questions upon that subject," exclaimed the prisoner. "That I do not rank you among my enemies has been made manifest upon more occasions than one. You have done me some few acts of kindness, and I am grateful for them; will you do one more for me ere I bid a final adieu to the world?"

"I will; name it, Somerton, and rely upon my zeal."

"It is," he replied, "that you will go and ascertain whether any tidings have yet been heard of my daughter. Let the news be good or bad, come to me when I am standing beneath the gibbet, and tell me of my child. Away—remember my words; and fail not in the performance of this last duty."

Lieutenant Granger gave the required pledge, and warmly pressing the hand of the unfortunate captive, he immediately took his departure from the prison.

CHAPTER XX.

The sky is changed, and such a change! Oh, night,
And storm, and darkness, ye are wondrous strong;
Yet lovely in your strength, as is the light
Of a dark eye in woman.   BYRON.

THE Manxmen, as the natives of the Isle of Man are termed, were stirring early in the morning that had been appointed for the execution of Luke Somerton. His approaching fate was regarded as an act of retributive justice, and a look of gladness was seen upon every countenance at the thought that he whose acts had occasioned so much dread was about to meet his doom. Even the women, on

this occasion, were vociferous in their expressions of satisfaction, and numbers of them mingled among the crowds which had assembled in various parts of the town, and its suburbs.

Upon the beach stood a group of persons, collected there to learn the earliest intelligence whether Louisa and James Somerton had escaped from the tempest which it was pretty well ascertained they had ventured to brave. Nothing certain, however, could be ascertained; for, although every one hoped that our heroine had escaped the fury of the waves, there was not a person among them who could throw the least light upon the subject.

By this time the wind had considerably abated in violence, and the sea, though still heaving and rolling its huge waves towards the shore, was calm in comparison to what it had been a few hours before. Many anxious eyes were directed over the vast expanse of waters in the faint hope of seeing the boat which had borne our heroine over to the main land. But they were doomed to disappointment, and every moment that passed away served but to increase the fears of the many anxious watchers.

"It's my opinion," said Dick Joyce, a sturdy blacksmith, "that we may as well give it up for a bad job. No boat could ever have lived in last night's gale, and the poor girl has gone down, like a good many others before her, to make food for the fishes."

"And what if she has?" exclaimed Nell Dawson, an Amazonian dame, who cared but little who sank so that she swam. "I've no patience with a parcel of fools making a fuss about this girl when there's others quite as good, if not a great deal better than she."

"Meaning yourself among the number, I suppose?" retorted Snizzle, the town crier, who had a mighty propensity to make people laugh. "But never mind, old woman," he added, 'when you put yourself into the same situation that Louisa Somerton has, we will all meet here, as we have now, and——"

"None of your sneers, Snizzle, if you please,'" exclaimed Nell, giving him a push that sent him flying into the arms of a venerable fish-wife, who made one of the crowd. "If I'm to be laughed at, it shall be by some one better than myself, and not by a half-starved, herring-gutted fellow like you."

"What the devil are you growling about now?" gruffly demanded Dick Joyce; "can't people be allowed to say that they're sorry for the poor girl, but it must raise the jealousy of an old harridan like you?"

"And who is this Louisa Somerton?" asked Nell, placing her arms a-kimbo; "ain't she the daughter of one of the greatest villains that ever lived? and is she to be pitied more than anybody else?"

"She can't help being the daughter of a bad man," interposed a pert little tailor, called Peter Prim. "The girl was always liked before it was known that Luke Somerton was her father, and I don't see why we should think any the worse of her now."

"Especially as it's not likely that we shall ever see her again," observed one of the by-standers. "The boat must have foundered in the storm, and even if she got a reprieve for her father, it will not be known till too late, for Luke's last hour in this world is now pretty well up."

"So much the better," exclaimed Harry Roden, a burly-looking carpenter, who had arrived just in time to hear the last few words. "Why, hanging is too good for such a villain as Luke Somerton, who, not satisfied with being a rebel against his lawful queen, must needs finish his crimes with one of the foulest murders that ever was heard of."

"Well, there's no denying that he's been a terrible fellow in his time," said Joyce, "but, for all that, I can't see why people should think any the worse of his daughter for it. She has always been a sort of pet favourite with the people hereabouts, and to turn our backs upon her now, is more than I can understand."

"Poor girl!" said Dame Findley, another of the females who formed part of the assemblage; "she was always kind and attentive to poor folks that couldn't help themselves. When I was laid up with the rheumatiz, who but she came to our cottage, and brought me flannel to wrap up my limbs, and all sorts of nice things that she had prepared with her own hands. I, for one, shall always speak a good word for her; and all I hope is, that she has not gone to the bottom, as most people seem to think."

"If she ventured out to sea, there's no other chance for her," exclaimed Dick Joyce. "Why, the largest ship in her majesty's navy would have a hard battle to weather out such a storm as we had last night; and what must have been the fate of such a crazy fishing boat as she went in, we may pretty well guess."

"Nothing, then, has been heard of her, I suppose," said Lieutenant Granger, who, at this moment, approached the spot, to ask if any tidings had been obtained.

"Nothing, your honour," replied Joyce; "but there don't seem to be much chance that we shall ever see her again alive—that is to say, if she was rash enough to leave Whitehaven, when the storm was brewing."

"And that she did so there can be no doubt," returned Lieutenant Granger; "for, whether she obtained her father's pardon or not, she would be equally anxious to return here with the least possible delay."

"And do you think it likely, your honour," asked Joyce, "that she would be able to speak to the queen?"

"*She* speak to the queen!" exclaimed Nell Dawson, contemptuously. "It's a very likely thing, indeed, that her majesty would stop in the middle of the street to speak to a girl like her. No, no, she would be taken into custody, and packed off to prison; and serve her right too, an impudent, ignorant hussy!"

"Well, well, we shall hear more about that by-and-by, I dare say," returned the young officer. "It seems, however, my good woman, that Louisa Somerton is no great favourite of yours—may I ask in what way she has ever given you offence?"

"Oh, in ever so many ways," replied the old woman.

"Will you name one of them as a specimen?"

"I don't see that you've any right to ask me," said Nell, "and as I sha'n't answer your question,

it's quite enough that I don't like her; and nobody frets more than I do about her going down to the bottom of the sea, there won't be much grief about her loss."

"You seem to have formed a most strange and unnatural antipathy against her."

"'Tipathy or no 'tipathy, I mean exactly what I says!" exclaimed the virago. "I never like people that set themselves up above everybody else. Pride always has a fall, and I knew well enough it would all come home to her some day or another."

"Don't mind what old mother Dawson says, your honour," cried Joyce; "she's one of them sort of folks that never has a good word to say for anybody, and the better people are, the more she seems to set her mind agin 'em."

"She's a reg'lar bit o' brimstone," said the town crier; but seeing that she was preparing to make another attack upon him, he dodged his way round three or four of the people, till he had placed himself in safety."

"Recollect, I owe you one for that!" exclaimed Nell, in a furious passion. "There's some people that fancy they can say just what they please to *other* people; but, I'd have you know that, woman as I am, I can take my own part against half-a-dozen such fellows as you."

"What occasion is there for all this anger?" demanded Lieutenant Granger. "All have met here, as I understood, in anxious expectation that tidings might reach them of poor Louisa Somerton. We know that she has risked much to save the life of her unfortunate father, and surely that circumstance might be sufficient to procure respect, even from her enemies."

"But her father's life ain't worth the trouble of saving," replied the woman; "hasn't he been the terror of all the people here, for I don't know how many months past—and oughtn't we to be glad instead of sorry, that Jack Ketch has at last got him in his hands?"

"As for Luke Somerton himself," exclaimed Harry Roden, "I don't think there's a person among us that cares about the fate he's brought himself to. He's been a regular bad chap for this long time past, and now that they've got tight hold of him, I think the sooner they put him out of the way the better. He has never been a friend to anybody, and I can't help thinking that the sooner they hang him, the better it will be."

"You wouldn't think so, if your own time was come," cried Dick Joyce. "Hanging is all very well for other people to talk about, but it don't bear thinking of when it comes too near home."

"Besides," added Dame Findley, "I always find, that people who talk most loudly about the faults of others, have got plenty of their own, if they would but take the trouble to ask themselves a few questions."

"If your sneers are meant for me, ma'am," exclaimed the virago, "I'd have you know, that I take 'em from whence they came. I dare say you ain't one of the very best folks in the world, for all your mighty airs; so now, Mother Findley, put that in your pipe and smoke it."

"Come, come, let us have no brawling, when we have matters of more consequence to think about," cried Lieutenant Granger, interposing himself between the two women. "We are now anxiously looking for news of Louisa Somerton, who, for aught we know, may have been the bearer of a pardon for her father, whose last hour in this world is at hand. The girl and her uncle, James Somerton, are still absent, and every moment that passes away seems to increase my uneasiness."

At this moment a man named Jack Martin approached the spot, and having made his way through the throng, advanced to the spot where Granger was standing.

"You were speaking of James Somerton," he said.

"I was; have you heard anything of him? Do you bring news that he has returned to the island?"

"No," replied the other, "and what's more, I don't think it very likely he ever will come again. By this time I should think he's at the bottom of

the sea, for I myself saw him in the boat struggling against the waves, and it seemed to me that there wasn't a chance for him."

"Did you make no attempt to save him?" asked Granger.

"Save him!" exclaimed the other; "why I might as well have attempted to fly. From the rock where I stood I could see the boat as it was buffeted about by the waters, but no human power could be of use in such a storm as was then raging."

"Yet, as they had crossed the sea from the main land, I should be inclined to hope that the boat could still weather the tempest," observed Lieutenant Granger. "But are you sure it was James Somerton that you saw?"

"I'm quite certain about it," replied Jack. "I know him well enough, and though it was not long after day-break, there was sufficient light to see the face of the two men that were in the boat."

"Are you sure Louisa Somerton was not with them?"

"I can swear she wasn't," replied the other, "for there was only James Somerton and one of the Whitehaven fishermen."

"And you think there is no probability of their having escaped from the peril they were threatened with?"

"For my part, I should say they must have had the devil's luck, and their own too, if ever they reached the shore, through the heavy surf that was running," replied Jack Martin. "In short, they seemed to have given themselves up for lost, and little is it to be wondered at, for the boat, which at one moment was down in the trough of the sea, was the next riding on the crest of an enormous wave, and the only thing which surprised me was that so small a vessel hadn't gone down before."

"Ah!" exclaimed Snizzle, "those Whitehaven fishermen are rare fellows on the water. They're used to rough weather, and can always keep afloat when almost anybody else would go to the bottom."

"When I saw them," continued Jack, "the owner of the boat was pulling at the oars with all his strength, for of course they had no sail up while the wind was blowing great guns. The other chap, James Somerton, I mean, had got the rudder, and he seemed to be pretty nearly exhausted with the fatigue he had gone through."

"What can have become of Louisa?" exclaimed Lieutenant Granger. "She was not with them, it seems, and yet I am sure no consideration would have prevented her return under the fearful circumstances in which her father is placed."

"I'll tell you what my opinion is about it," interposed Dick Joyce; "the queen wasn't best pleased with being interrupted in her way through Whitehaven, and the girl has been sent off to prison for her presumption."

"It is impossible!" exclaimed Granger indignantly. "The queen cannot be so destitute of all womanly feelings as to punish a heart-broken girl for a mere act of filial duty. She may, indeed, refuse to comply with her petition, but she would at least dismiss her without anger."

"The actions of great folks are not to be judged by what little ones would do in the same situation," replied Jack Martin. "It's likely her majesty has heard something of Luke Somerton's doings, and, if so, it's not to be expected that she would grant him a pardon after he has been found guilty of murdering one of the officers belonging to her service. If she does, the next man that kills another will expect to be let off the same way."

"The long and the short of it is, he deserves to be hanged as much as ere a villain that I ever heard of," exclaimed Harry Roden. "There isn't a man, woman, or child in the whole island but expects the sentence of the judge to be executed; and you may take my word for it there'll be a row in the place if he should be pardoned."

"You forget that there is a military force in the island," replied Lieutenant Granger, "and if any violence should be manifested it will be instantly suppressed. I speak this to all of you who are here present, that the consequences I speak of may be avoided."

"D—n the military," exclaimed Roden, sullenly, "there's men enough here, I should think, to set the red-coats at defiance,—aye, and they would do it too, or I am most confoundedly mistaken. Only let 'em set Luke Somerton at liberty, and I'd myself find some way to get rid of him, if my own hand took away his life."

"Then you would not hesitate to commit a murder?"

"How can it be called a murder, when the man has been condemned to die?" asked Roden.

"Nay," exclaimed Lieutenant Granger, "there must be some private feeling of malice in this. You owe him a grudge, and would seek unlawful means to gratify it."

"That I owe him a grudge ain't to be denied," replied the other : "but that has nothing to do with it, because the truth of it is we consider he's been justly sentenced to die, and there's no reason why he should get off. Besides, he's not liked for something he once did, and you may take my word for it, lieutenant, the people here would rise against him as one man."

"And serve him right too," vociferated Nell Dawson, "for I can't see why favour should be shown to him any more than to any other fellow that has committed a murder. It's all very well for his daughter to try and save him, because his death would bring shame upon herself, but the queen ain't to be bought over with fine words, so we sha'n't be cheated out of the pleasure we expected in seeing him mount the gallows."

"Is it possible that a human being can anticipate pleasure from seeing a fellow-creature suffer a violent death!" exclaimed Lieutenant Granger. "From women, especially, we generally expect sympathy and kindness: yet here is one who murmurs at the bare thought of mercy!"

"It's all very well for you to wish him to get off," retorted Nell, "because most of us know you have a sneaking kindness for the girl, and you hope to gain her favour by taking part with her worthless father."

"I'll tell you what it is, old Mother Brandyface," cried Snizzle, "you think you're everybody, and talk for the lot of us, just as if we were all of your own way of thinking. Ah! you may show your teeth, but you musn't bite now, for there's plenty here that will take my part against you, any day."

A loud laugh from the mob followed this valourous speech, and, taking the opportunity, Lieutenant Granger slipped away and directed his steps once more towards the town. This was quickly observed by Nell, who in a tone of exultation said,—

"Only see how I've made yonder *brave* soldier beat a retreat! Home truths don't do for some people, and I'll dare be sworn the lieutenant is by this time ashamed of the low-bred girl he was going to make his wife."

"Why, you surely haven't got anything to say against the girl?" exclaimed Dick Joyce. "She, at any rate, has never given you any offence, and if she has, I'll be bound to say she didn't do it intentionally."

"*She* give offence!" cried Snizzle; "why, she wouldn't have the heart to hurt a woman; and whatever people may have to say against Luke Somerton himself, there's no one but old Mother Dawson there that don't think all the better of the girl for trying to save her father from the gallows."

"It's all natural enough, I dare say," responded Harry Roden; "but, to my thinking, it's a pity any body should take so much pains about a murderer. There's one comfort, however, the queen ain't to be humbugged with fine words, so of course she'll not grant the pardon."

"And, as another matter of course, we sha'n't be disappointed of our day's pleasure," observed Peter Prim.

"I only wish I was as sure of a hundred pounds as that Luke Somerton will swing when the hour comes," said Roden. "It ain't very likely the girl was allowed to speak to her majesty; and, even if she was, there's no good reason for letting the murderer get off scot-free. At any rate, I shouldn't like to be standing in Luke's shoes."

"Well," exclaimed Dick Joyce, "if he really did commit the murder, there's no denying that he ought to suffer for it. But, for all that, the daughter's to be pitied, for she's done all she could to save her father's life; and the worst of it is, I'm afraid she's been lost coming back."

"There ain't much doubt about that, I believe," said Nell, with a malicious grin. "People shouldn't make themselves so uncommon busy, and then they wouldn't be getting into those awkward scrapes. If she's lost, folks will say it was a punishment upon her for trying to save the life of a shedder of human blood."

"It luckily happens that very few are such brutes as to think anything of the kind," exclaimed Snizzle, who was determined to have his say, now that there were plenty of people to take his part.

"What's the use of talking to people that haven't got any feeling?" asked Peter Prim. "The old woman was always fond of wagging that rancorous tongue of her's; but there's one thing to be said—the worst word she can utter won't make people think badly of Louisa Somerton."

"Peter Prim—Peter Prim! you had better mind what you say about me!" exclaimed the virago, shaking her clenched fist in the face of the little tailor. "It's bad enough to be talked to by a man; but such a paltry, under-sized wretch as you shall never say a word against me while I've hands and nails to protect myself."

"Hilloa, old woman!" interposed Dick Joyce; "this is coming out a leetle too stiff, I think. Report says you used to pitch into your poor husband, that's dead and gone, but you mustn't be threatening other people merely because they speak their minds freely."

These words raised a laugh at the expense of Nell Dawson, who retired from the scene of her discomfiture, vowing vengeance upon all who had taken part against her. These threats, however, had but little effect upon the persons for whom they were meant, and without taking any further notice of her, they once more returned to the subject that engrossed all their attention.

"I have heard it said," observed Harry Roden, "that even the governor himself is in hopes that a pardon may be granted to the prisoner. It don't seem very likely, to be sure, but if there is any truth in it, I can only say he might find objects more worthy of his pity."

"But maybe he knows something in the case that we don't," observed Snizzle, with all due deference, "Sir Charles Radcliffe has always given satisfaction here as governor of the island, and I don't think he'd shield a villain if he thought he deserved to die."

"But Sir Charles is as likely to fall into mistakes as anybody else," replied Roden; "and if he believes anything that Luke Somerton may say in his own behalf, he'll find himself very much mistaken in the end."

"People have been accused wrongfully before now," observed Dame Findley, "and none of us can say but what it may be the case with Luke Somerton; not that I'm going to take his part, only it would be a dreadful thing to hang him, and then discover by and bye that the murder was committed by some one else."

"Why, who, with a grain of sense in their brains, can doubt it?" demanded Roden. "Wasn't a dagger, marked with Luke Somerton's name, found in the cottage at the same time that the murder was committed?"

"To be sure there was," said Jack Martin, who now once more joined the group. "The weapon was dropped by the murderer after the crime was committed, and as there was good proof of its having belonged to Somerton, everybody felt satisfied directly that he had committed the deed. Why, even the judge said it was a strong proof; and that the jury thought so, is pretty plain by their having brought in a verdict of guilty."

"Yes; but judges, and juries, too, are sometimes wrong," exclaimed Dame Findley. "The dagger may have been stolen by the person who committed the crime, and a very fine reflection that would be after an innocent man had been hanged for the murder."

"It's no use talking to obstinate people," said Harry Roden impatiently. "You have taken it into your head that Somerton is innocent, but I, and a good many more, are equally certain that the crime was committed by no one else. At any rate, Luke has done many other things that deserve hanging, so that even if he should be innocent of this deed, there won't be much to complain of should it be proved the murder was committed by some one else."

"What's the use of argufying that topic now?" exclaimed Roden impatiently. "All our talk won't make any difference in the sentence, and as there is a man to be hanged, I mean to make one among the spectators. So follow me who likes, only let it be understood, that if the execution don't take place, I, for one, shall kick up a row that won't be stopped in a hurry by the governor nor all the soldiers he can bring against me."

With this threat Harry Roden made his way through the crowd, and was quickly followed by the greater part of the assemblage towards the place where criminals usually expiated their crimes.

CHAPTER XXI.

I know the inconstant people,—how their mind,
With every breath of good or ill report,
Fluctuates like summer corn before the breeze;
Quick in their hatred, quicker in their ire.
                                        SOUTHEY.

AFTER he had left the assemblage on the seashore, Lieutenant Granger made his way with all speed towards the castle, in order to see the governor, and exert what little influence he might possess to obtain a brief respite, so that it might be ascertained whether the queen had yielded to the entreaties of a daughter pleading for the life of her father. It must be admitted that his hopes grew fainter and fainter in proportion as the fatal hour came on; yet the object was one in the success of which he felt deeply interested, and he resolved to leave no effort untried whilst even the slightest chance remained. Absorbed by the thoughts with which his mind was harassed, he did not observe the approach of Caleb until the familiar tones of the latter assailed him.

"What cheer, your honour?" exclaimed the veteran; "how acts the wind now? has it shifted to a more favourable quarter than when I last saw you?"

"Everything remains exactly as it was," replied the young soldier. "The storm of last night has prevented the return of Louisa Somerton, and, to confess the truth, I begin to be almost afraid that she has fallen a sacrifice to the generous duty she undertook."

"Ah, sir, that's exactly what I've been thinking myself, only I did not put my thoughts into such nice words."

"You believe, then, that there is little chance of a boat living through such a storm as we had last night?"

"Lord love your honour!" exclaimed the sailor, "how can such a thing be thought of for a moment? Here have I been used to the sea fifty years—man and boy—and never do I remember a stiffer gale than the one that's just over. Why, a man-of-war wouldn't have been safe unless she had plenty of sea-room; but when you come to a cock-boat, such as Louisa Somerton went in, I should say she must have gone down to a dead certainty."

"And yet," sighed Granger, "I vainly flattered

myself with a hope that a small vessel, under good management, might have a better chance than a larger one."

"Well, I don't know but what it might," answered Caleb; "that is, if it was, as you say, under the management of an experienced sailor. They say innocence is under the especial care of Providence, and, in that case, I should say no harm has befallen Louisa, for a better girl than she is never lived. However, the storm must have been a bitter trial for her, and such as very few of your strong nerved men could bear without suffering severely for it afterwards. If they have escaped foundering, it must have been by keeping well out at sea, for a lee-shore is no place for either small boats or large ships when there is a heavy surf running."

"But even if they kept well out at sea I suppose there was danger to be apprehended?"

"That would depend upon what sort of craft the young lady was in," replied the sailor. "If she was all tight and trim, she'd float like a duck upon the water—'sometimes high and sometimes low,' as the old song goes. But if she warn't seaworthy, why there's no telling what might happen, though it's but too likely she'd go down, with all on board, to Davy Jones's locker."

"Heaven forbid that such a catastrophe should have occurred!"

"Amen, with all my heart!" responded the veteran. "The girl, your honour, was an especial favourite of mine, though, perhaps, not quite so much as she was of yours, seeing as how there was a sort of love affair between you."

"It seems, Caleb," said the lieutenant, without heeding the latter part of the sentence, "that she did not return with her uncle; or, at least, she was not in the boat with him when he was seen off this coast at an early hour this morning."

"So much the better," exclaimed the sailor. "Maybe she was warned against the tempest that was brewing, by some of the Whitehaven folks. They've got some chaps there that knows a little about nautical affairs, and if she took their advice she will have good reason to be thankful for it, after the night of tempest that has just passed away."

"Have you forgotten, then, the object for which she visited the mainland?" asked Lieutenant Granger.

"Why, to tell you the truth, I had almost forgot it at the moment," replied Caleb, "But you've soon brought it to my mind though, and now I come to think of it, your honour, it seems hardly likely she'd stay behind, knowing, as she does, that her father dies to-day, unless she has been lucky enough to get a pardon for him. Yet, with all reverence be it spoken, kings and queens ain't to be quite so easily got at as some folks think for. I know what it is to try and get a hearing from a lord of the Admiralty, and they're a sort of little kings in their own way."

"But Queen Anne has done many gracious acts during the short period she has been on the throne," answered Granger, "and upon that circumstance do I found my hopes. It is true, the crime charged against Luke Somerton is the most heinous in the black catalogue; but there is no actual proof of his having committed the murder, and her majesty may possibly grant a pardon on that ground, at least I trust such may be the case."

"Take an old man's advice, your honour, and never place your faith in princes," exclaimed Caleb. "Many of 'em are very good people, I admit, but, then, they can't attend to everybody's wants, and sometimes they give you reason to hope when there's no foundation for it."

"It may be so, my good friend," replied the lieutenant, "but in the present instant an immediate decision must be come to. The pardon must be either granted or refused, in consequence of so short an interval elapsing before the execution is to take place."

"Well, I dare say it was all done for the best," said the veteran; "and yet, between ourselves, it was a useless task for Miss Louisa to undertake. There were so many difficulties in the way, that I wonder a young girl like her could think of facing them."

"Filial duty is one of the strongest impulses in human nature," returned Lieutenant Granger. "It leads us on with a power that there is no resisting, and, fortunately, in many instances, with the most beneficial results."

"All that's very good argument, your honour," said Caleb, "and I'm sure there's no one wishes more than I do that the young lady may succeed. But supposing she should be lucky enough to find Queen Anne in a forgiving humour, what is to be done afterwards? Luke Somerton could never mix again in society, because all would shun him as a man that had been tried and convicted for murder. People are always inclined to look at the dark side of the question, you know, and then a man had better be hung out of the way at once than live to see himself scorned by his former friends."

"Your philosophy, Caleb," answered the young soldier, "will hardly serve to convince me that this attempt to save the prisoner ought not to have been made. He may be innocent, for aught we know to the contrary, and you would hardly advocate the punishment of a man for a crime that he has not committed."

"Certainly not, sir," replied the other; "but we can scarcely bring ourselves to believe the innocence of a man, after twelve men have found him guilty upon the evidence that has been brought against him. I was not present at the trial of Luke Somerton, but I've seen people that were, and they tell me that everything brought forward was as clear as a marlinspike. No one saw him kill Captain Aylmer, it's true, but, then, everybody knows that he bore the fiercest hatred towards him, and he has even been heard to say that he should never know rest till he had had his full vengeance!"

"Those were probably words spoken in the heat of blood," returned Lieutenant Granger. "In anger, we all of us speak words that we are ashamed of in our cooler moments, and we may fairly presume that Luke Somerton was also led away by the violence of his passion."

"I'm sure, sir, I don't want to make him out a bit worse than he is," exclaimed Caleb. "He bears but an indifferent name in other matters, though, perhaps, you'll say a man ought not to be hanged for any crime short of the one he has been found guilty of."

"Luke Somerton has been led away by the unbridled violence of his own temper," said the lieutenant. "He sustained many serious provocations from the man he is now accused of having murdered, and in disgust left the service to become that which rendered him an outcast from society. It is no excuse to say the persecution of a fellow-officer drove him into a life of error, but it may be urged, that had he never known Captain Aylmer, he would still have been honourably employed in the service of his country."

"And it's a thousand pities, your honour, that he should have been brought to the state he's now in," said Caleb. "It's bad enough that disgrace has fallen upon himself, but how much worse is it that poor Louisa Somerton will be pointed out by the world as the daughter of a man who was tried and convicted for murder!"

"For the honour of humanity, Caleb, I hope there are very few persons who would be guilty of so cowardly an act of injustice," said the young man. "Let what may happen, I will continue her firm friend, and unless met with a decided refusal, will make her my wife. She will then have a protector against all the shafts of calumny that may be directed towards her, and may thus be spared the annoyance of which you speak."

"But don't you think, sir, people will turn their backs upon you when they find you have married the daughter of a man that was executed for a murder?"

"I have said already that I care nothing for what people may think proper to say of me," replied Granger.

"Very good, your honour; yet you might think differently by and bye, when every friend has deserted you."

"Such friends are not worth the keeping," answered Lieutenant Granger. "They are mere common flies, that disappear on the first approach of a change, and are equally worthless."

"It certainly ain't for me to advise a man who, in most things, knows so much better than myself," replied Caleb, "and yet I should say you ought to look well before you take the leap. Miss Louisa is as kind a creature as ever trod God's earth, and yet she is no match for the like of you, because I feel certain, that much as she may love you, there will be a great deal of bitterness follow your marriage. Now, I never had a wife myself, and never mean to have one, yet I know pretty well what people ought to do, like a looker-on at cards, who can always see a great deal more of the game than those who are actually playing."

"At all events," said Lieutenant Granger, "you have erred most completely on the present occasion."

"It's like enough I may," replied the veteran, "because I feel anxious in your behalf, and too much anxiety begets distrust. It's very easy for a man to make a false step, but it's not quite so easy to set himself to rights again. As for Luke Somerton, I'll not give an opinion as to whether he is innocent or guilty of the crime brought against him. If he didn't murder Captain Aylmer it's very certain they oughtn't to hang him for it; but you may believe me, when I say it, that nothing will ever convince the people in this island that he didn't take away the life of his former foe."

"That is only a proof of their obstinacy and ignorance," replied the lieutenant. "Prejudice is too frequently paramount in such cases as this, and thus we find the innocent suffering as much from the evil opinions of their so-called friends, as if they had committed the most heinous offence in the catalogue of crime."

"I hope you won't think I meant to say anything against Miss Louisa, sir," exclaimed the veteran, "for I have the greatest goodwill towards her, and should like to see her as happy as she deserves to be. I was merely thinking it would be a pity for you to spoil your own prospects by marrying a girl who ——"

"I tell you, Caleb, she is worthy of a prince," interrupted Lieutenant Granger. "My opinions of her have not been formed suddenly or rashly; we have now been acquainted some time, and it is no little compliment to say that I love her more and more the older our intimacy grows."

"May I make so bold as to ask if you have popped the question to her yet?" inquired the old seaman.

"It's rather a singular one, certainly," replied Granger; "but as we have known each other some time, Caleb, I will be candid with you. I have mentioned my hopes to Louisa Somerton, and was gratified at learning that she regarded me with the warmest affection."

"No doubt of it," exclaimed Caleb; "a smart-looking young officer, like yourself, needn't look very far without finding some one that would be willing to be Mrs. Granger. Not that I think Miss Louisa is over vain or ambitious; but, of course, she has been looking after a good mate for herself, and where could she have been better suited than with Lieutenant Granger?"

"There are others in this island who seek her hand," replied the young officer, "ay, and good, eligible offers, too; yet she has rejected them all for me."

"Humph!" exclaimed Caleb; "very flattering, no doubt; but, considering that her father has been a ——"

"Not one word upon that subject, Caleb, I desire," interrupted Frederick. "Whatever may be the father's faults, the daughter can have nothing whatever to do with them. It is misfortune enough to know that affliction has fallen upon her parent, without being reminded of it by those who can have nothing to do with the affair."

"May I ask if Sir Charles Radcliffe is aware of your regard for the daughter of Luke Somerton?"

"He has formed a pretty shrewd guess upon the subject."

"And thinks of it pretty much as I do, I suppose?"

"He has no more right than yourself to think anything about it," replied Frederick. "It is true he has ever been my kind friend and adviser; but in an affair of this sort I do not choose to be guided by the counsels of any one. The virtue and many other excellent qualities of Louisa Somerton render her worthy to become the wife of one whose pretensions are higher than mine."

"Ah! this love is a strange, wayward fellow," exclaimed Caleb. "He has to do with every one, I believe, in the course of their lives, and terrible fools he sometimes makes of 'em. I was once pretty near getting spliced myself; but my own good fortune saved me just in time, and there's never been a chance of making a simpleton of myself since."

"What do you mean by good fortune saving you, Caleb?" inquired Lieutenant Granger.

"Why, the fact is, your honour, the girl didn't turn out to be quite such a model of virtue as I fancied her," replied the veteran. "I met with her at Portsmouth; and, lord, sir! to see her, you'd think butter would hardly melt in her mouth."

"It was lucky, Caleb, that you made the discovery in time."

"It was, indeed," answered the other, "for else had I been a miserable man for the rest of my days. I've heard people say that Love's blind; but I rather think it's the people that fall in love that's blind, or we shouldn't meet with so many people that are paired without being matched. Nance managed to deceive me by showing false colours; but no sooner did I find that there was another chap upon the same tack as myself, than I slipped cable and bore off under all press of canvass."

"But perhaps you were jealous of the girl without cause."

"I don't think I was, your honour; but, any how, I fancy myself better off as I am, for my life has been pretty well spent at sea, and, for my own part, I could never understand what we tars want with wives. We can wash our own shirts as well as make 'em, and, if we happen to be fond of the lasses—which most of us are—we find plenty of 'em at every port we go to, and they can help to spend the money for us quite as well as if the parson had made us one."

"But in old age, when you are rewarded with a pension, a wife is the best companion a veteran can have."

"Well, maybe your'e right, your honour; and yet, how can we tars be made happier than when we find ourselves in comfortable quarters at Greenwich Hospital? Most of 'em, it's true, have lost one or more of their limbs, but then they forget past troubles in the present comforts they enjoy, and, for happy inmates, I'll back Greenwich Hospital against any other inmates in her majesty's dominions."

"How is it, Caleb, that you are not yourself there?"

"Because I preferred being an out-pensioner, that the latter part of my days might be spent in my native place," answered the veteran. "I was born, sir, in the Isle of Man, and though there ain't much room in it to boast of, I think there ain't such another place in the world. Many a time have I fancied myself on the old spot, when I've been perhaps thousands of miles away from it, and I always fancied that, if God should spare me till the war was at an end, there would be no happiness like that of taking up my quarters in the place of my birth. So here I am, your honour, with a pension that is enough for all my wants, and, when death obliges me to strike my colours, I shall rest beneath the green turf of my old parish churchyard. So you see, lieutenant, I'm not much inclined to grumble, though I don't rank so high up as an admiral."

"You are an excellent fellow, Caleb," exclaimed the young soldier; "and I am, therefore, the more surprised that you are somewhat illiberal about Louisa Somerton."

"I never meant to be so, then," answered Caleb; "for I believe there ain't a person in the island thinks better of her than I do. She's as good a cretur as ever breathed; but that don't prove any the more that she's such a wife as you ought to look out for. Nay, don't look so angrily at me, for whatever I say is meant for your own good, and no disparagement to the young lady, whose misfortunes alone have made her no match for such as you."

"Such words from you surprise me a great deal more than if they had been uttered by anybody else," exclaimed Lieutenant Granger. "I always thought you a perfect model of what a British sailor ought to be; one who ever takes the part of the weak against the strong, and one who would rather assist a friendless female, than do aught that might involve her still lower in the depths of misery. Louisa Somerton has been the victim of circumstances. A few months ago, and there was not a happier girl in the whole island. She was respected by everybody, high and low, rich and poor; and so she would have remained to the last hour of her existence, but for the unexpected return of her father, and the events that have subsequently taken place."

"Well, sir," replied Caleb, "I don't say that the girl herself is any the worse for the evil doings of her father, but, if he's hanged, there's a slur thrown upon her name, and that ain't exactly the sort of wife that an officer in her majesty's service should wish to take to himself."

"And so I am to become unjust through a false feeling of pride!" exclaimed Lieutenant Granger indignantly.

"Avast there, your honour," vociferated Caleb, "I ain't argufying that you ought to turn your back upon the girl merely on account of her misfortunes; but my experience tells me that a man loses all chance of promotion if he forgets his own respectability. The girl deserves to be pitied because she's not brought these troubles upon herself, but there's other ways of doing her a service without leaping headlong into matrimony. For instance, she will no doubt like to live a retired life after the execution of her father, and, as I've heard say you have a good income besides what comes from your commission, you might make the girl an allowance that would save her from want."

"And so give the world room to say that my bounty was bestowed and received on dishonourable terms!" exclaimed Lieutenant Granger. "And yet why do we indulge in these idle fancies, when she of whom we are speaking has, in all probability, perished in her noble efforts to save the life of her parent? Had she lived, Caleb, I would have married her in spite of all that might have been said."

"I ain't particularly hard-hearted, lieutenant," returned the sailor, "but I'm of opinion that if she has gone to the bottom, it is through the mercy of Heaven, that would spare her from the miseries she must have endured after her father was hanged."

"How know you," demanded the other, "that she had not succeeded in the pious mission that took her hence?"

"It's rather unlikely, lieutenant, that's all," replied Caleb. "Those that shed human blood are not very often pardoned, and there's not much excuse for Luke Somerton, who killed the captain after he'd had plenty of time to grow cool."

"But there is a doubt whether Somerton's was the hand that committed the deed," exclaimed the young lieutenant.

"Ah, sir!" returned the other, "you speak as you wish, not as you really mean. The jury must have been convinced of his guilt, or they would not have returned such a verdict."

"Almost all the people in this island are the vowed enemies of Luke Somerton," replied Granger. "This is a fact that I can vouch for on my own experience, for no one speaks of his approaching fate but with exultation; and a crowd of persons from whom I have just escaped even threaten a resort to violence in case the queen, in the exercise of her royal prerogative, should spare his life."

"All vain boasting, sir," exclaimed Caleb. "They know we've military enough in the island to suppress any act of violence, and it's hardly likely they'd run the risk of being shot merely for an affair of this kind."

"At all events, it will be better to guard against their threatened outbreak," replied Granger; "and I am now on my way to the castle in order to warn Sir Charles Radcliffe of what may be expected. We shall then be prepared to give the rabble a reception they little expect, and if any should fall, it will be through their own fault."

"I don't think there's much chance of any mischief, sir," observed the old man; "for, if Luke is hanged, the people will be quiet enough; and, as no pardon has yet arrived, the execution will take place without doubt. But in case they should be inclined to begin a riot, I'll mingle among the crowd, and try what I can do to pacify them. In another hour, lieutenant, the execution must take place, unless it is stayed by the queen's royal authority."

"Poor Luke's allotted period does indeed approach towards its close," exclaimed Lieutenant Granger. "He himself, I believe, has not looked forward with the slightest feeling of hope; but the bitterness of death will be terribly increased by the uncertainty that envelopes the fate of his high-minded and beloved daughter. Here, however, I must leave you, Caleb, for we have reached the castle-gates, and I have something of importance to confer upon with Sir Charles Radcliffe. In the meantime, you will do all in your power to pacify the mob; tell them the danger they will incur by breaking into open violence against the laws; and, if you can, prevail upon them to think less harshly of the unfortunate man whose death they are so eager to witness. Perform these offices with zeal, and you will earn my lasting gratitude."

Lieutenant Granger then passed the sentry who was stationed at the castle-gate, and old Caleb, turning away, directed his steps towards the place where the gibbet had been erected, preparatory to the approaching execution.

In the meanwhile, Sir Charles Radcliffe was a prey to the most intense anxiety, as the hour drew nigh when his last painful duty was to be accomplished. His regret, however, was not so much occasioned by any doubt of the prisoner's guilt, as by the youth and devoted affection of the unfortunate Louisa Somerton. The doubt whether she had survived the fearful tempest of the preceding night filled him with inquietude, and after pacing the room for some time, he was about to summon a domestic to inquire whether anything had been heard of her, when the door opened, and Lieutenant Granger entered almost as soon as he had been announced as having arrived.

"You are a most welcome visitor, Frederick," exclaimed the governor; "for here have I been the last hour upon thorns, waiting to learn whether anything has been heard of Louisa Somerton;—has she yet returned to the island?"

"I am sorry to say we can obtain no tidings of her," replied the lieutenant. "One person, however, tells me that he saw James Somerton and a fisherman in a Whitehaven boat at an early hour this morning."

"Where did he see them?"

"Off the rocks at the east point," replied the lieutenant.

"Did they succeed in effecting a landing at that spot?"

"They did not," replied Granger; "and the man tells me there was no possibility of rendering them any assistance. The sea was running mountains high, and there is but too much reason to fear the boat was dashed to pieces upon the rocks that lie there concealed."

"And the girl, Louisa Somerton, was not with them?"

"She was not," replied Lieutenant Granger, "and therein lies a mystery that I cannot fathom. Had she obtained the pardon, she would have returned under the protection of her uncle, and her absence almost leads me to fear that she has failed in the generous attempt that took her hence."

"It was hardly to be expected otherwise," replied Sir Charles Radcliffe, "though I was unwilling to persuade her against a design that she seemed to have placed her heart and soul upon. The queen may delight in acts of mercy towards her subjects, but I do not see how she could interfere in a case where the evidence, though circumstantial, was tolerably conclusive."

"Do you, then, believe that Luke Somerton is guilty of having taken the life of Captain Aylmer?" asked Frederick.

"I am almost afraid to think seriously upon the subject," replied the governor. "I would fain believe him innocent, but the circumstance of Luke's dagger having been found in the house where the crime was committed, goes very far towards convincing me that the jury have come to a fair and impartial decision."

"Yet, supposing Aylmer fell by Luke's hands," interposed the lieutenant, "there may be extenuating circumstances that you do not seem to have considered. For instance:—a sudden quarrel may have arisen between them—an attack may, in the first instance, have been made by Captain Aylmer upon Luke—and the latter, in that case, would have been justified in defending himself. Should this view of the affair be correct, Somerton would be guilty only of manslaughter in the slightest degree."

Sir Charles Radcliffe shook his head doubtingly, and remained silent some little time. At length, observing that Granger expected a reply, he said,—

"Your theory, my dear young friend, is an ingenious one, but I fear it can avail but little at this the eleventh hour. If the facts had been as you have supposed, Luke Somerton had plenty of opportunities to have stated them at his trial. Nothing of the kind, however, was hinted by him, and it is therefore only fair to presume that the act was a wilful and premeditated one."

"Is that your deliberate and positive opinion, Sir Charles?"

"I am sorry to say, my dear fellow, I cannot conscientiously come to any other," replied the governor. "I am here placed in a situation of great trust, and it is expected that I shall perform my duty with the strictest impartiality. If there was but the smallest loop-hole by which I could give the prisoner the benefit of a doubt, I should be most happy to save him from his approaching fate."

"So I believed," answered Lieutenant Granger, "and my disappointment is all the greater now that I find you are still of opinion that Luke Somerton is guilty of the foul charge that has been brought against him."

"You must bear it in mind, Frederick, that I have no right to be prejudiced one way or the other. I do not presume to say that the prisoner is guilty of a cold-blooded murder, but a verdict to that effect has been returned by the jury who tried him, and I am bound to abide by it. Had their decision been a contrary one, it must be confessed I should have greatly rejoiced. Not but what Luke Somerton has led a reckless, lawless life, for some time past—making enemies of those who were once his friends, and bringing himself at last to this fearful strait."

"It is not my business to be his apologist," exclaimed Lieutenant Granger; "and yet I may perhaps be permitted to say, that he is not the only person to blame for the extremities to which he has gone. Had the conduct of Captain Aylmer been less marked with brutality, Somerton would never have left the service of his country, nor would this day have been marked as that on which a fellow creature is to die by violence. I may observe, too, that while Luke Somerton was an officer in the royal navy, his bravery and good conduct were the theme of admiration amongst all who belonged to his ship."

"That may be," replied Sir Charles, "for instances are not wanting in which men of previous good character have forfeited their good name in moments of sudden anger. With Somerton, however, there is still less excuse; for he seems to have brooded over his imaginary wrongs—nursing them, as it were, in his own bosom—and taking the first opportunity which offered to revenge himself on the man he called his foe."

"Why, every one knows the taunts and insults he had to endure from Captain Aylmer," exclaimed the young man. "On one occasion, a blow even was struck, and, if that is not resented, the man who receives it must be a coward, and unworthy of holding his commission."

"I see, Frederick, you are carried away by your own impetuosity," returned the governor. "That Captain Aylmer was a severe disciplinarian, I know,

and it may even be acceded that his conduct towards Luke Somerton was such as no man could bear with. But you know our military laws are exceedingly strict, and no officer is allowed to challenge his superior, however great the provocation may be. If he does so, the punishment is most severe."

"And equally severe ought they to be against the petty tyrant who abuses the power given him over those of rank inferior to his own," replied Granger.

"Your words are most bitter against Captain Aylmer," exclaimed the governor, "and, I must needs add, not altogether deserved. Let us at least suppose that Somerton, as well as the other, was in fault, and then, perhaps, we shall be nearer to the truth. At any rate, the quarrel has proved most disastrous in its results, for one has already perished by the hand of an assassin, and now the murderer himself is about to pay the fearful penalty of his crime."

The conversation was now interrupted by the entrance of the gaoler, to say the preparations were completed. The sudden intelligence seemed to startle Sir Charles for the moment, but, quickly recovering his usual composure, he made a sign for Lieutenant Granger to follow, and then immediately proceeded towards the condemned cell.

CHAPTER XXII.

I think we shall not meet again,
Till it be, in that world where never change
Is known, and they who love shall part no more.
SOUTHEY.

IT was observed by the prison attendants that, as the fatal moment approached, Luke Somerton became more and more restless, and the firmness which had hitherto supported him now gave way to the feelings which had struggled with in his breast. This was regarded as a certain token of terror; but little they knew of Luke Somerton, who imagined that he feared to meet the death he had been doomed to suffer.

The truth is, he had hitherto been supported by the hope that he should see, or, at least, hear something of his daughter, ere they led him forth from his dungeon towards the place of execution. At their last interview she had expressed it as her certain conviction that her errand would not prove a fruitless one, and no argument that he had used could convince her to the contrary. Since her absence he had himself almost began to believe that it was possible the queen's pardon might be obtained, though he would not confess as much to any other person. On the contrary, we have seen that he persisted in declaring it as his own conviction that the sentence would not be averted, and those to whom he had spoken on the subject believed he had made up his mind that his case was hopeless. The change that had taken place within the last hour or two was considered as confirmatory of this idea, and there were some who rejoiced at what they conceived to be signs of remorse for his past misdeeds.

When Sir Charles and his young friend entered the cell, they found Luke Somerton seated upon a bench, his arms pinioned behind him, and his head stooping forward till it rested upon his heaving bosom. Shortly after the entrance of the last-named personages, however, he was roused by the sound of their voices, and, starting from his seat, demanded in hurried accents, if all was ready."

"I have come to announce to you that the hour is at hand when the execution of your sentence is to be carried into effect," replied Sir Charles Radcliffe. "If there is any request that you have to make, I solemnly promise to carry it into effect, if not inconsistent with my duty."

"What mockery is this!" muttered Luke bitterly.

"You are about to send me to the gibbet, and yet affect the greatest commiseration for the victim you are to sacrifice."

"Nay," exclaimed the governor; "these reproaches become not a man in your unfortunate situation. It is the law, and not myself, that has adjudged you to death, and I have no power beyond that of affording what little consolation may be given in your last moments."

"Tell me of my daughter," said Luke Somer-

ton, wildly glaring round him. "Say that she has not perished in her effort to save the life of her father—say she yet lives, and my own fate will have lost its worst sting."

"Alas! we are at present uncertain what has become of her," replied Frederick Granger. "I have myself been down to the beach in hope of hearing some intelligence respecting her, but have been unable to obtain any tidings."

"Then she is lost!" exclaimed Luke, with fearful impetuosity. "Lost in her generous efforts to save the life of her parent."

"It would be too much to say that she has perished," returned the governor. "The storm commenced at an early hour last evening, and it is hardly probable she could bribe any of the Whitehaven fishermen to hazard their own lives by bring-

ing her over. In that case she would be obliged to remain there till this morning, when, the gale having subsided, she may make the passage in safety."

"And ere she arrives," murmured Luke Somerton, "her father will have been sent to his long account."

"Would that there were any way by which the execution could be postponed," said Sir Charles. "I myself would gladly wait till news arrive here from Whitehaven, but the law renders my duty imperative, and I dare not exceed the hour named in the warrant."

"Well, I cannot but submit," exclaimed Luke; "and I know not that life has ever been so pleasant to me that I need wish to prolong it by so much as a single minute. If my daughter had escaped, I leave her to the tender mercy of those who will not turn their backs upon her for the faults of her father. To you, Lieutenant Granger, I more particularly intrust the task of watching over her welfare, in the event of her uncle having perished on his return last night. If she lives, her future days will be filled with bitterness and sorrow, so that she will need the kindness of some friend who will endeavour to smooth down the thorns and brambles that will encumber her onward path."

"The charge you have entrusted me with shall be religiously obeyed," returned Granger, evidently moved by the melancholy scene that was passing. "You are aware of my anxiety to render myself agreeable in her sight, and should her present scruples be removed, I will give her that right to my protection which a wife has a right to claim from her husband."

"I have already spoken my mind freely on that subject," replied Luke Somerton. "That your present intentions are just and honourable, I do not doubt; but love may change to coldness, if not to hatred, when you find that the world's scorn follows the hapless daughter of a man who yielded up his life on a scaffold. Louisa has felt this, and I am assured that no consideration will ever prevail upon her to become your wife."

"What protection, then, can I afford her?" asked Granger.

"Place her in some family abroad, where her father's ignominious end has not been heard of," replied the convict. "I leave behind me money enough to supply her moderate wants, and all that is required of you will be to see now and then that she is under good and worthy protection. She will change her name, of course, and there is none better that I know of than that of Walford—the one lately assumed by her uncle. These, Sir Charles Radcliffe, are all the favours I have to ask. The hour appointed for my execution has, I believe, arrived—I am ready!"

"Will you now permit me to join with you in prayer for mercy?" asked the chaplain, who now advanced towards him.

"I have already tried to make my peace with Heaven, and have no need of your assistance," answered Luke. "You can follow me to the scaffold, if you please, and if your services are required, I will then ask them of you."

The prison bell now sent forth its solemn tones, warning them that it was time to move forward. Lieutenant Granger would have tendered his arm to support the prisoner, but he rejected all aid, declaring that he felt no terror at the approach of death, and only asking as a favour that the young man would accompany him to the foot of the gallows, in case he should think of any other request that he would like to make.

The procession then moved from the cell, winding its way through long subterranean passages that ran beneath the castle. At length they ascended to the courtyard, passing through which they made their way slowly towards the spot where the gibbet was erected. On perceiving the terrible engine of death the countenance of Luke Somerton became for a moment blanched. With a slight effort, however, he quickly resumed his former appearance of composure, and on reaching the scaffold, gazed round upon the throng of spectators that had assembled to witness the dying throes of the unfortunate convict. Luke fancied he could perceive exultation in every countenance, but all feelings of anger had subsided in his bosom, and, turning towards the governor of the island, he inquired if it was yet time for him to ascend the scaffold.

"There are not many minutes to spare," answered Sir Charles Radcliffe: "so if you have anything further to say, it must be in as few words as possible. Painful as it is, my duty admits of but little more delay."

"Aye," replied the prisoner; "and a man, Sir Charles, must do his duty. I know that; and yet, for a reason that I can hardly explain, I wish you and your duty could agree to give me a little longer time. Small as my chance is, I would not lose it if I could do better."

"Chance!" exclaimed the governor; "what chance is there?"

"Why, it is this," replied Luke Somerton, pointing straight before him. "Up yonder, on the rocks that overlook the ocean, I can see Caleb, who has been making signals for me to get as much delay as I can. There is something in it, or the old man would not be so anxious to get me the delay of a few moments."

"Perhaps some treachery is intended!" exclaimed Sir Charles.

"Treachery!" cried Luke Somerton, indignantly; "can you think a man like that, who has spent the prime of life in the service of his country, would blacken his character at last by one act of treachery. No—no; I have a hope of something better than that—he, perhaps, sees the boat that brings back my daughter in safety, and, if that should be the case, you may hang me as soon as you like after I have once more clasped her in my arms."

"Hurrah!" shouted Caleb from the lofty position he had taken. "She has just weathered the foreland; I know her by the rake of her mast, and the dark patch on her top-sail. It's one of the Whitehaven boats, and my life for it, she brings with her the daughter of Luke Somerton!"

At this announcement there was an evident movement of surprise and anger among the assembled crowd, some of whom would have rushed forward to despatch Somerton with their own hands, had they not been kept back by the guards. This, however, was not observed by the object against whom their fury was directed, who, shouting aloud to the old sailor, demanded what flag she bore.

"The red cross of old England," answered the veteran.

"Ah! then it's all over with me!" exclaimed Somerton, whilst his countenance assumed an ashy hue. "And yet," he added, after a pause, "why should I care about it now? I might have lived longer, and not died happier. But my poor Louisa! What a sight for her will this be when first she sets foot upon the island!"

"Prisoner," exclaimed Sir Charles, "it is my duty to inform you that the full time allowed by the law is up. You must now prepare for the immediate execution of your sentence—I have no other alternative."

"Let's drag him up the scaffold!" exclaimed

one of the mob. "The murderer deserves his doom, and why are we to be kept here after the time appointed for his execution?"

"Keep those people back as you value your own lives!" cried Sir Charles Radcliffe, addressing the guards. "If any man advances so much as a single step beyond the boundaries marked out, he will do so at his own peril!"

"Sir Charles," exclaimed the prisoner, "I must, of course, bow with submission to your commands; yet I cannot but think that you could, if you thought proper, grant me a few moments' delay, just to see if my daughter has succeeded in obtaining her Majesty's pardon. I hardly expect such an act of mercy, your excellency, and yet it is hard to die while there is the least chance left that the queen has been pleased to spare my life."

"You ask more than I dare grant," replied Sir Charles. "The dial now marks the exact time mentioned in the warrant, and my delay would be answered by my own dishonour. Lead him to the scaffold, and see that the execution instantly takes place."

These latter words were addressed to the gaoler and his assistants, who immediately advanced to lay hands on the prisoner. In the struggle that ensued, however, Luke burst the bonds which had confined his arms, and as the men drew back in alarm for their own safety, Louisa Somerton, bearing the queen's pardon, rushed through the crowd, and, as Luke seized the precious document, fell fainting on his bosom.

"I am saved!" exclaimed Luke Somerton, holding up the precious pardon at arm's length, above his head. "Saved when all hope seemed to be at an end! And by whom has this miracle been achieved? By my daughter, whose courage and filial affection have prompted her to brave dangers that few of our rougher sex would have dared to venture. Look at it, Sir Charles Radcliffe," he added, throwing it towards the governor; "you will see that it is signed by her majesty, and bears her royal seal. You do not doubt its authenticity I suppose?"

"It is the queen's signature, sure enough!" replied Sir Charles, after he had carefully perused the contents. "This document," he continued, addressing himself to the assemblage, "is a pardon granted by Queen Anne to Luke Somerton, who stood charged and convicted for the murder of Captain Aylmer. Her majesty is pleased to say that she has reason to believe that the prisoner has been found guilty on insufficient evidence, and directs that he shall be discharged from custody the moment I receive her commands. Luke Somerton, you are now free, and let me hope that from henceforth you will endeavour to prove yourself worthy of the gracious act of mercy that has been exercised in your behalf."

"I am thankful to her majesty," replied Luke; "but how much more so ought I to be for the heroic devotion of my dear daughter. Friends—if any there be amongst you—join me in one cheer for our liege lady, Queen Anne."

The governor, and those immediately connected with him, heartily responded to the call; but the assemblage maintained a sullen silence, only one here and there joining in the loyal cheer that was given.

"How is this?" exclaimed Sir Charles, looking round him with surprise. "Are her majesty's subjects on this island so disloyal that none of them will raise their voices in laudation after this signal act of mercy?"

"Mercy!" vociferated Henry Roden; "do you call it mercy, Sir Charles, to pardon a murderer after he has been justly condemned to die the death of a felon?"

"Who dares impugn the justice of her majesty's acts?" demanded the governor impatiently. "She has yielded to the prayers of yonder excellent girl, and we are all taught to believe that mercy is one of the brightest jewels in a kingly crown. Besides, it is her will and pleasure that execution upon the offender should not take place, and surely there are none among you so blood-thirsty as to desire the death of a fellow-creature?"

"Why, the truth of it is, we don't altogether see the justice of letting off a man who has been fairly tried and found guilty of a cruel murder," exclaimed Dick Joyce, who had caught the contagion from his discontented brethren; "her majesty seems to think Luke Somerton was found guilty upon insufficient evidence, and that being the case, she throws a slur upon the jury that tried him."

"There you are mistaken," exclaimed the governor. "Queen Anne knows the value of trial by jury too well to interfere in a general way, but there may be cases now and then when her interference may be called for. This is one of the instances, and even supposing Luke Somerton to have been guilty of the crime charged against him, we ought to rejoice that his life has been spared so as to enable him to retrieve his past errors."

"It seems I have not many friends here," said Luke, gazing round upon the multitude. "And yet it is scarcely to be wondered at, for they have all left their homes to see a man hanged, and doubtless 'tis a vexatious thing to return without having their curiosity satisfied. If this is to be taken as a sample of Isle of Man kindness, the sooner I leave it for some other place the better, I think."

"There's few here that will be sorry to be rid of you," cried Nell Dawson, at the top of her lungs. "The company of a murderer can't be much coveted by any one, and what's more, if you don't leave the island before you are many hours' older, you'll see good reason to be sorry for your own fool-hardiness."

"Let us seize upon the murderer and hang him up with our own hands," vociferated Henry Roden. "I'll be the ringleader if there's anybody game to follow me; so come along, my lads, and we'll soon see what sort of capers this fellow cuts when he is dancing upon nothing."

"Hold!" exclaimed Sir Charles Radcliffe, "and do not involve yourselves in a dilemma that you will afterwards have bitter reason to regret. There seems to be a determined spirit of mischief among you to-day, and that being the case, I shall take what precautions may seem necessary. Now, understand me, my lads, I am about to read the riot act, and all persons who do not disperse within ten minutes afterwards, must take the consequences of their own folly."

He then produced a paper from his pocket, which he read in a loud tone of voice, and having brought it to a conclusion, once more warned his auditors to return peaceably to their homes. But his words seemed to have very little effect, for the mob still continued immovable, and at length a stone, which was thrown with great force, passed within an inch or two of the still fainting Louisa Somerton.

"Bring before me the scoundrel that threw that missile, and I'll instantly make an example of him," exclaimed Sir Charles Radcliffe.

Still, however, the mob seemed to be disinclined to stir from the spot; it was evident they were bent upon mischief, and the governor, once more addressing them, earnestly requested that every person would return home, as at the end of the time he had named it would be his imperative duty to disperse the refractory, even though it might be at the sacrifice of life.

"Sacrifice of life, indeed," muttered Nell Dawson; "if you had done your duty in a proper manner there would have been none of us left here by this time. We came out to see Luke Somerton hanged, and if the executioner don't do his office, some of us here will perform it for him."

This threat had scarcely been uttered when another stone flew from the crowd and struck Luke on the shoulder. Incensed at this outrage, he looked round to see if he could discover the assailant; but he could not personally revenge the cowardly attack, as Louisa had not quite recovered from the swoon into which she had fallen.

"This is the second time a stone has been hurled at me," exclaimed Luke fiercely. "Beware how it is done again, for whoever the scoundrel may be, I'll make him remember it as long as he lives."

"You had better murder him as you did Captain Aylmer," shouted a voice from the midst of the crowd.

"The time is now expired," interposed Sir Charles Radcliffe, "and I shall be compelled to use violence if you do not at once proceed quietly to your homes. Lieutenant Granger, place yourself at the head of your dragoons, and chargeth e mob at your sword's point if they do not disperse without further warning."

The young officer promptly obeyed this command; his men were ranged up in order, and everything was ready for immediate action, when the crowd, taking to their heels, fled precipitately in every direction.

"The fellows have dispersed at last," exclaimed the governor to Lieutenant Granger; "but how long they will remain upon their good behaviour is more than I can answer for. You are in peril here, Luke Somerton, for the people evidently think your pardon an act of great injustice, and it is not at all unlikely they will find an opportunity to carry out their revenge. I should, therefore, recommend you to leave the island with as little delay as possible."

"That will be a matter for after consideration, your excellency," said Luke. "I am not such a coward as to be driven away by a rabble rout like that; and, as I am now at liberty to do as I please, I shall take time to reflect whether I shall remain in this island, or go somewhere else to pass the remainder of my days."

"Remember," exclaimed the governor, "after this warning, I shall hold you accountable for any mischief that may occur. For what reason it is I know not, but the people here have taken a most extraordinary dislike to you, and I am afraid they will never rest satisfied till you have been made to feel the full weight of their vengeance."

"I'm sure I can't tell what reason they have for it," said Luke Somerton; "but it is certain they were disappointed at not witnessing my execution, and, like an audience disappointed at a theatre, they have vented their disapprobation in the most unequivocal terms. Yet, confound the knaves! if I, and two or three more of my old companions, were to begin in real earnest, they'd soon see reason to repent the folly of beginning this outrage. There would be more broken heads in the island than have been seen at one time for many a long day past."

"Here's more good news, Somerton," exclaimed Caleb, who now came hurrying with all speed towards them. Your brother James has just come ashore, though in such an exhausted state that I have been obliged to leave him at a cottage just behind the cliff yonder. Confound the uncivil brutes though, they'd hardly give him a shelter, for no other reason than that he is your brother."

"Some of these savage islanders will smart for it before I have done with them," said Luke, impatiently. "They saw that I was not able to do anything because my poor Louisa required all my care. But let the rogues look out for themselves when I have my hands free, for if I catch 'em at any of their scurvy tricks, I'll play such a devil's tattoo on their backs that they shall never forget. One stone that they have flung nearly struck my daughter, and the other gave me so smart a blow on my shoulder that I have not got rid of the pain yet."

Luke's anger was at this moment interrupted by the slow and gradual recovery of Louisa, whose unconsciousness began to give way to returning animation. The father no longer thought of the rough treatment he had received from the people who had just made so precipitate a retreat; his every thought was now directed towards the perfect restoration of her to whose generous zeal he owed the preservation of his life, and, lifting her in his arms, he bade a hasty adieu to Sir Charles Radcliffe. To return to the cottage which he had never expected to see again was his next thought, and, having conveyed his almost unconscious burthen thither, he applied those remedies which he thought would effect the most speedy recovery.

CHAPTER XXIII.

Our rulers give us neither law nor justice:
The man was doomed to die—his guilt was proved—
Yet have they pardoned him, though why or wherefore
None deign to tell us.

The Sanctuary.

ON leaving the spot where the execution was to have taken place, the disappointed mob retired to a secluded valley about half a mile off, where they might confer together without fear of being overheard or disturbed. Here the ringleaders made a pause, and those who took a less active part in the proceedings of the day gathered round them, to hear all that was said, and to express their readiness to assist in any proposition that might be made in the course of the debate.

On this occasion Harry Roden took upon himself the part of playing first fiddle, and, mounting himself upon the trunk of a prostrate tree, he commenced by asking, in a loud voice, if there were any persons present who were satisfied with the mercy that had been shown to a criminal who deserved to have swung on the gallows. A vociferous shout of "No!" resounded from all sides, and the orator proceeded with his harangue.

"I am glad to see," he commenced, "that there are so many good fellows here of my way of thinking about this affair of Luke Somerton's. All agree with me in saying that he ought to have been hung, and, if a few stout chaps will only lend me their help, he shall not live to see the next sunrise. What say you, my hearties—shall we go back and execute the sentence, in spite of those that would save him from his fate?"

"Aye, aye," shouted the mob. "Lead the way, Harry Roden, and there isn't a man of us that will desert you."

"You forget, then," interposed Dick Joyce, "that the governor has got soldiers under his command; and, as Sir Charles ain't a man to be played with, we may look for warmer work than you seem to think for."

"Coward!" exclaimed Roden, "do you want to make these fellows as chicken-hearted as yourself?"

"I only want them to see the danger of following bad advice," answered the other; "and I *will* warn them, Harry Roden, though I die for it! What is it to us, I should like to know, if the queen chooses to pardon a man instead of hanging him? Mercy isn't shewn every day, and when we do see an instance of it, the least we can do is to be thankful to her majesty for sparing us an exhibition such as was to have been acted here to-day."

"You forget, then," exclaimed Nell Dawson, "that the villain deserves to die for his crimes?"

"That may or may not be," replied Dick Joyce; "but it should not be forgotten that there are a good many others among us who would not come off scot free if their evil deeds were brought to light. The law is severe against smugglers, and yet I can see a few in this assembly who are not over particular in the matter of cheating her majesty's revenue. Besides, if Luke Somerton has got off, I can't, for the life of me, see what anybody here has to do with it."

"My friends," interposed Peter Smalltext, the schoolmaster, "let me advise ye to refrain from breaking the law, lest your own heads are broken in return. We have armed soldiers in the island to preserve peace, and woe unto those who madly seek to raise a tumult!"

"Take your preaching to those that want it, Master Smalltext," exclaimed Harry Roden, "for here you'll not get many listeners, I can promise you. We know what the laws are, and can respect 'em when it suits our purpose; but if felons are to be let off without punishment, then, I say, it behoves every man to declare that though we may have laws we have no justice."

"And that's all through the queen's doings," observed Nell Dawson, who could not rest without taking a prominent share in the matter. "If the man had been hanged there'd have been an end of the matter, and we should all have returned peaceably to our homes. But no; Luke Somerton must needs be let loose upon us; and now that he finds murder may be committed without any notice being taken of it, we can't say who may be the next victim to his thirst for human blood."

"Woman!" vociferated Dick Joyce, "from one of your sex we might have expected pity instead of revenge. You howl for blood, and, by your own example, urge these infuriated men to commit an act of violence that must end in their own discomfiture."

"At any rate, Dick, nobody has yet asked you to make one of our party," cried Roden. "We want no cowards among us, so you may go home while we arrange our plans for revenging the murder of Captain Aylmer."

"How know you that Captain Aylmer was murdered!" again interposed the schoolmaster.

"Because we found him dead from the wounds he had received," answered Harry Roden.

"Humph! And is that any proof, my good fellow, that he died by the hand of an assassin?"

"I fancy it a very good proof, whatever others may think."

"You never heard, then, I suppose, of any man making away with himself?"

"Why, sometimes people are fools enough to do so," replied Harry Roden; "but, in the present instance, that's not very likely to have been the case, because, you see, we all of us happen to know that there was an old standing grudge between Luke Somerton and Captain Aylmer."

"Well," interrogated Peter Smalltext, "and it follows, because two people happen to have had a quarrel in the course of their lives, that one is to murder the other?"

"If I was in Harry Roden's place," exclaimed Josh Martin, "I wouldn't stand here to be questioned by an old prig like you, just for all the world as if I was a schoolboy. If you don't like what we're about, Master Smalltext, make the best of your way home, and blow up your young 'uns, that are obliged to be afeard on you."

"That's just what I was thinking myself," cried Nell Dawson. "We don't want advice from such as he, and when we do we can send for him, you know. So right about face, Master Smalltext, and don't stop here another minute, if you'd escape a ducking in yonder horsepond. Come, mizzle, will you—vanish!"

"Peter Smalltext will remain here under my protection," said Joyce, looking menacingly around him. "We have certainly as much right in this place as any one else that I can see here, and the first man that offers to molest us will get something he won't like for his pains."

"Why, I declare, if he don't mean to show fight!" exclaimed Snizzle, who, having a keen eye to his own safety, thought it most prudent to take the side of the strongest party.

"Oh, you may let him alone for that," muttered Harry Roden; "the odds are too great when they are a hundred to one, and Dick aint such a fool as to get a drubbing so long as there's a fair chance of escaping it."

"Then why don't he take a friend's advice, and go home about his business?" asked Nell Dawson.

" He ain't wanted here, I'm sure, for there's quite enough to do the business without him; and as for his advice, I should think, by this time, he's heard quite enough to convince him that he might as well talk to the winds. The long and the short of it is, we all came out this morning expecting to see Luke Somerton hanged, and hanged he shall be, unless he has the devil's luck and his own."

" Why, my good woman," cried Peter Smalltext, " you surely wouldn't be rash enough to take the law into your own hands—you wouldn't hang him after he's been reprieved?"

" It's a shame he was ever reprieved at all," exclaimed the virago; " and it's my opinion the queen hadn't any right to show him mercy. But Miss Louisa, forsooth! must go and ask pardon for her father—telling a parcel of lies, of course, about his innocence, and her majesty must needs believe it, though a judge and jury had no doubt about his being the murderer of Captain Aylmer. I've no patience to think of it; and, for my own part, I'll make one of a party to go and drag him out of his house, and hang him on a tree before his own door!"

" And are you aware," asked Peter Smalltext, " that by so doing you would render yourself liable to be tried for murder?"

" What! for giving a guilty man his deserts?" exclaimed Nell.

" Pray, Nell," demanded Joyce, " what right have you to persist in calling him guilty after our gracious sovereign has set aside the verdict? It strikes me there is a great deal of unnecessary warmth about this affair, and the sooner we separate from this place the better. If Luke Somerton is really guilty of the captain's death, it's proper that he should have time to reflect and repent; if, however, he is innocent, he has suffered so much already, that I'm sure that his worst enemies ought to be satisfied."

" That's all very fine talking," exclaimed Mother Dawson; " but what's to make amends for our disappointment, I should like to know? Didn't the governor say that Luke was to be hanged on this day, and ain't we all sent home like a parcel of fools, without seeing anything more than the gallows that he *ought* to have been swung upon? I've no patience to think on't, not I, no more than I have to hear fools prate and palaver, as you've been a-doing."

" Now, I'll tell you what it is, my lads," exclaimed Harry Roden, who had been for some minutes past engaged in earnest and whispered conversation with some of those who were nearest to him; " it seems to me that we are losing time when we ought to be making the most of it. I believe nearly all of us have determined to execute what they call Lynch law, and that being the case, I don't see much wisdom in wasting our time here, while the enemy will have time to make head against us. You all know that I'm for having our revenge on Luke Somerton, and every man that intends to give me his assistance will please to let me know it by holding up his hand."

At this moment a whole forest of dirty hands were held up, and immediately afterwards followed the vociferous exclamations of all who coincided with the last speaker. Joyce, Peter Smalltext, and two or three others, were the only dissentients,

and they might as well have held their tongues, for any good they did.

" I thought there wouldn't be many against us," observed Harry Roden, snatching a thick cudgel from a fellow who stood near him. " Master Somerton thought himself a lucky fellow when the queen's pardon arrived; but it won't be long before we let him know that not even her majesty herself can save his life when her subjects are determined to have justice."

" I would have you beware lest you meet the same fate you intend for him," said Joyce, making a last effort to avert the threatened violence. " Our governor, Sir Charles Radcliffe, is not a man to be trifled with, and if once his anger is stirred up there will be but little chance of mercy for any of you. He is bound to keep the queen's peace, and will do so, even if a hundred lives are sacrificed."

" Then run for your lives every one of you," exclaimed Sniggles, who had been endeavouring to make his escape from the crowd; " Sir Charles Radcliffe is coming this way at the head of a party of soldiers, and if we don't disperse there'll presently be bloodshed."

" Let those run that like," retorted Harry Roden; " for my part, I shall stay where I am, and as will every one else that's not a rank coward. The governor may threaten, if he pleases, but it won't frighten, I can tell him."

" Well, I'm not much of a coward myself," cried Josh Martin; " but hang me if I see much wisdom in resisting him when he is backed by the military. It may be all very well to have our revenge upon Luke Somerton; but I, for one, say it sha'n't be at the expense of my own life."

" Then let's hear what he's got to say," exclaimed Harry Roden, as the governor and his followers galloped up to the spot. " We needn't tell him exactly what we're here for, and if we can only pacify him for a bit, we may afterwards set about our task in good earnest."

" What is the meaning of this assemblage?" demanded Sir Charles Radcliffe, as soon as he had made his way through the opening that was made for him in the crowd. " Are ye met here to concoct some scheme of lawless violence, or will each man, at my bidding, quietly take his departure homewards?"

" I suppose there's no law against a few people talking together?" exclaimed Roden, insolently.

" That entirely depends upon their demeanour and the subject of their conversation," replied the governor. " The fact of *your* being principal spokesman certainly argues anything but peaceable intentions; and, as the representative of her majesty in this island, I hereby desire every man to depart without further ceremony."

" And what if we refuse to obey your order, Sir Charles?"

" Why, then you must take the consequence of your disobedience."

" What is the consequence?"

" Why, that I shall order these men who have accompanied me to clear the place, and if any resistance is offered the result will, in all probability, be bloodshed."

" But," exclaimed the fellow, tauntingly, " you can't draw your sword upon us till after the riot act has been read."

"I want no instructions in my duty," answered Sir Charles, firmly. "If you disperse not, the riot act *will* be read, and ten minutes' time allowed you for obeying its mandates. The wise will not refuse compliance,—the others must take the consequence of their obstinacy."

"Well, if this is law, it's not such as I can admire much," exclaimed Harry Roden. "First of all, a murderer is allowed to escape punishment, and then a few people mustn't meet together afterwards to say what they think about it."

"I am not here to argue upon the merits or demerits of the law," replied Sir Charles Radcliffe ; "neither have I the right or inclination to give any opinion upon the course that has been taken with Luke Somerton. The queen has exercised her undoubted right of bestowing mercy—that she has reason to believe the royal favour was merited I cannot doubt ; and, in truth, I am not sorry that her majesty was graciously pleased to yield to the prayers and supplications of an affectionate child."

"All that may be very fine," exclaimed Roden ; "but I should like to know if her majesty would have been as merciful had the case been mine instead of Luke's ?"

"At all events the queen cannot be charged with partiality," observed Sir Charles. "Personally, she cannot know anything of Luke Somerton ;—of his name she may certainly have heard ; but I believe all will admit that she has very little reason to regard him as one of the most faithful of her subjects. As a woman, she felt for the sufferings of an afflicted daughter, and, in my opinion, the royal prerogative has not been unwisely exerted."

"You haven't told us, Sir Charles, whether the queen pardoned Luke Somerton because she was convinced that he was innocent of the crime charged against him."

"It is a subject I had no right to inquire into," replied the governor. "The pardon that was placed in my hands contained the sign-manual of Queen Anne, and that was all I had a right to concern myself about. As a matter of course, the prisoner was immediately liberated ; and my most earnest hope is, that he will appreciate the leniency with which he has been treated."

"Not he," exclaimed Harry Roden ; "take my word for it, Luke Somerton murdered the captain, and it ain't likely he'll ever turn out any better than he always has been."

"Of course not, if you are suffered to have your own way," interposed Dick Joyce, who, turning to the governor, added, "you'll excuse me for what I'm going to say, your excellency, but there's more mischief brewing in this island than you are aware of. Luke Somerton has many enemies, who are disappointed because he was not hanged this morning like a dog. They have vowed to be revenged, and if the object of their wrath has not the protection that you can afford him, the mercy he has received from the queen will be of very little use."

"Do you mean to tell me ?" demanded the governor, "that these people would dare brave the queen's wrath for no other reason than that she has spared one miserable victim from a fate of shame and ignominy ?"

"That is exactly what I mean to say,' replied Joyce, "and I challenge any of those men to say

that I have given utterance to a falsehood about it."

"You have heard the answer," said the governor, addressing himself more particularly to Roden ; "and I now ask whether the violence you speak of is meditated ?"

"The truth is, that Joyce owes some of us a grudge," replied Roden, "so he don't care what he says to get us into a scrape. But I'd ask your excellency if it's likely that we would do an unlawful act, when we know that you have always got the red-coats to bring against us ?"

"The answer lies between yourself and your own conscience," replied Sir Charles. "However be that as it may, I am here to keep the queen's peace in this island, and I should be guilty of a neglect of duty were I to pass unheeded the warning that has been given me by this man. You will, therefore, immediately depart to your several houses, or I shall be compelled to use that power with which I have been invested."

"Will you take our words for it," asked Roden, "that, if left to ourselves, we will leave this place within ten minutes after you have ridden away?"

"I am not much inclined to make a treaty with you," replied Sir Charles ; "and yet, to prove that I will take any man's word who solemnly pledges it, your request shall be acceded to. Do not deceive yourselves, however, with a belief that my suspicions have been lulled ; I shall remain with the soldiers within sight of you, though beyond hearing. Ten minutes' time will be all that I shall give you, and if, at the end of that period, you have not dispersed, I shall take those means to compel obedience which I have been most anxious to avoid."

As he said this, he made his way through the crowd, and then, followed by the soldiers, rode to an eminence, from whence he could see all that was going forward. Harry Roden watched him for some few moments, and then addressing the mob, he exclaimed,—

"Whatever you do, my good fellows, don't talk so loud ; that chap yonder may hear what we've got to say. Joyce, like a coward and turn-coat as he is, has gone and split against us, so that we shall be obliged to be the more careful what we are about."

"He's sneaked away," cried Nell Dawson, "or, woman as I am, he should have had something to make him remember the trick he has served us ! But never mind, we shall catch him yet, and, if we do, I wouldn't stand in his shoes for a trifle."

"Do keep that fool's tongue of your's quiet, Nell," exclaimed Roden impatiently ; "we have only got ten minutes allowed us, and in that time we must plan among ourselves what's to be done. I suppose none of you have changed your minds on account of what the governor has been saying to us ?"

"No, no," murmured the crowd ; "death to Luke Someeton !"

"Hush ! or you'll be overheard," said Roden. "It seems that you are all determined to be revenged on this murderer ; and it now only remains to be seen how we can best bring our project to bear. In the first place, my good fellows, it is quite certain that we must find some other spot to meet at—what say you to the Long Close, about half way between here and Luke's cottage?"

"That will do," murmured nearly every voice.

"Very well," resumed Roden; "then let it be understood that we presently separate, and, in parties of not more than one or two, proceed to the place of meeting. Sir Charles Radcliffe will not know but what we are quietly returning to our homes; and, before the news can reach him, we shall have brought our business to an end. But mind, there must be no chattering among yourselves, or the governor may get hold of our secret."

"How the devil can he learn the secret," asked Jack Martin, "when you take good care to keep it to yourself?"

"I'm going to tell you all about it, if you'll only have a little patience," replied Harry Roden. "There can be no doubt that Luke Somerton and his daughter made the best of their way home after his escape from the gallows."

"Why, to be sure they did," said a bystander; "I took the pains to watch 'em, and never lost sight of 'em till I saw them fairly into the cottage."

"Then it will be our own fault if we ever let them come out of the cottage alive again," exclaimed Roden.

"Why, you would not go to hang Luke in his own house?" cried the man who had just given the information.

"The truth is, I don't mean he should be hung at all," answered the other.

"Not hung! why, just now, I thought you were in a greater hurry than anybody else to put him out of the way."

"And do you think I've turned my coat already?" demanded Roden. "No, no,—I'm not quite so changeable as all that, for Luke dies, though not by hanging."

"How then?"

"We will burn him in his house," replied the other.

"And so light up a fire that shall serve as a beacon to bring Sir Charles Radcliffe and the military upon us."

"It will be too late by the time they arrive," answered Roden. "Besides, it will be the safest plan for ourselves;—a report may be spread abroad that the fire was accidental, and thus we shall escape from all blame, while the death of Luke Somerton will be no less certain. As for the manner of his punishment, I see very little difference whether we roast him, or send him into eternity at the end of a rope."

"But his daughter?" questioned Jack Martin; —"we must find some way to save her from the flames."

"The daughter is no more to be pitied than the father," exclaimed Harry Roden. "If it had not been for Louisa Somerton there would have been no pardon, and we should have been spared the trouble of what we are now going to do. Besides, the girl seems to be so fond of him, that it would be a pity to let her live, knowing, as we do, that her heart would very soon break."

"This is a cool way of reasoning, at any rate," observed Nell Dawson. "However, I've no great fancy for the girl myself, and so, for my own part, I sha'n't say anything that might serve to mar so excellent a plot."

"There now, my friends," exclaimed Roden, "take example by this woman, and have done with scruples of conscience about an affair like this. It's agreed that Luke is to die, and his daughter must go with him to the next world."

"But how do you mean to set fire to the cottage?" asked Jack Martin, who did not seem very well to like a plan that was so utterly diabolical.

"Why, that part of our plan may be managed easily enough," replied Roden. "There's a stack of wood between this place and where we are going to. A dozen of you can each take a faggot, which afterwards will be piled up at the door of the cottage. Then the house must be surrounded to prevent the possibility of escape, and when everything has been properly prepared, I will myself set fire to the faggots. These being dry, will quickly rise in a huge flame, the thatch will next be in a blaze, and then the house itself. We may, perhaps, hear the shrieks of the poor devils within, but those whose nerves are more delicate than mine, can easily stop their ears till all is over."

"Upon my life, Harry, I never heard a piece of villany more coolly described," exclaimed Jack Martin. "Now I am not altogether against putting Luke Somerton himself out of the way, but, hang me, if I can sacrifice a poor innocent girl at the same time."

"Then leave us, and have nothing to do with it," growled the other. "We want no milk-and-water fellows with us, I can tell you; only remember, if you should afterwards turn informer, you'll know exactly what to expect. They may hang *me*, Jack Martin, but *you* won't be much better off; for there would still be somebody left behind to give a treacherous lubber his deserts."

"Your threats I laugh at," replied the other; "but for all that, I'm not going to turn informer. No, no, the thing may be done for aught I care, only I dont mean to have any share in it myself."

"Oh, then, you don't think there's as much sin in knowing of a crime that is to be done, as if you took a part in it!" exclaimed Harry Roden. "I won't ask any man to say anything against himself, so let the matter drop where it is. The fact is, we've all pretty well made up our minds as to what we've got to do, so those that don't like to join us may do t'other thing. Only I would advise any one that may be inclined to turn sneak, to mind what they're about, because it will be the worse for 'em, that's all. If anybody tries to do me an injury, I know what to do, and it won't be a trifle that will stop me, when I've made up my mind."

"Oh! I know you well enough," retorted Jack Martin; "you're a mighty fine fellow to talk of what you'll do, but you ain't got more courage than anybody else, when it comes to a push. Bullies are never the bravest fellows in the world, and if matters should turn out a little bit cross, we should see you among the very first to take care of yourself."

"If you go on so, there's no telling where this may end," whispered Dame Findley to the last speaker. "See how furious Harry looks; and when his cheek turns pale, I always know there's

mischief brewing. In the humour he's in at present, he'd no more mind plunging a knife into you, than he would into a sheep."

"You are right enough there, Mother Brimstone," exclaimed Roden, who had overheard the last few words; "I can put up with anything better than a doubt of my courage, and Jack ought to be the last man to say a word against me, seeing that we've been old friends together. But never mind, if he chooses to say we shall be foes from this time, I'll not cry nay to it, and by and by we shall see who gets the worst of it."

"And all this time," exclaimed Nell, "you seem to have forgot the business we've in hand. Joyce has gone away nobody knows where, and if he should happen to have told Luke Somerton what's in the wind, we shall find the birds flown, and there'll be an end of all our plans."

"Why, you're as thirsty after blood as a she-wolf," cried Jack Martin; "talk about the gentle nature of woman, indeed! Did ever anybody hear of such a specimen of female delicacy as we have in you?"

"I'll tell you what, Jack Martin," exclaimed Roden, in the cool, deliberate tone of a man who is bent upon mischief; "you and I, it seems, are no longer to be friends—you are one of Dick Joyce's sort, I can see, and I'll not have your as-

sistance even if you were to offer it me. Now, Nell, here, woman as she is, has a heart made of the right sort of stuff, and if you affront her, I shall take the quarrel upon myself. So now, as we understand each other, it would be best for you to make yourself scarce, and, above all things, take care that we don't meet together again, lest mischief should come of it."

"You forget," answered Martin, "that a word from me will put an end to the violence you intend to commit."

"But I know you dare not utter that word," retorted the other, fiercely; "only let one of the fellows here suspect that you would go and inform against them, and you'd never leave this place alive."

"Indeed!" exclaimed Martin; "and suppose I was to be murdered by your ruffians, how much the better would you be for it? The gibbet that has just been put up for Luke Somerton would have other victims before a month passed away."

"Oh, no, hanging seems to have gone out of fashion," answered Roden, with a sneer. "They've just let one murderer escape, and they can't well hang another person for the same sort of crime, unless they'd give the world cause to say that mercy goes by favour. Sir Charles Radcliffe has already given offence to the people here, and it wouldn't take long to drive our islanders into open rebellion against his authority."

"Come, come, it won't do to be talking treason in my presence," interposed Snizzler. "I am a man holding office under her gracious majesty, Queen Anne, whom Heaven long preserve! and the town-crier's place would soon be vacant, if it should happen to be known that I heard such words as these, without resenting them."

"Only hear how the fool talks!" cried Nell, with a loud derisive laugh; "he fancies himself somebody, I dare say; but I should like to see how he'd look, if we gave him a hoist from yonder rock into the sea."

"Why, you monstrous old woman, you wouldn't think of such a thing," returned the town-crier.

No. 12.

"Would you murder a man in cool blood—a man who has served his country as I have done?"

"Hold your tongue, or they'll lay violent hands upon you presently," whispered Martin to him. "I can see some desperate fellows here, that wouldn't mind what mischief they do; so take a friend's advice, and make the best of your way from this spot. You, at any rate, can have no business with people that are about to break the law."

"Then I'll run and tell his excellency that he and the soldiers are wanted here directly."

"You had better do no such thing," answered the other. "Harry Roden and his fellows talk very largely about what they'll do, but it strikes me there's more empty boasting about it than anything else."

"Oh! then you think they won't follow Luke Somerton and his daughter to the cottage down yonder?"

"Why, I don't know but what they may go that way, presently," replied Martin; "but I rather think they'll be glad to walk themselves back again without doing any mischief. At any rate, if any violence should be committed it will be easy then to send word to Sir Charles Radcliffe, who, with a few of the military, would soon be able to send the rest flying for their lives."

"Ah! that's a very good thought of your's," answered Snizzle. "By-the-by, they told me to make myself scarce just now, so I'll take the hint, and leave 'em while I've got a whole skin. But I won't lose sight of 'em for all that—I'll watch the rascals from a little distance off, and if I see 'em make an attack on the cottage, I'll take to my heels, and give the governor notice of it."

"You had better by half go and tell Lieutenant Granger," returned the other. "Folks say he has a bit of a sneaking kindness for the girl, Louisa Somerton, and if there's any truth in it, he'd lose no time in going to her rescue."

"That's a bright thought of yours," exclaimed Snizzle. "Yes, yes—I'll go to Lieutenant Granger as soon as I see that mischief is likely to begin, and he'll set them scampering like sheep over a common. But, between ourselves, Jack, don't you think it would be as well to give him a hint of what's going on, that he may hold himself in readiness in case he should be wanted?"

"No, that would spoil all," replied Martin, "for if you are seen going towards the castle, some of the people would be sure to watch you, and the whole affair would be known directly. Besides, I dare say the young lieutenant has his suspicions that violence may be used against Somerton and his daughter, and, if that's the case, you may be sure he'll be somewhere pretty handy in case of need. But see, Harry Roden is now leading the people away from this place, and, in half an hour or so, we shall know whether they mean to carry their threats into execution."

It was, indeed, as the last speaker had said, for, having addressed a few words to those who, like himself, were bent upon mischief, the ringleader placed himself at their head, and taking his way through the valley, led the mob towards the place where they expected to find their victims.

CHAPTER XXIV.

Whoe'er's been at Paris must needs know the Greve,
The fatal retreat of the unfortunate brave,
Where honour and justice most oddly contribute,
To ease heroes' pains by a halter and gibbet.

PRIOR.

IT was not without much difficulty that Louisa Somerton, even with the assistance of her father, wended her way back to the cottage in which they had sought a temporary asylum. The fresh air, however, served considerably to revive her fainting spirits, and, after having rested herself, she was able to reply to the questions of her father, as to the particulars of her journey in quest of the English queen. To her artless narrative, Somerton listened with breathless attention, but more especially to that part which related to the interviews she had had with the sovereign.

"I thought," he at length said, "the labour would have been a vain one, and that our royal mistress would have coldly rejected the prayers you uttered in my behalf. Indeed, my Louisa, I almost feared lest your rashness in presenting yourself before her might have brought you into trouble."

"There was little fear of that, dearest father," answered our heroine, "for I found the queen most kind, most beneficent. At first, my application seemed to startle her; but my warmest appeals in behalf of a hapless father, soon brought a favourable change, and in the end she assured me your life should be spared."

"And yet to what purpose has it been spared," exclaimed Luke, gloomily. "Had the law claimed its victim, I should now have ended my earthly troubles, instead of having before me the cheerless prospect that I now see. All hope of happiness is excluded—I am a marked and degraded being, at whom the finger of scorn will evermore be pointed."

"Nay, why do you yield to this black despair?" cried Louisa. "In this island, indeed, you may meet with coldness and neglect; but the world is still before us, and surely some place may be found where the errors and transgressions of Luke Somerton have not yet been whispered."

"Aye, girl; but what am I now more than the mere wreck of what I was a few months since?" asked her father. "Have I not got upon me the mark of Cain, and shall I not carry it with me, even to the grave?"

"But your own conscience acquits you of the crime they charged you with," answered Louisa. "The queen, too, has given credit to my assertions of your innocence, and surely others are not to charge you too harshly."

"Yet they have judged me, girl," he replied; "and you heard how the people murmured because they were disappointed of the show they came to see. I believe there was scarcely a person in that vast crowd, but went away muttering their imprecations upon her whose mercy spared me."

"Indeed, father, you judge them too harshly," cried Louisa. "There are few people, I hope, who delight in the ignominious death of a fellow creature, and surely none of those who were assembled to-day went away disappointed, because I happily succeeded in obtaining your pardon."

"That which I heard with my own ears I must

believe," answered Luke, gloomily. "You had swooned, and marked it not, but I witnessed the flashing eyes and burning cheeks of those by whom we were surrounded ; and some there were in that crowd, who even gave utterance to their savage yells of anger when the governor announced that my life had been mercifully spared."

"Then there is the more reason that we should leave this island," cried Louisa, eagerly.

"And what would men say if I left the place in the way you propose?" asked Luke. "None of these islanders are convinced of my innocence, and it would then be said against me, that I dared not meet the gaze of my fellow men—that I was obliged to quit this spot to seek a refuge among strangers."

"Let them say what they will—let them think what they will, so that you are removed far from them," exclaimed Louisa. "This is no longer a home for you and me ;—in some foreign land we may meet with friendship and hospitality, but even if we find neither, we may still be happy in the society of each other."

"I tell you, girl, there is no happiness for me on this side the grave," answered Luke Somerton. "Mine has been a chequered life, not altogether unmixed with evil ; and now the events which have recently taken place have added a load that neither time nor change of scene can ever remove. Once, indeed, I might have been happy in the society of my beloved child, but not after this nipping blight has fallen on my heart."

"So you may think now," urged Louisa ; "because recent events have left a chilling influence that cannot all at once be dissipated. A few months, however, will effect changes that you dream not of, and believe scarcely possible. Come then, dear father, let that gloomy look disappear from your brow ; smile upon me as you did in the days of my infancy, and though all the world beside should frown upon me, I can still be happy in so blessed a change."

"You are a kind, good girl, Louisa," exclaimed Luke, "and it grieves me to the very soul that I cannot make you as happy as you deserve to be. It was a luckless day for you, my daughter, that brought me back to the island, for I found you in the enjoyment of peace and repose ; yet now do I behold you drooping, like a flower that has felt the first chill blast of winter. Yet, cheer thee, my own Louisa, for I may not long be spared to this world, and when I am gone, you may, perhaps, soon learn to forget the misery I have caused you."

"Oh, speak not so, I implore you," cried the almost heart-broken girl. "I have no hope, no joy, no friend, but in you. If need be, I will traverse the wide world with you, and never murmur that I find the way too rough."

"Fool that I have been," muttered Luke, "to pass by a jewel like this for a pursuit that could bring me neither honour nor renown. Aye, and whose fault was it that I became what I am? Why, 'twas Aylmer's ! He it was that goaded me to madness—he it was that wrought the desolation and despair that now surround me."

"Oh, do not speak of that name which brings so many horrors to my mind !" cried Louisa, entreatingly. "He is dead, father,—he may have had faults, but of whatever nature they were, let them now lie buried in the grave to which he has so lately been borne."

"He has been my bane, my curse !" exclaimed Luke, gnashing his teeth with rage. "I endured his insolence as long as it was in the power of mortal man to do, as I thought the time would come when we should be separated, and I might forget the many wrongs he had heaped upon me. But it was my accursed fate always to be under his commands, and I could see the fiendish laugh upon his lips when he saw the torture his continued tyranny inflicted upon me. Thus we passed years together, Louisa, and during that whole period I never knew what it was to have a happy moment."

"Could you make no complaint against him, father?"

"It would have been in vain to have done so," replied Luke ; "or rather it would only have served to have rendered my future life even more insupportable. The murmurs of an inferior officer against one who is superior, are seldom attended to ; the man who utters them is looked upon as a discontented grumbler, and he is thenceforward treated with comtempt by all his former associates. I have seen men, Louisa, who have been suffering under this cruel species of torture, and never did I know one of them who could ever hold up his head again. Knowing the consequences of making a complaint, I nursed my wrongs in my own bosom, hoping and believing that a day would come when I should have my revenge. Well, girl, a day did arrive—I saw Aylmer in his bloody shroud—but I see my words are like poisoned arrows to your bosom. I add affliction where I ought to heal the wound which has been given by my own hands."

"Indeed, father, I blame you not for the past," answered Louisa ; "I would only ask you to remember that Captain Aylmer is in his grave, and his faults, great as they may have been, should now be forgotten, if not forgiven."

"That is Christian charity, my Louisa," replied her father, "but the wrongs and subsequent misery I have endured made my nature rather that of a wild beast than that of a man. And now you yourself are a witness of the sort of estimation in which I am held by my fellow-men, who, instead of rejoicing that my life has been spared for better things than the past, growl at their disappointment and curse the act of clemency that has spared me the ignominy of dying on the gibbet."

"But that feeling exists only among the ignorant," said Louisa. "I am sure Sir Charles Radcliffe is rejoiced at your escape, and as for Lieutenant Granger ——"

"Aye, girl," interrupted Luke Somerton I believe, is well pleased that your noble efforts in my behalf have been successful. It is but little I have seen of him, but somehow my heart is strongly prepossessed in his favour. I have watched the tenderness with which he regards you, and feel a cheering consolation in the hope that you will one day be his."

"Oh, do not encourage so vain a thought, dearest father," exclaimed Louisa, mournfully. "My regard for Lieutenant Granger is not less than your own, yet are there circumstances that must for ever forbid our union."

"You mean the disgrace I have brought upon our name."

"No," she replied; "I do not mean that; but the difference between our stations in life would render such a marriage imprudent in the eyes of the world. Lieutenant Granger has every prospect of rising in the honourable profession to which he belongs, and he should wed one who may be an ornament to the station he is destined to fill."

"And where could he hope to find a fairer ornament to fill his exalted station than in one so good and virtuous as yourself?" asked Luke. "I know his attachment for you, and have every reason to believe that he will never marry any other than Louisa Somerton."

"But we shall leave this island, dear father, and then he will in time forget me," answered our heroine.

"You are much mistaken in Lieutenant Granger if you think so," exclaimed her father. "He has declared to me his love for you, even when I was within a few hours of that fearful death from which you rescued me. I told him the disgrace that such an alliance would bring upon him, but all was of no avail, for he still vowed to have no other bride but yourself."

"Alas!" sighed Louisa; "he little dreams of the misery he is thus incurring both for himself and me. I have told him that I will never wed, and now that you have been spared, I devote myself to your service. A foreign land is destined to become our future home, and no other prospect remains before us, that I can see, but a life of poverty and toil. Am I, then, a fitting match for Lieutenant Granger, who may hereafter become the friend and companion of the great ones of our land?"

"All that depends upon his own thoughts on the subject," answered Luke Somerton. "By marriage you would become his equal, whatever may be the rank he attains, and who would then dare to point the finger of scorn at the woman he has made his wife?"

"Openly, none might do so," answered Louisa; "but who could prevent the whispers and scandal that would be uttered by false friends and envious people? That Lieutenant Granger loves me with a most pure and ardent attachment I will not attempt to deny; nor will I conceal the fact that my regard for him is fully equal to that which he bears towards me."

"Then why, in Heaven's name, do you put a restraint upon your affections, when so much misery will be the result?"

"It is to prevent misery that I do so," answered Louisa. "Lieutenant Granger perfectly understands my motives, and acknowledges that no blame is to be attached to them."

"Yet he still perseveres in urging a suit that you say is hopeless."

"He does, and bitterly do I regret it," replied our heroine.

"Well, then, hear what advice I would give you upon the subject," exclaimed her father. "It seems that he is still inclined to hope that the obstacles you have raised may be removed in the course of time; he still requests you to listen to him with a favourable ear, and I would myself join him in a prayer that appears to be so unob-

jectionable. At present it is not my intention to leave this island, and I would therefore prevail on you to permit his visits as often as he thinks proper to call upon us. He will be gratified by such a concession, and in time you may change the determination you have now come to."

"And why should I give him hopes that I feel assured will never be realised?" asked Louisa.

"Because I believe time will effect important changes in your present determination," replied her father. "The recollection of my trial and condemnation will gradually die away, and when that is the case, your principal objection to this union will be at an end."

Unwilling to carry this subject any further, Louisa remained silent, and ere she could change the conversation into another channel, a loud knocking was heard at the door. So sudden and unexpected was this that both Luke Somerton and his daughter stood irresolute whether to open it or not, till the knocking was repeated, when removing the fastenings with which it was secured, he gave admittance to Lieutenant Granger, whose agitation betokened that some new danger was at hand. With the quickness of thought he made all fast again, and then addressing himself to those in whose presence he stood, he besought them to fly without delay if they would save themselves from the violence of an infuriated mob.

"Who are our enemies?" demanded Louisa, terrified at the warning they had received; "oh, tell me, I implore you, who are they who would follow us to the humble home where we hope to find a refuge from our cares?"

"The mob," answered Granger, "consists of not less than an hundred and fifty persons—men and women. They are loud in their denunciations of Luke Somerton, and have sworn never to return home till they have executed upon him the full measure of their vengeance."

"Father—dear father! let us leave this place ere it is too late," cried Louisa, throwing herself upon his bosom. "I feared it would come to this, and now all my worst anticipations are about to be verified."

"How is it, Louisa, that I behold you thus suddenly become a prey to terror?" exclaimed Luke. "You, who but a few hours since were so bold in executing your task of filial love, are now become a coward because a brutal mob threaten me with their vengeance! You ask me to flee from our cottage, yet why should I do so when there is not one of those ruffians who can say I have injured him?"

"I would fain add my own entreaties to those of your daughter," said Lieutenant Granger. "This is no time to offer resistance where the force is so overwhelming, and I hastened hither to warn you of the danger, and conduct you and your daughter to a place where you will be secure from the violence of these lawless people."

"My daughter can accompany you, Lieutenant Granger, if she pleases," answered Somerton. "My own determination you have already heard, and I shall not depart from it. An Englishman's house has always been said to be his castle, and if any ruffians use violence to break open my door it will be at their own peril."

"That they will do so, I am assured," exclaimed

the young officer ; "they are excited to a fearful degree, and nothing short of your death will satisfy them."

"Why, then, has not Sir Charles Radcliffe taken means to prevent their coming here?" demanded Luke.

"He knows not what is passing," answered the other ; "and it was by a mere accident that I was informed of the design these people have formed against you."

"From whom did you hear these tidings of danger?"

"From a man—Josh Martin ; he sought me out about half an hour since, and gave me information of what was going on. I would have gone instantly to fetch a party of the military, but as there was hardly a possibility of doing that in time, I came here first that you might quit the cottage ere these ruffians arrive."

"I have already stated my determination," exclaimed Luke Somerton. "These bloodhounds have no right to pursue me here ; but, if they do so, I am resolved not to run away from them like a coward. This is not the first time I have faced danger, Lieutenant Granger, and these scurvy knaves will find to their cost that I can fight like an enraged lion when they drive me into a corner."

"But your own life will in all probability be sacrificed in the struggle," cried Louisa, in a paroxysm of fear. "There is yet time to escape the peril I so much dread to think of, and under the guidance of Lieutenant Granger we may find a place wherein to hide ourselves, until this terrible tempest of vengeance has passed away."

"Would you have me hide myself from them as if I feared their puny efforts?" demanded Luke Somerton.

"Aye, anything to preserve a life that is so dear to me," she replied. "Think, father, if you are taken from me, I shall have none to whom I can flee for protection."

"I tell you, Louisa," answered her father, "there are others who care for you more than you imagine. Lieutenant Granger, for instance, will be to you an honourable protector ; and, should you think proper to reject his kindness, there is your uncle James, who, it seems, was as fortunate as yourself in escaping from the perils of last night's storm."

"And think you either of these you have mentioned could compensate me for the loss of a beloved father?"

"Why, girl, you would be better without than with me," exclaimed Luke. "I have lived to be disgraced and loaded with infamy ; unhappily you share in the obloquy that has been cast upon my name and fame, but all may be well again when I am no more. The errors of Luke Somerton may then be forgotten, and his daughter restored to the station and respect from which she has been hurled from the time of Captain Aylmer's murder."

"Are there no arguments that I can urge to prevail on you to leave this place?" demanded Lieutenant Granger.

"All that you can say will be useless," replied Luke. "If my life is sacrificed, the loss to society will not be much ; to myself, it will be a mercy, since I have seen the wreck of every hope that I had in this world."

"That is more than you can say with certainty," cried Louisa. "Heaven has chastised you with heavy afflictions, it must be admitted, but the punishment has been endured, and there is reason to believe that the prospect before us is not so dark as you imagine."

"You cannot persuade me to that, Louisa," exclaimed her father ; "my faults have been punished heavily enough to be sure,—at least so you and I may imagine ; but these dogged islanders are of a different opinion, and, as you have heard Lieutenant Granger just now say, the growling savages grudge me the pardon you were at so much pains to obtain from our gracious queen."

"Then I am to understand," said the young soldier, "that you will not leave this house while there is yet time?"

"Such is my unalterable resolution," answered Luke.

"In that case there is but one chance remaining for us," replied Lieutenant Granger. "I will return with all speed to the castle and obtain such assistance as may seem necessary ; some of the soldiers are, I know, under arms in the guardhouse, and I will bring them here without loss of time, for even now it may not be too late to prevent the mischief these ruffians contemplate. In the meanwhile, Louisa, do you exert your influence to prevail on your father to leave this house ; you will be able to make your way without obstruction to the castle, by taking the private road that leads to it. On application, the sentinel on duty will direct you to the barracks, where, by making use of my name, you will receive shelter and protection. Luke Somerton, I again ask you to accept my offer without further hesitation ; your daughter has a right to claim this much of you, for, remember, by risking your own life in this instance, you also place her's in jeopardy."

With this parting counsel Lieutenant Granger took his leave of them, and having removed the fastenings, left the cottage with all speed. Again Luke Somerton made the door secure, and having closed the shutters, so as to prevent a sudden surprise by the enemy, he struck a light, and placed the lamp upon a table, while he examined his pistols to ascertain whether they were properly charged and primed. This done, he next took down a sabre that hung on the wall, over the mantelpiece, and laying it on the table, where it would be ready when wanted, he threw himself upon a seat to await the moment when he would be called upon to act resolutely in his own and his daughter's defence. Louisa had watched his every movement with an anxiety that she could not conceal, and when at length he had completed his arrangements, she once more earnestly besought him to seek safety in flight rather than risk the peril with which they were threatened.

"Nay, girl," he replied, "when once my determination is formed, even my love for you will not prevail on me to alter it. I could have wished, Louisa, that you had accompanied Lieutenant Granger from hence, because I have a firm reliance in his honour, and it would have been a consolation to me to know that, whatever may happen to myself, you, at all events, were in a place of safety. You have, however, chosen to share my danger, whatever it may be, and that thought will serve still more to nerve my arm against the villains who would hunt us out like wild beasts."

"But what, father, if they should succeed in obtaining an entrance to our cottage?" asked Louisa, in accents of terror.

"Why, then, my girl, you shall see how a British seaman can fight when he is driven to extremities," answered Luke Somerton. "This affair is none of my bringing on: I have returned, as I have every right to do, to my own roof, and these yelling hounds must needs pursue me to it. They have declared open war against me; let them now beware how they beard the enraged tiger in his own den!"

"Yet, how easily might all this have been prevented!" cried Louisa; "there could have been no disgrace in fleeing from the approach of an overpowering number of your enemies, and had we taken refuge in the barracks, as proposed by Lieutenant Granger, we might have gone abroad, where no such dangers would ever afterwards have threatened us."

"But I have no wish to go abroad," answered Luke; "at least, I will not be frightened into doing so by the yelping of these curs, whom I despise for the cowardice that prompts them to pursue me with their blood-thirsty hatred. It seems they want my life; and, Heaven knows, it is of so little value to me that they may have it, when I have shown them how much a single arm can effect against their numbers."

"Alas!" sighed Louisa, "can you, then, talk so coolly of bloodshed, when it might have been so easily avoided?"

"It is no fault of mine that I am driven to this alternative," replied Luke Somerton. "I am not aware of having committed any personal wrong to a single individual in this island, yet they must needs rise against me, for no better reason than I was not hung this morning for their edification and amusement. But they will yet see sufficient reason to repent the rash step they have taken, for this arm of mine shall not be weak in our defence, my girl; and if Lieutenant Granger only makes moderate haste in coming to our assistance, these ruffians will bitterly deplore the hour when they measured weapons with me."

"You have forgotten, then," cried Louisa, in alarm, "that Granger will hazard his own life in an affair that might have been easily avoided, had his advice been taken."

"Ah!" exclaimed Luke Somerton, "then I have at last got you to confess that you feel some interest in this young man, whom you have affected to regard with indifference?"

"I have never said that he was an object of indifference to me," answered our heroine, after a pause. "If I have refused to promise him my hand in marriage, it was because I feared to bring trouble and disgrace upon one whom I regarded with more than a sister's affection."

"Then, between ourselves, my girl, I think you have acted with some indiscretion," observed her father. "Granger could have suffered nothing in the world's esteem by your becoming his wife; and I should, at least, have had the satisfaction of knowing that my daughter would not be left to the cold charity of a heartless world. But why should I reproach you with this, now, Louisa, when we

are threatened with danger, and have need of all our wits for the coming contest. These people seek my life, and they shall have it, too, in welcome, on condition that they will promise to spare yours."

"It would be vain for you, dear father, to make such terms with them," exclaimed Louisa. "If you perish, I will not accept of life from your murderers; both must be suffered to leave this cottage in safety, or both will perish beneath the roof that now covers us."

"There is something of your father's dare-devil spirit in that, my girl," said Luke Somerton, glancing towards her a look of mingled pride and satisfaction. "I like to see courage even in a female, and if more time had been allowed us for preparation, we would have given these ragamuffins such a reception, that would not have been forgotten in the Isle of Man for many a long year to come. But it is useless to talk of what we *would* have done: the knaves will take us at a disadvantage, and all we can do will be to give them as much trouble as possible. They may, perhaps, at last, succeed in forcing their way into our house, but it shall be over the bleeding bodies of some of their own people."

"Nay," cried Louisa, "do you not think it possible that, if I speak to them, they will respect the prayer and entreaties of a helpless woman? I have always been a favourite among the lower classes in this island, and I have some hope that blood may be spared through my intercession."

"All that I require is, that they will show mercy to you," exclaimed Luke Somerton. "For myself, I am prepared for any emergency; if it should be death, my earthly troubles will have a speedier end than I anticipated; if I should escape from their violence, I will never rest satisfied till I have brought a heavy punishment upon those who have followed me with their vengeance."

"Hark!" cried Louisa, "I hear the sound of footsteps at the door. Our enemies are at hand—they are upon us, dearest father, and Lieutenant Granger has not yet returned to prevent their intended outrage!"

"I believe we can do without him," replied Luke, "for no doubt the cowardly knaves will fly the instant they find that I am armed and ready to give them a warm reception. They are here, sure enough, for I can plainly distinguish people whispering at the door, and no doubt they are holding a council of war among themselves as to their plan of operations."

Before Louisa could make any reply to this, the latch of the door was quickly moved up and down three or four times, and then it seemed that some persons from without were pushing with all their strength, in order to force it open. The door, however, being of good stout oak, resisted all their efforts, and then a voice was heard demanding immediate admittance.

"Who is it that makes the demand?" asked Somerton, snatching one of his pistols from his girdle.

"Open, and you will see," was the laconic reply.

"I will open to no man, till I have first been told his business," answered Luke. "I have been told there are foes abroad, and therefore it behoves me to be cautious lest I give admittance to any of them."

"It is in vain to set us at defiance," exclaimed a voice, that was at once recognised as Harry Roden's, "for we have mustered here in sufficient strength to force our way into this dog-hole, if any resistance is offered. Open, I say, or we will burst your door!"

"I would have you be careful how you do that," replied Luke, "for I am well armed, and resolute enough to defend myself against the numbers you boast of. Dare but to thrust your carcases against my door, and, as there is a Heaven above us, I will drill a bullet-hole through the hides of some of you!"

This threat seemed to have its weight, for a dead silence immediately ensued, though Luke Somerton deemed it ominous of fresh mischief.

"The villains are executing another scheme among themselves," he whispered to his daughter. "They like not my threat, and will now think of other means by which they may reach us."

"Would that Lieutenant Granger and his men were here!" sighed our heroine, despondingly.— "He has been gone long enough to have returned to us by this time, and I almost fear he may have fallen into the hands of these people."

"Not he," replied Luke Somerton; "a soldier would be careful not to fall into an ambush, and if I may venture upon an opinion, I should say he is somewhere close at hand, and only waiting for an opportunity when he can best carry his plans into operation."

"But do you not think these men may have gone away, after hearing you declare that you are armed, and prepared to offer resistance to their violence?"

"On the contrary," replied her father, "I know they are still about the place, for every now and then the sound of their footsteps falls upon my ear, though they move as cautiously as if they were stepping upon eggs. They are up to some devilish piece of mischief, Louisa, and if I don't look out, to see what they are doing, we shall be surprised before we are aware of it."

"Oh, for mercy's sake, do not show yourself to them!" cried Louisa, seizing her father's arm, as he was moving towards the window. "If these villains are still here, we may conclude that they have determined upon executing the vengeance for which they have leagued themselves together.— Yield to my entreaties, dearest father, or you will fall a victim to these savage men."

"But how am I to counteract their designs, unless I see what they are about?" asked Luke Somerton. "There is some danger in showing myself to them, I admit, girl; but in cases like this we must hazard something, or the enemy gain an advantage over us."

"At least, you may wait patiently a few moments," returned Louisa. "They cannot surprise us very suddenly, for both the door and windows are so well secured, as to defy their force for some time to come. Meanwhile Lieutenant Granger may arrive, and, in that case, our enemies will be speedily put to flight."

"Methinks he might have been here before now," said Luke Somerton, "for he knew our peril, and a little extra exertion would have brought him to the spot within half an hour from the time he left us. But perhaps it is as I said just now; he may be lying in ambush close by, and, if so, these scoundrels will find themselves in a snare when least they suspect danger."

"Hark!" whispered our heroine, tightly grasping the arm of her father; "I hear them again—they are piling something up against the door of the cottage. Surely they are barricading the place, to prevent our escape!"

"Then it is time I should do something towards our rescue," exclaimed Luke Somerton. "These wretches have concocted some new scheme of devilry, and we shall become their victims yet, if we do not take prompt means to counteract their designs. I will throw open the window, Louisa, and see what they are about, for I know well enough that they have some plan in view which will shortly place us in their power."

"Father! dearest father!" cried our heroine, in an agony of alarm, "they will slay you before my eyes should you be so imprudent as to appear before them."

"I must run the chance of that," answered Luke, in a tone of determination. "Danger enough we are in already, so I may as well die at once as to wait till they have completed this fresh scheme of theirs."

Resolved to hear no remonstrance, Luke Somerton strode towards the window, and, undoing the fastenings, threw back the shutters so suddenly that those without scarcely saw him till he had obtained a view of their operations. In one instant, however, several men rushed towards him, with the intention of entering by the window, and this purpose would no doubt have been effected had they not been terrified on seeing the pistols which Luke presented towards them.

"It is exactly as I suspected," exclaimed the latter, speaking to Louisa; "the villains have piled a heap of faggots at the door, and one stands by with a torch ready to set fire to them. Foiled as they have been in their purpose, they would now burn us in the place which we have sought as a refuge."

"And Lieutenant Granger?" she cried, in accents of terror; "do you not see him coming to our relief?"

"I see no one but the monsters who would destroy us," answered her father. "They are thronging round the house as thick as bees, and it seems to me that they intend to guard every place by which we might hope to escape?"

"You had better have surrendered yourself at once," exclaimed Henry Roden, "for it was of no use to oppose people that came determined to execute their purpose. So now, Luke Somerton, prepare yourself, for we will soon make this crazy old cottage too hot to hold you."

Roden, as he spoke these words, seized a lighted torch which one of his comrades held, and was advancing to set fire to the pile of wood, when Luke Somerton discharged one of his pistols at the inhuman monster who thus sought to satiate his revenge by a method as cruel as it was diabolical. The bullet took effect in the arm of the incendiary, who instantly dropped the torch, and reeling back a few paces, fell in the arms of his companions. At that moment, however, Nell darted forward, and snatching up the torch, hurled it amidst the dry wood which had been piled up against the door. In another few seconds the flames spread themselves, then rose up towards the thatched roof of the cottage, and presently the whole exterior part of the building was enveloped by the devouring element.

The scream of terror uttered by Louisa as soon as this appalling fact became known, was answered by the mob with a shout of fiendish exultation. Luke Somerton's first thought was to save his daughter from the horrible death with which she was threatened ; and, seizing her in his arms, he made his way towards the window, determined to force his way from the burning cottage at all hazards to himself. But in this hope he was doomed to be woefully disappointed, for the mob stood resolutely forward to prevent his exit, and encumbered as he was with his almost fainting burden, he found it impossible to make the only effort that afforded him any hope of rescue. The air around him grew hot and oppressive ; the smoke rendered his breathing difficult, and the thatched roof, which was now on fire from end to end, fell in a thick, sparkling shower around him. At this juncture despair came upon his heart like a heavy weight—not for himself, for he had no fear of death, but for his daughter, whose preservation was the only object of his care. He had, in short, abandoned every hope, when another shout was heard from the multitude, and, looking up, he perceived that his blood-thirsty enemies were scampering away in every direction. Taking this opportunity, he sprang from the window with his burden, and had scarcely done so, when Lieutenant Granger hastily advanced towards them.

"Thank Heaven, we have not arrived too late to be of service to you," exclaimed the young soldier, as he assisted Luke Somerton to bear the terrified girl to a place of temporary shelter ; "the villains have fled at our approach, but my men have followed in pursuit, and I am much mistaken if they do not return presently with some of the ringleaders."

"See !" cried Luke, pointing towards the burning cottage, "it has all fallen in now ; and, had your arrival been delayed but a few minutes, the wretches who set fire to my house would have seen the whole of their devilish project fulfilled. That they should have taken an hatred to me, Lieutenant Granger, I can perfectly understand, but why they should have sought to take the life of my daughter is not quite so easily to be accounted for."

"We shall know more anon," replied the officer, "for Sir Charles Radcliffe is incensed at the violence offered by these men, and he has said that those who were the chief agents in it shall be made an example of."

"And what good, Lieutenant Granger, would an act of vengeance do us ?" asked Louisa, who now began to revive from the swoon into which she had fallen. "My father and I are grateful for the preservation that has been vouchsafed us from Heaven through your means. We have escaped the fate designed for us, and the punishment of those lawless people can effect little good now."

"At any rate it will be a warning to these rebellious islanders in future," replied Lieutenant Granger. "This is not the first time they have broken out into acts of open violence, and it is now time they should be taught to respect the laws by which they should be governed."

"I have given one of the rascals something by which he may remember this day to the end of his life," replied Luke Somerton. "He has had a pistol bullet through his arm, and if that don't sicken him of getting into these sort of broils again, I don't know what will."

"It will only serve to make him the more revengeful against you, dear father," exclaimed Louisa. "I saw him at the moment you discharged your pistol, and recognized the features of a man they call Harry Roden."

"I know him for a violent, lawless fellow, as he is," said Lieutenant Granger. "He has always been more troublesome than anybody else in the island, and now, perhaps, we may find means to get rid of his annoyance. If any of my people fall in with him, he'll stand a chance of being cut to pieces unless he quietly surrenders himself."

"Oh ! do not speak of more bloodshed," cried Louisa, shuddering as she remembered the incidents of the last few hours. "Fortunately, these men have failed in their cruel designs against us, and neither my father nor myself have any wish that our enemies should be further punished."

"I don't exactly agree with you there," exclaimed Luke Somerton. "As far as my own life went, the villains might have taken it, and welcome; but they must needs include you in their savage thirst for murder, and that part of the business, Louisa, I cannot easily forgive."

"But I do," she replied ; "and, therefore, let me beseech you to think no more about an affair that, after all, might have ended so much worse for us. Besides, we can quit this island, and thus prevent the possibility of their making any further attempt to do us a mischief."

"Surely, Louisa," exclaimed her lover, "you are not in earnest when you speak of leaving this island ?"

"I was never more so in the whole course of my life," she replied.

"Yet there can be no reason for doing so now," he exclaimed. "Your father can dwell among us here as well as anywhere else ; and you, Louisa, I should have thought, can have little cause for wishing to leave a place where there are so many who regard you with affection."

"Why, the truth is, my wench has taken some strange notions into her head," interposed Luke Somerton. "I am in her confidence, and know the reason of this whim, and yet I am not at liberty to let you into the secret."

"Perhaps I can guess too well what this is all about," cried the young man. "Louisa approves not the attentions I have paid her, and would avoid them by banishing herself from my presence. If such is indeed the fact, I will from this moment yield up the pretensions which, it must be confessed, I had once formed."

"There is no occasion for it, lieutenant, that I can see," exclaimed Luke. "The girl likes you well enough, I know, but, like the rest of her sex, she has strange freaks and fancies, and, I dare say, a little time will serve to bring matters all right enough. At all events, she cannot forget that she owes her life to you this very day, and if that don't operate in your favour, I shall begin to think she is less grateful than I took her to be."

"Dear father, let us not speak further on this subject at present," cried our heroine. "Lieutenant Granger, I am sure, will not judge me too harshly in an affair that requires more than ordinary reflection. I ask him but for a brief period to reflect, and, if possible my reply shall then be as he and you seem to desire."

By this time they had reached the castle gates, from whence Lieutenant Granger led the fugitives to that portion of the building used as barracks for the soldiers. Here he left them in a comfortable room by themselves, and then went in search of Sir Charles Radcliffe, in order to report what had been done, and likewise to consult him as to what steps it would now be prudent to take.

CHAPTER XXV.

Ah, me! for aught that ever I could read,
Could ever hear by tale or history,
The course of true love never did run smooth!
Midsummer Night's Dream.

"AND SO," said Sir Charles, after he had heard the brief narrative of the lieutenant, "you arrived just in time to save Luke and his daughter from being roasted alive?"

"They had a narrow escape of it, indeed, Sir Charles," answered the other, "for they had scarcely left the cottage when the walls and roof fell in. But some of the scoundrels are, no doubt, by this time in safe custody, and I believe your excellency will agree with me in opinion that they merit a very severe punishment."

"Aye, and they shall have it, too, if I can only bring the guilt home to any of them," exclaimed the governor. "The lower orders in this island have, for some time past, exhibited symptoms of disloyalty that it is necessary to check. Make an example of the ringleaders, and, I'll warrant you, the rest of them will be as submissive as we can possibly desire."

"The ringleader in the present instance was, I understand, a man called Henry Roden," observed the lieutenant. "For some reason or other he has formed a bitter hatred against Luke Somerton, and, as he was saved from the gallows by the queen's gracious mercy, this fellow seems to have made up his mind that your late prisoner should not escape his doom. The scoundrel, however, has got something towards his deserts, for Somerton has wounded him severely in the arm with a pistol-bullet."

"It's a pity but what it had gone through his head, and so saved us all further trouble in the matter," exclaimed Sir Charles. "I have heard something of this Harry Roden before to-day; he is one of those idle, skulking vagabonds, who, being himself discontented with everything, must needs try to make every one else so. Such men are dangerous in a little community like this, Lieutenant Granger, and it is good policy to get rid of them whenever a favourable opportunity presents itself."

"But there is another who seems to have acted as prominent a part as he did in this affair."

"Indeed! and who was it, pray?"

"A woman."

"Ah!" exclaimed Sir Charles, "these women are either angels or devils, according as circumstances make them. I have sufficient gallantry to believe that the far greater portion of them belong to the first-named class, but when it does happen that they turn out bad, there's no being a match for them. I suppose, Mr. Granger, I know something of the female you allude to?"

"Oh, yes," replied the lieutenant; "she has been often enough before our magistrates here to make her name tolerably notorious—your excellency can hardly have forgotten the name of Nell Dawson?"

"I remember her very well," answered the governor; "why, it is not long since she was bound over to keep the peace for using threatening language to a poor woman, during one of her fits of drunkenness."

"Well, she has now gone somewhat further," exclaimed Lieutenant Granger; "for it appears, that after Roden was wounded in the arm, she snatched up the blazing torch, and applied it to the faggots that the fiends in human form had piled up against the door of Luke's cottage. The crime is one of the heaviest of which the law takes cognizance, and if the case is clearly proved against her, she will not be very likely to escape the gibbet."

"We shall see by and bye what proof there is against her," said the governor. "I have often thought that woman would come to a bad end, and now it seems probable enough that my anticipations were well grounded. But you have not yet told me about Louisa Somerton, lieutenant; hitherto, I believe, the young lady has not given you much encouragement to your wooing, but I should suppose, now that you have saved the lives of herself and her father, she will yield, if it is only out of gratitude."

"I am afraid not, Sir Charles," sighed the young man.

"Have you any reason for this despair?"

"Too much, as I imagine," answered Granger; " she fears that an union would bring discredit on me, and though I believe she returns my love, yet from motives of honour she rejects every overture that I have made. Even her father has added his entreaties to mine, though without avail."

"She is an extraordinary girl," exclaimed the governor; "but in spite of all this coyness, my young friend, I believe she is yet to be won. I have had more experience in courtship than you have, and feeling an interest in this affair, I will see whether I cannot persuade her that it would be cruel to keep you longer in suspense."

"I have no reason to complain of the suspense," replied Lieutenant Granger, "because she told me, from the time her father was first suspected of the murder of Captain Aylmer, that she would never consent to carry disgrace into my family."

"Disgrace!" exclaimed Sir Charles; "why, supposing her father to have been guilty of the crime, his daughter has no right to share in the obloquy attending it."

"So I told her," answered the young man, "but all was of no avail. It is evident that the cankerworm of grief is eating deeply into her heart, yet she will endure all rather than be guilty of what she deems a dishonourable act. Her heroism may in one respect be admired, but my own happiness can never be complete unless she consents to become my wife."

"Now, if I was in your place, young man," said the governor, "I should try to accommodate myself to circumstances; if the girl has made up her mind not to have you, why, there's an end of the matter, and as I don't see much chance of your succeeding, my counsel is, that you look elsewhere for a wife."

"Nay," exclaimed Lieutenant Granger, "where can I find another that I can love as I do her?"

"Ah! that's what all you sighing young lovers say," cried Sir Charles. "First love is impetuous, but, like everything else, will wear out in time. It is likely that she and her father will leave this island shortly, and, if they do, there will be an excellent chance of your forgetting each other. By the way, I almost wonder at her continued obduracy, after owing the preservation of her own life, as well as that of her father, to your exertions to-day. One would have thought such a thing as that might have brought about a satisfactory arrangement."

A servant now entered the room to announce that a party of soldiers had just arrived with a couple of prisoners—a man and woman, who were known to have been engaged in the recent attack upon the cottage of Luke Somerton. This intelligence afforded evident satisfaction to the governor, who, after a brief consultation with his young friend, desired that Luke and his daughter should be immediately brought into his residence.

"I thought it would not be very long before our people got hold of some of them," said Sir Charles, as the servant left the room. "If these prisoners turn out to have been chief instigators in the outrage, they will have cause to repent the violence they have been guilty of; but if they should have been misled by others, we may, perhaps, prevail upon them to give such information as will lead to the discovery of those who were most culpable."

"That we can ascertain from the evidence of Luke Somerton and his daughter," replied Lieutenant Granger. "There is no doubt that Roden and the woman I have spoken of took a leading part in this disgraceful attack, and something strikes me that those are the two parties who are now in custody."

Luke Somerton and our heroine entered the room at this juncture; the former approached with a firm and erect carriage, but the latter seemed to be bowed down with grief; she had been weeping, and on perceiving that Lieutenant Granger was in the apartment, she averted her face in order to hide from him the agitation to which she had given way. Sir Charles motioned for her to be seated in a chair that stood near the table, and then, making a sign for Luke to advance, he inquired if he would be able to recognise any of the persons who had taken part in the riot that had occurred that day.

"There were several of them I should know again if they happen to come across me," replied Luke; "but, to speak the truth, your excellency, I have no great fancy for turning informer against any of them."

"But it is necessary they should be punished," exclaimed the governor, "and I am determined to teach these turbulent people that I, as the Queen's representative, am determined to maintain peace and order within this island."

"I rather think they'll not give you much farther trouble, after what has happened," returned Luke Somerton. "One of them received a pistol shot in the arm, and as he seemed to be the leader of the rest, the example made of him will not be thrown away."

"Was there not a female who made herself very conspicuous during the affray which took place?"

"There was, Sir Charles."

"Then I have every reason to believe that woman is now in our custody," answered the governor. "Two prisoners have lately been brought in, and I rather think enough will be proved to send them both to the gallows."

"I hope not, Sir Charles," exclaimed Luke Somerton. "If you have got the two that were most inveterate against me, I think there is good reason why they should be let off without any more punishment being inflicted upon them."

"Why, what in the name of common sense can you have to allege in favour of these people, Luke?"

"The reason is plain enough," answered Somerton. "The man is certainly an errant scoundrel, and no doubt he would have roasted me and my poor daughter without the least feeling of remorse. But my own hand has punished him in a way that he'll feel all the rest of his life, so I fancy my revenge ought to be satisfied, as far as that part of the matter goes. As for the other prisoner, your excellency, I never yet warred against woman, and I don't want to begin now, when it might seem like a mere desire to satisfy a personal revenge."

"At all events I shall expect you to answer all the questions I put to you in their presence," said Sir Charles Radcliffe; then speaking to a servant who was in attendance, he desired the prisoner to be immediately brought before him.

"If you insist upon my giving my evidence there can be no help for me," exclaimed Luke; "but it will be given unwillingly, for I promised my daughter, not half an hour since, that I would do nothing by which these people could be brought to punishment."

"It was a strange request on her part," observed Sir Charles Radcliffe; "what could have been her motive for it?"

"Why, she has taken it into her head," replied Luke, "that if I appear as a witness against any of these rioters the others will make a second, and, perhaps, more effectual attack upon me. I am not very apprehensive of anything of the sort myself, but seeing Louisa's terror, I at last promised that I would not say a word upon the matter unless compelled."

"It is my duty most strongly to insist upon it," exclaimed Sir Charles. "But I hear them bringing the prisoners this way; I shall first put a few questions to them, and you will then, on your oath, reply to anything that I may deem it necessary to ask of you."

The two prisoners were then brought into the room under a guard of soldiers, and having been placed at the table, so as to face Sir Charles Radcliffe, the case was at once proceeded with.

"Before we go any further in this business," said the governor, addressing himself to the male prisoner, "it is necessary that I should know your name."

"Henry Roden," replied the fellow, in a low, sullen tone.

"And the females?"

"Eleanor Dawson."

"You are, of course, aware of the charge on which you have both been apprehended?" exclaimed the governor.

"Oh, yes," replied Roden; "we know all about that; but it's a hard thing that we are to be taken up for this business, when there's so many at liberty who have done quite as much as either Nell Dawson or I did."

"We shall see by and bye whether you have any just ground of complaint," returned Sir Charles. "At present, you are accused of being the ringleaders in the late riotous proceedings, and if such should turn out to be the fact, it is proper that the chief share of punishment should fall on you two. The others will not escape the consequences of their lawless conduct; but if it should be proved that they were led into the commission of evil by the counsel and advice of others, then the punishment inflicted upon them will be in a less degree. The charge against you is for conspiring to burn the house of Luke Somerton; that design you have carried into execution, though fortunately the whole of the crime you meditated was not accomplished—Somerton and his daughter escaped the death you intended for them."

"So much the worse," growled Harry Roden; "the man's life was forfeited beforehand; and as for the girl, if she was so fond of her father as she pretended, we thought the best way was to send them both out of the world together."

"Then you do not mean to deny your guilt, Roden?"

"Where's the use of denying what can be so easily proved?" demanded the prisoner. "I was first and foremost throughout the whole affair, and I should myself have set fire to the place if it had not been for the unlucky pistol shot I received in my arm."

"And then I finished the job that he couldn't go through with himself," exclaimed Nell Dawson. "As soon as the torch fell from his hands I snatched it from the ground, and in a few minutes there was a bonfire that might have been seen from one end of the island to the other."

"Woman," exclaimed Sir Charles sternly, "you seem to exult in this business as if the act had been a meritorious one. Have you no feeling for your fellow-creatures, more particularly when one of them happens to be of your own sex?"

"We don't want to be preached to, Sir Charles," retorted the woman. "We neither of us deny the act that we've been taken up for, so you can send us to our dungeons as soon as you please; or, perhaps, as the gibbet that was set up for Luke Somerton hasn't been pulled down yet, you may as well send us to it at once, and then there'll be no more trouble about the matter."

"If yonder fellow had been hung, as he ought, there'd have been no riot in the island," added Henry Roden. "If we are to be governed by laws, let 'em fall upon one person the same as another. Luke Somerton was sentenced to die for his crimes, and it was a shame to pardon him."

"The Queen of England is always glad when she can exercise the royal prerogative of mercy," exclaimed Sir Charles Radcliffe; "and in the present instance she had a double motive, having been supplicated by a grief-oppressed and nearly heart-broken daughter. The act which restored Luke Somerton to liberty has afforded satisfaction to many—myself being among the number—though it seems there were some in this island who hesitated not to proceed to acts of violence, for no better reason than that they were disappointed in not seeing an unfortunate fellow-creature suffer an ignominious death. You have chosen to place yourself at the head of these evil-disposed people, and must, therefore, take the consequences of your own criminal acts."

"May I not plead for them as I did for my father?" cried Louisa, breaking the silence which she had hitherto maintained. "These people could have had no previous ill-feeling against us; but they believed my father's guilt, and regarded the queen's mercy as ill bestowed. Let them then return to their homes, and all I ask of them for this intercession, is, that they will henceforth regard us with less malignant feelings."

"It is impossible to grant what you ask," replied Sir Charles. "The charge is sufficiently clear against them, and they do not attempt to deny it, so there is no excuse for letting them loose upon that society which they have so grossly outraged. When the proper time arrives they will be tried; and, if they choose to employ counsel in their defence, every opportunity for doing so shall be afforded them." Then addressing himself to Luke Somerton, he added: "Do you recognise in these two persons any of those who attacked and burnt your dwellings?"

"I can swear to both of them as being there present," answered Luke, with a slow and deliberate tone.

Louisa marked the fiendish look with which these words were listened to by Henry Roden, and dreading the future excitement that would prevail against her father, she buried her face in her hands, and gave way to the tears which she found it impossible to suppress.

"Can you swear," again asked the governor, "if it was Roden who set fire to your cottage?"

"I have already said that it was not him," replied Luke. "He was villain enough to try it, though, and was just in the act of applying the torch to some dry wood they had piled up against the door, when I discharged one of my pistols at him. You may see, by his wearing his arm in a sling, that my aim was a tolerably correct one."

"But that didn't prevent me from setting your dog-hole in a blaze!" exclaimed Nell Dawson, exultingly. "When I saw this poor fellow wounded, it stirred up a bit of savage nature within me, and while the rest of our cowardly people seemed inclined to run away at the first sight of blood, I stepped forward to revenge Harry Roden for the wound he had received. Aye," she added, shaking her fist at Luke and his daughter, "and if I could have had my own way for once, neither of you should have escaped."

"The crime you have committed is sufficiently heinous," said the governor, who had listened to her ravings with evident horror; "you have destroyed the home of those who have never injured you, and but for the fortunate interposition of Lieutenant Granger and his soldiers, you would have had the blood of these two persons to answer for."

"And if it had happened so, I should have been content;" exclaimed the virago. "I have owed Luke Somerton a grudge for many a long year before he returned to this island, but it seemed to me at one time that my vengeance would never be gratified. At last he appeared among us again, and then I thought to myself, 'now at least he shall not escape me!' Then came the murder of the captain; Luke was suspected of the crime and tried for it—they found him guilty and he was sentenced to be hanged! I fancied the revenge I panted for was certain. I counted every hour that passed between the sentence and the execution, and watched with a gleeful heart the setting up of the gibbet erected for his execution. When the moment arrived for the sentence to be carried into effect, I saw the prisoner led forth, and wildly clapped my hands in the fulness of my joy. But even at the twelfth hour I was to be disappointed—his daughter returned with a pardon, and the prisoner was set at liberty. Wonder not, then, that I incited the mob against the criminal who had escaped—that I urged them to complete the sentence which had just been revoked. Roden assisted me in it heart and soul, and if it had not been for the arrival of your military, both Luke Somerton and his daughter would by this time have perished in the flames that have reduced their home to a heap of mouldering ruins."

"I can hear no more of this raving," exclaimed Sir Charles Radcliffe, shuddering at the fearful vehemence with which she gave utterance to her words. "Let us hope you will repent your crimes, now that there will be time and opportunity for reflection. My chaplain shall attend you in your cell, and most earnestly do I entreat you to attend to the consolations it will be his duty to offer you, for, on your confession, there can be little doubt as to the result of your trial."

"Oh, we both of us know pretty well what we have got to expect," exclaimed Roden. "The queen's pardon can only be obtained for murderers, like Luke Somerton; we, of course, must be dragged to the gibbet, as a warning and example to others."

"I have pleaded for you, and would again go through that which I have done for my father," cried Louisa, rising from her seat and confronting the prisoners. "You have sought our lives, though Heaven alone knows in what we have given cause for this cruel hatred; I bear ye no malice for the past, but you have boldly avowed your guilt, and I fear that all efforts I might make in your behalf would be vain and fruitless."

"We don't ask anybody's interference for us," muttered Henry Roden. "For my own part I don't care what becomes of me, and I believe this old woman by my side is pretty well of the same way of thinking."

"I have just been informed that four more of these misguided people have been taken," said Lieutenant Granger, addressing himself to Sir Charles. "They are now in the guard-room, waiting their examination."

"Let them remain there for the present," returned the governor. "I will go to them after this business has been brought to a close, and if upon inquiry I find that they have not taken a very prominent part in these riotous proceedings, I shall not be hard with them. Security for their future peaceable behaviour will be all that I shall require if they seem penitent for what is past." Then addressing himself to the two prisoners, he added : "I am sorry it is not in my power to be equally lenient to you ; there is, however, a wide difference in your degrees of guilt—*you* incited an act of violence that never would have been thought of but for your evil example."

"And we are ready to suffer the penalty of it," exclaimed the female prisoner. "As for the other people that they've just brought in, I can only say they deserve punishment as much as we do, if it was only for their cowardice in running away, when, by making a bold stand against the soldiers, we could have kept them back till Luke and his daughter were buried in the ruins. If that had been the case, there would have been some satisfaction in going to the gallows."

"What reason you have for this deadly hatred is best known to yourself," said Sir Charles Radcliffe. "I seek not to inquire into the cause, though I suppose Somerton could explain it if he thought proper."

"It is some years since I have seen this woman," replied Luke, "but I now remember her features, changed as they are since the time I speak of. She was then as trim a lass as any in the whole island, and I believe I had half a fancy for making her my wife. She fancied something of the sort, I dare say ; but when I found that she gave as much encouragement to half a dozen other young fellows as she did to me, I thought it high time to sheer off, and take another tack. After that, we very seldom met, and before twelve months had passed away, I married the mother of my poor Louisa. Folks told me that Nell was furious at what she called my desertion of her ; but I thought nothing of that, and fancied she would forget me, and the affair too, before long."

"I never forgot either," exclaimed the woman ; "a slight such as you passed upon me I could never forgive, and I thought to myself, if ever a chance came in my way, I would have my revenge. Your wife—she who had supplanted me—died soon after the birth of this girl ; I saw her carried to the grave—I watched the grief with which you saw her laid in the earth, and I laughed aloud in triumph. You heard me not, Luke Somerton, because all your thoughts were in the grave that held my rival, but people there were who did hear me, and I believe some of them deemed me mad."

"And your rancorous feeling of hatred has never subsided from that time to the present ?" said Sir Charles.

"No," she replied ; "it grew within me stronger than ever, till at last my hatred reached his child also, who frequently stood before me, though she little knew the bitter feelings with which I regarded her. As for Luke, he went abroad in the service of his country, and folks said he was an honour to his profession. Whether he was so or not is no business of mine now—I only know that he afterwards got the character of being a pirate, smuggler, or something of that kind, and then the same people who had spoken so well of him before turned their coats, and said he would one day come to be hanged. There was some consolation for me in that, and I lived on in the hope that the prophecy would come true. And there was every chance of

its being true, till within the last few hours, when through the over officiousness of his daughter, he received the queen's pardon."

"It was a noble act, most nobly responded to," observed Sir Charles Radcliffe. "You seem to regard the conduct of this young female with disfavour, but I believe by everybody else she is looked upon as an excellent example, and deserving the success that attended her mission."

"Yet, what great credit is there due to me after all ?" cried Louisa. "My father's life was at stake, and surely no effort could be too great to avert the doom."

"Very true, my good girl," exclaimed the governor ; "but for all that, it is not every young female who converts herself into a heroine. You have done well, Louisa, and have fortunately received the reward you merited."

"But it seems," she replied, "that all are not inclined to take the same view of it that you do. Witness our home, reduced to a heap of burning ruins, by those who believe the royal favour was unworthily bestowed."

"Aye, but they who did it were the very scum and spawn of our society," answered Sir Charles ; "nay, almost the whole of them were led away by the evil advice of these two people ; and I'll be bound to say there is not one of them—now that the angry passion has subsided—but is heartily ashamed of the violence he has been guilty of."

"Aye," exclaimed Harry Roden, "but that is the consequence of having curs and cowards to deal with. The very people you speak of were as eager for the fray as I was, but the moment they are themselves defeated, they turn round and whine for mercy. It's well for them that I am not at liberty, for, though disabled of my best arm, I would teach some of 'em what it is to blow hot and cold with the same breath."

"A more savage and determined ruffian I never met with in my life," whispered Sir Charles to Lieutenant Granger. "This man must be carefully watched, or he will escape from us, and then there is no saying how far the ferocity of his disposition will carry him."

Then, addressing the corporal on duty, he added,—

"You will now convey these two prisoners to their cells, which are to be as far as possible apart ; they must hold no communication with each other, and the sentries must have strict orders to use the utmost vigilance, so that no chance is afforded them of making their escape."

"What chance is there, I should like to know, of my getting away ?'" demanded Harry Roden. "My right arm has been rendered useless by Luke Somerton, and without that I can't do anything, if I was ever so inclined."

"There is quite enough cause for the caution I have desired, at any rate," answered the governor. "These men understand the duty of obedience, and I shall hold them responsible for your safe custody. Your examination is now over, but should it appear necessary, I may desire you both to be brought before me again. In the meantime, Roden, I shall desire a surgeon to attend upon you, in order that your wound may be attended to."

The two prisoners were now led away, and Luke

and his daughter were about to leave the room, when Sir Charles Radcliffe called them back.

"Are you going to quit the castle?" he asked. Somerton bowed in the affirmative.

"May I ask where you are going?"

"To seek some place we may call our home," replied Luke. "Of our old one there is little left, except mouldering ruins; but I will seek my brother James, who I dare say will give us shelter during the brief period it is my intention to remain in the island."

"Your brother James's house is but small, and can scarcely afford the accommodation you require," observed the governor. "Now I have a proposition to make, which ought more properly to come from Lieutenant Granger, though he is too modest to urge it. The fact is, then, his own house is placed at your service so long as you think proper to accept a shelter there."

"It is kindly meant, no doubt," said Luke, "and for my own part I would gratefully accept his offer, but my daughter, Sir Charles, whispers me that we had better go and ask a lodging at her uncle's."

"Aye, aye," returned the governor, "I can understand whence the scruple arises, though I see no real occasion for it. Lieutenant Granger is of too warm and generous a spirit to make any favour of it, and I must needs say a refusal would not be very courteous, after the disinterested manner in which the proposition has been made."

"Still," said Luke, doubtfully, "I think, under circumstances, Louisa will hardly be prevailed upon to live in the same house with Lieutenant Granger."

"There will be no occasion for her to do so," replied the governor, "for it is already agreed between us that my young friend shall have an apartment with me in this castle. We foresaw that there would be some delicacy about it, and have prepared accordingly."

"Well," exclaimed Somerton, "as that is the case, I suppose you will hardly think of raising any further obstacle?"

"I trust Lieutenant Granger will not deem me either ungrateful or too prudish for the hesitation with which I have treated his generous offer," said Louisa. "He will perhaps believe me when I declare that I had but one motive for not at once accepting it."

"Though only about half in the secret, I know pretty well what you mean," said Sir Charles, smiling at the hesitation with which she spoke. "The fact is, Lieutenant Granger is a suitor for your hand, which you refuse, with that perversity which is the characteristic of some females. Now, I suppose, if the truth were known, she is unwilling to accept a favour from his hands, for fear it should be considered that he has a right to look for some return—in short, that he will become emboldened to ask her to be the mistress of his house, instead of a visitor."

"I dare say that's pretty near the truth of it," answered Luke Somerton; "though, judging from my daughter's looks, I rather think she wishes me at the bottom of the Red Sea for admitting as much. However, be that as it may, we will accept the kind offer of Lieutenant Granger, in full confidence that all parties are to stand relatively towards each other exactly as they do at the present moment."

"You have my solemn promise that it shall be so," exclaimed the young officer. "Nay, if Louisa desires it, I will not appear in her presence till she desires me to do so."

"That would be as great a privation to me as to yourself," answered Louisa, with downcast eyes. "I have said before, that I can ever regard you with a sister's love—be, therefore, as a brother, and there need be no restraint at our future meetings. Promise me thus much, Lieutenant Granger, and at some future time, perhaps ——"

"You will receive my visits upon terms more satisfactory to myself," said the young man, as she suddenly came to a pause. "Well, then, I agree to your terms, and should I ever break them, it will be for you to pronounce whatever doom you may think proper to punish me with."

"By the bye, young folks," exclaimed Sir Charles, "these little episodes of love are interesting only to the parties who are immediately concerned. The matter is now arranged, I believe:—Somerton and his daughter have accepted of their new place of abode, and you, Lieutenant Granger, are to make this castle your home so long as you choose to honour me with your company. So now, as my interference seems to be no longer necessary, I will go and look after these other prisoners, who have been brought in. They have been entangled in the meshes of more designing people than themselves, I doubt not, and if that should prove to be the case, I shall dismiss them, with a lecture to be more careful with regard to their future conduct."

So saying, the governor hastened from the room on his errand; and Luke Somerton and his daughter, with Lieutenant Granger for their conductor, left the castle, in order to take up their abode in the new home which had been offered for their temporary accommodation.

CHAPTER XXVI.

She does no work by halves, yon raving ocean;
Ingulfing those she strangles, her wild womb
Affords the mariners whom she hath dealt on
Their death at once, and sepulchre.—SCOTT.

LUKE SOMERTON at once fancied himself quite at home in the snug little abode which had been placed at his service by Lieutenant Granger. But it was far different with Louisa, who regarded herself as an intruder, notwithstanding the kindness with which the offer had been pressed upon them. The obligation, she thought, was such as they ought not to have laid themselves under to a person whose feelings towards her were well known, and who even yet hoped to remove the scruples she had so often expressed.

A fortnight passed away, and she was much gratified at observing the strictness with which Granger kept the promise he had given. During the whole of the period, he never once presented himself at the house—occasionally, it is true, he would stroll that way in the hope of meeting her, and on one or two occasions he succeeded in this attempt, but not a word escaped him that might be construed into a forfeiture of the promise he had given. He seemed anxious only to ascertain if they ere comfortable in their new abode, and then their conversation would revert to such subjects as a brother and sister might confer upon. Thus the confidence of Louisa became more and more established, and these meetings, which at first were submitted to with reluctance, became at length a source of pleasure, that she would not willingly have forgone.

Luke, though perfectly well aware of what was taking place, made no remark about them to his daughter, till he saw that she no longer sought to avoid them. Then, indeed, he began to speak about what had come to his knowledge, alluding to the subject with evident satisfaction, and finally urging her to keep the young man no longer in a state of suspense, that must be most irksome to him.

"It is in vain, dear father, that you urge me to change the determination I have already expressed," she replied to him, when he had, on one occasion, been more importunate than usual. "Lieutenant Granger loves me, I know, but never shall he share the stigma that rests upon our name."

"Psha! what stigma is there that either you or I need care about?" asked her father. "A few low ruffians, it is true, may choose to point me out as a man who has narrowly escaped the gallows, but even that, my girl, will wear away in the course of time. The governor himself does not hesitate to return my salutation as we pass each other, so we have not much to care about, if the mere rabble keep in their minds things that had better be forgot."

"But we know, from bitter experience, how far their frenzy will carry them," answered our heroine. "They have even sought our lives, and may do so again, if we remain much longer in this place."

"If they have any regard for their own necks, they will do nothing so rash," exclaimed Luke Somerton. "Experience has taught them that acts of violence will only recoil upon themselves, and you may take my word for it, there will be no more such cowardly attacks made upon us. Two of our worst enemies are already safe enough in the castle, and the example will, I dare say, be quite sufficient to deter others from getting themselves into a similar dilemma."

"Yet, on the other hand," cried Louisa, "the misfortunes of their comrades may serve only still further to exasperate those who want but an opportunity to wreak their vengeance on us. You have seen to what a fearful length their headlong thirst for revenge has carried them, and the danger, though arrested for the present, is, I fear, greater than ever."

"Then you still believe these people are so regardless of their own danger as to persist in their cowardly designs?"

"I see no reason to hope otherwise," answered Louisa.

"Have you no reliance, then, on the law, which is intended for the protection of her majesty's subjects?" asked Luke. "Is not Sir Charles Radcliffe the queen's representative in this island, and is it to be imagined that he will stand by inactive when our lives are threatened?"

"Sir Charles may mean well towards us," answered Louisa, "yet it might happen that the number of our enemies may prove too much for him. Besides, we cannot be upon our guard, if they should work in secret, and it is to avoid the danger I anticipate that I still urge you to leave this place."

"Humph!" ejaculated Luke Somerton, "that would be an act of cowardice, my girl, and never having yet showed the white feather, I am not inclined to do so on the present occasion. None of these fellows can say I ever did them an injury, and if they think proper to form an antipathy without rhyme or reason, I am not going to run away from them like a cur."

"Nor would I ask my father to dishonour himself, were my own life alone at stake," answered Louisa. "I could meet death without flinching from the blow, yet to see you perish by their violence, is a thought at which my heart sickens with terror."

"There is less reason for all this alarm than you imagine, my dear girl," said Luke Somerton, taking her hand, and pressing it to his lips. "The howling of these savage bloodhounds grows more and feeble every day, and I feel quite satisfied that, in a very short time longer, the danger which so alarms you will be at an end. Then, Louisa, I may perhaps listen to the suggestion you have so often thrown out—that of leaving a place which must constantly remind me of circumstances which it would be much better to forget."

"That resolve, I fear, will come too late," answered our heroine; "these men, I feel convinced, are still working against you in secret, and the blow they meditate will fall at a moment when you least expect it."

"So your love for me prompts you to imagine," replied Luke; "I, however, have formed a very different notion upon the subject, and by and bye you will acknowledge that I am right. At all events, you may depend upon it they will not venture to make another attack upon us like the last; and for anything else they may do, I shall be quite prepared."

"Alas!" cried Louisa, "how can you be prepared against the blow aimed at you by a secret assassin?"

"Why, I must take my chance for that matter, Louisa," replied her father. "My arm has not yet lost any of its strength, and if any villanous tricks are to be played upon me, I'll soon let the perpetrators see that I am a match for them."

"Aye, and here's somebody else that will always be ready to lend you a hand," exclaimed Christopher Dalton, who at that juncture suddenly presented himself before them. "You look surprised to see me, Captain Somerton—thought, I dare say, that I had gone to Davy Jones's locker?"

"I was indeed fearful that we should never meet again in this world," replied Luke. "In fact, your long absence, and the report that you had ventured to sea on the night of that fearful storm, seemed to confirm a rumour that went abroad of your having perished."

"And a very narrow escape I had of it," exclaimed Dalton; "for the boat was capsized soon after we had left the main land, and I was obliged to swim lustily for the shore. Thanks to a stout pair of arms, however, I succeeded, though the two poor fellows that were in the boat with me were less fortunate."

"They perished, then?" cried Louisa, sorrowfully.

"Aye, both of them went down before my eyes," replied Christopher, "and in a storm such as was then raging, I could not lend a hand towards saving either of them. Their shrieks are even now ringing in my ears, and what's worse than all, I saw their poor widows and fatherless children waiting for those they were never to see again."

"Why," asked Luke Somerton, "were you so rash as to venture to sea on such a fearful night?"

"I'll tell you how it was," replied Dalton; "the people at Whitehaven were assembled on the beach after your daughter had gone away in the boat, and from the conversation that was going on among them I found that they entertained the greatest fears for her safety. Somehow or other, the girl seems to have made a favourable impression on the minds of most people, for they admired the courage and earnestness with which she had sued to the queen for your pardon, and all regretted the danger that threatened her return to this island. So, at last, a couple of brave fishermen jumped into their boat, declaring that they would go in pursuit of you at all hazards; I accompanied them; we pulled through a surf that threatened us every moment with destruction, and you already know what took place when our little craft capsized. The gallant fellows deserved a better fate, Captain Somerton, and I would have saved them but that the winds and waves were too much for me."

"And you only just returned to this island?" asked Luke.

"Scarcely half an hour since," replied the other. "I heard, however, t'other side the water, how matters had been going on here, and as these mad islanders seem to have made up their minds to murder you, I came over by the first conveyance to see if you and I together can't teach them a lesson that they'll not be likely to forget in a hurry."

"If my father would but in this instance take my advice," said Louisa, "he will leave the place before any farther mischief can occur. I have repeatedly urged him upon the subject lately, and now, perhaps, you, Mr. Dalton, will join with me in endeavouring to prevail upon him to remove beyond the reach of danger."

"Why you see, miss," replied Christopher, with hesitation, "your father has been my captain for some years past. My duty has always been to obey him, and it would not become me now to be offering my advice to a superior. He knows I'd go through fire and water to serve him, but I can't run the risk of giving him offence, much inclined as I am to oblige you."

"The truth is, Dalton," exclaimed Luke, "my daughter has taken it into her head that I am no match for the ruffians who lately made an attack upon our cottage. You, at least, know that I am not a coward, and, by Heavens! these fellows shall discover it to their own cost if they attempt any more of their violence against me."

"Aye, aye, captain," returned Dalton, "you and I should be a match for a dozen or two of them so long as there's no treachery going on. Give us

a cutlass and a brace of pistols a-piece, and the rascals must keep a respectful distance off if they would save their miserable lives. We have been used to something of the sort when boarding an enemy's ship, and though a little out of practice of late, I dare say we could astonish these natives a bit."

"But why should such a risk be run when it is so easy to avoid it?" demanded Louisa, with anxiety.

"Why, for the best reason that a British sailor can give," answered Dalton. "Your father was never yet afraid of his enemies, and it's rather too late for him now to begin to show the white feather. If these people bear him malice without cause, he is in the right of it to show an independent spirit, and, should the worst come to the worst, he'll find that Kit Dalton is as ready to fight for him now as he was when they were serving together on board the same vessel."

"But then," answered Louisa, "you were fighting honourably in the cause of your country, and it would have been cowardice to shrink from the performance of your duty. In the present instance, however, no sufficient excuse can be offered, and I have, therefore, ventured to remonstrate against the fearful hazard he would run."

"That's nothing but a woman's argument, after all," exclaimed Christopher Dalton. "I can honour the feeling that prompts you to avert what you consider to be a great danger, but, at the same time, I can't promise to say a word towards changing the determination Captain Somerton has expressed. If these people have resolved to seek his life, he is in the right of it to let them see that he is not to be so easily frightened as they imagine."

"But it is well known," answered Louisa, "that they have resolved to avenge the death of Captain Aylmer."

"And that just proves the madness of the knaves," exclaimed Dalton. "Their prejudices lead them to believe that your father is guilty of Aylmer's death, and they must needs take upon themselves the office of being his executioner. As for the queen, I suppose they think she has no right to grant her royal pardon, even when thoroughly convinced that an innocent man has been unjustly condemned."

"The truth is," said Luke Somerton, "these people have been urged on by a few enemies, who, for some reason or another, have formed a deadly hatred against me. They will not believe me innocent of the crime laid to my charge, and the mercy which was extended towards me, through my daughter's exertions, is regarded as a favour of which I am unworthy. In short, Dalton, they still believe me guilty, and were I to leave the island clandestinely, these reports would appear to be confirmed."

"But their evil thoughts cannot injure you while such men as Sir Charles Radcliffe are satisfied of your innocence," replied Louisa. "He is one among many other persons who rejoice at your escape from an ignominious fate, and surely the favourable opinion of so exalted a personage as the queen's representative, is more than a counterbalance against the frenzied yellings of an ignorant rabble, such as your enemies are composed of."

"Yet for the present I must persist in the determination I have formed," answered Luke Somerton. "These people may, perhaps, desist when they find that I make a firm stand against them, and then it will be time enough to consider the proposition you have been urging. In a week or two this popular clamour may have subsided, and, if so, I will leave the island, probably for ever."

"But how is it that I have heard nothing about Lieutenant Granger?" exclaimed Dalton. "I thought he was the accepted lover of this young lady, and yet I now hear her urging you to leave the place where he has been stationed."

"Lieutenant Granger is quite aware of the necessary change that has taken place in our relative situations," replied Louisa. "He, himself, holds an honourable rank in the service of her majesty, and I will not tarnish his fair fame by an union such as he has urged."

"Well," exclaimed Christopher Dalton, "for my own part I think it would be an honour for him to possess for his wife the girl whose noble conduct won for her the admiration of the Queen of England. You will, perhaps, excuse my plain speaking, young lady, but I really think you look at this affair in a wrong light."

"It may be so," she replied; "I will not be so vain as to assert that my own views are correct, but Heaven witnesses that my intentions are for the best."

"May I be so bold as to inquire," said Christopher Dalton, "if the gentleman has expressed his acquiescence to your views?"

"Lieutenant Granger is too generous to oppose a request of my daughter's, though it may afford him both pain and disappointment," replied Somerton. "I have observed that he seldom visits us of late, and I suppose that we shall not again be honoured with his company till he has been assured that he may do so without being regarded as an intruder."

"Upon my life this is a most extraordinary affair," exclaimed Dalton. "The young folks seem to like one another well enough, I thought, and yet he is now discarded for no reason that I can at present understand."

"I have already said that I will not bring dishonour upon him, however painful this sacrifice may to be myself."

"Humph! I don't see any dishonour that can befal a man who marries a virtuous girl," exclaimed Christopher Dalton. "He has been acquainted with you long enough to have made up his mind upon that subject, and if he sees no reason to be dissatisfied, I should say the matter is upon a fair and right understanding."

"Do not, I entreat of you, let this subject be canvassed any further," cried Louisa, earnestly. "I have not come to this determination without anxious and serious reflection. Lieutenant Granger is fully aware of my decision, and if anything could add to the esteem with which I regard him, it is the generosity with which he has yielded to my views."

"Well, he's a noble-hearted fellow, and that's the truth of it," exclaimed Dalton. "I like the kind consideration that has prompted him to humour this caprice of yours; but, between ourselves, I think you might re-consider this decision of yours, if it was only to let him see that you can be no less generous than himself."

"I have myself urged this matter to my daughter quite far enough," interposed Luke Somerton. "She knows how anxiously I have besought her to accept the addresses of one to whom I could confide her in the perfect certainty that her happiness would be insured by it."

"Well," exclaimed Dalton, "as you are both content that the affair should rest where it is, I will not attempt to argue the point any further. I thought, perhaps, a little friendly advice might not be thrown away, but, as it seems I'm not likely to make any impression here, the subject may as well drop where it is. By the bye, Captain Somerton, I'm beginning to grow tired of this do-nothing sort of life,—this living among a parcel of land-lubbers don't suit me, and one of the objects that brought me here to-day, was to ask when you think of getting out to sea again."

"That is a question I cannot answer at present," replied Luke. "My daughter requires a protector, and who is so fit to take that part upon himself as her father?"

"Why, her uncle, James Somerton, was considered a sufficient guardian for years," answered Dalton; "and I should think you might again trust her to his care."

"There are more reasons than one against it," exclaimed Luke. "My brother is some years older than myself, and his health is now visibly declining. A short time may end his mortal career, and thus, in my absence, Louisa would be thrown upon the care of strangers."

"Why, that is the very reason why she should take unto herself a husband," exclaimed Dalton; "if the girl was married, she would ——"

"You forget that this is a forbidden subject," interrupted Luke Somerton.

"Ah! you are right there, captain," exclaimed Dalton, good-humouredly. "I had almost made a hole in my manners, and I humbly beg the young lady's pardon for being so forgetful. However, it can't be suspected that I urge this affair through any favour towards Lieutenant Granger, for I never saw him in my life till the unfortunate hour that brought us to this accursed island."

"At any rate I can speak of him from some little experience," said Luke, "and from what has passed under my own observation, I am quite certain that a farther acquaintance with him will serve to increase your regard. Even Louisa, with her usual frankness, will admit that he possesses every qualification that should obtain for him the esteem of the world."

"I have repeatedly said that I regard him with feelings of love, such as a sister can bestow upon her brother," answered Louisa. "He knows my thoughts towards him, and is content to resign all claims to my hand till I give him permission to become my lover."

"But it seems that is an event which is never to take place," said Christopher Dalton. "I am not going to urge this affair, because I've promised to remain mum about it, but I can't help saying the young fellow is placed in a very awkward situation, seeing that he don't know whether he is ever to have you for a wife or not."

"If his situation is an unpleasant one, I have not myself to blame for it," answered our heroine. "Lieutenant Granger will do me the justice to admit that I have requested him to transfer his affections to some female who is more worthy than myself of his love. He has declined my sugges-

tion, and is content to wait till better circumstances shall favour our union."

"And while he is waiting for that, you and he are not growing any younger," exclaimed Dalton; "your father would feel all the more happy for seeing you comfortably settled, and instead of wasting his time ashore, here, he would once more take to his favourite old element, and be again the man that I've known him in former times."

"I almost doubt the latter part of your assertion, Dalton," interposed Luke, "for, to tell you the truth, I hardly know how I can take the command of a vessel again."

"Why not?" demanded the other, with surprise.

"There are two reasons for it," replied Luke Somerton. "In the first place, I could not, as I have done before, fight against Queen Anne, now that I owe my life to her royal beneficence; and secondly, I could not enter her service, knowing, as I do, that all my future actions would be watched with suspicion. The brand of treachery is upon me, Dalton, and having once ranked myself under the banner of her enemies, it would be believed that I am still at heart a traitor to my queen and country.

"So, they would not give you the credit for gratitude, eh?"

"Have I not lost every friend whose esteem I once possessed?" demanded Luke gloomily. "That I have foes in abundance is but too evident; perhaps I deserve that it should be so, and, therefore, I will endure with patience that which has been produced by my own imprudence."

"Dear father, you view our present prospects in too melancholy a light," cried Louisa. "All of us are liable to fall into error at unguarded moments of our lives, yet we may hope to see our faults buried in oblivion when we endeavour to make amends for past indiscretions. An honourable profession is still open to you, the queen requires the services of experienced men like yourself, and a few months may serve to restore you to the confidence you have lost."

"We will speak upon this subject another time, my love," answered her father. "At present I am little inclined to argue upon a topic upon which I do not see my way very clearly, but I promise to give it my most serious consideration, and, perhaps, you will hereafter have cause to rejoice at the temporary delay I have asked for."

"By the bye," exclaimed Dalton, "while we are upon this subject, I should like to ask you just one question. There is a mystery connected with the earlier period of your life that I could never properly understand. Once you told me that I should hear and know all whenever a favourable opportunity arrived. It seems to me that we have now leisure for it, and, if quite agreeable to yourself, you will, perhaps, let me know something of your early life."

"My promise has not been forgotten," said Luke Somerton, "nor am I inclined to withdraw it now that you have reminded me of the circumstance. In fact, I have at different leisure times written out rather a voluminous description of past events, which I will place in your hands for perusal. You will find that it is written in the third person, a course that I adopted for reasons which I may explain at some future period."

"Have you the manuscript by you?" asked Dalton.

"No; but it is in safe custody," replied Luke; "it was given to the care of the negro, Scipio, soon after we came to this island, for I thought it would hardly be safe in my own possession, at the period when my troubles came crowding on so thickly. To-morrow I will entrust them to your keeping, with the one condition, that you do not divulge any portion of the contents without having my leave to do so."

"You have my word for that, Captain Somerton," answered the other. "I'll never mention the subject to any one except your daughter, who, of course, knows all about it."

"My daughter is as much in the dark upon that subject as you are," replied Luke. "I will to-night relate to her all that it is necessary she should know at present. You will perceive, on perusing the manuscript, that the earlier part of my career was passed in the military profession, but it is unnecessary for me now to explain why I changed it for the one that made us acquainted with each other. The document is rather more bulky than I originally intended it to be, but wherever the narration grows tedious, you can either pass over a few pages, or throw aside the manuscript as unworthy any further trouble."

After a little further conversation, Christopher Dalton took his leave, and went round the neighbourhood to ascertain if the danger which threatened his friend was as great as had been imagined. These inquiries proved to be tolerably satisfactory, and on visiting Luke next morning, he received from him the promised manuscript, which, with some abridgement, ran to the following effect.

CHAPTER XXVII.

Now treason stalks abroad throughout the land,
Yet are there gallant hearts whose honest zeal
Will urge them into action. In honour's cause
'Tis fit that we should rouse.

The Rencontre.

It was about five-and-twenty years since that a person, named Deville, dwelt on one of the islands near the coast of Ireland. Deville, however, was but an assumed name, his real one being Luke Somerton. He was the last member of a once noble family; his father had sought refuge in retirement, but possessing all the high spirit of his family, he determined to conceal his rank from the few persons with whom he associated.

One day, when Luke had strolled beyond his usual haunts, the weather suddenly changed, the clouds rolled heavily along, and large drops of rain foretold an approaching storm. Alone, and on foot, Luke was pressing on to gain some place of shelter, when, before a cave, he perceived a steed, gaily caparisoned, near which sat a young female, apparently overcome with terror. Instinctively he sprang forward, and gently raising her in his arms, he beheld a countenance of surpassing loveliness. In a few moments she recovered herself, and observing the presence of a stranger, would have withdrawn herself from his support.

"Fear nothing, lady," exclaimed Luke, in accents of gentleness; "my poor services, humble as they may be, are at your command. Accept of me as your guide, and I will lead you to my parents' cottage, where you may find a shelter till your own friends have been apprised of your destination."

After a little hesitation she acceded, and having been assisted into her saddle, she accompanied him from the place where she had sought a temporary shelter. At length they arrived at their place of destination, where they were equally surprised and rejoiced to find that her father, Sir Richard Bolton, and his attendants, had arrived there before them.

Having dismounted and received her father's congratulations, she presented Luke, and stated her obligations in such glowing terms as almost overpowered him, though he could not but exult at the thought that his parents heard the praises which were bestowed upon him. To the questions of Sir Richard, the elder Somerton gave replies so evasive that but little could be gathered from them. His manner, so superior to his lowly station, evinced a pride which could not be mistaken, while his wife's attention to their guests showed she had moved in a sphere of life very different from the present.

In the character of Sir Richard Bolton, pride was, perhaps, the strongest marked feature. His family consisted of only one daughter, Eveline, whose mother had died in giving birth to her, bequeathing her infant to the care of a father, to whom a son would have been far more acceptable. He did not long grieve for the loss; other cares engrossed his attention, and a journey to court being necessary, he set out, accompanied by his young daughter. In the metropolis he resided some years, during which lapse of time but few circumstances occurred that need be recorded here.

As soon as Sir Richard and his daughter were sufficiently rested, they prepared for their return home, and the former, judging that a pecuniary reward would be rejected by his host, proffered his interest for the future advancement of Luke Somerton. The offer was accepted, and the baronet and his daughter took their leave. During the remainder of the day Luke was unusually thoughtful and abstracted, and when he retired for the night, the occurrences that had taken place floated before his fancy in feverish dreams of what had been, and what might be.

Some short time elapsed, when Sir Richard Bolton, not unmindful of his promise, and wishing to be considered the patron of a youth whom he had many reasons to believe was of superior birth, procured him a commission in the army. The predilections of Luke had always been for the sea, but he was not inclined to throw any obstacles in the way of his preferment, and when the mandate for his departure arrived, he lost no time in setting out for the mansion of his patron. On his way, in crossing a part of the domain, he perceived a small building, the walls of which were covered with richly flowering shrubs; the last cadence of a song breaking through the quiet beauty of the place, and the soft accompaniment of a lute, skilfully touched, struck upon his ear. He paused, in anxious expectation of a repetition of the delicious sounds, when a female approached the window,—it was Eveline! She started, and would have retired, when Luke, respectfully saluting her, apologised for the intrusion he had been guilty of.

"I was about to return home," she replied, "but the pleasing solitude of this spot is so in accordance with my feelings that I have remained longer than I intended." Then changing to another subject, she added,—"I have been particularly remiss in deferring my visit to your parents, to thank them for the attention they bestowed upon me. To you, also, I owe a heavy debt of gratitude which neither time nor absence can ever make me forget."

"Oh, name not the trifling service it was my good fortune to render you," answered Luke. "If my life had been sacrificed in your behalf, it would have been of little consequence so that your safety was the result. To your father, for his liberality, I am much indebted, since he has placed me in a situation of honour such as I could never have attained by any exertions of my own."

During this conversation they were advancing towards the mansion, on arriving at which, Eveline desired a servant to conduct Luke to her father's presence, and then, having again thanked him for the service he had performed, she retired to her own apartment.

Seated at a table which was covered with books and papers, and evidently absorbed in business, was Sir Richard Bolton, who was, however, soon aware of the presence of his young visitor, who he motioned to a seat, and then addressing him in a tone of kindness, said :—

"I am happy, my young friend, that it lies in my power to bestow some remuneration for the assistance you afforded my daughter. But there are two questions that I would first ask of you—from what family are you descended, and what has induced your parents to adopt the obscure life they at present lead ?"

Luke Somerton, who had been desired not to afford any explanation on family subjects, merely replied that the Irish rebellion had led to all their troubles ; that their rank had been respectable, and that, having collected the wreck of their property, they had selected the island as a place best adapted to their altered fortunes.

Sir Richard now produced the commission, with a letter from Lord Derry, the commander of the regiment ; it required the immediate attendance of Luke, as the rebels had collected in considerable numbers, and some warm work was immediately expected. An equipment being necessary, Sir Richard offered a sum of money sufficient for that purpose, but the pride of Luke could not yield to this obligation, and, thanking the baronet for his kindness, he replied that his father had made arrangements for the new career he had been called upon to follow.

Eveline now entered the apartment, and Luke could scarcely withdraw his gaze from her beautiful countenance. At length, however, with faltering accents, he was about to take his leave, when Sir Richard expressed a wish for him to remain the day with him ; this invitation, so agreeable to his wishes, was promptly accepted, and he sat down to a repast, during which his eyes were more fully occupied than any other sense. Placed opposite to Eveline, every glance rivetted the chains firmer ; and as, almost unknown to herself, her heart beat with a congenial feeling, it soon became evident to each of them that the separation which was to take place, would afford pain to them both.

When the time for retiring arrived, Luke was ushered into an apartment in the west wing of the castle. As he trod the lofty corridors, preceded by a servant with lights, he was struck with the splendour that reigned throughout the building. The gallery was hung with paintings, which had belonged to the former proprietor, but retained by Sir Richard Bolton, that any person not acquainted with his family history might imagine they were portraits of his ancestors.

On the door being thrown open, Luke Somerton entered the chamber, and being left alone, approached the window, which opened on a balcony. The apartment had the same air of luxury as the others ; the rich silk drapery of the bed was festooned with silver, and armorial bearings above the canopy ; the panels of the wainscot were cedar, and the numerous mirrors gave it altogether the appearance of a palace in fairy-land.

He passed into the balcony. To rest was impossible, and the loveliness of the night tempted him to wander amongst the beautiful grounds that lay spread before him. Descending a flight of steps, he reached a terrace that ran along the principal front of the building. Slowly he paced it with folded arms, when, passing a window, the curtain of which was not entirely drawn, he perceived a female seated at a table, evidently buried in thought ; a veil half concealed her countenance, when, on turning towards the light, it proved to be Eveline. She rose and approached the window, while Luke, fearful of being observed, retired within the shadow of a buttress.

Presently she opened a window which was on a level with the terrace, and, stepping out, bent her course along the walk. The young man, who had been watching, longed to throw himself at her feet and avow the passion she had inspired in his heart, but the fear of being considered too presumptuous withheld him. Still concealed, he attentively observed her, while in passing, a sigh and half murmured exclamation, which sounded like his name, escaped her lips.

When she had proceeded some distance, he came forward, that he might be observed on her return, but he waited in vain—she had regained her apartment by a different way, while Luke, unable to seek repose, lingered in the open air till the morning began to break.

At the conclusion of the morning's repast, at which he only met Sir Richard Bolton, he was on the point of taking his leave, when his host requested him to look at some horses that he had recently purchased. Luke followed him to the court-yard, where the horses were led out for inspection ; but one among the rest struck him as being a particularly handsome animal ; the fire of its eye, its flowing mane, and impatience of control, proved it to be of high blood. His opinion of the steed was asked, and the reply being satisfactory, Sir Richard requested his acceptance of it. The manner in which the gift was urged upon him admitted of no refusal, and the offer having been accepted, the baronet presented his young friend with a letter to his commander, Lord Derry, and then ordering the horse to be saddled on the instant, he dismissed his visitor without affording him an opportunity of paying his parting respects to his daughter.

Anxiously did Luke Somerton direct his gaze towards the windows, but no Eveline greeted his view; and, as there was not any possible excuse for his lingering in the neighbourhood, he spurred his horse forward at a rapid pace, in order to drown the feelings with which he was tortured.

At length the humble dwelling of his parents appeared before him, and his father beheld him with joy, in all the pride of youth, rein in his steed, spring from the saddle, and throw himself into the arms of his mother, who had been anxiously awaiting his return home. After a brief explanation of what had taken place, he exhibited the commission he had received, as well as the letter of introduction to his commanding officer. Thus everything was so far satisfactory, and, as it was desirable that he should join his regiment as soon as possible, the following day was named as that on which he should take his departure. The necessary preparations were few, and his father, taking down the sword which had belonged to his ancestors, said,—

"Take this weapon, my dear son, and use it nobly to suppress the unnatural rebellion that distracts our unhappy country. Never let it be drawn in a private quarrel, unless the insult is of a most aggravating nature; a brave man cannot add to his laurels by taking the life of one who has perhaps been his dearest friend. You are now, my dear Luke, about to quit your parental roof for a life of dangers and difficulties, but where the honour to be acquired, should you survive, will far surpass the risk you have to encounter. Be cool in all your actions; never be hurried on by a false desire of fame—a soldier should never be too rash. Remember, your condition will be a subordinate one. Till I give permission, do not divulge our rank. You have much to learn; but, if I judge correctly, Luke Somerton will never forget the honour he is bound to protect."

Such was the old man's advice. His mother strove to calm her agitation; to part with her son was a severe trial, but, combatting the natural feelings of a parent, she in time became reconciled to the separation.

Next morning, at early dawn, Luke rose, and, accompanied by his father, proceeded to the seashore, where a ferry-boat was ordered to be in readiness. Here he bade the old man adieu, and his horse having been previously embarked, he was conveyed across to the opposite mainland. Then mounting his steed, he proceeded on his journey, determined to reach as far as he could by nightfall. At the close of day he found himself near a small village inn, where he dismounted, and called for some one to lead his jaded horse to the stable. Not, however, receiving any reply, nor perceiving any trace of inhabitants, he fastened the bridle to a ring in the wall of the building, and, passing through a door which he found open, entered what appeared to be the public room for travellers. The apartment was large and lofty; rough beams of timber formed the roof, which was darkened by smoke; the remains of a fire at the further end threw a glimmering light on the objects around, as well as on a door leading to some other part of the house.

Luke seated himself, uncertain how he should next proceed, when the sound of human voices struck on his ear. The persons approached, and entering, proved to be the host and his wife, who had been to a neighbouring village, and had left their house in charge of a boy, who it seemed had not been very attentive to his duties.

On perceiving his unexpected guest, the host paused, took off his cap, and making his obeisance, began to stammer out a thousand excuses for the little attention he had met with; at length, finding that his apologies were hardly needed by his visitant, he added, to his wife:—

"Hasten to the larder, Nelly, and see that the lamb, trout, and chickens which are left there are immediately prepared for this gentleman's meal, and take this key, which, as you know, unlocks the third wine cellar on the left; let our son come here directly, in case we should want him to run of any errands, and desire Rob to make haste and get the gentleman's horse in the stable."

The hostess having disappeared to obey these orders, her husband seated himself opposite Luke, and proceeded, after a short pause, in his usual garrulous strain:—

"You are most fortunate, sir, in having secured lodgings for the night at my house; for the roads are far from safe, and in no other village for miles round could you meet with accommodation equal to what you will find at my inn. Have you travelled far?—but I know you have, for your horse seems to be nearly knocked up. Ah, sir, you now see me landlord of a house of public entertainment; but I was better off in the world once. I have been in the army, like yourself; you are an officer, I perceive, and no doubt are going to join your regiment?"

Luke Somerton, though much amused by the inquisitiveness of the old man, merely replied that he was travelling for pleasure, and a desire to see some of the places so celebrated in Irish scenery. He then asked him the nearest way to Kildare, and if he could procure a guide for the following day's journey. The host paused for some little time at the mention of a guide, and then again breaking forth, he exclaimed:—

"How very lucky you are to-day, sir; why, I know the very man that will suit your purpose. Here, Rob," calling to his son, who not replying immediately, the host started off his chair, and ran to the door, just as a man was entering, and against whom he ran with so much violence as almost to send him off his feet.

"Is this the way you welcome your friends?" asked the newly arrived visitor, a little ruffled at the rudeness of the shock he had received.

"Oh! my dear Terence!" cried the landlord, "I was just going to send off an express for you. Here is a gentleman who is in want of a guide to Kildare, and as you are well acquainted with all the short cuts, I have recommended you." Then turning to the traveller, he added, "This is my excellent friend Terence, sir, as worthy a fellow as you could meet, and one who can travel blindfolded to Kildare without going out of his way."

Luke now turned his attention towards the man whose praises were thus sung; in height he was of the middle size, square and strongly built; his limbs appeared active, and his countenance indicated a fair share of boldness and daring. The only weapon he carried was a long-bladed knife which was stuck in his belt.

"Aye, sir," he exclaimed, after the host had finished his recommendation, "the old chap knows me well enough, and I believe you could not have found a guide better acquainted with the road. However, sir, if you don't like the look of me, there are several other men to be found that would be glad to have the job."

"There is no occasion to take any further trouble about the matter," answered Luke; "the host here has strongly recommended you, and I wish you to be ready to attend me in the morning. But say, my good fellow, since you know the country so well, are there any straggling parties of the insurgents in our track?"

"There may be, sir," replied the man; "but trust to me, who knows the country so well. Those you speak of lie in ambush near the main road; but we shall take bye-paths that lead across the country."

"Let him alone, sir," interposed the host, "and I'd answer for him he conducts you in safety. But what, I wonder, keeps my wife so long preparing the supper? I'll go and see, and be back in a few minutes."

Although he entertained doubts and misgivings regarding his future conductor, Luke carefully concealed them. He was well armed, and except from superior numbers or treachery, he had not much to fear. However, he determined to keep a watchful eye on the man.

His reveries were interrupted by a violent altercation, and presently the host entered, with an enraged countenance, dragging in his son, a strapping youth, who seemed to be half strangled from the grasp of his father. To Luke's inquiry of what was the matter, the host exclaimed :—

"Ah, sir! matter enough, in all conscience. The lazy, worthless scoundrel, whilst I and my wife were absent, let two fellows who stopped here eat most of the provisions we had in the house. But I'll punish him for it—he shall starve for the next week; and it's only out of respect for you, sir, that I have not given him a worse thrashing than he's had."

"Well, well," interposed Terence, with a significant smile; "it's a bad job to be sure, but I dare say, under the circumstances, the gentleman won't mind putting up with what you can procure. I suppose you have got some bread and cheese in the house?"

"My good friend," exclaimed Luke to the host, "a very little will satisfy my appetite, nor am I at all particular as to its quality. I, however, should like to have it as soon as possible, having far to travel to-morrow, and being much in need of rest after my day's journey." Then turning to his guide, he said, "I shall expect you here at sunrise."

The host now busied himself in preparing what little his larder actually afforded, for the truth is, the lamb, trout, and chickens, had existed only in his own fruitful imagination. Having, therefore, spread a table with bread and cheese, and a couple of poached eggs, he put before his guest the bottle of wine which had been long since ordered. This frugal meal was soon despatched, after which he was conducted to the cheerless-looking chamber in which he was to pass the night. When the hostess

had retired, he fastened the door, and having placed his sword and pistols on a chair within reach, he threw himself upon the bed, where, in spite of its wretched accommodation, he soon fell into a sound slumber. His rest was undisturbed till day-break, when, starting up, he dressed, and descended to the lower apartment, where he found the host, his wife, and the guide, awaiting his presence. · He was surprised at the change of dress and appearance of the latter, who now wore a cap of steel and a breastplate, as if in anticipation that their journey was likely to prove a dangerous one. He was armed, too, with a sword, a dagger, and pistol, and at the door stood a good horse ready saddled.

Having paid the expenses of the over night, Luke mounted his steed, and, accompanied by his guide, set forth on his journey towards Kildare. He was pleased to see the soldier-like bearing of the man whose services he had engaged, and after riding some distance he broke the silence by inquiring of Terence if he would like to join him in the expedition he was about to take.

"I am about to join the troops under the Earl of Thomond," he added, "and shall be attached to the division commanded by Lord Derry."

"I shall be most glad to accept your offer, sir," replied Terence. "I will serve you to the best of my ability, and I trust you will see no reason to repent having taken me into your service."

Having proceeded some distance further, our travellers entered a mountain path; above, the lofty trees threw a gloom over the narrow and rugged way, which only allowed one horse to pass. In the valley below, and through the vistas in the wood, a river was perceptible, stealing its silent course along. Having continued along this path some time, they arrived at a broader part of the road, which led to an entrance in the forest; scarcely, however, had they reached this place when they heard the distant clash of arms, and the shout of combatants.

Luke and his attendant paused to ascertain the direction the sounds came from, when, urging forward their horses, they soon arrived at the place of conflict. On a small plain, nearly enclosed by trees, they beheld a party of soldiers in fierce conflict with a superior number of insurgents, whose repeated and desperate charges had nearly broken in upon the regular troops. Luke and Terence immediately galloped to the assistance of the royalists, who, gathering hopes from this trifling addition to their numbers, made one more effort to charge the rebels. Terence slew one of the ruffians, and Luke singled out the leader of the band, who, after a hard conflict, fell beneath his sword, not, however, before Luke was sorely wounded in the shoulder. The chief officer of the royal party instantly rode up, and almost breathless with exertion, exclaimed :—

"Gallant friend, you and your follower shall ever receive my warmest thanks for your timely aid. Henceforth your fortunes shall be my especial care, and I trust you will ever consider Lord Derry as your friend."

At the name of the nobleman Luke was agreeably surprised; the discovery that he had been instrumental in the rescue of his future commander was an unlooked-for and happy occurrence; therefore, taking Sir Richard Bolton's letter from his pocket, he handed it to his lordship, saying, that it should be the sole happiness of his life to serve under so distinguished a leader in the cause of his sovereign.

In the meantime Terence had joined the soldiers, amongst whom he recognized, and was joyfully welcomed by, some of his old acquaintances. Having washed off, in the neighbouring stream, the marks of their late fray, they sat down on the green sward and partook of the provisions with which they had been provided.

Lord Derry and Luke, apart from the rest, conversed upon a variety of topics, until, to a question from the latter, his lordship replied, that having led his men that way, they had been attacked by a party of insurgents, who must have waylaid them, in order to prevent them joining some troops to whose assistance they were going. It was further remarked, that though the dress of the party was that of the peasantry belonging to the country, yet the fact of many of them having horses was a proof that they belonged to a class of persons superior to most of those who had risen in rebellion against the government. At length, sufficient time having been allowed for rest and refreshment, they were summoned to horse, and commenced their march just as the moon was rising above the distant mountains.

A march of about four hours brought them in sight of the camp to which they were journeying. As this scene burst on the view of Luke Somerton, the nobleman turned his eyes upon him, to observe the effect this novel sight had on him; he perceived a flush mount on his cheek, his eyes sparkled, and his bosom heaved violently under all the ardour of a youthful soldier.

Altogether the scene was most picturesque; our travellers were on the brow of a hill; beneath them was a verdant plain, beyond which was a gentle acclivity, on which the tents were pitched, ranged in lines, and defended in front from any attack by trenches and pallisading; the camp extended to the brow of the hill, where the commander's tent stood, and near it the royal standard of England unfurled its broad expanse, and floated majestically on the breeze.

Lord Derry ordered the trumpets of his party to sound, and they were almost immediately answered from the camp. Three officers then issued from the general's tent, and appeared observing the party as they descended into the plain, which, when they reached, they spurred their jaded horses onwards, and soon arrived at the entrance of the encampment, where they were received by a number of their comrades, who anxiously inquired the cause of their diminished numbers, their pale and wounded appearance; and the detail of the insurgents' treachery inflamed their hearers, who vowed to avenge their slaughtered comrades.

Leaving Terence with the troop, Lord Derry and Luke Somerton rode on, until they arrived at the general's tent, where, having dismounted, Derry addressed the principal person present by the title of the Earl of Thomond. He then presented Luke to him, saying :—

"You may thank this gallant youth, my lord, for our safe return; the insurgents came suddenly upon us, and we were nearly overpowered by numbers, when he and his attendant rushed to our aid,

and rescued us from a defeat that would otherwise have been inevitable."

Somerton regarded with a scrutinizing eye the nobleman to whom he was presented. He was about middle aged; his stature tall and majestic; his visage bold and commanding; his glance, quick and penetrating, evinced a firmness and decision of character; and his whole appearance was such as to secure for him the respect of those whose duty it was to obey his every command. Having glanced towards the young man who had been thus flatteringly introduced to him, he turned towards Lord Derry, and said :—

"Your recommendation of this young stranger shall not be forgotten, and an early opportunity, I doubt not, will be afforded, in which he may prove that your high character has not been misplaced."

As soon as this interview was ended, Lord Derry conducted Luke to his tent, where, having refreshed themselves with a few hours' repose, his lordship directed his attendants to bring the arms and regimentals he had ordered. "My friend, Sir Richard Bolton," he continued, "has requested me to take this duty upon myself, and I trust it will have been performed to the satisfaction of all parties."

Nor was Terence forgotten, for in reply to Lord Derry's inquiries, Luke gave a slight sketch of his follower's story, and spoke so highly in his favour, that he was appointed to the same division of the army as his master; and, being an old and experienced soldier, was made a non-commissioned officer.

The camp now presented a scene of the greatest bustle; the tents were struck, and the soldiers, forming under their different leaders, commenced their route towards the place where it was reported a great gathering of the rebels was going on. They continued onwards till evening, and as the Earl of Thomond was anxious to rest his troops at a town that laid in their way, after delaying a few hours to refresh themselves, they resumed their march.

The inroad of the royalist leader, with so great an armed force, into a territory where the insurgents thought themselves safe, was deemed a sufficient excuse to commence hostilities in earnest. Plans were therefore hastily formed, and a large party having been brought to bear upon one particular point, they made a sudden attack upon the advanced guard and slew nearly every man composing it. This news was quickly brought to the Earl of Thomond, who, upon holding a council of war with his officers, determined to make an immediate attack upon the foe.

It was evening when the news arrived, and the clouds rolling heavily and dark along the sky, portended a stormy night. Luke, wrapping himself in his cloak, accompanied by Terence, directed his steps through the camp; all was hushed in silence, save the sentinel, who, while he kept his lonely watch, thought of those who were anxiously waiting his return at home, and of the dangers which might prevent him ever seeing that home again.

Giving the pass-word, Luke and Terence moved onwards, when their whispered conversation was suddenly checked by a light appearing close to them, and much were they surprised at finding themselves under the walls of the town it was intended to besiege. The place from whence the light shone was a window, in a building immediately inside the walls, which in this part were only a few feet in height. Noting the place, and retreating with the greatest caution, they were returning to the camp to give notice of the discovery they had made, when a footstep sounded in their ears, and no reply being given to their challenge, our two adventurers rushed forward, and seized the stranger, who proved to be a servant belonging to the chief officer in command of the town.

Terrified by the suddenness of his surprise, notwithstanding the repeated assurances of Luke that he should not be injured, they conveyed him to the camp, where Somerton, leaving him in charge of his attendant, hastened to acquaint Lord Derry with the circumstance. He found him and the other officers just leaving the general's tent, the council having dissolved without coming to any decision. On hearing this fresh piece of intelligence, Lord Derry instantly returned to the general, and mentioning the late discovery, proposed the immediate surprise of the town, and capture of its disloyal inhabitants; then, sending for the other officers, the prisoner was brought in for examination.

At first, terror prevented him from replying to a single question, and safety and reward were promised him. He then acquainted them that the town was but weakly guarded, and the few undisciplined troops very inattentive; that the wall might be easily surmounted, and finally, that he would act as guide, if they felt disposed to send a party to surprise the town.

The present opportunity being considered a favourable one, the earl immediately directed one hundred men, under an experienced officer, to advance for the assault. Luke and Terence were ordered to join this party. The troops were got ready in silence, and leaving the camp, they proceeded on their enterprise. All was according to their wishes; their guide, secured between Somerton and Terence, led them to the low part of the wall, where the light had been observed. They mounted it, and descended into the town without the least interruption. Having passed through some narrow streets, they arrived at the citadel, the wall of which they mounted.

The last of the besieging party had mounted the platform, and the rest directing their way to the entrance, when a sentinel, who had been slumbering on his post, suddenly awoke, and uttered loud cries of alarm, which had scarcely passed his lips, when he fell to the ground mortally wounded.

At this juncture lights appeared in various parts of the citadel, and a party of insurgents, hastily armed, rushed tumultuously to oppose the assailants. The combat was short and decisive, the desperate efforts of the rebels were in vain; the shouts of the combatants, groans of the dying, and glare of torchlight, had alarmed the other citizens; and now there was once more an obstinate enemy to cope with. Lord Derry's opportune arrival with his detachment turned the scale of victory. Each street, however, was sharply contested; the English were assailed with missiles of every description, from the windows and roofs of the houses, and several of the soldiers were in this manner slain.

The Earl of Thomond, having been informed of the opposition offered, immediately led on the remainder of his troops, and forcing the gates, entered the town with such an overwhelming force, as at once to end the contest; and determining to make an example of the place, he gave it up to immediate plunder.

Luke and Terence strove to curb the rapacity of the soldiers, but to no purpose. A party of the military having entered a house, were rushing up the staircase, as Somerton, borne in with the crowd, attempted in vain to reason with them, when a youth, belonging to the insurgents, armed with a cutlass, opposed himself to the foe.

"Ye pass not here, save over the body of Arnold Lorimer," he exclaimed, resolutely.

The soldiers paused for a moment, until, allured by the hope of plunder, they were about to rush furiously upon the gallant youth, when Luke Somerton forced his way through the crowd.

"My brave sir," he exclaimed, "opposition is useless,—your town is taken, and if you yield to us, I solemnly pledge myself for your safety."

"Saxon!" replied the young insurgent, "I care not for myself; but a parent lies breathing his last within yonder chamber—my sister tends him—let not his dying moments be disturbed—assure me of my sister's safety, and I will then yield myself your prisoner."

Partly by entreaty, and partly by command, Luke then cleared the house of all except four soldiers, whom he kept in the event of any sudden attack. He then succeeded in easing the apprehension of Arnold Lorimer, who led them onward to an apartment. As they passed the chamber occupied by Arnold's parent and sister, Luke could distinguish the low and languid utterance of the invalid, frequently interrupted by the hysterical sobs of his daughter. Somerton pitied them, and determined, as much as he could, to soften the misery to which they had been reduced.

He had lingered a short distance behind his companions, when passing a curtain that was suspended before an archway, and turning to ascertain the cause of a slight rustling behind him, a dagger was suddenly plunged into his side. Staggering beneath the stroke, he beheld the assassin, with the direst malice in his visage, preparing to repeat the blow, when Terence rushing to his aid, cut down his assailant; then supporting Luke in his arms, he loudly called for assistance. Arnold and the English soldiers returned and bore him almost fainting to an apartment, where, after some time, they succeeded in staunching the blood that flowed from his wound, while the suffering youth, pale and motionless, gave but few signs of animation.

Some days elapsed after Luke received his wound, but as yet he evinced no consciousness of those around him; he was placed upon a couch, supported by cushions, and every care seemed to have been taken in the sick chamber. Terence, after watching by him all night, lay buried in sleep, at the farther end of the apartment, while upon a chair beside the couch a female was seated; a thick veil shaded her countenance, her dark hair had escaped from its folds, and flowed in loose tresses over her shoulders; her arms bare, and of dazzling whiteness, and her waist confined by a girdle, the length of which could scarcely have exceeded a couple of spans.

Softly drawing the curtains, and gazing with anxiety upon Luke Somerton, who drew a deep and heavy sigh, she beckoned to Arnold, who stole to her side. A flush passed over the countenance of the wounded youth; and, half opening his eyes, he uttered a few incoherent expressions.

"Heaven be praised! our deliverer will recover," was the exclamation of Arnold and his sister Honor, who was the only female that had with such careful anxiety tended Luke during the period of his insensibility.

Aroused by their joyful exclamations, Terence started from his slumber, and kneeling by the couch of his master, poured forth the gratitude with which his heart overflowed. He then hurried away to acquaint Lord Derry, who speedily paid a visit to the sick chamber.

Luke was gently raised and supported by pillows. Honor left the chamber, nor was the wounded man aware of his having had so fair and attentive a nurse. Arnold, however, remained, and received Lord Derry with an ease that proved he had been accustomed to superior society. His lordship congratulated his young friend on the probability of his recovery, and promised, the moment his health permitted, that he would prevail on the Earl of Thomond to recommend him for promotion. He

also mentioned an expectation that the insurgents would make an attempt to re-possess themselves of the town, and expressed his regret that Luke would be prevented taking an active share in its defence.

The first use Somerton made of his recovery was to express his thanks to Arnold for the care and attention that had been bestowed upon him during his illness, and assured him of using every means in his power to alleviate the captivity he and his sister were placed in. Inquiring for his parent, Arnold informed him that he had died on the evening when the town was surprised; his sister, Honor, he said, was so deeply affected at her loss as nearly to have sunk under her grief.

"It's all true enough, sir," exclaimed Terence; "but that did not prevent her showing you all the attention in her power. When she heard you had saved her brother's life, and was so near losing your own, she roused from her griefs, and watched and prayed by your bedside."

In an apartment, handsomely furnished, Honor Lorimer reclined upon a sofa, apparently absorbed in thought; her head reclined upon her hand, and her veil thrown back, disclosed a countenance strictly beautiful, though impressed with a haughty air of command; her forehead high and polished, her nose slightly aquiline, arched eyebrows, her mouth small, and adorned with teeth rivalling in whiteness the finest pearls; her figure was rather above the usual size, and when she moved there was an air of majesty in every action that commanded homage and respect. Plunged in thought, a deep sigh at intervals burst from her bosom, and tears chased each other down her cheek.

"Merciful Heaven!" she exclaimed, clasping her hands, "teach me to smother feelings that I have done wrong in encouraging. Is it for this I was reserved, to love an enemy of our country, our religion? He was wounded, and I tended him. Alas! I have myself fallen! Numbers of my countrymen fell by these foes, yet *he* saved the life of my brother."

"Why do I find you thus agitated?" demanded Arnold, as he suddenly entered the room. "Our guest expresses his gratitude to you; he is much better. But say, dear Honor, from whence proceeds the silence and abstraction you have shown of late? There was a time when gaiety and health shone in your smile, and beamed upon your cheek. 'Tis true, we have been conquered; but, mark me, sister, 'tis but for a time. Our friends are already gathering to attack the town, and if numbers may avail, the victory is certain to be ours."

"Dearest brother," she exclaimed, "if you conquer, let me entreat you to spare the life of him who might have taken yours. We owe him a heavy debt of gratitude, for much I doubt if any other than himself could have checked the soldiers in their deadly rage."

"Honor," replied her brother, "you speak with feeling of this wounded stranger; 'tis true, he saved me from the swords of these English; but, were it not for thee, who, as a brother, I must ever protect, life were of little heed; but let not pity carry thee beyond the duty we owe to our country, and the religion they would trample on"

With these words he left his sister, who, torn by conflicting passions, sought the cool and refreshing shade of the garden, to strive and collect her wandering ideas.

A week afterwards, Luke Somerton finding himself sufficiently recovered, prepared to join Lord Derry, who had proceeded to Kilkenny. From the time he had expressed his thanks to Arnold for his sister's attention, the name of Honor Lorimer seemed forgotten; yet once, when he touched upon the subject, Arnold changed the discourse. To an inquiry from Terence he was informed that some days had elapsed since she had been seen, and even her attendants seemed at a loss to account for her absence.

Grateful for the attention that had been bestowed upon him, Luke Somerton determined by every means in his power to soften the rigour of Arnold's captivity. He, therefore, proposed taking him to Kilkenny, and that he should adopt the English garb, to prevent recognition. To this proposition, after some hesitation, Arnold agreed; and the morning of their departure saw him habited in the manner that had been recommended.

He requested that Luke would permit a youth to accompany him as an attendant, an orphan reared up in the family; his affection for Arnold would not allow him to remain behind, and as Luke knew it would be a solace to Arnold to have one of his own country people to converse with, he readily agreed to the proposal; and commencing their journey, they in due time arrived at Kilkenny.

Entering the town, they passed a group of officers who were engaged in earnest conversation, one of whom, turning towards Luke, proved to be Lord Derry, who hastened over, and congratulating him on his recovery, led him and his party to the quarter of the town where his troops lay; and having seen them safely lodged, he, accompanied by Luke, retraced his steps to the place he had come from.

On their way Somerton informed his friend of all that had occurred since his departure, and pleaded for Arnold with such effect, that Lord Derry advised him, as the safest course, for the young captive to keep up the disguise, till a satisfactory arrangement could be made. After some little further conversation on this subject, his lordship rejoined the party he had left, while Luke, who had promised to wait on his commander on the following morning, hastened to rejoin Arnold Lorimer.

He found him very anxious to ascertain the result of his conversation with Lord Derry, and on being informed, he fully concurred in the advice which had been given.

Arnold's attendant happened to be in the apartment; and, advancing to his master, he expressed a few words with a strong and marked energy. Luke had not particularly observed this youth before; but now he remarked his slight and elegant figure. His features were beautifully moulded, but his skin was somewhat darker than is generally to be found in this country. Having listened to a remark to that effect, Arnold replied that Basil was a native of Spain; and the youth, being aware that they spoke of him, turned his eyes toward Luke Somerton, and hastily withdrew them; and after spreading a repast upon the table for the two friends, he suddenly retired from the apartment.

CHAPTER XXVIII.

For thee they fought, for thee they fell,
  And their oath was on thee laid;
To thee the clarions raised their swell,
  And the dying warriors pray'd.　　PERCIVAL.

THE next day Luke Somerton, being alone, was seated in anxious meditation upon certain mysteries that he could not in any way clear up. In the midst of these thoughts, however, he was interrupted by a slight sound in the room, and turning, he observed Basil standing within a few paces of him. Calling the youth to him, he inquired his birth and parentage, and how one so delicate in figure and manners could endure the rude scenes and hardships of a soldier's life.

"Alas, sir," answered the youth, "you little know the firm devotion to a cause Basil is capable of. Yes, I could follow him whom I have vowed to serve through danger unto death itself; and happy should I be, if the sacrifice of my life could shield him from the dangers to which he is exposed."

"You are, indeed, a faithful servant," exclaimed Luke, "and it is to be hoped your master appreciates the noble affection you have manifested. And now there is one question you will, perhaps, be able to answer,—in short, I have long desired to know what has become of the long absent Honor Lorimer?"

On hearing that name a flush passed over the countenance of the youth, and after a few moments' hesitation, he hastily replied,—

"I cannot give you any information upon that subject, sir; but this I believe, that her present place of retreat is known only to myself."

"She is happy, no doubt, and she highly deserves to be," replied Luke. "I have been most anxious for an opportunity to express my thanks for the generous attention she bestowed upon me in the hour of need."

"She needs them not, sir," answered the youth, warmly. "Thanks, did you say? Ah! how cold a term! Could you not change it for one she better deserves?"

"Boy! you grow presumptuous!" exclaimed Luke, with more sternness than he usually displayed. "The name of Honor Lorimer should be uttered with respect."

"By me it always shall be," replied Basil; "may the Holy Virgin guide her in her present purpose!"

Having uttered these words, the youth abruptly quitted the apartment, and Luke Somerton was again left to wander in all the mazes and labyrinths of an inextricable mystery. That there was some strange secret yet to be divulged he could not doubt; yet not the slightest clue could he find by which he might hope to discover to what all this tended. For nearly an hour he remained pondering over the various circumstances that had occurred since he left the humble abode of his father, and at length, wearied with conjectures, he was about to rise from his seat, when a deep sigh near him interrupted the silence, and raising his eyes, he beheld a female, closely veiled. Starting from his seat, surprise prevented his utterance for some few moments; he had not observed any females in the house before, nor could he imagine how, or for what purpose, she had gained admission. At length, recovering from his surprise, he approached her with a gesture of profound respect.

"Lady," he exclaimed, "although I am not aware of what has occasioned me the honour of this visit, yet, if I can in aught assist you, command me. Or, perhaps, you have mistaken the apartment; I am a perfect stranger, and have been here but a short time."

The female still kept her veil over her face, but at last sank into a seat; while Luke could perceive from her agitation and audible sobs that she was deeply affected. At length, in broken accents, she exclaimed,—

"Pity me—oh, forgive me! Yet surely you will do so, when you find that you alone have been the cause of my present unhappiness."

"Me!" cried Luke, with astonishment; "good heavens, I know not that we have ever met before. Lady, explain this mystery; you must mistake me for some other, for here I pledge my honour and my faith, that until now we have never met together."

She dropped her veil, and Luke Somerton started back with astonishment when he beheld the features of Basil, but not in male attire, and rid of that dusky hue that had marked the visage of the youthful attendant. The figure now before him presented graces and feminine charms rarely equalled, and impossible to be surpassed; glossy raven hair, confined by strings of costly jewels; the large and brilliant eyes darting rays of bewitching lustre; the high, commanding forehead, slightly aquiline nose, and exquisitely formed mouth, all betrayed a lady of no common rank; conviction flashed over his mind—it must be Honor Lorimer!

How flattering to the vanity of a youth at his age, to find himself loved by one possessing such superior attractions; yet an innate sense of honour and delicacy prevented him from evincing, by his countenance, any elation at the extraordinary discovery he had made. The image of the beauteous Eveline was too indelibly imprinted on his memory; and as, at this period, the fortunes of his family

required to be rescued from the unmerited obloquy that had so long hung over them, he had no place in his bosom for other feelings.

Seating himself beside Honor Lorimer, he took her hand, and, with a chastened, brotherly affection, addressed himself to her with forced composure.

"I should indeed be ungrateful," he exclaimed, "could I forget the kind and unremitting attention you bestowed upon me during my illness, and it would be ill repaying your favour were I not to act with perfect candour. Long before I beheld you, my heart was yielded to another. When I first loved her my prospects in life were far different to what they are at present, and she was placed by fortune so far above me, that I could only hope for some auspicious change in my own prospects. That period seems to be at no great distance, and I may now aspire to the hand of her I have so long worshipped in despair. Deign, then, dearest Honor, to bestow your friendship on me; permit me to consider you in the light of a beloved sister."

He paused—a pallid hue overspread the countenance of Honor Lorimer; her eyes were closed, her head drooped, and her hand was pressed to her heart; yet, through her dark eyelashes, Luke perceived the tears trickling; she clasped her hands, and starting from her seat, stood for a few moments as if buried in thought.

"Mr. Somerton," she at length exclaimed; "it is well—you reject me; I have merited your scorn—I, who have rejected the offers of men who ranked far above yourself. You know not what you have sacrificed—wealth beyond the highest of your ambitious hopes, and love, the most devoted. But mark me! love will turn to hate!—aye, hate the most deadly; and when a woman knows she has a rival, revenge is sweeter far to gratify than love itself. We shall meet again; and she, for whom I am scorned, shall bitterly rue the hour when she crossed my path. Nay, speak not—nor approach; we now part, but not for ever!"

She then passed from the apartment before Luke Somerton could sufficiently recover himself to reply. He reflected whether he should acquaint Arnold with the disguise his sister had assumed; but when he considered again, he recollected that Arnold must be aware of it already. Her avowed passion for him, however, only strengthened his resolution of constancy to Eveline, and he determined, the instant he returned home, to acquaint his father with his passion, and then to throw himself at the feet of his mistress and declare his feelings.

His further thoughts were interrupted by the entrance of Arnold, to whom he related as much of his family affairs as would account for his intended journey; and he strongly advised his young friend, during his absence, to act with caution, and not to embroil himself in any party affair. He should now probably have it in his power to offer him an asylum, and his influence might effectually serve Arnold, provided he had sufficient policy and command of temper not to oppose the English Government.

Somerton then went in search of Terence, and bade him prepare for an immediate journey; that night a letter from the ministry, inclosing an order for his father's recall, was sent to him, and Luke, next morning, accompanied by Terence, left Kilkenny to pursue his homeward journey. The attendant, however, was not to proceed the whole of the way, and leaving him at the village where they had first met, Luke set forward, after promising to call for Terence on his return.

It was evening when Somerton arrived within sight of the cottage where he had passed his childhood. The sun was fast declining, its mellow tints deepening into shade, when two figures were perceptible through the dim twilight; nor did it require a second glance from Luke to discover the forms of his father and mother. The clattering of the horse's hoofs caused them to turn, when they beheld their son throw himself from his steed and fly towards them. His father held him back for a few moments, that he might gaze his fill, and view with parental admiration the changes that absence had wrought in his son, while his mother threw her arms around him, and reclining her head upon his breast, gave vent to all the tender emotions of a mother.

In a few minutes Luke Somerton once more found himself seated with his parents at their humble board, where he had scarcely taken his place, when, drawing from his bosom the mandate of King William the Third, for his father's recall, he placed it before them, and hastily recapitulated the circumstances which had led to so happy an event. Having related all the events that had occurred to him during his absence, with the exception of that part connected with Honor Lorimer, he at last ventured to make inquiries after Sir Richard Bolton and his daughter.

His mother informed him that Eveline had usually visited her every day, and the more she saw of her, the more excellent in every respect did she appear to be; she added also, that Luke was often the theme upon which they discoursed, and that at all times Eveline mentioned him in terms of esteem.

This intelligence was most gratifying to Somerton, but his pleasurable anticipations were damped by finding that Eveline and her father had been for some time in London. A pang thrilled through his heart as he reflected on the numerous rivals he would probably have. However, this he did not even allude to, and after some time, taking leave of his parents, he retired to his chamber, where his conflicting thoughts were soon buried in slumber.

On the following morning they made the necessary arrangements for beginning their journey on the following day. But little preparation was necessary; they had been so faithfully served by their attendant, a young peasant, that, as a reward, they bestowed the cottage and ground upon him. They then proceeded to the village where Terence was waiting the return of his master, and from which place they set forth for the place of their destination. On the second night of their journey they arrived within sight of the camp; the road in several parts was rough and broken, and it was with no little difficulty that they could proceed. At last they reached an outpost, but not being acquainted with the watchword, they were detained by the sentinel, until a party, headed by an officer, coming up, they were passed onward. In the course of half an hour more they arrived near the royal pavilion, when suddenly a light shot up, and it was discovered that the king's tent was in flames

Luke was the first who recovered from his surprise, and throwing himself from the vehicle, he rushed forward, and darting through the burning canvass, was in a moment lost to view.

The whole camp was now in a state of commotion; soldiers crowded from all sides, and the tent was quickly divested of its burning drapery. Luke had been so fortunate as to rescue the queen from the flames; and soon, under the care of her female attendants, she was recovered from the terror into which she had been thrown. But the alarm did not cease here; the fire had doubtless been the work of some incendiary in the camp, and the outposts, now rapidly retreating, giving information that the insurgents were approaching to attack the royalists.

The courage of King William now shone forth; half dressed, with no arms, save his sword, and mounted on horseback, he placed himself at the head of his troops and opposed the rebels who had now approached him. His firm position, and the dauntless appearance of the English, awed the partizans of James, who, having abdicated the throne of England, was now striving to regain it, by stirring up the Irish to rebellion. They retreated to a distance, and were satisfied with watching the progress of the conflagration, which lasted through the greater part of the night. By dawn, however, it was extinguished, and the insurgents, once more disappointed, retired within the walls of the town which they still held possession of.

Sir Philip Somerton had joined the party led on by the king, who could not recognise him during the darkness, but when daylight shone over the field, the monarch discovered by his side his former favourite. Notwithstanding the lapse of years, he recognised him at once, and held out his hand. As Sir Philip pressed it to his lips, he felt his heart bound with delight at being again in favour with his sovereign, whom he had always regarded with love and veneration. The result of this interview was, that Sir Philip had a distinguished command bestowed upon him; nor was Luke forgotten—the queen expressed her gratitude to her preserver, and loaded him with costly presents; she also retained Lady Somerton in her suite.

From this period the situation of the insurgents became more and more desperate, and by and bye they had a more appalling enemy than the English army to cope against. Famine, that direst of calamities, and frequent attendant on war, presented itself in all its horrors; cooped up in their town, and viewing from the walls the constant supplies of provisions that poured into the English camp, their state was truly pitiable; thus, assailed at once by war and hunger, without any prospect of relief, they made frequent sallies, but without success, for the strength of the besiegers' fortifications defied them, and King William patiently waited till famine should compel them to yield.

At length no other alternative remained, and a capitulation was agreed upon. The terms, however, were severe, and strictly enforced, so that the result was a temporary return to the peace which had been so long desired.

*   *   *   *   *

We may now suppose a period of two years to elapse, when we find Sir Philip Somerton in possession of his estates, and Luke about to be united to Eveline.

The disappearance of Arnold since the night of the conflagration in the English camp had caused much surprise to Luke, who regretted his absence exceedingly. Nor was the mystery that hung over the fate of Honor Lorimer cleared up. He often remembered her, and could not help feeling interested for her welfare.

The castle inhabited by Sir Philip Somerton was considered to be almost impregnable. Seated upon an elevated situation, its dark battlements frowned in awful majesty; it was encompassed by a deep moat, and from its lofty towers commanded such a view, that no foe could approach it without being discovered. It had been built at a period when civil war raged with fury, and was admirably calculated, in case of a siege, for sudden sallies, and, even if surprised, afforded numerous places of concealment for its inhabitants.

Winding subterraneous passages, to which there were outlets in different parts of the surrounding forest, and the entrances within the castle so contrived, that, unless perfectly acquainted with the secret, chance would never lead to a discovery. The apartments were wainscotted with oak, dark with age, highly polished, and richly carved; the windows gothic, and admitting a scanty light through their small panes of stained glass.

The family were all seated one evening, when the hoarse murmurs of the rising wind, pattering of large drops of rain, and flashes of lightning at intervals, denoted the coming of a storm of more than ordinary violence. The roaring of the wind increased, the rain fell in torrents, and sheets of intensely vivid lightning illuminated the sky.

At length a peal of thunder shook the castle almost to its foundations, and a crash, as if part of it had been struck by lightning, was quickly succeeded by loud and continued screams along the corridor. Luke and his father sprang from their seats, and, followed by Sir Richard Bolton, who was then at the castle, rushed from the apartment to ascertain the cause of such fearful cries of alarm. Scarcely had they reached the passage when Margaret, the attendant of Eveline, came rushing towards them.

"Oh! save me!—save me!" she wildly exclaimed. "Look! there it is! see, it approaches nearer!"

Turning towards the spot to which she pointed, they saw a figure, clad in a dark mantle; its face being turned towards them, disclosed a visage more resembling a tenant of the tomb: a pale unearthly flame flickered around its forehead, and, with outstretched hand, it seemed to forbid their nearer approach.

Margaret crept closer to her protectors, and clasped the knees of Sir Philip Somerton, while Luke stood gazing at the figure for a few moments, when, rousing himself to action, he hastily moved forward, determined to ascertain whether it was an earthly or a supernatural being, when suddenly it seemed to sink before their eyes, while a loud peal of thunder and a fresh outburst of the tempest followed its disappearance.

All were now involved in darkness, and calling loudly for lights, they examined, with the strictest scrutiny, every niche and panel of the corridor. The floor was also narrowly investigated, in order to satisfy themselves, but neither joining nor trap-door was to be found.

Returning to the apartment, the extraordinary incident furnished conversation for the remainder of the evening, and, before he retired to rest, Sir Philip Somerton gave strict injunctions to the servants to be on the alert, as he could not be persuaded that the singular appearance he had seen was supernatural.

While Eveline was preparing for bed, her attendant, Margaret, was particularly loquacious upon the subject that had filled the whole place with consternation.

"Ah, miss!" she exclaimed, "this is a strange house, and terrible stories they tell of it. Only think, dear lady, that horrible monster, King Richard the Third, stopped here one night, when he and his party were tired with hunting; and it is positively said that his infernal majesty pulled him out of bed, and dragged him, by a great iron chain round his body, along the corridor, flogging him all the way; indeed, some said afterwards, that it was the king, who found one of his hounds in his bedchamber and whipped him out; but old Thomas has assured me that the mark of the devil's foot is burnt into the floor, and he ought to know something about these sights, having lived in the old castle, man and boy, upwards of sixty years."

She would have talked on much longer, had Eveline felt disposed to listen to her rambling narratives, but, being fatigued, she dismissed Margaret and composed herself to rest. Her sleep was far from refreshing; she dreamed that she and Luke were walking in a delightful garden filled with the choicest and most fragrant flowers, when, stooping to pluck a blooming rose, a serpent issued from beneath it, and slowly winding round her, approached towards her face; then suddenly the scaly coat fell off and discovered a human countenance; a fearful convulsion of the earth shook all around, and a yawning chasm separated her from Luke. Then the serpent changed to the figure of a man, masked, and who held a poniard to her breast. She strove to scream; all power to do so was denied her; cold drops stood upon her forehead; she trembled with excessive fright, and, awaking, could not be convinced, till some time afterwards, that all she had witnessed was merely a vision.

Luke Somerton also passed the night in a state of feverish anxiety. He was convinced that some enemy of his family was concealed in the castle, and a thousand plans were revolved in his mind to discover who the intruder was. At the earliest opportunity that offered itself, he, accompanied by Terence, explored every part of the castle to which he could gain access; but all was in vain, for he made no discovery that could in any way throw a light upon the mystery he was so anxious to elucidate.

Wearied with the thoughts that pursued each other through his busy brain, and desirous of forgetting, as much as possible, the events that had occasioned him so much uneasiness, he at length strolled forth from the castle. Scarcely, however, had he proceeded a mile, when he and Terence were startled by a piercing scream that sounded from the forest which they had been approaching.

Immediately afterwards both of them sprang forward to ascertain the cause of this cry of terror, and, striking into a bye-path, they beheld a female supported in the arms of a man, who, on advancing nearer, proved to be no other than Arnold Lorimer.

The two friends recognised each other with joyful surprise, and Luke springing forward discovered that the fainting girl he bore in his arms was Eveline. He started and looked to his friend for an explanation of the mystery.

Arnold then stated that he was on his way to the castle, and when within a short distance, he had suddenly come upon two ruffians, masked and armed, who were bearing away a female wrapped in a cloak. He had immediately drawn his sword and assailed the ruffians, who were forced to turn and defend themselves, but who fled on hearing that other persons were approaching the spot. In their haste, however, they had left behind them a mask and cloak.

As soon as Eveline was sufficiently recovered from the fright into which she had been thrown, she informed her friends that, having taken a book from the library, she had strolled out, and seating herself beside the rivulet, was completely absorbed in the interest of the volume, when she was suddenly lifted from the ground and borne rapidly along. She contrived, however, to throw aside part of the envelope, and screamed for assistance, when by struggling she disengaged herself but fell to the ground, and, from the violence of her agitation, became insensible, until. on recovering, she found herself surrounded by friends. She could not describe the ruffians, but imagined there were more than two.

By the time she had finished her brief narrative they had arrived at the castle, when Luke Somerton, leading Arnold to a chamber where it was not likely they would be disturbed, requested an explanation of the events which had led to his sudden disappearance from the camp, and his unexpected visit to the castle.

"After you left Kilkenny," began Arnold, "there appeared a blank in my existence; there was no one I could call my friend, and I scarcely knew how to employ my time. I took long and frequent rides, and explored the country all round, but hostilities again commencing, I was forced to confine myself within certain limits. I could not take an active part in the siege, nor war against my own countrymen, and Lord Derry, who fully entered into my feelings in that respect, left me at uncontrolled liberty.

"But that which afforded me more serious annoyance than anything else, was the sudden disappearance of Basil, my youthful attendant; and, although I made every inquiry, I could not gain any intelligence respecting him. The hours thus passed on, and I anxiously looked for your return. When that fire broke out in the camp, and the sudden attack of the insurgents took place, I could not remain an idle spectator, and yet I did not know which side to take—love of my country combatting against a sense of honour. Before either of these feelings could obtain ascendancy, I was struck by a bullet, and fell senseless to the ground. At the moment, however, I thought I heard your voice, but it could only have been imaginary.

"I remained in a stupor, and it was long afterwards ere I could bring to recollection the events which had taken place. When I recovered, I found myself in a hut situated amongst the mountains. I glanced round the miserable hovel, and discovered a hag, nearly bent double with age, mumbling over a few lighted sticks, which were under a vessel that seemed to contain some herbs. A burning thirst parched my lips, and with some difficulty I made her understand that I required drink to moisten my parched throat. She hobbled forth, and soon returned, accompanied by a man of venerable aspect: a snowy beard descended to his girdle, and his wrinkled forehead denoted that he had lived beyond the usual number of years allotted to man. He felt my pulse, and taking a small phial from his vest, poured out a few drops of a dark liquid, which, after mixing with some water, he gave me. I drank it, and soon sank into a deep sleep, and the next day found myself so much recovered as to be able to sit up, when the first inquiry I made was respecting the old man to whose kindness I was so deeply indebted.

"The old woman told me that he was called Father Edward, and that he was the universal benefactor in the neighbourhood. Several years since, he had taken possession of a cave at the side of one of the mountains, and formed it into a hermitage. A fountain of the purest water streamed from the rock near his door; his food consisted of the fruit and bread bestowed upon him by the peasantry, as a return for his religious instruction and medical assistance afforded to the people.

"At this juncture the old man entered; his countenance beamed with unaffected pleasure, when he beheld me so far recovered; and he assured me I might be certain of an immediate restoration to health. To my inquiries as to how I had been placed under his care, he said,—

"'That, one dark and stormy night, the trampling of horses outside his cave announced a party of travellers. To their repeated calls he at length appeared, when I was borne into the cave, insensible, by some of the party. From the nature of the wound, he thought it advisable to have me removed to the hut, whither he accompanied me. Those who had brought me then retired, and, as he had taken but little note of them, he could not describe them sufficiently so as to give me any means of discovering who they were.'

"In a few days, I was strong enough to walk to the hermitage, and thither I bent my steps. I entered, and beheld Father Edward just rising from his devotions. He placed me upon a seat hewn out of the rock, and I then repeated to him my thanks for the kindness he had bestowed upon a perfect stranger.

"'You owe me no thanks, my son,' he replied, 'for the religion I follow teaches me to afford assistance to all who may need it.'

"'Yet,' I exclaimed, 'it cannot be denied that my life has been preserved by your care and attention.'

"'It is possible,' answered the old man, solemnly, 'that you may be reserved for the endurance of yet greater trials. You are but just entering on the path of life; but when you have passed through such sorrows as mine, and drained unto the very dregs the bitter portion of adversity, you will then learn to regard life as only a weary pilgrimage to a better world. I perceive, my son, your curiosity is excited; my tale is melancholy, and the sad relation is more than I could bear. During my leisure hours, however, I have sketched the story of my eventful life, and but little more remains to conclude it. Come to me to-morrow, and I will commit it to your hands for perusal.'

"I returned to the hut, and anxiously awaited the following morning, when I hastened to the cave. A gloomy silence reigned round the entrance—the day was cloudy, and all nature seemed to prognosticate that some great evil was at hand. I entered; a lamp, just expiring, stood on the table; I called upon the name of the old man, but received no answer; I passed onwards—stooped over the pallet whereon he lay; I listened for his breathing—all was silent; I brought the light close to his countenance—his eyes were fixed and glazed—his cheek pale and cold—his hands clenched—he was dead! Upon the table lay a heap of papers; I possessed myself of them, and quitted the abode of death. I then acquainted some peasants with what had occurred, and they hastened to bestow the rites of sepulture upon the old man.

"Next day, finding myself able to undertake my journey to Kilkenny, I hired a horse and guide for that city. It was then I became aware of all the changes that had occurred, and after remaining some few months in the city, I left it, to make the best of my way to your father's castle. Of my journey I have nothing particular to relate, but, as you are already aware, I arrived just in time to rescue the lady who, it seems, is shortly to become your wife."

"For which act," exclaimed Luke Somerton, "I can never sufficiently express my gratitude. There is, however, one thing that remains to be done—the ruffians who endeavoured to drag her away must be discovered. The whole world shall be ransacked, but what I will find the villains who sought to perpetrate this great wrong. If they have been but the instrument in the hand of another, I will sift the matter to the very bottom, and then woe be unto the traitor who has sought to betray a female whose hand is already betrothed to another."

A few evenings after this conversation had taken place, Sir Philip Somerton and Luke expressed a curiosity to hear the history of Father Edward; and Arnold, having produced the manuscript, read from its pages the following remarkable narrative.

CHAPTER XXIX.

Beware! to childhood's spirits gay
Is added more than childhood's power;
And you, perchance, may rue the hour
That saw you join his seeming play —GRIFFIN.

"THE only male heir to a noble family and splendid fortune, I looked forward to every enjoyment that this world could afford. England was the place of my nativity, but, under my present assumed name of Father Edward, I must conceal the noble one that my vices would render infamous. My father held a distinguished command in the French wars, at which period I was very young, and being over indulged by my mother, every wish that I expressed was immediately gratified.

"As soon as the intelligence of my father's death reached us, I became aware of my own importance. Unable to restrain my naturally violent temper, my mother, when too late, saw the fatal result of her misapplied indulgence; so that she at last called in to her assistance the chaplain of our family;—had she sought for one more adapted to counteract her views, she could not have done so.

"Cold, selfish, and hypocritical, this man had the consummate art to appear a saint; and so well cloaked were the worldly lusts and fierce passions that struggled in his bosom, that in after times I have remembered his actions with amazement. Methinks even now I see him—his hands crossed upon his breast—his eyes meekly bent downwards—his strongly-marked features displaying calmness and resignation to the will of Heaven.

"When first placed under the discipline of Father John, I resolved to try how far he chose to exercise the power my mother had delegated to him. I was then sixteen years of age, possessing strength and activity, and addicted to hunting and other manly sports. Father John and I soon began to understand each other; what would have been considered slight offences in a layman, but heinous offences in a priest, placed him completely in my power, and then he at once threw off the mask he had assumed. He had now no concealments from me—his real character stood confessed; and although he was a wretch in every respect, and rendered me as great a villain as himself, yet to him I owe a considerable share of worldly knowledge.

"Father John had not always been a priest; in early life he had mixed in the highest circles, from whence he was obliged to fly, and conceal himself under the cowl. He had caused the assassination of a most intimate friend, whose wife he betrayed into a breach of her marriage vows; and yet compunction never seemed to strike him for his misdeeds.

"To a youth like me, who never had strayed much beyond the limits of our own estate, the glowing description he gave of the enjoyments of life excited in my bosom an anxious desire to taste the pleasures so artfully pourtrayed, and without hesitation he promised to prevail on my mother to permit a visit to London, under the plea that it was necessary for the completion of my education. She agreed to the proposal, and as her health would not permit so long a journey, Father John and I travelled by ourselves, and without any material incident we arrived within a short distance of London, when we perceived a party on horseback a little in advance of us; they were laughing loudly, and as we approached soft and feminine tones struck upon my ear with a charm that was till that moment unknown to me.

"The party consisted of two gentlemen and three ladies, with their servants; the road being rather narrow for so many to pass, they drew up on one side, and as I came near the youngest of the ladies I gained a full view of her countenance. Never shall I forget its exquisite beauty—a face oval, blue eyes, and light auburn hair; her lips were small and pouting, and her age apparently about my own. Struck with the lovely vision, I gazed, unheedful of the road, when my horse stumbled, and I, unprepared for such an accident, was flung off.

"The party all crowded round me to render their

assistance. Fortunately the house of Sir Thomas Rivers, the eldest of the strangers, was near, and thither I was borne in a state of insensibility. I soon, however, recovered upon being bled; but having received a severe contusion on the shoulder, I was forced to remain quiet and keep my chamber. I was soon visited by my kind host, and his son Alfred, who conveyed the regrets and inquiries of the ladies for my accident. At last they and my tutor retired, and left me to repose; but rest was denied; the fair vision hovered round my pillow, and I passed a feverish and unrefreshing night.

"Father John visited me early the next morning, and he soon became aware of my feelings; he promised to become my friend and mediator, and to further my views in every respect; what they were at that period I scarcely know myself. He left me for the purpose of making inquiries, and Alfred Rivers visited me in the interim.

"'My father has only just now been made acquainted with your rank, my lord,' he said, 'and he is most happy that his house is honoured with the presence of one whose father he knew and greatly esteemed. But he is here,' cried Alfred, as Sir Thomas entered; who, coming to the side of the couch, took my hand.

"'I knew your father well,' he exclaimed, 'and none regretted his loss more than I did; but he fell in the moment of victory, and his name is honoured by all who remember his worth. You are on your way to London, I understand, where I hope you will frequently visit us, as it is our intention to be there in the course of a short time.'

"'I am indeed most happy in your kindness,' I replied, 'and also make my acknowledgments to your sisters, for the interest they have taken in my behalf,' turning towards Alfred Rivers.

"'To my sister, you mean,' he exclaimed; 'two of the ladies are not related to us. I shall not feel surprised if your heart acknowledges the power of her who caused your accident, for Kate Raymond has excited no slight sensation among the gallants of the day, I assure you. The other lady acts the double part of her governess and companion!'

"Father John now came in, and Sir Thomas and his son retired; my cunning tutor had obtained every intelligence from one of the female attendants, whose assistance he required to prepare a lotion for my bruised shoulder. Kate Raymond, she told him, was an orphan, reared up in the family, and educated with Sir Thomas's children, he making no difference between them. Still there was an air of mystery about the birth of Kate, that caused some to report that she was his natural daughter. He had, several years before, on his return from London, brought her with him; she was then an infant, and he gave strict injunctions to all his household to treat her with the same respect as one of the family; and even if he had not given such directions, from her engaging manners, she would have rendered every one her friend. The servants idolized her; and Alfred Rivers and his sister felt for her the sincerest regard. It was indeed whispered among the domestics that their young master looked upon her with the eye of a lover. But this report had been confined to their own family.

"Father John assured me of his willing co-operation, and laughed at what he sneeringly termed my honourable feelings.

"'No, no,' said he, 'never shackle yourself with the marriage ties; you will obtain her on much easier terms; she will not long resist the allurements you can hold forth. Besides, in any alliance that you form, you must consider high connexion, nor contaminate your blood by a low or base-born marriage.'

"'But,' I said, 'you have not reflected that she is supposed to be prepossessed in favour of Alfred.'

"'Leave that to my management,' he replied; 'trust me I will bring such strong and damning proofs of her infidelity, that he will give her up without a sigh. And how know you,' he exclaimed, 'that his intentions are more honourable than those I have proposed for yourself. At any rate she will benefit by the change—a lord for the son of a knight. Ambition will sway her; and you may depend on it, that before we leave this house she will be yours. I caution you, however, to be coldly polite before all the rest, warm as you please when alone with her. Prudence works much with women. You must, if possible, appear to-morrow; languor interests the sex, and pity is so near akin to love, that the sooner you awaken it the better.'

"He then left me, and I strove to compose myself; my hopes of success in a great measure assisted, and I enjoyed better rest that night. Next day, when dressed, I was supported down stairs, and entered the apartment where the beautiful Kate Raymond was seated. How much Julia Rivers sank in comparison before her, although she, too, was considered beautiful! The two ladies were the only part of the family present. When I was seated, Julia, turning to her companion, said archly:—

"'You have much to answer for, Kate; behold yonder wounded youth, struck to the ground by the magical rays of your beauty. Say, what recompense can you possibly make him?'

"'I know not,' replied the blushing girl; 'all I can offer are my fervent wishes for his recovery.'

"'No, no,' cried the lively Julia, 'he must wear your colours when he goes to court; but what am I saying?—it is too dangerous a request; you will have to accept many a challenge with the competitors for her smiles.'

"'Ladies,' said I, 'be pleased to weave the colours of both, and I pledge myself to wear the scarf, and uphold your beauty and accomplishments against all others.'

"'What say you, Kate?' cried Julia; 'shall we grant his request? But here comes my brother Alfred, and I fear he will not consent to my proposition; he, if I have any penetration, is desirous of a similar favour.'

"Alfred Rivers manifested much pleasure at finding me so much better; while I, with close and guarded observation, watched his manner towards Kate. Had I never beheld her, it is more than probable that Julia would have made an impression; but, as it was, my entire soul was entranced, and I had no thoughts upon any other subject than my own wayward passion.

"Father John and Sir Thomas Rivers returning from a walk, the conversation became general, and I could perceive that my tutor had already made deep inroad in the favour of our host. Whenever I addressed myself to Kate, she replied to me with distant politeness; yet how different I thought was her manner towards Alfred! To him there was an attention, a suppressed tenderness, that sunk deep into my soul. I fancied I could construe Sir Thomas Rivers' manner into a desire that Julia should make an impression on me ; and, to speak without the vanity of youth, there was a flattering approval of all my sentiments upon her lips ; her eyes, also, I could perceive frequently seeking mine, and when our glances met, her cheek was covered with blushes. Yet I felt no more for her than I should for an utter stranger.

"Thus our evenings passed until I was suffi-ciently well to proceed to London. Bidding farewell to our hospitable entertainers, I lingered for a few moments, to catch a parting glance, unobserved by other eyes than Kate's. I failed, and bowing to both ladies, sprung upon my horse, and followed Father John down the venerable avenue.

"We arrived in London, and found apartments prepared for us ; after resting a few days I recommenced my course of studies ; love and ambition seemed now to incite me, and most anxiously did I look forward to the expected arrival of Sir Thomas Rivers.

"With the natural passions of youth, and free from any control, I gave full scope to every indulgence ; and I had strong reasons for believing that scarcely a night elapsed that Father John did not divest himself of his religious garb, and, in the dress of a layman, revel in those pleasures that are forbidden to his class.

"I was returning home one night, rather elevated with wine, when, turning the corner of a street, I heard the clash of swords. It was moonlight, and drawing my weapon, I hastened on to render assistance to the assailed party, when a man rushed past me, and, a short distance further on, I perceived a gentleman supporting a female. With much astonishment I recognised Alfred Rivers, who had arrived in town that evening, and was on his way to me, when a female requested his protec-tion from a person who persisted in following and annoying her.

"Alfred insisted upon the man leaving her, which was immediately replied to by the stranger's unsheathing his sword and attacking him. After a short contest Alfred disarmed him, and he fled, leaving his weapon upon the ground. I took it up, but what was my surprise and consternation to find that it belonged to myself! It then immediately struck me that Father John had been on one of his usual nightly excursions, but, as there was no probability of Alfred's recognising his assailant, I had not much fear on that account ; however, I flung the sword into a garden.

"By this time the female had recovered ; and returning us thanks, she was going towards her home, when Alfred insisted upon seeing her safely

No. 16.

there. I followed, and we left her at the door of an humble habitation, in a narrow and apparently deserted street. Alfred insisted upon my accompanying him home, to which I made no objection, as I was again to behold Kate Raymond.

"Sir Thomas Rivers welcomed me in the most friendly manner, and the two ladies held out their hands. As I touched Kate's, a thrill shot through my frame, and I could scarcely conceal my agitation. The conversation that ensued turned upon the war that was then raging against France; and Alfred, I found, was soon to join his countrymen on the continent, and he and his father endeavoured to persuade me to accompany him; however, I was in no humour for this, and made the best excuse I could.

"I confess the prospect of his absence afforded me much pleasure; I should then have full opportunity to carry into execution my plans relative to Kate Raymond, and no sacrifice seemed too great to gain possession of her. At the mention of Alfred's intention, a pallid hue overspread her countenance, and had she not been seated in the recess of a window, shaded from general observation, her distress would have been manifest.

"After remaining there some time, I made my adieus, and hastening home, immediately sought the chamber of my tutor. I found him lying upon a couch, his arm bandaged. At once I declared my suspicions to him, and he could not deny being the individual, but imprecated curses and vows of vengeance against Alfred Rivers, who, in the defence of the female, had inflicted a severe sword wound in his arm.

"I mentioned having seen the female home, and a smile of demoniac satisfaction passed over his countenance as I named the street. After talking over our future plans, I left him, his wound becomingly exceedingly painful.

"The next day I called upon Alfred, and, although he was a year older than me, yet I soon found he possessed but little discernment, and scarcely knew anything of the world. My first plan was to estrange him from home as much as possible, by introducing him amongst my gay associates, to give him a taste for dissipation. In this I was much assisted by a fear of ridicule, which rendered him all the more easy to bend to my purpose.

"However, I was not always his companion, and the moment I found him engaged in company, I flew to his father's house, where, seated beside Kate Raymond, I seized every opportunity of whispering, in glowing language, my admiration of her surpassing beauty. Julia Rivers was most provokingly in my way, and I had no means of getting rid of her. At last Sir Thomas was seized with a severe fit of illness, and his daughter watched unceasingly by his side. This was an advantage too favourable not to be taken advantage of.

"In a short time I could perceive that Kate was much hurt by the visible neglect of Alfred, and, under the appearance of palliating his errors, I rendered them the more apparent. His father became highly incensed at the dissipated course of life he was pursuing, and often regretted that his son, Alfred, did not follow the excellent example I set him. Alas! he little knew that I was the chief instrument, the exciting cause that urged his too confiding son to his own destruction and loss of character.

"The extravagance and pecuniary difficulties of Alfred increased, and I helped to embarrass him still more; when, with reluctance, he applied to me for assistance in his emergencies, I pretended that it was not in my power. His presence in England was my chief obstacle; for, such is the power of woman's love, that it requires the most convincing proof of her admirer's unworthiness before she can be prevailed upon to believe he is in error.

"In short, I closely followed the treacherous advice of Father John, and no one could boast a more willing coadjutor. Still, I was far from being advanced in the favour of Kate Raymond, and at last I began to fear that she suspected my designs and was preparing to circumvent them.

"One morning, rather earlier than usual, I called, and was waiting for Kate, when a paper, within the leaves of a book, attracted my attention; it was a half-finished letter, in the following words:—

"'DEAR ALFRED,—I have a sad presentiment that fate is unpropitious to us; for your father's, for your sister's, for your own sake and mine, refrain from your present reckless pursuits. I have often feared that Lord —— is not so disinterested in his friendship as he pretends. Beware, then, of treachery; naturally noble-minded and unsuspicious as you are, you may find, when too late, that under the mask of kindness, a base and false friend was concealed.'

"Here it broke off, and Kate just entering, I had scarcely time to return the letter to the place from whence I had taken it. After some unimportant conversation, she requested permission to finish a letter, which proved to be the one I had just been perusing. When it was concluded, she left the room for a few moments, and during her absence I had written the following, and folding it like her's, substituted it instead.

"'DEAREST KATE,—Meet me this night at the usual place of assignation, that we may concert means for our future uninterrupted happiness. Were I inclined to be jealous, I would ask you why Lord —— is so constantly with you, only I know him to be the admirer of another. Farewell, love—fail not.'

"Unsuspicious of what had taken place, she returned to the room, and despatched the letter to Alfred by a confidential servant. I soon afterwards took my leave, and arrived just at the moment that Alfred was puzzled by the letter; perceiving that he knew not what to think of it, I asked him, with an appearance of indifference, what was the matter with him, and proffered my assistance, if he was in need of it. Totally unsuspicious, he let me at once into his confidence; told me the story of his love, and laughed at his former jealousy of me. Then, showing me the letter that had just arrived, he asked my opinion of it. I smiled on perusing it, and replied that it was evidently a mistake, as she had directed to him a letter addressed to herself.

"'Do you know such a person as the writer?' I inquired. 'Have you ever seen the person?'

" 'I have,' he replied; 'and his character is that of an unprincipled libertine. But how came Kate to know him? He does not visit in our circle of acquaintance.'

" 'Egad, my dear fellow,' I exclaimed, ' one would imagine you knew nothing of the sex. Excite a woman's curiosity and she is sure to gratify it.'

" 'I have been a most consummate fool !' cried Alfred; 'it is all my own fault, or, long ere this, she had been mine. My father had no objection to our union, and had it not been for my own reckless folly, I should now be possessed of a prize that I deem inestimable.'

" 'Retrospection will be of little avail, Alfred,' I exclaimed. 'You must now look only to the future; and it would be too galling to let this rival triumph over you. I will be with you to-night; we will seek this person, and depend upon it he will not escape very easily.'

"We then parted, but not till I had promised to meet him in the evening.

"Returning home, I sought Father John, and after stating all that had occurred, solicited his advice. Cool, and unbiassed by youthful feelings, he recommended me to work upon the jealous passions of Alfred, and urge him on to a quarrel with his supposed rival.

" 'No matter,' he added, 'whether he or his adversary falls; in either case you will be rid of Alfred Rivers, and I advise you to take advantage of his absence.'

"On leaving the artful priest I hastened to my appointment with Alfred, who I found in a high state of excitement from the wine he had been drinking. Taking his arm we hurried off to the several taverns I knew to be the haunts of the man who had excited his jealousy. At length we found him just rising from table; and Alfred, without any prelude, rushed forward, and struck him a blow in the face.

"The blood at once rose in the countenance of the person who had been thus assaulted; his eyes darted fire; and in an instant his sword was drawn from his scabbard. They fought for some time without any marked superiority on either side, when the cloak of the imaginary rival (which he had not time to divest himself of) encumbered his right arm, and threw him off his guard; that instant was fatal—Alfred's sword had pierced his heart !

"There were none present but ourselves and the master of the tavern, so that we quitted the spot without any interruption. But Alfred, now brought to a sense of his rashness, was deeply affected; so soon as he reached home his danger became manifest. I advised him to remain beneath his own roof till dark, in the meantime, to make preparations for his departure, and that I would have a vessel in readiness to convey him to the coast of France, and above all things I cautioned him against rendering his sister or Kate unhappy by acquainting them with his proposed departure, stating that I myself would break it to them with the greatest care and circumspection. I then took my departure, and did not return till the evening.

"In the meanwhile I had arranged with the owner of a French fishing smack, and Alfred being in readiness, proceeded with me to the water side, where he embarked. On taking leave, he pressed my hand warmly, and exclaimed,—

" 'To you I commit the care of my sister, and her whom I hold dearer than life itself—my own Kate. Watch over them both as a brother; and be to my poor father, what I, alas! have never been—an affectionate son.'

"We parted, and as I drew my cloak around me, I could not help feeling that I was a villain—one who was about to violate the sacred ties of hospitality.

"On the following day Sir Thomas Rivers became aware of his son's absence, and the reason that had led to it. The affair made a great stir, and the venerable baronet finding that all eyes were directed towards him, deemed it advisable to retire for a time to his country-seat.

"Previous, however, to his quitting London, I determined to put my project into execution, and gain possession of Kate, let the consequences to myself be what they might. My plans, however, were retarded by the unexpected arrival of my mother from the country. Would to Heaven that that period could be blotted entirely from my memory—that I had not lived to behold her! and my hands would not have been stained with human blood—I should not have borne the damning sin of matricide !

"But my narrative now draws to a close; I wanted money to carry on my diabolical schemes; I asked my mother for a sum, when, surprised at the large amount, she required to know for what purpose it was required. I refused to acquaint her; she denied my request, and I flung from her presence.

"Rage had taken entire possession of me; I dared to curse the author of my being—the parent who had watched over my childhood—whose hand had smoothed the pillow of sickness—whose tears had flowed for the pain I had endured. Madly I flew from her, and rushing into the library where my tutor was seated, I stood breathless before him; even he was surprised by the fiendish expression exhibited in my countenance.

" 'Why, what is the matter with you?' he exclaimed; 'what has occurred to ruffle you so much ?'

" 'Ask me not,' I angrily replied, 'for you cannot assist me; gold—accursed gold I want, and must have.'

" 'How know you that I cannot render assistance ?' he demanded; 'you are not aware of my resources.'

" 'My mother has peremptorily refused me,' I replied. 'I am now desperate, and will carry Kate off this very night, or perish in the attempt. Money I must and will have, for those whom I have engaged to assist me are clamorous in their demands for payment.'

" 'Your mother's health has been but indifferent of late,' said the wily villain; 'she is religious, charitable, and as such, fitted for Heaven. Now it is taught that human nature, prone from birth to sin, errs every day; but those who best know your mother, deem her most pure. Before she possibly can fall, were it not right, if we, as humble instruments, obtained her Heavenly happiness ?'

" 'I do not comprehend the import of your

words,' I exclaimed; and yet a vague suspicion thrilled through my mind; a cold shudder ran through my frame, though I scarcely knew for what reason. At length he thrust his hand into his vest, and producing a small phial, he exclaimed,—

"'Behold! this is the elixir of everlasting life —but it is in a future state.'

"I threw myself upon a couch, covering my face with my hands; my brain whirled rapidly; Kate, all lovely as she was, stood in fancy before me; then madly starting up, I grasped the arm of the incarnate fiend.

"'Give it me!' I exclaimed, with desperation.

"'Be patient—be cautious,' he replied. 'We must carefully avoid giving the least suspicion of what is going on. Your mother has sent for medicine to give her rest; her female attendant will be here in a few moments: I shall mix the potion, and before morning dawns you will be the free master of your own actions.'

"I recollect nothing of what passed during the next few hours. At length, however, I stole to my mother's chamber; there was no sound of breathing. I passed the bed—I dared not turn my eyes towards it. I reached the cabinet which contained the accursed gold that I had so fatally coveted; I touched a secret spring—clutched a bag of money, and returned with faltering steps to my apartment. There I threw a cloak over my shoulders, and then proceeded to the spot where the hired ruffians were waiting my commands. Giving them the reward agreed upon, and every instruction how to gain admittance to the house of Sir Thomas Rivers, I saw them depart on their enterprise.

"Long and impatiently did I wait their return. At length, borne in their arms, and rendered senseless by terror, Kate Raymond was placed in my power. Quickly I conveyed her by a secret way to my chamber; the moment I entered, I placed her on a couch; she was still insensible; her eyes were closed, and her cheeks pallid as the hue of death. At last she partially revived, and looking round her, exclaimed wildly,—

"'Where—oh, where am I? for what purpose am I brought here? Ha! my lord, did you rescue me, or are you the ——? But no—no; you cannot be the base employer of those wretches who have torn me from my home.'

"'Dearest Kate,' I exclaimed; 'calm your fears, and behold at your feet one whose heart, whose fortune, is at your command. Oh, be not cruel, then, but yield to me that love which I thus earnestly implore!'

"'Are you indeed so lost to every feeling of honour?' she exclaimed; 'but no—no, it is but a frightful dream; the friend of Alfred Rivers could not act so falsely.'

"'Alfred,' I hoarsely ejaculated, 'shall never call you his.'

"'False, perfidious villain!' she cried, 'I now see thee as thou art—the vile cause of his absence from the land of his birth. But for thee, he would now have been in England, free and innocent. But I will be thy accuser—for even wealth and title shall not save thee from the fearful consequences of thy guilt. Is there no help at hand?' she continued, in a louder tone. 'Ah! I hear

footsteps—save me from this wretch whom I loathe and execrate!' As these latter words were pronounced, Father John entered the room, and she threw herself into his arms, claiming protection and safety.

"'Are you mad, that you have brought her here?' he exclaimed, addressing himself to me; 'I heard the sound of her voice from my study, and you know what awaits you to-morrow.'

"'I do,' I exclaimed, recklessly; 'but whither would you have me convey her?'

"Terrified as she was, Kate Raymond could not utter a word; apparently struck motionless, her eyes upturned to Heaven, her hands clasped, she looked the picture of agonized despair. In truth, had not my tutor and I been so far plunged in guilt, we could not have resisted her earnest appeal to our pity and generosity.

"'You wear the garb of religion,' she said, addressing herself to the monk; 'as you hope for mercy in the world to come, protect me from this danger, and I solemnly promise never to divulge the names of those who now stand before me.'

"'I will myself take care to prevent any mischief,' answered Father John; 'for, when you go from hence, your silence will be secured.'

"'What mean you?' said I, addressing him in a low, subdued tone.

"'Our safety is concerned,' he replied, 'and she must be disposed of. You know the dungeons underneath the gardens; the entrance is unknown to all save me. I will convey her there forthwith. Nay, start not, nor raise objections, for you will find that in this, as in every other instance, I can be paramount.'

"'Never!' cried I. 'I now, when too late, behold thee as a wretch, stained with every mortal crime, but henceforth thou wilt meet me as a deadly foe.'

"Pale, speechless, and nearly fainting, Kate gazed at us with terror, until suddenly a scream so loud and shrill burst from her lips, that never will it quit my memory. Maddening under the disappointment, and determined not to lose her by the monk's interference, I drew a concealed dagger, and with wild impetuosity rushed upon him. I made a plunge at the bosom of the villain—Kate was in his arms—the dagger pierced her heart! The next blow was more true—it struck to the heart of the false friar.

"The weapon fell from my hand—my hair bristled with horror—my feet were rooted to the ground. I stood like an image of mute despair.

"The crimson blood streamed fast from the bosom of the unfortunate Kate Raymond. My tutor had fallen to the ground, he was in the agonies of death; he spoke with extreme difficulty, while slowly raising and supporting himself with one hand, he pointed to the murdered girl.

"'She is my daughter!' he exclaimed. 'I knew it not till this night; fly, or justice will overtake you. I have already spread abroad a rumour of your mother's death.'

"Frantically I rushed from the scene of iniquity; bare-headed as I was, I braved the pitiless storm that was then raging. On reaching the wharf I found a small boat with passengers on the eve of departure. I leaped in without knowing or caring where they were bound; we rowed down the river and were taken on board a trading vessel, and after a rough voyage, I found myself next day an outcast on the French shore.

" Since that period years have rolled away, but those moments of horror are often presented vividly to my imagination. I entered the army, and have courted death in any and every shape ; for a time it eluded me, but at last I fell dangerously wounded.

" Upon recovering, I found, to my surprise, four years had elapsed unconsciously to myself. I had been a maniac—had strayed through the greater part of France—had subsisted on the charity of the humblest peasants. Such was the fate of one who was heir to a title and immense wealth. But after all, my sufferings have been nothing in comparison with the enormity of my crimes. A shameful and ignominious death ought to have been mine, and yet, perhaps, after all, it was the mercy of Heaven that has allowed me ample time to repent the heinous offences of which I have been guilty.

" But to bring my narrative to a close. One evening I found myself, fatigued and overpowered with travel, at the entrance of the cave which has ever since formed my habitation ; there, under the assumed name of Father Edward, I have carefully concealed myself from that world which I have so foully outraged. Yet years of prayer and penitence have failed to calm my feelings, or expiate my heinous offences, nor do I yet dare to look for that pardon which it has been my earnest desire to obtain."

CHAPTER XXX.

But ill he lived, much evil saw,
With men to whom no better law
Nor better life was known;
Deliberately and undeceived,
Those wild men's vices he received,
And gave them back his own.
WORDSWORTH.

For some time all was quiet, and no recurrence of the disturbance took place ; in short, it was nearly forgotten, when one night Luke Somerton was awoke by a slight sound in his chamber, that seemed to him like the quick opening of a sliding panel. He raised himself from his couch, and grasping his sword, which he invariably kept near him, could plainly distinguish a figure wrapped in a dark coloured cloak.

" Speak, or I strike !" he exclaimed, and darting forward, aimed a blow at the apparition, which, however, eluded the blow. He was not superstitious, yet he could not help feeling a more than ordinary sensation, from the mystery in which the circumstance was involved. He searched all round the chamber, striking with his sword in every direction, and at last woke Terence, who lay in the next room. A diligent search was then made for some time without success, but, at last, on crossing the chamber, Luke, perceiving a paper on the ground, picked it up, and, to his amazement, read the following lines :—

" Presumptuous stranger ! dare not to wed Eveline ; if thou do so, thy life will be the forfeit. A power that controls the fate of both forbids the union."

Somerton could scarce believe his senses ; the mysterious paper trembled in his palsied hand ; but by degrees his astonishment gave way to suspicion

that it might be a trick of some secret enemy. In this belief he renewed his search, but without avail, and the morning's dawn found him pacing his chamber with feverish anxiety. The late attempt on Eveline, added to the other extraordinary events that had occurred, made him determined to use every means in his power for the elucidation of the mystery. He sought for Arnold Lorimer, and having acquainted him with what had taken place, it was arranged that they should keep watch that night.

Eveline, conscious of the friendship that existed between Luke Somerton and Arnold, always treated the latter as the confidential associate of her affianced husband. Her beauty struck Arnold as surpassing that of any other woman he had ever beheld. On the other hand, her manner to him was always polite, but distant, for there was an expression of freedom in his countenance such as she had never till then been accustomed to.

One day she strolled into the garden, and was engaged in plucking some beautiful flowers, when a rustling among the shrubs that grew round a small pavilion caused her to start with surprise. In another second, Arnold, emerging from his concealment, suddenly stood before her. Surprised, yet not wishing to appear offended, she timidly inquired why he had not gone to join in a hunting excursion to which Luke had set out early in the morning.

" Nay, wonder not at it," exclaimed Arnold, approaching and taking her hand, " for long have I struggled with a passion that each moment becomes more and more uncontrollable. Nay, do not let pride lour upon thy brow, for in birth and wealth I am at least thine own equal. List to me, lady. The enemies of those I side with are lulled into a feeling of repose ; conquest has made them too secure, and ruin hangs above them ; fly, then, ere it is too late ; I will remove thee to a richer soil—place thee where loveliness like thine will meet the true devotion which is its just meed."

He would have continued in this strain, but waving her hand indignantly, she turned away from him.

" It is, then, as I have often thought," she said, reproachfully. " Luke, too confiding in his friendship, has nourished in his bosom a deadly viper. Begone, ingrate that thou art, and never more approach my presence."

" Hear me, lady, for we will not part thus," exclaimed Arnold ; " it is true Luke has saved my life, yet better had it been sacrificed than that I should now be doomed to drag on a wearisome existence. You must and shall be mine ; aye, and preserve strict silence, or your lover—my rival's life shall be the forfeit !"

Overcome by her terror, and the threats which had been uttered, Eveline sank, fainting, upon a seat. In a few moments, however, steps were heard approaching, and the well-known voice of Luke calling upon her, restored her to recollection. She endeavoured to conceal her agitation, but could not entirely succeed, and Somerton, when he came up, surprised at finding her in company with Arnold, hastened forward, and eagerly demanded the cause of her trepidation.

" Alas !" cried Arnold, with affected concern, " the young lady requested a narration of the dangers you have encountered, and, perhaps, as I too minutely described them, her terror became insupportable."

Eveline darted a glance of scorn at Arnold, which, however, was not observed by her lover, and, supporting herself on his arm, they together quitted the garden. The other gazed after them so long as they remained in view, and, muttering vows of deep and deadly revenge, rushed from the place to form plans by which he might carry out his design,

The maiden soon forgot the bold intrusion of Arnold, and, when they met again that evening, her countenance only betrayed a cold and distant expression. Luke did not remark any particular change, and all passed on as usual, nor did they receive any further interruption from the mysterious intruder. But, alas! the happiness they enjoyed was not of long duration.

One morning they waited longer than usual for Lady Somerton's appearance at the breakfast-table; no suspicion of evil, however, had crossed their minds, when suddenly a female attendant rushed into the room, and rapidly exclaimed to Luke,—

"For Heaven's sake, sir, hasten to your mother! She is sick—sick, I fear, even unto death!"

Luke started from his seat, and hastened to the apartment, where he found his father plunged in the deepest affliction, seated beside the couch on which lay all that remained of his unfortunate parent. Some of the female servants were on their knees round the couch, whilst the surgeon, who had been called in, was watching a vein which he had opened without effect.

Lady Somerton's features, always calm and placid, now presented in death a striking difference. They wore an expression of mingled surprise and horror. When Sir Philip Somerton had entered the room, he found her seated in a chair, her hands upraised as if in supplication, but death had already seized upon its victim.

As soon as possible, Luke conducted his grief-stricken parent from the chamber of death, and, leaving him with the chaplain in the library, he hastened with all speed to make inquiries after Eveline. She, however, had been led to her chamber, where she was plunged in sorrow for the irreparable loss which had occurred. Lady Somerton had been to her as a tender mother. Even Sir Richard Bolton participated in the general grief, for, although selfish in matters connected with worldly affairs, yet he could feel when the approach of death was made so manifest.

Where all had been gaiety and happiness, now reigned deep gloom and melancholy silence. For the present all preparation for the nuptials were put a stop to, and Luke was compelled to endure, with what resignation he could, the postponement of his happiness.

The chapel, which had been prepared for his bridal, now served for the solemn ceremony of his mother's funeral, and, as she was consigned into the family vault, he could not avoid—in fact, did not attempt to repress the tears that flowed for her memory. Afterwards, when he and Eveline met, his mother's name was not mentioned, for she feared to open afresh the wounds that were scarcely healed, and Luke could not think of her without sadness and regret.

The chaplain was now continually closeted with Sir Philip Somerton, and the result of his advice was quickly apparent. As soon as he was recovered from his illness, he declared his intention of retiring into the monastery to which the chaplain belonged, and there, secluded from the world, to prepare himself for that change which he felt assured would ere long take place.

Luke and Sir Richard Bolton endeavoured to prevail on him to abandon this purpose, but the resolution he had formed was invincible. In deference to them, however, he postponed putting his plan into execution till after he had witnessed the marriage of his son and Eveline.

Arnold Lorimer had not ventured to urge his suit since the period when he had met so unexpected a rebuff; yet an observer might have discovered a dark malignant expression in his countenance whenever he glanced at her. She, on the other hand, was well aware of the fatal consequences that would follow if Luke should ascertain the baseness of his pretended friend, and well the latter knew that he owed his safety to her silence. Not but that he possessed sufficient courage to scorn any danger he might be threatened with; yet he could not forget that he owed his life as well as his present asylum to Luke Somerton.

In the course of two or three weeks, everything at the castle began to assume its wonted appearance; still the death of Lady Somerton had left a melancholy void that was felt by everybody, and Sir Philip looked forward impatiently to the period when he should see no further obstacles to his retiring from the world. At length this wish, together with an earnest desire for his son's happiness, determined him to urge the speedy celebration of the nuptials which had been deferred.

At length arrived the auspicious morning that was to give to Luke the possession of that treasure which he had so long sought. Sir Philip Somerton had given intimation of the event to the neighbouring nobility; and on the morning of the ceremony the courtyard was crowded with the retinues of the different visitors, and there was scarcely a chamber in the spacious edifice unoccupied. On the green, the peasantry celebrated their rustic games with all the mirth inspired by the joyous occasion that had assembled them together. Some danced, some played music; the young romped merrily, and the old seated themselves a little aloof, where they could watch all that was going on without being in the way.

By-and-bye the chapel was filled with company, who formed lines on each side the principal aisle. Luke and his bride, attended by Sir Philip Somerton and Sir Richard Bolton, entered; the ceremony proceeded, and the chaplain was bestowing the final blessing, when an arrow, evidently directed at Eveline, grazed her side, and stood quivering in the altar; and a shield, belonging to the statue of an armed knight, fell down with a heavy crash, and rolled to the feet of the bridegroom.

Instantly a cry was raised of "Treachery!" "Close the doors!" "Search the chapel!"

It was some few minutes ere Eveline recovered from the terror into which she had been thrown; she was then led from the chapel to the grand hall, and for the remainder of the day the occurrences of the morning furnished ample food for conversation and remark.

The instant the nuptial ceremony was over, Arnold hastened out of the building, and, repairing to the darkest recesses of the forest, gave free vent to the violence of his passion. Curses the most deep and deadly trembled on his lips ; his hands were clenched—his eyes fixed upon the ground, when a rustling noise at no great distance off aroused his attention, and a masked figure stood before him, a bow in one hand and a quiver of arrows in the other.

"How fares it with thee now, Arnold?" exclaimed the mysterious intruder ; "so, all thy hopes are fled, and thy rival possesses the prize which should have been thine ;—aye, I say should, for one there is who would yield worlds to separate them. But Eveline's doom is sealed. Curse on this trembling hand, or my arrow would, not long since, have found its way to her heart. We are both disap-pointed, Arnold, but, mark me, we will both be satisfied, if vengeance, deep and deadly, can be gratifying."

Arnold Lorimer stood transfixed with astonish-ment ; he passed his hand across his eyes to ascer-tain whether it was a vision. He looked again— no figure was before him. Had it dissolved into air, or sunk into the earth? He examined every bush and thicket, but without effect.

At length, returning to the castle, he entered the banquetting chamber, where, surrounded by the noble and the gay, he beheld his fortunate rival, and that lovely and innocent being who had that day bestowed upon him her hand. However, suppressing the evil passion that combatted within him, and assuming a pleased and friendly aspect, he advanced to offer his congratulations.

"Believe me, dear Arnold," exclaimed Luke, as he took his offered hand, "that, next to Eveline and my father, you hold the highest place in my esteem. My fair bride, too, I am assured, feels the truest friendship for you."

Scarcely daring to trust a glance at Eveline, he at last raised his eyes ; and when he beheld her pure, confiding innocence of aspect, he was almost shaken from his purpose ; but the evil one con-quered, and he made a secret vow to blight the happiness they so fondly anticipated.

The festivities continued at the castle for several days. At last, the guests by degrees returned to their different homes, and Luke was left to the calm enjoyment of uninterrupted happiness with his beauteous bride.

Arnold Lorimer again mixed in society, and Luke was delighted at perceiving the gloom which had hung over his spirits gradually pass away. But this change lasted not for any long time, for, ere many days had elapsed, he gave an intimation that in the course of a short time he should take his departure from the castle. The truth is, he still nourished an unholy flame within his breast ; and often was he on the point of making another declaration of his love, but from the affection that existed between the bride and bridegroom, he could see but slender hopes of success. At length, his passion changed to revenge, and he determined no longer to hesitate as to what step he should pursue.

We may now pass over an interval of nearly twelve months, at the end of which period Eveline gave birth to a son. Flying to her chamber, Luke knelt beside her, and with unutterable joy found that all danger was at an end. But, alas! how fleeting was his happiness ! for, within a few days, how large was the share of bitter grief that fell upon the hapless Luke Somerton !

On the evening in question, loud shrieks were heard from the chamber occupied by Eveline, and when her husband rushed in, he found her nearly insensible—the nurse in a strong fainting fit, and the child nowhere to be seen. When, at length, the female attendant came to herself, she stated that, having fallen asleep, she was suddenly awoke by cries from her mistress, who, when she went to render her aid, she found suffering from the most poignant agony and grief, for the infant had been conveyed away nobody knew how or whither. The unfortunate husband was overpowered by this se-vere blow, and, as if fate had not yet done its worst, Eveline expired a few hours after it had been ascer-tained that her child was nowhere to be found.

Reckless as to the misery of his friend, Arnold secretly exulted at the blighted happiness which he thus witnessed. Of this, however, Luke was unconscious, for affliction had bowed down his spirit, and he was now lying under the influence of a raging fever.

One evening whilst he was tossing uneasily upon his bed, a strain of music stole upon his ear ; it gradually grew louder, until it seemed to be within the chamber in which he was lying ; he started up ; a female form, robed in white, stood near the couch ; it was veiled, but the form resembled that of the lost Eveline. His senses were entranced ; with clasped hands he gazed upon the vision ; it receded from him ; he started from the couch to clasp it in his arms, but it instantly vanished. Overcome with emotion, he sank upon the floor, where he remained in a state of insensibility till discovered next morn-ing by the faithful Terence.

Upon recovering from this state of torpor, he perceived Arnold Lorimer seated beside him, and his faithful valet in anxious attendance. At the moment he opened his eyes, the latter flew to the bedside, and falling upon his knees, bedewed the hand of his master with tears of joy for his recovery.

From this time forward Luke acquired strength, but it was many days ere those about him could venture to speak of the dreadful catastrophe which had produced such fatal results. As soon as Arnold thought he had sufficient strength to bear the shock, he informed him of the discovery of his infant's body, which had been found floating in some water near the castle. Upon Luke's inquiry what had become of the child, he was told that it had been interred with its mother during his illness.

Thus heavily afflicted, Luke Somerton deter-mined to travel ; and, by visiting foreign climes, wear away the remembrance of those miseries which had so deeply afflicted him. But there were other troubles awaiting him, of which he little dreamed.

It was so long a time since Luke had paid his respects at court, and he was so partial to retire-ment, that his solicitation to be excused attending excited suspicions in the minds of the sovereign, who, through some secret channel, had become aware of the story of Arnold Lorimer, and that he, although a rebel, had been for some time residing with Luke. This friendship for one of the procribed, was a heinous offence in the eyes of the monarch, and he dispatched an order for the confiscation of his estates, and the close imprisonment of Luke Somerton and Arnold Lorimer.

Fortunately Terence had been at a neighbouring village, and was on his return home, when he fell in with the party on their way to the castle. From their expressions and inquiries as to the road, he suspected the nature of their business, and directing them in a contrary path, he took the nearest way home ; and, hastening to his master, acquainted him with what had taken place.

Fully aware that the innocence of his intentions would not shield him whilst this prejudice existed, Luke resolved upon retiring to some other country, and, as he had purposed travelling, it was only hastening the period of his departure. He had arranged for Arnold and Terence to accompany him, and was much disappointed and surprised, when the former declined.

" I would accompany you," said Arnold, " but one object so completely binds me to this country, that I cannot on any consideration leave it. You need feel no sort of fear for me ; I am perfectly aware, and will immediately assume a disguise that they cannot penetrate. Farewell, Luke ; when next we meet I trust it will be under far happier auspices."

So saying, he coldly extended his hand, and presently afterwards quitted the room.

Luke Somerton had scarcely time to reflect upon the peculiar manner of Arnold towards him, when Terence returned, ready equipped for their sudden journey. The horses were ready saddled, and Luke, having secured his money and jewels, summoned the steward, whom he informed that urgent business required his immediate absence, and, as it was uncertain when he should return, the care of the castle would, for a period, devolve upon him.

He then hurried out, and mounting their horses, he and Terence were soon at a considerable distance from the danger they were fleeing to avoid. For several days they continued their journey with little intermission, when, upon arriving at a seaport town, they embarked on board a vessel that was on the point of sailing, and after a quick passage reached Lisbon, where they took a lodging in an obscure and retired street.

A few evenings after his arrival, Luke, to wile away the time which now hung so heavily, strolled into a tavern, where he had been seated no great while when a loud and angry discussion in the next room attracted his attention ; it appeared to be an argument as to the merits of a naval expedition that was preparing to sail from the Tagus, one party being in favour of the object in view, and the other declaring that it was a mere waste of the public money. Luke, who was already tired of the monotonous life he was leading, immediately resolved to offer his services in this expedition, and having made a few inquiries of the host, he gathered sufficient information to enable him to put matters in progress. In short, there was not the slightest impediment in the way ; he, under the assumed name of Deville, accompanied by Terence, went on board the vessel, and a few hours afterwards they were sailing towards their new place of destination.

We must now return to the Irish rebels, who, having secretly assembled, and consulted on the best and most advisable means of retaliating upon the victorious English, proposed fitting out a number of piratical vessels to scour the seas, and attack and capture all merchant ships that might happen to fall in their way.

Foremost among these rebels was Arnold Lorimer ; he possessed jewels to a considerable amount, which being disposed of, he fitted out and equipped a vessel which, for size and armament, seemed well adapted for the purpose required.

Arnold was now in the prime of life, bold, active, formed for the toils of war, and burning with a desire to signalize himself against those whom he regarded as his deadliest foes. He determined to show no lenity to those who fell into his power ; and as his vessel sailed from the port, on her first cruize, he stood upon the stern, and proudly gazed upon the force under his command. The crew consisted of one hundred and fifty men, and in every respect the vessel was more than a match for any other of her own size.

For several days they sailed about without meeting anything to attack ; and, amongst such an assemblage of adventurers, no better than banditti, who had all separate interests to influence them, this want of success in their first enterprize was rather dispiriting.

Seven days had elapsed, and their vessel lay upon the calm bosom of the sea, with but little motion ; their sails were lowered, and the men gave themselves up to scenes of disorder and intemperance. At length, " A sail ! a sail !" was shouted by one of the crew ; the wine-cup was thrown aside ; sails hoisted, and soon they approached the strange vessel which had caused all this commotion among them.

Arnold, surrounded by some of the most daring of the crew, stood prepared for the assault, which was momentarily expected. The strange vessel was of English rig, but her defective cordage and damaged sails showed that she must lately have suffered from a severe tempest ; her hull also was much damaged, and the crew, who stood crowding on her deck, appeared haggard and toil-worn. The piratical vessel ran athwart her bows, passed her, and then, running up, ranged close alongside of her.

" Whence come you, and to what country do you belong ?" demanded Arnold Lorimer.

" Who is it that questions me ?" asked a man of bold and noble aspect. " Say, by what right do you inquire ?"

" By right of force," answered Arnold ; " we are the strongest, and demand reply."

" What if we refuse ?"

" Why, then a broadside will, perhaps, teach you the folly of this vain resistance."

The deck of the strange vessel was now cleared for action, but the weak and sickly appearance of the men did not promise much effectual resistance. Arnold now ordered preparations to be made for boarding, and in a short time the pirates stood upon the deck of the vessel they had thus boldly challenged. The struggle that ensued was short and decisive ; the English, after considerable slaughter, were compelled to yield ; when Arnold Lorimer, advancing towards the commander of the ship, said,—

"It is the fortune of war, sir;—to-morrow my fate may be similar to your own. However, you may rest satisfied that you and your crew shall be well treated till the ransom for your release arrives."

The English captain could not avoid showing how deeply mortified he was by the defeat he had sustained : but, compelled to submit to his hard fate, he merely replied, that he trusted to the generosity of his enemies, whom, in his own thoughts, he deeply regretted to be rebels.

Some of the pirates who had gone below to examine the cargo of their prize, returned with a man whom they had found chained and a prisoner in a small and dark cabin. When they brought him upon deck the English captain could not control his vexation, while the unfortunate being gazed on him with a smile of bitterness and contempt.

"Why hast thou been made a prisoner?" demanded Arnold of the unhappy being before him. "Art thou a robber or a murderer?"

"Neither," answered the other. "I have ever upheld my good faith to man—fought and bled for my country and my king—risked life and fortune —and what has been my reward? Behold these fetters—these white hairs—look at this care-worn visage, and then say if I merit a fate like this."

Struck with these words, and the tone with which

they were expressed, Arnold desired the old man's chains to be removed, and then addressing his crew, he said,—

"My brave fellows, I can judge your feelings by my own ; they speak the warmest pity for this oppressed and falsely-accused man. Though our hands are raised against his nation, we should gain but little by his captivity—old man, you and your companions are free."

He then sent for refreshments from his own vessel, and having paid the most honourable attention to the venerable captive, he restored him to the command of his vessel, and shortly afterwards they parted company, each setting sail towards his own destination.

The weather, which, for the last few days, had been exceedingly calm, now assumed a threatening aspect ; the sea birds screamed wildly as they swiftly flew around the vessel, and the dark scud was impelled rapidly through the sky. The pirates, well acquainted with these symptoms of an approaching tempest, prepared for the gale ; and as the wind was blowing towards the shore, they took in all sails, and kept up a most strict watch lest they should get among the breakers, which they could perceive at no great distance off. At length, finding a place well suited for their purpose, they cast anchor, and early next morning, having discovered a strange sail, they once more weighed anchor, and gave chace. She proved to be a merchant vessel, laden with a variety of commodities, and she was captured after some little resistance and the slaughter of part of her crew.

Amongst the passengers on board her was one, who, offering resistance to the pirates, had nearly fallen a victim to their fury, when a little girl, springing forward, clung to his knees, and by the most piteous exclamations and gestures, implored the mercy of the assailants. Arnold, upon entering the prize, and perceiving the old man's danger, directed his own people to desist, and ordered the prisoner to be brought before him.

"Whence come you, stranger?" he asked; "declare your name fearlessly, and say why you

No. 17.

offered resistance, which it was evident could avail you nothing?"

"Pirate," answered the old man, haughtily, "it was not for myself I contended against your superior numbers, nor for the paltry gold that lies within this casket. I sought to protect my only child from the captivity which would be far worse to her than death itself. But fortune has deserted us, and I resign myself to my fate."

Then folding his arms, he stood, seemingly indifferent, while the pirates were dividing their spoil.

The captives having been removed on board the victorious vessel, and the prize completely stripped, they set her on fire, and left her to drift wherever the wind and tide might carry her. A wish was now generally expressed by the crew to have a short respite from their toils, and as Arnold's own inclinations pointed the same way, they directed their course homewards, and in the course of a few days reached the coast of Ireland.

But Arnold, however, was far from being happy, though he endeavoured to appear so in the presence of others. Often would he pace with hurried steps the walks of his garden, or, throwing himself upon the ground, give vent to his agonized feelings; then, suddenly rising, issue orders for his band to prepare for another cruise, and hastening on board, in the noise and tumult of his departure, strive to recover his customary ease and self-possession.

He had no confidant—none who were aware of the cause that plunged him into these fits of melancholy. He was alone in the world—wrapped up within himself—a mysterious, isolated being; brave to desperation in action—mild, and apparently calm in peace.

There was one, however, who could mould him as he pleased—who addressed him in tones of freedom that none others dared venture upon, and of whom he appeared to stand in the greatest awe—that one was Denzil, the stranger who had been taken prisoner. Arnold had never treated him as a captive. His years, his venerable aspect, brought to the mind of the pirate the remembrance of his own father; and he could not treat with harshness one for whom he felt a filial respect.

It is a singular fact, that in some of the most recklessly cruel minds we frequently find gleams of virtue, which probably their course of life has prevented ever shining forth sufficiently to be moulded and rendered subservient. The child, too, who had been made captive with Denzil, was reared with the tenderest care. Arnold, when he sailed on any of his cruises, left strict injunctions for every respect and attention to be shown his prisoners, but at the same time they were not to be allowed to go beyond certain prescribed limits.

CHAPTER XXXI.

Then is not youth, as Fancy tells,
Life's summer prime of joy?
Ah, no! for hopes too long delayed,
And feeling blasted or betrayed,
The fabled bliss destroy.   SOUTHEY.

THE course of our narrative now requires that we should change the scene of action to Granville, a small town in the kingdom of France. The night to which we desire to draw the reader's attention was stormy and dark, the rain fell in torrents, while, at quick intervals, the vivid flashes of lightning served to guide through the narrow streets a man well protected from the fury of the elements, by his ample cloak and broad-brimmed hat.

In person he was tall and commanding, his form athletic; and although a gloom sometimes passed over his countenance, there was a certain glance in his keen, dark eye, that would excite interest in his behalf, even in the mind of a stranger. From the boots and spurs that he wore, it was evident that he had just come off a journey.

By degrees the storm died away, and the moon, which had hitherto been concealed, burst forth, and gave sufficient light to guide him towards the place to which he was making his way. Continuing his route, he presently afterwards turned down a narrow street that branched off from the main one, when a female suddenly made her appearance, and with extreme difficulty tottered towards him.

"Oh, save him!" she cried, seizing the arm of the astonished stranger—"save him ere it is too late. Quick, I implore you, ere it is too late. He has not tasted food these two days, and perishes with want and ——"

Here excessive weakness overpowered her. She sunk into his arms; her head fell back; her dark hair, wet with the rain, hung cold and disordered down her neck. Her supporter gazed upon her, and started with horror and remorse; for she who now lay senseless in his arms, had once been the dearest object of his affections. Young, beautiful, and, alas! too confiding, he had sought, gained, and at length deserted her.

Yet she spoke of one perishing with want and hunger. Perhaps a child of hers—his own—dying for want, like its unfortunate mother! He looked upon her countenance. None but himself could have recognized the once beauteous Lucille in the insensible form he now clasped in his arms.

A light faintly flashed from a half-open door, affording him some hopes of a place of shelter being at hand. He called, and in a short time saw an old woman approaching him, and cautiously shrouding with one hand the light which she carried in the other.

"Who is it that calls, and what is wanted?" asked the dame, in a voice of terror.

"Fear not, my good woman, but come quickly hither," replied the stranger. "Speed, in Heaven's name—speed! and I will amply reward you."

"Alas!" cried the old woman, who had by this time come up, "the poor thing is gone as well as her poor boy. Had she taken my advice, she would ——"

"Cease, cease, woman," interrupted the stranger, sternly. "Conduct me to the place where her child is, and let me lay her in a chamber."

"Ay, ay," muttered the old woman. "She would have had a fine one of her own, if she would but have taken my advice."

Carrying the inanimate form of Lucille in his arms, and conducted by the old woman, he entered a narrow doorway, and ascending a flight of stone steps, entered a large and dilapidated chamber. Cold damps covered the walls; the windows were without any protection from the inclemency of the weather, while a half-expiring faggot smouldered dimly on the hearth. A heap of old rags collected in one corner formed a miserable bed, and thither the stranger bore the corpse of the hapless woman who had just expired in his arms. He was on the point of laying her upon it when he heard a faint cry, and beheld, nestling before him, a fair and beautiful child. One hand was thrown above its head, and the other was placed between its lips, as if to lull the horrible cravings of hunger.

"Alas, my child!" groaned the stranger, "what a villain have I been to her who brought thee into this world of pain and misery."

Then gently laying down the unconscious form of poor Lucille, he lifted the child in his arms, and, throwing off his cloak, wrapped up the infant, to afford it that warmth for which it seemed to be on the point of perishing. The richness of his attire afforded a subject of astonishment to the old woman, who, taking from him a purse of gold, proceeded immediately to procure such necessaries as were most required at the moment.

By degrees the attentions bestowed by the stranger seemed to revive the nearly expiring child. Opening its dark blue eyes, it gazed upon him for some moments, then faintly raising its head, called for its mother. Long and ardently did the traveller gaze upon the child, until he became affected even unto tears.

Soon afterwards the old woman returned with a basketfull of refreshments; and having given the child some warm bread and wine, which threw it into a deep sleep, the stranger once more wrapped it in his cloak, and telling the woman that he would make arrangements the following day for the interment of her deceased lodger, he directed his steps to the principal inn, where, upon arriving, he gave the infant in charge of his servant, and directed that it should be conveyed to the chamber next the one he himself occupied. In a short time afterwards he retired to his own apartment, where, in loneliness and bitterness of heart, he gave way to the poignancy of his feelings.

Sir Edmund de Lancy, as he paced his chamber, thought over the days when she whom he had that night seen breathe her last, had been the admiration of all and the envy of many. Brought up in seclusion, uncontaminated by the vices of the age, and devotedly attached to him who was her first love, he thought himself happy in having the entire possession of her heart.

Chance had led to their first acquaintance; in humble guise he had sought and gained her regard; nor was it to be subsequently increased by the riches and splendour with which she was surrounded, when it was ultimately discovered that her seemingly humble lover was the wealthy and powerful baronet, Sir Edmund de Lancy. Yet a pang often thrilled through her heart as she reflected that all prospect of being his by the holy bonds of wedlock were now for ever blasted—the daughter of a peasant would never presume to aspire to an union so far above her.

She was, however, now doomed to meet the severest of trials. De Lancy saw the Lady Celia Montrose. She was of rank equal to his own. He thought not of the anguish he was about to inflict on the unfortunate Lucille, who, long neglected by him, was now scarcely remembered. He wooed the wealthy heiress, and was accepted.

Lucille, although the daughter of a peasant, had a woman's pride—a woman's feelings. She quitted the castle of her betrayer, and fled into another country, where, in sorrow and shame, she give birth to a son. Yet she still regarded her seducer with tenderness; and as she hung over her fair child, she traced in its infant features the lineaments of its heartless father. It grew, she reared it tenderly, laboured for her own and its support, while her betrayer, in the arms of another, forgot the vows with which he had brought her to the lowest depths of misery.

In a very short time after their marriage his wife died, without leaving him any issue. In a few weeks after which event, he left his native land, to journey on a secret mission; in the prosecution of which he arrived, as we have seen, in the town of Granville. What, then, must have been his surprise at discovering the dying Lucille and her child! A kindly feeling found its way to his heart as he gazed upon his offspring; and he resolved to have his newly discovered son conveyed, by a trusty servant, to his mansion, from which he had set out a few days previously.

Early on the following morning he hastened to the miserable hovel where he had left all that remained of his once beautiful Lucille. He entered the chamber, approached the corpse, and gazed upon those features now sadly changed, but once so exquisitely beautiful. He thought of that evening when, in the rustic arbour of her father's garden, she first listened to his insidious vows of love—first owned that he was the possessor of her heart, and placed her hand in his, with these confiding words:—

"Take, it, Edmund; for though thou art poor and humble as myself, yet what is wealth and rank without affection?"

Passing the chamber of death with hurried steps, he awaited with impatience the arrival of the old woman, that he might make more minute inquiries respecting the hapless female whose fate he so bitterly deplored. At last he heard her as she ascended the stairs, and no sooner did she perceive him, than, uttering an exclamation of welcome, she exclaimed,—

"Oh, sir, you are welcome—most welcome. I am glad you are here, for, Heaven help me, a poor lone woman. When you left last night, I went away too; not that I was afraid of that poor dead creature—no, no—not I, indeed; but then you know, sir, there is something very awful in being left alone with a corpse. As for poor Lucille, she was as quiet a soul as you could find; indeed, too quiet, I fancied—always taking care of her child, and sometimes when I came in I found her crying. 'Why, Lucille, my girl,' I would say to her, 'what do you make your eyes so red for? Is not our landlord there, who would do anything for you, if you would but agree to the terms he has proposed?' But the poor creature, sir, would never listen to me till she was taken ill, and then what little money she had went; and you know, sir, a poor lone woman like me must take care of herself, so that, however my heart might be inclined that way, I had not the power to assist her."

"My good woman," said De Lancy, "it is too late to talk of that now. But, tell me, did she never see any person, or receive any letters?"

"Never, sir," answered the dame; "in this little

box of hers, amongst other things, is a letter, which I know to be her writing, because, on one occasion, when she was ill, she told me so ; it is directed to some great man, though I cannot tell how she came to know him."

"Where is the letter? Shew it me," exclaimed De Lancy, with impatience.

"It is here, sir," answered the old woman, who, after having rummaged the box, found the letter, and presented it to him.

He eagerly snatched the letter, which was directed to him, and was dated at the period when she fled from the castle. The epistle ran in the following words :—

"I intended, but cannot upbraid you for the past —no, I have loved you too well, and ever shall continue to do so, however great my sufferings may be. Yet, for your own sake, we must part. Your bride must not be offended by the sight of Lucille's offspring. Farewell, Edmund, we shall meet in another and a better world—in this, never again. The past shall be pardoned, and all I ask in return is that you will sometimes think with kindness of your long-suffering and heart-broken

"LUCILLE."

Sinking upon his knees, the once proud but now deeply humiliated De Lancy solemnly vowed, before Heaven, to be the future protector of the lost Lucille's child.

"Ay, ay," muttered the old woman, "that was all the poor soul was anxious about ; she had no other thought nor care but for her poor little Reginald. I'm sure the promise you have just made is a great comfort to me, for what could a poor old woman like me have done for the child, when I scarcely know how to get one meal in the course of a day."

De Lancy, after a few moments' consideration, gave the old woman a further sum of money, and directed her to have all things arranged for the funeral, promising that he would himself follow it to its last resting-place. Then, returning to the inn, he found that his servant had taken such good care of little Reginald, that he already appeared to be quite a different being—proper food and a good night's rest having made a most material change for the better. But the poor little fellow was, nevertheless, restless, and repeatedly called for his mother. How those words pained the feelings of De Lancy.

"Rest satisfied, my boy," he said, taking Reginald upon his knee ; "your mother is gone a long, long journey, and she has asked me to take you where you shall have fine horses to ride, and wear a sword when you are old enough."

"And when shall I be old enough ?" asked the child, eagerly ; "give me a sword now, for I could use it, so that it was not so large a one as that you wear."

Towards evening, again intrusting the child to the care of his servant, De Lancy retraced his steps towards the place where lay the body of the hapless Lucille.

Wrapped in his cloak, and his countenance shaded from observation, the baronet, plunged in gloomy silence, followed the bearers of the corpse ; as he stood by the grave, and saw the cold earth heaped upon her who had once listened confidingly to his vows, and felt happy in his smiles, he shud-

dered, and made a solemn vow to Heaven to watch over her motherless child, and guard him, as far as possible, from future ills.

The last melancholy rites having been solemnized, he returned to his hotel, and the next morning he set forth, accompanied by little Reginald, for his own castle. On arriving there, however, he was much at a loss as to how he should act with respect to the child. Intending that he should receive an education to qualify him for the court or camp, he yet determined to conceal their relationship, even from Reginald himself ; and he was one day debating in his own mind how to arrange matters for the best, when a servant announced a visitor, and the Baron Heinbach immediately afterwards entered the room.

"How, now, Sir Edmund!" he exclaimed ; "how is it that I find you so gloomy and thoughtful? Have you heard aught from France, or has our friendly intercourse of late caused a suspicion of our purpose ?"

"Neither," he replied. "Since I last saw you, a dear friend has died, and left me guardian to a child, whose safety affords me no little concern. In a short time the service of my country will demand my absence, and then my poor little Reginald will ——"

"Suffer no uneasiness on the boy's account," interrupted the baron, "for it will be hard, indeed, if between us we cannot provide for his well-doing. To-morrow I return to my home, where I shall remain a month ; come with me—bring the boy, and leave him there, and when we return his education shall be properly attended to."

"Most gladly do I accede to your proposition," exclaimed De Lancy ; "I will accept your invitation, since, in the privacy and seclusion that we shall enjoy at your house, we may consult at ease, and form such plans for the future as may seem best."

Baron Heinbach possessed all that fearless intrepidity and open generosity of disposition that characterised the Swiss. Owner of a vast extent of the Valais, he could bring a considerable body of his own retainers into the field. His principal Castle of Bautzen was seated upon a lofty eminence, and commanded an extensive view of the surrounding country. Its high and massive towers frowned with awful majesty, and their dark outlines were reflected in the magnificent lake which lay far beneath in the valley. The outward wall had small towers at equal distances, flanked at each corner by larger ones from where the principal defence could be made.

It was always well stored with warlike ammunition, and upon its towers and platforms were planted cannon of various kinds, each being admirably adapted for the special purpose intended. A strong body of men was always kept within, and a discharge of three guns successively and the hoisting of the standard was the signal by which his retainers were called in from the neighbouring villages. He was much beloved by all ranks in the canton, and kept up such a degree of military splendour that his castle was the resort of all who visited that part of the country.

After an easy journey, De Lancy and Heinbach, with Reginald and the attendants, arrived at Bautzen, where all his vassals were drawn up to receive the baron, and their acclamations of joy at his return fully denoted the love they bore their liege lord.

As the party entered the castle, De Lancy, with the eye of an experienced soldier, observed the well-planned fortifications, and expressed his admiration to the baron. Neither could he fail remarking the well-appointed troops that were drawn up.

Passing onwards, they reached the chamber where refreshments had been laid. It was a lofty apartment, arched overhead, having a raised platform at one end, whilst the walls on every side were curiously ornamented with various military trophies. It was brilliantly illuminated, and the table that was placed for the travellers gave evident proofs of the hospitality that reigned within the castle. Near the fire-place stood an elderly female, who strove to restrain the youthful impetuosity of a beautiful girl, who, with affectionate anxiety, sprang forward and threw herself into the arms of the baron.

"Dearest father," she exclaimed, "how I have longed for the moment of your return. I have reckoned every day since your departure, and worried Jeanette enough to make her cross, to tell me when I should see you."

"You see, my dear Mildred," said her father, leading Reginald forward, "I have brought home a young playmate for you."

Mildred drew back with diffidence, not having perceived the stranger before, while poor Reginald, fatigued with his long journey, was more inclined for rest than the formalities of a long journey.

Perceiving how matters stood, Heinbach directed Jeanette to take the boy to the chamber prepared for Sir Edmund de Laney, which contained a small pallet for the child. Then leading the way to the table, the baron prepared to do the honours of hospitality.

Next day, Heinbach and his guest, after visiting every part of the castle, and surveying the fortifications, rode out together. Being within his own wide domain, the baron did not consider attendants necessary. During the private conversation that now ensued between them, they arranged to collect as many soldiers as possible, and although they were not to appear openly in arms, they were to hold themselves in readiness for any sudden emergency. It was further agreed that Reginald should be left at the castle, where his education was to be carefully attended to by the chaplain. Besides, he would be a playmate for Wildred, who was quite delighted to have a companion so near her own age.

After dinner, when the two friends were left to themselves, Sir Edmund made some remark upon the infantine beauty of Mildred; but in a moment he regretted the want of caution he had been guilty of, for he perceived the quivering lip and changing countenance of Heinbach, as some painful recollections seemed to pass through his mind.

"Pardon me, my dear baron," said De Lancy, as he observed the effect produced by his words; "I fear I have touched upon a subject which reminds you of circumstances that had better be forgotten. I knew not that I was treading on dangerous ground, or I would have been more cautious."

"The pang is over, my dear friend," answered Heinbach, assuming a forced appearance of serenity. "You spoke just now of Mildred's beauty; but, had you seen her mother—had you beheld her as she truly was, glowing with health and beauty, your regret for her early death would indeed have been great. My father, as you are aware, was the owner of this castle and estate; attached to home and a country life, he lived within the bosom of his family, whilst I, with all the ardour of youth, preferred a wandering life, visiting by turns all the important places around us. Generally attired as a hunter, I mingled a great deal in humble life, sharing the peasant's hut and fare; nor could they for a moment have supposed they entertained the heir of an almost princely estate.

"Returning, on one occasion, through the mountains, at the close of a dark, wintry day, I found myself at fault; I had missed the path, nor could I bring to mind ever having been there before. Fatigued as I was with a long day's journey, I knew not where to seek shelter, when suddenly the gleaming of a distant light directed me which course to pursue. In the course of half an hour I arrived before a cottage, and knocked at the door for admittance. A man of venerable aspect opened it, and learning the object of my visit, invited me to walk in and share such hospitality as he had it in his power to bestow.

"The offer was gladly accepted, and in a few minutes I was seated by a blazing fire, with such refreshments before me as the cottage afforded. For some time I saw no one but the person who had admitted me; but at length, suddenly issuing from a side door, burst upon my view a vision of loveliness such as I had never till then beheld. Entranced I gazed upon the beauteous being, whom my host introduced as his daughter.

"Meanwhile the maiden, unconscious of the admiration that her charms had excited, paid me every attention that hospitality could dictate. Her father, I found, had been a soldier, who had served with honour throughout a long war, and at length had found that peaceful quiet which he so well and justly merited.

"I passed several days at Moran's cottage; but Stella, it must be confessed, was my sole inducement. The lovely girl had so entwined herself around my heart, that I did not strive to resist my passion, well aware that my father was much too affectionate to oppose my wishes in a matter so nearly concerning my future happiness. They were not aware of my rank, deeming me, in fact, as one moving in their own humble sphere; however, when I had fully gained the affections of Stella, and the good opinion of her father, who approved of my addresses, I made an excuse of urgent business, and taking my leave of them for the present, returned home.

"I at once stated all that had taken place to my father, who, much pleased with my candour, assented at once to my wishes, and planned a surprise for Stella. It was arranged, as one of our band of hunters, I should, with the rest, call at Moran's cottage to claim my bride, under the character of my father's retainer, espouse her, and then declare my name and station in society.

"We, De Lancy, seek for virtue more in humble life than in the palace or the castle. Like our native hills, we are rough and uncouth to appearance, yet to the mind that penetrates will be found virtue and sterling worth. But to proceed with my narrative :—

"On the third day after my departure from the cottage, attired as a hunter, I joined my father and the party ; we soon arrived at our place of destination, where we found Moran seated at the door ; he raised his eyes as we approached, and rising up, welcomed my return.

" 'Ah, my son,' he exclaimed, 'how happy you will make Stella! She has been most anxious since your departure, and scarcely hoped to see you again so soon. But who are these companions you have brought with you ?'

" 'Oh! some friends of mine,' I replied ; 'some of the retainers belonging to the Baron Heinbach, who you see yonder.'

"As my father approached, I perceived a peculiarly anxious expression in the countenance of Moran ; a flush passed over his visage, as if the recognition which had taken place was far from favourable. My father looked equally astonished, and grasping the old man's hand, he exclaimed,— 'By Heavens 'tis he—the preserver of my life !'

"I looked surprised, and was about to inquire the meaning, when a signal from my father checked me.

" 'Long have I sought you, Moran,' he exclaimed ; 'ever since that day when, wounded and deserted by my men, left to the vengeance of an infuriated foe, your sword defended me, your home afforded me shelter.'

" 'Oh, name it not, my lord,' interrupted Moran. 'I only did my duty as a soldier and a man. Heaven forbid I should ever have been so base and dastardly as to refuse assistance to an enemy when conquered. But those days are passed, and you and I, my lord, must give way to younger spirits.'

" 'True,' answered my father, 'and that reminds me of the business which has brought us here ; this youth, in whom I take much interest, having informed me of his passion for your daughter, has sought my permission, and solicited my presence at his nuptials. Now, as it has always been my wish and practice to reward a faithful servant, I purpose that the ceremony shall take place at my Castle of Bautzen. What say you, Moran, to my proposition ?'

" 'What reply can I make to you, my lord ?' exclaimed the old man ; 'what return can I give but my thanks for your noble generosity ?'

" 'It seems we are so far agreed, then,' said my father. 'Call the damsel, and let me behold her to whom I am about to yield 'one whom I regard with as much affection as a son.'

"Stella had not been visible till now, when she made her appearance, and never shall I forget the joy that flashed across her beautiful countenance when she saw that I had once more returned to her father's cottage. Regardless of the spectators who stood around us, she flew, with a cry of rapture, into my arms.

"I could instantly perceive that my father was struck and pleased with the simplicity and devoted attachment of the artless girl. After our first congratulations were over, Stella hastened to prepare refreshments for our party, and soon afterwards all the provisions that the cottage afforded were place before the visitor.

"While my father sat conversing with Moral I assisted Stella, but was apprehensive that sh would 'discover my rank, in consequence of th respect with which I was treated by our follower After they had partaken of the refreshment, requested Stella and her father to prepare to retur with us ; and in due time our happy party arrive at the Castle of Bautzen.

"Stella and her father were shown to a cham ber, while I retired to prepare for the ceremony and as soon as all was ready, I led my bride t the chapel, accompanied by my father and Moral It was the chaplain who performed the ceremony and as soon as it was concluded, and that I foun myself indissolubly united to the only femal whom I had ever truly loved, while I clasped he in my arms, a shout of joy burst from th assembled retainers, 'Health, happiness, and ever worldly good attend our noble lord and his lovel bride !' resounded in one loud, deep chorus.

"Moran, taken as he was by surprise, stoo speechless with astonishment, alternately gazing a his daughter and me, while Stella, who was sti pressed to my heart, by her quickly varyin blushes and panting bosom, denoted her surpris at finding me so high in rank ; yet she had love me when I was deemed humble as herself, and could not do her such injustice as to believe th discovery which was now made had any othe effect than that of rendering me more dear to he than ever.

"When Moran had sufficiently recovered fror the surprise into which he had been thrown, h turned to my father, as if seeking an explanation c the occurrence which had just taken place.

" 'Is it possible, my lord,' he at length ex claimed, 'that I behold your high-born son th husband of my child ! This is, indeed, a day c joy to me, for now shall I sink into the grav happy and satisfied that my dear Stella has n longer reasons to fear the frowns of the world.'

" 'And you, too, my brave and generous pre server,' returned my father, 'resign your cottage come and rest you here among us. Our ages ar nearly alike ; we have both looked on death, an now can find a pleasure in retracing days of old It was to ensure my son's happiness that I gave m free and hearty sanction to his marriage with you daughter. But why do we thus waste our time The nuptial banquet waits, and there are friend assembled in the hall who will marvel at ou longer absence.'

"But I will not lengthen my story unneces sarily, and since that which follows is melancholy I will dismiss it in as few words as possible. Ou wedded life was, as you imagine, passed in unalloye happiness, till fate began to frown upon me, an then the bitterness that followed was greater tha any words of mine can possibly describe. After few months, my father was suddenly removed fron us by death. Deeply we grieved for one who wa so dear to us, but scarcely had we recovered fron that blow when Moran also languished, and in few days he also was conveyed to the tomb. Ye the heaviest blow of all was to come ; my wife— the very idol of my soul, was snatched from m shortly after having given birth to my littl

Mildred, and I was thus left to deplore the utter annihilation of all the fondest hopes I had ever pictured in my fancy.

"However, to quit' this melancholy subject: soon after the death of my wife, I, the better to forget my griefs, plunged deeply into the politics of the time. I did not, however, neglect the education of my daughter, who I left under the matronly care of a tender and affectionate female. Jeannette has had the care of her for the last four years, and the chaplain has undertaken the completion of her education. Your young charge, Reginald, therefore, has an admirable opportunity of benefiting by the instructions of a teacher who is well qualified to render him for that course of life which it is most likely he will follow. He may remain here while you and I are engaged in the service of our country, and when the proper time arrives you can remove him to that sphere for which he may seem best adapted."

This arrangement, in every way so satisfactory, was cheerfully acceded to by De Lancy, and shortly afterwards the conversation turned to subjects of more varying interest.

CHAPTER XXXII.

Spirit of love! soon thy rose-plumes wear
The weight and the sully of canker and care;
But one bright moment is all thine own,
The one ere thy visible presence is known!
L. E. L.

WE must now pass over a considerable time, for some years had elapsed since Reginald had seen his father, though he frequently received letters from him. Meanwhile, reared up with Mildred, whose charms were daily increasing, although he regarded her in the light of a sister, yet we may well imagine that warmer feelings by degrees found their way to his heart, when the lovely girl, radiant in youthful beauty, presented herself to his imagination. She was now sixteen, and was regarded as the fairest maiden of a district that is justly celebrated for the beauty of its daughters.

Baron Heinbach, delighted at the youthful prowess exhibited by Reginald, was still more gratified in observing the increasing partiality with which the young folks regarded each other; and not having any male heir to succeed to the rank and honours of his house, he looked forward with pleasure to the anticipated marriage of Reginald and his daughter.

But the time had now almost arrived when it was expected the youth of Switzerland would be called into action. The confederates had been for some years so jealous of the increasing power of France, and so totally averse to the levies that had been made by that power, that they resolved to oppose with all their force the continuation of a league they deemed adverse to the interests of their country.

Arnheim, a personage who will now be rather conspicuous in our pages, although somewhat beyond the middle age of life, was still a wily political intriguer, and his religious character and vows of celibacy had not quenched those evil passions that had marked his youth, and rendered him abhorrent to all those who detest the character of a hypocrite.

He had heard of the charms of Mildred Heinbach, and resolved to lose no opportunity by which he might gratify a passion that his religion should have taught him to subdue. He had the art, however, to appear most sanctimonious; when he walked forth from his convent, he was clad in the humble garb of his order, his eyes bent upon the ground, his lips moving in apparent prayer, and a rosary of large beads suspended from his waist.

He had been for some time residing in the abbey of St. Nicholas, about two miles distant from Rome, but had come into Switzerland upon private and confidential matters which required the utmost caution and circumspection. One evening, when he was thoughtfully pacing the cloisters of the convent, he was startled by hearing footsteps near him, and turning to ascertain who was near, perceived at some little distance a figure clad as a pilgrim.

"Your pardon and your blessing, holy father," said the stranger; "I have journeyed far, and now, fatigued with travel, and drooping for want of food, I have dragged my way hither to crave charity and relief."

"You shall have it," returned Arnheim; "follow me, and I will see that proper care is bestowed on thee. You say you have travelled far," he continued, as they pursued their way towards the refectory.

"I have visited several countries, holy father."

"And no doubt have made yourself acquainted with the policy and government of each?"

"As far as lay in my power," answered the pilgrim. "I have visited the English, French, and Spanish courts; penetrated the cabinets of each; dissolved the mystic knots tied by the ministers of state—nay, think not that I boast, or speak at random; even I, simple as I appear, have been the sole adviser and promoter of many a daring plan which has afterwards surprised the world."

A light from a lamp flashed upon the countenance of the pilgrim; his eyes gleamed with fire, his countenance was agitated, but his action energetic. Suddenly pausing, he folded his arms upon his breast, while his staff fell upon his shoulders.

"Forgive me, holy father," he added, in a more subdued tone; "for sometimes these reminiscences will excite me."

Arnheim gazed upon him for an instant, and quickly through his fertile mind flashed the thought that he would prove an able auxiliary in his present and future schemes; and from his habit and appearance he would not excite any suspicion. On reaching the refectory, Arnheim gave directions that the pilgrim should be taken every care of, and if he felt sufficiently refreshed after partaking of some food, to be at once conducted to his presence. He then retired to his apartment, where he anxiously awaited the pilgrim's appearance.

At last he came, and of the many countenances Arnheim had seen, he had never before met with one so inexplicable as the stranger's; the features delicate, yet marked; the eyes quick and penetrating; the mouth beautifully formed, but, when closed, an accurate observer would detect a bitter and scornful expression. The figure was slightly formed, but rather above the middle size, and the skin was sunbrowned with travel.

"Draw near me, and take a seat," exclaimed Arnheim, after a pause of a few seconds; "I have desired this interview for the sole purpose of furthering the interests of our holy religion. I have long wished for an able, willing agent, one whom I could could confide in, who knows the world, whose thoughts are not developed on his brow, whose words are not the picture of his mind. Such a one have I sought, but long in vain, and, until the last hour, I had despaired of success; but say, what is your name, country, former occupation, and causes that have led to your present pilgrimage? None can overhear us, therefore you need not be apprehensive of confiding in me."

While Arnheim was thus speaking, the stranger had placed himself upon a seat, his eyes fixed upon the ground, as if in profound reflection; at length raising them, and steadily gazing at the monk, he said,—

" You shall be informed, holy father, of my story as far as relates to those events which have rendered penance requisite; yet I may not reveal either my country or my name. In early youth no one was more happy, gay, or innocent; my first sad loss was when death deprived me of my parents, a misfortune which threw me upon the world, and that, too, at an age when I was incapable of acting discreetly for myself. Thus circumstanced, I met with one whom I regarded as the only being calculated to bestow true happiness upon me; often when I gazed upon those eyes of piercing lustre, that face of matchless beauty, I have rushed forth into wild and deep seclusion, there to mourn over the vain hopes I had formed. Another was preferred—my love turned to hate—dark, hellish, hateful. When first I heard the death-blow to all my expectations, I fell to the earth—my brain whirled—my tongue clove to the roof of my mouth —my lips were parched—I thought not—heard not a sound. Suddenly revenge flashed across my mind. I was alone, yet methought some one whispered in my ear, ' Revenge !' I arose and returned home an altered being—the canker was in my heart, though a treacherous smile played upon my lips. I first thought of seeking the friendship of my rival, then changed my purpose, and determined on concealment. I always bore about me a poniard and a deadly drug, both instruments to glut my fiendish revenge. I gained admittance to the chamber of my rival, mingled the bowl, and concealed myself in a place from whence I saw it raised to his lips and drained to the very last drop. A chill ran through my veins. I shuddered at the act I had committed, and dreadful sounds of accusation rang in my ears. I stole from my lurking-place and sought security in a deep and lonely cavern. Alas ! I could not flee from my own terrible feelings—conscience still kept pace with me, my revenge was satisfied, but my peace was for ever lost. I had yielded myself to the arch fiend ! Say, father, does your religion hold out hopes of pardon to such a criminal as me ?"

" Despair not, my son," answered Arnheim; " we will receive you into the bosom of our church, which ever pours a healing balm into the wounds of the afflicted; but say, will you enter into the service of our holy faith ?"

" Most willingly, holy father."

" What is your name ?"

" You may call me Julio."

" And your country ?"

" Nay, I crave your pardon there, holy father,"

exclaimed the pilgrim, " for there are reasons which render it impossible for me to divulge that fact at present. I will serve you most zealously, but you must bear with me, for I have suffered much, and often feel as if the maddening stings of conscience would turn my brain."

Arnheim having revolved within his subtle brain the first mission upon which he should despatch his new adherent, arose from his seat, and, ringing a bell, a lay brother made his appearance, whom he directed to conduct the stranger to a cell.

" And when you have sufficiently reposed," he added, speaking to the pilgrim, " let me see you upon the subject of this night's conversation."

Then, bestowing his benediction upon the unfortunate wanderer, they parted.

We must now return to the Castle of Bautzen, where events are about to transpire that will have considerable influence towards the development of our narrative.

" Dear Reginald, how anxious I have been for your return," said Mildred, one morning, as the youth entered an apartment which she solely appropriated for her studies.

" You could not be more desirous for my return than I was myself, dear Mildred," answered the youth, approaching and taking the hand of the beauteous girl.

" I dare say you will laugh at my fears, Reginald," she said; " but, after you quitted me this morning, I left the castle upon my accustomed walk, when suddenly, on the path before me, I saw a figure lying in a state of insensibility. On approaching closer, I heard a groan, and words indistinctly muttered. With all speed I returned home, and, directing a party of the servants, had the stranger conveyed into a chamber, where he now reposes. While they were carrying him along, I marked his countenance; it was fine, but hunger, care, or evil passions, had so changed his features, that a cold chill crept through my veins as I gazed upon him. Do, dear Reginald, visit the poor sufferer, and offer him an asylum here so long as he chooses to remain."

The youth promised to obey her request, and immediately hastened to the chamber where the stranger had been previously conducted. Entering the apartment, he approached the couch, beside which sat an attendant. The stranger seemed to be in a restless slumber; the heaving of his breast, flushed brow, and clenched hand, all betokened the visions that were passing before his disturbed fancy.

To Reginald's inquiry the attendant replied, that the stranger had been very incoherent in his speech, —that he had spoken of assassins, and muttered in a foreign tongue, but that latterly he had sunk into a doze.

In a few minutes afterwards, the sleeping man appeared to be much agitated; his arms were thrown about; he started up on his couch; his eyes glared wildly; then, fixing them upon Reginald, he grasped the arm of the youth, and steadily perusing every lineament of his countenance, he sank back upon the couch, and buried his face in his hands, while sobs, deep and convulsive, burst from him.

Reginald raised him from the couch, and, with the assistance of the attendant, supported him to an open casement. As he wiped the cold drops from the forehead of the stranger, he could not forbear gazing with wonder and admiration upon the fine contour of his features.

"Thanks, youth," he faintly murmured, "may Heaven reward you! But, say—where am I? By what name am I to know my hospitable entertainer?"

"You are in the Castle of Bautzen," answered the youth, "belonging to the Baron Heinbach, and where you will receive every care and attention."

"And your name," said the other, "is, if I mistake not, Reginald?"

"It is."

A shudder passed through the frame of the traveller, and he sank fainting upon the shoulder of his supporter, while tears chased each other down his

cheeks, and soon relieved him. Still feeling excessively weak, he requested to be led back to the couch; and Reginald having complied, retired to the chamber where Mildred was anxiously awaiting the report as to the state of the invalid.

"I cannot account for it," he said, "but I feel much interested for this stranger; and he regarded me as if I brought to his mind the image of a former acquaintance. Alas! I must soon leave all that is most dear to me."

"What mean you, Reginald?" cried the astonished maiden; "what reason is there for you to leave us?"

"The words I have just uttered are but too true," answered Reginald; "my father's commands hasten me away, and another week will see us separated—perhaps for ever. Ah, say then, dearest Mildred, that you will not be offended if I now divulge a secret which, until this moment, has been confined to my own bosom."

"How can I be angry?" she asked. "Are you not to me as a fondly-loved brother, and have not our wishes ever been as one? Ah! never till now did I feel the pain that afflicts my heart!

"Our separation, dear Mildred, will be but for a time," exclaimed Reginald. "My father writes with certainty of a glorious destiny and a bright career. But do not let my absence change those feelings that you now possess.

Mildred was about to reply, when her father entered the room. He had just received a packet, and he presented a letter to Reginald, while his countenance wore an appearance of extreme chagrin.

"It seems," said the baron, "that your father wishes you to join him. He is now at Paris, and the journey is so long and dangerous, that he is desirous you should join the next body of soldiers who are going that way. I expect a few here to-morrow on their way to France, and with them is a young officer, Henri Longville, to whose care and guidance I can safely entrust you."

While Heinbach was thus speaking, Mildred had sought her chamber, where in solitude she gave way to the feelings which had taken possession of her heart. Never until now had she felt how dear Reginald was to her ; till the present time, she had regarded him as a fondly-loved brother—never bestowing a thought upon the passion of love for one who had been her constant companion from childhood.

A light step in the chamber aroused her, and, turning, she beheld the object of her thoughts. Flying to her side, and seating himself, while one arm encircled her waist, and the other pressed her hand to his own throbbing heart, he said,—

"Mildred—dearest Mildred, hear me ere the sad moment of parting arrives. I must leave you —Heaven knows with how much reluctance—but a father's command compels me. Think not, however, that either time or absence will banish your loved image from my mind. Let us, then, look forward to a happy re-union, and offer up to Heaven your prayers—your fondest wishes—for my safety."

Tears choked her utterance, and, soon afterwards, Reginald was obliged to leave her, in order to commence the necessary preparations for his journey.

The stranger, who had been thrown upon the hospitality of Baron Heinbach, was Julio, the private agent of Arnheim. He had received instructions to gain admittance to the castle of the baron, and it was rather extraordinary that his plans were furthered, without trial on his part. He had made the journey to Bautzen on foot, and had sunk exhausted with fatigue. On recovering, he found himself an inmate of that castle whose secrets he had been instructed to gain a perfect knowledge of. As soon as he was able to collect his thoughts, he revolved within his mind the best mode of carrying his designs into effect.

In his interview with Reginald, he had nearly betrayed himself, for the features of the youth had struck him as bearing a striking resemblance to a female whose remembrance was like a thorn in his bosom. Expressing, therefore, to his attendant his desire for another interview with Reginald, he waited with intense anxiety till the young man made his appearance. Then, raising himself on his couch, he said,—

"Again, sir, I tender you my thanks for the hospitable manner in which I have been received. A wanderer, such as I have been for many years, must now seek out a quiet spot for shelter. It was for this purpose that I have now sought your counsel and advice. Would the noble Baron Heinbach, through your intercession, grant me an asylum within the walls of his castle, my utmost wishes would be gratified, and perhaps my poor abilities and knowledge might be of some avail to him."

"The Baron Heinbach," answered the youth, "never yet refused shelter or hospitality to the unfortunate, and you may rest assured he will agree to your request. I leave this place early to-morrow, and will not fail at once to name your wishes. When I return, I hope to find you happy beneath this hospitable roof."

"Stay, young sir," said Julio ; "pardon my boldness—but tell me by what other name, beside Reginald, I am to know you."

"I am called De Lancy."

"You belong, then, to a French family?"

"I do ; my father holds military rank under the French monarch."

"These inquiries may appear impertinent," said the other, after a brief pause, "but, believe me, it is not mere idle curiosity that has prompted them. In short, your features so closely resemble one whom I knew in former days, that I could not resist the desire to discover if my surmises were well founded."

"Are they well founded?"

"I think it is impossible you can be related," answered Julio ; "however, as you leave this place to-morrow, do not refuse a request that I have to make. I was not always what I now appear to be ; early in life, I moved among the gay and wealthy of the land, but long since have I learned to look upon and think of riches with contempt. Yet I have here a gem, with which some circumstances of a peculiar nature are connected. Accept it— wear it for my sake."

As he placed the ring upon Reginald's finger, he gazed at it, clasped his hands, and, bowing his head, made a sign that he wished to be alone.

Upon quitting this mysterious being, Reginald hastened to the Baron Heinbach, whom he found busily engaged writing letters to his father and other friends. The request of Julio was now mentioned, and readily acceded to ; for the castle was ever open to those who were in need of a shelter, and the necessities of the present applicant seemed to be too urgent to be met with a refusal.

After dinner, Heinbach informed the young man that he expected the party with whom he was to travel would stop for a few hours the following day at the castle, and advised him to make every preparation without delay. He did not think an attendant necessary, but presented him with one of the finest horses from his stable.

When Reginald returned to his chamber for the night, he found a packet upon the bed. Hastily opening it, he greedily devoured its contents ; then taking a tress of dark hair from its folds, he pressed it fondly to his lips.

"Yes, dearest Mildred," he exclaimed, "you shall be obeyed. It were, indeed, better for us both not to seek a parting interview. Thy heart thy affections are mine, and most confidently thou mayest depend upon the plighted vows of Reginald This precious gift shall be worn next my heart, and the hand that tears it from me must first deprive me of existence."

Then enclosing the lock of hair in a silver case from which he took a relic that had been given him by the chaplain, he attached it to a small gold chain, and suspended it round his neck.

Scarcely had the sun risen on the following morning, than he was roused by the sound of a bugle, and starting from his couch, he hastily dressed himself, and passed through the corridor to the hall, where he found Heinbach welcoming an officer who, at the head of a small party of soldiers had just arrived. This was the companion of whom he had been told ; and upon advancing the baron introduced him by name as Henri Longville, who frankly extended his hand to Reginald, saying,—

"I can already esteem you for your father

sake. There is not among us a more valiant soldier, or a wiser politician. If your future life and conduct be moulded after his, your fame will be most certain."

"It delights me," said the baron, "to hear these just praises of one whom I am proud to rank among my friends. And you, Longville, let me hope you will stay some little time, to share my hospitality."

"For two hours I will remain your guest," answered the officer; "and in the meantime, my young friend can make whatever preparations are unfinished."

Then following the baron, who led the way to a chamber where refreshments were placed, the short time which had been limited soon passed away in conversation. The adieus being over, Reginald mounted his horse, and, riding by the officer's side, was some distance from the castle ere he could recall his scattered ideas. Longville forbore to interrupt his meditations until he saw that the regret at parting with his friends had in some degree subsided, when, breaking the silence, he launched forth into encomiums upon the soldier-like manners of Baron Heinbach.

"He is regarded as one of our stanchest friends," he continued, "and soon, I hope, will join us with all the levies he can muster. But tell me, my young friend, for you have lived long at Bautzen, is the report too flattering, or does the Lady Mildred possess all those charms so often and so glowingly described?"

"Report has not done her justice," answered Reginald, earnestly. "She is surpassingly fair, and as excellent as she is beautiful."

"Bravely spoken," exclaimed the officer. "You love the girl? Nay, do not seek to deny it, for your tell-tale countenance betrays you."

"All who know the Lady Mildred will bear witness that I speak the truth," exclaimed Reginald. "Is it, therefore, to be wondered that I, who have been all my life at Bautzen, and always regarded by her as a brother, should feel an interest for her such as I have manifested?"

"Ay, ay—it is natural enough, I admit," answered Longville. "At your age I thought and felt as you do; but the sterner occupation of war has long since driven all love-notions from my head."

Thus conversing, they pursued their journey, and as evening approached they halted at a village, where the soldiers having been dispersed in the different cottages, Longville and Reginald found excellent entertainment in a small farm-house near the entrance of the village.

They had remarked this snug abode on their entrance into the place, and their attention was afterwards further attracted to it by the owner himself, a man of venerable aspect, who was led by a youth towards the group of peasants who had been assembled by the arrival of the soldiers. Approaching Longville and his companion, he tendered his house for their night's rest and refreshment.

"You will honour me, gentlemen," he said, "by accepting the shelter of my humble roof. I have myself been a soldier, and my heart warms whenever I meet those who devote their lives and services to their country."

The offer so generously made was at once accepted; and having partaken of a repast, which, although different to what they had been accustomed to, yet their long journey had seasoned it with a good appetite, they retired to rest, and, stretched upon their humble pallets, enjoyed the blessing of a refreshing slumber, that even a monarch might have envied.

CHAPTER XXXIII.

Has thy heart sickened with deferred hope?
Or felt the impatient anguish of suspense?
Or hast thou tasted of the bitter cup
That Disappointment's withered hands dispense?
SPENCER.

THE stately Castle of Bautzen had now no longer charms for Mildred, deprived as she was of the society of Reginald; her harps and books were her only resource—even her favourite palfrey was no longer regarded as the means of chasing away melancholy. In her confession to Father Ambrose, though she avoided stating the passion which had taken possession of her heart, she could not entirely conceal the regard in which she held the absent Reginald. This discovery troubled him not a little; and whilst reflecting upon what step he ought to take, he recollected the pilgrim, Julio, who had now recovered from his illness, though, for some reason or other, he seemed to avoid mixing with the family. He, however, lost no time in seeking him out, and at once declared that he was desirous of consulting him upon an affair of no little difficulty.

"Let me hear what it is that troubles you," said Julio, "and you may afterwards freely command my services."

"The difficulty I speak of is this," said Ambrose: "Lady Mildred is well versed in the learning adapted to her sex, but her father is desirous that she should be acquainted with the history of various countries—the manners and customs peculiar to each. Now you, I believe, have travelled much; and your descriptions, couched in an easy, lively style, would serve to divert her mind from other thoughts that at present distract it."

"You would have me become her tutor?" exclaimed the other, eagerly. "I understand your meaning, and will cheerfully undertake the task. Gratitude, at least, demands thus much of me, and you will find me ready to commence whenever I receive orders to do so."

This point being agreed upon, they separated, but again met at the dinner-table, when Julio entered into conversation with the ease and freedom of one who has seen much of the world. Among other subjects the departure of Reginald was mentioned, and the utmost regret at his absence expressed. Julio's eyes were instantly directed towards Mildred, and he could not fail to remark the blush that glowed upon her cheek, as she held down her head to conceal the confusion of which she was conscious.

Already the baron began to regard him as a valuable acquisition, not only as an able master for Mildred, but, acquainted as he appeared to be with politics and court intrigue, he would also be a valuable auxiliary in the approaching crisis of affairs. However, these thoughts he kept to himself, and listened with much pleasure to the conversation that was carried on.

We must, however, leave them for awhile, and follow Reginald and his companions, who, having journeyed as far as the Lake of Lucerne, paused to view the truly magnificent scenery that lay spread on every side around them. The place reminded Reginald of the peaceful calm he had enjoyed at Bautzen, and heaving a sigh to the memory of departed pleasures, he expressed an earnest wish that the war, which had so long been carried on, was brought to an honourable conclusion. Longville was about to reply to this, but at the moment a low, solemn chant was heard, and then the deep peal of an organ added to the impressiveness of the moment.

Looking round them, the two friends now discovered that they stood at the entrance of a monastery, and it was the evening hymn which they had just heard. Fatigued after a long day's travel, the officers advanced, and knocking at the gate, soon brought the porter to demand their business. A request for shelter and refreshment was then made, and the gate was once more closed until the superior had been informed of their arrival.

In the course of a few minutes the abbot, attended by two subordinate monks, appeared to welcome the travellers. An hospitable invitation to enter was then given, and leaving their followers to the care of some of the lay brethren, Longville and Reginald accompanied the superior into the abbey.

A table was now spread with refreshments, and the wine produced by these holy fathers showed that they were not altogether regardless of the creature comforts of this life. Having somewhat appeased their hunger, the travellers found time to observe their entertainer. His cowl was thrown back, and disclosed a countenance at variance with his sacred garb. Instead of meek resignation and sanctity, the expression of his visage was bold and daring; his hair was grey, yet time had not subdued the fire of his eye; his forehead was broad and expansive, his eyebrows heavy, and his nostrils curved with an expression of contempt. He courteously attended to his guests; and his manners, easy and polite, evinced an intimate acquaintance with courtly society. His caustic and penetrating remarks fixed the attention of even the volatile Henri Longville, who had now began to feel himself quite at home.

"Holy father," he exclaimed, "I must do you the credit to declare that your wine is excellent, and, egad, you are no niggard with it."

"Why should I bestow it with a grudging hand?" asked the abbot. "All that we enjoy in this life is for our use and benefit, and to distribute amongst those of our fellow-creatures who are in need of it. I cannot, therefore, claim any merit for simply performing my duty."

Reginald now gave evident tokens of fatigue, having been for some time nodding in his seat. At length his friend woke him, and bidding the superior good night, they were shown to their sleeping chambers. Early next morning our travellers were up, and prepared to continue their journey.

"What think you of our late host?" demanded Henri Longville, after they had ridden some distance in silence.

"I am but an incompetent judge," answered Reginald, "but to me he appears to wear an assumed character, and seems more accustomed to wield the sword than to govern a fraternity of monks."

"He certainly is a man of strong mind and penetrating judgment," returned Longville, "and had I time to prosecute my inquiries, the result might be worth all the trouble. You perceived how he avoided the subject of—but psha! I forgot that you had been asleep at least half an hour when that topic was commenced."

Reginald was not sufficiently acquainted with the subject to offer any opinion. He now anxiously looked forward to the meeting with his father, under whose superintendence he was to make his essay in the honourable profession of arms.

At length they reached the French encampment, and much was our youth delighted with the exciting scene that broke upon his view. The lines of white tents, with gay streamers floating above them—the soldiers sitting in groups, or furbishing their arms—parties of cavalry going through their military evolutions,—all conspired to render it a sight of extraordinary interest.

As the two friends rode along, Longville viewed the spectacle as one with which he was familiarized; but Reginald's flushed cheek, and sparkling eyes, gave token of those feelings which only required an opportunity to be brought into display. As Longville had to communicate important news to the king, he directed one of the soldiers to conduct our youth to Sir Edmund De Lancy's tent, and then hurried away.

Reginald had not seen his father for a long time, and he pictured to himself the change that had in all probability taken place. On arriving at De Lancy's quarters, he dismounted, and gave his name to one of the soldiers who was loitering near the place. This was scarcely done, when a part of the drapery was thrown aside, and Reginald was once more clasped in the arms of his father.

We must now return to Mildred, who, from the period when her lover quitted Bautzen, had changed in appearance much for the worse; the healthful glow upon her cheek gave place to a pallid hue; and her eyes, hitherto so bright, and beaming with content and happiness, were now heavy and melancholy. The companion of her youth was gone—he had embarked in a hazardous profession, and her fear was that she might never again behold him. Her father, anxious as he was in her behalf, was the last to discover the sad change that had taken place.

Although she submitted to receive the instructions of Julio, it was with evident reluctance, for a gloomy presentiment of future evil had taken possession of her mind. She would shudder when she gazed upon him, nor could she avoid a superstitious feeling that he would be in some manner connected with her future destiny. Often had she observed him gazing upon her with a look of invidious meaning; so that she never felt at ease in his presence, and most happy was she when the hours of instruction were past, that she might escape to the seclusion of her own chamber.

At length a circumstance occurred which considerably increased her fear of Julio. She had sat up one night later than usual to finish the perusal of a volume in which she felt deeply interested, when her lamp by some accident fell, and the light was extinguished. Not wishing to awaken her attendant, and as she knew a lamp was always kept burning in the corridor, she proceeded to re-light it herself. She had succeeded, and was returning to her chamber, when a low, rustling sound startled her, and turning she beheld Julio stealing along with a lamp and dagger. Rooted to the spot, she lost all power of speech or flight, while he approached where she stood, but did not appear to observe her. As he came nearer she could distinguish broken sentences, which he muttered; and it now struck her that he was walking in his sleep, and that the consciousness of some wicked deed had disturbed his dreams, and caused him thus to wander. The sentences he muttered were broken, but sufficient of them was heard to increase the apprehension under which she suffered.

"Yes—yes," he muttered, "poison will be best—a dagger—then there would be blood, and that would discover all—psha! what should I fear? they know me not; but how to administer the deadly potion! I have it—yes—I'll do it on the instant!" and onwards he proceeded towards the library.

It was some time before Mildred could recover from the terror into which she had been thrown. When she did, however, she hastened to her chamber, and sinking into a seat, gave free utterance to her feelings.

"Merciful Heaven!" she cried, clasping her hands, "how shall I conceal this fearful discovery? To think that the garb of sanctity should cover such a monster! If I relate what I have witnessed to my father, his anger may be such as to excite vengeance in Julio; and yet how shall I in future bear to receive instruction from one who meditates taking the life of a fellow creature? yet I must not by word or look permit my knowledge to be suspected, or I may myself be the next victim of his deadly fury."

The next day, when she met Julio, she strove as much as possible to conceal the feelings that agitated her; but to him who was so deeply versed in the human countenance, the internal struggles she endured were but too perceptible.

"What is it, my daughter, that thus agitates you?" he said, in his blandest accents. "Confide your troubles to me, and fear not but that I will give you such counsel and advice as will calm your mind. But surely you have not yet been exposed to the vicissitudes and annoyances of this life?"

"No, believe me, no, Father Julio," she replied; "my days are yet unalloyed with care or trouble."

"So were mine at your age," he replied, in a hollow voice; "I was then free from care; but what have I not endured since—what do I not endure now!"

Mildred shuddered as she remembered the scene of the previous evening; she could not avoid glancing at Julio, as he paced the room; his arms folded, and his breast heaving with the violence of his agitation. At last he approached the table, and seating himself, went through with her the daily course of instruction. As soon as this was concluded, he quitted the room without asking any further remark, and Mildred hastened to her own chamber, delighted that the much dreaded hour had passed away.

When Arnheim had instructed Julio to act as a spy over the actions of Baron Heinbach, he had furnished him with papers and documents, purporting to be a correspondence between Heinbach and the French king, relative to the levies, and also proposing the total subversion of the countries, and assuring the monarch of all the aid in his power, upon the appearance of an invading army. These papers Arnheim had instructed Julio to place in a cabinet in the sleeping chamber of the baron, and thither his agent hastened, and succeeded in secreting them. He then sought the solitude of the forest, where, stretched upon the ground, he gave way to the various reflections that forced themselves upon his mind. So deeply, indeed, was he buried in thought, as not to observe the baron, who had been regarding him for some time, and who at length advanced.

"I have observed, holy father," he said, "that you are not at peace within—that, in short, some unhappy circumstances recur to your thoughts, and keep up continued agitation. If I can in any way assuage your sorrows, you may command me."

"I thank you, my lord," answered Julio, "but in no way can you be of the least assistance. It is true I have griefs—griefs so profound, that nought but death can ease them." Then starting suddenly from the ground, he continued. "But we will, for the present, wave the subject, my lord baron. In short, I fear I must now quit your hospitable mansion, though, perhaps, it may be only for a short period."

"I shall much regret your departure," said the unsuspecting baron. "My daughter, I find, has much benefited by your instruction, so that I must insist upon your accepting this purse of gold as some slight recompense for the trouble you have taken. Nay, refuse it not, for, on your journey, it will prove most useful."

Still, however, the wily priest put aside the bounty that had thus been proffered.

"No, my lord," he said; "it is true I have done my best, but my humble exertions for the instruction of your daughter have already been amply rewarded."

"Nay, I request you to accept it."

"I neither can nor will accept your offer, baron," exclaimed Julio, resolutely; "and now, as, it is probable we shall not meet again, at least for a very long period, again receive my thanks for the hospitality which you have been pleased to bestow upon me."

Then making a low obeisance to the baron, he quickened his pace, and made his way towards the castle.

Heinbach had not received any letters of late from De Lancy, and was anxiously looking forward to an account of the movements of the French. He knew that the monarch was near Florence, but was not aware that Arnheim, by his intrigues had excited the Swiss confederates to resistance. These thoughts were passing through his mind as he paced his chamber, when a servant entered with the long-looked for despatches.

Heinbach received them with a trembling hand, and immediately proceeded to peruse them. Astonishment at the boldness of Arnheim's movements gave place to pleasure at the intelligence that all the intriguer's schemes had been foiled in a battle which had been gained by the French army; and, rom some passages in De Lancy's letters, the baron decided upon an immediate journey to Bern. Giving directions for a small retinue to be in readiness the following morning, he hastened to Mildred to gladden her with the intelligence of Reginald's safety, and the honour he had achieved in his first affray with the enemy. These praises she heard with undisguised rapture, but could not repress her alarm when the baron mentioned his intended journey. No entreaties, however, could induce him to abandon a project which he felt in honour bound to follow up, and he hastened from the room, leaving her a prey to the thousand fears which her own apprehensions had conjured up.

But she had not been long left alone, when her maid, Josephine, entered the room, wearing an expression of more than usual satisfaction.

"Joy, joy, my dear lady," cried the abigail, as she came bustling into the room; "we are about to loose that proud, gloomy-looking Father Julio; and glad enough I am of it; for never could I meet him but he frightened me almost out of my life, stalking along as he did in that black habit of his, and looking for all the world like the pictures I have seen of the *old gentleman!*"

"When does he leave us?" inquired Mildred.

"To-morrow, my lady," answered Josephine; "and then we are to be left to ourselves; for my lord, the baron, is also going a journey, and ——"

"Go to my father," interrupted Mildred, "and ask him if he is at leisure, as I much wish to see him before he takes his departure from hence."

Josephine left the room, but soon returned to say that the baron was in the library, where he was waiting to give her the interview she requested.

"What is it my daughter desires?" asked Heinbach, as she advanced towards him.

"To see you and receive your blessing ere you depart," she replied.

"You have it, my child," he replied, pressing her to his bosom; "but have you no message for your friend and playmate, Reginald, whom I shall soon see?"

"I have not, my dear father," she replied, as a blush suffused her countenance; "but, when you see him, bear my regards, and say that he is not forgotten."

"And is that all my dear Mildred would have me say to him," asked her father. "Nay, that tell-tale blush discloses the secret you would keep from me. Well, it is as I and De Lancy wished. Your tutor, also," continued he, "speaks of business that requires his absence. Whilst I am away, I would not wish you to venture much abroad without attendants; for though our neighbourhood has been undisturbed of late, yet it were better to be cautious in these troublous times. Now, farewell, my dearest child,—unto Heaven's choicest care I commit your safe keeping."

Then pressing her to his bosom, and kissing her with all the warmth of paternal affection, he once more bade her adieu, and hurried from the apartment.

Anxious as he was to perform the task he had undertaken, Heinbach journeyed on towards Bern, totally unsuspicious of the plots that were forming against him; indeed, in cunning and duplicity he was no match for the crafty Arnheim, who had woven his web with such art, and apparently patriotic feelings, that the honest burghers of Bern were made the instrument of his malice.

It was evening when the baron reached the city, Arnheim having received notice of his movements had urged the inhabitants to have him seized, and, in consequence, a party of soldiers waited in readiness to arrest him soon after his arrival.

Scarcely had he entered the gates, than he and his party were surrounded. They made a show of resistance, but against so superior a force there was but little chance; and, at the baron's command, the attendants followed his example by surrendering themselves. It was then with astonishment that Heinbach found himself branded as a felon, and conveyed to a dungeon where, having been rudely thrust in, he was left to his own reflections. Here, far distant as he was from any friends, and in the power of his most inveterate foe, he felt the hopelessness of his situation, and although he bore his misfortune with manly resignation, yet would he have yielded the best of his estates—even Bautzer itself, to be at liberty.

The instant he had been arrested, a messenger was despatched to notify the event to the council, as well as to Arnheim, the latter of whom exulted with fiendish joy at the prospect of thus being revenged upon the man whom he so bitterly hated. He then began to arrange the evidence against him, and as the forged papers, which were at Bautzen, formed a material part of the charge, he resolved to make a journey there for them himself, and a few hours afterwards he set out on this nefarious errand.

Heinbach was purposely kept in ignorance as to the extent of the accusations against him. He was several days without seeing any one, except the keeper of the prison, who preserved a gloomy silence, scarcely replying to any of the common inquiries made by the baron.

At length, one evening, the sound of footsteps in the passage leading to his cell awoke him from a slumber, and, the door being thrown open, four men entered, one of whom informed him that his first examination was about to take place. He was then led through several dark passages, which terminated in a spacious hall, dimly lighted by a lamp, which threw around a sickly light, sufficient only to disclose the stern, angry countenance of seven burghers, who sat round a table covered with black cloth. On one side was placed a piece of machinery, and before it stood a tall and muscular figure of a man masked, his arms bare, and folded on his bosom.

Upon his entrance, the baron made a slight inclination of respect to the assembled burghers, and then drawing himself up with the erectness of conscious innocence, he awaited the questions from the tribunal. At length, the president addressing him in a sonorous tone, said,—

"Prisoner, you are charged with traitorously conniving at, and assisting levies of troops, not only in this country but in others, and carrying on a secret correspondence with our enemies, the French, for whose assistance those levies were raised. We wait your answer to the charge thus preferred."

"Bring forth my accusers — produce your proofs," answered Heinbach, firmly. "Let me behold the hand which has thus in the dark struck the blow. Besides, I question the authority you have thus taken upon yourselves; I am an independent noble, and am not thus to be seized, and led before a self-created tribunal. Such is my answer, nor shall I give any other until my enemy is placed before me."

"That cannot be," replied the president. "You have heard the charges, and if you refuse to answer them we have the means at hand to enforce your compliance. Again, we ask, will you make such confession as may induce us to extend our mercy towards you?"

"Never!" exclaimed the baron; "desire your minister of torture to exercise his utmost cruelty; my lips are sealed!" Then, folding his arms, he sternly regarded the rack and executioner.

The president waved his hand, and Heinbach was immediately seized, stripped, and bound to the rack; yet, although his limbs were stretched to an extent nearly bordering on dislocation, not a groan escaped his lips. Still, his agonies were such that his writhing features could not but denote the pangs he suffered. At length, so severe was the torture applied to him, that nature could no longer endure it, and he became insensible to all that was going forward.

He was then unbound, and being partly revived, was conveyed to his dungeon, where, stretched upon his hard couch, he lay for some hours, scarcely evincing any animation. Meanwhile, his judges, who remained in deliberation, though they were desirous of Arnheim's presence with the written proofs of the prisoner's guilt; yet, as they deemed the obstinacy of Heinbach a proof of his guilt, it was determined, that if the accuser did not arrive before the expiration of three days, the prisoner should be publicly executed.

From the intelligence De Lancy and Reginald received, they saw but too much reason to be apprehensive for the life of Heinbach. At length, Reginald obtained permission to go and see what he could do towards the preservation of his kind friend and benefactor. Adopting the habit of a citizen, and attended by a servant, he quitted the camp, and proceeded to the city. No adventure of any moment occurred until he reached the place of his destination; when, putting up at an inn, he sat down to partake of refreshment.

There was not any one in the room when he entered, but soon after he had seated himself, a man of middle age and commanding aspect, came in, followed by four soldiers. The stranger, advancing to Reginald, accosted him, and inquired his name, whence he had come, and other particulars. From the air of authority he assumed, the young man supposed he must be a person of some authority in the place, and therefore replied that he was an inhabitant of the canton, travelling upon his own private business.

"I am well aware of your purpose," said the stranger, "and my earnest prayer is that Heaven may prosper your errand. But this is no place for conversation; accompany me home, and there we shall be free from interruption."

Reginald was undecided how to act; the stranger's manners and words were fair, but he knew enough to guard against the folly of implicit confidence. However, he kept his suspicions within his own breast, and bowing his head, intimated that he was quite ready to attend him. They then quitted the inn and passed through several streets, till they reached a house which, from its size, appeared to belong to a person of consequence.

Here Reginald's conductor took a key from his pocket, and unlocked a small door at some distance from the principal entrance. A narrow passage lay before them, lighted by a lamp at the end, which threw an uncertain light, but which, nevertheless, was sufficient to guide them up a flight of steps which led them into a chamber of large dimensions. Here the stranger threw aside his cloak, and holding out his hand to Reginald, said,—

"You do not recollect me, I perceive; but I knew you at the gate to-night, and your purpose in coming here flashed at once upon my mind. It is some years since I saw you at Bautzen, whither I went on business to the baron. You know not how happy I am to have it in my power to facilitate his escape; but we must act with caution, not only to avoid suspicion, but in consideration to his present state of weakness and exhaustion. Two days more only remain, young man, and then the sentence of death is to be put in force."

"Good Heavens!" exclaimed Reginald, "is, then, the danger of my friend so urgent as you have said? Oh! save him if you can; rescue him from this peril, and our everlasting gratitude, our unceasing prayers shall be yours."

"The task is by no means an easy one," said Ritzen—for such was the stranger's name; "but no effort of mine shall be wanting to save the baron. Arnheim is his bitter enemy; he has vowed his ruin, and nothing but instant flight to the Valais, and close seclusion in his castle, can avail him."

"When may I see him?" asked Reginald; "when assure him that there is yet a hope of his liberation?"

"We must be cautious," answered Ritzen. "The plan I have laid is this—you shall appear as one of the prison guards; under my usual dress I will wear another, in which Heinbach, when disguised, can quit with us. Then, your horses being ready, you can pass him off as your servant, and thus all suspicion will be lulled till the danger is past."

Then, after arranging for the plan being put into execution the following night, Ritzen accompanied Reginald back the inn, where he found his servant in much perplexity and trouble for his safety, knowing that his master was a perfect stranger in the town.

Nothing of any consequence passed during the next day; and, as soon as darkness had set in, Reginald called for the young officer, and, conducting him to the same apartment where he had been on the previous night, assisted in putting on the disguise, which he wore over the clothes he purposed travelling in, and he intended divesting himself of the soldier's habit as soon as he quitted the prison. They were quickly admitted to the dungeon, and, as they entered, the heart of Reginald throbbed violently, and a dizziness seized him, as the fear of a discovery, and the consequent failure of their plans, struck him. At length, nerving himself for the task, he followed Ritzen into the dungeon, and the door closed on them.

Stretched on a bed, and in a broken slumber,

lay the hapless prisoner. As Reginald approached, he heard the name of Mildred murmured by her father. The sound of their footsteps, however, quickly roused him, and, starting with surprise, he rose and gloomily demanded who it was that had come to visit the miserable captive in his den.

"Do you not know me, my lord?" asked Reginald, in sorrowful accents. "Do you not recognise the son of De Lancy, who has come to effect your liberation from this abode of wretchedness and despair?"

"And who is he that accompanies you?"

"A friend," replied the youth, "who pities your condition, and has arranged with me a plan for effecting your escape from hence this night."

Ritzen now advanced, and briefly stating the arrangements that had been made, earnestly besought the captive to lose no time, since all depended upon the speed with which they effected their departure from the city.

Having in some degree recovered from the surprise into which he had been thrown, Heinbach aroused himself, and, although his sufferings were so recent, he was quickly habited in the disguise, and they quitted the prison without challenge or interruption, as Ritzen had free access to it at all times. On reaching the house of the latter, Reginald threw off the military garb and appeared in the travelling costume, and Heinbach, disguised as his servant, followed him to the place where their horses were standing ready saddled for the journey.

Passing through the city gates, they urged on their steeds and soon left the town far behind them. Then, reining in their horses, the baron proposed that they should proceed to his own canton, where he was resolved to raise such a force as would set his enemies at defiance, and particularly Arnheim, against whom he had vowed the most inveterate hatred.

At length they arrived within sight of a town, upon entering which they rode up to the door of an inn, and, having given their horses to a servant, were shewn into a room appropriated to the use of travellers. Here refreshments were placed before them, which, having partaken of, they sought that repose which their long journey had rendered necessary.

Next morning they continued their journey, and on arriving within sight of the Castle of Bautzen, gave themselves up to the pleasing anticipation of a speedy meeting with Mildred. At length they entered the fortress, upon which loud shouts of recognition were raised by the retainers, though, at the same time, their countenances were expressive of gloom and despondency. Heinbach looked anxiously around him, yet no Mildred appeared to welcome his return. A feeling of sickness stole over Reginald—a presentiment of evil struck to his heart while he followed the baron, who, accompanied by his steward, demanded an explanation of the gloom which was evident in the countenances of his retainers, and why the Lady Mildred had not yet appeared to welcome him.

"Alas! my lord," answered the old man, "you must summon all your resolution to support the evil tidings I have to relate—the Lady Mildred has suddenly disappeared, nor know we in what manner."

"Gone!" exclaimed the baron and Reginald in a breath; "whither has she fled?"

"That none of us can learn," replied the steward. "About a fortnight since, a person, bearing the appearance of a priest, came to the castle, and spoke of having a message of importance to deliver to our young lady. Supposing he came from your lordship, he was admitted and ushered to a chamber, where the Lady Mildred soon waited on him. Some time elapsed, when one of the servants hearing groans he gave an alarm, and, bursting into the chamber, we beheld the stranger stretched upon the floor, bathed in blood, and exhibiting scarcely any signs of life."

"And your young lady?"

"Was nowhere to be found," answered the steward. "The wound of the stranger was deep and dangerous, and for some days he lay nearly insensible. About a week since, however, a party of men came, and inquiring for him, the principal one was shewn into his chamber. He soon assisted the wounded man to rise and dress, when, having distributed some money among the servants, he was conveyed away in a carriage that was waiting for him at the gate. We would have detained him until our young lady was discovered, but he assured us he knew nothing of the cause of her extraordinary absence."

The feelings of both the father and the lover, on hearing this recital, may be better imagined than described. Heinbach knew not what course to pursue, nor upon whom to rest his suspicions. We shall, however, leave him and Reginald planning measures for the recovery of Mildred, while we, in as few words as possible, explain the mystery of her disappearance.

Arnheim having determined upon visiting the Castle of Bautzen, for the purpose of obtaining the papers to produce in support of his charge, and partly that he might see Mildred, of whose beauty he had heard such glowing descriptions, left his retinue at some distance, and presented himself alone at the castle. He obtained admission in the manner that has already been mentioned, and obtained the interview with Mildred that he had sought. From his travel-worn appearance, she imagined that he had come from her father, and with intense anxiety demanded the news of which she supposed he was the bearer.

"He will not return for some time," answered Arnheim, "and he has commissioned me to conduct you to him, as his stay at Berne must necessarily be much longer than he at first anticipated."

"Had he not time to write to me?" demanded the maiden with surprise.

"He was so much engaged that he was obliged to send me with a mere verbal message," answered the other, in his most plausible manner. "As a proof, however, that my mission is from him, he directed me to ask for a packet of papers that you will find in a private drawer belonging to his escrutoire."

"When are we to take our departure from hence?" again asked Mildred, with hesitation.

"This very hour," replied Arnheim; "there is much need of haste, and the baron requires your immediate presence."

"Liar! your doom is sealed!" exclaimed a voice

close by. "Your villany is discovered, but there is one at hand to punish the hellish treachery!"

Two rapid strokes of a dagger stretched Arnheim upon the ground, whilst Julio stood over him, with vengeance in his countenance, and his dark eyes flashing with demoniac fire.

Mildred trembling, and unable to move, caught his attention, and striding up to her, he grasped her arm, while brandishing in one hand the poniard which was still reeking with the blood of his victim:—"Scream, or resist, and you die upon the spot!" he exclaimed, as he dragged her to-

wards a flight of steps, at the bottom of which was a small chamber, passing through which they reached a cavern of vast extent. A distant glimmering of light denoted an outlet in that direction, on arriving at which, Mildred was surprised at perceiving the habit of a page and a large cloak lying upon the ground. These Julio directed her to assume, in exchange for her female attire, and whilst she dressed in these, he waited for her at the entrance of the cavern.

As soon as she was disguised in the page's habit, Julio conducted her into the midst of the forest, where two horses, ready saddled, were tied to a tree. Upon one of these he assisted her to mount, then throwing himself upon the other, they struck into a wild, and apparently unexplored path, by which they at last emerged from the forest, and found themselves in the high road.

Although Mildred was most anxious to effect her escape, yet, when she hazarded a glance at her strange conductor, and beheld his dark eye glanc-

ing at her, hope sunk within her breast; and although she did not wholly give way to despair, yet she could not but fear that a protracted absence from her father would lead to some disastrous results. Yet Julio's manners towards her were friendly—he had rescued her from imminent peril, and this circumstance alone gave him a claim to her gratitude.

At last they arrived at a town, where they rested two days. Julio did not prevent her from walking out while they remained there, for he was well aware that she had no means of escape, and, therefore, did not keep that strict watch over her that he had during the progress of her journey. They seldom conversed; indeed, Mildred preferred the solitude of her own thoughts.

Now that she was completely in his power, Julio did not think it worth his while to wear any longer the mask of hypocrisy, and he candidly admitted that he was bearing her away from, instead of to her father. At the same time, how--

ever, he desired her not to be alarmed, as it was his intention to place her among friends, with whom she would be perfectly safe.

The inn at which they had rested, had originally belonged to a nobleman of high rank, but who had lavished away his wealth, so that his estates soon passed from his possession into the hands of those to whom he had become indebted. As his fortune decreased, so did the pretended friends of his prosperity; when, maddened with himself and the ungrateful world, he was supposed to have rushed unbidden into the presence of his Maker. The mansion was soon afterwards taken by the present occupant, and converted into a tavern.

Such was the story related to Mildred by the girl who officiated as her attendant, and who timidly looked round the chamber, and started at the slightest noise caused by the rattling casements, or low moaning sound of the wind through the lofty arched corridors. She hurried through her attendance on Mildred, and leaving the lamp in the chamber, quitted it, trembling at the idea of passing through the house alone.

Next morning Mildred took a more careful survey of her apartment than she had on the previous evening. It was lofty and spacious, and evidently had not been intended as a sleeping-chamber. The walls were tapestried, and the windows long, narrow, and of the Gothic shape. As she passed her hand over the hangings, in one part it felt as if there was a space behind; this aroused her curiosity, and she attentively examined every part, to ascertain whether there was any concealed entrance, until lifting one corner of the tapestry that was loose, she discovered a recess behind, which afforded her some faint hopes of escape. At that moment, however, Julio suddenly entered the room.

CHAPTER XXXVI.

All, when life is new,
Commence with feelings warm, and prospects high,
But time strips our illusions of their hue.

BYRON.

IT is now necessary that we leave them on their road towards the sea-coast, in order that we may return to Heinbach and Reginald.

The visit of the stranger, and the subsequent mysterious absence of Mildred, led to continued inquiries, which eventually proved that the stranger was no other than Arnheim. The baron vowed the most deadly vengeance against his implacable foe, but, not to place himself at the mercy of his enemies a second time, he filled his castle with troops, and had soldiers stationed upon the surrounding eminences, to give notice of any hostile approach; and having furnished the castle with sufficient provisions for a lengthened siege, he awaited letters from his partizans, whom he had despatched to Bern, to gain intelligence of the enemy's movements.

Distracted with a thousand fears for the safety of the idol of his affections, Reginald could not conceal his feelings from the baron, who gladly discovered the partiality that existed between his his daughter and the companion of her early life. But now the sad interruption to their mutual happiness was doubly felt; all inquiries proved unavailing; but they returned without bringing any favourable tidings, and had not the Baron Heinbach some active pursuits to employ his time, he would inevitably have sunk under his misfortunes.

In the midst of all this confusion and dismay, Reginald received a letter from his father, desiring him to join him without loss of time, as he was engaged in a mission to England, where a treaty of some little importance was in progress. In another letter, which was addressed to Heinbach, he arranged a correspondence, so that all his future plans might be communicated.

It was with much regret that the baron parted with Reginald, who could not but feel severely upon leaving Bautzen, uncertain as he was of the fate of Mildred—to leave Switzerland, unknowing when it would be in his power to revisit it. Without the occurrence of any particular incident he joined his father, with whom he shortly afterwards landed in England.

As our travellers and their train advanced towards London, they became aware of a figure, seated by the roadside; the man rose as they approached, and addressing De Lancy said,—

"If you are not above taking counsel you will change your route; for, three miles hence, you will be waylaid by a band who are now lying in ambush to attack your party. Resistance would be useless, as their number far exceeds your own."

"How came you to know this?" demanded the knight.

"When you passed me a short time since," replied the stranger, "I could not avoid feeling much interested by the features of this noble youth who rode beside you; he bears so close a resemblance to one whom I formerly valued as my dearest friend; this excited my attention to the conversation of two men, who spoke in a suppressed tone of De Lancy, plunder, and attack, and prisoners' ransom, and reward from their employer. It struck me that some evil must be intended to you and your party; I therefore joined their conversation, pretending I was a man willing to embark in any deed of darkness so that my services were well paid for. This obtained their confidence, and having pressed me to join them, they declared their purpose. I acceded to all their wishes, and agreed to meet them at the place of ambush."

De Lancy's attendants were too few to cope with their enemies, and the only means they had of eluding them was to take a different road. None of the party, however, could act as a guide, until fortunately a peasant approached, who, upon being questioned, informed them that he knew of a circuitous road by which they might reach the metropolis. Under present circumstances, this difference in the distance was of no consequence, and the peasant, having agreed for his reward, was mounted upon one of the spare horses, while the traveller from whom they had received the timely information was similarly accommodated. Turning to the right, they crossed a bleak moor of some miles in extent, upon attaining the further borders of which they arrived at a town, where they dismissed their guide, and reached London without any further adventure.

De Lancy offered a liberal remuneration to the stranger for the valuable service he had rendered them; but he respectfully declined the gift, and solicited instead a situation in the knight's household. To this Sir Edmund acceded, and he was appointed to be the attendant of Reginald, with directions to accompany and guard him whenever he went out.

We must now follow Julio and Mildred upon their rapid journey. After they had quitted the last place where we left them, they travelled without interruption until they reached the sea coast, when Julio informed her that business of moment would require his absence for some months; and having arranged with the superior of a convent for the temporary residence of Mildred there, whilst he was away, he left strict injunctions not to allow her to leave the walls of the edifice. The reason of his sudden departure was intelligence he had received from the captain of a merchant's vessel, and who was about to return immediately to England. Agreeing, therefore, for his passage, he was soon afterwards on his way to Britain.

Left to the free indulgence of her own thoughts, Mildred wandered through the gloomy building in which she was a prisoner; and the only time she felt a gleam of happiness was when in the garden, from whence a magnificent view of the ocean was to be obtained. As she gazed, tears would fill her eyes; the happy days passed at Bautzen would flash across her mind; now separated from her parent, home, and lover, without a congenial mind to participate in her feelings.

The superior was haughty and repelling in her manner; the nuns were elderly females, and had she been inclined to exert the flow of spirits natural to her, it would have been regarded as a most heinous crime, and ill in accordance with the strict propriety of the convent. With the sisters, therefore, she had but little communion; the gloomy bigotry of their countenances, and the solemnity of their deportment, threw a damp over her existence. Still she cherished the fond hope of being soon restored to her former happiness.

She was one day seated in the garden, enjoying the cool refreshing breezes from the ocean, when, at a distance, she perceived one of the nuns. As she approached, her veil, being drawn aside, disclosed a countenance fraught with the remains of exquisite beauty, but now presenting traces of care and ill health; her figure was tall and slight, and a mournful expression passed across her features, as her eyes rested upon Mildred.

Taking a seat beside her, she made some remarks upon the beauty of the scene; her tones were mournfully sweet, and her language of the most refined description. Mildred was agreeably surprised when the stranger addressed her; her superiority above the other inmates of the convent was evident, and she promised to be a desirable acquaintance where all the others were so cold and haughty.

While these thoughts were passing in the mind of poor Mildred, the attention of the stranger was fixed upon a vessel just entering the bay; her white sails filled with a favourable breeze, which wafted her towards the shore, and her gay streamers floating upon the gale. The nun sighed as she thus gazed, and, after the silence of some few moments, she said,—

"I have been reflecting, my dear child, upon the situation you are placed in at your early age. You must, however, bear up against the vicissitudes of this life, and remember that you are not the only one who suffers from cruelty and injustice."

"I am quite aware," answered Mildred, "that there are thousands of others as unhappy as myself. Half the troubles of life, however, are removed, when we have friends with whom we can converse, and, with you, even this dull convent may not be without its charms. Be, therefore, my friend and adviser; let your words comfort me, and I shall in time learn to bow with entire submission to the will of Heaven."

The friendship thus commenced increased with each succeeding day, and Mildred found that the solitude she had been doomed to had lost half its terrors. Her mind was now comparatively happy, though she anxiously looked forward to the return of Julio, from whom she hoped to hear intelligence of her father and Reginald. At the close of each day, when the sun moderated its scorching rays, when the cool breeze of evening threw around a refreshing calm, she and the nun would seek the terrace in the garden, from whence they could view the bay, crowded with boats and presenting an ever varying prospect.

One day, when she was seated in this place alone, she was suddenly seized upon and hurried away in the arms of one of the men composing a band of ruffians who had unexpectedly stolen upon her. Whither they were carrying her she knew not; fear chained her tongue, and although she strove to ascertain what her captors were speaking about, she could not understand their language, though she was aware that they spoke in Italian.

At length they reached the sea coast, and found two boats waiting, into one of which she was carried, and conveyed on board a vessel that lay at anchor; the darkness of the night prevented her remarking the appearance of her conductors; but when she was placed upon the deck of the vessel, she found herself surrounded by men whose fierce looks assured her but too truly that she had fallen into the hands of pirates. A sickness came over her, and she lost all recollection, until she recovered to find herself in a cabin belonging to the vessel, and attended by a female. The remembrance of her situation again flashed upon her mind, and once more she sank back upon her couch in a state of insensibility.

In this situation we must now leave her, whilst we convey the reader amidst far different scenes and characters.

With hurried steps and glances impatiently cast seaward, Nadoc paced the platform before his castle, heedless of the cold blast, or the salt spray which dashed over the parapet. His eyes ever and anon sought for some looked for object. It was the close of a winter's day, and dark clouds spread quickly through the sky; the sea looked wild and angry, and the boisterous surge broke in foaming waves over the lower rocks upon which the castle stood.

The figure of Nadoc was large and muscular, his countenance dark and fierce, while his eyes darted their fiery glances from black, shaggy brows. His mantle was thrown around him, and his arms were folded as he paced to and fro.

"Stephen comes not," he muttered to himself;

" he was not wont to be so tardy, yet he is a friend, and such as I can trust. My plans, too, are well laid, and when I land my golden cargo hither, I'll bid defiance to my foes from this sea-girt spot."

A bright flash at this moment gleamed upon the horizon, and although to others it might appear like lightning, yet the experienced eye of Nadoc at once recognized it to be a signal gun from the vessel he was expecting. Raising a whistle to his lips, a shrill blast was sounded, and the clank of armed men was immediately heard.

Upon the arrival of the soldiers upon the platform, he directed the beacon on the watch tower to be fired, and lighted torches to be held by the whole band. Another flash, and the report of a gun now heard, denoted the vessel to be near, and soon the white sails were distinguishable as she approached.

The bark was now entering the harbour, and a shout of welcome from those in the fortress was echoed by a corresponding burst from those on board. Sweeping majestically before the gale, she shot past the castle, and was at once in smooth water. A heavy plash announced the fall of the anchor, and Nadoc and his band hastened into the castle to await the presence of their comrades.

The chief anxiously paced the hall listening to every sound, whilst bursts of noisy merriment broke from groups of men who were assembled together. At length Stephen, the lieutenant of the band, entered, accompanied by his crew.

" What news, Stephen ?" exclaimed Nadoc, impatiently ; " say briefly what intelligence you bring me."

But Stephen, by a sign, notified that he had a communication to make in private, and they withdrew together.

Whatever the intelligence might be, when they afterwards assembled at the evening's repast, several of the band perceived that some plan of moment was in agitation. Nadoc was unusually silent, and a sullen melancholy was on his visage.

Meanwhile, the noise of revelry and mirth sounded through the hall. The party who had just returned entertained their comrades with an account of their exploits, and the plunder they had gained. In the midst of this, Rodolphe, a ruffianly-looking fellow, drew a dagger from his belt, and exultingly pointing to the stains on its blade, exclaimed,—

" Look ye, comrades ; this bit of steel has brought more to the cause than any other in the band ; no one can tax me with being chicken-hearted ; but methinks were one in want of a confessor, Oliver here would do well for the service ; witness the last affair in which ——"

" What would the prince of cutthroats with Oliver ?" demanded the person alluded to, addressing himself to Rodolphe ; " I am not easily moved, but when my blood is once up, even those that sneer at me may be made to tremble for their worthless lives."

" Why is all this anger ?" demanded Nadoc, for the first time interfering.

" Oh, it's nothing unusual, captain," said Lawrence ; " Oliver protected a female from the dagger of Rodolphe, and they have been snarling at each other ever since."

" For shame !" cried Nadoc ; " are you a man, Rodolphe, to raise your dagger against a woman. But where is the female you speak of ?"

" Aye, there's the rub, captain," replied Lawrence ; " we would have brought the damsel with us, and truly she is a present fit for an emperor, but she escaped through Oliver's interference, and we could not delay for a pursuit ; besides, we know not who we should have had to cope with."

" Where is she supposed to be ?" demanded Nadoc.

" In one of the islands off the Scottish coast," answered Lawrence ; " we stopped there to take in water, and landing met her near the coast."

" We will go thither in search of her," exclaimed the captain. " Now, my lads, fill your goblets ; here is ' Success to the pirate's life, and may we never meet a foe stronger than ourselves !' "

Three tremendous cheers rang through the hall, and might have been heard even outside the massive walls of the ancient fortress.

" Where will our gallant captain lead us next ?" exclaimed Lawrence. " Methinks we have been rather idle of late."

" Perhaps so, but it is no fault of mine," answered the leader ; " and I promise you ere long a prize that shall make amends for the little we have hitherto been doing. You all know the Castle of Danebury, where Lord Dalmeny has lately caused the greater part of his wealth to be conveyed. It is but weakly guarded, and even were it twice as strong, I should have little doubt as to the result. But I must first reconnoitre, and arrange my plans accordingly. Lawrence, you are a good musician, and disguised as a wandering minstrel shall accompany me to-morrow. Stephen, how many do we at present muster ?"

" Scarcely fifty," answered the lieutenant, " besides those who are required on board the vessels.'

" The force will be strong enough," exclaimed Nadoc ; " and next week, when there will be little moon to mar our purpose, we will try our fortune."

So saying, he took a lamp from the table and sought his chamber, while the remainder of the pirate band kept up their scene of revelry till a late hour.

We must now return to the solitary cottage inhabited by Luke Somerton and his daughter, Louisa, as mentioned in a former part of this work. The young female gazed frequently towards her father, who was apparently occupied in reading, but whose mind was, in reality, filled with thoughts that occasioned him the greatest uneasiness. At length, closing his book abruptly, he rose and paced the room for a few minutes, then suddenly pausing, he exclaimed,—

" My dearest Louisa, you must be upon your guard, and not extend your walks so far as you have been used to do of late. Even here you are scarcely safe ; but I tremble lest you should again be exposed to danger such as you escaped. Had I been present, girl, I would have resented the insolence of those who intruded upon you."

" Dear sir," she replied, " I am most thankful that you were absent, or your life might have been sacrificed in an encounter with the ruffians."

" Had they the appearance of sailors ?" he asked.

" They had, though not such as I have been accustomed to see,"

"Heaven shield us, my child, from such ill-omened visitors!" cried the old man; "I can well believe that they belong to a band of pirates, who have for some time infested this part of the coast but whose haunt has hitherto eluded the search instituted by government."

At that moment, Richard, the humble follower of Luke Somerton, entered the cottage, exclaiming with alarm,—

"Master, dear master, make haste down to the sea-shore, for there's a number of ships approaching the coast, and I fear lest their errand should prove a dangerous one for yourself!"

Startled by this intelligence, Luke hurried from the place, and quickly beheld a scene as novel as it was animating. Five vessels under sail had passed the extreme point of the island, and were about to anchor. This was a sight Louisa had never seen before, and her father called her to view it. The sea was beautifully calm, and a light breeze barely curled the blue surface, whilst the waves, as they sluggishly rolled upon the beach, had not sufficient impetus to break into foam.

"Observe those ships, Louisa," he exclaimed; "by their rig and appearance, they belong to England. Would that they may have come from Ireland, for then might I know how matters are going on, and whether the time has yet arrived when I may recover my lost rank and wealth."

"And yet, dearest father, what is fortune without happiness?" she demanded.

"True," he replied; "but it will be unwise, if now that an opportunity should offer itself, to reject it. Besides, I am thy only protector, and, were I to be called from this world, to whose care could I leave thee? But see—some boats are quitting the vessels; retire, my love, and see prepared whatever refreshments we have to offer; for we must show these strangers, as far as lies in our power, the rites of hospitality."

On hastening down to the beach, Luke found a group of islanders, hazarding various conjectures as to who the strangers could be, and the purpose of their visit, while Richard having launched a boat was waiting for his master; for this, however, there was no occasion, as shortly afterwards a number of sailors, accompanied by an officer, had reached the shore. The latter was attired in his uniform, yet, though his appearance had been much altered since their last meeting, Luke immediately recognized the countenance of an old acquaintance, and eagerly advancing, he exclaimed,—

"Do my eyes deceive me, or is it indeed Terence who thus once more crosses my path?"

"Sir Luke Somerton!" ejaculated the officer, "to what extraordinary chance do we owe this most extraordinary meeting? Do I indeed again behold him whom I have long mourned as lost? But say," he continued, "how is it that I find you in this island? Your garb, dear sir, informs me but too truly that your circumstances are not what they were when I last saw you."

"The narrative is somewhat long," answered Luke; "but if you will accompany me to my cottage, I will there relate all that has occurred during the long interval of our separation."

"I have some few orders to issue, and shall then be at your service," replied Terence. Then addressing himself to the sailors, he directed them to return on board, and tell the lieutenant that two of the vessels must weigh and stand on for the coast, and that he would join them on the following day. Then accompanying Luke Somerton, they took the path that led towards the cottage.

The night, which by this time had set in, was one of those dark and cheerless ones that we sometimes find in summer, when there is not a breath of wind stirring, nor a sound, save the bark of some watch-dog. On such a night it was that a boat shot through the gloom, and ran upon the beach in the river Shannon. It contained two persons, one of them a youth of fair and open aspect; the other, a man whose visage denoted the presence of various conflicting passions. As the light boat grated upon the beach, the elder of the two sprang upon the shore, and was speedily followed by his companion.

"Now," exclaimed the eldest, "know you where you are?"

"How should I, mysterious being?" demanded the youth; "plunged into a deep slumber by a drug, and borne from my home and friends, and kept closely confined, how can I know whither you have conveyed me?"

"Reginald," answered the other, with vainly suppressed emotion, "didst thou ever hear of thy mother?—didst thou ever hear of her melancholy fate?"

"Why do you ask me that question?" demanded Reginald; "I once put that question to my father, but he evaded a reply, as if there was some mystery which I had no right to penetrate. Tell me, then, do you know aught of her who brought me into this world of wretchedness and woe?"

"Know her!" cried the other, bitterly. "Oh, merciful Heaven, what terrible thoughts does her name awaken in my mind! But away with this weakness. Take this purse and sword, Reginald, and follow this line of beach until you arrive at a dark and massive building, to which you will obtain ready admittance. When asked your business, say that you are the stranger who was expected, and then demand a packet, which you will open at the first opportunity that offers, and you will therein find all the directions which are required."

"I will obey your instructions," answered the youth; "but ere I go on my errand, tell me if we have not met in days gone by?"

"Why do you ask that question?"

"Because your voice seems familiar to me."

"At present," replied the other, "there are reasons why I cannot satisfy your curiosity. Follow the instructions I have given, and ere long we shall meet again."

Landed, as he was, upon a strange shore, and left to himself, Reginald felt completely at a loss to account for the mysterious agency and purpose for which he had been brought from Italy. There was much in this last adventure that he was unable to account for. From a long and unnatural sleep he awoke and found himself on shipboard; the cabin door was secured on the outside, and no means were left by which he could communicate with those in the other part of the vessel. Whenever the man who afterwards brought him refreshments entered the cabin, he perceived that another was stationed outside, and no information could he obtain from his mute attendant, who never opened his lips, however strongly he might be appealed to. Glad, therefore, was he when at length the anchor was cast, and he found himself once more permitted to breathe the fresh air, of which he had so long been deprived. There were none upon the deck save himself and his mysterious conductor, whom he now beheld for the first time. He was directed to enter a boat which had been lowered alongside; the stranger followed, and they reached the shore, where the foregoing conversation took place.

Following the directions he had received, he slowly made his way along the dark and rugged path, and after a wearisome walk of more than an hour, he found himself in front of a ruined entrance of a large constellated edifice. The piers at each side of the gate were formed of roughly hewn stone, nearly overgrown with ivy, and through whose thickly tangled leaves the night wind mournfully rustled.

The rising moon, however, gave him a distinct view of the building from the gate. A broad roadway led to the mansion, the gate of which had fallen from its hinges. He passed on, and was crossing the hall when a gleam of light caused him to start involuntarily, and immediately afterwards a deep-toned bell sounded the hour of midnight. Arriving at the opposite door, he knocked loudly, and after waiting two or three minutes, a voice from the other side demanded his name and business.

"I am here for a packet," answered the youth.

"Whence came you?"

"From the sea."

"'Tis well. Enter."

And the door was immediately thrown open for him. Reginald gazed around him, but the torch he bore only faintly disclosed the vast extent of the chamber which he now entered. The attention of Reginald was next directed to his conductor. Ruffian was legibly stamped upon his countenance, and traits of the deepest cunning marked every feature. His figure was of gigantic proportions, and as the light gleamed upon the various weapons he carried, he stood, in appearance, a declared bandit.

Reginald's suspicions were aroused, yet concealing them within his own bosom, he followed the man up a broad flight of steps, and at length entered a chamber, in which was a blazing fire, a table spread with wine and provisions, and every appearance of comfort that a weary traveller could desire. The man made a sign for him to be seated, when, going to a large chest that stood on one side of the chamber, he took out a packet and handed it to the visitor. Reginald hesitated not, but breaking open the seal, he read the following lines, which only served to increase the wonder and anxiety he already felt:—

"If you desire to behold your father, and one whom you regard as most dear, implicitly follow the directions of him to whom you will be conveyed. But ask no questions, nor express your astonishment at anything you may see or hear."

Reginald was much perplexed by the mystery which still involved him; however, he determined to wait with what patience he could the appearance of the individual whom he had yet to see.

"Come, young sir," exclaimed the man, "the night is none of the warmest, and a cup of this good liquor will send your blood tingling through your veins."

The hint thus thrown out was too inviting to be rejected, and, as his appetite had been somewhat sharpened by the night air, Reginald did not fail to do ample justice to the excellent viands that had been placed before him. At length, breaking the silence, which had lasted some time, he inquired of the man if any one else dwelt in the place besides himself.

"At present, sir, I have the whole of the building to myself," answered the other; "you must know that this place is a kind of depot of ours; the rest of our people are farther up the river, but I expect them home before the sun rises."

"My arrival here," said Reginald, "was, I believe, not altogether unexpected?"

"Ay, our lieutenant expected you."

"Who is your chief?"

"That you will know all in good time."

A loud and very shrill whistle outside now interrupted them, and the man, starting from his seat, exclaimed, "Here they are," and immediately hastened down stairs.

In a few minutes the sound of several footsteps was heard approaching along the passage, and the door being thrust open, the man who had given admittance to Reginald entered the room, accompanied by another.

"You are welcome, my young friend," said the person who had last arrived. "I have expected you some time, and began almost to despair of your coming. Of course," he added to his companion, "you gave the young gentleman the packet according to the directions?"

"I did."

"Then now leave us," said the lieutenant; "and mind that all is in readiness by daybreak."

CHAPTER XXXV.

It was a ship, and a ship of fame,
Launched off the stocks—bound for the main;
With an hundred and twenty brisk young men,
All picked and chosen every one.—*Old Song.*

THE action, which it is our present purpose to describe, commenced with equal resolution on both sides. The English ship was much better worked than her opponent, and nothing but the desperate courage of the pirate crew would have withstood the desperate force with which they were attacked. They neared each other, and their yards and rigging becoming entangled, a party of British sailors poured irresistibly upon the deck of the pirate vessel. Prepared, however, to oppose them, stood the others, much reduced in numbers indeed, but led by the captain, Nadoc, whose fierce courage was of itself a host.

The contending parties met in furious collision— the pirates receiving fresh courage from the example that was set them by their leader. At length, however, he suddenly paused; his upraised arm was suspended, and a shudder thrilled through his frame, as before him stood a youth, who, armed only with a sword, was contending fiercely with the enemy. He had already struck down two of the pirates, and was advancing with unhesitating step to attack their leader.

The English had began to retreat, when this unexpected auxiliary inspired them with fresh hope; the crowd of combatants hid Reginald—for he it was—from Nadoc, who now, summoning all his energies, headed a furious charge with his surviving crew. So resistless, indeed, was this last effort, that they drove the enemy back to their own vessel, and a breeze springing up, by a sudden filling of the only sail they had remaining, the pirate swung clear from her opponent.

To account for the sudden disappearance of Reginald on board Nadoc's vessel, it must be remembered he accompanied Stephen to the place where the pirate vessel lay—upon going on board which he was placed in a cabin secured upon the outside. Fortunately the door was of slight materials, and much exertion was not required to force it open; so that, upon hearing the preparations for an engagement, he hastily dressed himself, and rushing upon deck, snatched up the sword of a fallen combatant.

When the vessels separated, and he found himself with the English, he relinquished his weapon, and addressing a person who appeared to have command of the ship, he asked in what part of the world they then were.

"For," he added, "I have been seized and borne from my friends in so mysterious a manner, and without any apparent object, that I am most anxious to let my friends know where I am at present."

"You are now," said the officer, "on board a vessel of war belonging to Queen Anne of England. I have the honour of being her commander, and for the service you lately did us, I now return my thanks."

The officer and Reginald now descended to the cabin, and a slight wound of the former having been dressed by the surgeon, the young stranger communicated his name and rank to Captain Danvers, between whom and himself a feeling of friendship had been already established.

"Your story is certainly a singular one," said the captain, on hearing it to a conclusion. "At present I can see no clue by which we may hope to unravel it, and you can only look for an explanation from him who brought you from your native land."

"Where can I seek him?" demanded Reginald.

"That is a question rather difficult to answer," returned the captain, "though I have no doubt he is a confederate of the band we have just encountered. With us you should have good quarters and honourable treatment while you remain, which, I suspect will be some time, as I fear there will be no opportunity of landing you in France for some time to come. In the meanwhile, consider me as your friend, and do not refuse—as a loan, if you would rather it should be so—a sum sufficient to provide against immediate necessities."

This generous and well-timed offer was at once accepted by Reginald, and he would now have felt himself happy, had not the remembrance of Mildred flashed across his mind. When he thought of the days of undisturbed felicity that he had passed at the Castle of Bautzen—the dangers he had escaped in battle—and the fond and pleasing anticipations he had indulged in of ultimate happiness, the retrospection threw a gloom over his spirits, and, hastening to the deck, he stood gazing upon the blue waters around him, though his thoughts were wandering amidst the fertile districts of fair Switzerland.

At length the vessel having reached the coast of Ireland, they cast anchor, and the captain proceeded on shore to report his arrival to the queen's deputy. Reginald did not accompany him, but, retiring to his cabin, was still buried in profound thought, when Captain Danvers, having returned in the interim, once more presented himself before him.

"I have seen the Lord Lieutenant," he exclaimed; "and, from what has passed, it seems necessary that you should conceal the fact of your being a native of France. Our queen is now at war with your nation, and you may be suspected, however innocent, of being a spy. In short, none here, except myself, must be in your confidence."

The young man willingly acceded to this proposition; and then proceeding to the deck, they entered a boat which was lying alongside, and were immediately rowed towards the shore. The low land to the south and east of the town, and forming the head of the bay, was thickly wooded, the trees growing to the water's edge, and as the tide was full in, they appeared as if sprung out of the sea. Towards the north the shore presented a different aspect, steep cliffs and promontories jutting into the sea, upon whose rugged summits there was scarcely sufficient earth to nourish the heath and stinted grass that was the only verdure it afforded.

Immediately in front of the town, a number of the inhabitants had assembled upon the beach to gaze upon the strangers, whose arrival had occasioned no little sensation among them. No obstruction, however, was offered, and having landed, Captain Danvers ordered his men to return on board, and bring him some packages to the inn, where he intended to put up for a short time.

The sound of the minstrel's harp rang through the spacious halls of the Castle of Dalmeny, and there sat the noble proprietor, surrounded by his friends and adherents, whilst the wine-cup was frequently emptied to do honour to his various patriotic toasts.

"Success to the Lord Dalmeny," was one of them, "and may the brave sons of the west be victorious over those who would fetter their limbs in iron!"

"We will be victorious, my friends." exclaimed Dalmeny, looking triumphantly around him. "What though I have been made captive by the bright eyes of Clonberlie's fair daughter, think you, in the battle's heat, my sword would spare her brother Robert, knowing, as I do, that Ireland has not within her a spirit more subtle or vindictive. Think you that I forget the field of mortal strife? No, by Heavens, though my wounds are healed, they have left behind a pain that neither time nor circumstances can cure. And now, forsooth! who has the English queen set above us? Why, this very man, who, traitor to his name and country, mingles his blood with the Saxons. One act of mine I shall ever regret—I mean that of joining the English in my plans, and seeing them afterwards fail me in the hour of need."

"Well, well," cried O'Brien, "think no more of the past, but rather look forward to the revenge that is in store for us. You all know the high and mighty Hugh Macnish carries the sword of state before the Lord Lieutenant, who already fancies himself the lord of Ireland."

"Curses upon him !" exclaimed Dalmeny.

The entrance of two strangers here interrupted the conversation. By their habits they appeared to be a couple of wandering native minstrels ; their figures were tall, and the countenance of the elder one possessed a rather pleasing, though, perhaps, forced expression. They had no arms of any kind ; each wore a short cloak, which, when brought over the shoulder, served to cover the harps which they carried. Upon advancing up the hall, they gazed round them, which being perceived by Dalmeny, he demanded, in a haughty tone, who they were, and what had brought them to his castle.

"We are travellers," answered the elder one, with assumed humility, "and having heard a good report of your lordship's hospitality, have ventured to request food and shelter, till the morrow's dawn enables us to pursue our way."

"Ye shall find both," exclaimed Dalmeny, as he directed one who appeared to be a favourite attendant. "Let these strangers be attended to, and see that they receive the best my castle affords."

Nadoc, for he it was in disguise, accompanied by one of his band, did not quit the hall without taking due note of the number and state of those who were assembled, not did they seem likely to offer any very formidable resistance. From one of his spies he had received intelligence of a considerable quantity of treasure having been conveyed to the castle, and his present visit was to reconnoitre previous to the meditated attack. They followed the attendant to another apartment, where an abundance of provisions were placed before them in obedience to the commands given by Lord Dalmeny. During the progress of the repast Nadoc began to sound the servant.

"Doubtless," he exclaimed, " you are happy in the employ of so good and generous a master ?"

"So much so," replied the man, " that I shall never desire to transfer my services to another."

"My Lord Dalmeny," continued the pirate, "has the character of being an indulgent master, a generous friend, and an invincible enemy. Now, however, he is at peace."

"Yes," replied the man, " we are at peace just at present, though Heaven knows how long it will last. Be that as it may, however, we are prepared for the worst."

"Do you always keep up a sufficient force in the event of a sudden attack being made ?"

"That depends upon the number of the enemy by whom we might be assailed," answered the servant ; "at present we number only one hundred armed men ; but in a week we shall have ten times as many."

"And your leaders ?"

"Are men of high reputation—soldiers who have been tried in the field, and may, therefore, be relied on."

"Think you Lord Dalmeny would enlist us in his cause ?" demanded the pirate chief.

"That is more than I can undertake to answer for," replied the man, " though I have no doubt he would, because he is in want of all the assistance he can procure. So, if you know the use of arms, you will assuredly receive a hearty welcome, and such honourable treatment as your merit may deserve. However, as you appear to be fatigued, defer your offer till to-morrow, when I will lead you to his presence, and you may declare your wishes to him. So, now, remain here awhile till I make the necessary arrangements for your accommodation."

The man hereupon quitted the chamber, when Nadoc, having ascertained that no one was listening, stepped up to his companion, and in a low tone said,—

"By heavens ! Lawrence, this is beyond my hopes ; the garrison is weak, and our band more than doubles them in number. To-morrow night shall see this castle attacked and pillaged, its halls and chambers desolate, and my Lord Dalmeny's coffers emptied, and divided amongst those who join me in the expedition."

At this juncture the attendant returned and informed them that a chamber was prepared for their reception. The two friends had presence of mind enough to change the subject of their conversation as the man entered, and presently afterwards they followed him to the sleeping room where they were to pass the night.

*   *   *   *   *

"Och, Patrick ! honey dear,—what a gossoon you are to be standin' there, scratchin' your head whilst the poor cratur, drippin' wet as she is, will take her death with cowld,—run for the smallest taste of whisky in the world."

Such were the words uttered by Patrick O'Gorman's wife, as she was trying to restore animation to a beautiful female, who had been discovered upon some floating wreck off the coast near where their cottage was situated. She had been brought to land, and as yet had shown few, if any, signs of life. At length a slight pulsation gave some faint hopes of recovery, and as soon as Mrs. O'Gorman got the spirits from her husband, and a few of her female neighbours had come to her assistance, she pushed her better half out of the room, and then closing the door, afforded every assistance she could think of to her guest.

Divesting her as quickly as possible of her wet habiliments, and bringing her own bed near to the fire, she dried her well, and applied the spirits externally as well as forcing a small portion of it warmed down the throat of the poor lady, who soon opened her eyes, and gazing with astonishment, closed them again, as if the objects she beheld were only in a dream.

"Spake to me, honey, there's a dear," cried the dame, " spake to me, I say, and tell me how you feel after the whisky I've been pouring down your throat ? Take another drop, and maybe you'll then be getting better of the cowld water that has found its way to your stomach."

Again the stranger opened her eyes, and spoke, but her language was incomprehensible to the good women by whom she was surrounded.

"What is she after saying, Mrs. O'Gorman ?" asked one of them who happened to be rather hard of hearing.

"Bad manners to me, if I can tell," replied the old woman ; " but stop a bit, a bright thought has just struck me ;" and, opening the door, she went out to look for her husband, who, upon finding, she directed to go and bring Father Manesty, the parish priest, "who," she observed, " was just the man they wanted, for he spoke a power of languages."

Father Manesty was soon found ; and, as the

news had by this time spread abroad that a beautiful foreign lady was at Patrick O'Gorman's, the good-natured priest, guessing the occasion of his being sent for, hastened as quickly as possible to the cottage where his presence was required. Having first satisfied himself how the lady had come there, he next proceeded to speak to her in French, and as she was by that time much recovered, she immediately replied to him in the language he had used. The priest now became curious to learn where she came from, and she did not keep him any very long time in suspense.

When Mildred had been borne from the convent on board the strange vessel, they immediately hoisted sail, and for some time pursued their voyage under tolerably favourable circumstances. As the female who attended her did not understand French or Italian, Mildred could not gain any information as to whither they were bound. When she went upon deck and viewed the vast expanse of waters upon which their solitary vessel appeared as a speck, fears that she would never again behold her father, or the friends of her youth, would frequently cross her mind. But again she placed her full reliance upon heaven, and with resignation yielded herself to the protection of a superior power. The strange and wild appearance of the

crew of the vessel had at first terrified her; but by degrees her fears subsided, and she felt anxious for their arrival at whatever place they were destined for.

One morning she was awoke by the violent motion of the vessel, the roaring of the tempest, and the hurried confusion of the mariners as they quickly moved from place to place on the deck. Rising from her couch, with much difficulty, she reached the deck; but as she did so, what a sight of horror met her view!—the deck strewed with broken fragments, and several of the dead bodies of the crew, who had been killed by the falling of the masts. The devoted vessel, tottering on the ridge of a mountain wave, would suddenly dart down into the dark abyss, apparently never to rise again; then, gradually mounting to the summit of another billow, she would appear amidst the white foam that crested the wave. Without sail, and urged on by the fury of the wind, she scudded before the gale; the crew, unable to work, and worn out by the fatigue of the previous night, threw themselves upon the deck, resigning themselves to whatever fate was in store for them.

Mildred gazed upon the scene with more composure and resolution than might have been expected; but her spirits were broken by the hapless condition in which she had been thrown, and death, in any shape, would have been preferable to the misery she was then enduring.

The evening again came on, and all around them was threatening; above the horizon, and in the direction of their course, there appeared to be what some of the crew declared to be land, but they could not ascertain it to a certainty ere the darkness of night again closed upon them; and all, therefore, was conjecture. Still Mildred remained upon deck, even through the storm of night, till at length a tremendous shock was felt throughout the vessel, and a wild cry of horror burst from the whole crew. The timbers of the ill-fated ship grated harshly upon the rocks, and then came the foaming surge, rushing and boiling through her riven planks. Floating upon part of the deck, which still held together like a raft, she was borne along towards the shore, and next morning was fortunately discovered by some Irish fishermen, who rescued her from a fate that appeared inevitable, and she was then conveyed to one of their cottages, as we have already mentioned.

While Father Manesty was conversing with Mildred, Mrs. O'Gorman and her neighbours, with countenances expressive of impatience, were waiting to hear all the particulars about the strange young lady.

"Be quiet, will you?" exclaimed the priest, "for I've no time to tell you yet what you are all so anxious to hear. But take care of the poor dear creature, and don't give her any more of the whiskey, or you'll send her into a burning fever, that will end her life in less than no time. Here, give me the bottle; for, now I think of it, prevention is always better than a cure."

So saying, the worthy priest snatched the bottle from Mrs. O'Gorman, applied the neck to his lips, and, turning the bottom upwards, seemed to relish the contents, if one might judge by the long continuation of the draught, and the loud smack he gave as soon as the whole of the contents had found their way to his stomach.

"Ah!" he exclaimed, puffing and blowing with the exertion he had just gone through, "see what I have done, out of good nature and humanity."

Upon leaving the cottage, the priest gave strict orders that their guest should be kept as quiet and free from interruption as possible. He then returned home to comfort himself with his favourite pipe, when a sudden thought struck him, and he hurried out, directing his way along a bye-road till he arrived at a straggling pile of buildings, which had formerly been a nunnery, but was now occupied by a person to whom we are about to introduce the reader.

Geoffrey Dunholm, the present head of his family, had attained much fame in the court of France by many gallant acts that he had achieved. He was a most accomplished gentleman, and a perfect courtier, in the strictest sense of the word. Still there was much haughty superiority in his manner, and from his long residence in foreign countries he had formed so light an opinion of females, that he only regarded them as agreeable trifles to wile away his lighter hours. This defect in his character gave much serious annoyance to his mother, the Lady Rachel Dunholm, whose character had ever been most praiseworthy and exemplary. From the time of her husband's death she had secluded herself from society, and resisted every argument of her friends to mix once more with the world.

It was to this lady that Father Manesty took his way, and, upon being shown into her presence, he at once stated the purpose for which he had come. Relating, as nearly as his memory would serve, the story he had heard from Mildred, he submitted that the cottage where she now was could not be deemed a fit place for the daughter of a nobleman, and proposing that, till she could be conveyed to her friends, she should be provided with an asylum at the nunnery.

Actuated by her own generous feelings, Lady Rachel at once agreed to the proposal, and a party of servants, with a letter, and under the priest's guidance, was despatched to conduct Mildred from the cottage where she had found present refuge. This change was an agreeable one, for, although the people where she was had treated her with undeviating kindness, yet, from not being able to comprehend their language, or to make herself understood, she was much at a loss. She therefore willingly acceded to the proposition that was made, and, proceeding to the nunnery, experienced the welcome and hospitality that had been promised by Father Manesty. Here, however, we must leave her for a time, while we return to other persons connected with our narrative.

As soon as Nadoc thought the inhabitants of the Castle of Danebury were buried in sleep, he and Lawrence gently stole through the long corridors which led towards the main entrance of the building. Descending with caution, and screening their lamps to escape detection, they passed along with noiseless tread, until they reached a door which they had previously taken notice of; this was opened without difficulty, and they then entered a low square chamber, which having crossed, they found themselves in the armoury. Here Nadoc looked anxiously round him for a shield, with an eagle for its device, which had belonged to one of Lord Dalmeny's ancestors. Upon finding this, he pushed it aside, and, pressing upon a brass knob, a panel in the wainscot flew open, through which he and his follower passed, and then descended a flight of narrow steps, which led to a vault beneath the castle.

One side of this dungeon was formed by the castle wall, and after some trouble they discovered an iron door, strongly bolted on the inside, but which they at length unfastened, and then quickly found themselves outside the building. The night was pitch dark—not a star was to be seen, and the gloom with which they were surrounded seemed well fitted for the purpose they had in contemplation. For some few moments they paused to listen, when, distant sounds striking upon their ears, they each uttered an exclamation of joy, and waited for the arrival of those whom they expected.

At length, all being assembled, the pirate band, led by Nadoc, entered by the door we have just spoken of, and, without interruption, gained the castle hall, where, having lighted their torches, they divided themselves into four separate parties. Leaving one of these in the hall, he despatched the other two to guard the different places of egress, and with the fourth proceeded to the chamber of Lord Dalmeny. Aroused from their slumbers, some of the retainers rushed into the hall, resolutely determined to defend their lord or perish in the attempt.

Whilst this conflict was going on, Nadoc had endeavoured to effect an entrance to the chamber of Lord Dalmeny; but the latter, upon the first alarm being given, had sprung from his bed, and, having hastily armed himself, had, by means of a secret passage, gained a different part of the castle, where some of his retainers had already assembled. These he found were still faithful to him, and, placing himself at their head, he resolutely charged Nadoc and his formidable band. Stoutly did both parties continue the contest, but the strife seemed to be evidently against the pirates, many of whom fell beneath the weapons of their gallant adversaries.

Overpowered by the resistless force by which they had been opposed, the pirates were in the act of retreating, when fresh succours from their vessels poured into the castle, and turned the contest in their favour. Lord Dalmeny and his followers were at length forced to retreat through an open postern, and Nadoc and his band found themselves masters of the castle.

Fearing lest, with the return of daylight, a larger force might be sent against them, the pirates compelled one of the prisoners to lead them where Dalmeny kept his plate and money. The coffers, heavy as they were with treasure, were quickly conveyed on board their vessels, and, having also stripped the armoury, they hoisted sail before the sun had risen above the horizon, and were merrily bounding over the waves towards the island in which they had fixed their chief retreat, where we will for the present leave them to the enjoyment of the carouse which usually followed their expeditions, whenever they proved successful.

We must now return to Luke Somerton, who, it will be remembered, conducted Terence to his cottage. Here it was found that Louisa had been employing herself most diligently in preparing refreshments against their expected arrival. As soon as the meal was over, the maiden retired to her own chamber, and Somerton at once proceeded with his promised narrative.

"You remember," he commenced, "the evil presentiment I expressed to you on the morning of the battle. I knew the weakness I was guilty of, yet found it impossible to throw off the feeling, or to conquer the depression that weighed upon my spirits. Separated as we were from each other, I looked round in vain for you, and was urging my way towards a distant part of the field, when I received a pistol bullet in my side, and the next moment my treacherous enemy struck me to the earth with the butt end of his weapon. I lost all recollection for many hours, and it was not till evening had set in that I opened my eyes. All was silence around me, save the groans of a dying soldier, who lay a little distance from me. My brain whirled round; I was sick, and a burning thirst parched my throat.

"With much difficulty I arose, and supported myself on a musket, with the assistance of which I crawled towards a thicket of trees, at the entrance of which I again fell to the ground, and lost all sense. How long I remained in this state I am unable to say, but, on recovering, found myself stretched upon a heap of dried leaves, and an old man seated beside me. He had bound up my wound, after extracting the bullet, and, although I was stiff and unable to rise, I yet felt that the assistance thus rendered had saved my life. Gratitude for this service prompted me to give utterance to the feelings of my heart, but he desired me to refrain from speaking in my present exhausted state, and, giving me a cooling draught to allay my thirst, I soon afterwards fell into a sound and refreshing sleep.

"Next morning, when I awoke, he was about, but soon returned with some provisions which he had been sent to procure. In this asylum I continued for several days, during which period I learned the story of my kind benefactor. He had, it seems, led on a band of his countrymen against our troops, but, as usual, they were unsuccessful. At length, however, a reinforcement came up; we were driven back, and the fortune of the day was completely changed. After the battle was over, he had found me, and I was conveyed to the place in which I afterwards found myself.

"Upon being sufficiently recovered, I bade adieu to my generous protector, intending to return home with as much despatch as possible. My greatest regret, Terence, was having lost sight of you, nor could I ever ascertain whether you had fallen in the action in which my own life had been so nearly sacrificed. You were returned as missing, but no trace could be obtained whether you had been slain or were made a prisoner.

"No event of any consequence occurred during the early part of our voyage home. At length, however, we discovered a small vessel making towards us. Upon nearing it, we found that it was running before the wind, without any one apparently to guide it; so, as the water was smooth, we lay to, and lowering one of our boats, rowed alongside the strange vessel. Upon stepping on board, a melancholy sight greeted our eyes—a man of venerable aspect, exhausted, and nearly expiring, lay upon the deck, while a lovely female child was weeping beside him.

"Gently raising the stranger, we placed him in the boat, and, with his young companion, gained our vessel, when he was laid upon a couch and restoratives administered. As I sat beside him, he grasped my hand, and faintly articulated his thanks.

"'I feel,' he said, 'the hand of death pressing heavily upon me; when I am gone, and my child thrown upon the world without a protector, will you promise to convey her to a safe asylum?'

"'Most willingly,' I replied; 'I accept the sacred trust, and solemnly vow to obey your wishes.'

"'Thanks—a thousand thanks!' he gratefully exclaimed; then, addressing himself to the little girl, he added,—'Leave us for a little time, my child, for I have something to communicate to him who has thus generously undertaken to be your future protector.'

"Then taking from his bosom a packet, and handing it to me, he exclaimed,—

"'When my child arrives at the age of twenty, this will disclose to her the name and rank of her father. Wherever you place her, let this packet be given with these my last injunctions. You will find in this,' producing another parcel, 'jewels of value adequate to her support. It is but right that you should know him whom you thus oblige is no unworthy object. Remember,' he added, more faintly, after a convulsive spasm had taken him; and with a deep sigh of anguish his spirit took its flight and passed away. I did not attempt to check the first burst of grief from his daughter; but having explained to her the dying request of her father, she promised to be guided by my advice.

"The weather, which had hitherto been exceedingly favourable, now suddenly changed, and a strong gale blew us several leagues out of our course. We had intended to bury the stranger on shore, but under present circumstances it was deemed better to commit the body to the deep.

"For several days the gale continued with unabated fury, and we were driven before it, unable, from the shattered state of our rigging, to make our way for any port that would be advantageous to us. At length, however, we arrived off the coast of Ireland, and anchored just in sufficient time to save ourselves and whatever articles of value we had on board. In fact, the storm had rendered our vessel so leaky, that within three hours after we had quitted her she sank in deep water.

"Upon effecting our landing on this island, we were most hospitably received by its few inhabitants, who, although poor and unpolished, yet manifested a degree of kindness such as I have rarely experienced from people of greater pretension. There I have remained during the last ten years, watching anxiously over my youthful charge, and feeling for her an affection as strong as if she were my own offspring. In another year she will reach the age when her name and birth are to be disclosed to her.

"I have now related all the principal events that have occurred to me. You well know my early afflictions, and believe me, were I now to have an offer of those honours of which I was deprived, I would refuse them, rather than return to that world, the false pleasures of which I have learned to despise. Yet Louisa, I feel assured, is of noble birth ; and, to establish her rights, in whatever country her family be, is a duty that I voluntarily took upon myself, and will perform, however great may be the sacrifice."

"Depend upon it happier days than you imagine are yet in store for you," exclaimed Terence, as this narrative was brought to a conclusion. "I dare say you are surprised at meeting me here, and in the possession of such rank as I at present hold. But in some respects my adventures have been similar to yours. On the same field I also fell severely wounded, and upon recovering my consciousness, found myself a prisoner. When I expected nothing less than death, I was kindly treated, though still detained as a captive. When many months had thus elapsed, I was liberated by a party of my own countrymen, and returning home with them, I rendered such service to a French nobleman, that he took me into his house. Thus I had an opportunity of being about the court, which led to my introduction to great men, by whom I was patronised till my present elevation was attained. But the many benefits received from you are not forgotten, and be assured I am now anxious to repay them in any way that may be most gratifying to yourself."

"Not yet, Terence," replied Somerton; "but when I want the assistance of a tried and trusty friend, I will then not hesitate to seek your aid."

Luke then accompanied the officer to the beach, from whence the latter once more embarked for his own vessel.

CHAPTER XXXVI.

Ah, mischief! thou art quick
To enter into the thoughts of desperate men.
SHAKSPERE.

UPON a piece of gently rising ground, and facing the broad Atlantic, a figure upon its knees, its face turned upwards, its hair streaming upon the breeze, and the tears coursing each other down its pallid cheek, attracted the notice of Nadoc. Advancing with rapid strides, he grasped the arm of the unfortunate, who, turning round, gazed upon the intruder, and rising, wrapped his dark cloak more closely round, and walked towards the fortress.

For a few moments Nadoc gazed after the retreating figure—a shade flitted across his brow, and a momentary pang of regret seemed to strike upon his heart.

"Psha !" he muttered at length, "was not I far more guilty?—and yet I feel not the stings of conscience ; nor do such fearful images as he speaks of flit before my path. No - no ; the earth conceals the deed ; though some weak fools there are, who swear that blood, if shed, or life by violence destroyed, call loudly to high Heaven for vengeance. I believe it not, or long ere this I should have had numberless proofs to convince me of its truth. And yet, though success has ever crowned my wishes, there is a subject I have but lately turned within my thoughts—this isle is wild and romantic, and owns me for its chief; my gallant band obey me, and respect me as their leader. Wealth I possess, and fame, such as it is—for who is there but trembles at my name? And, now I remember me, did not Oliver say there was a beauteous maiden in yonder isle? She shall be mine, unless Dame Fortune should prove fickle when most I need her services."

As the ruffian pursued his way, this last plan gave animation to his dark and generally repulsive visage, his eyes lighted up with anticipation of an exploit that promised the indulgence of his passions, and as he stood upon the pinnacle of a rock, and threw a glance around his sea-girt territory, he gave utterance to a laugh of triumph that seemed almost fiendish.

Meanwhile Rupert, for such was the name of the person who had been disturbed by Nadoc, gained a small creek which lay to the northward of the castle, where a boat was secured to the beach. Into this he leaped, and immediately pulled across toward the main.

We must now return to Mildred, who we left at the hospitable mansion of Lady Rachel Dunholm, and where she would have felt herself most happy in the society of her newly found friend, had not the marked attention of Sir Geoffry Dunholm given her much uneasiness. Seizing every opportunity that offered, he poured forth his unmeaning compliments in a style to which she had never been accustomed, and which, when compared to the silent, but deep and respectful admiration of Reginald, she was often almost tempted to turn into ridicule, had not a consideration for his mother checked the inclination.

Knowing the distinguished family to which Mildred belonged, Lady Dunholm would willingly have received her as her daughter-in-law. She, indeed, wished her son to become more domesticated, as she was fearful he would eventually join in the disputes that were constantly occurring amongst the different factions into which Ireland was at that time divided.

From the moment of his introduction to Mildred, he determined to leave no means untried to win her to his love ; and, even if force were required, he was one who would not hesitate to use it. Still, however, he had the art to conceal the dark part of his character from his mother, who thought that his faults proceeded more from the gaiety of youth than from any very deeply settled principles of evil.

One evening Mildred had strolled forth unaccompanied by Lady Dunholm, and had not proceeded any very great distance when she was suddenly encountered by Sir Geoffry.

"My dear Mildred," he exclaimed, "this good fortune is indeed beyond my hopes; long have I sought such an opportunity as this to confess a passion that till now has been pent within my own bosom. Nay, do not turn from me—do not throw disdain into those eyes, which should beam only with love and tenderness I can assure you, fair damsel, mine is a heart that ——"

"Forbear, sir, I intreat you!" cried Mildred, assuming a firmness that she did not really feel. "I cannot, must not, listen to such language from the son of my kind, my generous benefactress. I shall ever esteem you, and regard your friendship, but a warmer feeling it is impossible for me to bestow."

"May I ask the reason?"

"Simply, sir," she replied, "because my heart is already bestowed upon another."

"But that other you may never again see."

The colour fled from her cheek as he hinted at this possibility, but again Hope whispered her to place her reliance in Heaven, and that she would not be disappointed. At length, after a pause of some little duration, she said,—

"And if I never do behold him again, Sir Geoffry, still my heart cannot be yours."

"Why so, Mildred?"

"Because," she replied, "it is too firmly in the possession of one whom I have known from childhood."

Anxious as she felt to put an end to a conversation so painful to herself, Mildred turned and retraced her steps towards the mansion, while Sir Geoffry walked for some time beside her in silence.

"How unfortunate I am," he said, at length, "to be rejected by the only one I ever really loved! —Yet even now I will not yield myself to despair. Would it be too great a favour to ask the name of this my favoured rival in your love? And yet, why need I put the question—the name of Reginald, traced beneath the sketch you dropped the other day, affords me all the information I require. But from this hour let him regard me as his bitterest foe. Should we meet, do you think my sword will spare him? No, one or both of us shall perish, for ever, while I live, shall he possess your hand. Farewell, Mildred; when next I sue it shall not be thus vainly."

These words, together with the tone in which they were uttered, alarmed Mildred, who determined to remain within doors as much as possible. That there was danger to be apprehended from the evil passions of the young libertine she could not doubt, and she now urged the immediate departure of the messenger whom Lady Rachel had proposed despatching to Baron Steinbach.

But little aware was the last-named lady of the deep political schemes in which her son had embarked. The French monarch, upon declaring war against England, secretly despatched an agent with private letters to Sir Geoffry Dunholm, in which, after promising his future favour, he instructed him to sound the feelings of the different Irish noblemen, and, if possible, to prevail upon them to enter into an alliance with them for the purpose of rendering the projected conquest more easy.

This proposal was most flattering to the vanity of Sir Geoffry, who, however, determined not to give up the designs he had formed against Mildred. He now manifested the semblance of a respectful bearing towards her, and thus succeeded in completely lulling the suspicions which had arisen in her mind; for she was not sufficiently acquainted with human nature to know that the countenance is seldom the index of the heart, when self-interest is in the way.

Reginald and Captain Danvers fixed their residence in a place convenient for their purpose, till Lord Tenby should return to his estate. The more Reginald knew of Danvers, the more reason he saw to esteem him, for he was not only brave, generous, and talented, but a safe companion and a true friend. From the present aspect of political affairs, Reginald deemed it prudent to conceal the country of his birth, and although he determined never to draw his sword against the interests of the French monarch, yet he agreed to accompany Danvers in any expedition against the insurgent Irish, whose turbulent and unruly spirits had, for some time past, loudly called for an efficient check.

The Earl of Clonmel, whose powerful influence and chivalrous bearing had impressed the English government much in his favour, was now likely to rise to that eminence which his great talents merited. Like all other men, however, he was subject to human weakness, and the favours showered upon him so filled him with vanity, that upon his return to Ireland he conducted himself with such hauteur towards those chiefs who deemed themselves his equal, that the Marquis of Aboyne eagerly seized the opportunity to forward accusations to the English court against a man whom he had begun to regard as a dangerous rival. The principal charge thus brought, was that of having shielded one of another faction, who had slain a favourite attendant of Aboyne's, and, as it was further asserted, unfairly.

This the English sovereign could not avoid taking notice of, and a trial, by special commission, was ordered to take place before commissioners appointed by the government of England. As may be anticipated, the result was in favour of Lord Clonmel, who, immediately afterwards, was nominated Lieutenant of Ireland, in the room of the Earl of Aboyne. The change was, of course, hailed with joy by the Clonmel party, who looked forward to many advantages from the well known liberal sentiments of the new governor-general.

It was at this period that the rebellion of the Earl of Carrick broke out, and the English minister, prompt in all his actions, at once despatched a force to assist Clonmel in suppressing the disturbance which threatened the peace of the whole country. At the same time private instructions were sent over to make Carrick a prisoner, even though treachery might be employed for the purpose.

Danvers and Reginald, with three hundred soldiers, joined Clonmel, while Terence, with four hundred more, was left to keep peace in the provinces.

Meanwhile, the Earl of Carrick had drawn all the disaffected nobles that he could assemble to his standard. Amongst these was a large body of Sir Geoffry Dunholm's vassals, collected and headed by himself.

The insurgents pitched their camp upon the banks of a lake, where, in case of attack, they had a strong castle to retire to, as well as some vessels which it was expected would prove of great service in the event of a decisive engagement taking place near that spot. Here they remained for some days, during which period various ships came in with intelligence that the Earl of Clonmel had crossed the river, and was rapidly approaching them by means of forced marches.

Sir Geoffry, desirous of ascertaining by personal observation the strength of the lord lieutenant's force, put on a plain riding suit, and, without any attendant, directed his course towards the spot where it was reported the enemy was to be found.

But the troops of the government had not been marched in such haste as was represented, for he did not wish to fatigue his men unnecessarily, and after a consultation with his officers, it was resolved to halt at a village every night, in order that they might at length reach the rebel camp, ready for an immediate battle.

On the evening that they reached Kilsayne, Reginald felt inclined to indulge himself with a stroll. Leaving Danvers, who pleaded fatigue, he took a path which, from its unbeaten appearance, seemed to promise the solitude he required. The evening was warm and beautiful, and he had continued his walk some time, when the sound of a horse near him disturbed the train of his thoughts, and raising his eyes, he beheld a stranger, who, as he advanced, asked him the name of the village to which he pointed.

Having replied to this question, Reginald passed on, and in about an hour's time returned to his quarters, where he had left Captain Danvers. Upon entering the public room of the inn, he found the traveller he had before seen, seated at a table, and apparently enjoying the good fare which had been placed before him. Danvers jumped up from his seat as he entered, and welcomed him back with as much warmth as if he had been absent on some distant and very dangerous expedition.

"Where have you been?" he exclaimed; "invoking the sylvan deities, I'll dare be sworn, though, between ourselves, I have not had the good fortune to meet one of them since my visit to this island. You shake your head; then I cannot be very wrong in believing that you have been ruminating on your lady-love."

"On the last point you are right," answered Reginald, "for I have indeed been thinking of one whom I value far beyond all else in the world."

"Well answered, sir," exclaimed the stranger; "your candid avowal does you honour, and evinces the truth and sincerity of your passion."

"Genuine love needs no concealment," answered the young man; "indeed, I see no reason for denying that I have loved for many years a young and beauteous female, who is no less lovely in her person than noble in the rank to which she is born."

"Then by all means give us her name," exclaimed Danvers; "come, come, my dear Reginald, there should be no concealment among friends, you know."

At the name of Reginald, the stranger, who was no other than Geoffry Dunholm, started, and fixed an inquiring glance upon the young man. But, when the magical name of Mildred Heinbach escaped his lips, the baronet, with a trembling hand, raised the glass, and quaffed off the wine. Fortunately, however, for him, no one observed the agitation that had seized him.

"Truly, the name is a most noble one," exclaimed Danvers, gaily; "'tis one I have often heard, though I suppose she is no relation of Baron Heinbach, who ——"

"She is his daughter," answered Reginald.

"Then," continued his friend, "if report speaks truth, she is of peerless beauty."

"Flattering as the report is, it has barely done her justice," answered the young man, earnestly.

During the time this conversation was carried on, Sir Geoffry was pondering on the most effectual method of picking up a quarrel with Reginald. Sitting, as he now did, in company with his rival, against whom he had so lately uttered threats of vengeance, he closely scanned the handsome but firmly knit proportions of his figure, and was gratified to find that he would have no unworthy adversary. Priding himself, as he did, upon being an expert swordsman, and having generally come off victorious, he had not the least doubt of similar success in the present instance. The plan thus hastily formed, was no sooner thought of than put into execution.

"You have," he said, pointedly addressing himself to Reginald, "spoken highly of the beauty of the Lady Mildred's person, but you have omitted to speak of the ease and elegance of her manners, the fascination of her smile, and the music of her voice—all of which are, of course, equally worthy of admiration."

"You speak to me in mystery," said Reginald.

"Then I will most readily explain myself," answered Sir Geoffry, with an ill suppressed sneer: "I have seen the Lady Mildred Heinbach—nay, but a few days since, I spoke to her of love—wooed her—need I say that my wooing was successful?"

At the commencement of this latter speech Reginald's cheeks flushed with the sudden anger that had seized him, and no sooner had the braggart concluded than the other sprang on his feet, exclaiming, fiercely,—

"Villain! whoever thou art, I give thee the lie in thy teeth. The Lady Mildred may, by some miraculous chance, be in this country, but that she should listen to thee, as thou hast said, is beyond belief. Nay, had it even been as thou hast boasted, thou must be a base, unmanly slave, thus to betray a secret that should have been inviolate. But I now stand forth to avenge the insult thou wouldst cast upon her. Come forth, then, if thou art not a coward, and answer for the base falsehoods thou hast thus given utterance to."

"I am quite at your service, young stripling," answered Sir Geoffry, with cool contempt. "Your blood seems to be soon heated, but the lesson I shall give you will, I hope, act as a future caution never to be quite so hot-headed again without greater provocation than you have now received. Your vanity, sir—your overweening vanity, sir, will get you into frequent quarrels."

Captain Danvers had been wholly unprepared for such a case of extremity as the present, but upon hearing the sarcastic words that fell from the lips of Sir Geoffry Dunholm, he stepped forward.

"Were I not confident," he said, "that my young friend is well able to chastise your insolence, I should feel myself called upon to avenge the reproaches that have been undeservedly heaped upon him. But now, sir, I shall attend you both to the ground, and pledge myself, as an officer and a gentleman, that no unfair advantage shall be taken on either side, and, if the fortune of the field should declare in your favour, you shall be at liberty to retire without further molestation."

Hastily quitting the house, they soon reached a spot suitable for their purpose, when, drawing their swords, the two principals advanced to the onset. At first Sir Geoffry Dunholm held his adversary at too cheap a rate, and a slight wound in the shoulder taught him not to be too sanguine as to the result. From that time, therefore, he fought more cautiously; but it was in vain that he tried the most dexterous points, for Reginald contrived to foil him, until, becoming the assailant, he so hotly pressed upon him, that Sir Geoffry would have inevitably fallen beneath his sword, had not a figure at the moment rushed forward and struck up the weapon.

Reginald at once recognized Julio, whom he had left at the Castle of Bautzen, and in him also the mysterious being who had landed him from the vessel.

"How comes it," said Julio, sternly, "that I find thee here leagued with the enemies of France, instead of joining those to whom I had directed thee? I find thee too raising thy sword against the life of one who should be thy friend! The sword thou wieldest, boy, should be employed only in the service of that monarch whose cause thou hast adopted."

"I would know," exclaimed Reginald, "by what authority you seek to exercise this power over me. In the first instance I obeyed your instructions, joined those persons whom you wished, but found them such as I determined to quit on the first favourable opportunity that should offer. Think you a son of a De Lancy would herd with pirates? But fortune aided me in extricating myself from the thraldom in which they would have bound me. Upon our way we fell in with an English vessel, engaged, and boarded her; when the two vessels parted, I was left on the deck of the English ship; and at once found myself among friends instead of enemies. As to my present conduct, the name of one, whom you are well aware is pure as virtue itself, has been assailed by one whom I deem a coward—she of whom I speak is the Lady Mildred Heinbach—I would not sit tamely by and hear her lightly spoken of; for, even had I a thousand lives, all of them should have been hazarded in defence of her honour."

"Boy," answered Julio, "thou hast spoken well and generously; but this stranger is wounded, and we must not leave him without rendering the assistance he needs, lest he should bleed to death."

So saying, he knelt beside Sir Geoffry, who was supported by Reginald. Having bandaged up his wounds, they bore him back to the inn, where he was placed in bed, and proper restoratives administered. This done, Julio led the young soldier apart, and conversed for some time with much earnestness.

Reginald's cheek flushed as this conversation proceeded, and he exhibited strong marks of surprise at the communication that was made to him. As they parted, Julio said,—

"By that gem you wear, and which was once your parent's, I charge you to obey me!" Then quitting the inn, he struck into a by-path, and was soon lost amidst the quickly gathering shades of night.

On returning to the room Reginald found Captain Danvers partaking of some refreshment, which he invited his young friend to join him in; but this was declined, as his mind was too much occupied with the recent interview in which he had been engaged. The intelligence, too, that Mildred was in Ireland, filled him with astonishment and dread. What could have brought her there? Violence must have been used to bear her from the Castle of Bautzen, which she so dearly loved as the cherished home of her childhood. The more he pondered, the more bewildered did he become, and, at length he determined to ascertain from his late opponent where he had seen Mildred, and whether she was detained a prisoner.

Danvers, perceiving that his young friend was meditative and thoughtful, retired to his own chamber, though not before he had advised Reginald to follow so prudent an example. The latter however, seemed scarcely to heed him, and as soon as his friend had retired, he stole gently to the door of the room in which lay the wounded stranger. But upon opening it and looking in, he found that he was buried in so deep a slumber, that he deferred making his intended inquiries until the following day. Proceeding, therefore to his own chamber, he threw himself upon the bed without undressing, and fell into an uneasy and broken slumber, from which he was at length roused by a voice calling out to him to rise, and at the same time a strong light flashed before his eyes. Starting up, he discovered to his no small amazement that it was Danvers, ready dressed and armed, standing by his bedside.

"Hear me, Reginald," he exclaimed, "an express has just arrived from the lord-lieutenant, commanding us to hasten our immediate march, as, instead of laying seige to the castle of Lord Carrick, we are to assist Morley against some of the factions of Ulster, who are now, it seems, in arms against us."

This summons was quickly obeyed; the horses were immediately got ready, and the troopers having mounted, they quitted their halting-place, just as the sun was rising above the horizon.

Reginald was much disappointed at not having been able to prosecute his inquiries about Mildred; for, as he had not even learned the name or rank of his late adversary, all clue to him would now be lost. These fears he communicated to his friend Danvers, who agreed with him that it would have been better had inquiries been made respecting the present abode of Mildred, but at the same time expressed his suspicions that but little confidence could be placed in the word of a man such as his late opponent appeared to be.

"I, myself," answered Reginald, "scarcely give credit to his assertions, and yet I cannot make out what his motive could have been for fastening a quarrel upon me. He appeared to be courteous enough till the name of Mildred was uttered, and then you were a witness of the means he took to excite my wrath. Would that I had an opportunity to quit this place and return to France, or, at least let my father know to what place my wanderings have led me."

"Nay," answered his friend, "it may be many months before such a chance as you speak of occurs. Besides, this country is so disturbed by factions, that a stranger's road is not the safest. Be advised by me, therefore, and rest patiently as you are for awhile. How know you, Reginald, but that some enchanter holds your lady love in his strong hold, and that it will be your high privilege at some future time to rescue her?"

But no raillery could remove from Reginald's mind the painful impressions that recent events had left there. He felt assured that Mildred was in danger, and it was, therefore, his duty to rescue her whenever he could ascertain the place in which she was abiding. Leaving them, therefore, to pursue their journey, we will now once more shift our scene, and return to the pirate chief.

CHAPTER XXXVII.

I have great comfort from this fellow; methinks he has no
Drowning mark upon him; his complexion is perfect gallows.
If he is not born to be hanged, our case is miserable.
TEMPEST.

ELATED by the success that had attended him, Nadoc deemed his retreat inaccessible, and his band not to be overcome even by a greatly superior force. Indeed, the entrance to the harbour was so narrow, and so well defended, that even if his enemies had vessels of sufficient size to attempt his overthrow, the chances were that a terrible destruction would fall upon themselves.

His daring attack and plunder of Lord Dalmeny's castle had struck terror throughout the length and breadth of the land, and the pirates were looked upon as a desperate and sanguinary band, against whom it would be in vain to contend. Still, Nadoc, although in his element of war and devastation, was far from being so happy as he would fain have had it believed. A fixed gloom appeared upon his brow, and although at times the exhilarating effects of wine, or the smiles of the fair would throw a brighter gleam across his countenance, yet it would again, ere long, relapse into its usual settled, stern expression.

The disturbed state of Ireland had prevented the lord-lieutenant from directing his energies towards the suppression of the pirate band; but at length their outrages became so alarming that he issued orders to fit out three or four vessels with the intention of suppressing, without further delay, a band of ruffians who had set all laws and power at defiance.

No sooner was this design made known than the rebellious faction, under the Earl of Carrick, determined to enlist the pirates on their side. Sir Geoffry Dunholm had by that time recovered from the effects of his wounds, and having received instructions from the insurgent leader, he embarked in a small fishing vessel, and proceeded without delay to the pirate's isle.

The day when this expedition was undertaken was a very fine one, and as the little vessel glided past the rock upon which the stronghold was seated, Dunholm could not but gaze with admiration upon the well-constructed fortress, upon whose platform frowned several pieces of artillery, while lighter ones peered from the battlements. Within the harbour, too, were anchored four large and well-armed vessels, which being moored so as to secure the entrance, opposed an almost impenetrable barrier to any who might attempt to attack them. Several of the pirates were upon the platform, while others were strolling about the rocks, as if keeping a watchful look-out lest the enemy should make any attempt to surprise them.

As soon as Sir Geoffrey landed, he ascended by a flight of steps cut out in the rock, which led to a green plain before the castle, when, having declared that he came on urgent business with the chief, the guards gave him admittance, and he was conducted to the presence of the person he desired to see.

Upon the visitor being announced to him, Nadoc raised his eyes from some papers that he had been perusing, and after slightly glancing at the person who had been thus introduced to him, he desired him to be seated. Sir Geoffry had been accustomed to the society of nobles, but he was struck with astonishment when he beheld the commanding figure and deportment of this far-famed pirate chief. At length, having somewhat recovered from his astonishment, he entered upon the subject of his mission, stating that several nobles, amongst whom was the Earl of Carrick, dissatisfied with Clonmel's conduct as lord-lieutenant, and desirous of liberating Ireland from the English yoke, had assembled large bands of patriots, and would soon be able to take the field, but that they were anxious to secure the alliance and co-operation of Nadoc and his followers.

"Are you aware, Sir Geoffry," said the pirate, after a pause, "that amongst those chiefs who seek my assistance, there are many against whom I have, ere now, levied war? What surety, then, have I that they would not, at the first favourable opportunity, turn their force against me and my people?"

"The honour of an Irish nobleman ought to be a sufficient surety for his good faith," answered Sir Geoffry. "When all are leagued against the common enemy, private feelings must be forgotten. In short, there are many in our ranks who, if they were disbanded, would turn their arms against each other; yet these will fight against the friends of the English, side by side, brothers in arms, to aid the common cause."

"I can believe your assertion, Sir Geoffry," exclaimed the pirate chief; "but my men, accustomed as they are to a life of war and plunder, will not, perhaps, feel quite as well satisfied with this suggestion of yours as I should myself. However, I will give the matter a night's reflection, and to-morrow you shall know my final determination. Meanwhile allow me to act as your host." Then ringing a small bell that was placed upon the table, a youth, habited as a page, entered the apartment in which they were seated. To him orders were given for refreshments to be prepared without delay, and when the youth had retired, Nadoc invited his guest to walk with him upon the platform.

If Sir Geoffry Dunholm had admired the strength and appearance of the fortifications from the boat, how much more gratified was he now that he had obtained a nearer view of them. Within the parapet were ranged all the requisites for the cannoniers—balls piled in pyramids, powder, levers, rammers, and a good store of swords and pikes, so secured as to be protected from the inclemency of the weather. The martial and dauntless appearance of the band next attracted his attention, and certainly, to look upon them, a more hardy set of men it would be impossible to find assembled under the command of one leader.

Dunholm viewed the fortress and his garrison with the experienced eye of one accustomed to war, and judged, from all appearances, that Nadoc and his band would prove most efficient allies. Nor was the pirate chieftain opposed to the plan suggested; for his subtle mind at once perceived the advantages that might result to him from joining the disaffected, who were strong enough to

afford a reasonable hope of proving victors in the contest. At any rate it would assist him in his predatory excursions, which might be regarded as warlike reprisals upon the party to whom they were opposed.

When the Earl of Clonmel marched against the rebellious forces of Carrick, he left troops in Galway under the command of Terence, as well as the vessels in which the soldiers had been sent over from England. These latter were anchored close to the shore, and a sufficient force kept on board to prevent surprise. As a further precaution, Terence also erected a small fort upon the beach, to the north-west of the town, which, in the event of an attack by water, would prevent the landing of troops. He had also several boats in readiness

upon the lake, in which troops could be transported across whenever they might be required; and a chain of outposts was kept up for several miles, to give notice of any hostile approach. The town, too, was well provisioned, and the men under admirable discipline, so that it must be a formidable force that would venture to make any attempt upon it by means of a surprise.

Terence frequently visited Luke Somerton in his secluded abode, and as often entreated him to quit the solitary island and reside at Galway, as he argued that Louisa would soon be made acquainted with her name and rank; and the wild peasantry of that district were but indifferent companions for a young and beautiful girl to associate with. Kind in manners as she was, there were none who did not regard her with esteem; were any of them sick or in trouble, like a ministering angel she flew to their immediate relief, soothed their sorrows, and poured the balm of sympathy upon their afflicted spirits.

It is generally acknowledged that there are no people in the world more grateful than the Irish peasantry. A kind word, a benevolent act, will bind them to your service for ever. Yet they are in extremes, for where they fix their hatred it is deep and deadly. Cheerful in their dispositions, and seldom giving way to much reflection, the troubles of life are forgotten almost as soon as they are felt. This, however, does not proceed from any apathy, but from a light-hearted manner much to be envied, and which prevents the frequent occurrence of many evils that are to be met with in all other countries.

To an enlightened and inquiring mind, such as Luke Somerton possessed, the study of these children of nature was a pleasing gratification. Here he beheld a race of beings happy and contented upon fare that would be rejected with disdain by most other people—here he beheld their firm devotion to their land and chieftain, whose quarrel they always looked on as their own. Fierce and savage they were at times, it is true, but nevertheless, in their unenlightened minds existed the purest gems of hospitality, true courage, and genuine kindness. Could these be improved by art? it was possible, yet, becoming more polished, would not their real worth be utterly destroyed?

In his fits of gloomy retrospection, Luke was in the habit of strolling to the shore, on the northern side of the island, where a sandy bay stretched between two headlands, forming a romantic amphitheatre. There, while he paced to and fro, he thought of his early days, the wife of his bosom, his child—both torn from him; himself an exile—none to regard him but the child of his adoption, and his old and long-tried friend, the faithful Terence.

One evening, when he was in this secluded place, he beheld a figure, apparently that of a monk, seated upon a fragment of rock, close to the margin of the sea. Prompted by curiosity, he approached the stranger, who, being seated with his face towards the water, was not aware of any one being so nigh. Luke had stood beside him some little time, when the stranger, suddenly turning round, started, sprang to his feet, and while his countenance became as pallid as the hue of death, he faintly exclaimed,—

"Wait but a brief space longer and I will be even as thou art. I know thine errand; but thy spirit is blest, while mine is doomed to the endurance of everlasting torture. Let me not gaze on thee! I cannot bear the horror of thy reproachful glances!"

So saying, and covering his face with his hands, he rushed from the beach, and was quickly lost to sight, amidst one of the rugged paths that led to the interior of the island. Luke thought the countenance was familiar to his memory, and the voice was certainly one that he had heard before; but he could not bring to his recollection when or where. A folded paper, which had been evidently dropped by the stranger, caught his eyes, and taking it up he perused the few lines that it contained; the handwriting was such as he had seen before, yet, with all his efforts he could not call to remembrance the person who had so mysteriously fled from his presence.

The figure and habit of the stranger were different from any that he had ever seen in the place, nor had he heard of the arrival of any one answering his description. The occurrence changed the current of his thoughts from brooding over his own circumstances, and with slow steps he returned to his cottage, resolving, at the first opportunity, to seek out the stranger, and, by his counsel and sympathy, strive to alleviate the sorrows to which it was evident he was a prey.

"Whither have you been, dear father?" asked Louisa, as she met him at the door; "I have waited most anxiously for your return. Here has been a messenger from Galway, with a packet for you."

The letter was from Terence, advising him to provide for Louisa's safety as well as his own, by quitting the island without delay, since it was likely to be visited by the pirates, and inviting him to repair to Galway, which was now strongly garrisoned, and where he and his daughter might hope to find shelter from the troubles which had broke out. Luke could not but agree with the counsel thus given him, and, acquainting Louisa with the proposed change, he added,—

"You will mix in society, my dear child, and thus I may hope to see you regain that cheerfulness which of late has been changed for a look of despondency. With my friend we shall be safe from the terrors that may pursue us even here, and ——"

He paused as a wild shout sounded outside the cottage, and then remembering the hint he had just been reading about respecting the dangers of a visit from the pirates, he added, with much earnestness,—

"Dearest Louisa, retire, I implore you. Conceal yourself—let me alone meet those ruffians, who, if they possess one spark of generous feeling, will not attempt to injure innocence like thine."

"Never, dear father, will I quit you," answered Louisa, resolutely. "Can you, indeed, think that I would hesitate to share your fate, whatever it may be? If there is danger threatening us, I will at least have the consolation of perishing with my friend—my benefactor."

Snatching up a sword, Luke Somerton was about to quit the house, when the door was suddenly burst open, and in moment or two afterwards the room was filled with a party of Nadoc's band, headed by Stephen, their lieutenant.

"This is the girl," he exclaimed; "bear her away to the boat, and let not a moment be lost, as you dread the vengeance of our chief."

"Approach not as you value your own lives!" cried Luke Somerton; advancing a pace towards the intruders, and presenting his sword towards the throat of their ruffianly leader.

"We want not you, sirrah!" exclaimed Stephen, with a terrible oath; "it is your daughter for whom we are sent, and nothing shall induce us to leave this place without her. Nay, be not so much alarmed, for the destiny of the girl is an enviable one, seeing that she is destined to become the honoured bride of our gallant leader. Come on, my men," he added to his men, who stood irresolute whether to retreat or advance, "Come on, I say, and if he still resists, let his blood be upon his own head!"

The words of the lieutenant were abruptly brought to a termination by a vigorous thrust from Luke Somerton. But what availed one against so many? Although long unaccustomed to the use of arms, he resolutely contested the victory, and it was not until three or four had fallen beneath his weapon, that he at length fell exhausted with the loss of blood that flowed freely from the wounds he had received.

"Quick, to the boat!" cried Stephen, wrapping a scarf round his own wounded arm; then, bearing Louisa to the beach, he soon conveyed her on board the vessel which was to transport her to the Pirate's Isle.

*   *   *   *

In her present peaceful abode, Mildred now passed her time in the society of Lady Rachel Dunholm. The more she knew of that excellent woman, the more fortunate she deemed herself thus to be thrown upon the protection of one who was in every respect so well fitted for the charge she had undertaken. Still, there was one cankering thought which nothing could ever efface from her mind—the remembrance of Reginald was still vivid in her memory, and most anxiously did she look forward to the time when she might be permitted to retire with him, to that home in which all the first, and certainly the happiest, years of her life had been passed.

The absence of Sir Geoffry Dunholm was a source of no little satisfaction to her; she had not quite forgotten his threat, and it was her determination, when he returned, to preserve that distant manner which would at once quench any hopes that he might have formed. Nor was it very long before her resolution was put to the test, for, having completed his negociation with the leader of the pirates, he returned to the Earl of Carrick, who, being pleased with the success of his last mission, sent him to rouse the people of the province in which his own large estates were situated.

This was a task for which Sir Geoffry was excellently adapted, his long residence in that district had made him acquainted with the minds of the persons he was employed to tamper with, and he well knew that to flatter their ruling passion was the only way to gain the confidence he was desirous of securing.

Ere he proceeded on his mission, however, he could not resist the opportunity of paying a brief visit to his home. Mildred, though unwittingly, had enslaved him as far as it was in the power of beauty to charm a reckless and heartless libertine. But he, who had seldom sustained a defeat in the prosecution of his wishes, perceived that in the present instance it would be necessary to act with extreme caution and deliberation. His chief fear was that she should ascertain the fact of Reginald's being in Ireland, and the most ready way of preventing this was speedily to convey her to some secluded spot, where she could be detained until he had either quitted the country, or the maiden herself had consented to become his bride.

Adopting an appearance of the utmost humility as a cloak to his real designs, he paid her the most devoted attention ; and Mildred, who was but too easily deceived by this, gradually abated the cold reserve with which she had been used to receive him.

To his mother's eager questions, as to where he had been, he replied on a visit to Sir Edward Carrol, an old friend of the family, whose lady had been very particular in her inquiries after his mother, and anxious to receive a visit from her with as little delay as possible.

"She has been ill," he proceeded to say, " and therefore hopes that you will wave all useless ceremony, and visit her. Lady Mildred, too, can accompany you, and as it is dangerous travelling in these times of trouble and disorder, I will, if permission is granted, act as an escort on the occasion."

This was a deep-laid plan of Sir Geoffry. The illness and invitation of Lady Carrol were indeed true, and he had himself arranged matters that a party was to attack them on the road, seize Mildred, and bear her to a place which he had fixed upon for her, while he and his mother, with their retinue, would be permitted to proceed on their journey.

The invitation thus sent was readily accepted, and with inexpressible joy, Sir Geoffry heard his mother give orders that immediate preparation should be made for the anticipated journey.

At about the distance of ten miles from home, high rocks bounded the path on each side, and these being surmounted with trees of large growth, which hung over, formed a verdant but gloomy arch across the road. Indeed, the sun never pierced through this leafy roof, and for a considerable distance it seemed like travelling by twilight.

It was in this spot that Sir Geoffry Dunholm had stationed a band of ruffians, headed by a man of desperate character, whom he had long retained in his confidence, and who had been, on many previous occasions, accessory to his master's deeds of violence, and pandered to his worst vices. The orders he issued were to separate Mildred from the rest of the party, all of whom they were 'to secure, not omitting even Sir Geoffry himself, in order to give a colour to the transaction. They were then to convey the younger female to the lonely retreat provided by Sir Geoffry Dunholm, to which place he was to follow her as soon as he could quit his mother, under the pretence of going forth to seek the maiden who had been thus torn from them.

The morning on which the party set forth on their journey was one of those clear, bright days, when not a cloud was perceptible in the blue sky, and scarcely was there the slightest breeze to rustle the leaves that hung listlessly above them. Our travellers commenced their journey ; the Lady Dunholm and Mildred rode in a carriage, and were followed by Sir Geoffry and half a dozen of their attendants on horseback.

At length they entered the gloomy defile we have spoken of, and had reached about midway, when, at a preconcerted signal, the ruffians rushed from their place of ambush, seized the servants, and with little difficulty succeeded in binding them. Their leader then advanced to the carriage, and throwing open the door, commanded Mildred to descend without delay.

Trembling with apprehension, she was compelled to obey the ruffians, while Lady Dunholm, also descending, threw her arms round the weeping girl, and mingled tears with her entreaties. But all was unavailing, and Mildred was torn from the arms of her benefactress, who was immediately afterwards forced back to the carriage, in spite of the earnest prayers with which she pleaded for the restoration of her young favourite.

Meanwhile Mildred was compelled to mount a horse that stood in readiness close by, and being then surrounded by the band, she was led off at a rapid pace, so that in less than a quarter of an hour they were beyond all chance of a successful pursuit.

*   *   *   *

The sudden move that Lord Robert Tenby had made northward, instead of following up his instructions to make a prisoner of the Earl of Carrick, had not only surprised his own followers, but astonished his opponents. With all the readiness of wily cunning, the moment Sir Geoffry heard of this movement, he secretly despatched a letter to the English sovereign, charging Tenby with being in league with the French king, and adducing, as a proof, the fact that a son of Sir Edmund de Lancy was actually at that time amongst the troops of the lord lieutenant.

This was a sudden and unexpected blow to the Earl of Clonmel, who repelled the charges with disdain, and demanded to be immediately confronted with his cowardly accusers. But this was not granted by the king, and a summons was issued, calling upon Tenby to repair, without loss of time, to England, where, upon his arrival, he was placed in close confinement during the changes which subsequently took place. And although Reginald was recognised as the son of Sir Edmund de Lancy, one of the chief councillors of the French king, yet, from some political cause or other, the government did not deem it necessary, just then, to follow up the knowledge of an enemy being in its power, and he was, therefore, still permitted to remain with his friend Danvers.

We must now accompany Louisa, who, upon being, as we have seen, torn from the protection of Luke Somerton, sank into a torpor, from which she did not fully recover until she found herself in the pirate's fortress. There, extended upon a silken couch, and in an apartment furnished with luxury, she became fully aware of the extent of the misery to which she was doomed. By degrees the last view she had of her protector, as he sunk, pale and wounded, beneath the swords of his fierce assailants, flashed upon her recollection.

"Alas—alas! he has fallen!" she bitterly exclaimed. "He protected me even to the very last —he has faithfully kept the vow made to my dying father, and has resigned the trust only with his life. Oh, Heaven, forsake me not, but throw around me your protection, that I may be shielded from the wild and savage race of men by whom I am now surrounded."

"Not so wild or savage, fair lady," exclaimed a voice close to her, "as to be totally insensible to the charms of a lovely female. Pardon, then, what may have appeared as an act of violence to you; but view your beauty, as reflected in yonder mirror, and then say, if you can blame the man who would encounter every risk rather than yield up a fair prize on which he has set his mind."

"If, as your appearance bespeaks," replied Louisa, "you have command in this prison, you will not refuse to say for what purpose I have been torn from my home, why detained here against my will, and when I am to take my departure from hence."

"Thou dost blame me, girl, and yet the fault is scarcely mine," answered the pirate. "The fame of your beauty reached me even in this lone nook of the world, and, unused to bridle my own passions, I determined to possess the prize at whatever cost it might be. I therefore sent a party of my men to bring thee here, though with strict orders to exert no more violence than might be necessary for the due accomplishment of their purpose. If they have exceeded my directions, the knaves shall suffer for it, though I doubt not the happiness that

is in store for you here will soon chase away the remembrance of a scene which was the first step towards making thee the mistress of all you now behold around."

"Villain, desist!" exclaimed Louisa, in a tone of peremptory command. "Your present garb bespeaks you for a soldier—one whose honourable profession should render you the protector, rather than the oppressor of a woman. Let me then return to that peaceful home from which I have been cruelly forced—let me seek for my father who I left wounded by your ruffians in his own house, and who sorely needs the assistance which there are none but myself in the wide world to render him. Alas! I almost fear lest he may have perished in the protection of her who has been to him as a loved daughter!"

"Lady," answered the chief, "you may, perhaps, deem me cruel when I say you must not quit this island; yet such is my decree, and, if aught of cruelty there is in it, the fault rests entirely with yourself. Smile but encouragingly upon me —approve my love—let me but call you mine— and, once possessed of such a treasure, you may command every favour that it is in my power to bestow upon the beautiful object of my heart's worship."

"Never!" answered Louisa, resolutely; "never shall my heart or hand be yielded to one who could even contemplate the foul wrong you have sought to inflict upon me."

"Of what can you accuse me?"

"The probable death of my father."

"Nay, my hand is innocent of the crime."

"Thy hand may be," she replied, "but not so thy heart. Though yours was not the sword which has bereaved me of a father's protection, yet the villains who slew him acted under your commands."

"These reproaches are most cruel and unjust," he exclaimed; and as he spoke, the fierce expression of his countenance softened into one of deep and earnest tenderness. "Bid me but hope, fair maiden; say only that there is a prospect of reward, and I will wait for it with patience, however distant the time may be."

"Restore me to the liberty of which I have been unjustly deprived," she exclaimed. "Think you I can regard the man who has committed this violence, or that I will hug the chains which render me your captive? But I am not so utterly defenceless as you imagine;—Heaven never yet deserted the oppressed, and even now I am not without hope of escaping from the thraldom you have thus vilely sought to impose upon me."

Thus defied, even within his strong lair, Nadoc paused for awhile in sullen thoughtfulness. His countenance gradually assumed its usual fierce and fiery character, and at length a low, exulting laugh, broke harshly on her ear.

"Ay," he exclaimed, with bitter triumph, "thou mayest invoke the aid of Heaven, but thy prayers can bring no fleet of vessels, no troops of soldiers to conquer him who commands upon this rock. Remember, girl, I am not often used to be thus thwarted, nor will I, beyond this day, endure the reproaches you have thus heaped upon me. A few hours I will give thee for reflection—when the proper time arrives I will again summon thee to my presence, when I shall expect thine answer to be favourable to my wishes."

Having uttered these words, he waved his hand for her to depart ; this she willingly did, and at the door was met by a private attendant, who immediately conveyed her to an elegantly furnished chamber which had been evidently fitted up for her reception.

We left Luke Somerton severely, and, to all appearance, mortally wounded by the ruffians who had suddenly set on him. But life, although quivering, and upon the wing, was not wholly extinct, and the fluttering spark became once more gradually kindled. Upon recovering the use of his senses, he found that his wound had been carefully tended, and that he had been removed from the place where he had fallen, to his bed. A monk was seated beside him, and as he opened his eyes he beheld the holy man just rising from his knees as if he had been offering up his prayers to Heaven.

" Where is my daughter Louisa ?" he eagerly exclaimed ; " why comes she not to me in this hour of trouble and suffering ?" Then pressing his hand across his feverish brow, he faintly exclaimed, " But alas ! now do I remember all—she was ruthlessly torn from me by ruffians, and ——"

" Have patience, my dear son," interrupted the monk, in a low and solemn tone. " Heaven often exercises its holy prerogative, and dooms us to severe trials, that we may become the more pure and chastened. Your daughter may yet be restored to you. Nay, I myself possess power, which shall, in good time, be exercised in your behalf."

" Alas !" exclaimed Luke Somerton, " you perhaps have never felt what it is to lose the object of your fondest affection. Your calm and holy mind views with placidity all worldly trials ; reared in the secluded cloister, and devoted to the service of Heaven, your life has passed without those ills and crosses we are doomed to bear during our progress through this life."

" Thou hast judged my lot too favourably, my son," replied the monk. " I have had my cup filled to the brim with sorrow. The draught has, indeed, been a bitter one, but the dregs will soon be finished."

" There is a solace in relating our afflictions to others," exclaimed Luke Somerton. " May I ask from thee a narrative of the sorrows thou speakest of ?"

" Not at present," answered the monk ; " you now require rest and composure ; but when returning health permits, I will relate the melancholy history you have asked from me. May Heaven support me in a task that I dare scarcely venture to think of. Farewell, my son—follow the instructions I have given, and in a short time you will recover from the effects of your wounds."

The road by which Mildred and her conductors travelled was wild and craggy ; large fragments of rocks frequently obstructed their path, and they were often compelled to dismount, while their horses were led through the defiles. As she viewed the ruffian band by whom she was surrounded, a chill struck to her heart, and she could not but believe that Sir Geoffry Dunholm was concerned in the cruel outrage. After travelling several miles through a country presenting no appearance

of inhabitants, and scarcely any signs of vegetation, they arrived at the summit of a hill, from which a prospect burst upon her view, which, had she been differently situated, would have amply compensated for the cheerless way she had passed. In the vale beneath them, an extensive lake spread its clear blue surface ; flowery meadows garnishing its fair margin, and several beautifully wooded, green islands studding its bosom as with gems of emerald. High upon a promontory stood a noble castellated mansion, on one of the lofty turrets of which floated the national standard, whilst several boats were moving about between the shore and small vessels that lay at anchor.

The party remained for a few moments upon the brow of the hill, before they descended the winding path that led to the castle, whither Mildred now ascertained, from some of the men, that they were bound to. As they descended, a cloud of smoke issued from the battlements of the castle, and in a few seconds the reverberating echoes denoted that artillery had been discharged, and a distant shout from a body of soldiers, who appeared upon the shore as the boats reached the strand, announced the landing of some person of consequence.

In about half an hour afterwards Mildred, and the party she had been guarded by, reached the castle, where the latter were hailed in terms of recognition by several of the soldiers who were gathered about the entrance. To the inquiries that she ventured to make of one of her escort, she received a surly reply, intimating that she must defer her questions till introduced to the person who alone could answer them.

Crossing the drawbridge they entered a courtyard of considerable extent, where dismounting she was conducted up a flight of steps and through a lofty door into a spacious corridor, which terminated in a handsome presence-chamber, when a person in military garb advanced to meet her.

" You are most welcome, young lady," he exclaimed, as he led her towards a seat. " Nay, do not tremble thus, I beseech you, for though there has been some violence committed in separating you from your friends, yet rest assured no ill shall befal you beneath this roof."

" If you indeed pity me," cried Mildred, " I intreat you, by the honour of your profession, to see me safely returned to the protection of Lady Rachel Dunholm. I cannot but believe that her son, Sir Geoffry, has been the instigator of this cruel outrage, and cannot but express my wonder that he has found a person, such as you appear to be, to aid him in so dastardly an act."

" Think not so harshly, fair lady," exclaimed the other, " for believe me I would not lend my assistance towards any enterprise that I deemed a dishonourable one. But pardon my forgetfulness, for, after your long and fatiguing journey, you must require rest and refreshment."

Then beckoning to a female attendant who stood near the door, he bade her conduct the young lady to a chamber, and to see that every care and attention was paid to her.

Mildred gladly followed her conductress, from whom she determined to obtain information, if possible, as to where she then was, the name of the present host, and the purpose for which she had been conveyed thither. Having led her to the chamber prepared for her reception, the female tendered her assistance, and from the expression of her countenance Mildred began to entertain hopes that she would find a friend in her. Fearing, however, that a direct question would mar the object she had in view, she, after some little hesitation, inquired if Sir Geoffry Dunholm had yet made his appearance at the castle.

"No, miss," replied the attendant, "but the Earl of Carrick expects his arrival here to-night."

"It was the Earl of Carrick, then, whom I saw just now, and who received me so courteously?"

"It was, miss," replied the woman. "We are all confusion here, as you see, officers and soldiers crowding in every day; we thought before this the place would have been attacked, but now all is prepared, and we do not fear any number that may be brought against us."

By this Mildred found that she was in the head-quarters of the Carrick faction; and, to her inconceivable horror, there was every certainty of her sharing all the dangers of a siege. Soon afterwards her attendant retired, and Mildred, wearied with the exertion she had gone through, retired to rest.

The vessel which had been despatched by Terence to convey Luke Somerton and Louisa from the island to a safe asylum in Galway, stood off and on, while a boat was manned and despatched on shore under the command of a confidential officer. Terence would himself have hastened to show every respect to his former master, but he knew he would be excused from this task, when his presence in another place was so much needed.

The moment the officer landed, he hastened onwards towards the tower, followed by a part of his crew. The door was standing open, and he paused for a moment, and called upon the name of Luke Somerton; no answer was, however, returned to this, and believing that the silence which reigned everywhere around portended some evil, he proceeded to enter the cottage.

Here everything seemed to be in a state of the greatest confusion; the furniture overthrown and broken, and the stains of blood, newly shed upon the floor, filled him at once with dread for the safety of the person of whom he was in search. Directing some of his men to keep a careful watch below, to prevent a surprise from any enemy that might be lurking in the neighbourhood of the place, the officer ascended the stairs, and entered a chamber which was darkened.

At the farther end, however, a bright flame was rising from an iron vessel, over which a figure was leaning, and muttering in a jargon that was not understood by the intruder. At length, raising its head at the noise made by the entrance of the officer and men, and pointing with its hand towards a couch in the corner of the room, it exclaimed, in a sepulchral tone,—

"Approach, and fear not. Behold him whom you seek, saved from the jaws of death. Be silent, for he slumbers; his strength is now sufficient to enable him to bear a removal from hence. Tell him, when he wakes, that his late attendant will meet him soon, on the arrival of an hour of trial which he little anticipates."

The flame sunk; a slight tremulous motion shook the chamber, which was now left in utter darkness, and when the window shutters were thrown open, and light admitted, none but the invalid, the officer, and men were in the room; nor was there any appearance of the vessel from which the flame been seen to issue.

In spite of the usually strong nerves of the soldiers, they felt awed at the sudden and mysterious injunction, and subsequent disappearance of the singular being, whom they verily believed to be neither more nor less than an agent of his satanic majesty. However, Luke Somerton turning upon his couch, awoke, and with much surprise beheld his chamber filled with armed man. His first and most natural supposition was that the pirates were returned to finish the work of death which they had begun; but he was soon undeceived, when the officer approached, and bidding him not be alarmed, announced the fact of his having been sent by Terence.

Luke Somerton, then, having somewhat recovered himself, described accurately the attack of the band, and the bearing off of his daughter.

"Such is the situation in which you find me," he exclaimed, "but, let Heaven nerve my arm once more against these fiends in human shape, and dearly shall they rue the day when they ventured to set foot upon the shores of this obscure island. But come," he continued, springing from his couch, "let us not lose another moment by delay; I know my faithful Terence, when he hears this narrative, will send a yet stronger party of his men to root out and destroy these villains who have borne away my hapless child."

Then quitting the cottage, and proceeding with them to the shore, Luke Somerton accompanied them on board their vessel, and in less than half an hour afterwards they were speeding, under a favourable breeze, towards the coast of Galway.

Mildred had been several days at the place to which she had been forcibly taken, yet during all that time she saw nothing of Sir Geoffry Dunholm, whom she was anxious to obtain an interview with, in order that she might tax him with the cruel perfidy he had been guilty of. All her wishes, with the exception of being set at liberty, appeared to be anticipated; a handsome suite of apartments had been allotted for her sole use, and the Earl of Carrick, to whom the castle belonged, treated her with the utmost respect and attention, evidently regarding her as the intended bride of Sir Geoffry Dunholm, whom he much wished to attach as closely as possible to the cause he had espoused.

Frequently, during those days of captivity, did she stroll along the ramparts of the castle, the view from which was magnificent in the extreme; the lake extending its broad bosom for several miles, while many a green promontory, and bold, rocky cape, jutted into its waters; ranges of lofty mountains formed the distance, and rendered the scene an earthly paradise.

Mildred had, as usual, been viewing the enchanting prospect, when the shrill notes of a bugle sounded at a distance; and as she turned her eyes to the quarter from whence the sounds proceeded, she perceived a body of men surmounting a hill, about a mile from the castle, while the setting sun glittered upon their arms, and the light breeze scarcely served to waft abroad the flags and banners which were borne by some of the men. The sentinels who had been stationed on the different towers were now aroused, and ere many minutes had passed, the utmost activity was manifested in all parts of the place.

Before she descended to her chamber she could perceive preparations making for an encampment upon the hill, and soon its green surface was whitened by a multitude of white tents. Upon questioning her female attendant, the woman replied that it was part of the lord-lieutenant's forces, who had marched hither for the purpose of besieging the castle.

"It's a sad thing for us women," she continued, "to be placed here in the midst of war and strife; but there is no way left for us now to leave the place, and I suppose we must run the risk of being shot, or cut down with sabres. From what I can learn, though," she added, in a less doleful tone, "they must bring a great many more men than they seem to have at present, or they will go back quicker than they found their way here."

Mildred was possessed of sufficient heroism not to fear the result of a siege, as, in the event of the castle being taken, she would be liberated from the restraint under which she now laboured. The interior of the edifice presented a scene of active preparation. Boats had been dispatched across the lake, and provisions of every kind brought in. At the same time messengers were sent round to all the leaders favourable to the insurrection of Earl Carrick; and, by the dawn of the following morning, the garrison was fully prepared to offer an obstinate defence.

In the interim the besiegers had been no less active in their preparations. A battery had been erected during the night, and six pieces of cannon, which, by great manual exertion, had been brought up the hill, commenced pouring forth volley after volley upon the castle. The artillery was well served, and pointing, as it mostly did, to one focus, appeared to make a sensible impression upon that part of the building. Still the guns from the castle gave much serious annoyance to the forces of the enemy, and the first day's bombardment passed with no loss to the castle garrison, whilst almost thirty of the English were slain, and more than double that number wounded.

The Earl of Carrick, like an active and experienced general, as he was, kept up the spirits of his men, praising and rewarding the excellent skill manifested by his gunners—ridiculing what he termed the puny efforts of the besiegers, and confidently prognosticating their entire overthrow at the first sally that could be made. He was most anxious for the return of Sir Geoffry Dunholm, whose gallantry and experience he fully appreciated, particularly as he meditated the sally which he so much desired to make against the enemy; and, although there were several officers of ability in the garrison, he was so much prepossessed in favour of Sir Geoffry as not to deem it prudent to carry his scheme into effect till his return.

Unable to view the proceedings from the battlements, where she would have been exposed to too much danger, Mildred sought a narrow window in one of the towers, from which she beheld the side of the hill and the plain covered with soldiers. They appeared as if about to make some grand military movement; their leaders rode along the ranks, and as they addressed the soldiers on the duties they had to perform, a loud cheer ran through the lines. The Earl of Carrick, from the battlements, viewed the enemy, and, calling his principal officers around him, he said,—

"We must now be prepared to resist the attack I see they are preparing to make upon us. Let the bugles immediately sound, hoist all our colours upon tower and battlement, and give the enemy such a salutation as they little expect. Ha! who is that I see coming?" he added, as he directed his eyes towards the lake, and beheld several boats crossing, evidently filled with troops, and who, as they approached nearer, he distinguished by the green flag to be of his party.

In a few minutes afterwards they landed, and, to his extreme gratification, he discovered in their leader the long and anxiously looked-for Sir Geoffry Dunholm.

With this accession the garrison was sufficiently strong to attack the enemy in their entrenchments, and the Earl of Carrick having collected his officers around him, decided upon making a sally on the following day against the invaders of his domain. This arrangement being made, he addressed himself particularly to Sir Geoffry, and after stating the plans he had formed for defence, he informed him of the safe arrival of Mildred at the castle.

"Indeed, my lord," answered the other, "I am much indebted to you for the warm interest you have manifested in my cause. Would that our opponents were driven far from hence, for then might I turn my thoughts from war to love; but now the ruder mistress must claim all my attention. However, meanwhile, I will find time to visit the fair Mildred."

"In truth she is surpassingly beautiful," exclaimed his lordship, in a tone of admiration; "and but that I regard her as the affianced bride of my most esteemed friend, her charms would doubtless have kindled a flame in my heart that would have rendered me a formidable rival."

"Believe me, my lord," answered Sir Geoffry, "in trusting her to the care and protection of the Earl of Carrick, I fully estimated the honour which ever guides him."

"You are too flattering, my dear Dunholm," exclaimed his lordship; and he then added, as he was quitting the battlements, "I trust you will not fail to induce the young lady to honour us with her company at the banquet which I have ordered to be given this evening to all the officers belonging to our garrison."

Without sending a message, or giving any other notice of his approach, Sir Geoffrey Dunholm entered the chamber where Mildred was seated, in anxious suspense. His entrance caused her to raise her head, when, starting from her seat with surprise, she exclaimed, in a tone of surprise,—

"Methinks, Sir Geoffry, after the violence already perpetrated against my liberty, you might have felt ashamed thus to appear before me, unless your object is to restore me to the protection of the Lady Rachel Dunholm, who has been to me as a mother."

"Indeed, fair Mildred, you are much mistaken," said Sir Geoffry; "for I can assure you no such motive has been the occasion of my present visit. I will restore you to her protection, it is true, but it will be as my wife. I have vowed, and my word was not lightly given, that you should be mine—aye, even if the braggart, Reginald, whose sword has lately crossed with mine—even if he, I say, supported by a host, opposed me, I would either gain you, or perish in the attempt."

"Merciful Heaven !" cried Mildred, "do I hear aright ?—is Reginald indeed in Ireland ?"

"He is."

"And think you," she added, "that, base as you are, threats will force me into compliance, when my heart shrinks from you with loathing and abhorrence ? But you have yet to learn that I can be firm in spite of the power you have assumed over me, for Heaven will not desert me ; and you may be assured that Reginald, slightingly as you may think of him, will yet rescue me from the evil hands into which I have fallen."

While Mildred was uttering this words, with all the animation of offended pride, Sir Geoffry was calmly regarding her, conscious that she was in his power, and certain in his own mind that he had but little to fear from the person of whom she spoke.

"I have patiently listened to you, charming Mildred," he at length replied, "and must express my regret at having fallen under your severe displeasure. Do not look thus coldly upon me, but grant me your forgiveness, and let me go forth to the ensuing battle shielded from danger by your prayers and good wishes."

"Deserve them, Sir Geoffry—give me safe conduct to where Reginald de Lancy, the friend of my childhood, my adopted brother, now is, and you will, indeed, merit and receive my warmest gratitude."

"That can never be," answered Sir Geoffry ; "so I would at once have you abandon a thought that is altogether hopeless. I have, too, the satisfaction of informing you that Reginald de Lancy is among the troops who have been brought to besiege this castle, and should he fall a prisoner into our hands, I will afford him the exquisite pleasure of being present at our nuptials."

He quitted the room with these words, and when he had retired she secured the door of the chamber, to prevent his return, and then, throwing herself upon her knees, she invoked the aid of Heaven to deliver her from the peril into which she had fallen. The knowledge that Reginald was so near gave her fresh hopes, in spite of the threats which had just been uttered, and most ardently did she hope that the besiegers might prove victorious in their next attack upon the castle.

The besiegers, with unabated vigour, continued the bombardment until the cannon balls had battered down a considerable portion of the southern bastion, against which it was proposed that an attack should be made on the following day. Could it have been possible to make the assault by water, as well as by land, the castle could not long hold out ; but the vessels the Earl of Carrick had upon the lake prevented any attempt being made in that quarter.

The morning was black and portentous ; dark, heavy clouds rolled overhead, and fierce gusts of wind, accompanied by wind and sleet, flew in the faces of the besieged, who, ranged along the battle-

ments, and upon tower and turret, awaited the approach of the enemy.

On the previous night a deserter had been brought into the English camp, and was immediately led into the presence of Captain Danvers, who commanded the troops. Reginald was sitting with him at the time, and felt but little interest in the information given by the soldier, until the mention of a beautiful foreign lady, who had been brought to the castle, and who, the man said, was to be espoused to Sir Geoffry Dunholm. It then at once flashed across Reginald's mind that it must be Mildred ; and from the description given he recognized Sir Geoffry Dunholm as his late opponent. At length the deserter was led away, when Reginald mentioned his suspicions to Captain Danvers, who, after weighing all the points, agreed in the probability.

"At length, then," exclaimed Reginald, "my wishes will be gratified, and I shall have it in my power to restore Mildred to her father, and punish the miscreant who has dared to slander her fair fame."

"At any rate you shall have every opportunity afforded you," exclaimed Danvers ; "and, what is better still, you will not be kept long in suspense, since the assault is fixed to take place to-morrow. There is our plan of attack," he continued, opening a roll of parchment on which was described the castle, and the manner in which the soldiers were to approach it ; "our artillery shall cover our advance. Our first body consists of three hundred chosen men, who will so contrive it, as to keep the breach clear of the enemy, so that our own men will have comparatively but little difficulty in obtaining access to the castle."

"The plan seems to be admirably arranged," said Reginald ; "and I have now to crave permission to join the party which is to lead the attack."

"Anxious as usual, I see, for the post of danger," exclaimed Captain Danvers. "Well, then, be it as you desire ; and you have my fervent good wishes that you may punish this Sir Geoffry as he deserves."

When the appointed hour arrived, the English troops advanced under cover of an incessant fire, and, encouraged as they were by their leaders, they seemed resolved to take the castle, or perish nobly in the attempt. Reginald gallantly led them on to the breach, and with wondrous good fortune, escaped the musket balls, which, however, levelled many of his brave companions. The troops that defended the breach formed themselves into a solid square, and seemed to bid defiance to every attempt that might be made to drive them back. Numbers of them, it is true, perished, but the places of those who fell were immediately filled up, so that little or no progress was made by the attacking party.

Finding that his men were dropping fast around him, Reginald at length determined to try the effect of a feint. Drawing off his soldiers by degrees, he pretended to retreat, for the purpose of drawing the enemy into a pursuit. This, however, proved unsuccessful, and turning, he was about to re-commence the attack, when a large portion of the bastion fell with a tremendous crash. At that moment Captain Danvers advanced with the remainder of his troops, and joining those led by Reginald, charged over the ruins and gained the first court-yard, where the conflict continued for a length of time, without any decided advantage to either party.

The Earl of Carrick, with the rest of his faction, opposed the English, and gallantly he fought, though in a bad cause, in that day's strife; his sword seemed charged with certain destruction, and, ever in the thickest of the throng, he seemed to bear a charmed life. Once he and Captain Danvers crossed swords, but they were quickly separated by the rush of combatants, as they impetuously advanced to the work of destruction.

Reginald sought everywhere for Sir Geoffry Dunholm, knowing, as he did, that he was second in command. His sword had already proved fatal to three whom he mistook for him, when he found himself engaged with the very person of whom he was in search. The recognition was immediate and mutual, and deadly was the hatred with which they engaged each other. Before they could decide their quarrel, however, the Earl of Carrick charged at the head of a large body of his men, while Captain Danvers and his men boldly sustained the assault, and, by their steadiness and valour, obliged the earl to retreat.

The English had now so far gained the fortress that both the Earl of Carrick and Sir Geoffry Dunholm saw that it was useless to defend it any longer; but this casualty they had provided against by having several vessels and boats upon the lake, into which they retreated, having first well secured the gates leading to the water.

As Reginald and some of the men made their way through the castle, the former sought in every chamber he came to for some trace of Mildred. At length the sound of steps hurrying on before him, gave speed to his advances; a shrill scream and the closing of a door was then heard, and on approaching yet further, he discovered that the gate was securely fastened on the other side. This effectually checked the pursuit of Reginald, whose rage and despair may be imagined when, looking through the iron grating,

he beheld Mildred borne to a vessel in the arms of Sir Geoffry Dunholm.

"Turn, coward!" he loudly exclaimed; "turn, and meet him who has thus long sought you in vain."

A loud insulting laugh was the only reply made to this, and Mildred was carried on board one of the vessels, and in a few moments more they were rapidly speeding their way to the opposite shore.

Now that the troops of the lord lieutenant were in possession of the castle, they posted sentinels on the walls, whilst the great body of the men busily occupied themselves in repairing the breaches. Within the castle they found an abundance of provisions and military stores, which the Earl of Carrick, not anticipating a defeat, had collected for future use.

Captain Danvers strove in vain to console Reginald. To have his beloved Mildred snatched from his grasp at the moment when they were so near each other, and to know that she was exposed to the insulting offers of Sir Geoffry Dunholm, was madness to him, and he determined to disguise himself, and trace her, wherever she might be.

"What though I should fall?" he said, mournfully, to Captain Danvers; "I may not be alone, and can I perish in a better cause than for her who is dearer to me than all the world beside?"

His friend endeavoured to persuade him against so rash an attempt, but all was in vain, and within an hour afterwards he beheld him depart in the disguise of an Irish harper.

Meanwhile Carrick and his troops retreated in good order after landing. Sir Geoffry rode by the side of Mildred, and frequently addressed himself to her without being able to obtain any reply. But she had recognised the voice of Reginald, and at length endeavoured to move the pity of Dunholm; but he, maddened at the delay and the victory which had been gained over them by the English forces, determined not to be again thwarted, and expressed his resolution to have the nuptial ceremony performed at the first convenient place they arrived at.

CHAPTER XXXVIII.

Dangers shall not daunt me,
For I've vowed to execute my holy errand.
There is no spot on earth but I will visit
Till she I seek is found.—*Rivalry.*

THE habit that Reginald had assumed was a sufficient protection to him from the wandering parties of soldiers, amongst whom his approach was always gladly hailed, nearly all of them being much pleased with the martial songs, of which Reginald knew several, and which he sang with a spirit that gained him pretty general applause. He was, however, compelled to use much caution in his inquiries, and was often obliged to pretend attachment to the Earl Carrick and his followers.

With unabated vigour he continued his route through the wild county of Kerry, where he felt himself much at a loss, often mistaking the different roads that lay in his way, and becoming entangled amidst the dark forests that extended along the foot of the lofty mountains which abound in that district.

At length, faint and exhausted, after a long day's travel, he threw himself beside a stream, in whose cool waters he bathed his swollen limbs; then, placing his harp near him, he threw himself once more upon the greensward, and sank into a slumber, which lasted some time, and from which he was at length roused by the sounds of music. Scarcely awake, the sweet sounds, floating on the gale, seemed like a choir of spirits, when, raising his head, he beheld with astonishment a man of venerable aspect seated at a short distance from him, who, with a masterly hand, swept the chords of his harp, accompanying the music with a voice that had considerable power and sweetness.

In a few minutes he ceased, and laying down the harp, passed his hand across his eyes, as if some powerful emotion had been awakened in his bosom.

"You look at me with surprise, my son," he at last said; "and the words you have just heard must have acquainted you with the misfortunes that have driven me into a tedious exile. Here, amidst the wild scenery, far from the haunts of my fellow-men, I feel a melancholy solace in breathing forth my sorrows. Your harp tempted me to try my hand, now long unused to harmony. My hut is near, and as you appear to be fatigued, accompany me home to where I can afford you both rest and refreshment."

"I thank you, father, and most gratefully accept your generous offer," said Reginald; then rising from the ground, he accompanied the recluse through a thick grove of trees, until they reached a low and comfortable-looking cot. Upon entering, the stranger placed a seat for his visitor, who now looked round at the interior of the humble dwelling. Within a recess stood a bed of rude construction, whilst the remainder of the furniture consisted of such articles as were absolutely necessary, but nothing more.

In a very short time the table was spread with such homely fare as the house afforded, of which Reginald partook with a good appetite—the old man performing all the rites of hospitality in a manner that was sufficiently expressive of the hearty good will with which it was bestowed. The meal being over, a flask of excellent wine was placed on the table, when the host, filling two cups, handed one of them to Reginald, exclaiming,—

"Drink, my good young friend; wine enlivens the heart of man; and although I have withdrawn myself from the world, still I have not thought it necessary to adopt all the manners of an anchorite."

They then began to converse upon various matters, and the old man having gathered the motives which had led to his guest's journey, said,—

"It seems likely, my son, that I may be able to afford you some intelligence of importance. Not many hours since, a party of soldiers passed this way; one of them was severely wounded, apparently in a recent affray. Unable to proceed with his companions, he remained with me; but, becoming much worse, he prepared himself for death, and confessed his sins. Among other things, he mentioned the assault on the castle of the Earl of Carrick, and spoke of a knight he called Sir Geoffry Dunholm, who was carrying off a beautiful female to the stronghold of a pirate, whose name and daring deeds have reached me even in this seclusion. Contrary, however, to his own expectation as well as mine, the soldier recovered sufficiently to pursue his way, and I believe he followed those in whose company he had been when I first saw him."

"And what would you have me do?" asked Reginald.

"My advice is," replied the old man, "that you hasten with all speed to Galway, and claim the aid of the lord-lieutenant's troops, which are there stationed. Your having been at the taking of the castle of the Earl of Carrick will certainly procure you this favour."

With this advice Reginald at once agreed, and as the night was by this time far advanced, he threw himself upon the bed which had been prepared for his reception and obtained the refreshment he so much needed. In the morning when he awoke, he found that breakfast was prepared for him, and having partaken of it, he bade farewell to his kind host, and immediately pursued his journey in quest of Mildred.

The harbour of the Pirate's Isle afforded an enlivening spectacle as the vessel, bearing Sir Geoffry Dunholm and Mildred Heinbach, entered the anchorage ground. The entire naval and military force of the pirates were assembled; seven large and well-armed gallies lay at anchor, and all the band who were not otherwise engaged on duty mounted the walls of the fortress. The vessels were moored so as to command with their guns the entrance of the harbour, and the soldiers were under review by Nadoc when Sir Geoffry Dunholm arrived. The moment he landed, he retired with the pirate leader, and, having closed the door of the chamber, turned towards the outlaw with a perturbed and anxious look.

"What has procured me the favour of this visit, Sir Geoffry?" demanded the pirate; "is there aught in which my services may be of use?"

"There is," replied the other.

"'Tis well," exclaimed Nadoc; "for it seems then we are likely to be of mutual service to each other. In truth, I need the counsel and advice of an experienced soldier like yourself."

"All shall be at your service," answered Sir Geoffry; "and in the first place, I must congratulate you upon finding that you are so well prepared to greet the visitors who soon intend to set foot upon your soil."

"What visiters do you speak of?"

"Even the forces belonging to the Lord Lieutenant of Ireland," replied the baronet. "They will be here anon, accompanied by a fleet that will require the exercise of all your courage and skill to subdue."

"Indeed!" exclaimed the pirate; "then, to say the truth, I am not sorry to hear the intelligence you bring me, for, once more, I shall find myself in my own element of war and bloodshed. Behold yonder men," he continued, throwing open a casement, and pointing to his well ordered band, who, at the moment, were going through their usual military evolutions. "Each of those men will sell his life dearly, ere he perishes, for those who enlist in my service know that if in action they are taken alive, no mercy will be shown by their captors. Therefore do they fight to the very last, neither asking nor accepting mercy. Under your command, they will prove their gallantry, for, having landed upon our isle, you must now, perforce, become one of us."

Sir Geoffry Dunholm did not feel much gratification in the prospect of becoming a member of so notorious a fraternity; but he deemed it prudent to be silent, and, therefore, changed the subject to one of more paramount importance to himself.

"I can scarcely venture to hope," he said, "that you have a priest in your island; yet, if I knew where to light upon one at this moment, he might render me a most important service."

"You are most fortunate, Sir Geoffry," said the other; "for it so happens that we have beneath this roof a monk, though, it must needs be confessed, his manners are not such as I can exactly approve of. Few here have ever had an opportunity of seeing his countenance; but those who have been so highly favoured, speak of it with marked curiosity and wonder. So much for the monk;

and now I would fain know for what purpose you require his priestly services?"

"To perform the rites of marriage."

"Indeed! between whom, I pray?"

"Myself and a young female," answered Sir Geoffry.

"Does she consent to the union?"

"No," answered the baronet; "she is perfectly aware of my views, though, yet, in spite of all my entreaties, she wilfully rejects the offer I have made."

"Then she must be taught the duty of obedience," exclaimed Nadoc, with a hideous grin. "In truth, Sir Geoffry, I also am about to wed, and she upon whom my choice has fallen seems to be as full of whims and fancies as the wench you speak of. Still, I shall enforce compliance, as I suppose you intend to do."

"Aye," exclaimed Sir Geoffry; "for why else is power bestowed upon us, if we are not to be permitted to exercise it when there seems to be occasion."

"Oliver," shouted the pirate to one of his men, "instantly summon Father Julio hither, and if he seems unwilling to obey, force him to my presence at the end of half a dozen bayonets. I have only seen the priest twice," he added, as the man went away on his errand, "and then he flitted past me wrapped in his dark habit, so that I know not what sort of a fellow he is."

At that moment the figure of the monk approached the doorway, and, on being desired to do so, he entered the apartment in which the consultation had been held.

"I have sent for you, holy father," said Nadoc, "to mumble your prayers, and assist in uniting me and my friend to our respective brides. Do you freely consent to do that which we have the power to enforce?"

"You may command my services," replied the monk. "When shall you require them?"

As he spoke, the tones of his voice seemed to strike the pirate, as if they were familiar to him.

"Have we ever met before, priest?" he hastily exclaimed; "for, methinks, if my ear deceives me not, we are no strangers."

"It has been my lot to travel through many climes," answered Father Julio, with some slight show of perturbation. "Where think you we have met before?"

"That is what I cannot now recal to my mind," replied Nadoc, after a pause of anxious reflection.

The monk moved closer to the pirate chief, and whispered in his ear. The effect of his communication was instantaneous. The face of Nadoc became ghastly pale, and his eyes glared wildly.

"Speak!" he exclaimed; "man or fiend, or whatever thou art, speak without an instant's delay! Where couldst thou have learnt that secret?"

"Ask me not," replied Father Julio; "but rest satisfied that I am acquainted with much concerning thee that thou would'st not willingly have known. But my time is precious, and I must away from this island before to-morrow's dawn. Say, then, the hour and place where the marriage ceremony is to be performed?"

"At ten to-morrow night."

"And where?"

"In the hall."

"Fear not that I shall fail to meet you there," replied Father Julio, in a tone of peculiar meaning, as he passed quickly away from their presence.

"You appeared to be astonished at the monk's strange communication," said Sir Geoffry Dunholm, at length breaking the silence which had followed the priest's departure.

"And well I might feel surprised," answered the pirate ; "for the secret he pronounced was one that I thought was unknown to all the world beside myself. But enough of this—for the present we part, Sir Geoffry, and when next we meet it will be to go through the ceremony yonder monk has promised to perform."

We must now return to Mildred, who had been conducted to a small, though not ill-furnished chamber, where, being left to herself, she gave way to a burst of affliction that she could no longer suppress. Plunged as she was in sorrow, she threw herself upon a couch, and yielded to the emotions of grief and despair.

"Daughter, why weepest thou ? Hast thou resigned all trust in Heaven?" asked a voice near her, when turning, she beheld standing near her Father Julio, her former tutor at the Castle of Bantzen.

Joyfully she hailed the appearance of one so familiar to her. For, although she might attribute her present unhappy situation to his bearing her from her father's castle, still his voice and manner gave her hopes that he would yet endeavour to rescue her from the power of Sir Geoffry Dunholm. Happily in this respect she was not doomed to be deceived.

"My child," he again exclaimed, "I know your sufferings, and that the nuptial ceremony which is to make you the bride of Sir Geoffry Dunholm, is fixed for ten o'clock this night. Yet, fear not, for you shall be saved from the much dreaded sacrifice."

"May I depend upon you?"

"You may, Mildred," he replied. "Have you sufficient courage to cross a wild and stormy sea in a small, frail vessel, such as the least movement would be sure to overthrow ?"

"Oh, give me but the chance of an escape from this dreadful place," she eagerly exclaimed, "and were the foaming waves to raise themselves threateningly, I would rather brave their worst fury than give my hand in marriage to the hated Sir Geoffry Dunholm."

"Since such is your resolution, my daughter," he replied, "I think there will be no great difficulty in our way. An hour before the time appointed for the marriage ceremony I will convey you across the bay to a lone cave, known, as I believe, only to myself. There thou mayest remain, until I can find means to further your journey as far as Galway, where I have friends, under whose protection, when thou art once placed, no future fears need torture your repose."

To this suggestion of Father Julio, Mildred at once and most willingly agreed ; and it was then further arranged that she should be prepared to accompany him an hour before the time which had been appointed by Nadoc and his friend.

The pirate chief, when he quitted Sir Geoffry Dunholm, sought the apartment of Louisa, whom he found seated at the open casement, gazing wistfully over the blue expanse of waters, and sighing for the home from which she had been so lately torn.

"Come, come, Louisa," exclaimed the outlaw, as he observed the melancholy expressed in her countenance. "Let hope cheer thee, my girl, for thou wilt be far happier here than at the miserable cottage from whence I took thee. This night thou art to become mine, and, at the same time that I lead thee to the altar, my noble friend, Sir Geoffry Dunholm, will wed a lady who is now within this fortress. Thus will our double nuptials infuse a feeling of joy throughout this isle, such as it has never before witnessed."

"Leave me," she exclaimed ; "I may be in your power for a time, but will never become yours."

"Nay, you must—you shall be mine," he cried ; "fate has ordained it, and no human aid will be sufficient to rescue you from my hands."

The excesses of the pirates had of late become so alarming, that the Lord Lieutenant determined to send a considerable force against them, and thus, by one determined act, root out the nest of robbers who had so long bid defiance to every effort that had been made to suppress them.

Collecting, therefore, twelve vessels and a proportionate number of men, the command was given to Terence and Danvers, who had by this time returned from their expedition against the Earl of Carrick. Luke Somerton also accompanied them, and Reginald most opportunely arrived just as they were on the eve of sailing. With much surprise he recognised in the commander of the troops the traveller who had given his father and their attendants information of the meditated attack, when they were proceeding to London.

While Terence seemed to derive much information from this meeting, Reginald burned with impatience to rescue the unfortunate Mildred from the pirate's hold, and the expedition sailed with the confidence of success which superior force and numbers rendered almost certain. The soldiers, too, were eager with the prospect of plunder, for the fortress of the pirate chief was said to contain vast wealth, and consequently the booty to be divided would be immense.

It was the first dawn of morning, when they beheld the rugged cliffs of the Pirate's Isle rising in dark masses above the horizon ; a council of the officers having been called, it was resolved to anchor close in shore, and await the dusk of evening ere the attack was commenced. Lowering their sails, they came to the southward of the island, and prepared everything in readiness for a contest that they had every reason to believe would be resisted to the very last.

As Reginald and Danvers paced the deck together, their conversation turned upon the present commanders of the expedition, and Reginald was much pleased to find that he was by all parties held in high estimation both for bravery and skill.

"Would that this unfortunate Irish war was over," said Danvers, "and that I might once more return to England. When that is the case, Reginald, you must accompany me, and pass some time at my uncle's hospitable mansion. Trust me, you and the fair Mildred, who, I hope, you will be able to bring with you, shall be most welcome."

"I have little doubt of it, my kind friend," replied Reginald, " and shall be delighted to avail myself of your kind invitation. But, to our present purpose—are you acquainted with the localities of this Pirate's Isle ? And are we to bombard him from the sea or land, and carry his stronghold by escalade ?"

" We are strong enough to do it both ways," answered Danvers. " It has been arranged that six of our best vessels shall take their station opposite the fortress, while the remainder land their troops in a deep and narrow rocky creek, that lies a little to the northward of the castle. Thus, while his attention is engaged by the bombarding vessels, the troops from land shall scale the walls, and take him in the rear when least prepared for such an attack."

" The plan seems to be an excellent one," exclaimed Reginald. " At any rate, our numbers are so great, that we can hardly fail in effecting our purpose."

" With troops and sailors such as we possess I think there is no doubt of success," replied Captain Danvers. " On the other hand, if report speaks true, the pirate chief is a man of superhuman strength and courage, cunning in his plans,—sudden and bold in execution,—a hand that spares not in the hour of battle,—a sword that never yet has been conquered. At least, so say those who, having been engaged against him, are most likely to report correctly."

" I have myself heard much of his prowess," exclaimed Reginald; " but I pray Heaven I may not be disappointed in the purpose that has brought us here ! Let me but meet that villain, Sir Geoffry Dunholm, once again, and either he or I shall never leave the field alive."

By this time the shades of evening were fast approaching, and the vessels quickly weighed anchor ; when, urged on by a favourable breeze, they soon arrived within gun-shot of the castle walls. By the time all this had been done it was dark, and the vessel in which Reginald sailed was astern of the rest. As he leaned over the quarter, and watched the undulating waters, he reflected how soon he was about to mingle in the contest which it was to be hoped would restore to him his beloved Mildred ; still he was liable to the dangers of the field, and, in common with the rest of his companions, would be exposed to the dangers of the coming strife.

As these and other thoughts passed through his mind, a dark object at a short distance off attracted his notice. It was a skiff, which now passed close under the quarter, and, as it shot by, a torch placed near the bows threw a gleam of light across the waves, and gave to Reginald's astonished view Mildred seated in the stern of the boat, while a figure, habited as a monk, plied the muffled oars. Prompted by the momentary impulse, the youth would have instantly plunged into the sea and swam in pursuit of her, had not Captain Danvers at that moment sprang forward to prevent him.

" What madness is this you are about to commit ?" he exclaimed. " Know you not that certain death would be the consequence of the plunge you were about to make ?"

" Saw you not who was conveyed past us just now in yonder boat ?" demanded Reginald.

" No ; who was it you speak of ?"

" Mildred Heinbach."

" Psha ! you must have been deceived," exclaimed his friend. " Believe me, Reginald, you have thought so much upon this subject lately, that your imagination must have played you false."

" But I am most positive it was her."

" Others have been equally deceived though no less positive than you seem to be," answered Captain Danvers. " Besides, who do you think is likely to have aided her escape ?"

" That is more than I can say."

" The supposition is too ridiculous to be entertained for a single moment," continued Danvers. " Nay, to venture out at this hour of the night across the bay in a small boat such as the one I descry yonder, would be an act of fool-hardiness that few people would be guilty of. And, hark ! there is the signal gun for us to sail without delay towards our place of destination. Now, my men, the moment of strife is at hand, and you must be ready to man the boats the moment we cast anchor."

The pirates had allowed the vessels to approach the island without offering the least interruption to them ; but scarely had they reached the spot from whence they were to bombard the fortress, when a single bugle note was heard, and all the artillery from the castle burst forth with most tremendous fury. For a moment platform and ramparts assumed one horrid mass of living flame ; while the pirate's vessels, that were moored across the entrance of the harbour, poured forth a most destructive fire upon the besieging ships.

Thus placed between two fires, their situation was rather precarious ; their men began to fall fast, and their hulls were dreadfully shattered by the cross-fire they had to sustain. Still the courage of the invaders was not to be subdued, and in spite of the disadvantage they were placed in, the men fought with all the hardihood and gallantry of British sailors.

The troops had by this time landed in the creek, and having assembled and silently marched along the road that led to the front of the castle, they commenced scaling the walls with the assistance of the ladders they had taken care to provide themselves with. Whilst one party of the men affected an entrance, another stood at hand with their muskets, prepared to keep the walls clear of any enemies who might advance to repulse those who were surmounting the walls.

This double and well-planned attack was promptly met by Nadoc, whose trumpet immediately summoned a strong body of his men about him. These he addressed in a few energetic words, and being assured of their continued fidelity to his his cause, he rushed forward to the point of attack, resolved either to repulse the foe, or perish in the attempt. Scorning the cover of the parapet, he sprung upon it, and hurling two of the soldiers from the top of a ladder, he clove a third through his thick cap, and spurned the body with his foot to the ground beneath.

Although a mark for the entire of the assailants, he escaped unharmed, while none dared to approach within the sweep of his death-dealing sword. Sir Geoffry Dunholm had been left in charge of the platform towards the sea ; and stoutly he defended it until the English vessels were obliged to cut their cables, and, as well as their shattered state would permit, bring the point between them and the fort, which sheltered them from the battery and the shipping.

As soon as they got near the remainder of their fleet, they anchored, and landed the surviving troops who were still left in the six vessels. One hundred and fifteen had been slain, and eighty wounded; these latter were left on board, and Terence, with Luke Somerton, joined Captain Danvers, at the head of two hundred and fifty men, burning with a desire to avenge the slaughter which had been committed on their unfortunate comrades.

The moment Terence advanced, and beheld the situation of the troops, he determined upon gaining some commanding position, from whence he could with tolerable safety bombard the fortress. He, therefore, instantly despatched a party to convey four pieces of cannon from one of the vessels, with the necessary ammunition; and casting his eyes across the harbour, made choice of an eminence which completely overlooked the pirate's hold.

Withdrawing his troops from before the walls, the moment the guns were landed, he despatched a party with them, commanded by Captain Danvers, and in a short time they were drawn up the hill; and, when morning broke, they commenced their fire upon the fort. This was an unexpected attack for Nadoc; but one of his officers, who was on board one of the vessels, ran his ship close to the land, and, with the crew, leaped on shore, for the purpose of silencing or spiking the guns. But they were repulsed with considerable loss, so that out of seventy men but fifteen escaped, and all of them severely wounded.

The English guns had by this time battered down a great portion of the square tower. And now upon the battlements was beheld a young and beauteous female, who, with dishevelled hair, and hands upraised in supplication, was gazed at by the English with surprise and sorrow, for they feared that every shot would immolate her amongst the ruins of the tower. Suddenly a loud shout was heard, and Luke Somerton, rushing forward, exclaimed frantically,—

"It is my child! my lost Louisa! Soldiers! let no cowardice unnerve ye at a moment like this! rescue my child, and all I possess in the world shall be yours!"

"Fear not, but she shall yet be saved," cried Terence, who at that moment happened to be standing by. "My friends," he added, to his soldiers, "you see the peril of yonder female—on to her rescue, and believe me that your reward shall be great."

With a loud shout, expressive of their determination, the English now advanced, and in justice it must be admitted that they were met with equal bravery by the pirates. Nadoc still struck down all who opposed themselves to his sword, when, with an activity and resolution that surprised every one, Luke Somerton rushed up a ladder, and engaged the chief of the outlaws. This act seemed to excite others to renewed courage; for the English now mounted the walls in every direction, and the combat became more fierce and desperate than it ever had been before.

The pirates, rendered desperate by the determination with which they were attacked, closed round their ship, and Terence, Luke Somerton, and Reginald, with the bravest of their followers, charged the foe as they retreated in the wildest disorder before them. The tower, beneath which they were now fighting, had been much shattered by the English cannon from the opposite hill; English and foemen were mingled in fierce strife beneath the walls, when a considerable portion of the battlements fell with a tremendous crash, burying a number of both sides under its sides.

This unlooked-for event caused an instant cessation of hostilities. The pirates were deprived of their leader, for Nadoc was amongst those overwhelmed; and, throwing down their arms in consternation, they yielded to their conquerors, and were at once placed under a sufficient guard of the English troops.

Luke Somerton's first care was to seek the entrance to the tower, and as he mounted its tottering stairs, his heart sank within him, at the fear of beholding Louisa among the victims of that day's strife. But Heaven had watched over her, for, as he reached the summit, she sprang into his arms, and, overcome with gratitude for her preservation, fainted on his bosom. At that moment Luke seemed to be endowed with superhuman strength, and bearing her to a lower apartment of the tower, he met Terence and Reginald, whose congratulations he received on the restoration of her whose safety had been at one time so much doubted.

The ruins having been cleared away, the body of Nadoc was extricated from the heap of dead that covered him. Luke Somerton was among the first to approach and look upon the pirate chief, when, starting back, he exclaimed, with amazement,—

"Merciful Heaven! what do I behold? That face—that form, are but too faithfully impressed upon my memory. Let him be conveyed to a chamber, and every care that can be bestowed upon him." Then drawing Terence on one side, they conversed for nearly half an hour in a tone so low that none others could hear what passed between them.

    *   *   *   *

To all appearance dead, and stretched upon a couch, Nadoc lay, surrounded by Luke Somerton, Terence, Reginald, and Captain Danvers. A reviving cordial having been administered, the almost exhausted flame of life lighted up his eyes, and supported by pillows, he gazed wildly around him; till Luke Somerton advancing, took his hand, and, in accents of wonder, exclaimed,—

"Do my eyes deceive me, or has the lapse of years caused a change as that I now behold, that Arnold Lorimer can have forgotten one he once esteemed as a friend?"

Nadoc, or, as we shall now call him, Arnold Lorimer, turned his eyes on Luke Somerton, as he replied, slowly and with much difficulty,—

"I knew you once as such, but times, since last we saw each other, have marvellously altered. It is true, you saved me from the uplifted sword of an enemy—but what of that? You crossed my path—possessed yourself of her who, of all others in the world, I could most have loved. But I loved in vain; her virtue, cold as the ice that bounds the northern pole, resisted all the entreaties of Arnold Lorimer. Yet did I conquer in spite of all;

yes, this hand mingled the drug—these eyes beheld her charms fade beneath its blighting power. I beheld the bitter anguish of your soul as she slowly perished, and gloried in the sight !"

Unable for some time to reply, Luke Somerton at length exclaimed,—

"Monster! fiend of mischief! could you indeed have exulted in the crime you committed? Oh, gracious Heaven! do I live to hear that my beloved Louisa fell beneath thy hand? My child, too! had he but lived, there might yet have been some consolation for me."

"Rest satisfied he does," said Arnold, with difficulty. "Yes, Luke, the heir of thy wealth lives, but never will have it in his power to claim his birthright. With peasants he was reared as if their own offspring, and all the honours of your house are doomed to pass away into obscurity. Ah, revenge! revenge! how precious art thou even at the dread hour of death! Luke, I see thee writhing with torture beneath this terrible stroke; yet have mercy, and do not curse me in thy madness! Oh, I cannot call on Heaven! Louisa—see! she shews my fate—points to the flames in which my guilty soul will soon be plunged! Oh, for one moment! In vain—hell is before me—I sink—I burn! Oh, maddening torture!"

Spasms now choked his utterance; his visage became livid and frightfully distorted; foam burst from his lips; and, ere he could utter more, his guilty soul fled to the realms of darkness.

Overpowered by the dreadful confession of Arnold Lorimer, the unfortunate Luke Somerton remained for some time plunged in the deepest affliction. The wounds time had nearly healed were again opened, and he mourned afresh for his murdered Louisa. He had named the orphan whose protection he had undertaken after his beloved wife, and now she strove to soften the tide of sorrow that bore all before it. Terence, too, strove to console him; and Reginald felt the most sincere pity for the unhappy man, whom affliction had thus bowed down to the very earth.

The body of Nadoc was committed to the grave by some of his own band, a small portion of whom only survived, and even of them the greater number were wounded. The plunder of the fort was immense, and amply rewarded the soldiers and sailors who had been engaged in the perilous undertaking. It consisted of almost every valuable that could be conceived—embroidered stuffs, gold and silver vessels, arms of all kinds, and jewels, which had been years collecting. In short, the excessive avarice of the pirates must have proved their own destruction, for they could have long since abandoned their predatory course of life with an ample sum of money for their future support.

During the heat of the battle's strife, Reginald had sought everywhere for Sir Geoffry Dunholm, but in vain; and it was not until the prisoners were examined that he was found disguised as one of the band. Upon being led into the presence of Terence and Captain Danvers, his courage and haughty bearing seemed to have forsaken him. To be led a prisoner before Reginald, whom he had so deeply injured in the person of Mildred, was galling in the extreme; and when he entered the apartment he folded his arms, and remained sullenly regarding those who were his judges.

"Sir Geoffry Dunholm," said Terence, "how is it that I find you—a subject of the English crown—leagued with pirates, and opposed in arms to the faithful soldiers of the sovereign you have forsaken?"

"I was detained a prisoner," he replied, after pausing a few moments to frame an excuse; "and when the fort was attacked, the pirates compelled me against my will to take an active part in defence of the place."

"Do you dare pledge your word to the truth of the assertion you have made?"

"He dare not!" cried a voice from the door of the chamber; and one of the pirates, led in by soldiers, entered, and, confronting Sir Geoffry Dunholm, said,—

"Disgrace to the arms you bear! you were our ally—not a prisoner! You came hither to aid us; and although our chief, Nadoc, has fallen deservedly for his numerous crimes, long since committed, yet, could he now start up from his grave, and here confront you, you would not deny the words I have uttered."

Reginald here ventured to interpose :—

"You cannot but admit, Sir Geoffry Dunholm," he exclaimed, "that at the capture of Lord Carrick's castle you were in arms against us."

"Although I have full power," added Terence, "to bring you to instant trial, and the doom your traitorous opposition well deserves—yet I will at present consign you to close confinement, until the pleasure of our gracious sovereign has been made known."

Sir Geoffry Dunholm was then conveyed away, closely guarded, while the man who had so boldly charged him with falsehood attracted the attention of the judges; his figure was tall and commanding, combining strength with activity, and his well-proportioned limbs appeared to much advantage in the uniform of the band to which he belonged. Terence gazed upon him for a few moments, and then demanded his name.

"Lawrence," answered the other.

"Do you confess yourself to have belonged to the dangerous horde of men we have just defeated?"

"It would be in vain to deny it," replied the other; "nay, more—I am one who was bound by every tie of gratitude to Nadoc, and, could the sacrifice of my life have saved his, most gladly should it have been made. He is, I know, charged with crimes of the deepest dye; yet to me he was ever kind and beneficent. He once saved my life at the hazard of his own, and gratitude would have prompted me to return the obligation."

"How came he to fix his residence in this island?" demanded Luke Somerton. "When last I saw him he was in yonder mainland. Since then I have lost sight of him, though I heard rumours that he had quitted his native country to join a horde of pirates who infested the African coast."

"It was there I passed my youth," answered Lawrence. "Taken in a foreign vessel when yet a boy, Arnold Lorimer retained me about him as a page—carried me with him on all his expeditions —nurtured my youth, and trained me to the use of arms."

"Do many of your people now survive?" asked Terence.

"None," replied Lawrence; "in the last attack all were either slain or mortally wounded."

"Are you willing to enter among our troops, and fight for the English sovereign?" demanded the officer.

"I am most willing," he replied.

"Then from this moment you are free."

Upon the pirate retiring, Terence, turning towards Captain Danvers, exclaimed,—

"Methinks, were we to disperse our prisoners among the troops, the sovereign we serve would gain some hardy soldiers; and mercy shown where they have reason to expect the harshest treatment —nay, death itself—will bind them still more firmly to our service."

"I entirely agree with you," replied Captain Danvers; "and have no doubt they will thankfully accept the mercy we offer them. With regard, however, to Sir Geoffry Dunholm, we must keep him strictly guarded until his fate is decided by our sovereign."

These matters being thus arranged, Luke Somerton, Terence, Captain Danvers, and Reginald de Lancy, assembled in the large dining hall, where a repast was prepared, at which Louisa appeared, bursting upon the already enamoured sight of Captain Danvers with charms that soon captivated his heart; he was indeed disgusted with warfare, and being anxious to retire to the rural shades of Devonshire, his native county, he pictured in his mind how sweetly such a companion would solace his calm retirement, believing her, as he did, to be the daughter of Luke Somerton.

He therefore endeavoured to render himself as agreeable as possible to her supposed parent, and succeeded to the full extent of his fondest hopes; for Luke, naturally open and candid, was gratified at the prospect of his young ward's forming so eligible an alliance, and was much pleased with the gay and gallant manners of Captain Danvers. As for Louisa, she was above all deception, and knowing the wishes of her protector upon the subject, she exhibited no disinclination to receive his addresses. He was the first person who had spoken to her in the language of love—the first who had gained an interest in her affections.

When Reginald contrasted the happiness of Danvers with his own present unhappiness—when he thought of the fair Mildred, so mysteriously rescued from the power of Sir Geoffry Dunholm, and subsequently conveyed he knew not whither, it rendered him gloomy and abstracted. To every inquiry which he made of the means by which Mildred had quitted the island, he could not obtain the slightest information, and this last stroke of an adverse fate completely overwhelmed him with despair.

"Be more resigned to the will of Heaven, my dear young friend," exclaimed Luke Somerton, on one occasion, when they were together. "Had you suffered as I have—had you seen the early hopes of happiness nipped in their bud, and each succeeding year adding to the afflictions—then indeed there might have been some reason for thus giving way to despondency and grief; but hope should never be lightly resigned, and I have no doubt that you will, ere long, receive the most gratifying intelligence of your Mildred's safety."

As had been anticipated, the pirates gladly accepted the offer of serving the English monarch,

and after much anxious deliberation it was arranged that they were to be sent to Galway, while a sufficient number of the English were to remain on the Pirate's Isle, which was to be repaired and fortified as heretofore, it being deemed a commanding situation, and one well adapted as a depot for troops and vessels engaged in quelling the disturbances in the neighbouring districts.

Upon the return of Terence to Galway, he was accompanied by Luke Somerton and Louisa, who took up their residence in a house allotted to them by the former. In a short time afterwards, Captain Danvers and Reginald followed them. The latter was still unable to discover any trace of Mildred and her mysterious conductor, and he at length determined to take the earliest opportunity that offered to return to France.

As Louisa had now reached the age when Luke Somerton was to open the packet consigned to his care by her father, and which contained the secret of her name and family, he acquainted Captain Danvers with so much of her story as he knew, and appointed a day when the important packet should be opened.

*   *   *   *

The ship was now ready for sea, and Luke Somerton, Louisa, and Reginald, prepared for their departure. Captain Danvers had been some time in England, and the last messenger he had sent informed them that he would visit Ireland the ensuing year, and meet them at Dublin, where Luke Somerton proposed spending some months. Terence parted with his old friend and former master with much reluctance; however, now that Luke Somerton had a prospect of being re-established in his rank and honours, Terence willingly accepted an offer that he had made him, and had written to the English court, resigning his command, and only waited the arrival of the officer appointed to succeed him, when he would follow Luke Somerton, and pass the remainder of his days beneath his hospitable roof.

The spacious bay of Galway was lighted by the first rays of morning, which glittered upon the clear blue waters of the broad Atlantic, as the gallant vessel saluted with her cannon the fort, on her departure, and was greeted by them with a similar compliment. Majestically she glided over the waters, and as they passed between the Arran islands, Luke Somerton bestowed a parting glance at the humble cottage so long inhabited by him and Louisa, during their retirement.

Reginald felt much pleasure in the society of Luke Somerton and Louisa, whose company indeed seemed to be almost essential to his happiness. With them he could speak without restraint of former days; and both, if they could not avoid the subject, at least endeavoured as much as possible to banish from his mind the bitterness of the disappointment which he endured at the separation that had taken place between him and Mildred.

At length, as they were passing an island which reared its lofty pyramidical rocks several hundred feet above the sea, Luke Somerton inquired of the captain who lived upon so rugged a crag, which scarcely appeared capable of affording food or shelter to some goats which they could observe bounding on the hill sides.

"I will tell you all I know about it," replied

the captain. "Upon the first voyage I ever made hereabout, I anchored in the harbour, the entrance to which you may perceive round that bluff headland, to the north-east. While there I fell into company with the superior of a convent, who seemed to be a most religious and enlightened man ; indeed, so well pleased were we with each other, that I visited him often during my stay, and derived much gratification and instruction from his society.

" 'We lose one of our number to-morrow,' he said to me, one morning, as I was seated with him in the convent parlour, 'and I shall consider it a favour if you will allow one of your boats to convey our brother to his destination.'

" 'Most willingly,' I replied ; 'where does he go to ?'

" 'Upon the largest of the rocks you see yonder in the distance, for a period of twenty days, and then he will be relieved by another of our fraternity.'

" 'What is the object of his residing there ?' I asked.

" 'An ancient custom of our order ; its object being, by means of a beacon light, to warn the

mariner of the dangers which in that place surround him. But the origin of the custom will be more fully explained in a legend which you shall be at liberty to peruse.'

" I accompanied him to the library, where, opening the ancient manuscript which he placed in my hands, I found many parts so decayed and obliterated as only to be able to decipher a small portion of it. The purport of the narrative was, however, that a vessel had been wrecked, and, of all the mariners she contained, one only was brought on shore alive. He appeared to have been the captain, and had a bag fastened round his body, which contained a large amount of valuable property. In three days after he had been brought ashore he died, leaving all he possessed in the world for the convent, on condition that a light-house was erected on the rock where the vessel had been placed, and that the monks resided there in turn to afford relief whenever it might be required."

A breeze springing up, the sails filled, and the vessel soon glided past the rock, soon after which Luke Somerton and his party descended to the cabin.

At the period which we have now reached, William the Third, of England, desirous of strengthening his own cause by engaging the affections of his nobility and wealthy subjects, directed commissioners to consider the claims of Luke Somerton, and give in their report with as much expedition as possible. The commands of their monarch were gladly obeyed, particularly where the restoration of a noble name was in question ; and the proud and honourable feeling inherent in true nobility prompted the commissioners to report so favourably, that Luke Somerton was immediately restored to his rank and honours. The estates, too, which had been sequestrated, were given back to him, and as large a sum of money as the treasury could well spare, refunded, in lieu of the rents which, during the last two or three years, had been received by the crown.

Thus situated, Luke was most anxious that Reginald de Lancy should participate in his change of good fortune, for he had taken a liking to the youth, and could not endure the thought of a separation, which it was likely would prove an eternal one. But he deemed that it would be unjust to prevent his meditated journey to France, where the Baron de Lancy then was, and he therefore furthered, as much as possible, his departure, and presented him with a horse for himself, as also another for his servant, one of his own domestics being desirous of returning to France, of which country he was a native. They parted from each other with much regret, and had it not been that filial duty claimed his attendance abroad, it is probable that very little pressing would have induced him to remain with friends whom he so much esteemed.

CHAPTER XL.

NOTHING worthy of particular remark occurred to Reginald during his journey, and in safety he arrived at Paris, where he had once more the happiness of being pressed to the bosom of his parent. Time had scattered his snows upon the head of De Lancy, and his step was less firm than when the youth had last beheld him.

The baron received his son with the warmest parental affection, and regarded his manly form and bearing with the most sincere pleasure. He had none but Reginald to leave his vast wealth to, and depending upon his interest with the French monarch, he intended soliciting the legitimatizing the young soldier, so that he might, in some measure, make amendment for the injuries he had in early life inflicted upon his mother.

After the baron had been gratified by a brief relation of Reginald's adventures during the interval of their separation, he informed him that he intended despatching a messenger the following day to the Baron Heinbach; "when," said he, "you can communicate to him whatever intelligence of his daughter you have become acquainted with."

"Alas!" replied the young man, "must I inflict yet deeper pangs upon him, by letting him know that, in a far distant place, away from home and friends, his daughter, reared in the enjoyment of every domestic comfort, now wanders amongst strangers, and without the power of returning to her father's home?"

"And yet her situation may not be so bad as your fears lead you to imagine," exclaimed De Lancy.

"Do you then see any hope?" demanded his son.

"A faint one, it must be admitted," returned the other. "May not the mysterious being you have described as accompanying her in the boat, have rescued and conveyed her to her father ere this? But, my dear Reginald," he continued, "you must at present turn your thoughts towards the completion of a plan nearly matured. I am now advanced in years, and unfit any longer to endure the trials of war. You are in the bloom of manhood, the bearer of my name, and, I trust, the future inheritor of the title I have won by a faithful discharge of my duty to my king and country."

"That the day you speak of may be far, far distant, is my most ardent prayer, my dear father," exclaimed Reginald, pressing the hand of the old man to his lips. "Long may you enjoy the rank and honours you are so well fitted to bear, and if it should indeed ever be my lot to succeed you, may I support them with no less honour and worthiness than you have done."

"I have no doubt you will, my dear son," answered the old man, "for I have ever watched thy progress with joy and satisfaction. Reginald, thy mother was an angel of goodness, and my own conduct regarding her now inflicts a pang that I can hardly endure. But why should I now recur to that which I would fain bury in oblivion? She was my wife, Reginald—bound to me by the ties of God and man. Yet, to gratify ambition, that worst of all the human passions, I wooed another, whose wealth and high family tempted me beyond the power of resistance. My suit was readily adopted, and thy mother deserted, made to believe that the ceremony which had joined us was an illegal one. She bore thee with her; and I, along with bitter feelings of remorse, felt myself most unhappy with my wife—though wife, in truth, she was not. But fate so willed it that she shortly died. Never shall I forget the night I met thy mother—famishing for want, Reginald; she died in these arms,—nay, thou, too, would'st have perished had I chanced to arrive an hour later. Years of penitence and sorrow have passed, but that night can never be obliterated from my memory. Thou art legitimate, my son, though the world has deemed thee base-born. Hadst thou not proved worthy of the name of De Lancy, I never should have acknowledged that which I now declare to thee; but as thy claims must be made known to the French king, I will take fitting opportunity at as early a period as possible. Your gallant conduct in the field has attracted his favourable attention, and often has he mentioned you, and regretted that so accomplished a soldier should be lost to his service. My wishes, therefore, are, that you should at once again resume your station as my acknowledged son, and the heir of my wealth and titles."

Reginald promptly yielded obedience to the wishes of his parent, for he anxiously desired to raise for himself an honourable name among the defenders of his country's honour. Yet ambition did not prevent his thoughts from wandering ever and anon to his lost Mildred.

"Dearest girl!" he would murmur to himself, "when shall I again have the happiness of clasping thee to my bosom? when behold thee in the mansion of thine ancestors, gladdening with thy smiles and presence the father who now mourns thee as dead?"

Reginald's desire for active employment and warlike pursuits soon appeared to be upon the point of being gratified, for the flames of discord had already begun to spread, and he resolved to espouse a cause in which there was every chance of his attaining the honour to which he aspired.

*   *   *   *   *   *

Brightly shone the sun upon the castellated mansion of Luke Somerton, while music sounded through its halls; and issuing from the gates appeared a troop of servants in the richest liveries.

Two travellers, descending a hill half a mile from the castle, checked their steeds to gaze for a few moments upon the enchanting prospect. Not a cloud was perceptible in the clear, blue sky, and the light air of morning was scarcely sufficient to rustle the leaves of the trees, which spread forth their shadowy wings.

"What think you of Ireland?" said the elder of the two travellers, after a long pause.

"It is an earthly paradise," replied the other, in a tone of admiration. "Where will you behold more verdant plains than these—where groves of richer hue than those with which we are surrounded? In good truth, Captain Terence, your beautiful country wrests the palm of excellence from any that I have yet seen."

"Ay, Danvers," answered the other; "and our damsels, too, are no less beautiful than the country they inhabit. Thou seest yonder mansion—is it not a noble edifice? Hear you the sound of music wafted on the gale?"

"I do, I do," replied Captain Danvers; "would that we were near the house of our friend, Luke Somerton; for I have reasons to wish our journey at an end, and you, I know, will pardon the impatience of a lover."

"Most willingly," said the other, smiling at these words; "and in order that you may not be kept in suspense longer than necessary, I at once declare yonder mansion to be the end and aim of our present journey. 'Tis the favourite retirement of our friend Somerton."

By this time they had been met by some of the servants who had been sent forth to ascertain if it were Terence and his friend Danvers who approached, as, not perceiving any attendants with them, they did not imagine them to be the persons expected. This, however, was easily explained as having been occasioned by the impatience of Captain Danvers to reach the place of destination.

They were met at the entrance by Luke Somerton, who greeted them with all the ardour of a sincere friendship, and gave his guests a hearty welcome to his abode. Then directing a servant to show them to their apartments, and see that they were properly attended to, he hastened to acquaint Louisa with their arrival. This news was, indeed, most gratifying to her, and blushing as she thought of once more seeing her lover, she arose from her seat, and giving her hand to Somerton, was conducted to the drawing-room, where, by this time, Danvers and his friend were awaiting them. The former advanced, and leading her to a seat, placed himself beside her, while Luke Somerton and Terence, unwilling to impose any restraint upon the lovers by their presence, passed out upon the terrace, and descended to the garden.

The accents of love flowed ardently from Captain Danvers, and they both felt gratified in recapitulating the occurrences that had befallen each other during their late separation; the hopes and fears that had agitated them, and the reward of constancy which their present meeting afforded to both. In short, so successful was Captain Danvers in his suit, that, with little difficulty, he prevailed upon Louisa to name a day in the following week for the celebration of their nuptials.

On the return of Luke Somerton and Terence they all adjourned to the dining-room, where a splendid repast had been placed upon the table in honour of the arrival of their visitors. In the evening they sought the cool and refreshing shade of the garden, where, seated in a beautifully trelliced arbour, Captain Danvers related to Luke Somerton and Louisa the miserable end of Sir Geoffry Dunholm, who, unable to endure the contumely attached to his traitorous conduct, and despairing of obtaining the pardon of his offended

sovereign, had finished his career by committing suicide. The keeper of the prison, one morning, on entering his cell, found him stretched upon his couch—a phial in his firmly-clenched hand, and his visage horribly distorted by the anguish occasioned by the deadly drug with which he had terminated his mortal existence.

Thus fell a man, who, had he controlled his passions, and remained true to his king and country, would have been an honour to his name, as well as the land of his birth. As it was, no one regretted his fall. His base conduct had, some time previously, sent his mother broken-hearted to the grave; and a mound of earth, with a rude stone cross at the head, was all that marked the spot where the once gay and gallant Sir Geoffry Dunholm found his last resting-place on earth.

Captain Terence confessed that he had but little to relate. His application to the English monarch was granted with extreme regret, as he found his services so valuable in Ireland, where he had been chiefly instrumental in checking the rebellion which had broken forth with so much fury. But no reason could be found for refusing the favour he asked, and the request was accordingly acceded to, after some little hesitation. On leaving the sovereign's presence, he had hastened over to Ireland at the earnest solicitation of Luke Somerton, intending to pass the remainder of his days with the valued friend by whose side he had so often fought.

As the day for the nuptial ceremony was fixed, Luke Somerton proposed a grand hunting party during the interim, and early one morning the cheerful notes of the bugles, intermixed with the loud baying of the hounds, roused all within the house; and soon the party on horseback crossed the, as yet, dewy plains, and sought the spot where the wild boar made his lair. Louisa was among the riders, and, as a matter of course, Danvers rode closely by her side.

The cries of the dogs, and the shouts of the huntsmen, soon roused the infuriated animals from their shelter, and then commenced the spirit and enthusiasm that belongs so exclusively to the chase. The horse which Louisa rode bore her some little distance in advance of her companions, and she was just reining back the steed, when a huge boar rushing from a thicket close by startled the horse, and, ere the rider could recover her presence of mind, she was thrown to the ground. At that fearful juncture the boar made furiously towards her, and in another moment all would have been over with her, had not Danvers perceived her perilous situation, and rushing to her aid, plunged his hunting sword full in the throat of the infuriated animal, which instantly fell gasping to the earth. The rest of the party coming up congratulated Louisa upon her fortunate escape from a fate that seemed to be certain.

They were thus occupied, when suddenly the clouds, dark and gathering, gave notice of an approaching storm, and large, heavy drops came pattering through the foliage beneath which they were assembled. Fortunately, at this juncture, one of the servants discovered a cottage at a short distance off, and thither the party repaired to request the shelter they so much needed. On approaching, they were met by an old man, who bade him welcome to such humble accommodation as his place afforded.

"And yet," he added, after seeing his visitors seated, "you have come to a house of sorrow and mourning, for a fellow creature lies upon the bed of death in the room that adjoins the one we are assembled in."

A low groan of agony sounded near, and the old man, starting, prayed them to excuse his absence, while he went to see after his patient. In a few minutes afterwards he returned, but his countenance was expressive of a strong emotion of horror; he staggered towards a seat, and remained for some few moments unable to utter a word. At length he exclaimed,—

"Leave this place, I entreat you; hasten from my cot, ere its roof fall and crushes the innocent with the guilty. I have heard such a narration—so replete with horror, so fearfully dark, that even now I can scarcely believe but I am suffering from the effects of a dream."

The curiosity of Luke Somerton, Danvers, and Terence having been excited by these words, they entreated the old man to acquaint them with the terrible revelation to which he so mysteriously alluded.

"Enter and behold the wretched man," exclaimed the cottager; "and if your prayers, offered up to Heaven, can gain forgiveness for a miserable sinner, prostrate yourselves, I implore you, in his behalf."

Upon advancing into the chamber in which the dying man lay, they beheld, by the faint rays of a lamp, a figure stretched upon a pallet, the sickly light tinging the hollow cheek, the eyes gleaming with unearthly lustre, and the hand grasping at fancied objects, conjured up by the expiring visions of fading fancy, a sure indication that death is near.

As the party entered, a bright ray of reason flashed across the sufferer, who, in a tone of voice, hollow and broken, exclaimed,—

"Approach! and let me quit the world while I can have the prayers of those whom I have deeply injured. Yes, injured!" repeated the sufferer, as those who were present looked at each other with astonishment. "Luke Somerton, hast thou indeed forgotten the miserable object who now lies dying before thee?"

Luke started with surprise as these words sounded on his ear; then stooping forward he looked earnestly into the countenance of the person by whom he had been addressed. That one momentary look was sufficient, and wildly clasping his hands, he exclaimed,—

"What do I behold! Is it, indeed, Honor Lorimer whom I then find at the point of death?"

"Who calls upon my name?" he faintly demanded. "Who names that wretched being, fallen from his name, religion, country. No; call me Julio, for as such I have long been known. Luke—your hand," and firmly grasping it, he pressed it to his lips. "Oh, Luke, Luke! I have injured you past all forgiveness!"

"No, no," he exclaimed; "I forgive you—freely forgive you, though Heaven knows what I have lately suffered. Your brother—Arnold Lorimer ——"

"Ah, name him not!" he exclaimed, interrupting him; "he it was that urged me on to all the wickedness I have been guilty of. His lawless passion for your wife, and mine for you, were the foundations of misery and suffering. Oh, Heaven! none can tell but those who once have known the maddening tortures of rejected love. Luke, it was I who aided Arnold in the terrible deed of vengeance—your mother was our first victim—but I grow fainter, raise me, that I may complete this fearful revelation of crime!" Then after a pause of a few minutes, she added,—" Your son still lives—he is most worthy of you—seek Reginald de Lancy—he is your child—his affianced bride is now in Munster, and I believe safe. Luke Somerton, your hand once more. My eyes are dim! Louisa beckons me! She offers poison!—no, 'tis blood—human blood that fills the cup! Ha! who is that yonder? 'Tis he! I hear the rustling of his wings—a hellish smile of triumph is on his lips. Satan, avaunt! Pray for me, Luke Somerton—the fiend drags me with him—mercy!—mercy!"

And with a long, fearful groan of mortal anguish, the soul of Honor Lorimer took its flight. Those who were present stood for some few moments as if deprived of the power of speech and motion; but at length Terence, advancing towards Luke Somerton, said,—

"Yonder unhappy woman's words remind me that long since I was struck with the wonderful resemblance the youth, reared as De Lancy's son, bears to your departed wife. When I first beheld him in England, the likeness appeared to be so perfect, that I sought for a situation in the train of his reputed father. How he first came to be taken under the protection of the Baron de Lancy, and treated as his son, I never was informed."

"This packet," said the old man of the cottage, "which I forgot till this moment, may, perhaps, serve to clear up all that at present appears so mysterious. I see it is directed to Luke Somerton."

The certainty that his son lived—that he had, indeed, beheld him, and that he was in every respect worthy, conveyed a solace to the breast of Luke, which banished from his mind some of the painful impressions it had just before received. Receiving the packet from the hands of the old cottager, he exclaimed,—

"My friends, Danvers and Terence, to you I commit the last sad offices to the unfortunate Honor Lorimer. Let her be interred with all respect becoming the station she once occupied in life. She is now no more, and although she has injured me most deeply, anger must not be suffered to exist when the object of it has passed beyond the grave. Danvers, you will, as soon as you have given the necessary directions to the servants, attend Louisa to my house. As there are obvious reasons for it, you will excuse my hastening on before."

When Louisa, accompanied by Captain Danvers and Terence, arrived at home, they found Luke Somerton much agitated. He had perused the manuscript left behind by Honor Lorimer, and it had revived the remembrance of his early sorrows, opening anew those wounds which time had nearly healed. Handing the manuscript to Captain Danvers, he exclaimed,—

"Take this, my dear friend, and read its contents to Louisa and Terence. Alas! I am unfitted by the horrid tale from joining you for the present.

But the recovery of my long-lost son shall be my first care, and early to-morrow preparations shall be commenced for our immediate departure for the French capital. It will for a short period necessarily delay your nuptials ; but, if I am not much mistaken, you will feel more happy when my gallant boy, and your esteemed friend, is witness of your happiness."

"Let us not delay an instant, my dear sir," replied Danvers ; "I long to meet once more with my friend, Reginald,—or by what other name shall I call him ?"

"Call him Luke, from henceforth," answered the father. "But remember what I have requested you to do—peruse that packet carefully, for you will find in it much to astonish and perplex you."

Captain Danvers having quitted the presence of Luke Somerton, hastened to Louisa, and having acquainted Terence with the wishes that had been expressed, he seated himself beside his future bride, and opening the manuscript, commenced perusing it as follows :—

"Luke, dost thou remember my oath of vengeance ? Dost thou remember when my love was scorned, and I quitted thy presence breathing revenge ? Full dearly have I kept that fatal vow ; my brother, too, aided my purpose ; he beheld thy wife—loved her to madness—was rejected, and became her bitterest foe. In close disguise I hovered round the castle—often beheld Louisa in the grounds—often did I grasp the dagger I had armed myself with, with the fell purpose of plunging it into her heart. Yet even this I deemed a poor revenge for hatred like mine. I vowed to ruin thee, and all connected with thy name and family ; thy mother was my first victim ; she, by some means or other, contrived to penetrate my disguise, as I gave utterance to my imprecations against thee.

"I and my brother, fearful of discovery, entered her chamber early in the morning. Arnold's hands fixed the fatal scarf round her neck. Methinks I see her struggling—I hear her suffocating supplications—the fearful gurgling in her throat, that told us nature was almost exhausted. I fainted at the feet of our victim, and in that state Arnold bore me from the apartment ; he ridiculed what he called my weak and womanly fears.

"'Are they not,' cried he, 'the enemies of our race ? Have they not wrested from us our wealth, our rank ? And is it not just that we should retaliate at the very first opportunity that offers ? Oh ! could our father now look down and behold his children, would he not smile approval at our having slain one who was a foe to us ?'

"Louisa, at that time about to become a mother, was next doomed to destruction, and long did Arnold and I consult together as to the means by which this could be best effected. At length poison was decided on. She had a son, and I entered her chamber by a secret way ; the nurse was absent ; a light was burning near the cradle ; I stooped over thy child, and in its infant features could trace a perfect resemblance to thyself. A tear of pity moistened my eyes, but my fiendish brother, closely following on my footsteps, whispered in my ear :—

"'Quick ! lose no time, but instantly despatch the offspring of those we have doomed to vengeance.'

"In a moment my dagger was unsheathed ; I raised my arm ; a scream rang through the chamber ; it was Louisa, who, beholding the danger of her infant, sprung from her bed, and rushing forward, threw herself on her knees, imploring mercy for her innocent offspring. Alas ! she little knew the ruthless nature of those whom she was thus supplicating.

"At this juncture Arnold took a phial from his vest, and presenting it to her, exclaimed,—

"'Drink this instantly—drain it to the very dregs, or behold the life-blood of your child flow through your own accursed obstinacy !'

"'Ah ! restore to me my child,' she wildly exclaimed. 'What would I not do to save my blessed babe from the cruel fate you have doomed it to !'

"She seized the deadly drug, and swallowed what, had she possessed ten thousand lives, would have extinguished all. A shudder thrilled through her frame ; her countenance assumed an ashy paleness ; drops of agony hung upon her brow, and the most frightful convulsions immediately followed. Seeing her thus helpless, Arnold bore her to the couch she had just left, and placed her upon it.

"'Quick, Honor,' he exclaimed to me ; 'convey that child from hence without a moment's delay.'

"I hastily wrapped it in my cloak ; I felt its warm breath on my cheek ; its fingers clasped my hand, stained with the blood of its murdered parent. At length, opening its eyes, it smiled in my face. Oh, Nature ! who can control thine impulses ? I was a woman, and though my heart was nearly callous to the feelings of humanity, still, when I beheld the innocent babe smile in the face of its bitterest enemy, I could not have harmed it even to save my own life.

"Once more wrapping it in my cloak, which I had closely bound about me, I quitted thy castle, and, mounted upon horseback, took the first road that offered. I cared not whither I fled to, so that I was borne far from the haunts of man. Long I debated within my own mind how best to dispose of the child I bore in my arms.

"At length I crossed over to France, and stopping one evening at a farmhouse, beheld a female in great affliction—a stranger and a traveller like myself. Upon making inquiry I found that her child had died that very day, and, being exceedingly poor, she possessed not the means to give it burial.

"I could not, hard-hearted as my nature was, behold one of my own sex thus sorely distressed, where I had the power of relieving her. I therefore handed her my purse, and she most thankfully accepted a portion of its contents. Her child was buried, and she willingly undertook the care of little Luke ; though not till I had first noted down her name, and the place where she intended to reside.

"She related to me her melancholy story : seduced from the care and protection of her friends —imposed on by a false marriage, and then forsaken when the betrayer's passion had been gratified. Although her heart was nearly bursting with the intense agony she endured, she still had sufficient pride remaining to spurn his offers of a provision for herself and child. She quitted him, and preferred dragging on a life of misery and want to one of splendid ease, allied as it must have been to the most disgraceful infamy.

"Still my revenge was not fully satisfied. Luke, know that it was I who wrote those letters to the monarch, charging thee with treachery and disaffection. Then, when I beheld thee stripped of all thine honours, compelled to flee from thy native country, thy name attainted, then did I feel a joy long, long unknown to me. In disguise I followed thee—took passage in the vessel bound to foreign lands.

"Dost thou recollect the voice that awoke thee from thy slumbers, when an ambush stole upon thy camp? It was my voice: I could not, although I hated thee, behold thee slain without a struggle. Thou wert wounded,—I sat by thy couch, moistened thy lips, heard thy frenzied ravings, and my detested rival's name.

*   *   *   *   *

"I sought the woman to whom I had entrusted the infant where she had mentioned, but found that death had claimed its victim; and from an old female, who had witnessed her expiring agonies, I learned that the child—which had been deemed her own—was taken under the protection of the Baron de Lancy, a powerful French nobleman.

"I was satisfied so that the boy was lost to thee. I well knew how impossible it was that thou shouldst ever become acquainted with his existence. Disappointment and sorrow, with the fatigues of travel and exposure to different climates, had so altered my appearance, that even Arnold would have failed to recognise in me his sister, Honor Lorimer. I made mankind my study; I passed into various countries; I found ambition the leading star to which all persons directed their course; I beheld the churchman's sanctity a cloak beneath which the strongest passions struggled; the warrior ambitious of fame; the merchant yearning after the acquisition of great wealth, that he might surpass his less fortunate competitors; the females ambitious of admiration; until, turning with disgust from this selfish picture human nature afforded, I thought of myself and of my deeds; I shuddered, for I felt how culpable—how guilty a creature I was.

"I plunged into politics. Smile not when you read this; few are better able to conduct affairs requiring secrecy, promptitude, and manœuvring, than females. You will ask—Why? They have not the impetuosity of men—they are more cool and calculating—they possess equally firm resolution—and who can attain the knowledge of a secret like a woman, if she uses those enticing charms nature has gifted her with?

"I joined in Arnheim's schemes, and was induced to co-operate with him against the Baron of Heinbach. It was in the castle of the latter that I again beheld thy son, placed there by the Baron de Lancy, who had given him his name, and, as I understood, deemed him his child. I had fainted from excessive fatigue near the castle, and as the youthful Luke stood beside my couch, methought the spirits of thy murdered mother and wife hovered round me, and, pointing to thy son, bade me render him justice.

"I found him kind and humane, and with him ministered to the wants of a beauteous girl. Although neither of them were acquainted with each other's feelings, yet I could perceive that a mutual affection existed, and that, although they thought they felt as brother and sister, yet a few revolving years would ripen into the warmest love. I therefore arranged my plans; I bestowed upon Luke a ring, which you must remember, from having seen it frequently in my possession. I had so arranged it, that he was to be brought into thy company, and thy recognition of the jewel would cause an explanation; for, believe me, Luke Somerton, years of sorrow and of penitence at length had conquered that hellish passion for revenge which had so long raged within my breast.

"After I met thee upon the island of Arran, and fled from what I deemed no living man, by chance I heard thee mentioned in terms that could leave no doubt upon my mind of thine identity. Thy daughter, too, was mentioned, but I well knew she could be no relation of thine.

"I accompanied Arnheim to the Castle of Bautzen; he had vowed the destruction of Heinbach, and determined to possess himself of Mildred, the chosen bride of thy son. But I foiled him in this last plan; I plunged my dagger in his breast, and fled from the Castle of Bautzen, bearing with me the unconscious maiden. Then, leaving her at a convent, I hastened upon other matters, which prevented my accompanying her to Ireland, whither I determined upon sending her in charge of one whom I knew, and I gave him full instructions as to the means he should use for getting her away from the convent. This man, who commanded a vessel, was about to join my brother Arnold immediately.

"I witnessed the battle in which your son was engaged, and beheld him nobly perform his duty, until he fell grievously wounded, and fainting from loss of blood. Assisted by a soldier, I bore him from the field—tended upon him until he began to revive—when, administering a powerful sleeping potion, I had him conveyed on board ship. I was in the same vessel, but kept out of sight, until we reached the coast of Ireland. Upon our arrival in the Shannon, I landed him at dark, giving him instructions by which I knew he would reach a depot of my brother's band, from whence he would be conducted with as little delay as possible to the Pirates' Isle.

"Think it not strange that I should place thee and thy son in my brother's power. I had determined upon the destruction of the pirates, and regarding my brother as the cause of all the crimes I had committed, I cared not whether he fell or was saved. My intentions once accomplished—thy son restored to thee, and he united to Mildred Heinbach—it was my resolve to flee to some solitary place, and there, in penitence and prayer, expiate my offences. But Fate ordered that such should not be my destiny. The vessel Mildred had been on board for some time past was wrecked, and she alone, of all that sailed in her, was saved.

"At a subsequent period she fell into the power of a Sir Geoffry Dunholm, who, captivated by her extraordinary beauty, and meeting a decided refusal, had her borne to my brother's retreat in the Pirates' Isle. It was from thence I rescued her, and fearing that my original plan might fail, as an opportunity offered for landing on the Dutch coast, we journeyed towards Switzerland, when circumstances occurred to change my determination, and I led her back to Ireland, though without being able to procure for her any permanent residence. She is now, however, at the German town of Munster, but I fear sadly needs the assistance of those who have long sought her in vain."

Luke Somerton, after perusing this extraordinary confession, lost no time in preparing for his journey; and, leaving Terence to manage his domestic affairs, he and Captain Danvers set off for France with a sufficient number of attendants. It was part of Luke's design to visit the mansion of the Baron de Lancy, but as he did not know in what part of the country this lay, he took the road to Paris, where, if he did not find him at his town residence, he could at least obtain all necessary information from his servants.

On arriving in the French metropolis, the residence of the Baron de Lancy was easily found. An eager impatience to behold his child would have urged Luke Somerton at once to hasten to the mansion; but Danvers, with some difficulty, prevailed upon him to remain behind, whilst he first of all went to break the affair which had taken them thither.

This being at length acceded to, he left Luke at the inn, and, guided by one of the landlord's servants, soon reached the noble mansion of the Baron de Lancy. It was a spacious structure; large folding gates opened into a handsome courtyard, within which stood the building itself; and to the principal entrance of which a broad flight of marble steps led the visitor. Here Captain Danvers, addressing himself to a grey-headed porter, who stood in the hall, asked if Reginald chanced to be at home.

"He is, sir," replied the man.

And calling to another servant, who was passing along, he desired him to acquaint his young master that a gentleman desired to see him immediately.

"What name am I to give?"

"It is unnecessary to mention any name to him," replied Captain Danvers; "but say that a friend from Ireland has taken an early opportunity to call and pay his respects."

The visitor was now ushered into the reception room, where he had not waited many minutes ere Reginald entered. Starting with mingled joy and surprise at beholding his friend, he uttered an exclamation of welcome, and then, springing forward, clasped him in his arms.

"You are most welcome," he exclaimed, as they seated themselves; "for nothing could have afforded me so much satisfaction as thus meeting with you in a place where I can entertain you as I wish. But I must now introduce you to my father, who has expressed a most anxious wish to be introduced to you, in order that he might return his grateful thanks for the many acts of kindness bestowed upon me during my sojourn in Ireland."

"Say no more, my dear friend, I beseech you," interrupted Captain Danvers; "for you do but overrate thus an act, which can be deemed no more than a soldier's duty, and such as I may, perhaps, some day or other, look for in return. I shall be most happy to be acquainted with the Baron de Lancy, but it must not be till I have explained the object of my present visit to France. So now, my dear Reginald, listen to me, I entreat you, and do not let any surprise you may feel cause an interruption, till I have concluded my narrative."

Captain Danvers then, as concisely as possible, commenced with the eventful history of Luke Somerton—his marriage, and subsequent happiness, until blighted by his mother's death, so closely followed by the loss of his infant son, and the wife whom he tenderly loved—the false accusations brought against him—his deprivation of rank and fortune. These various incidents excited exclamations of pity and regret from Reginald; but when Captain Danvers detailed the meeting with Honor Lorimer, and her confession, and that he who had always been considered the son of the Baron de Lancy was the long-lost child of Luke Somerton, all power of utterance for a time forsook him. At length, having in some degree recovered from the effect of his surprise, he exclaimed,—

"Oh, let me fly, my friend—let me hasten without delay to embrace a parent whom, meeting as a stranger, I esteemed most highly, but, viewing as a parent, must fondly love! And my second father —he who generously protected my youth, and trained me up to arms—how shall I break to him the intelligence that I am not his son? His affections have been warmly enlisted in my behalf, and I much fear this unexpected news will fill him with sorrow and regret."

"Let it be my task to prepare him for that which it is necessary he should hear," said Captain Danvers. "Introduce me to the Baron de Lancy, and I will repeat the story to which you have just now listened."

This being agreed to, the two friends hurried up stairs to the library, where De Lancy was seated. He raised his eyes as they entered, and perceiving a stranger with Reginald, cordially welcomed him as the friend of his son. After a few other complimentary explanations had taken place, he addressed himself to the young man:—

"You have just come at a fortunate moment, my dear Reginald," he said, "for I was on the point of sending a message, requesting your immediate presence here. Our friend, Baron Heinbach, has written to me, and requests to see you at his castle without delay. In short, I am most anxious you should go, as your presence will solace him, under the afflicting and mysterious absence of his daughter Mildred."

"You will ever find me most obedient to your wishes," answered Reginald; and then taking the baron's hand, he added:—"Allow me to introduce to you, my friend, Captain Danvers, with whose name you are familiar, and who, in Ireland, did me so many acts of kindness."

"I am indeed most happy to see one of whom I have heard so favourable a report," exclaimed the Baron de Lancy, presenting his hand to the young officer, who had been thus introduced to his notice. "The obligations my son was under to you can never be forgotten, and I therefore trust you will make this mansion your residence during your stay in our capital."

"I fear, my lord," he replied, "that it will not be in my power to accept your hospitality. I come to Paris with a friend upon matters of a private nature, which will shortly be concluded, when it is our intention to depart without further delay from France."

"Why cannot your friend accompany you here, and share in the welcome we extend to yourself?" asked the baron.

"Ay, why not, indeed?" added Reginald. "With your permission I will accompany you to the house where you have taken up your residence, and endeavour to prevail upon your friend to come back with us."

Captain Danvers offered no objection to this, and, taking leave of the baron, the two friends hastened to the inn, upon arriving at which, Reginald found himself clasped in the arms of his long-expectant father.

"My dearest boy," he exclaimed, with emotion, "to hold thee to my heart gladdens my soul with pleasure long unknown. And you, Danvers, who will one day know the force of fatherly affection, receive my heartfelt thanks, for to you do I owe all my present happiness."

As soon as the first joyful feelings had become somewhat moderated, Captain Danvers informed Luke Somerton of the arrangement he and Reginald had entered into. It was then agreed that Somerton should accompany them to the baron's mansion, and being introduced, was, at a fitting opportunity, to relate the singular events which had proved Reginald to be the son of another person.

De Lancy bitterly grieved at discovering that he was to be deprived of the blessing he had so much relied on, and it was a long while before he could become reconciled to the thought of resigning the hope which had inspired and supported him for years. Luke Somerton observed the struggle which was going on in his bosom, and endeavoured by every means in his power to assuage his grief.

"Nay, compose yourself, my dear baron," he exclaimed, "and permit me to point out the means of happiness that are still in your power. You have ever acted as a fond father to my son, and having been thus deprived of the solace, I would fain prevail upon you to accompany me back to Ireland, where you can pass the remainder of your days amongst friends whose chief care will be to render you happy and contented with your lot."

"I accept your generous offer, my dear sir," answered the Baron de Lancy, after a few moments had been given to consideration. "From henceforth the world is nothing to me, and the chief part of the wealth shall be given to Reginald—pardon me—I can scarcely yet prevail upon myself to call him by his new name of Luke."

At this moment the young man, who had left the room unobserved, returned in a state of the greatest agitation.

"Father," he exclaimed, "and you, my dear baron, give me your advice how I should act in this new difficulty that has sprung up. Mildred Heinbach is detained as a prisoner in the city of Munster, which being now besieged, renders the horror of her situation worse than death. I must at once hasten to her aid, for oh! think of her father's agonizing feelings were he to hear that I knew of her sufferings, yet stirred not to attempt her rescue."

"I rejoice to find thee so ardent in the cause of a suffering and oppressed woman," said Luke,

smiling at the ardour with which the young man had spoken. "Thou hast my free permission to do as thou mayst think best in this affair, and may therefore depart on the errand as soon as the few necessary preparations can be made. Captain Danvers, I dare say will accompany you, whilst the Baron De Lancy and I return to Ireland, where I hope you will shortly join us, after having achieved the object which separates us so soon after this discovery has been made."

"And methinks," observed De Lancy, "it would be a good plan to take Switzerland in our way, in order that we may visit the Castle of Bautzen, and let our good friend Heinbach learn such intelligence as we may have to give him of the daughter whose absence he so deeply grieves."

This being decided on, the two young men, with a considerable number of attendants, set forth; and, joining a large body of troops raised by the German princes, for the assistance of the citizens of Munster, resolved to make every effort in their power for the rescue of Mildred. They were amongst the first who entered the city after the gates were thrown open to the besieging army.

The obstinate defence of Munster had filled the streets with melancholy proofs of famine and misery, and the victorious troops, though accustomed to scenes of blood and warfare, could not withhold their commiseration from those whom they beheld around them. Mothers clasping their famished and expiring children in their arms, parents and children struggling with each other for the last particle of food, whilst heaps of unburied dead lay in the streets, the enfeebled survivors being unable to give them burial.

Now that Reginald—for we must still call him by that familiar name—had rescued Mildred from the horrors of her situation, he lost not a moment in despatching a messenger to her father, announcing her safety, and their intention of hastening to the Castle of Bautzen with the least possible delay.

The happiness of the young man was now at its height; and the only addition, if any could be made, was to be surrounded by those friends who were absent, that they also might participate in his joyous feelings. The ties of friendship between him and Danvers were bound yet more closely by the generous sacrifice the latter had made in thus absenting himself so long from Louisa. But when the interest of Luke Somerton was at stake, in the recovery of his long lost son, Captain Danvers found it impossible to hesitate between duty and inclination.

Mildred, Reginald, and Danvers were one evening conversing upon several occurrences that had tended to separate them, and relating numerous adventures that had occurred to each during the interval. In the course of her detail she mentioned the convent in which she had passed some of the time, and deeply regretted the sufferings of the Countess de Rougemont, whom she had left there. On hearing this name both the young men uttered an exclamation of wonder and astonishment.

"Tell me," at length exclaimed Danvers, "does she yet live? does the deeply-injured and innocent woman you have named still exist?"

"She does," answered Mildred; "at least, I can

declare that a female bearing that name was living up to the period when I left the convent."

"This discovery is a most fortunate one," exclaimed Captain Danvers, "for she of whom you speak is the mother of Louisa, the adopted child of Luke Somerton. Her story is briefly this :— The Count de Rougemont, plunged into embarrassments by his treacherous friend, Rodolph Dumas, listened too readily to his false insinuations against the countess. He quitted the castle in disguise, carrying with him his infant daughter. Upon reaching the shores of the Mediterranean he found a vessel ready to sail for Gibraltar, and taking his passage in her, he was captured by the vessel commanded by Arnold Lorimer, and conveyed to a prison on shore, from whence, during one of the pirate's cruises, the count, with his child, escaped in a small open boat. But fatigue and illness had so far weakened him that he was unable to guide the vessel, when they were discovered from the ship in which Luke Somerton was returning home."

This was the substance of what Captain Danvers related, and Mildred and Reginald were, by other confirmatory circumstances, convinced that the countess was indeed the mother of Louisa. This determined Danvers to proceed at once to the convent, and, if possible, prevail upon the countess to return into the world once more, and accompany him to Ireland. Taking with him, therefore, a few attendants, he set off on his errand, and immediately afterwards Mildred and Reginald directed their course towards the romantic valleys of Switzerland.

Upon the arrival of Luke Somerton and the Baron de Lancy at the Castle of Bautzen, they found Heinbach suffering under a dangerous illness. His known partiality to the French interest had excited against him the jealousy of the German emperor, who, deeming him an opponent too dangerous and too powerful, issued orders for his banishment to a foreign country.

It was upon the eve of his departure, and though his medical attendant loudly exclaimed against his quitting the Castle of Bautzen in his present state, yet the emperor's orders being peremptory, they could neither be questioned nor postponed. Agonizing as it was to his friends to behold him worn down by sickness, and compelled to quit the castle of his ancestors, they yet prepared to accompany him in his banishment. His money and jewels he secured and gave them into the charge of his friend, the Baron de Lancy.

As he was assisted into the carriage which was to convey him away, he gazed around upon the house he had been thus driven from, and could not refrain from shedding a tear as he thought of the many happy hours that he had passed beneath that roof. He then sank back exhausted, and, covering his face with his hands, seemed anxious to shut out a scene that awoke so many recollections which now but added to his sorrow.

They made short stages, travelling slowly on to accommodate the patient, whose friends endeavoured by every means they could think of to assuage the anguish which he in vain endeavoured to conceal. Up to this period they had not mentioned the name of Mildred to him, nor did they deem it prudent in his present precarious state to agitate his mind any more than it already was. Thus they continued, until arriving at one of the frontier towns, where his illness increased so alarmingly, that the medical attendants gave up all hopes of being able to preserve him from that doom to which he was hurrying.

"I have but one regret in quitting this life," said the dying man. "It is that an impenetrable mystery hangs over the fate of my poor daughter. Unhappy child! perhaps at this moment thou art wandering far away, and unable to return."

"Do not despair so readily, but place all your reliance in the mercy of Heaven," exclaimed the Baron de Lancy. "There is more reason to hope than you imagine, my dear Heinbach, for even now she is near, and will soon be restored to your arms. But tell me, could you receive her with calmness nor agitate yourself with this unlooked-for happiness?"

"She is here, then?" exclaimed the dying man, faintly pressing the hand of his friend. "Tell me that I am not mistaken, and let me behold her while I have yet sufficient strength to endure the interview. Fear not, De Lancy, for I can be calm, even though I see death is ready to grasp upon his prey."

He had scarcely uttered these words when the door opened, and De Lancy, beckoning to Reginald, he entered, accompanied by the pale and trembling Mildred. The eyes of the Baron Heinbach sparkled with most unusual lustre at the appearance of his long-lost daughter; he took her hand, placed it in that of Reginald, and pressing them, thus united, to his heart, he faintly murmured, "Bless you, my dear children," and then sank into their arms, as his soul passed for ever from its mortal tenement.

When Mildred became aware that her father was no more, she required all the consolement of her surrounding friends to reconcile her to the melancholy bereavement she had sustained. Long and deeply she mourned the affliction with which it had pleased Heaven to visit her; but by degrees she felt the kindness of those whose incessant task it was to banish the recollection of the past, and her grief became more moderate. Every possible mark of respect was paid to the memory of her father; Luke Somerton, his son, and De Lancy, saw the body committed to the earth, and ere they left the country, directions were given for the erection of a splendid monument in memory of the deceased.

As there was now no further obstacle to delay their return to Ireland, the whole party commenced their homeward journey, and after a tedious, but unobstructed travel, they arrived at the mansion of the former. Here a surprise awaited them. Upon entering the hall they were received by Terence; and Danvers, descending the flight of steps which led to the principal chambers, advanced with a lady leaning on each arm; one of whom was Louisa, who hastened forward to welcome her beloved guardian; while, to the surprise of all, Mildred was seen to rush with an exclamation of joy into the embrace of the other lady.

"Allow me, my dear Somerton," cried Captain Danvers, "to introduce to you the Countess de Rougemont, mother to my Louisa, who has at length listened to my entreaties, and returned once more into the world to yield happiness to her children, by becoming a partaker in theirs."

Luke Somerton congratulated his foster-daughter upon the discovery of her mother, while the latter poured forth her thanks to him for the generous protection he had afforded to the child of his adoption.

And now a happier company could not have been found than was assembled together at the mansion of Luke Somerton. The recent loss of her father had given a pensive softness to the countenance of Mildred, that rendered her more deeply interesting than ever; while the sportive features of Louisa, decked with smiles, betokened a heart free from guile, and unclouded by care.

After a few days had given the travellers sufficient rest, the marriages of Reginald and Mildred, Danvers and Louisa, were fixed to take place. It was at that altar where Luke's nuptials had been celebrated, that his son received the hand of Mildred Heinbach—a prize that he had long coveted, and which, now in his possession, he would not have changed for worlds.

But little more remains to be added to this part of the narrative: Danvers and his bride, after a few months' sojourn in Ireland, proceeded to England, accompanied by the Countess of Rougemont, Luke Somerton, and the Baron de Lancy, in social and friendly intercourse, away from the intrigues of court and camp fatigues, passed their time in uninterrupted happiness. Terence, the faithful and attached friend of Luke Somerton, being raised to a more familiar rank by his services in the English army, fixed his residence under the roof of the man he so much regarded, while Reginald and Mildred, happy with each other, still sought to make others so, by the exercise of those virtues which alone lead to happiness in this world as well as that which awaits us hereafter.

But the calmness enjoyed by Luke Somerton was not to be of very long continuance. He married a second time, but within twelve months afterwards the lady died in giving birth to a daughter. That child (the heroine of our story) was named Louisa, after Mrs. Danvers, but early in life she was doomed to vicissitudes and misfortune. Luke again became an object of suspicion to government, his estates, without the slightest foundation, were confiscated, and he, himself being reduced to poverty, was compelled to enter the navy as a subordinate officer. It was thus that he became subjected to the tyranny of Captain Aylmer, which at length compelled him to quit the ship, after which he became disgusted with the world, and reckless as to the course of life he pursued.

In an evil hour he associated himself with a number of men who were engaged in an extensive system of smuggling. He became captain of the vessel in which this illicit traffic was carried on; and, as we have said at the commencement of our narrative, soon made for himself a name that carried fear and distrust wherever he went. At length, in a sharp encounter with one of the revenue ships, his own vessel received so much injury that he and his people were obliged to land on the Isle of Man. Here, as we have shown, he met with his daughter, who, since their last meeting, had grown into womanhood. His fatal encounter with Captain Aylmer has been related, and we have also seen the filial anxiety with which

Louisa Somerton sought the presence of Queen Anne, and obtained from her the pardon she supplicated.

CHAPTER XLI.

Never did horrid shapes,
Compelled by some magician's mighty charm,
Break through the prisons of the solid earth
With more strange horror.

MARLOW's "*Lust's Dominion.*"

CHRISTOPHER DALTON was deeply musing upon the events recorded in the narrative of Luke Somerton, when he was abruptly accosted by Scipio, the black cook, who had approached him without being observed. His countenance was indicative of more importance than usual, and finding that his presence was unheeded, he at length broke in with,—

"Massa Dalton, de gubernor's been axing for you, and you must go to him dis berry minute."

"What does he want with me, Scip?" demanded the other.

"Him no tell me dat," answered the negro; "Massa Luke Sumerton neber speak him mind to poor Scipio. He tell me to come his errand, and now you know as much 'bout it as I do."

"Has he received any bad news?"

"Don't know; but shouldn't wonder if him have. He walk up and down de room wid him arms folded; and den such a look as him gave me! oh, lor! I run away quite frightened."

"More ill news, I suppose," muttered Christopher Dalton to himself; and then addressing the negro, he inquired where the captain was to be found.

"At him own house, Massa Dalton."

"Was his daughter with him?"

"Iss; but she was crying, and den he told her she'd better go to her own room. Poor ting! I pity her, she look so berry unhappy and miserable."

"I suppose there is some new source of affliction," said Christopher, musingly. "Confound this infernal island, say I, for there's been nothing but misfortune ever since we first set foot upon it. First, our captain must needs meet with that fellow Aylmer; then he is charged with having murdered him; and afterwards, for no other reason than that he has been fortunate enough to escape hanging, the savages of this place must needs take the queen's pardon in high dudgeon. Egad! I believe they're enraged enough to hang him themselves, if they could only lay hands upon him!"

"Humph! den why does he stay here, Massa Dalton?"

"That's a question, Scip, that I've asked myself a thousand times," replied the other. "Our vessel is now repaired and ready for service, yet he must needs stay ashore as if he had grown heartily tired of a sea life."

"Maybe he don't like to leave Miss Louisa behind him," observed Scipio, with a most sagacious grin.

"Then he had better give up the command to somebody else," retorted Dalton. "His men are all grumbling at the inactive life they are leading, and I've had enough to do to prevail on them to wait with patience a little longer."

"And some of 'em hint dat dey wouldn't mind having you for dere captain instead of Massa Somerton," observed the negro, with a sly look at the chief mate.

"The scoundrels had better never let me hear them speak upon such a subject," exclaimed Christopher Dalton. "We have all sworn to be faithful to our captain, and the first man that turns traitor shall have an ounce or two of lead through his brains by way of warning to the others."

"Good!" exclaimed Scipio; "and I'll stand by you if de fellers should prove false to dere captain. I want to be on de sea again as much as our chaps do, but Scip knows his place, and can wait till it suits de captain to give de word ob command."

"There's a half-crown piece for your honesty, Master Blackie," said Dalton, thrusting the coin into the negro's hand. "Luckily your heart ain't so black as your skin, Scip, so you and I will be faithful to Luke Somerton, even if all the rest of our fellows are base enough to desert him. Not that I think the chaps would venture quite so far as that, though they do give way to grumbling a bit now and then."

As he said this, he left the room, and directed his steps towards the house where Luke Somerton had found a temporary asylum. During his walk he devised a thousand schemes for pacifying the men for the present; resolving, however, to urge upon Somerton the necessity for going on board ship again with as little delay as possible. He was still in the midst of these thoughts when he reached the house, where he found Luke pacing up and down the room, and evidently in no very good humour. He, however, seemed pleased at the arrival of his friend, and having desired him to be seated, inquired if he had met any of the islanders in his way.

"Not one of them," answered Dalton. "At least, if any of them crossed my path, I was too much occupied with other thoughts to take any heed of them. But you seem disturbed, sir; has anything happened to make you uneasy?"

"Aye; a threatening letter has been sent, warning me to leave the island directly, or denouncing vengeance if I do not take immediate notice of their peremptory command."

"They can't forget that affair of Captain Aylmer's then?" exclaimed Dalton. "The hounds will be satisfied with nothing else than your blood; but it only wants a little coolness on our part, and when they find that we are not afraid of them they will become more quiet."

"But in the meantime," observed Luke, "there is reason to fear they will inflict upon me a most grievous injury."

"Would the villains assassinate you?"

"Their feelings in that respect have already been made pretty manifest," answered Somerton. "That, however, is not the cause of my present uneasiness; for, not satisfied with threatening to take away my life in the event of my not departing from their accursed island, but they must now direct their vengeance against my poor daughter, whose only offence consists in having sued for and obtained my pardon from the queen."

"But," answered Dalton, "the scurvy knaves forget that she has friends who are both able and willing enough to protect her."

"I am not so sure about being able to guard my

poor Louise against these ruffians," exclaimed Luke Somerton. "Those enemies of ours work in the dark, and I fear some terrible evil will befall the girl when neither you nor I are present to avert the mischief they intend."

"Then remove her to some other place, where she will be safe," exclaimed Christopher Dalton.

"I have thought of doing so," replied the other; "but, after all, the act would look too much like cowardice. Neither you nor I were ever much inclined to run away from enemies, and I should be loth to sneak out of the island, merely because a set of infuriated wretches have chosen to raise a cry of vengeance against us."

"Better do that than stay and be murdered."

"But Louisa herself is unwilling to leave a place in which nearly the whole of her life has been passed," said Somerton.

"And yet she is aware of the danger by remaining."

"She is," answered Luke; "but we have already seen an instance of her unconquerable resolution; and it is scarcely half an hour since she declared her determination to remain here, unless I positively command her to depart with me."

"Which, I suppose, you do not feel inclined to do?"

"I have before said that I do not like the idea of being driven from the island by a brutal mob," answered Luke Somerton. "My daughter is well aware of the threats that have been used, yet still is she resolved to remain, trusting that the law is strong enough to protect us from the violence with which we have been threatened."

"But Scipio told me just now that she had been weeping."

"And he spoke the truth," replied Luke. "Poor girl! she shed tears indeed; but they were caused by apprehension for my safety, and not through any fears for herself."

"Where is she now?"

"In her own room. I would not let her remain here, lest my uneasiness should serve to increase hers. The truth is, Dalton, I have too much reason to suppose that before the lapse of many hours our house will be attacked."

"And yet," exclaimed the other, "you have taken no steps to prevent it."

"I have arms enough in the place," replied Luke Somerton, "and shall not fail to use them against an enemy, in the event of being driven to desperation by the frantic violence of these people. Every precaution shall be taken, but if they proceed to force an entrance into my house, it will be at the sacrifice of some few lives."

"By which," replied the other, "you will risk another trial for murder; and on the second occasion can hardly expect to be so fortunate as you were in the first."

"But where there is no alternative, how is it possible for me to act otherwise?" demanded Luke Somerton.

"I will tell you," exclaimed Christopher. "Our people are tired of the inactive life they have been leading for some time past, and nothing would please them so well as giving them something to do. Have eight or ten of them to remain in the house with you, and, in case of an attack being made, they would be found of real service. They will keep off any mob that may venture to come for any illegal purpose; and, depend upon it, if once they should be routed with a few broken bones among them, they will not be inclined to pay a second visit, that might prove even yet more disastrous."

"Your plan is not a bad one," answered Luke; "but the question is, whether our fellows will feel inclined to undertake the service. They are not very well satisfied with me of late, and are as likely to refuse their assistance as not, merely out of a spirit of revenge for the quiet life I have compelled them to lead for the last few weeks."

"Then go with me down to the cave by the seashore," exclaimed Christopher Dalton. "We shall find them assembled there, and I think very little persuasion will be required to bring them round to our views."

"But how can I leave my daughter here unprotected?"

"Scipio will soon return," answered Dalton, "and I can depend upon his fidelity, either to yourself or your daughter. Besides, the distance is not very great, and we may be back again in a couple of hours."

"In that case I will go with you," exclaimed Luke Somerton; "not, however, that I think the fellows will be very willing to lend a hand in our difficulties; but my daughter's life depends upon prompt measures being taken, and I will, at least, make every effort in my power to rescue her from the threatened wrath of these accursed islanders."

"And our men can find a good night's lodging in the barn behind the house," returned the mate. "They'll be as comfortable there as in the cave, and an extra allowance of grog will put them in good humour again, I'll warrant you."

"I'll go and tell Louisa what our present plans are, and instruct her how to act in case an attack should be made during our absence," said Luke, who, by this time, had recovered some of his usual composure. "The girl has spirit enough to protect herself in case of need, and if the doors and lower windows are kept fastened, there is little fear of the mob being able to gain admittance to the house. At any rate, she will manage to continue the siege till our return, and then, I think, there is little doubt that we shall teach them the madness of interfering with people that have never harmed them. Or, suppose I was to go to Sir Charles Radcliffe, and, after representing the danger we are in, claim his protection against the frenzy that has seized the minds of the people?"

"There's no doubt the governor would do all in his power to assist you and your daughter," replied Christopher Dalton; "but, for my own part, I never saw the use of asking other people for aid when we are well enough able to help ourselves; and I am sure, with eight or ten of our chaps to back us, we could put to flight all the people that may collect together, to pull the house down about your ears."

"At all events the experiment shall be tried," exclaimed Somerton; "for when people are urged to extremities, they are authorised to defend themselves in the best way they can. I have no vindictive feelings against these men, who howl like ravenous wolves for my blood; but they must beware how they urge me too far, for I will defend myself and my daughter, even though it may be at the sacrifice of some few lives."

"And yet how easy it would have been to avoid coming in collision with them," exclaimed Dalton. "You and your daughter might have left the island long enough before this time, and she could have been placed with some family abroad, whilst you appeased the impatience of our men by taking another voyage with them as usual."

"But my daughter has an invincible objection to leaving a spot that is rendered dear to her by many associations," replied Luke Somerton. "Besides, she half suspects the sort of traffic we have been engaged in, and probably thinks her influence over me is sufficient to terminate a dishonourable course of life that she regards with horror."

"Or, rather," exclaimed the other, "she is unwilling to go far away from Lieutenant Granger."

"There you entirely mistake her," answered Luke Somerton ; "for, sincere as her regard is for Lieutenant Granger, I have reason to know that she is resolved never to marry him."

"Then why not quit a place where they must frequently meet each other, and thus encourage a passion that ought rather to be conquered, if she is so resolved never to become his wife ?"

"Because there is every probability of his going abroad with his regiment, in the course of a very short time," answered Luke Somerton. "An order from head-quarters is expected almost immediately ; and as he will most likely be abroad for some years, his love will become cool, and then it is to be hoped he will place his affections upon another."

"Is he aware," asked Dalton, "that she has made up her mind never to become his wife ?"

"Oh, yes," replied Luke Somerton, "she has candidly told him that, though she must ever continue to regard him with esteem, it is impossible that she can give him her hand in marriage."

"And yet," observed the other, "fond of him as she seems, it is strange that she can inflict so much pain and anguish."

"It is not at all singular, when you come to reflect upon the position in which she is placed," replied Luke. "My name has been branded with dishonour, ever since the murder of Captain Aylmer was attributed to me. She shared in the disgrace, and is resolved not to carry the stain into a family which has always held a high station in society. That she ardently loves Lieutenant Granger I know, but selfishness forms no part of her character ; and she would rather pine in secret over her own griefs, than commit an act which she conceives to be one of dishonour."

"Upon my soul," exclaimed Christopher, "this daughter of yours is a noble-spirited girl. I admire the feelings that prompt this self-denial, and yet, as the young man seeks her hand, I think she might yield her own consent."

"I seldom speak to her upon the subject," answered Somerton, "and never urge my own opinion about it, because I know she would feel the more grief at refusing my request ; in short, Lieutenant Granger has at length yielded to what he finds is her firm determination, and though they continue to meet each other as often as usual, it is as a brother and sister rather than as lovers."

"And the young officer, I suppose, thinks none the worse of you for that unfortunate affair of Captain Aylmer's ?"

"From the very first," replied Luke Somerton, "he expressed the firmest conviction of my innocence, and took every means in his power to convince others that I was the victim of a cruel persecution. I am, indeed, deeply indebted to him for the warm interest he manifested in my behalf, and nothing would have afforded me so much satisfaction as to have seen him the husband of my daughter."

"Oh, you may depend upon it matters will turn out all right enough by and by," exclaimed Christopher Dalton ; "the girl has got good sense of her own, and if the young fellow returns to the island again, she will have forgotten this affair that hangs so heavily upon her mind at present, and Granger will not have much trouble to persuade her to make him happy—that is, you know, if they are both determined to remain single so long."

"Louisa has declared her intention never to marry," answered Somerton. "Her heart, I know, has been irrevocably given to Lieutenant Granger, and never can it be given to any other."

"Then I can only say it's a great pity that she don't marry him," replied Dalton ; "indeed, I can see no reason why she should have refused him, for he knows all about that affair of Captain Aylmer's ; and, believing as he does, that you are perfectly innocent of it, she can have no excuse for making the rest of his life miserable."

"At all events, her motives are most pure and honourable," exclaimed Luke Somerton ; "and for that reason I cannot urge her so much as I should otherways have done. But here is our faithful friend Scipio, so we may now safely leave the house in his charge, while you and I go down to seek the fellows at the cavern."

After a few directions had been given to the negro, Luke Somerton and Dalton left the place, and taking a circuitous route, proceeded to the seaside, and entered the retreat where they expected to meet with the men who formed the crew of their vessel. No one was, however, there, and they were about to proceed in another direction in search of them, when Dick Lowrie, one of the most turbulent and disaffected of the men, suddenly confronted them.

"Ho ! ho ! Captain Somerton ; so we have met at last," he exclaimed, in a tone of insolence. "After weeks of idleness in this accursed island, you begin to grow tired of doing nothing, and I suppose you have come to say that we are to prepare for sea without further delay ?"

"My errand is for no such purpose," answered Luke Somerton. "At present there are reasons why I must remain where we are ; but I hope you and our other people are not going to turn mutinous to your captain ? Surely we have known each other long enough to continue friends after the many perils and adventures we have gone through."

"You had better hear what my comrades say about it," replied Dick ; "they are in no very good humour, I can tell you, and nothing will satisfy them but a promise to set sail from this place without delay."

"Which promise I am not just now prepared to give," exclaimed Luke Somerton ; "I have matters of importance to settle before I leave the island,

and unless you and your companions have turned traitors to me, you will remain with patience till I give the word to depart."

"How long is it likely to be first?"

"That it is impossible to say at present," replied Somerton ; "a week may make an important difference in my affairs, though it is likely that time will not be sufficient to bring everything to a settlement."

"Nor a month neither—nor two months—nor yet three, if we go on this way," muttered Dick. "I'm tired of waiting here doing nothing, and, what's more, shall cut the concern entirely before many more days have passed away."

"I'll tell you what it is, Dick Lowrie," exclaimed the mate, who had listened to this conversation with great impatience ; "you and the rest of us have sworn to obey the orders of Captain Somerton, and the man that goes from his oath is no better than a traitor."

"Ay ; but we are ashore now, and can do as we like about it," answered the other. "We promised to obey Captain Somerton as long as we were afloat, but if he brings us to the land, and keeps us there longer than is necessary, we are not bound to waste any more of our time than we may think proper to agree to."

"Would you have me leave my daughter among strangers?" demanded Luke Somerton.

"There's no occasion to leave her, that I know of," replied Dick ; "take her on board with you—she may live there like a queen, and be quite as happy as on shore.'"

"She shall never enter our ship," exclaimed Somerton, resolutely. "It is no place for a young and innocent female ; and, if no other alternative remains, why, I will give up my command of the vessel, and pass the remainder of my days in any place where she may choose to reside."

"Now, then, listen to me," interposed Christopher Dalton ; "you have heard our captain's determination, and it is high time we should come to a proper understanding together. He has affairs to attend to that make it necessary for him to remain in this island for some little time longer ; and it is now for you to say whether you will continue faithful, or prove so many traitors to the man you should serve."

"Then the long and the short of it is," said Dick Lowrie, "that we are all heartily tired of doing nothing."

"If that's all, we will soon find active employment for you," exclaimed Luke Somerton ; "these islanders have taken a mortal dislike to me, and there's likely to be warm work with them before many hours are over our heads."

"Humph ! Is there any chance, think you, of having a brush with them?"

"It is almost certain that we shall," replied Somerton. "Already they have burned down my cottage, and now they threaten to attack the place in which I and my daughter took refuge. In short, Lowrie, I believe they will never rest till I have been sacrificed to their furious hate."

"Then why haven't you called upon us to come to your assistance before?" demanded Richard Lowrie.

"Because I was unwilling to risk an affray with them that might have terminated in bloodshed."

"And hasn't the governor power to protect you from these people?"

"I have not spoken to him upon the subject," replied Luke Somerton ; "and as my enemies keep their projects pretty close, I suppose Sir Charles Radcliffe is not aware of the dangerous schemes they have in contemplation ; nay, I have no wish to claim the assistance of the military, because I know my own people are able enough to ward off any danger with which I might be threatened, and I believe if it were known that a party of you were in the neighbourhood of my house, the cowardly rabble would not venture to come anywhere near us."

"Now I understand what you mean," exclaimed Dick. "Some of us chaps are to keep guard over you and your daughter ; and if there should be need for it, we are to have a bit of a brush with the fellows?"

"That's exactly it, Dick," answered the mate. "You have been complaining of want of employment, and now here's as pretty a chance as a man need to wish for."

"Very true," exclaimed Dick ; "only it so happens that we shall not be fighting in our own element. However, even this is better than nothing, so you may depend upon it we shall not hesitate to follow any command that may be given."

"Where are the rest of our people?" asked Luke Somerton.

"Wandering about different parts of the island, I believe."

"That is unfortunate, for I wanted some of them immediately."

"How many?"

"Eight or ten."

"Well, I think I can muster that number for you," answered Dick Lowrie. "A party of 'em, I know, went to the public-house yonder, and they'll be pleased enough to hear that there's something for 'em to do, especially if there's a chance of having a fight with the surly fellows hereabouts"

"I hope there will be no occasion for coming to that," exclaimed Luke Somerton. "My foes are numerous enough, and would murder me if they could find a favourable opportunity for executing their vengeance ; but that they are rank cowards I have found by experience, and no doubt, when they find that I am well guarded, they will give up their sanguinary project in despair."

"But, perhaps, after all, they have no such intentions as you imagine," observed the sailor.

"There can be very little doubt that they mean mischief," exclaimed Christopher Dalton. "Our captain has received a threatening letter, and the fellows may be expected to make an attack upon his house to-night."

"Well, then, I hope they will not fail to come," returned Dick. "It would be a pity to spoil such sport, for, if they only show their faces near the spot, they'll meet with such a reception as they little expect. I myself owe some of these people a grudge, and will not fail to pay it."

"There must be no fighting, I tell you," interposed Luke Somerton ; "at least, there must be none till we are forced to use our weapons for our own protection."

"And why not, when we know they come for mischief?"

"Because, in the event of a skirmish taking place, Sir Charles Radcliffe would send a party of the military to quell the tumult, and should any lives be lost among these islanders, we should have a fair chance of being arrested for murder."

"That is to say, if they could lay hold of us," answered Dick.

"Would you be mad enough to risk a fight with the soldiers?"

"To be sure I would," replied the other. "We have got good stout hearts among us, and if there should be any danger of our getting the worst of it, why, we could retreat to our boats, and be on board the ship before they would be able to pursue."

"You forget that I could not leave my daughter behind."

"And why not?—they would not harm her."

"I am not quite certain about that," exclaimed Luke. "These people hate her as much as they do me, and in their blind fury they would sacrifice her in revenge for those who might be slain or wounded in the conflict."

"But I suppose she is not without friends here?"

"There are those who would defend her to the utmost, but it is not certain that they would be able to afford her the protection she requires. Sir Charles Radcliffe has offered her an asylum in the castle, but that, for reasons of her own, she has refused."

"And how about Lieutenant Granger?"

"He would sacrifice his life in the defence of hers," replied Luke Somerton; "but why should we urge him into so dangerous a position when there is no real necessity for it?"

"Then it seems," observed Dick Lowrie, "that you only want us to keep watch about your house?"

"That is all I require," answered Somerton. "If the rabble should come, as I expect, they would immediately disperse upon perceiving that we are prepared for them, and thus our safety would be insured without much trouble or difficulty."

"Aye, but don't you think it would be as well to teach them a lesson for the future?" demanded Dick. "Let some of the rascals feel that we are not to be trifled with, and you'll never be bothered by 'em again."

"You have heard our captain's commands upon the subject," exclaimed Christopher Dalton; "and it is not for us to dispute them. All that he wants is to prevent the mischief they have threatened, and, if matters go on pretty smoothly for a time, there is no doubt he will soon go on board ship again, and then things will go on as usual."

"If I only thought that," replied Dick, "I shouldn't mind staying here for a week or two longer. My fellow shipmates love our captain, and all they want is to see him as he used to be, and the moment he takes his place in the vessel, he will see that there aint a man but will obey his commands as in days gone by."

"Then you'll tell the men that they are wanted to protect Captain Somerton against his enemies?"

"I will, and you may depend upon it they'll undertake the task with pleasure."

"In an hour, then, you will despatch them to their place of destination?" exclaimed Christopher Dalton.

"Aye, aye, they shall march there in a body, and so frighten the scurvy knaves from the place."

"Nay, that would be too dangerous a display for us to venture upon," answered Luke Somerton. "Were that to be done, the governor would deem it necessary to send out a party of soldiers against us, and we should defeat the very plan we have in view."

"Well, then, tell me how you would have us proceed, and I'll take care that everything is exactly according to your wish," replied Dick.

"You must go singly, then," exclaimed Luke Somerton; "and, by so doing, no one will suspect that we are preparing ourselves against an emergency. My house must be your rendezvous, and, being once assembled there, I will place you in a position where you may be at hand in the event of any assistance being required. I am most anxious to avoid coming in collision with these people, and do not wish them even to suspect that I am prepared for resistance till they come to hunt me from my home."

"And suppose they make an attack upon the house?"

"Why, then I will try fair words," replied Somerton; "and, if they should fail to have any effect upon them, I must have recourse to other means."

"That is to say, you will give us leave to commence an attack, even if some few of the scoundrels should fall?"

"Nay, I should be unwilling to proceed to such an extremity under any circumstances," replied Luke Somerton. "These people are brutally ignorant, and their enmity has been engendered against myself by a notion that the pardon of their queen was misapplied. I have no wish to quarrel with them for a mere matter of opinion, and my only desire is to prevent any violence they may meditate against me and my daughter."

"There's nothing that would convince them of their folly so well as a few hard blows, sir," exclaimed Dick Lowrie. "If they're as ignorant as you say, they want a little good teaching, and, depend upon it, their thick skulls would be none the worse for such knocks as we would give 'em. So leave it to me, Captain Somerton, and I think you'll see no reason to be sorry for it afterwards."

"Humph!" ejaculated Dalton; "methinks you presume rather too much, Master Dick. It is our duty to obey, and the man that acts against orders will deserve any punishment that he may get for it. So now, having heard my opinion upon the matter, perhaps you'll just tell your fellows that Captain Somerton will consider any man as his enemy who acts against the commands that are given."

"And you may also say," exclaimed Luke, "that I shall not fail to reward them for their services in the event of their acting in strict compliance with my wishes. There can be little fear of violence when I am surrounded by friends; and, if we only succeed in deterring these fellows from doing me the injury they meditate, my purpose will be completely accomplished."

"It shall be exactly as you have said, then," replied Dick. "I'll send them all to your house, so that they shall arrive there one at a time; and as for the chaps acting according to orders, you needn't be afraid of their going astray, for they still respect their captain, though, it must needs be confessed, they have lately grumbled a bit at being obliged to waste their time ashore."

"Their grumbling, then, will soon be at an end, as far as that goes," exclaimed Christopher Dalton. "Tell them that another fortnight will see us afloat again, and if that don't satisfy them, I know of nothing that will."

"Enough has now been said to explain our plans, and the mode in which we wish them to be executed," interposed Luke Somerton. "You will, therefore, go and collect the men together, whilst Mr. Dalton and I return home to make what further arrangements may seem necessary. Within two hours I shall require you all to be assembled at my house, where you will receive further orders; and I have no doubt the steps we are about to take, will answer all the purposes I have in view."

Luke Somerton then left the cavern, and was proceeding towards the path by which they had come, when Christopher, taking his arm, exclaimed:—

"Not that way, captain, if you please. Let us return over the heath, for I have to introduce you to an old friend that you have not seen for some years."

"Who is it?"

"Nay, that is a question that I do not wish to answer just at present," exclaimed Dalton. "I anticipate the pleasure of giving you a surprise, and you will surely not wish to prevent so harmless a wish."

"As you please," answered the other, and, following the direction pointed out by his companion, they soon reached the borders of a heath, the desolate appearance of which was anything but tempting for them to proceed.

"Why have you come this way when the night is set in?" demanded Luke Somerton. "There scarcely seems to be a path to guide us, and, to confess the truth, I like not the appearance of the place."

"Psha! there's no danger to be apprehended," answered Christopher Dalton. "I have been across this heath many times lately, and have never yet seen any person except the one I came to meet."

"Why do you practise this mystery?" asked Somerton.

"Merely for a pleasant conceit of my own," replied the other. "I like these little surprises, and fancied that perhaps it might be agreeable to yourself."

"Yet I must not ask who it is you are taking me to see?"

"Where would be the pleasure I expect from the surprise, if I blabbed the secret?" demanded Christopher Dalton. "Besides, we have not very far to go before you'll learn all about it; and I am much mistaken if the person you are going to see is not the very last you would guess, if you were to rack your wits for a month."

Finding that it was useless to inquire any further, Luke Somerton walked on for some little time without speaking. The darkness of evening rapidly gathered around them, and consequently the difficulties of their way increased with every step they took, so that Somerton at length expressed his apprehension that they were in danger of wandering about the heath all night.

"Don't make yourself uneasy about that," replied Dalton, "because I know quite enough of the place to promise that I will take you home safe enough in less time than it took us to go to the cavern."

"But I see no sign of a human habitation," exclaimed Luke, "and yet you said ——"

"That you were to see a friend," interrupted the other. "Such was my promise, and I'll keep my word, or never place reliance on the promises of Kit Dalton again."

"But my daughter will be alarmed at our long absence."

"Psha! I tell you we shall be no longer than if we had gone the other road," answered Christopher. "This wild-looking heath has grown familiar to me of late, and, if you will only take my word for it, I'll guide you safely enough to your home. So come—don't begin to doubt me after all the years we have known each other, for if I have made a mystery of the object that has brought us this way, you will presently acknowledge that I have not failed in accomplishing my promise."

"I heartily regret having come with you," exclaimed Luke Somerton, "for something strikes me that the surprise you meditate will not be a very agreeable one."

"A few minutes, at any rate, will prove whether it is or not," said Christopher Dalton, laughingly.

"But why refuse to tell me the name of this person?" demanded Luke Somerton, with increasing impatience.

"Because you will be able to guess my motive when you have seen the person," answered the other. "Another minute or two will bring us to the place."

"I see no house, nor even the sign of a human habitation," exclaimed Luke Somerton, glancing round him.

"Truly, I should wonder if you did," answered the other; "for the place I am taking you to lies behind yonder piece of rising ground. A couple of hundred paces will take you to the spot, and then all the wonder and curiosity I have excited will be at an end."

"And, after all, it may be some one that I have no wish to see," observed Luke Somerton.

"I have said that it is a person you have known."

"That is possible, but I may not have respected him."

"Judge for yourself," exclaimed Dalton, suddenly pausing, and laying his hand on the shoulder of Luke Somerton. There was a solemnity in his tone that was truly appalling, and no sooner had Luke directed his gaze in the direction pointed out, than a cry of horror broke from his lips, and after reeling a few paces, he stood, with his face buried in his hands, as if transfixed to the spot. Dalton regarded him, for a moment or two, with wonder, and then exclaimed:—

"What ails you, captain?—There is the friend I brought you to see, and surely it don't seem a very kindly act to shrink back as if the look of him had blasted your sight."

"I see nothing but the body of a man swinging

upon a gibbet," exclaimed Luke Somerton, shuddering.

"Well, and know you not who it is?" demanded the other.

"How should I?" exclaimed Luke. "The countenance scarcely exhibits a trace of human features."

"Do you not remember Henry Everton?"

"My second mate?"

"Aye—that carcase is all that remains of him," replied Christopher Dalton. "He and you had a quarrel about two years since, and he left the vessel as soon as we arrived at Malta. You have never heard of him since; but, by a mere accident, I heard that he took the command of a smuggling vessel that carried on an illicit traffic between Holland and England, and that in a very short time he earned for himself a name that was likely, before long, to bring him into trouble."

"And how was it that he came to meet the terrible fate of which I am now a witness?" demanded Luke Somerton.

"By a murder."

"Who did he kill?"

"Only an officer belonging to the Government Preventive Service," replied Dalton, in a tone of indifference.

"There was an affray, then?" observed Luke Somerton; "or was the crime committed with deliberation?"

"It was not thought of a moment before it took place," replied Christopher Dalton. "The facts of the case were these:—Poor Harry was obliged to make for this island through stress of weather, but mistaking the right harbour, he was attacked by a revenue cutter, and after a severe engagement, was boarded by some of the queen's officers. Still, however, he was determined not to be conquered without an effort, and meeting the lieute-

nant in command of the boarding party, he engaged him in a desperate broad-sword combat. A short time served to prove that they were nearly equal both in respect of courage and the use of their weapons; but chance gave the advantage to Harry, and his adversary at length fell mortally wounded at his feet. This served but to increase the fury of his adversaries; the attack was continued with redoubled determination on both sides, and at length the smugglers were completely overpowered, so that they were compelled to submit at discretion."

"And were afterwards tried, I suppose?"

"Yes; the whole of them were brought before the Admiralty Court, and found guilty of the murder of the officer in command of the revenue cutter. It was, however, thought unnecessary to hang the whole of the crew for the act of one man, so they ordered poor Harry to be executed, and the rest of the men were sent to Botany Bay, to be drilled into good behaviour for the future."

"And you have brought me to this wild, desolate spot to look upon the ghostly remains of a man whom, two years ago, I parted with in a quarrel."

"Why, the truth is, I thought you might like to see him, though you were not the best of friends the last time you saw each other," said Dalton. "At any rate, you once respected him, and ——"

"Had no wish to see him under such circumstances as the present," interrupted Luke Somerton. "His doom may seem a hard one, but it was one which might have been expected, from the violence he has manifested on more occasions than one, and I have ever thought that his life would end in ignominy and disgrace."

"Well, I myself had a notion that something of the sort would take place," answered Christopher Dalton ; "yet I hardly expected when we came to this island that I should find him here, hanging in chains, and food for the ravens. Poor fellow! he and I have spent many a happy hour together, and little did I then think of the horrid spectacle I was one day to witness."

"Then it was by accident you heard the story you have just been relating to me?" said Luke Somerton.

"Why, the fact is," replied the other, "everybody on this island can tell his whole history. It is notorious to everybody, and the first time I asked whose body it was that I had seen hanging upon a gibbet, the whole facts, as you have just heard them, were related to me. I could hardly believe at first that it was poor Harry they were telling me of ; but, at length, one circumstance or another convinced me of it, and so, as we happened to be out together, I brought you round to have a look at him. Perhaps the sight of him is not very pleasant, but nothing is too great a sacrifice for old friendship's sake, and I hope you won't grudge the little time it has taken to look at him once more."

"I had rather been spared the sight you have been at so much trouble to show me," replied Luke Somerton ; "but since you have brought me here, I will not quarrel about the means you have taken to bring me to the spot. The sight of death is never an agreeable one, but still less so under the circumstances under which I now behold it."

"You don't look upon him with any unkindly feelings, I hope?" exclaimed Christopher Dalton.

"No," answered Luke ; "any quarrel that I may have had with him is from this time forgotten. I had certainly many things to complain of him when we were both on board the same vessel ; but his fate has been a most deplorable one, and I cannot do otherwise than regret that his end has been so disgraceful."

"Aye," exclaimed Dalton, "hanging upon a gallows is a dog's doom, that few people can envy."

"Let us not speak upon this subject," exclaimed Luke Somerton, with emotion. "I have myself endured all the horrors and agony of suspense, and would fain banish from my mind the recollection of an event so fearful in my existence."

"Pardon me, Captain Somerton," cried the other, "for I had no intention of reminding you of an affair that I would gladly forget myself. Egad, I had almost given you up for a dead man at one time, and so you would have been, too, if it had not been for that jewel of a girl of yours, who saved your life by an act of heroism that is worthy of all praise."

"I owe her my life," exclaimed Luke, with emotion ; "and never can I forget the heavy obligation."

"Well, we won't talk any more upon this subject now," cried Christopher Dalton. "I'm sorry, indeed, that I brought you over the heath to look upon the body of poor Harry swinging on the gibbet ; so now let us make our way towards your house, for I should think by this time Dick Service and his companions are on their road there. At all events, your daughter is anxiously looking for our return, and if the rabble should have shown themselves she will be terribly alarmed."

"She has too much nerve and courage to be alarmed," replied Luke ; "but her danger is not the less on that account ; and I, therefore, feel the more anxious to return home, lest a tumultuous mob should already have assembled round my house."

"Still the danger would not be very great, seeing that some of our people will be there before long," exclaimed Christopher Dalton. "Besides, half an hour will take us to your own door, and if any of the ragamuffins should happen to be there they will stand a fair chance of finding out the sort of metal I am made of."

"Let there be no violence, Dalton, or there is no saying where the mischief will end," cried Luke Somerton, alarmed lest the zeal of his friend should hurry him into an act that might lead to mischief. "For my own part, I am reckless of all danger ; but my daughter must share in whatever perils I encounter, and should these people be excited by any act of intemperance, there is but too much reason to fear that it will terminate in the most disastrous consequences."

"Which would fall most heavily upon themselves, remember," exclaimed the other, "for Sir Charles Radcliffe bears the character of being a stern judge, and should these islanders break the law, he is bound to visit their crimes with the severest penalty of the law. In short, a few of them would have a very pretty chance of hanging, by way of an example to their rascally companions."

Shortly afterwards they reached home, where they found Louisa waiting their return with intense anxiety. Scipio had in vain endeavoured to keep up her courage, but the absence of her father and Christopher Dalton had filled her with apprehension, and their return at a juncture when she was yielding to the most gloomy apprehensions, filled her with joy. The first question put to her by Luke was whether she had seen or heard of any of the people who had threatened to attack the cottage.

"I have not seen anything of them myself," she replied ; "but Scipio tells me that about half an hour since he saw three persons pass by, whom he recognized as being among the deadliest of our foes."

"Iss, massa. Dam ugly fellows," exclaimed the negro.

"Were they armed?"

"Only wid big sticks."

"Did they seem as if they had any mischievous object in view?" demanded Luke Somerton.

"Him don't know much about dat," answered Scipio ; "but dey look bery hard at dis house, and den dey all laid dere heads togeder, as if something was wrong."

"They have been sent as spies, to see if we are prepared to resist an attack," exclaimed Christopher Dalton. "The knaves expect to meet with a warm reception, and, like cowards as they are, will not venture to make an attack until they find us unprepared."

"But may they not come to-night?" asked Louisa, who could not conceal the alarm she felt.

"I rather think not," replied Dalton; "for it so happens that we shall have more friends here than they would like to encounter. Eight or ten fellows would be able to scare away a couple of hundred of such white livered rascals; and they are not likely to risk an attack when they know not how many there might happen to fall. Why, I myself, with only this brace of pistols and a cutlass, would not mind meeting a score of them."

"I begin to think these fellows are more inclined to talk than to act," observed Luke Somerton. "It is true they have broken out into violence against me before; but having got the worst of it, they will be more cautious how they run themselves into peril again."

"It is towards you, my dear father," said Louisa, "that their principal malice is levelled, and I fear that, being disappointed in their present object, they will afterwards lay wait for you, in order to destroy the object of their vindictive hatred."

"I must take my chance about that," observed Luke; "for it will never do to hide myself, as if I were afraid to venture out of my own house. Besides, I don't think there is so much fear as you seem to imagine, Louisa, for they know that I always go out well armed, and whenever they have seen me coming the fellows ran away like so many startled deer."

"Yet, being resolved upon your destruction," she said, "they will have recourse to other measures. There is no trusting them, and I shall henceforth look with the utmost terror to your leaving the house alone."

"Why, as to that, Miss Louisa," exclaimed Dalton, "there is no occasion for your father to go out alone, seeing that it is a part of my duty to share in any peril that may threaten him. I will be his companion, unless he gives me orders to the contrary, and even then I don't know but I should prove mutinous for once in my life."

"And Scip will go wid you," interposed the negro; "for he can fight as well as one here and dere."

"You are a faithful fellow, Scip," exclaimed Dalton; "and, as a reward for your good conduct, I'll see that, next voyage, our fellows do not illuse you, as they did in the last. You have made a friend of me, old fellow, and, from this time, you and I will be sworn companions together."

"Tankee, Massa Dalton," said the negro, grinning, till he showed nearly the whole of his white teeth. "Scipio much oblige by your offer ob friendship; but p'rhaps you won't forget to order de cat ob nine tails quite so often as you did de last time we sailed togeder."

"I'll remember your conduct to-day, Scip," replied the mate, "and be merciful, even at the expense of justice. But you must be more careful of the grog, old fellow, and then you and I shall not have much chance of falling out."

They were now interrupted by a knock at the door, which being opened, Dick Lowrie presented himself.

"Where are all the rest of your men?" asked Somerton.

"Outside, waiting for further orders, your honour."

"How many do you muster?"

"Only seven," replied Dick. "I've been beating up for the fellows half over the island, and could only meet with the few that I have brought with me."

"And they, I suspect, will be more than enough for our purpose," replied Luke Somerton. "These half-savage islanders have not yet ventured to show themselves; and I rather think we shall have less trouble with them than was imagined. But tell me, Lowrie, are your men well armed, in case of emergency?"

"Ay, ay, sir," exclaimed the sailor. "Every man has got a cutlass, a brace of pistols, and a double allowance of powder and bullets. I looked to that before we came away, or you would have seen me here before now."

"The next thing to be considered," said Christopher Dalton, "is, how we shall stow these men of ours away, so that they shall not be seen by the enemy; for I don't want to frighten them away, if they come with a hostile intent, since it is only fair that they should have a good peppering, to teach them better manners in future."

"Would it not be better," interposed Louisa, "that they should be aware of our defensive state, in order to prevent a conflict that must prove disastrous."

"By no means," exclaimed Dalton; "if men choose to come here to do us an injury, we have every right to punish them for it; and I therefore propose, with Captain Somerton's permission, that our men shall be concealed, so that they may rush out suddenly upon the rabble, if they should venture to come near us."

"And do you propose this," said Louisa; "when the consequences must prove fatal to many of these ill-advised people?"

"If they are ill-advised, Miss Louisa, it's no fault of ours, and they must needs take the consequences, whatever they may be. They have already burnt a house down about your ears, and if we suffer them to go on much longer, the next thing will be that they will murder your father, and perhaps yourself into the bargain."

"The truth is, Louisa," said her father, "that our dangerous position renders it absolutely necessary that we should take vigorous means to save ourselves from the fury of these incarnate fiends. If they come here, there can be no doubt that it will be with the intention of murdering us, and, therefore, whatever happens to them will be justly merited. I have no desire to be the cause of bloodshed, and still less to be the victim of a cruel persecution, such as I have endured, from the first moment that I set my foot upon the island. They have driven me to this desperation, and now the consequences must fall upon their own heads."

"And they shall have such a reception as they little expect," cried Christopher Dalton, rubbing his hands as if in joyful anticipation of some great pleasure. "I have long wished it to come to this, and, by Neptune and all the Tritons, I'll be one of the foremost to give them their deserts! They shall have cause to remember the hour when they came to interfere with harmless people. So, now," he continued, to Dick Lowrie, "do you take our men round to a large shed that you will find at the back of the house. Provisions and rum shall presently be sent you, but mind, not a man among them must be the worse for what he drinks. We must have clear and cool heads, Lowrie, and, above all things, see that at least two keep watch while the others sleep, for if these fellows come down upon us at all, it is likely they will steal to the place like so many wolves upon a flock of sheep."

"I'll take care they sha'n't have much chance of that," exclaimed Dick, "for I'll act the part of a sentry myself, and will keep such a look-out that not so much as a mouse shall stir without my seeing him."

"Then now away to your hiding-place," said Christopher. "I will myself keep watch from the windows of this house, and if you should hear a pistol shot, you may be sure that an attack has been commenced, and that one at least of the fellows has fallen. Then rush out from your place of concealment, and make such a sudden attack upon our enemies, that they shall be glad to beat a hasty retreat."

Having received these instructions, Lowrie took his departure, soon after which the quick, regular tramping of the men, announced that they were marching round to the place in the rear of the premises.

"We are all right now, captain," exclaimed Dalton, as soon as the sound had died away; "the men are housed safe enough, and if you like to go to bed, I'll rouse you up the moment danger seems to be approaching."

"I shall take no rest to-night," answered Luke, "nor do I indeed need it, for the excitement produced by this affair is quite sufficient to deprive me of all inclination for sleep. However, I hope you, Louisa, will lie down, for it will be weary watching for you, poor girl, when every moment we may expect the arrival of our enemies."

"I cannot sleep, my dear father," she exclaimed, "and would rather, with your leave, watch with you, lest these people should come suddenly upon us. Nay, do not refuse me a request upon which I have confidently relied, for I should only become a prey to my own fears were I to be absent from you in the moment of danger."

"Well, then, you shall take your place in that large chair," said her father, "and, perhaps, when all is quiet, you may obtain a few hours' slumber. Dalton and I will keep watch through the night, and even if the worst should happen, you at least shall be saved from the fury of these men."

"Aye, aye; you may make yourself perfectly easy about that, Miss Louisa," exclaimed Christopher Dalton, "for we shall be upon the look-out all night, and at all events, you shall be safe, whatever may come of this. I owe these fellows something for the mad pranks they have already been guilty of, and it shall be no fault of mine if the debt is not paid on the very first opportunity they give me."

He and Luke Somerton then busied themselves in getting together the refreshments that had been promised the men, and having first looked out to ascertain that the coast was clear, Christopher Dalton took the hamper containing the provisions, whilst Luke remained at the door, to prevent the possibility of anybody entering the house. In less than a quarter of an hour the mate returned with intelligence that the men were well satisfied with the fare provided for them, and anxiously waiting to have a brush with the foe, should they venture to come near the place. The two watchers then took their post at the window, but though more than once they fancied they heard the sound of approaching footsteps, the night wore away without the threatened attack being made.

CHAPTER XLII.

Revenge is but a frailty, incident
To crazed and sickly minds; the poor content
Of little souls, unable to surmount
An injury—too weak to bear affront.
OLDHAM.

Two hours after sunrise, Louisa Somerton awoke from the uneasy sleep into which she had sunk, and perceiving that her father and Christopher Dalton were still looking out, she inquired if anything had been seen of the people whose expected visit had filled her with so much dismay. To this she received a reply in the negative, and feeling somewhat assured by their non-arrival, she ventured to express a hope that all danger from them was at an end.

"Why, as for that, Miss Louisa," exclaimed Dalton, "there's no saying yet what mischief may be in the wind, though their keeping away does certainly look as if they were a little bit frightened at the preparations we have made for their reception. However, it's early times yet to fancy ourselves secure, for it seems the fellow that was put into prison for the last affair has contrived to escape, and as he was always one of the most violent among the mob, it's hardly likely that his feelings towards your father have been improved since his committal to gaol."

"How did he contrive to escape?" asked Louisa.

"By cutting his blanket into strips, and tying them together," replied the other. "He then let himself down from the window, which was almost at the top of the building, and was off some hours before his escape was discovered."

"But surely he will not venture to show himself, lest he should be again captured by the officers of justice."

"I suppose not," answered Dalton; "but he will find a refuge among some of his companions, and, it's likely enough, will urge them never to desist from their evil designs till they have been accomplished."

"Then, my dear father," exclaimed Louisa, earnestly, "let me again implore you to leave this island ere our worst apprehensions are accomplished. Here you will be in continual danger of assassination; and, should you fall by the cruel machinations of these men, my future misery would be too great for endurance."

"I know it," answered Luke, "and have all night been thinking what step I ought next to pursue. It must be confessed, I like not the idea of running away from the place like a coward; but your happiness depends upon the result of my determination, and at length I have come to the decision that my absence from this island is necessary."

"Oh! what a relief it is to my heart to hear you say so!" exclaimed Louisa, throwing her arms round his neck. "I will be your companion, wherever it may please you to go, and, though the most abject state of poverty may be our lot, no murmur—no complaint shall ever escape my lips."

"Nay," answered her father, "my present arrangements render it necessary that you remain here for a while. You will be safe after it is known that I am gone, and by-and-bye we shall be able to rejoin each other."

"But why cannot I accompany you?" she asked.

"Because I am going a voyage," answered Luke, "and our ship is no place for a young, pure-minded girl, like yourself."

"Not when you are by as my protector?"

"Do not urge me further upon this point, my dear Louisa," exclaimed her father; "I have well considered the subject, and the determination is one that I can never depart from."

"And the captain is in the right, depend upon it," interposed Christopher Dalton. "The crew of a ship are not the best companions for a young lady at any time, but ours happens to be a roughish lot, and their language would not be at all times such as you ought to hear; besides, we are likely enough to have an engagement or two with the enemy, and women are always best out of the way when fighting and bloodshed is going on."

Louisa betrayed much alarm at this intelligence, which being observed by her father, he said,—

"The truth is, my dear girl, the vessel I command is a privateer, and it is our business to attack all vessels which there is a probability of taking. Our career, therefore, is one of continual danger, and such as no female can be allowed to share with us."

"And what think you, then," she asked, "will be my feelings, when you are absent, and exposed to all the perils of war?"

"You must think of such matters as little as possible," answered her father. "I have been long engaged in the same pursuit, my dear girl, and have hitherto escaped with a few slight wounds, that are scarcely worth remembering."

"But it may be your fate to fall at last," she exclaimed.

"That is looking at the blackest side of the picture, Miss Louisa," interposed Dalton. "Your father has hitherto escaped, though always exposing himself in places where the greatest danger lay; and I can see no reason why you should fear that his good fortune is about to fail at last. By Jove, I'm delighted to hear the captain say that he's going to sea again, for our fellows have been grumbling at the idle life they lead in this island, and when once they receive orders to go on board ship, we shall see nothing but smiling faces among them, instead of looks of ill nature and discontent."

"In fact, Louisa," resumed her father, "I have too long delayed my departure, through an unwillingness to leave one who is so dear to me. Seeing, however, the furious hatred of these islanders towards me, and the danger in which it involves you, I have at length determined to take another trip to sea. To you these people have no particular aversion, and when it is made known that I have left the place, you will have nothing further to fear from their violence."

"And when," cried Louisa, "do you leave me?"

"This very day," he replied. "I shall presently go on board my ship, though it is possible we may not sail for two or three days. In the meantime Mr. Dalton will remain on shore to observe what effect my departure has on my enemies in this island. If things turn out as I anticipate, I shall go away with a perfect assurance of your safety; or if, as seems likely enough, the war should end in the course of a few months, I shall return to England, and we shall meet together in some place where the remainder of our days may be passed in happiness and tranquillity."

"Aye, aye, always look forward to the best," exclaimed Christopher Dalton. "Trouble enough you have had, it must be confessed; but misfortunes don't last for ever, and it's your turn now to have a share of better. So, don't be downhearted about it, miss, but remember you are the daughter of a sailor, and let the world see that you have the fortitude and resignation of a heroine."

"Since we must be separated," answered Louisa, "I will endeavour to bear my troubles without complaining. Hope shall support me during the absence of my father; and should we ever meet again, I shall think all my misfortunes have at length come to an end."

"That's spoken like a sensible girl," exclaimed Dalton. "There's nothing like being resigned to what can't be helped, and as there is every reason why our captain should go to sea again, the only way is to let him go, without saying anything more about it. As for fighting, he's not such a coward as to be afraid of having a brush with the enemy, and as he has always had the good luck to escape from danger, we may hope that he will do so this time, and in that case you will meet again before long."

"But I have heard it rumoured," said Louisa, speaking with hesitation, "that the vessel commanded by my father is engaged in contraband traffic."

"Why, I dare say people may have said so," answered Dalton; "and even if there is any truth in the report, I see no great harm in a man bringing foreign goods to England free of the duty. People like to outwit the government, if they can, and I never yet knew any one that thought a drop of brandy or hollands any the worse for not having paid a heavy tax. Besides, smuggling, my dear girl, is carried on by people in high life, for there is scarcely a lady or gentleman of rank that goes abroad without bringing over goods of foreign manufacture; and all sorts of schemes, too, they try to get them ashore without coming under the eyes of the custom-house officers."

"That may be true," answered Louisa; "but there is a heavy punishment for those who keep vessels for that purpose."

"Which punishment your father is not likely to feel," exclaimed Dalton; "for he has only done it three or four times, when we had nothing better to occupy our attention, and, from what I have heard him say, he will never run the risk again, though the profits attending it are certainly tempting."

"That, at least, is some consolation," said Louisa. "It is bad enough to know that he will be hourly risking his life against the enemies of his country, but still worse to exist in the certainty that he is doing that which, if discovered, would bring him to shame and ignominy."

"Which I will never do, if it is only for your own sake, my dear girl," exclaimed Luke Somerton. "I have, it must be confessed, till very lately, taken up arms against my lawful sovereign, but it was in revenge for injuries inflicted upon me, when I was doing all that either honour or loyalty demanded of me. Since then, however, my life has been preserved by the mercy of Queen Anne, and she shall now acknowledge that she has not a more faithful subject in her dominions. Through her grace and clemency I have been saved from a shameful death, and the debt I owe her can only be paid by devoting the rest of my life to her service."

They now sat down to breakfast, in the course of which Christopher Dalton inquired of his captain how soon he would be required to join him on board the ship.

"In that," replied Somerton, "we must be guided by circumstances. My daughter may need your services after I am gone away, for it is by no means certain that these people will cease from their persecution, and if there should be any appearance of danger, it must be your task to remain and protect her."

"Which I shall do with all my heart and soul," exclaimed Dalton. "These Manxmen and I are not upon the very best of terms, and if they should show themselves inclined to any of their cursed tricks, it will be high time for me to let them see who they have to deal with. Egad! I only wish they had paid us a visit, as we expected, last night, and then we should have seen what sort of faces some of them would have put on about it this morning."

"It is much better as it is," replied Luke Somerton, "for the fact of their not coming proves pretty clearly that they were afraid of the consequences. They had a notion, I dare say, that we were prepared for them, and had they ventured to make the threatened attack, they would have found, to their cost, that we were able to encounter double the number that they could have brought against us."

"But if any lives had been lost," said Louisa, "they would never have rested satisfied till you had been made to answer for them with your own."

"That may be," exclaimed Luke; "but they must have caught me before they could expect to work out their vengeance. That, however, is rather unlikely, for we have always a boat lying in readiness for us on the beach, and, in case of there being any necessity for it, I and the rest of our people should have made our way to it, and we should have been on board ship before a pursuit could have been made; so you see, Louisa, our danger was not quite so great as you have been inclined to imagine."

"You see, miss," said Christopher Dalton, "people that are used to danger generally take the best means they can to prevent it. We were well enough aware that all the lower order of people were against us; so not feeling inclined to trust ourselves too much to their tender mercies, we made preparations for defeating any evil designs they might form against us."

"Which," observed Louisa, "had they been aware of them, they might very easily have frustrated."

"True," answered Dalton; "but we took good care that they should not be aware of them. Our people are no babblers when they know a secret is to be kept that concerns themselves; so the boat has remained on the beach, and none of these islanders had the least suspicion that it was intended for our escape in case of being wanted."

"Or it would most certainly have been either stolen or destroyed," observed Luke Somerton. "However, I must now go to the ship whilst the opportunity offers; for delay may render my retreat impossible, and it will be better that I get on board before the bloodhounds again assemble to track me out."

"Alas!" sighed Louisa; "must we indeed part with the terrible uncertainty whether we shall ever be again permitted to see each other?"

"Our separation will not be so long a one as you think," exclaimed her father; "nor is there so much danger as you imagine, though it must be admitted some few are doomed to perish in every hostile encounter that takes place. A few months will serve to restore us to each other, and it is likely I shall not afterwards be required to leave you."

"Excuse me, captain," exclaimed Christopher Dalton, "but as a third party don't seem at all necessary here, I'll just go and send two or three of our men to get the boat ready against you arrive at the beach. These parting scenes are not much to my fancy; so, when you are gone, I'll return home and wait with the young lady till she is quite safe from any further attacks of the enemy."

With this he left the house, and passing through the garden, proceeded to the shed in which the men had obtained a shelter for the night. On reaching the place, he found them engaged in a consultation together, and both their looks, and the few words that met his ear, proved that they were not in the best of humours at the duty which had been imposed upon them. Dick Lowrie was the first to speak, and in a sullen tone he demanded how much longer they were to be kept there.

"No longer than you like, Dick," answered the mate. "I've come to say that there's no occasion for any more watching, for the devil a bit has any one made an appearance all night, and I'm inclined to think these thick-headed fellows have at last made the notable discovery that their riotous proceedings will only involve them in trouble."

"Whether they have or not, I don't mean to waste any more of my time hulking about the island, when there's plenty to do on our own element," exclaimed Lowrie, sullenly. "The captain seems to be tired of the old way of life; so I shall offer my services elsewhere, and in four and twenty hours I hope to be far enough from the confounded place."

"That's likely enough," exclaimed Dalton; "but it won't be under a new captain, though, for Luke Somerton has made up his mind for another cruise."

"He has?"

"Ay, as true as my name's Kit Dalton."

"And when does he sail?"

"In a few hours, I believe; at any rate, he goes on board a ship directly, so the sooner you and the other fellows get things in readiness, the quicker we shall weigh anchor and after the enemy."

"And who's he going to fight for this time?"

"Queen Anne, to be sure," answered Dalton. "He owes his life to her, you know, and it's hardly likely, after receiving a pardon, that he will fight for a foreign power."

"But it was the English government that robbed him of his inheritance," observed Dick Lowrie.

"He don't want reminding of that," replied the other; "but between ourselves, Dick, it's likely enough they may restore him to it when they see he is returning to his allegiance. The queen has done him a good turn already, and I'm much mistaken if she don't do him another before many more months have passed over his head."

"Well," exclaimed Dick, "it don't much matter to me which side I take, so that we get out of the idle life we are living in this place. But how soon did you say it would be that he goes on board the ship?"

"Immediately," replied Dalton, "so a couple of you fellows run down to the beach and get the boat in readiness, for he don't want to be delayed a moment when he gets there, lest these people should happen to hear of what he's going to do."

These words were scarcely uttered before the men hurried out to make their way to the sea-side, and Dick Lowrie was about to follow them, when he was called back by Dalton.

"Are yonder men to be relied on as formerly?" he asked.

"Ay; they are true to the back-bone; but what makes you think they're not faithful, Mr. Dalton?"

"I thought they seemed to be grumbling just now, when I came in."

"So they were," replied Lowrie, "and it ain't to be wondered at, when they've been leading an idle life against their own inclination. They were saying that as there wasn't much chance of getting to sea again in a hurry, they should enter themselves under some other captain without further delay."

"Then it's a proof they've no regard for their old commander."

"Just try 'em, Mr. Dalton," exclaimed Lowrie. "Wait till they get on board; and as soon there's a chance of earning prize money, you'll see 'em the same smart, active seamen that they used to be. The truth of it is, they wanted employment; and you saw how delighted the fellows were as soon as they heard you say we were under sailing orders."

"Didn't we find employment for them last night?"

"Yes; to sit up in this ricketty old place, and watch for an enemy that never came," exclaimed Dick. "The chaps grumbled enough about it, I can tell you; and it was as much as I could do to persuade 'em that it was their duty to obey the orders of their captain, however disagreeable it might be to keep watch in a tumble-down barn, through a long dreary night. But they're satisfied now, and I'll answer for it there won't be any reason to find fault with the way they do their duty."

"Well," returned Christopher Dalton, "if they have such a fancy for fighting, I can answer for it they'll have enough before another month passes away."

"But there's a talk of the war coming to an end," observed Dick; "and if England and France should shake hands and make it up, what's to become of us jolly tars, I should like to know?"

"Why, you must wait patiently till a war breaks out again," replied Dalton. "The two countries are never at peace very long together, and then those that like fighting will have an opportunity of indulging their propensity. However, let that be as it may, we have a fair chance at present, and if we should be lucky enough to take a few of the enemy's vessels, we may get prize money enough to keep us ashore till another row breaks out, and then, hey for the sea again, and more fighting."

"But not under the same captain, I'm thinking?"

"Perhaps not," answered the other. "Luke Somerton conceives that the care of his daughter is superior to every other claim, and he intends, at the first opportunity, to settle himself in England, and take her under his own eye. And he's right enough, too, I think, for she's a fine spirited lass, and deserves all the kindness and attention he can bestow upon her. In short he owes his life to the exertions of that girl, and he can do no less than make the rest of her days happy and comfortable."

"And yet," observed Dick, "I have heard it whispered that it was his hand that spilt the blood of Captain Aylmer."

"Have a care how you utter such a hint in his presence," exclaimed the other. "Luke Somerton is himself silent upon the subject, but he knows the suspicions that are abroad, and the thought sometimes drives him almost to madness. If he was indeed guilty, a conscience ill at ease is a punishment worse even than death itself, though it might have been on a public scaffold."

"Well," uttered the other, "if he really did kill Captain Aylmer, I can say there was a fair excuse for it; for they do say that the provocation was beyond all bearing, and that no man could have put up with the insults our captain received when they were officers on board the same ship."

"That's true enough," answered Christopher Dalton; "for I have myself heard insulting remarks that made my blood boil with indignation. Luke Somerton, however, refrained from making any retort, because his rank in the ship was inferior to that of Aylmer's; but at length he left the vessel, and they never afterwards saw each other till they unfortunately met in this island. That Captain Aylmer died by violence is certain; but, in my opinion, he may have committed suicide, for a pistol was found lying close to the body, and to that circumstance our captain was indebted for the merciful consideration given to his case by the queen."

"And his daughter acted like a heroine," exclaimed Dick Lowrie. "I shall never forget what a stormy ocean she had to cross over, and yet go she would, though death was staring her in the face all the while. Well, Heaven reward her, say I, for her father would have been hanged, sure enough, but for her interference."

"And the good queen that pardoned him deserves fighting for," exclaimed Dalton; "and as far as I am concerned, she shall find that her royal mercy is not forgotten. I was in despair when the morning of execution arrived, for the mission of Louisa seemed to be but a wild-goose chase, after all, and when, at the last moment, the announcement of a reprieve was made, I couldn't believe my ears."

"I'm sure our captain never expected such a piece of luck," exclaimed Lowrie, "for, with the sea raging as it did at the time, there seemed no possibility of the girl returning in time, even supposing she had been fortunate enough to obtain the pardon. However, she possessed more courage than a good many men would have had, and Heaven protected the messenger that had gone on so holy an errand. But what is to be done with her, Mr. Dalton, while her father's away on this voyage of ours?"

"She remains here, of course?"

"What! when the rabble are so incensed against her?"

"It is not against her that the evil feeling exists," replied Dalton. "Her father, it is true, has many enemies here; but when it is discovered that he has left the island there will be no further attempt to injure her."

"I'm not quite so sure about that, Mr. Dalton, for they look upon her as the person that disappointed them on the morning of the intended execution."

"Even if they are inclined to continue their persecution," said the other, "they will find themselves opposed by one that is not to be trifled with. Lieutenant Granger is the girl's lover; and, if need be, he would die in her defence."

"And what good would his dying do?" exclaimed Lowrie; "he had better marry her at once, and then the scoundrels would know that it would be a dangerous experiment to try and do her an injury."

"But the girl is not disposed to marry him."

"Humph! she don't like him, then, I suppose?"

"She is devotedly attached to him," replied Christopher, "but refuses to give him her hand, lest the union should bring dishonour on the man she loves."

"What dishonour would it bring, Mr. Dalton?"

"None, to my thinking," answered the other; "but she, poor girl, happens to think very differently. In short, she believes that affair of her father has brought discredit on his name, and she has declared that nothing shall ever induce her to marry Lieutenant Granger until it is satisfactorily proved that her father was not guilty of the death of his old enemy, Captain Aylmer."

"Then, I'm afraid there's very little chance of the affair ever coming off at all," said Dick, "for no one saw how Captain Aylmer came by his death, and where there's no witnesses, there can be very little chance of matters turning out much better than they are at present."

"Sensible enough, Master Lowrie, considering where it comes from," exclaimed Dalton. "There are certainly no witnesses in the case, but sometimes strange things turn up to bring things to light, and who knows but some lucky chance or other will prove that Luke Somerton is innocent of the crime he was accused of? Be that as it may, however, Lieutenant Granger is willing to marry the girl, and I'm in hopes, when the remembrance of her father's misfortunes has somewhat faded away, she will consent to become his wife."

"Between ourselves, Mr. Dalton," said the other, "I can't help thinking her a simpleton for

holding out as long as she has. If he don't mind being twitted afterwards with having married the daughter of a man that was sentenced to death for murder, I don't see that she ought to put a stopper to his hopes. Why, even the Queen of England herself was not too proud to speak to her, and that's an honour that very few people can boast of."

"See!" exclaimed Christopher, pointing towards the house, "Luke Somerton has just left his daughter, and is making his way towards the sea-shore. I must go and speak to the poor girl, for I dare say she's melancholy enough at the parting that's just taken place."

He then left the sailor, and, re-crossing the garden, entered the house, where, as he had anticipated, he found Louisa weeping at the separation which had taken place between her and her parent. For some time she took not the slightest heed of his well-intentioned efforts to relieve her despondency; but at length, raising her head, and wiping away the tears that bedimmed her eyes, she said,—

"It is in vain that you would persuade me that my father incurs no danger in this new enterprize of his. I know his courage will not allow him to take any other place in battle than the post of danger, and there is a fearful presentiment in my mind that our recent interview was the last we shall ever have."

"The daughter of a brave man ought surely to have more courage than you seem to possess on this occasion," exclaimed Dalton. "He is called away by both duty and honour, and his remaining longer in this place would have led to the desertion of all the men that have hitherto obeyed his command. Nay, in less than two days, they would have left the island and transferred their services to some else."

"Would that they had done so," exclaimed Louisa, "for then would my father have remained with me."

"Which would have been done at the expense of his honour," returned Christopher Dalton. "People would not have believed but that he had become a coward of late, and I know he would rather throw away his life in battle than give his enemies an opportunity of throwing out hints disparaging to his honour."

"And who is there," demanded Louisa, "that would dare utter a word in contradiction of his courage?"

"He has unfortunately many enemies," replied Dalton; "and there is not one among them but would have been glad of such a chance. He is now going a voyage that is not likely to prove a very long one, for we are on the eve of a peace with France, and when that is concluded, your father will return to England, and it is more than likely he will never leave you again."

"Such is the hope you would inspire me with," answered Louisa; "and yet no arguments that you can make use of will ever make me believe that it will be our happiness to meet again."

"That's only because you haven't yet got over the sorrow of parting from him," said the other. "But time wears away our troubles, as it does everything else; and before a week has passed away, your fears will give way to hope, and then you'll be looking forward with as much anxiety as any one, for the day that is to bring your father back again."

"Not when I know that every hour will expose him to the peril of battle," answered our heroine.

"It is my duty, however, to endure all this uncertainty with fortitude and resignation, and whatever may be my own sufferings, I will conceal them from the knowledge of all the world."

"That's spoken like the daughter of Luke Somerton," exclaimed Dalton. "I knew your courage could not give way just when it was most required, and since there's no help for what has taken place, it behoves you to put on a cheerful countenance, instead of making it appear that you have not courage to endure the trials of life."

"And yet," observed Louisa, "I have already afforded proof that my energies are not to be easily depressed by difficulties."

"True," exclaimed the other; "you have done that which few females would have had the resolution to attempt. Your father owes his life to your unparalleled exertions, and the affair is not likely to be forgotten in a hurry, I can tell you. The people here speak of your conduct with admiration, and ——"

"Some of them," interrupted our heroine, "have since rewarded me by burning down our house, and threatening death and destruction to both my father and myself."

"Merely the rabble, my dear Miss Somerton,"

exclaimed the other. "For some reason or another they were incensed against the captain, and would have slain him in their blind fury; but towards yourself they bear not the slightest animosity. In short, now that your father has left the island you have nothing more to fear from the violence of these people; and even if you had, there is a certain gentleman that I know of, that would risk his own life any day to save yours."

"You mean Sir Charles Radcliffe?"

"No, I mean a younger person than him," replied Dalton, laughing. "Lieutenant Granger is the person I allude to, though it's hardly necessary for me to say what a vast deal of interest he takes in your welfare."

"I am indeed much indebted to him for many

acts of kindness," replied Louisa. "He has even risked his life to preserve me from the fury of a brutal mob, and the only regret I feel is, that it is totally out of my power to make any recompense."

"There is one way at all events to show your gratitude," said Christopher Dalton, slily. "Consent to become the young gentleman's wife, and he will be more than repaid."

"This is a subject which I have requested even my father to abstain from," said Louisa, with firmness. "He knows that my determination is fixed and unalterable, and he has now ceased to importune me upon that point. Lieutenant Granger has also consented to abide the result of my further consideration, though it is upon an understanding that at present there is no prospect of my ever reversing the decision to which I have already arrived."

"Well, it's no business of mine to be sure," exclaimed Dalton ; "only I respect my captain, and as for his daughter, I should like to see her as happy as she deserves to be. However, there is an end of the matter as far as I am concerned ; so, as I see our friend Scipio is close at hand to give his assistance in case of need, I'll just run down to the beach to see if your father has managed to get safely off in the boat."

Without waiting a moment longer the warm-hearted fellow hastened out of the house, and having first looked round to satisfy himself that there were no enemies lurking in the neighbourhood, he took the road across the common, and once more passing by the gibbet, soon reached the sea side. But the person he was in search of had not yet arrived, and he therefore bent his course towards the more frequented road, not doubting that he should soon fall in with his captain.

In the meantime Luke Somerton had been pursuing his own way, in the course of which he was met by Lieutenant Granger, who was at that moment on his way to the cottage on a message from the governor. Luke would have been glad to have avoided an interview just at this moment, but the other stepped hastily towards him.

"By Jove! you are the very man I was in search of," he exclaimed. "Sir Charles Radcliffe has sent me to say that he has something particular to speak to you about immediately."

"Upon what subject?"

"That is more than I am perhaps warranted to explain," answered the lieutenant. "You may, however, guess that it relates to yourself and the riotous people he finds it so difficult to keep within the bounds of peace and moderation."

"As far as I am concerned he is likely to have less trouble then heretofore," replied Luke. "In a word, I am now on my way to the boat, in order that I may once more embark on board my vessel."

"Are you going to leave the island, then?"

"I am."

"For how long?"

"In all probability for ever."

"Humph! the old profession has such charms for Captain Somerton, that he cannot make himself happy on shore, even though it may be that his daughter will be left almost without a friend to protect her."

"The truth is," answered Somerton, "I have found little here that can render the island a pleasant home to me. Discord has followed my footsteps ever since I have been in the place, and as my daughter shares in the odium that has been cast upon me, I have resolved to take another trip to sea, under the impression that they will suffer her to rest in peace and quietude after it is known that I am no longer here."

"Singularly enough, my message from the governor bears upon this very point," exclaimed Lieutenant Granger. "He has seen, with mingled feelings of grief and anger, the revengeful feelings of these people towards you, and as nothing but violent means—which he does not mean to resort to—will ever bring them to submission, he wished to see you in order to suggest the prudence of your leav-

ing the island till this vindictive feeling has been forgotten."

"You will tell him, then, that his wishes have been anticipated."

"Assuredly I will," replied Granger ; "he will be rejoiced at hearing of your safety ; yet let it not be imagined that he has any wish to send you from the island. He only fears that your life is endangered here, and will be glad when the opportunity for your return arrives."

"I shall never again set foot upon this accursed spot," exclaimed Luke Somerton. "It has been the scene of my disgrace—the hotbed from whence my worst enemies have sprung, and when I quit the place it is with the firm determination never to return."

"But the mad fury of your enemies will subside in the course of a little time," observed Granger, "as will the anger their persecution has excited in your bosom, and then you will surely be anxious to return to your daughter."

"How know you that she is not going with me?"

"I merely judge so from the improbability of your taking her to share the perils you are about to encounter."

"The perils," observed Luke, "can scarcely be greater than those she has had to encounter here. The devotion she displayed in behalf of her condemned father has created foes as numerous as they are revengeful ; even her sex has been no safeguard against the attack of these cowardly assassins, nor were their hearts touched with sympathy by the heroic ardour with which she braved every danger to obtain the queen's pardon for a father whom she believed innocent."

"But really," exclaimed Lieutenant Granger, "you will not condemn every person in the island for the intemperate acts of an ignorant and misguided rabble?"

"Certainly I do not include all in my censure," answered Luke Somerton ; "for I have found many good and warm-hearted friends—yourself amongst the number—of whose kindness I must ever retain a lively remembrance. But all that is bad in the past I would now fain bury in oblivion, and I know not of any way so likely to effect my purpose as by taking the cruize I meditate."

"And on which side do you mean to draw your sword?"

"For Queen Anne."

"Excellent! you will thus regain her favour, and may, in all likelihood, obtain the restoration of your lands which were forfeited some years since."

"Misfortunes, my dear young friend," exclaimed Somerton, "have obliterated every trace of ambition from my heart. The loss of all my wealth was assuredly keenly felt at first, but I have long ceased to regret it ; and, were not my daughter more interested than myself, I should refuse the restoration of my lands even were the offer made to me."

"Have you, then, no wish to return to Ireland, which I hear is the land of your nativity?"

"Not with a name tainted by crime," answered Luke. "I have been accused, tried, and convicted of murder—nay, I have stood upon the very scaffold where the supposed crime was to be expiated, and a few more seconds would have seen me hanging like a dog, but for the generous devotion of my child. She saved me from a death of shame, Lieutenant Granger, but I feel that people will remember what has taken place, and that the finger of scorn will ever more be pointed at me. The land of my birth, therefore, can possess no charms for me, and all I can most desire is to die in some lone spot, where none have ever heard of Luke Somerton or his misfortunes."

"And would you take Louisa into the retirement you seek for yourself?"

"I would not," answered Luke Somerton; "would to Heaven she had accepted the generous offer you made her, for then could I have ended my days in peace, if not with happiness."

"Then why not have been more urgent in backing my entreaties?" demanded Lieutenant Granger. "Surely the sincerity of my offer was not doubted, when I offered to forego all earthly considerations, on the solitary condition that she would bestow upon me her hand and heart."

"Louisa knows and acknowledges your worth," replied Somerton; "but you are aware of the one reason which has dictated the conduct she pursues, and I believe there are none but will esteem the motive as an honourable one."

"I am inclined to give her all due credit for it," exclaimed Lieutenant Granger, "though the determination has deprived me of the fond hopes I had ventured to form. She fears the alliance would bring disgrace upon my name; but what disgrace can attach to our union with a high-minded girl who has obtained the applause of even the queen herself?"

"The truth is, I have hinted as much to her," replied Luke Somerton; "but no arguments can prevail with one who is resolved to act with the most perfect honour. That her heart is fondly attached to you I know, yet it is not in the power of human persuasion to prevail upon her to consult her own inclinations to what she conceives to be a paramount duty."

"Do you think there is a chance that she will at any future time be inclined to accept my addresses?"

"That will depend upon circumstances," replied Somerton. "I may recover my lost name— may once more be restored to society, and attain the station from which I have been driven. These things may come to pass, and if so, Louisa will no longer withhold her consent to the union."

"Then I will yet venture to indulge my hopes," exclaimed Lieutenant Granger. "A few months may serve to bring all these things about, and during that period I shall have an opportunity of convincing Louisa that the professions of love I made to her were neither hollow nor insincere."

By this time they had reached the sea shore, where the boat was lying in readiness, a couple of sailors being seated in her as if prepared to depart the moment their captain took his place with them. There were idlers upon the beach, and, amongst others, Harry Roden, whose violent doings had on a previous occasion got him into a prison, from which, however, he had found means to escape.

"That fellow's impudence is marvellous," whispered Lieutenant Granger to Luke. "He has broken from prison, yet here he stands as unconcerned as if his liberty was not in peril by a recognition.

However, I shall keep my eye on him, for he is watching us as if there was mischief in the wind; and besides, he and I must have a word or two before we part."

"Oh, don't trouble your head about him," exclaimed Luke, "for depend on it he'll not come near enough to run himself into any danger. Besides, if he has injured anybody, it has been me, and, as I am going to leave the place, there's no need to punish him for what's gone by."

"Depend upon it he will not get off with Sir Charles Radcliffe upon quite such easy terms," answered Lieutenant Granger. "He has been long known as one of the roughest vagabonds in the whole island, and it was a subject for general congratulation when he was thrown into prison for that affair of yours. By some means or another, however, he managed to make his escape from us, and it was imagined that he had got away from the place altogether. But yonder he stands, and I should be remiss in my duty were I to fail in restoring him to the place from whence he came."

"The fellow deserves all he may meet with, that's certain," returned Luke Somerton. "Not that I wish him to be persecuted from a mere spirit of revenge, but because he waged war against my daughter—a helpless female, whose only crime consisted in obtaining the pardon of her condemned father."

Whilst speaking, Luke advanced towards the boat that was waiting for him, and, as he did so, Harry Roden sprang forward, and presenting a pistol at him, was about to pull the trigger, when Lieutenant Granger struck up the assassin's arm, and the contents were instantly discharged in the air. In another moment the would-be assassin was seized and secured, though not without some resistance on the part of the culprit.

"Villain!" exclaimed Granger, "had not my arm interposed, you would now have had to answer for the life of a fellow creature! What motive had you for this violence?"

"Ask me no questions, for I am resolved to answer none," returned the ruffian, sullenly. "You have saved the life of yonder man, for which he owes you a heavy debt of gratitude; but from me you have earned nought but curses and imprecations."

"'Twas a cowardly act, to say the best of it," exclaimed the officer. "He was unprepared for the attack, and yet, assassin-like, you stole upon your victim, and would have immolated him to a cruel spirit of revenge."

"I should only have served him as he did Captain Aylmer," replied Harry Roden in the same tone of dogged indifference. "He slew his enemy unprepared, and surely I am as worthy of the queen's pardon for this offence as he was when the law had sentenced him to death for his crimes."

"This bravado will not serve you," exclaimed Lieutenant Granger. "You were detected in the very act of attempting to take away the life of a fellow creature, and the punishment will be as certain as it is terrible. Let him be instantly conveyed before the governor," he added to those who had charge of the prisoner; "and, above all things, let him be strictly guarded, for he has escaped once already, and, should he do so a second time, those who permit it will suffer a penalty so heavy that they will not be at all likely to forget it in a hurry."

Harry Roden was about to growl out his defiance, but, ere he could half complete the sentence, he was dragged away and conducted towards the castle.

"You have saved my life," exclaimed Luke Somerton to the young soldier, "and that act of itself will endear you more than anything else to my daughter. Make what use you please of the advantage it gives you, and add, if you think proper, that my wish for your union is fully equal to your own."

"Nay," answered Granger, "I will seek no advantage from an act of duty that affords me so much real satisfaction. That I saved your life, is indeed true, but what would have been the misery and despair of poor Louisa had I not been present to arrest the arm of the assassin."

"That is well thought of," exclaimed Luke Somerton. "My daughter will most likely hear of this attempt upon my life, and, as the rumour will of course be full of exaggeration, I should wish you to see her without delay, in order to lull the alarm into which she will be thrown."

"Had you not better return," said the other, "and by your presence convince her that the treacherous design has failed?"

"Nay," answered Somerton, "I could not endure a second parting from one whom I so fondly love. She clung to me just now, so that I could scarcely break from her embrace, and it was only when she had nearly swooned from the excess of her emotion that I was able to leave behind me all that I hold most precious in the world. You, however, will see her, Lieutenant Granger, and to your care do I commit the task of assuring her of my safety."

"I accept your task," he replied, "and will lose no time in acquainting her with all that has transpired."

"And do not fail, from over modesty, to state the heavy debt of gratitude you have placed me under," exclaimed Luke. "There is no harm in a man sounding his own praise in such a case as this, though I do not hold at all times with people uttering that commendation of their own actions, which would be better left to others. However, we are now losing time that is too precious to be wasted—hasten, therefore, without delay to my daughter, and assure her of my safety, though no thanks to the miscreant who sought my life."

Fully impressed with the importance of speed in such a case as this, Lieutenant Granger required no further bidding, and, having taken farewell of Luke, he hurried away on the errand he had undertaken. As Somerton gazed after him tears of gratitude glistened in his eyes, and then turning once more towards the boat, he was about to step in, when the well-known voice of Christopher Dalton struck upon his ear.

"Hilloa, captain," he exclaimed, "what cheer after the broadside the piratical ruffian was going to pour into you? No harm has happened to you, I hope?"

"Thanks to Lieutenant Granger I have escaped without the slightest injury," replied Luke. "He struck up the arm of the assassin just in time to save my life."

"All honour to him for the noble act," exclaimed the other. "Somehow or another I always had a liking for that young fellow, and now, hang me if I wouldn't walk barefoot through the world to show my regard for him. But now, captain, tell me how all this comes about."

"Step into the boat, then, and I will tell you as these men row us to the ship," replied Luke. "I have lost too much time already, but, as for you, if there is anything to do ashore, why you can return in the morning."

To this suggestion Christopher Dalton was perfectly willing to agree, for he wished to be on board the vessel that night. The two then took their seats in the boat, and the rowers applying themselves to their task, soon left the shore.

<hr/>

CHAPTER XLIII.

Why dost thou ever haunt me thus—
Dogging my footsteps where'er I go,
As if some hellish purpose prompted thee
To seek my life?

The Court Favourite.

AFTER having seen the prisoner conveyed to a place of safety, Lieutenant Granger proceeded to visit Sir Charles Radcliffe, in order to apprise him of what had taken place, and consult with him as to what ought to be done to prevent the possibility of any further attempts being made against the life of our heroine. On reaching the castle, he found that the governor was already engaged with some other person, and turning away, he was about to proceed to Luke Somerton's cottage, when he was accosted by old Caleb, the weatherbeaten tar, to whom the reader has been already introduced.

"Good evening to your honour," exclaimed the veteran, with his very best sea bow. "Wanting to see the governor, I suppose?—another mutiny in the island, I hear—people vow vengeance against Luke Somerton, and they'll have it too, if he don't make haste and leave the place."

"He has already left it," replied Granger.

"Then he's not such a fool as I thought him," exclaimed Caleb. "Some one told me he was determined not to be frightened away, which would have been sheer madness, seeing that the enemy was too strong for him."

"I believe he was not frightened away, Caleb," answered Granger, "but the truth is, he went away out of consideration for his daughter, because it became pretty certain that all antipathy towards her would cease the moment it was ascertained that he was no longer in the island."

"Who told him so?" demanded the veteran.

"More than one person, I believe."

"Then, they know nothing at all about the matter," exclaimed Caleb. "The people here are as savage as so many wild Indians, and are not to be quite so easily pacified as some folks may imagine. They are howling for his blood like so many famishing wolves, and will never give over following him till he has been hunted to death."

"There, at least, they will be disappointed," replied Lieutenant Granger; "for, as I said before, he has left the island, and, I believe, never intends to return to a place where he has so many foes."

"May I ask where he is going to, your honour?"

"Wherever fortune may lead him," replied

Granger. "At present his home is on the waters, and will be so for some time, if the war is not put an end to."

"Hah! going to the old trade again, I suppose?"

"Luke Somerton will no longer rank himself among the enemies of his sovereign," answered Lieutenant Granger. "He has received too great a favour ever to be ungrateful for it, and henceforth we shall hear of him only as fighting in behalf of his country. He will thus achieve honour, and wipe away the stain that recent events have thrown upon his name."

"And is his daughter to remain here?"

"She is."

"That's a pity," answered Caleb, "for I'm afraid the place is almost too hot to hold her. They think she had no right to sue for her father's pardon, and as she was the means of disappointing them of their revenge, they have taken a dislike to her that ain't likely to be forgot in a hurry."

"How do you know all this, Caleb?"

"Because I mix a good deal among the people here," he replied, "and oftentimes get valuable information through being among them so much. They fancy I hold with all their wicked ways; and it's a good thing for me that they do, for if it hadn't been for that, they'd have killed poor old Caleb with as little remorse as they'd hang a mad dog."

"But you," said Lieutenant Granger, anxiously, "you, I hope, Caleb, would raise your hand for the protection of a female who has few that she can call friends."

"Why, to be sure I would, your honour," answered the veteran, with enthusiasm; "I've always liked the girl as if she'd been my own daughter, and I'd lose the last drop of my blood rather than see her ill-used by a parcel of ragamuffins like Harry Roden and his crew of incarnate fiends."

"I hope there will be no occasion for anything of that sort," returned the officer, "for the example that will be made of this fellow, Roden, will be sufficient to strike terror into the minds of the rest of his brutal companions."

"That is to say if you can catch him again, your honour."

"He has been caught."

"What! is he in prison again?"

"Aye, and with little chance of breaking out of it as he did last time," replied Lieutenant Granger. "I have only just returned from seeing him delivered into safe custody, and am now anxious to see Sir Charles Radcliffe, in order to learn from him what is the next step to take."

"And does his excellency know what has happened?"

"I suppose so; at any rate, I sent him a messenger to that effect, and then came hither according to my promise."

"Then depend upon it he won't keep you waiting very long, Mr. Granger," exclaimed Caleb. "The governor has been terribly vexed ever since he heard of the escape, and it was only this morning that I heard him say he wouldn't mind giving fifty pounds out of his own pocket to have that fellow once more under lock and key."

"Which he now fortunately is," replied the officer, "and that, too, upon a charge that is likely to rid us of his turbulence for ever afterwards."

"You mean his escaping from the prison, in which he was confined I suppose?"

"That is one thing, certainly," replied Granger; "but there is another charge even more serious than this against him. He has attempted the crime of assassination, and was only prevented by my fortunately being near enough to prevent his villanous design."

"Why, that's the second time he's attempted to take the life of the same person," exclaimed the veteran. "Does your honour happen to know what reason he has for all this spite?"

"I believe it is only because he received the queen's pardon, instead of being hung according to the sentence," answered Lieutenant Granger. "The fellow has never ceased to breathe forth vows of vengeance, and not long since would have accomplished his diabolical purpose, but that his pistol was struck into the air at the moment when he was about to discharge it at his intended victim."

"And you say Luke has since left the island?"

"Yes; but not on that account, though," replied Granger. "He was about stepping into a boat, in order to return to his ship, when the attempt was made, and, therefore, cannot be suspected of having run away in consequence of the brutal outcry that has been raised against him."

"Let people say what they please about Luke Somerton," answered the old sailor; "there's no one that can accuse him of being a coward. I was as much against him as any one a little while ago, but the daughter's anxiety to save his life, and her noble conduct in braving every danger to procure a pardon for him, has completely altered my feelings towards him. Besides, I never heard of his doing any harm to these people, and their wild outcry only shows that they have less of human nature about them than brutal ferocity. However, Mr. Roden has gone the entire length of his tether now, and when he's sent abroad, he'll have time to reflect on the evil deeds he has committed."

Further conversation between them was here interrupted by the sound of voices behind them, and Sir Charles Radcliffe having taken leave of the person with whom he was in conversation, beckoned for Lieutenant Granger to enter the room in which he usually transacted business.

"So, the fugitive has been taken?" he exclaimed, as soon as the young man was seated; "Roden is once more in our custody, and it shall be no fault of mine if ever he contrives again to evade our vigilance."

"He is," replied the lieutenant; "but the violence of these people is not yet quelled, though, for a time, they may not openly demonstrate their evil passions. They will all look upon this Harry Roden as a martyr to their cause, and I am afraid we shall yet see them attempting to wreak their vengeance upon the innocent daughter of the man against whom they have formed this prejudice."

"Then Louisa Somerton has not accompanied her father on board ship?" exclaimed the former.

"No," answered Granger; "she would have done so, I believed, but Luke himself was opposed to the step, and she has consented to remain here till he quits his profession, which I believe will be at the close of the present war."

"Poor fellow!" exclaimed Sir Charles; "his

has been a most unfortunate career, indeed. Born to high rank and wealth, he has been deprived of both by the treachery of supposed friends, and has since languished under wrongs which have been too heavy for endurance."

"You believe him innocent, then, of the crime for which he had so nearly suffered?" cried Lieutenant Granger.

"I have no right to think otherwise, since it has been the pleasure of our gracious queen to extend her royal mercy to him," answered the governor. "She must have placed implicit reliance upon the story told her by Louisa Somerton, or the sentence would never have been reversed. In truth, I was heartily glad when the pardon arrived; for the fate of the unfortunate man had filled me with grief, though I was bound, by virtue of my office, to see it carried into full effect."

"Depend upon it, Sir Charles, that man will soon regain the station he has lost," exclaimed the lieutenant. "He has more than the common share of bravery, and having resolved henceforth to devote all his services to the honour of his queen and country, we may hope ere long to see him restored to the good opinion of his fellow men. At all events, he will lose no opportunity of doing so, and there are yet persons who will gladly hail his return to society."

"But, in the meantime, what becomes of his daughter?"

"She will remain in the cottage that I placed at their disposal, after their own was burned down by the mob."

"And thus run the risk of a similar act of violence."

"I rather think that there is not much to fear from that now, Sir Charles," answered the lieutenant. "The fury of these people was directed against the father, and when it is known that he has left the island, they will cease to pursue her any further. At least, such is my hope, and if I should be mistaken, the consequences of their violence will fall heavily upon themselves."

"Have a care how you proceed in this matter," exclaimed Sir Charles Radcliffe. "I am armed with sufficient power to quell any outrage that may be committed in the island, and am prepared to put down these turbulent people, even if it should be at the cost of a few lives. Already has the queen's peace been broken, but if ever it is attempted again, I shall order out the military, and then heaven only knows where the mischief may stop."

"Then, with your permission, Sir Charles," exclaimed the young man, "I would suggest that a proclamation to that effect be issued. It would deter the timid or wavering; and even the boldest among them would pause ere they involved themselves in the destruction that must follow any further demonstration of their mad fury."

"Your advice, young sir," answered the governor, "is taken in such good part, that I shall not hesitate to follow it. The proclamation shall be issued with the least possible delay, and in the meantime I wish the rumour of my intention to be spread as widely as possible."

"Which can easily be done," returned Lieutenant Granger. "I have only to mention it to Caleb and one or two other persons, and it will soon spread from one end of the island to the other.

Ill news flies apace; and if this don't frighten them into peace and quietness, I know not what will."

"And what about Louisa Somerton?" demanded Sir Charles. "She must feel lonely in the cottage, now that her father has left the place; and I would fain offer her an asylum in this place till she can return to the protection of her father. As I am an old man, Lieutenant Granger," he added, smiling, "there can be little scandal from such an arrangement."

"I believe your well-intended kindness will not be accepted," answered the other. "She has no fears for herself, and will remain where she is till Luke Somerton has fixed upon some abode where they may together pass the remainder of their days in that peace which they have not been able to find here."

"But, surely, she will not object to the offer of a home where she will be perfectly free from all interruption?"

"I believe her mind is made up on that point, Sir Charles."

"Nevertheless, you may as well see her about it," answered the governor; "and I need not say that it will be your duty to urge it as much as possible. The girl's heroic conduct lately has inspired me with a high esteem for her; and I should grieve to see any harm befal one whose heroism and filial love prompted her to an act that few females would have had the courage to perform."

"Yet she regards it only as the performance of a solemn duty," replied Granger, "and forbids any mention being made of it in the way of praise. Even her father has scarcely ever alluded to the subject, because he knows that the recollection of the circumstance fills her with a feeling of melancholy, that it is not easy to remove."

"There is one good likely to result from it," exclaimed Sir Charles, "and I trust my anticipations in that respect will not prove ill-founded. The queen has more than once spoken of the maiden who so earnestly sought the life of her father, and there is but one circumstance that prevents the entire restoration of Luke Somerton to the high station he formerly held in society."

"And that, I suppose," observed the other, "is the fact of his having fought against his country on a late occasion?"

"Exactly so," replied the governor. "There are people possessing high influence, who, in her presence, are continually branding him with the name of traitor; so that, if her majesty was ever so much inclined to forget the past, ungenerous foes are resolved not to let it escape her memory. Still, however, time may work wonders in his behalf; and as he is now going to retrieve his errors by siding with his own countrymen, it is to be hoped she will, before long, see the justice of restoring him to her royal favour."

"More particularly," observed Lieutenant Granger, "as his fault, great as it may have been, was undoubtedly provoked by the injustice he had received from his own countrymen. This, you will say, is no excuse for a man who takes up arms against his own native land, but it may be a palliation of the circumstance, that will henceforth lead to his entire restoration."

"He shall have whatever influence I myself

possess," exclaimed Sir Charles ; "and sometimes a few words, well applied, have a marvellous effect. I shall see the queen at the next levee, and if, in the meantime, Luke Somerton has done anything worthy of reward, I will present a petition to the throne in his favour."

"And that we shall soon hear of his being engaged in a gallant action against the enemies of England, I am quite certain," replied Lieutenant Granger. "He appears to be most anxious to retrieve his lost honour ; and as that can only be done by the execution of some daring exploit, he will never rest satisfied till he has made his valour talked about from one end of the country to the other. People will then forget his past transgressions, and even his worst personal foes will be obliged to yield to the popular cry that will be raised in his favour."

"My dear fellow," cried the governor, "your anticipations are great, and most heartily do I hope they may prove well founded. In truth, I have a notion that Luke Somerton will do his best to regain the ground he has lost in the estimation of his fellow-men, and time will show whether those expectations are to be realised or not. However, to return to our original subject, you will see Louisa with as little delay as possible, and deliver my message with respect to her immediate removal to the castle ?"

"I will go there immediately," he replied.

"And, of course," continued Sir Charles, "it is unnecessary to say that you must urge, to your utmost, her acceptance of my offer. Tell her of the danger she will run by remaining alone and unprotected, and, above all things, represent the agony that would afflict her father should aught happen to her during his absence from the island."

"All that I have said to her over and over again."

"Well," returned the governor, "and by frequent repetition she will at length see the necessity there is for accepting my offer. There can be no selfish motive attributed to me, for none, I believe, will do me the injustice to imagine that I am actuated by any dishonourable design. Nay, even you yourself, Lieutenant Granger, the professed lover of the girl, will, I should think, acknowledge that she ought not to hesitate to accept an offer that is in every way so advantageous to her."

"I do indeed acknowledge it, Sir Charles," answered the other ; "and so convinced am I of the importance of her taking the step you have proposed, that I shall urge the necessity of her compliance, by every means in my power."

"Yet you think it will be of no avail?"

"I am fearful it will not," answered Lieutenant Granger, "and the more particularly as, in the event of her coming to this place she would be frequently thrown in my way."

"A very curious reason, by-the-bye, for her refusal," exclaimed the governor. "You love the girl, and, if I have not been misinformed, she does not look upon you with any disfavour, yet, for some unaccountable cause or another, she must needs treat your advances as if they were made by some person that she could not love."

"In that respect she is less to blame than you seem to imagine," answered the other. "Louisa Somerton has candidly acknowledged that her heart can never be bestowed upon another, and it is only a pure sense of honour that has prompted the step she has taken in this affair."

"And that, too, in utter disregard of the pain she may inflict upon you by the refusal," observed Sir Charles.

"Nay," answered the other, "that is judging of her motives too harshly, for Louisa Somerton is sacrificing her own peace of mind to a strong sense of duty. She has not forgotten the accusation of murder brought against her father, and, therefore, refuses to bring dishonour upon me by what she calls a disgraceful alliance."

"A mere romantic notion, that ought to be driven out of her mind as quickly as possible," exclaimed Sir Charles. "The girl, I dare say, means all for the best; but in this instance her happiness, as well as your own, depends upon her coming to a different conclusion, and were I permitted to speak to her upon the subject, I should most plainly express my opinion as to the folly of sacrificing so much to a feeling of mistaken duty."

"I have myself tried to convince her of it, Sir Charles," replied the young man ; "but hitherto I have not been able to remove the impression she has received."

"Then I will take an early opportunity of speaking to her about it," exclaimed the governor. "You may, perhaps, think me rather meddling in this affair, Mr. Granger, but when I see so much at stake, I conceive it to be my duty to interfere for the advantage of both parties."

"But she may, perhaps, think you have been urged to interfere by something that I have said."

"And she will be right enough, too," answered Sir Charles, smiling at the alarm with which these last words were uttered. "The girl ought to know that you are inconsolable at the foolish determination she has expressed, and it shall be my task to point out to her the cruelty she is guilty of in suffering you to pine away your existence, when she has it in her own power to render you the happiest of mortals. I know the humour of womankind better than you do, Lieutenant Granger, and can assert that most of them want humouring as much as spoilt children do."

"But," answered the other, "you are mistaken in supposing that Louisa Somerton is to be judged of by the rest of her sex."

"Ah ! that's exactly the notion of all the lovers I ever came near," laughed the governor. "I never came near one yet that did not think his own mistress the most perfect being upon earth, and for this especial reason, that no one can see a fault in those they love. Perhaps I was once as great a fool myself, but, even admitting that to be a fact, I have a right to argue you into something like good sense."

"Perhaps you will tell me in what I have erred, Sir Charles."

"Why, in being too subservient a lover," he replied. "Women expect, and perhaps have a right to all the consideration and respect that men can pay them ; but then we ought to be governed by something like discretion, and not lead them to suppose that we are to be the victims of their caprice and folly."

"I have nothing to complain of in that respect,"

answered Lieutenant Granger, " for however I may feel inclined to regret the decision she has arrived at, I must allow her to have the same freedom of inclination that I claim for myself. She has not said that my love is not returned, but that she will never give her hand to one she regards till she can do so with honour and her own free approbation."

" Ah! I see!" exclaimed the governor; " there's that old story of her father and the trouble he got into, acting as a regular mar-peace, when, in point of fact, it ought to have nothing to do with the business. You have told her that you are willing to make her your wife in spite of all that has taken place, and surely that ought to be enough for a girl who does not wish to give unnecessary pain."

" Indeed, Sir Charles, you entirely mistake her."

" I hope I do," he replied ; " but, if that is the case, she will very soon come into my way of thinking with respect to this projected marriage. By the by, I suppose her father has no objection to the union, provided both the other parties are agreeable to it ?"

" He is scarcely less anxious that it should take place than I am myself," answered Lieutenant Granger.

" Then why the devil don't he insist upon her consenting ?"

" Because he well knows her motives," replied the other, " and cannot but respect feelings that are dictated by the most exalted notions of honour. Luke Somerton has, however, spoken his mind, on previous occasions, very freely, but where once a determination has been firmly made, it is not even the command of a parent that can effect any very material alteration."

" Then she has positively refused to obey his wishes ?"

" She has protested against his interference," answered the officer, " but has declared her intention to yield her own inclinations, if he refuses to accept the terms she has proposed."

" And pray," demanded Sir Charles Radcliffe, " what are the terms she has dictated to her father ?"

" They are not altogether unreasonable," answered the other ; " but, on the contrary, are such as he was at once disposed to yield to. In short, Sir Charles, the only request she made was, that some delay might be granted."

" Ha! she wants time, and by and by will evade the affair altogether."

" That will depend upon circumstances," replied Granger. " If her father is restored to the honourable position he once enjoyed, she has expressed her willingness to bestow her hand upon me ; but if, on the contrary, he remains under his present stigma, she is determined never to change her condition in life."

" Psha !" ejaculated the governor, impatiently, " the girl's head is crazed, surely. Did any one ever hear of such nonsense, that a woman should throw away her every chance of happiness in this life for no other reason than that her father happened to be under a cloud ?"

" Do you give her no credit for good intentions, sir ?"

" Good intentions, my dear fellow, are sometimes very mischievous things," exclaimed the baronet. " An immense deal of harm may be done by them, though the parties themselves may mean nothing but good. The present is a notable instance of the truth of my assertion ; for, had Louisa Somerton been less fastidious, she would ere now have rendered you one of the happiest, instead of one of the most miserable fellows under the sun. But women are headstrong creatures at times, and between ourselves, my boy, I rather think she'll repent of it now before she's much older."

" What makes you think so ?" demanded the lieutenant.

" Because, if she really loves either you or her father, she must regret the unhappiness she causes both."

" But having acted from a good impulse, she may think us to blame in this affair rather than herself."

" Well," exclaimed Sir Charles, " the truth is, I hardly know which is the greatest simpleton, you or the girl. She for refusing a good offer, or you for being put off, when it requires only a short seige to take the fortress. However, it's no use talking, I see ; so away with you, my boy—see the girl, and try if you can't make up for lost time. Gain some sort of confession from her, if you can ; but if that is impossible, you may, at all events, prevail upon her to take up her residence in this place."

" I will see what can be done, Sir Charles," replied the young man ; " but I rather think both attempts will prove equally hopeless. She asks only for time before she answers the first question you have proposed to me, and as for the second, I know she will refuse it, on the grounds that she apprehends no fears for her safety."

With this he took his leave of Sir Charles Radcliffe, of whose kind intentions, in spite of his bluntness, he was fully aware ; and, leaving the castle, took his way towards the more humble abode of our heroine.

In the meantime we must return to Louisa Somerton, who, full of grief for the departure of her father, sat herself down near the window to commence the perusal of the manuscript history of his life, with the contents of which the reader has already been made acquainted. She was deeply absorbed in the introductory passages, when a slight noise caused her to start, and turning round she thought she perceived the shadow of a man pass across the window. Somewhat alarmed, she rose to ascertain the cause of this ; but the examination proved fruitless, for though she looked round in every direction, there was not the slightest appearance of any person being near. By degrees the natural courage of her disposition returned, and believing that there was no reason whatever for the alarm she had experienced, she once more sat down, and taking up the manuscript from the table upon which she had thrown it, resumed the narrative at the point where it had been so abruptly broken off. She was thus engaged for some little time, when a sound similar to the former one again startled her, and turning hastily round, she perceived a man of ruffianly aspect, threatening her, with his clenched fist, through the open casement, near which she was seated. A low exclamation of terror burst from her lips as this apparition met her view, and sinking back into her chair, she remained for some few minutes incapable of moving from the place. At length, however, she was again roused by hearing steps in the apartment, and looking up, she perceived, to her infinite delight, that her visitor, on the present occasion, was Lieutenant Granger.

"What ails you to-night, Louisa?" he demanded, taking her trembling hands within his. "You have been alarmed—something more than usual has occurred to terrify you."

"I have indeed been frightened," she replied, "foolishly so, perhaps; and yet I could not resist the alarm, when I beheld those fearful eyes glaring revengefully upon me."

"Nay, be more composed, dearest Louisa," said her lover, soothingly; "you have seen some one whose presence forbodes evil, and I would fain know who it is, that I may pursue the villain to his lurking-place."

"No, no, no," exclaimed Louisa, wildly, "for mercy's sake do not follow the footsteps of that dreadful being."

"What dreadful being are you speaking of?" he demanded.

"I know not who it was," she replied; "but as I was just now reading, a noise at no great distance off startled me, and looking up, I perceived a ferocious-looking being standing at the window, and using gestures that but too well assured me of the malignancy of his purpose. As soon as I turned round he fled, and from that moment till your entrance into this house, I have been unconscious."

"And you have no idea who the man was, Louisa?"

"I have no recollection of ever having seen him before."

"Did he give utterance to any threats?" demanded Granger.

"A low, hoarse murmuring sound escaped his lips," she replied, "but the import of them I did not catch. That they were threats, however, there can be no doubt, from the gestures with which they were accompanied, and the only explanation I can give is, that he must be one of my father's enemies, who, knowing of his absence, would take the opportunity of sacrificing me to his feelings of vengeance."

"Then the message I am charged with by Sir Charles Radcliffe may not prove so vain a one as I imagined," replied the young man. "He has heard of your father's departure from the island, and apprehending that some imminent peril awaits you in this unprotected state, he has sent me to offer you an asylum beneath his roof."

"I have already said," answered Louisa, "that no consideration shall ever induce me to leave this cottage till I am summoned to join my father in another land."

"But such a resolution was uncalled for," exclaimed her lover, "and, therefore, I trust you will not consider it to be immutable. Remember, Louisa, the danger with which you are threatened in this unprotected state, and do not, I implore you, throw yourself in the way of people whose fiendish desire for vengeance is not yet gratified. They have sought your father's life, and will never rest until they have destroyed either him or you."

"Let it be my life, then, that is sacrificed," exclaimed Louisa, "for I am most willing to give it up on condition that my dear father is spared the further persecution of these savage people."

"But your death would not appease them," answered Lieutenant Granger. "They desire blood; but the shedding of yours, instead of satisfying them, will only make them the more anxious to take the life of your father."

"Then Heaven preserve us!" cried Louisa, shuddering; "for if they are resolved to perpetrate crime, it is beyond my power to prevent them. Had my life been sufficient, it should have been willingly given, so that, in my last moments, I could have known my father was safe."

"Am I, then, to tell Sir Charles Radcliffe that you reject the generous offer he has sent to you?"

"You will say that it is impossible for me to accept it," replied Louisa Somerton; "but, at the same time, I would have you convey to him the expression of a grateful heart for the favours he would bestow upon a stranger."

"Nay, not a stranger, Louisa," he replied, "for Sir Charles Radcliffe has seen you many times, and from the hour when you undertook the almost hopeless task of procuring your father's pardon, he has felt for you the most exalted friendship and esteem. It is, therefore, from motives of kindness that he has desired me to state his proposition, and it would appear almost ungrateful on your part to reject an offer made under such circumstances."

"I have already given an answer from which I shall never, on any consideration, depart," answered our heroine. "That I am ungrateful, Sir Charles Radcliffe cannot do me the injustice to believe, and it is my most earnest request that you will tell him I am actuated by far different motives. Say that I have made a vow not to leave this place till I am called upon to rejoin my father, and surely after that he will not urge me to take a step against which I have expressed so much repugnance."

"He will urge nothing for which there is any reasonable ground for opposition," replied Lieutenant Granger. "He is only apprehensive for your own sake, and most anxiously does he expect that you will answer in the affirmative."

"It is a pity," sighed our heroine, "that so much kindness should have been thrown away upon one who can scarcely be regarded as worthy of it. You will, however, be pleased to make the best excuse you can in my behalf, and he will then, perhaps, forget from that time the humble girl whose only desire is that she may remain unheeded and unremembered by both friends and foes."

"Then," exclaimed Lieutenant Granger, "having failed in one part of my mission, may I be permitted to urge a request that more immediately concerns myself?"

"In full reliance upon your honour, sir," she replied, "I can venture to say that, at least, I shall feel no anger at the request, whatever it may be."

"Why, then," he exclaimed, "it was to urge a suit that has already been denied. Nay, do not suffer a frown to cloud your brow, dearest Louisa, for if aught could, more than another, add to my unhappiness, it would be the giving you cause of offence. But I have loved you—long and tenderly loved you, Louisa, and would now urge you to become mine."

"I have already requested you not to speak to me again upon this subject, until circumstances render our union possible," interrupted Louisa Somerton. "I am, myself, unhappy enough even as it is, but it will add to the bitterness of my regret if I should know that my refusal will occasion you one moment's uneasiness."

"And yet how can I do otherwise than feel despair, when I see all my hopes of happiness destroyed at a blow?" demanded Lieutenant Granger. "We have known each other long, and I believed the affection was reciprocal, though now I am awakened from my dream to the dreadful consciousness that the treasure I have so long and anxiously sought can never be mine."

"Nay, I have never yet gone so far as to say that," replied Louisa Somerton. "I have requested you to think as little as possible of me at present, but at the same time I declared that the time might come when I could give you my hand with the free concurrence of my heart. That moment has not yet arrived, Lieutenant Granger, and yet you again urge me, as if the moment I fondly anticipated had already arrived."

"And if I have done so," he replied, "it was because I saw you surrounded with dangers on every side, and no other hope of avoiding them presented themselves to my mind. In the first place, however, I delivered the governor's message, offering you an asylum beneath his roof, and it was not till you refused, that I ventured once more to urge my own claim to your consideration."

"I am well aware of the generosity that has prompted you to this course," exclaimed Louisa; "but though, while confessing my own strong attachment towards yourself, I am compelled to decline the kindness you propose."

"May I inquire if it is for the same reason that you mentioned on the last occasion when this subject was alluded to?" demanded Lieutenant Granger.

"Precisely so," she replied. "I have resolved never to give my hand whilst the name of my father is stained with dishonour, and no earthly consideration will ever induce me to change that determination."

"But," answered her lover, "even Sir Charles Radcliffe has given me his unasked opinion that your father's dishonour has been removed by the free pardon that was vouchsafed at your request by Queen Anne. It was an act of grace tantamount to declaring him purged of the crime, and from that moment his daughter could have no reason to believe that she should carry disgrace into any family who might seek an alliance with her."

"Such may be the opinion of Sir Charles Radcliffe, and so may think many more besides himself," answered Louisa Somerton. "The argument is capable of being looked at in more lights than one, but my own impression is adverse to our union at present, and, therefore, do I again most earnestly entreat that this may be the last occasion on which the subject is spoken of, till you have heard that my father, by some act of extraordinary bravery, has redeemed the character which he once bore."

"But suppose, in the meantime, you should be exposed to danger through the violence of these people?" asked the young man. "They have already shown a revengeful feeling towards yourself as well as to your father, and there is but too much reason to fear that ere long you will be placed in imminent peril."

"The same providence," she replied, "which has hitherto protected me, will, I trust, continue to do so. Be that as it may, however, I am perfectly ready to die, should my enemies seek my life, though it must be confessed I felt no little terror just now when the ruffian presented himself at the window."

"And the probability is, that the villain intended to have murdered you had he not been disturbed by my approach," exclaimed Lieutenant Granger. "He could have been here for no other purpose, and, therefore, do I again most earnestly implore you to accept the offer made to you by Sir Charles Radcliffe, who has both the power and inclination to protect you against lawless violence."

"I am not quite so unprotected here as you appear to imagine," replied Louisa Somerton. "My father was well aware of the danger I was exposed to, and he left behind him two brace of pistols, well loaded and ready for immediate use, in case they should be needed."

"But should you have the courage to use them?"

"A Somerton never lacked courage when there was occasion to exercise it," she replied. "I have practised with loaded pistols before now, and can venture to assert that there are few persons whose aim and coolness in the moment of danger are better than my own. You smile at me, sir, and look incredulous, yet if you need convincing I can exhibit a proof of my prowess before you leave this house."

"Not upon myself I hope, Louisa?" he said, smiling.

"By no means," she replied, "for though I may appear to be somewhat stern towards Lieutenant Granger, I am the last in the world who would do him a mortal injury, whatever offence he might give me."

"So far I am indebted to your candour," he exclaimed, "though I should have been better pleased had you placed more reliance in me than upon those pistols."

"You think my boast somewhat too masculine?"

"I have not yet thought that," he replied; "but the truth is I had rather you gave me a right to guard you against those evils with which you are threatened. Sir Charles Radcliffe has been kind enough to say that he would countenance our union, and surely that circumstance alone would be sufficient to disarm the ill-nature of any one who might make remarks about it."

"It is my own conscience that I think of, more than of what people may say," answered Louisa. "I know enough of the world to be aware that if once a man brings disgrace upon himself, he is lost beyond all hope of redemption. This is a solemn fact, Lieutenant Granger, and were I to act directly in the face of it, I should deserve my own as well as the world's execration."

"Pardon me, dear Louisa," he exclaimed; "but believe me you take too serious a view of this matter. In what respect can you bring disgrace upon me?"

"Am I not the daughter of a felon?"

"You are the daughter of a man who was tried for a felony, but who ——"

"Escaped the penalty of the law when all hope seemed to be denied him," interrupted Louisa Somerton. "There is no disguising the fact whichever way you may put it, for my father was accused of a murder, he stood arraigned before the judges to answer his accusers, was found guilty, sentenced to die upon a scaffold, and would have met the ignominious doom but for the mercy of his gracious queen."

"Which," exclaimed Lieutenant Granger, "would never have been exercised but for the earnest application of the warm-hearted daughter of the convicted man. The queen heard the story, was struck with certain important truths, became convinced of the innocence of the accused, and granted him a free pardon. Thus the facts run, Louisa—the world has resounded with your praise, and yet you still persist in believing that people regard your father as a murderer."

"Perhaps I am wrong," she replied, "but, at all events, my motives are such as you have little cause to complain of. I am myself most unhappy in the fallen condition in which I find myself—the finger of scorn seems pointed towards me whithersoever I go, but Heaven save me from the injustice of ever dragging another into the same gulph in which I am involved."

"But there can be no shame where there is no disgrace."

"Is it no disgrace, then," she asked, "to have one's nearest and dearest relative tried as a common felon at the bar of a criminal court? Is it no disgrace that the world whisper of him certain things, the commission of which would exclude him from all honourable society?"

"You allude, I suppose, to the report of his having engaged in some smuggling transactions?"

"I do."

"Then in that case," he exclaimed, "how many are there who are equally culpable as himself? Smuggling, my dear Louisa, is an offence against the laws of the country, but the crime is not so serious a one as you seem to imagine. That it sometimes leads to acts of violence, I admit, but in the absence of such violence, the offence is much less than over-rigid people are apt to believe. However, be that as it may, your father has never been a professed smuggler, nor do I suppose he will ever again join in such expeditions."

"But people will look to the past," she replied; "however, I will speak no further upon this subject at present; you have been sent hither by the governor on a message, and I decline, though with many thanks, the kind offer he has made. I am content to remain where I am, and as for your own equally generous offer, Lieutenant Granger, I must also request you to wait a little longer till I have ascertained whether my father retrieves his honour by some action against the enemy worthy of record."

"Your father's honour is already retrieved," he replied; "for surely he who has received favour from the hands of his sovereign, need care but little for the envy of those who are in no respect superior to himself. Sir Charles Radcliffe is among the first to show this world how highly he esteems you, and yet you refuse to dwell beneath his roof, though, by so doing, there would be an end of that malevolent feeling which at present exists against you."

"My actions are actuated by the best motives," answered Louisa, "and, therefore, am I content to abide by the consequences, be they what they may. I am not, however, ungrateful for the courtesy shown me by the governor, and shall carry the remembrance of his kindness to me even to the grave."

"But I am fearful that the violence of these people has not yet reached its utmost height."

"I myself scarcely think it has," replied Louisa; "and yet I fear them not, for, as I said before, I am prepared to defend myself or perish in the attempt. You smile, Lieutenant Granger, and, perhaps, deem my words merely those of a girl who knows not the dangers she has to encounter. But my resolve has not been formed without careful consideration, and should an attack be made upon me beneath this roof, the ruffians will find that I am well prepared to receive them."

"Why, Louisa," exclaimed her lover, "you are, after all, the very wife for a soldier. Your spirit pleases me, and I should consider myself the happiest of mortals if you would only take my case into your merciful consideration."

"I will do so," replied Louisa, "but you must be content to wait my favourable answer with patience. It is probable that a few weeks will serve to show which way I ought to act, and surely that is not too long a time to ask you to wait the result of my deliberations."

"Were it years, instead of weeks," returned Lieutenant Granger, "I could wait your reply, if there was a certainty that after all you would not reject my offer. Remember, Louisa, my wish is backed by that of your father, who has said that nothing could afford him a higher gratification than to see you the wife of the man he calls his friend."

"All that I admit," she exclaimed, "but, at the same time, he has given me permission to act in this affair exactly according to my own inclination."

"Then your inclination is not favourable to me?"

"Nay, I have not said that," answered our heroine, "for, on the contrary, I have expressed myself with sufficient clearness, so as to convince you that my heart can never be given to another. All I ask is delay, and yet that single favour you are disposed to murmur at."

"You shall have no further cause to reproach me with being dissatisfied," exclaimed Granger; "for, since it is your wish, I will e'en wait till the time comes when you can give me a more decided answer. I shall, however, make one little reservation—you must not be offended, Louisa, if I now and then refresh your memory upon the subject."

To this proposition Louisa silently acquiesced,

and after a little more conversation upon general subjects, Lieutenant Granger took his leave, in order to be present at the examination of Harry Roden before the governor. Our heroine parted from him with regret, but her fortitude did not so far forsake her that she manifested even the slightest sorrow at the separation they were doomed to endure.

CHAPTER XLIV.

A bold and reckless villain—
One who committed crime, and gloried in't
As 'twere a deed deserving laud and praise
From all mankind.

The Pilgrims.

THERE was great joy, and no small degree of exultation in the castle, when it became generally rumoured about that Harry Roden had once more fallen under the strong arm of the law, and that this time he would stand a fair chance of meeting with his deserts. Indeed, the domestics had been in commotion among themselves ever since his escape, lest he should take it into his head to revenge his supposed grievances upon any of them, and few of them had ventured out of the place, since he had so unceremoniously left it, lest by any evil chance they might happen to fall in with him. It was, therefore, a subject of congratulation amongst them, when it became certain that he was no longer at large, and so rejoiced was Mr. Binley, the butler, that he condescended to invite Randal, the head gardener, into his room, in order that they might discuss the matter over a bottle of the governor's very choicest wines. The latter was, or affected to be, more than usually sagacious upon the occasion, and shaking his head at the butler's expressed opinion that all danger was now over, he, with a half suppressed groan, declared it as his opinion that neither stone walls, nor iron fetters, would keep the fellow a prisoner longer than he thought fit.

"Then, begging your pardon, Randal," said the butler, "you are a great fool for your pains. The fellow will be carefully guarded this time, so, if he gets out again, it must be with the assistance of a certain old gentleman down below."

"And that he has dealings with him I've no doubt," replied the other, "or he would most certainly have broken his neck the other night when he let himself down from the window. I've had the curiosity to go up and look at the place, and for a hundred guineas I wouldn't try the same feat even by the broad daylight."

"But having got off once there's the less chance of his doing so again," exclaimed Mr. Binley, who, like other great men, had a mighty high opinion of himself. "Now I can tell you a secret, friend Randal, that you could never have guessed if you had tried at it for a month; but the fact is, our governor sometimes condescends to make a confidant of me, and from his own lips I have heard—what do you think I've heard?"

"I can't think at all about it," answered the other, gruffly; "but I happen to know that you have a confounded habit of exciting people's curiosity, and then keeping them in suspense till you think proper to explain yourself."

"That's because I don't like all the pleasure to

come at once," replied Mr. Bayley. "However, as you are so impatient, I'll tell you what the governor said to me in confidence. He said, 'Binley, my boy, I'm afraid it's all over with me; I've got enemies at court, and they are trying to set the queen against me, because that scoundrel has contrived to break out of his prison.'"

"Did he speak it in that familiar way?"

"Neither more nor less than I tell you," replied the butler. "He's always uncommonly polite to me, but on this occasion he was more so than ever, because I suppose he wanted to have a little good advice from me. He praised me for my long and faithful services, and said there were only two persons in his employ; one, of course, was myself ——"

"And the other?"

"Was you."

"Then I wonder he's never told me so," exclaimed Randal, who was not inclined to believe above one half that he heard from the butler. "He hardly ever condescends so much as to look at me, and never speaks, unless it is to give me any new directions about his gardens."

"Ah!" returned Mr. Binley, "you don't know his ways quite so well as I do, my boy."

"May be not; but what has all this to do with Henry Roden, or his safe keeping in future?"

"A great deal," replied the butler; "Sir Charles has once very nearly lost his governorship, so he won't be likely to run such a chance again. The capture of this fellow will restore him once more to the queen's favour, and even if Roden was, as you say, assisted by the devil, he'd be puzzled to find his way out of the castle, till his time come to be either hanged or transported. So I think we may consider ourselves pretty safe at last, and it was in the joy of my heart that I invited you to come in and partake a bottle of wine with me."

"At our master's expense, eh?"

"Why, who has so much reason to rejoice as himself?" demanded Binley. "Don't he get out of a confounded scrape, and isn't it our duty, as faithful servants, to rejoice at the good fortune of their master? and how, let me ask, can we show our gratitude so well, as by drinking his health over a bottle of the best wine his cellar affords?"

"True," exclaimed the gardener, pouring out for himself another glass of wine; "I like to show my gratitude, and certainly this is the most pleasant way of doing it that I ever tried. But how about the prisoner, Mr. Binley, have they got him safely in his cell yet?"

"No; he's in the guard-room, with about a dozen soldiers. The governor has ordered him to be strictly guarded, and presently he will have him called into his room for examination on this new charge."

"What, for attempting to murder Luke Somerton?"

"Yes; and if that don't hang, or send him out of the country for the rest of his life, I'm a Dutchman."

"But I've heard he didn't draw so much as a drop of blood."

"And you heard very rightly," said Mr. Binley; "but what of that?—he intended to do more—he meant to kill the man, and the law can punish the scoundrel for it, just as much as if he had accomplished the crime."

"And where is Luke Somerton?"

"Gone on board his ship."

"Then there's an end of the business," said the gardener, with a look of self complacency, "for if he goes away the principal witness against him will be absent when he's wanted."

"Very true," replied Mr. Binley; "but are there no other charges against him? Isn't he an escaped convict, and can't he be transported for life? which, I take it, will be quite sufficient protection for you and I."

"Was he very violent when they took him?" asked Randal.

"Uncommonly."

"Did he hurt anybody?"

"He tried very hard to do so," replied Binley; "but there were too many for that, so at last he was obliged to cry quarter and submit himself to his fate. He had fallen into wrong hands, you know, when he had to deal with Lieutenant Granger, for the young man has a sort of sneaking kindness for Louisa Somerton, and of course he would resent any attack upon the man he wants to make his father-in-law."

"It signifies very little what he wants to do," retorted the other; "for it seems the girl has made up her mind not to have him, and so, if he's of my way of thinking, he'll be for looking after somebody else."

"But suppose he can't fancy another so well as he does her?"

"Psha! love wears out in time, like everything else," replied Randal; "she's a pretty girl, and a very good one, I believe, in the bargain; but the world contains many others of the same sort, and I should think Lieutenant Granger, who is a handsome young fellow enough, will not be long before he's suited."

"The truth of it is, old boy, you never happened to be in love—at least, I heard you say as much,—and so of course you can know nothing about the tender passion." Here Mr. Brinley heaved a deep sigh, and in a few seconds afterwards proceeded:—I have been in love, friend Randal, and, as an experienced man in such matters, can solemnly declare that no man can feel the tender passion so strongly the second time as he does the first. I once made up my mind to be married—the happy day was named—the ring bought, and, dressed in all my wedding finery, I stood an expectant bridegroom at the altar. But, alas! the fickleness of woman was to be that day proved to me. I waited in vain—the lady jilted me,—and instead of making me her husband, she eloped the night before with a journeyman baker."

"Then," observed Mr. Randal, "you ought to have thanked your lucky stars that you have got rid of a bad bargain."

"Why, so I do now," answered the butler, "for I have since heard that she turned out such a complete virago, that her unhappy husband was glad to jump into the water to escape her eternal abuse. But at first I thought it very hard, and in a rash moment I made a vow never to pay my addresses to another woman."

"A *rash* vow do you call it?" exclaimed the other. "Now, I think it was about the best thing you could do, for having been jilted by one woman, you would have been a fool to try another experiment. Excuse my freedom, Mr. Binley, but I always speak my mind, and more particularly when I've been taking a glass or two of wine, which happens to be the case on the present occasion."

"But all women are not bad alike?" said the butler.

"It would be a pity if they were," answered Randal; "but marriage is a sort of lottery, in which there are a great many more blanks than prizes. The chances are that you may get hold of a shrew; and when that is the case, away goes a man's happiness for ever. Now, Louisa Somerton may be a very good sort of girl, but if she won't have the lieutenant after he's asked her, I should advise him to think it's all for the best."

"But it seems," said Mr. Binley, "that she likes him well enough, only she won't have him at present."

"Then he should have his revenge."

"How so?"

"By letting her live a few years longer in single blessedness, and, when she becomes an old maid, nobody will have her. That's fair revenge, isn't it?"

"I don't know about that," replied Binley, "for as he is really fond of the girl, I've a notion he would suffer quite as much pain and disappointment as herself. However, to end this argument, there goes the governor's bell, so I suppose he wants some of us to be present at the examination of the prisoner."

Taking another glass of wine, he appointed to meet his companion in the evening; he left the room, and proceeded to the Hall, which he found thronged with a number of persons, who were anxious to hear the proceedings that were going on. Sir Charles Radcliffe was seated at one end of the table, and the secretary was by his side with writing materials before him, ready to take down the evidence that was about to be offered against the prisoner. Harry Roden had not yet made his appearance; but, in a few moments afterwards, a bustle was heard outside the door, and presently he strode in, casting around him a sullen look that seemed to bid defiance to all who were present. At length, being placed at the end of the table, so as directly to face Sir Charles Radcliffe, the business of the day commenced.

"Prisoner," exclaimed the governor, "there are circumstances in this case which might have rendered it unnecessary to pursue any further inquiry, for you are an escaped convict, and therefore liable to the punishment to which you have been already sentenced. But you are charged with a fresh crime of great magnitude, and it is therefore my duty to hear whatever evidence may be brought against you."

"It was my own fault, or you would never have had the chance," replied the prisoner, doggedly. "My arm had lost its usual strength, or in spite of the numbers that were against me I should have escaped, and that, too, not without leaving marks behind me to prove that it is a dangerous thing to have to do with a desperate man."

"You are hardened in iniquity, I know," exclaimed the governor; "but I will yet warn you

against carrying off this affair with so much bravado. It would be well for you to show repentance for the past; for by that alone can you hope for any remission of your punishment."

"I ask for neither favour nor mercy," replied the criminal. "You have now got me in your power, and all I ask is, that you will deal with me exactly as I would have done with Luke Somerton. I would have slain him; send me to the gibbet if you please, and then we may cry quits. But I don't see the principal witnesses here, and without them I know not how you can proceed against me with this charge. May I ask your excellency who is the prosecutor in this case?"

"Luke Somerton."

"And he is not here!" said Roden in a tone of taunting exultation. "He has no doubt set sail by this time, and so you can only deal with me upon the old charge."

"There you are mistaken," replied Sir Charles Radcliffe, "for we have a sufficient number of witnesses who saw the attempt made upon the life of Luke Somerton, and upon their evidence I can commit you for trial. In a short time he is expected to return, and then these proceedings can go on."

"Who is your principal witness?"

"Lieutenant Granger."

"And he is not here."

"He will arrive shortly," answered the governor, "and in the meantime we can proceed with the examination of the other persons. You seem to treat this affair very lightly, but it may prove more serious than you at present seem to think for."

"I'm not to be frightened by anything that you can either say or do," replied the prisoner. "I know exactly the situation in which I'm placed, and can boldly defy you to do your worst. I've got plenty of enemies here, no doubt, but if I was at liberty, there isn't one of 'em that would dare stand up and face me."

"This bold insolence of bearing will not serve you," exclaimed Sir Charles, vainly endeavouring to make an impression upon the mind of the prisoner. "You have long been the terror of this island—have set the law at open defiance, and it is high time that an example should be made, in order to deter others from following in your footsteps. There are several, besides yourself, who have, on frequent occasions, broken the queen's peace; but I am armed with power by my sovereign, and will yet teach these misguided people that their outrageous conduct will not be permitted with impunity."

"I see how it is," muttered Roden; "there's some that may commit any crime without fear of punishment, while others may not look nor speak without being hanged or transported. If you'd ask what I mean by it, I say, look at Luke Somerton, —a man that was tried and convicted for as cruel a murder as ever was committed; yet he gets clear off, and that, too, because the queen chooses to listen to the prayers of an artful girl."

"She of whom you speak," replied Sir Charles Radcliffe, "proved herself to be anything but artful. It was through her possessing the very reverse qualities that procured for her the sympathy and kindness of the queen, who, upon further inquiry into the case, granted a free and unconditional pardon to the unfortunate man who was lying under sentence of death."

"But he was convicted upon as good evidence as you afterwards had against me," exclaimed Roden ; "and yet murder can be excused, though for a little bit of a riot I must needs be sentenced to transportation. It is true that through the carelessness of your guards I was able to make my escape, but it is my own fault that I remained long enough in the island to fall into your hands again. However, I was determined to have my revenge upon Luke Somerton, and if I had only succeeded in that, it isn't even the gallows itself that would have made me sorry for what I had done."

"Has he ever injured you, that you entertain this bitter animosity against him?" asked the governor.

"Why, I can't say that he ever did me any harm," replied the fellow ; "but that was, perhaps, because he never had an opportunity. But I like to see justice dealt alike to all people, and if he had had his deserts, I should not at this moment have been standing here to answer for what I've done."

"It was the queen who thought proper to pardon him," answered Sir Charles ; "and you may be assured she would not have done so but upon certain evidence that her mercy was properly and wisely bestowed."

"And what does her majesty know about the case?" demanded Roden. "She has had no chance of making any inquiries that would bring the truth before her, and so she must needs take the word of a blubbering girl that throws herself upon her knees before her in the streets of Whitehaven? It was that that made my blood boil, because I knew well enough that a favour of the same kind would not have been granted to myself."

"How can you affirm that which has never been tried?" demanded Sir Charles Radcliffe, with impatience.

"Because I know it to be the truth," answered the culprit. "If you doubt my word, let some one go and ask her to pardon me, as she did Luke Somerton. Let 'em try it, I say, and you'll find that they would come back with a very different story to the one that was told by the girl I'm speaking of."

"Then it would be because your innocence was not satisfactorily made apparent," replied the governor. "In Luke Somerton's case there was no direct proof of his guilt, though circumstances certainly inferred it. But instances have been known where juries have come to wrong conclusions, and, therefore, her majesty acted with merciful discretion in saving him from an ignominious fate that there is every reason to believe he did not deserve. However," he continued, as the door was suddenly thrown open, "Lieutenant Granger is now present, and we can, therefore, go on with the examination."

"Am I to be judged by his evidence?" demanded the prisoner.

"You will hear what he has to say," exclaimed Sir Charles ; "and rest assured your case will meet with all the consideration it merits. If he fails to establish the fact of your having made an attempt upon the life of a fellow creature, your punishment will be so much the less, as transpor-

tation for a shorter term will satisfy the ends of justice."

"He will be sure to swear anything against me," exclaimed Roden, with a vindictive scowl at the young officer.

"Let Lieutenant Granger be sworn," said Sir Charles, and when that ceremony had been gone through, and the witness had taken his station at the table, the governor, addressing himself to him, said,—

"Do you know the prisoner who stands before you?"

"I do," was the prompt reply.

"What is the charge you have to make against him?"

"That of attempting the life of Luke Somerton."

"What weapon did he use?"

"A loaded pistol," replied Granger. "It was levelled at him, and there is little doubt would have taken deadly effect, but that I rushed forward and prevented the murderous design. The weapon was consequently discharged in the air, and the intended victim escaped."

"Have you any means of knowing whether the pistol had been charged with bullets?"

"I can swear most positively to that fact," replied Lieutenant Granger ; "for the weapon was afterwards carefully examined by myself, and, from my own experience in such matters, I can declare that a bullet had just before been discharged through the barrel."

"Are you aware," asked the governor, "of any hostile feeling on the part of the prisoner towards the person who was placed in this danger? Was there, in short, any old grudge subsisting in the mind of the accused against the man whose life he is charged with having attempted?"

"There can be little doubt about that, I believe," replied the witness ; "for it was not many days before that he headed a riotous multitude, who attacked the cottage of Luke Somerton, and burnt it to the ground. Nay, so determined were they upon the fulfilment of their murderous design, that they surrounded the burning house, for the express purpose of preventing the escape of the inmates."

"And I believe," said Sir Charles, "they were only saved through your fortunate intervention at the moment when all hope of succour appeared to be at an end."

"I was happily the means of rescuing them," answered Lieutenant Granger, with diffidence.

"Really, Sir Charles," exclaimed Roden, who had sufficient tact to conduct his own case with some little adroitness, "I don't see what all this has got to do with the case. You are not examining the witness now about what took place some little time ago, for the truth is, I have been tried and convicted upon the charge already, and if you have anything at all to do, it is to prove whether I attempted the life of Luke Somerton."

"The examination is perfectly correct," answered Sir Charles Radcliffe ; "and whilst the purposes of justice require it, I shall make no alteration in the course I am at present pursuing. My object is to ascertain whether you bear an ill feeling towards the party you are accused of attempting to assassinate, and, if we succeed in fully establishing that fact, the case will be so much the more clear for a jury to decide upon. You will, therefore, proceed, Lieutenant Granger, to narrate any circumstances that may appear to bear upon the point."

"There are several other instances that I could mention," answered the witness, "all of which go to prove that there was a decided hostility on the part of the prisoner towards Luke Somerton. Nay, even his unoffending daughter was included in the savage act of revenge that was meditated; and even within the last few hours, since her father has left the island, a villain was seen lurking close to the cottage, with the evident intention of watching for an opportunity to assassinate her."

"Do you know who the fellow was?"

"I cannot speak positively upon that point," replied the young man, "but from the glimpse Louisa Somerton obtained of him, she is able to state most certainly that he was one of the persons who accompanied Roden when the attack upon her father's cottage was made."

"The fellow must have been a fool and a coward to boot," exclaimed the prisoner, "or he would have made sure work of it, so as to prevent the possibility of her appearing against him at some future time. Had I been there, the end of it should have been different."

"Do you dare boast of your villanous purposes?" cried Sir Charles, astounded by the boldness with which this declaration was made.

"I am not afraid of speaking my mind," he replied, "even if you hang me for it afterwards."

"What injury has the poor girl ever done you?"

"What injury? Why, is it not through her that I am now standing here a culprit before you?"

"In what way has she been instrumental in rendering you the unfortunate object I now gaze upon with horror?"

"Why," replied Roden, "it was all through her that Luke Somerton was saved from the gibbet, at the very moment when he ought to have been turned off. I swore to be revenged for it, and I would, too, before now, if it hadn't been for the meddling fool that now stands yonder as a witness against me."

"You ought, rather, to feel grateful that you have been spared the perpetration of so foul a crime," exclaimed the governor. "The girl, convinced as she was of her father's innocence, performed but an act of duty in exerting herself for the preservation of his life; and yet there are fiends in human form who would revenge themselves upon her for an act which nearly all the world must regard with admiration."

"But we are not all obliged to think alike," answered the prisoner. "You and the lieutenant here, may have reasons for praising her conduct, but I can only curse her for it, and that, too, the more heartily because I happen to know that it is through her I have been brought to this pass. As for the fellow that it seems has been seen watching about the house, I could serve him as I would have done Luke Somerton, if I was only permitted to have my liberty for about a couple of hours."

"Which I will take care shall not be case," exclaimed Sir Charles Radcliffe. "Your threats are sufficiently convincing to prove the necessity for keeping a strict watch to prevent the possibility of a second escape; and as there appear to be no signs of contrition on your part, I cannot recommend any remission of the sentence which has already been passed upon you. What additional punishment a second conviction may entail upon you I cannot say, but whatever it may be, the fault will rest entirely upon yourself."

"And for all this I have to thank Lieutenant Granger."

"You have rather to blame the perversity of your own disposition," answered Sir Charles. "By your own good fortune, or, rather, through the carelessness of the people who were set to keep watch, you contrived to escape from prison, and might easily have left the island without hindrance. You would, however, remain, in order to satiate your revenge upon Luke Somerton, and the consequence has been that you stand in your present perilous situation."

"Which I only regret because I have been defeated," cried Roden, fiercely. "Somerton deserved hanging as much as any man ever did, and as the executioner was spared his trouble, I thought the duty belonged to myself, and I would have carried it into effect, too, but for the interference of a meddling fool that has thwarted me in more instances than one. But don't let him make himself too safe because I happen to be no longer able to raise my arm against him, for there's people in this island that will revenge the fall of a comrade, and Lieutenant Granger will find that out to his cost before he is many days older."

"These threats only render your own case worse," said the governor, "because they prove the necessity of removing you from a spot where you meditate such mischief."

"Remove me as soon as you please," exclaimed the ruffian. "Send me away to a foreign country —banish me for the rest of my life, and then see how much better you will be for it. Why, there's plenty to do the work I've cut out for 'em, and it ain't because I'm punished that they are to be frightened out of what they mean to do. Lieutenant Granger, I believe, professes to be desperately in love with Louisa Somerton, but all his care and all his watchfulness will not save her life, now that she has been marked out for a victim. She'll fall, and then you'll see how this young officer will repent the moment when he took part against me."

"He has only performed a duty," cried Sir Charles Radcliffe, "and, having done so, I will take care that his life shall not be hazarded by your lawless ruffians."

"Then the task of punishing him shall fall upon myself," exclaimed Harry Roden, and drawing from his pocket a large clasp knife, which had been secretly handed to him by a confederate in the room, he rushed towards Lieutenant Granger, and would have buried it to the hilt in his bosom, but for the interposition of the persons who stood close by. In an instant the ruffian was seized upon by three or four men, and having been securely bound, he was placed in the spot from whence he had escaped.

"Villain!" exclaimed the governor, "this audacity exceeds all bounds of belief. I had ordered that your limbs should be left at freedom, and yet this is the return for that which I meant as an act of kindness. But you have now forfeited all claims to consideration, and from this time you will remain securely bound to prevent a repetition of this violence."

"Do with me as you please, since I am to be thwarted at every turn," muttered the wretched man. "I have been foiled, and it may be that I shall never have another opportunity of taking revenge into my own hands ; yet, for all that, I feel some little satisfaction that what has been left undone by myself, will be performed by others. Lieutenant Granger has had a lucky escape, but his triumph will not be a very long one."

"Let those who meditate the crime take example by your own fate," returned Sir Charles. "That there may be people in the island almost as wicked as yourself, I can believe, but the same power which has saved him from your violence will, I trust, still preserve him in the hour of danger. You have now placed yourself beyond all hope of mercy, and banishing pity from my mind, I shall henceforth look only to the means by which any further mischief may be frustrated. A solitary cell will be your place of confinement till the day of trial comes, and then, should a conviction take place, you will leave this country never to return to it."

"It will not cause me much grief to leave this island," answered Roden, "though I would rather have done something that would have sent me to the gallows at once. It is an easy way for a man to get out of his troubles, and for that reason I suppose you will take care that I shall live in misery?"

"Your crimes deserve no better fate," answered the governor. "Several heinous offences were already laid to your charge, and now you have added to them by an attempt that had very nearly been consummated. And for what reason did you attempt the life of Lieutenant Granger? Was it because he came here to give testimony respecting your former outrages?"

"I am not obliged to answer your questions," exclaimed Roden ; "but, to speak the truth, I owe a grudge to yonder officer that nothing but his death could have satisfied. I once had a notion that Louisa Somerton might, with a little persuasion, have become my wife—perhaps I presumed too far, but such was my hope, and I indulged in it up to the moment when she was first known to Lieutenant Granger."

"Did she ever afford you the slightest encouragement?"

"I can't go so far as to say she ever did that," replied the culprit ; "but it seemed there was a fair chance for me, and that chance was destroyed as soon as ever a rival came and stood between us."

"Her's has, indeed, been a most fortunate escape," said Sir Charles Radcliffe ; "we have had ample proof of the wickedness and natural depravity of your heart, and had it been your fate to have been united, I shudder to think of the endless misery she must have endured."

"Not so much misery as you seem to imagine," retorted Roden. "I should not have been the wretch you now see me, had she been my wife; so whatever sin I may have committed can be safely laid at her door."

"And so, because you were disappointed in an ill-placed affection, you must needs become a villain and a stabber!"

"I do not say it as an excuse," returned the prisoner, folding his arms and assuming a look of yet greater indifference, "but to let the world know who is most to blame in all that has occurred. It is at least some satisfaction to me that I can inflict pain upon those that have caused my ruin, for both Louisa and her lover must henceforth feel that they have been the means of making me what I am."

"Wretched man!" exclaimed the governor; "even there your venom will prove less mischievous than you intended. There is no reason for them to reproach themselves with the crimes you have so wantonly committed, for it is the natural depravity of your heart that has led to this result, and not the mere disappointment, of which you have no right to complain."

"Was I then to endure my misery in silence?" he asked.

"The misery was of your own bringing on," replied Sir Charles Radcliffe, "and, therefore, these young people have no occasion to bestow a moment's uneasiness upon the subject. Louisa Somerton had at least as much right as yourself to a free choice in the matter—she exercised that privilege in rejecting an offer and accepting another, yet you would deny her the same right that you have claimed for yourself. In short, time has proved that she exercised a wise discretion in the matter, for had she yielded to your proposition, it is certain she would have sealed her own unhappiness."

"I didn't expect to hear anything else come out of your lips," muttered the criminal; "of course you'll take their part against me, because they happen to be favourites, and I am unfortunate. But, say you as you please, Sir Charles, they must feel that I have been driven to desperation by their own conduct, and they will suffer many an hour of reproach for having made me what I am. There is a satisfaction for me in all this, and you shall not deprive me of the pleasure I feel by any preachment you may make."

"My motive," replied the governor, "is not to deprive you of any gratification, but to place the matter before you in its true light. You glory in the malevolent thought of having made a declaration calculated to inspire them with feelings of self-reproach, and it therefore becomes my duty to show that whatever your crimes may have been, they had nothing to do in causing them. I take the sting from your words in order that they may not give ear to a charge that has not the slightest foundation in truth."

"Perhaps you think that I never loved the girl?" said Roden.

"I neither know nor care whether you have," replied the governor; "since it is sufficient for my purpose to reflect that Louisa Somerton had as much right as anybody else to refuse or accept the offer. She had, perhaps, seen or heard of your violent conduct on previous occasions; and, if so, she is to be commended for not having risked her future happiness by so ill-judged an alliance."

"All this will not convince me that I do not leave the poison to rankle in the wound I have made," replied Roden. "I know they must both often think with bitterness of the charge I have brought against them, and the certainty of that will serve to cheer many an hour when I am dragging on the life of misery you have doomed me to. Lieutenant Granger," he added, turning towards the young officer, "may my eternal curses light upon and slowly consume your future life—may you lose the respect of friends as I have done, and die unnoticed, unregretted, like a dog."

"These bitter wishes happily have not the power to harm him, though it is your fiendish wish to inflict upon him the misery of a reproving conscience," exclaimed the governor. "He has had nothing to do with causing the evil actions you have been guilty of; but, on the contrary, will have the consolation of knowing that, through his means, a most atrocious criminal has been punished."

"Ay, that's always the way when a man gets into trouble," returned the ruffian. "Give him a bad name, and you may as well hang him at once, for the world will never look upon him with kindness, let him deserve it ever so much. Louisa Somerton and her favoured lover have driven me to what I am, and all that you and the whole world put together can say, can never take from 'em that comfortable reflection. For my own part, I know the worst that can happen to me, and that's my consolation. You may send me over the water, and make a slave of me for the rest of my days, but no one shall ever see that I feel my punishment, however hard it may be."

"You are little aware of the excessive hardships you will have to undergo when you leave this country for another," exclaimed Sir Charles Radcliffe. "In the penal settlements our convicts endure a life of misery such as no conception can picture to those who have passed their days in this happy country. Men there, whatever may have been their former situations, lose all their rights of citizenship, and become the slaves of those who are seldom inclined to treat them with the slightest kindness. Their days are passed in toil that is measured to the extreme of human endurance, and their nights, instead of being soothed in refreshing slumbers, are occupied with thoughts that are more harassing than the labour they have to go through. Most of them, hardened as they may be, have left behind them friends whom they have loved, but whom they are doomed never more to behold, and that reflection alone is enough to drive them to the very verge of despair."

"At any rate, I shall not leave any one behind me that I care a rush for," answered Roden, in a tone of indifference. "Since I was scorned by Louisa Somerton, I have lived without loving or being loved, so that one part of the world is the same to me as another. And as to the toil you speak of, I have been used to labour hard enough here for a scanty bit of bread, and the change I meet with over the water, will be scarcely felt, or, at least, no one shall ever hear me make any complaint about it."

"You are over bold now," said Sir Charles, "because you have never had experience in the sort of life it will be your destiny henceforth to lead. A short time, however, will effect a wondrous change, and though you may not be induced to acknowledge your repentance, I feel well assured that you will heartily regret the violence that has brought you to so terrible a punishment."

"When I grow tired of it," exclaimed Roden, "I can do as others have done before me, make away with myself, and so put an end to my miseries at once."

"Not so," answered the governor, "for suicides from despair were at one time so frequent that a strict watch is now kept to prevent desperate men from rushing unbidden into the presence of their Maker. Even the attempt at self-destruction is subjected to a severe punishment, and those who are guilty of it are sentenced to an additional share of labour, besides being deprived of their chance, which good conduct affords, of a remission of their doom. But the opportunity which you speak of will not be afforded, so depend not upon it, lest you be deceived."

"I can starve myself to death, I suppose, if I choose?"

"That would be regarded as a heinous offence by those in authority there, and the lash would be unsparingly used to bring you to repentance."

"Let 'em try it, that's all," exclaimed Roden. "Death I could endure, but if ever a stripe should be laid upon my back, it should be revenged in the blood of him that gave the blow—ay, and of him too that ordered it, if my arm could but reach him."

"Enough of this," said Sir Charles Radcliffe, who perceived that neither argument nor persuasion had any good effect upon the hardened criminal before him. "You will now be conveyed back to your solitary cell, there to await the decision of the queen's secretary of state, as to what shall be done with you. It may appear to him sufficient to punish you for the offence of which you have been already convicted; and if so, there will be no necessity to keep you in this country till the return of Luke Somerton. Let him be conveyed away," he added to the gaoler and his assistants; "and remember, should he be suffered to escape again, the punishment will fall most heavily upon yourselves."

These orders were immediately complied with, and as soon as he had been removed, Sir Charles, accompanied by Lieutenant Granger, retired to another apartment, and the hall, which had been so closely thronged, was quickly cleared of its inquisitive spectators.

That evening, according to previous appointment, Mr. Binley and his friend Randal met together in the snug room belonging to the former, where, over another bottle of wine, they discussed the events of the day.

"Did you ever hear of such a scoundrel as that Harry Roden?" asked the latter. "Why, the fellow talked to Sir Charles as if he had been his equal; and, as for the punishment he is going to receive, I verily believe he cares less about it than I do for this glass of wine."

"Sir Charles was wrong to lecture a fellow that wasn't likely to profit by his good advice," replied the other, after lighting his pipe, and giving three or four whiffs that filled the room with a dense smoke. "If I'd been in his place I should have contented myself with asking a few questions, and then packed him off to his cell, where he'll have plenty of time to repent what he's done."

"And after all," observed Binley, "I don't think they'll give him a bit more punishment for his attempt against the life of Luke Somerton. To be sure, he was sentenced to transportation for life, and that's no joke, though people are apt to make rather light of it."

"But if they don't look sharp he'll escape after he gets over there," returned the other. "He's the sort of chap that would run any risk rather than be deprived of his liberty; and, if he should get into the bush, they'll have a customer to deal with that will give 'em a good deal of trouble. They ought to hang him at once, and then there'd be an end of him."

"Very true," replied the butler, with a knowing nod; "but as he didn't murder the man, I don't see how they could hang him."

"For the attempt, to be sure," said Randal; "didn't he present a loaded pistol at Luke Somerton, and wouldn't he have killed him if it hadn't been for Lieutenant Granger, who knocked the weapon out of his hand?"

"Well, I dare say he would," answered Mr. Binley; "though for the life of me I can't see why he has taken such a hatred to the man. Somerton was lucky enough to obtain a pardon, and because he wasn't hanged, the whole riff-raff of the island must rise up in arms."

"That's because they believed him to be guilty of having murdered Captain Aylmer."

"Psha! what does it matter what they believe?" demanded the latter. "The governor don't think anything of the sort, that's very clear; no more does Lieutenant Granger, and if the respectable inhabitants of the place are inclined to think the evidence was not sufficiently clear against him, I don't see what a parcel of ignorant folks have to do with it. And yet, there they are, howling like so many wolves that have been disappointed of prey."

"Well, it's nothing to me, certainly," exclaimed the gardener, "but there's a good many queer stories told about this Luke Somerton, and, among other things, people say he has been a good deal engaged in smuggling between the French coast and this country."

"Suppose he has," retorted Binley, "is he worse for it than a good many other people that hold their heads higher in the world than he does? Besides, by all accounts, he's left that off to fight honourably in the cause of his queen and country, so that he may soon wipe away any stain that might be upon his character. Sir Charles Radcliffe, too, is not ashamed to own him as a friend, so I don't see what other people have got to talk about."

"Fiddle-de-dee!" ejaculated Randal; "how can you stop people's mouths when they've a mind to go preaching among their neighbours? The truth is, Luke's got a bad name in this place, and, perhaps, the wisest thing he could have done was to leave the island."

"And I suppose the people here will be fools enough to think he has been frightened away by their clamour?"

"I don't believe he'll care much about what they think," answered Randal, "for I heard Sir Charles telling Lieutenant Granger that Somerton don't intend to return to the island. He's sick of the people, it seems, and, when the war is over, he means to find a home somewhere else, and his daughter Louisa is then to join him."

"At which time," observed the butler, "we may expect to hear of the young folks being married."

"Don't make too sure of that," exclaimed the other, "for the girl don't seem to be one of the marrying sort. Leastways, she won't give the lieutenant any hopes, so he goes moping about, and looks as melancholy as if he had been cashiered for some offence."

"Maybe she don't like him?"

"Quite the contrary," answered Randal, "for, by all accounts, she's uncommonly fond of him, only some foolish notion has got into her head about not being his wife till her father's honour has been cleared up. Did you ever hear of such romantic stuff? As if the young fellow would have asked her to marry him, if he hadn't been willing to make her his bride."

"There's no accounting for people's fancies, particularly when they happen to be of the female sex," retorted Mr. Binley. "I've had some little experience that way in the course of my life, so you may take my word about it."

"But there don't happen to be anything in the way of their union," exclaimed Randal. "She has declared that she will not marry any one except Lieutenant Granger, and her father is as anxious as any one can be to see the union take place without delay. Yet, with all that, she must keep everybody in suspense, though a single word from her lips would make all of 'em happy."

"Never fear, but it will all come right enough in time," replied Mr. Binley. "The young fellow will have opportunities enough of seeing her, and if he don't make good use of them, he's not half the lad of mettle I take him for."

"Because he's a soldier, I suppose you would have him lay a regular siege to her heart?"

"To be sure I would," replied the other. "Some girls want a deal more persuasion than others do, before they can make up their mind to accept an offer, and if that should be the case with Louisa Somerton, I hope the young gentleman won't lose her for want of carrying on his love suit with spirit."

"Between you and I, she's a simpleton for dilly dallying with him so long," said Randal, with a sagacious shrug of the shoulders. "She's not such a great catch after all; for, though a pretty wench enough, there's no fortune to be expected with her, and it isn't every girl in her station that can boast such a chance."

"I rather think you reckon her a little too cheaply," answered Mr. Binley, "for I've heard her father is likely to get his estates back again, and if so, she will be as wealthy an heiress as you'll find here and there."

"Ah! then Luke Somerton has once been rich, has he?"

"Did you never know that before?" inquired the butler. "Did you never hear that he had large estates in Ireland, that were forfeited as soon as he took part with the French?"

"I've heard something of the kind," replied the other; "but never believed there was any truth in it. But what was it that made him fight against his own country?"

"Why, they say that it was all owing to the quarrels he had with Captain Aylmer, when he was an officer under him," replied Mr. Binley. "Be that as it may, however, everything was swept away when he sided with the enemies of old England, and then it was that his daughter Louisa was entrusted to the care of her uncle James."

"Who, by-the-bye, has left the island rather strangely," observed the other, in an inquisitive tone.

"He has," replied the butler, "but I believe that may be accounted for by the fact that he felt disgraced after Luke was sentenced to the death of a felon. They say he is now living somewhere on the Cumberland coast, and is trying to make all the friends he can, to obtain a reversal of his brother's attainder, which can only be done by means of the most powerful court influence. However, we have finished our bottle, Will Randal, and now, if you please, we will break off our conversation for the present."

The butler rose from his seat as he said this, and, quitting the room, left his friend to smoke out his pipe, and ruminate upon what had passed between them.

CHAPTER XLV.

Among the crew
Are spirits bold and daring—desperate men,
Who, with unbridled passion, would enforce
Their own tyrannic sway.

BARBILLON.

LUKE SOMERTON had not been at sea many hours before he began to discover that there was a spirit of disorder and insubordination among the crew, that had never on any previous occasion manifested itself. This, at first, he affected not to notice, hoping that a short time would serve to restore them to their former submission; but in this he was mistaken, for the men became more and more unruly, and it was evident that strong measures must be taken to subdue the feeling that had grown up among them. There was, however, one friend who still remained firm to him—this was Christopher Dalton, who had always possessed considerable control over the crew, though at present he acknowledged himself sorely perplexed as to what course it would be best to adopt in order to subdue the refractory spirit that had shown itself.

It was on the evening of the second day after they had set sail, that Luke Somerton was pacing the quarter deck, gloomily meditating on the prospect before him. His own resolute disposition at once suggested the employment of the most decisive means, in order to restore discipline among the crew, and he was turning to descend into the cabin, when he was suddenly confronted by his mate.

"How now, Mr. Dalton," he exclaimed; "what news bring you from these unruly scoundrels now?"

"Little that is good," answered Christopher, "though I have nothing more to report than you know already. The men are sullen and reserved, but hitherto they have not ventured to break out into open remonstrance."

"Know you what cause they have for complaint?"

"I know nothing to a certainty," replied the mate; "but from what I have gathered by chance, it seems that they like not the cruize we are going on."

"Have they turned cowards, then," asked Luke, "that they are afraid to encounter the foes of their country?"

"The truth is," answered Dalton, "they are disinclined to fight against the French, with whom they so recently sided. They accuse you of deserting the cause, and declare that they are not bound to change their opinions merely because you have seen reason to do so."

"The scoundrels! dare any of them tell me that to my face?"

"I should hope not," answered Christopher; "but we must be prepared to meet any remonstrance they may make with boldness and determination. I have myself taken care to give them a hint that bloodshed will be the certain consequence of the first appearance of mutiny, and I rather think, for the present, my threats have not been thrown away."

"But I suppose they do not go to their work cheerfully?"

"Not so well as I could wish," answered the mate; "yet a few hours' reflection may serve to work a better change in them. At any rate, they shall see that their numbers do not terrify us into yielding to their desires."

"Who is the ringleader?"

"Thomas Bowyer."

"Let him be instantly put in irons."

"It ain't my place to remonstrate against your orders, Captain Somerton," exclaimed the mate; "but I do think it would be better to wait till we see how they mean to proceed, before we go to extremities. They may see the folly of their ways, and return to their duty, if we only show ourselves firm and resolute."

"And that," said Luke, "we cannot do, without taking means for the suppression of this threatened mutiny."

"I only wish we had brought out a fresh crew with us," exclaimed the other, "for these men have been so used to a different sort of life, that they are unwilling to change it."

"You mean that they would rather be smugglers than fight honourably in the cause of their country?"

"Honour they care little about," replied the mate; "for all they desire is to lead a wild and reckless life, such as they have been used to. There is not a man among them that would have come this cruize, had it been known beforehand what your intentions were, and no sooner was it ascertained that you were looking about for French vessels to capture, than they began to murmur and give other unequivocal signs of disapprobation."

"Have any of them dared to disobey the orders that have been given?" demanded Luke Somerton, sternly.

"They have not exactly disobeyed orders," answered Dalton, "but they have not performed their duties cheerfully."

"Then flog the most refractory," said Luke; "and the others, if they are wise, will profit by the example."

"True; but we must be as firm as a rock, or, you may depend upon it, these fellows will very soon begin to imagine that we are afraid of them."

"Then will they find themselves most confoundedly mistaken," exclaimed Luke Somerton; "for I have controlled their fiery spirits before, and the same means are still open to me. Let the actions of this Thomas Bowyer be carefully watched, and if I have sufficient reason to believe that he is trying to mislead the others, I will have him hung up to the yardarm without little form or ceremony. Let us but punish the ring-leader, and, I'll answer for it, his comrades will soon benefit by the example."

"I rather think they would rise as one man to save him from the punishment, Captain Somerton," answered the mate. "These fellows have led too reckless a life to be intimidated by the death of one or two of their number, though I rather think a little display of firmness and determination on our part will not be without a good effect. They like to see boldness in those who are placed above them, and would probably yield obedience when they see that it is useless any longer to resist."

"But are such men to be depended on in the event of our having an encounter with the enemy?" asked Somerton.

"I think so."

"What! with all their predilection for the French?"

"The fact is, sir," replied Christopher Dalton, "they care less about the French then they themselves imagine. Just at the present moment, perhaps, they may feel disinclined to fight against their former allies; but only bring them broadside to broadside with them, and you would soon see that there was little cause to fear any falling off in their duty. They are no cowards, Captain Somerton, though I must needs say their conduct just now affords sufficient reason to doubt their fidelity."

"I trust your opinion of them may prove correct," exclaimed Luke; "and yet I must needs say the course you have persuaded me to adopt is the last I should have thought of myself. However, I will give them the advantage of a fair trial, and, if they deceive me, it will then be expedient to adopt more resolute means to show them that I will not be trifled with."

"They shall be closely looked after," said Dalton, "and you may depend upon receiving a faithful report from me, should there appear to be any good ground for supposing that their evil designs are still in progress."

"Are there none whom we may regard as friends?" asked Luke Somerton, "or are all of them infected alike with this spirit of mutiny and insubordination?"

"I believe there's about half a dozen that would hesitate to join their companions if matters came to the worst," replied Christopher Dalton. "I have seen them wavering when others have worn a stern and moody brow, and have had hopes that from them at least we had nothing to fear."

"Have you ever ventured to speak to them upon the subject?"

"No."

"Would it not have been better to have done so?"

"I thought it most prudent to conceal from all of them my knowledge of what is passing in their minds," replied Dalton. "They believe their designs are kept secret from both you and me, and will, therefore, be the more taken off their guard should matters by-and-bye come to a more serious pass."

"Let the first favourable opportunity be taken to show them that we have it yet in our power to punish the refractory," exclaimed Luke Somerton. "If any man hesitates to obey orders, the lash shall bring him to his senses—that will at least show them that I am not to be trifled with, and, perhaps, the others will learn from it a lesson that will be useful to themselves and beneficial to me."

"You may depend upon my obeying your orders, Captain Somerton," answered Dalton. "Menacing as these fellows are, they know I have not the slightest fear of them, and that will serve to curb their spirits more than the severest punishment that we could inflict."

"And do you always go well armed?" asked Somerton.

"Behold," exclaimed the other, throwing aside the thick wrapper with which he was covered, and displaying a couple of brace of pistols, besides a cutlass, and the long knife which was used only in engagements. "You see, Captain Somerton, I am not unprepared for any case of sudden emergency; and, if these fellows should play us any foul tricks, it will be the worse for some of them, whatever may be the issue of the business. I may possibly fail if assailed by numbers, but it would not be before I mowed down a few of them, by way of teaching the rest what it is to have to do with a British bull-dog."

"Your precaution is well-timed, and I shall not fail to follow the example," returned Luke. "Egad! I know not why we should be alarmed at their menaces, for, though they may surpass us in numbers, I will defy them to do so in courage. We will at least be true to each other, and the chances are that we shall overcome our enemies, numerous as they may be."

"Then you think it will be better not to let them form a suspicion that we have an idea of the evil designs they are meditating?"

"Upon that subject we must be silent," replied Somerton; "for, if they know we are upon our guard, they will only dissemble, and we may be attacked at a future time when we are not so well prepared. There is but one way to encounter such scoundrels as these, and that is to deceive them into fancied security."

"But they may suspect that we are aware of them."

"Let them do so," exclaimed the captain, "for in that case they will be always in fear of us. Every man who has a guilty conscience is a coward at heart, and we should have but little to fear from men who believed that their mischievous designs are suspected."

"Why, as for fear," exclaimed Dalton, "I may say, without boasting, that few people know less what that feeling is than myself. I have been in dangers quite as great as this threatens to be, and have always managed to fight my way through them without coming to much harm. Even among those savage islanders that we have left, our lives were continually placed in jeopardy, yet the fellows saw plainly enough that I heeded them not, and it's my belief that to that circumstance alone I am indebted for my safety."

"Did they not threaten you with violence, then?"

"Ay, several times."

"For what reason?"

"Because they knew I would stand up for you against all their villanous doings. Several attempts were made upon my life, and it was only two days before we left the island that my hat was pierced with a bullet, sent after me, I suppose, by some rascal that intended it for my head."

"Yet you never mentioned the circumstance to me."

"What would have been the use of doing so?" demanded Christopher Dalton. "I knew well enough that you had got sufficient troubles of your own to think about, so I kept the affair to myself, thinking that—vainly enough, perhaps—I could take care of number one better than any other person could do it for me."

"Do you know who it was that attempted your life?"

"The same ruffian that attempted yours," replied Dalton.

"Then it is hardly likely," observed Luke Somerton, "that he will ever have it in his power to make a similar attempt, for he was secured by Lieutenant Granger, who, I believe, took him back to the prison from which he had somehow contrived to escape."

"And I dare say he'll not have much chance of getting out of it a second time," exclaimed Dalton. "There was fuss enough made about the affair as it was, and it was even rumoured that Sir Charles Radcliffe had got into trouble with the secretary of state about it. However, they have taken him back to his prison, and, for the sake of all persons that are better disposed than himself, I hope he will be sent to pass the remainder of his days at Botany Bay."

"Of that you may rest assured," answered Luke Somerton. "His first offence of aiding and assisting in burning down my house will secure for him at least banishment from his native place for life. However, leaving him to a fate that he so richly merits, I must now once more charge you to keep a vigilant watch upon these fellows of ours, lest their treacherous designs should prove successful."

"Ay—ay," answered Dalton; "I'll not give 'em a chance, depend upon it; and they are aware of that, too, or they would have broken out into open mutiny before now."

"If it be possible, consistently with our own safety, to spare the shedding of human blood, I should wish to do so," observed Luke Somerton. "With all their faults, the fellows have served me well and faithfully on former occasions, and, in return, I would not deal too harshly with them, unless it should appear that there is no other alternative."

"Why, just now, captain, you were for hanging up the ringleader to the yardarm!"

"The words were spoken hastily, and I thought no other way presented itself to insure our own safety," said the commander. "Reflection, however, has convinced me that boldness and vigour may stop this discontent, and if the men return to their duty, I believe there will be little chance of a second outbreak of their violence."

"That will depend upon circumstances, Captain Somerton," exclaimed the mate. "I never place much reliance upon men who have once forgotten the duty they owe to their superiors, and as I know they have a strong aversion to fight against the French, we may reasonably suppose that much dependence cannot be placed on any of them."

"But we may at least appear to do so," answered Luke, "and that will serve to lull their suspicions that the plot is known to us. In the meanwhile, your conduct towards them must not be different to what it always has been. You will thus have frequent opportunities of observing them when they least suspect that their designs are anticipated, and we may be so prepared as to frustrate any attempt that they may intend to make against either our lives or liberty."

"I shall obey your orders, captain," replied Dalton; "for you may depend upon it I have made up my mind not to give a chance away now that I know the sort of scheme the fellows have got in their heads. D—n 'em! I thought at one time there was not a braver or more faithful crew than that you commanded; but they can neither have courage nor fidelity to turn against their captain for no better reason than that he is going to fight against the enemies of his country, instead of siding with them as he had before."

"How know you," asked Luke Somerton, "that that is the only motive for their mutinous conduct?"

"Because I heard three or four of them talking together, when they little thought I was so near to them," replied Dalton.

"Did they mention how they meant to attack us?"

"No."

"Nor when?"

"They only said that matters could not go on much longer as they are," answered Christopher Dalton. "They spoke of you as a renegade to the cause, and I could have found it in my heart to rush from my place of concealment and punish them for it on the spot."

"It is well that you were prudent enough to restrain your impetuosity," exclaimed Luke; "for, had you discovered yourself to them at that moment, it is more than likely they would have instantly sacrificed you to their vengeance."

"That is to say, captain, if I would have let them," answered Dalton. "You forget already how heavily I have armed myself; and if the traitors had dared to have raised an arm against me, there is not a man among them that should have lived till this time."

"But they would have raised an alarm, and, against the numbers that would have come to the assistance of their comrades, there would not have been the shadow of a chance for you. In all probability I also should have fallen a sacrifice to their fury, and if once the vessel had come under their command, they would have directed her course to some distant part of the world, where they might have carried on a piratical traffic, with little chance of ever being taken and punished for their crimes."

By this time they had reached the companion-ladder, which Luke Somerton descended, leaving his mate to keep watch upon the deck, with a strict injunction to look closely after those whose evil intentions there was much reason to dread. But Dalton scarcely needed the directions thus given to him, for he was fully alive to the danger of being unguarded even for a moment, and, pacing up and down, he kept a sharp look-out, though in such a manner as not to rouse the suspicions of the men that they were at the period the objects of his watchfulness.

In the silence and solitude of his cabin, Luke Somerton could freely indulge in those thoughts which anticipated events gave rise to. With respect to his own fate he was utterly careless, for life had few charms for him; and had it not been for his daughter's sake, he would rather have perished than drag on an existence that so many circumstances served to render miserable. But to her he owed a duty that was paramount to everything else; he was her only protector, almost her only friend, and, though severed for the present, he knew she looked forward to happier times, when they would again meet to pass the remainder of their days in each other's society.

When, however, he turned his thoughts to the new peril with which he was threatened, he began almost to doubt whether her eager hopes would ever be realized. The overpowering force opposed to him was appalling, for he well knew the desperate characters of the men he had to deal with, and there was but one in the whole vessel upon whose assistance he could, with any certainty, reckon. Yet Christopher Dalton, with his indomitable courage, was a host in himself, upon whose powerful aid he could place the utmost reliance, even though they might have to contend against the whole ship's crew. But he felt assured that among so many men some few would prove waverers when the moment of danger came, and some of these might even be expected to side with him, so that there was a tolerable fair chance of quelling the mutiny, even if it should break forth as he expected.

Having satisfied himself in this respect, he seated himself at the table, and busied himself in examining the charts and maps by which to direct his course towards those distant seas in which he intended to cruise. Occupied by his calculations, his mind was totally absorbed in this one subject, when suddenly he was roused by hearing a low moan, as if some one was gagged and endeavouring to raise an alarm. He listened with suspended breath, but all was now still and silent as the grave, and believing that it was the howling of the wind among the rigging of the vessel, he was once more applying himself to his task, when the sound was again heard, though more feebly than at first. He felt convinced that the impending danger was about to burst forth, and was rising from his seat in order to make his way to the deck, when the cabin-door was suddenly forced open, and several men, armed with pistols and cutlasses, rushed tumultuously into his presence.

"Stand back, all of ye!" exclaimed Luke Somerton—"stand back, I say! for the first man who advances another step shall perish like a dog!"

"Mind that fate don't befall yourself, Captain Somerton," said Thomas Bowyer, who acted as ringleader of the mutineers. "We have not come here without being well prepared for resistance, and, if we are forced to it, your blood shall be shed as if it was so much water."

"Where is Mr. Dalton?" exclaimed Somerton, looking anxiously around him.

"We are not here to answer questions, but to make certain demands, that you must agree to," returned the ringleader, in a tone of insolent authority.

"I will not hear you till my doubts have been first satisfied respecting Mr. Dalton," exclaimed the captain. "You have, perhaps, murdered him, and, if so, I care not what fate you may have in store for me."

"He's alive at present," answered one of the fellows; "but it will depend upon you and him how long he will be so. We have bound and gagged him securely enough, and there's plenty left to watch over him, to take care that he don't come to your assistance."

"It was his moan, then, that I heard a short time back?"

"I dare say it might have been," replied Bowyer; "but that ain't the business we've got to talk about just at present."

"What is it you want of me?"

"To alter the ship's course, and, instead of fighting against the French, to side with them."

"That I'll never do."

"If that's the case, you must take the consequences."

"Whatever they may be, I am prepared to meet them," exclaimed Luke Somerton. "You are numerous enough to carry your murderous purposes against one man; but be warned, I say, for I am armed, and will never yield while I have power to resist my enemies."

"We don't want to harm you, Captain Somerton," returned the ringleader; "but there isn't a man among the ship's company that don't feel dissatisfied at the way we are going on. The thing don't suit 'em at all, so the sooner you consent to make an alteration the better."

"Am I to be dictated to by my men?" demanded the captain.

"If you are wise, you'll submit to it, rather than make matters worse," replied Bowyer. "We have been used to a hardy, reckless sort of life, and don't feel inclined to fight against our principles, merely because you do."

"Then quit the ship at the next port we come to," said Luke Somerton, "and I will engage fresh hands, who will serve me more faithfully than you are inclined to do."

"That'll never do!" exclaimed the mutineer. "Leave the ship, indeed! And pray what is to become of us, if you desert us in a foreign country? Do you take us for fools?"

"I take you for a set of scoundrels, that would desert your commander at the moment when he has most need of your services," replied Luke Somerton, unawed by the danger with which he was threatened. "You have broken in upon me un-

bidden, and certain demands are made which I can refuse only at the peril of my life."

"That's because there was no other way left to us," answered Tom Bowyer. "We waited patiently enough till we saw that you were determined upon fighting against our old friends, and then we thought it was high time to let you know our minds upon the subject. So, to sum all up, Captain Somerton, you must give up this plan of yours, and for once suffer us to dictate what is to be done."

"And suppose I comply with your demands," said Luke; "think you I should not do all in my power to bring you to punishment when we return to England?"

"I dare say you would be inclined to do so," replied the fellow, carelessly; "but, in the event of your falling in with our views, there is a little ceremony to go through, that will make us tolerably safe. In short, Captain Somerton, you would be required to take an oath never to take any future proceedings against us."

"And what if I refuse to comply?"

"Why, then, having gone so far in this business, we must take care to prevent mischief coming of it."

"By murdering me, I suppose?"

"That's as it may happen," exclaimed the mutineer. "We don't want to kill you, but, if there's no other way left to make ourselves safe, I suppose it must be done."

"What's the use of talking about it, when we all know that it was agreed on to kill the captain, and take possession of the ship?" demanded one of the ruffians. "We are losing time parlavering here, when the job ought to be done and over; and, for my own part, if no one else will do it, I'll send a bullet through his brains, and so bring the affair to a conclusion at once."

"Ay, ay—down with him!" murmured several other voices.

"If any man attempts to do it till I give the word of command, it will be at the cost of his own life," exclaimed Bowyer, advancing a step or two, and glancing fiercely round upon his companions. "I was chosen to undertake the management of this affair, and no man shall dare to take the business out of my hands."

"To end this affair at once," interposed Luke Somerton, "I will now tell you that my mind is made up as to the course I mean to pursue. Overwhelmed with numbers, it may be impossible successfully to resist you, but force shall never make me yield against my own inclinations; and if it is my life you seek, you may take it, but it shall not be sacrificed till I have shed the blood of some of those cowards who have taken me at this disadvantage. Approach, then, he who dare, and I will make him a terrible example to his comrades."

As he said this, Luke Somerton placed his back against the panelling of the cabin, and drawing a pistol from his belt, presented it threateningly at his assailants. The men were evidently unprepared for this defiance against their superior numbers, and shrunk back with dismay, all of them fearing to advance, lest the threat which had just been uttered should be put in execution. Luke Somerton smiled scornfully as he perceived the terror which a little resolution had occasioned; and, addressing himself to the crouching ruffians, he exclaimed,—

"Why do ye not approach to perpetrate the foul deed ye came hither so intent upon? Are ye afraid of me, alone and unfriended as I now stand among ye?"

"They are not so easily to be frightened as you think for, captain," retorted Tom Bowyer. "The fellows know what I threatened them with just now, if they disobeyed my orders, and it is well that they have taken heed of my words, for if any man had advanced but a single step to injure you, till I gave the word, I would have laid him dead at my feet, even if it had been my own brother who attempted it."

"Then why have you not given the word?" said Luke.

"Because I would rather try and persuade you to come to our terms," replied the ringleader. "We bear you no particular malice, Captain So-

merton; but the truth is, we are all determined not to follow the course you seem inclined to pursue, and so we have combined together in order to bring you to our way of thinking."

"Which you will never be able to do."

"More's the pity," answered the other, "because it will drive us to do what we wished to avoid. In short, we do not wish to kill you, Captain Somerton."

"What brought you here, then?"

"To show, that we have sufficient strength among us to compel you to fall into our plans."

"Your strength I despise!" answered Luke. "It is not sufficient to force me to do aught against my own inclination, even though I may know that instant death will be the consequence. I fearlessly tell ye that ye are cowards all; and since Christopher Dalton is either dead or doomed to die, I am willing to share the fate of the only true friend that I have on board the vessel."

"Mr. Dalton, as well as yourself, may save his life, if he chooses to agree to our terms," answered Bowyer. "We have always respected him, because he was a good man and a brave officer; but we know how far his friendship for you would carry him, and, in order to prevent mischief, we have bound his limbs and put a guard over him, so that he may not come to your rescue."

"And it is well for yourselves that you have done so," exclaimed Luke Somerton; "and had he been free ye would not have been suffered thus long to insult me with your presence. The triumph is, however, yours for the present, though I would not have ye exult too much at it; for, whether I live or perish by your hands, the violence that has been this day committed will be fearfully avenged."

"By whom?"

"By those who administer the laws in your own country," replied Luke Somerton. "The crime you have committed will be certainly known, and yourselves will be made a terrible example of, as a warning to all others who may feel inclined to mutiny against their superiors."

"That we must take our chance of," exclaimed Bowyer; "but they must catch us before they hang us, and that I fancy will give them more trouble than you think for. We shall take care never to trust ourselves in any place where the English laws are obeyed; and as for our vessel being taken in any engagement, I'll take care that shall never be the case—even if, to prevent it, I, with my own hand, throw a torch into the powder room, and blow the ship and all her crew into the air."

"And it is to lead this reckless life that you have entered into this mutiny?" said their captain.

"Anything is better than fighting in a cause that we don't like," exclaimed the ringleader. "Men are not to be so easily driven as you seem to imagine ; and, for my own part, I care not what becomes of me, so that I lead a life such as I have always been used to. There is not a man among us but what took to smuggling because he had done something that prevented his remaining in England ; so, having very little to do with what the world calls *conscience*, we took to a profession that secured us plenty of profit, with no great deal of trouble. As for the danger we were continually exposed to, that was a mere trifle, since a man can die but once, and it may as well be in following our own course, as anyhow else."

"Are you going to preach all day?" demanded one of the ruffians ; "or are we to go through with the job that brought us to this place?"

"We will now come to that point at once," said the ringleader. "You hear how impatient the men are to bring this matter to a close," he added, to Luke Somerton. "They are athirst for your blood, and I shall not be able to restrain them much longer if you don't come to our terms."

"You have had my answer," said Luke, firmly. "So, now, let your blood-hounds rush upon their prey as soon as they like. I have, however, warned them of what they are to expect, and they shall find that I am not worse than my word, if they can summon courage enough to advance upon me, for the completion of their murderous purpose."

"If that is your final answer," exclaimed Tom Bowyer, "I will take all the risk of the consequences upon myself. You have refused the terms we offered you, and, in order to save ourselves from the punishment that might possibly follow, I will myself strike the blow that shall rid us of all fear on that score. You shall die, Captain Somerton, even if I also perish in the attempt."

So saying, he raised his cutlass, and was rushing towards his intended victim, when the loud report of a pistol was heard, and the next moment the ringleader of the mutineers fell to the floor with a heavy groan. The men were instantly struck with alarm when they perceived the fall of their leader ; but one of them, more bold than the rest, rushed towards Luke, with the intention of cutting him down with his sword. Somerton, however, was prepared for every extremity, and ere the ruffian had advanced three paces, he also fell mortally wounded by the side of his dying companion. At that moment Christopher Dalton came hurrying down into the cabin, and placing himself beside Luke Somerton, he held himself in readiness to slay the next mutineer that should venture to approach. They, however, stood for a moment, as if petrified, and then, having thrown down their arms, fell upon their knees, and loudly implored forgiveness for what they had done.

"A pretty set of cowardly scoundrels you are, truly," he exclaimed, gazing upon the abject wretches before him. "You thought to deprive the captain of my services, but you see I have broke from my bonds, and you shall soon find to your cost what it is to mutiny, and threaten death to all that are not of your own infernal way of thinking."

"Down with him!" cried several voices, menacingly, and at the same moment every man was ready to rush upon the one who had just destroyed their leader. But Christopher Dalton was prepared for the violence they threatened him with, and giving a preconcerted signal, eight of the crew, well armed, made their appearance, and so vigorously attacked those who were already in possession of the cabin, that the whole of them were soon made prisoners, and securely bound to prevent any further mischief from them. Towards effecting this object both Luke Somerton and his mate rendered good service ; and the whole of the fellows having been thus secured, the former, addressing them, said,—

"The cowardly conduct ye have been guilty of merits but little mercy from me, and yet I will not inflict death upon any of ye, till I have had time coolly to weigh the matter, and form a deliberate judgment upon each man's case. I will take two hours for reflection ; during which time it will be well for all of ye to prepare yourself for another world, for an example must be made, and at present I know not which among you will be doomed to die."

"And what is to be done with their ringleader?" exclaimed Dalton. "He is not dead, I see ; but, judging from the position of the wound, I think he is not likely to survive the injuries very long."

"Let him be conveyed to the cockpit," answered Luke. "He will there receive such poor surgical skill as we happen to have among us, though, methinks, it would be better for him to die at once, than meet the fate that will certainly be his, should he happen to recover."

An order was then given to convey the prisoners to a place where they might be safely guarded ; and the cabin having been thus partially cleared, Bowyer, still in a state of insensibility, and bleeding profusely, was carried away, with little chance of surviving the wound he had received. Luke Somerton and his mate were now the only persons left ; and a silence of some little duration ensued, which was at length broken by the latter inquiring what was to be done with the prisoners who had just been taken away.

"That," replied Somerton, "was the subject that just now occupied my thoughts. All of them deserve death, and yet I do not want to abuse my unexpected good fortune by an act of sanguinary vengeance."

"But you surely will not set them at liberty after the threats they just now uttered against yourself, captain?"

"I must either do so, or give orders for some of the worst of them to be executed," said the other. "To keep them all in custody throughout a long voyage is impossible, and I have been thinking, Mr. Dalton, whether an act of mercy towards them may not have the effect of securing their zeal and faithful services in future."

"What! without making an example of any of them?"

"They have already a terrible example in the fate of their ringleader," answered Luke Somerton. "You have given him his death wound, I rather think, and if that does not prove a warning to them in future, I know not what will."

"And, egad! it was lucky that I came to your assistance just in the nick of time," exclaimed Dalton ; "for, if my presence in your cabin had been delayed another moment, you would have been murdered by the ruffians, and before now they would have had the ship under their command."

"They told me your limbs were bound," said Luke, "and that a guard had been placed over you, so as to prevent the possibility of your coming to my assistance."

"Ay," answered Christopher Dalton, "but I was not to be overcome quite so easily as they thought for; so, having removed the gag that they had placed over my mouth, I began to try what sort of stuff the hearts of my guards were made of."

"And, of course, you found that the scoundrels were no better than those who had left them in charge of you?"

"They were a good deal better, or matters would not have turned out quite as well as they did," replied Dalton. "To be sure, at first they did not seem inclined to listen to me, but when I spoke of the fearful risk they were running, and the certainty of being rewarded by you if they rendered any assistance, they began to treat the affair differently."

"Were those the men," inquired Luke Somerton, "who afterwards accompanied you here to my rescue?"

"They were," answered the mate. "I told you in our last conversation that there were some of the men that, either from cowardice or a better feeling, would be glad to get out of this mutiny, and by good fortune those happened to be the very fellows left to keep watch over me. At first they were afraid of bringing down upon themselves the vengeance of their comrades, but I made it pretty clear to them that, with their assistance, we could utterly defeat the mutineers, and then they began to waver, till one of them proposed that they should enter into our plans."

"And you were then unbound, I suppose?" said Luke.

"Not immediately," answered the mate; "for as all were not quite agreed upon the matter, a long consultation took place between them, during which I could observe that there was a great difference of opinion among them, for some were still in fear of their comrades, and it was not an easy matter to produce arguments sufficiently strong to prove that their safest course would be to lend their assistance towards restoring order in the ship."

"In the end, however, I suppose they were more unanimous?"

"Yes," replied Christopher Dalton; "but it was not till I had put another spoke in the wheel, and convinced them that punishment must follow sooner or later if they kept on in the course they were steering. I thought they seemed rather inclined to laugh at this, but luckily I was mistaken, for soon afterwards one of the fellows came to me, and asked if I was ready to take an oath that you would pardon them on condition that they did as I proposed."

"Which you, of course, readily agreed to."

"What else could a poor devil in my situation do?" asked Christopher Dalton. "I could plainly hear the scoundrels threatening and abusing you below, and feeling very certain that you would be murdered if prompt measures were not taken to pre-

vent it, I told the men that they might not only make sure of your pardon, but of a handsome reward as well, if they would do their duty faithfully."

"Upon which they set you at liberty?"

"The cords were cut in the twinkling of an eye," replied the mate, "and, snatching up a cutlass that was lying close to me, I called upon them to follow me to your rescue. The fellows acted even better than I expected, for in a moment every man was close upon my heels, when, rushing down the companion-ladder, I arrived here just in time to save you from the deadly attack of Tom Bowyer."

"The service you have this day done me, Mr. Dalton, can never be sufficiently rewarded," exclaimed Luke Somerton. "I was in the hands of those villains, and must have perished by their violence but for the means you took to rescue me."

"And the men that assisted me deserve no small share of your gratitude," observed the other. "To be sure, the fellows did it with the view of saving themselves from the consequences of this mutiny; but your life was saved through it, and that being the case, I don't know that we have a right to look too deeply into the motives of your preservers."

"I will not fail to reward them for what they have done," exclaimed Luke Somerton; "but it is necessary that we should now decide upon the course we ought to pursue against our prisoners."

"Well, then," said Christopher, "I should say, hang the two worst of them, and after keeping the rest of them in confinement for a week or so, you will see what sort of punishment is best for them; and if they seem to repent the evil of their ways, you can set them at liberty, with a threat of sending them up to the yard-arm in the event of their making a second attempt at mutiny."

"You had better go and speak to them, Mr. Dalton," said Luke, "and if you find them sorry for what has passed, offer them my pardon and forgiveness, on condition that they do not make a second attempt, such as the one we have just frustrated. A little kindness may not be thrown away upon them; but should I find them ungrateful, they will discover, on the next occasion, that I can be as terribly severe as I am now inclined to be lenient and conciliatory."

"Upon my word, captain," exclaimed Christopher Dalton, "I would not give them their liberty till it has first been seen whether they are to be trusted."

"There you and I differ most materially," answered Luke, "for I think there is now less danger to be apprehended than before this mutiny took place. The fellows know well enough that our suspicions will ever be directed against them —that their every action will be watched with the most jealous care, and that, at the first appearance of revolt, such active measures will be taken as to prevent the possibility of their succeeding in it. Besides, they have now learnt by experience that no reliance is to be placed upon one another, for already have some of their comrades turned against them and brought confusion and dismay into the midst of their camp."

"Well," exclaimed Dalton, "there may be some truth in all that; but hang me if I like trusting people that have once deceived me. Then, too, we are very certain that they are unwilling to fight against the enemies of England, and supposing we should have an engagement with a French ship, what dependence have we on these fellows of ours? Why, they might suddenly turn against us, and after delivering us into the hands of the foe, we should find ourselves prisoners, with very little chance of regaining our liberty till the end of this war."

"You are a Scotsman, Christopher," said the captain, "and are more wary and circumspect than I could ever pretend to be. However, I give you credit for good intentions, though I am not inclined, in the present instance, to follow your advice. You will, therefore, go to these mutineers, Mr. Dalton, and tell them the conditions upon which I will consent to restore them to the liberty which they have forfeited by their own crimes."

"I'll tell them, captain; but, between you and I ——"

"Have the kindness, sir, to do as I have requested," interrupted Luke Somerton. "I may be wrong, but it is a fancy of my own to try the effect of kindness upon these misled men of ours, who, after all, may prove grateful for the favour."

Christopher Dalton made no further objection, but left the cabin to go upon the errand he was desired. During the period of his absence Luke paced uneasily up and down the cabin, and never did time seem to pass so long as the interval which now elasped. He had, indeed, begun to think that something was wrong again, and was about to go in search of the mate, when footsteps were heard descending from the deck, and presently Mr. Dalton stood before him.

"Well, captain," he exclaimed, "I believe the fellows see their fault, for they acknowledge themselves to have been in the wrong, and express themselves much obliged to you for the leniency shown to them. Somehow or another though, I can't fancy they are sincere, and it will, therefore, be well for us both to be upon our guard, lest, in a careless moment, they should make another and more successful attempt to murder us."

"You have executed your task well, Mr. Dalton," said the captain; "and I trust your suspicions of their future movements are groundless. We will, however, look after them sharply, and, if necessary, repress any further mutinous conduct before it is too late."

Luke Somerton then left the cabin, accompanied by his mate, and paid a visit of inspection over the ship. On reaching the cockpit they found that Bowyer had just breathed his last, and, as the chief instigator of the revolt was no more, the men declared that all ill-feeling between themselves and Luke was at an end.

CHAPTER XLVI.

Fierce and vindictive,
E'en the approach of certain punishment
Fails to appal him. He is a-thirst for blood
To quench his rancorous hatred.

The Greek Slave.

GREAT was the consternation amongst the lower orders of the Manx people when it was rumoured abroad that Harry Roden had again been captured and carried before the governor, for examination on a charge of having attempted the life of Luke Somerton. Had the latter named personage been in the island, there is little doubt that he would have been immediately sacrificed to their immoderate fury, who could only believe that he was the cause of all the misfortune that had befallen their favourite champion. It was, however, known that he had gone to sea immediately after the attack had been made upon him; and it was then seriously argued among themselves, whether, as the father was beyond their reach, they should not wreak their vengeance upon his daughter. By some, this suggestion was hailed as a very proper act of retribution, and full two-thirds of the crowd would have proceeded to the cottage instanter, had there not been a few among them who thought it rather too bad that she should be made to suffer for the supposed delinquencies of her parent.

"Are ye all mad," said Dick Joyce, "that ye must condemn a poor girl to death merely because ye happen to have taken offence against her father? What harm has she ever done you that four or five hundred people should vow deadly vengeance against a weak and helpless girl?"

"I'll tell you what it is, my fine fellow," retorted Nell Dawson, "this is not the first time you have interfered with us when your advice has not been asked, and if everybody here was of my way of thinking, I'd soon see if you should disappoint us again as you've done once or twice before."

"Ain't other people as much right to give their advice as you have?" demanded Snizzle, the town-crier, who thought himself tolerably safe when he was under the protection of Dick Joyce. "But I'll tell you what it is, Mrs. Dawson, you're a regular shrew, and ——"

"I a shrew!" vociferated the beldame; "only let me catch you alone one of these days, you little whipper-snapper, and see what I'll give you for calling me ugly names."

"Ay, ay; quarrel among yourselves as much as you like," exclaimed Joyce, "for, after all, I don't know but it's the best way to keep you out of worse mischief."

"Do you mean to say, then," demanded the virago, "that we sha'n't go and pull down the house about the girl's ears if we have a mind? Who are you, I should like to know, that we are to submit to be schooled and lectured like so many children?"

"And who are you," retorted Joyce, "that you are to go and threaten this poor girl, who has never been guilty of an unjust act towards any of us? The worst that you can say of her is that she procured her father's pardon when you were looking anxiously forward to his execution, and from that time till the present moment you have done nothing but vow vengeance against Luke and his daughter."

"Why don't you feel a little pity for poor Harry Roden, instead of giving it all to the fellow that has caused him to be thrown into a prison?"

"Because Harry has been a mad, hot-headed fool, and deserves whatever may befal him," answered Dick Joyce. "He should have kept himself quiet and minded his own business, and then he would have had nothing to complain of now. But it's always the way with people that interfere with matters that don't concern them; they are sure to get into hot water, and then grumble when they find out the pain and inconvenience of it."

"Well, you may say as you like of Henry Roden," exclaimed the virago; "but as they didn't think proper to hang Luke Somerton, I, for one, say no harm shall happen to the other, who hasn't done more harm than the man who was tried and convicted for a murder."

"How will you prevent it?" demanded Joyce.

"Why, ain't there enough here to go and get him out of prison?" demanded Nell Dawson. "The governor could feel a great deal of pity and compassion for a fellow that was guilty of shedding the blood of a human being; but he can see no excuse for a poor man that has been guilty of no more crime than helping to burn down the house of a blood-thirsty assassin."

"But if the queen was pleased to pardon him," said Joyce, "we have a right to suppose she believed him innocent of the crime. Besides, for my own part, I don't grudge the man his life; for, if he really committed the murder laid to his charge, he will now have more time to repent the evil he has done."

"How very compassionate some people can be when it suits them," exclaimed Nell Dawson, with a sneer. "This Somerton seems to be a mighty favourite of yours; but if anybody else had done half as much to deserve punishment, we should have heard your voice raised against him as loudly as any other person."

"Not half so loud as your voice is," interposed Snizzle, who delighted in saying something to tease her, when he could do so with impunity. "I'm sure," he added, "you have been making noise enough with that confounded tongue of yours, to last anybody for the next twelve months to come, at the very least."

"You are determined not to let me alone," exclaimed Nell, shaking her huge, red fist threateningly at him.

"There you are mistaken, old woman," retorted the town crier, "for you happen to be the last person in the world that I would have anything to do with."

"Then why do you interfere?"

"I merely follow your example," replied Snizzle. "You happen to take one side of the question, and I the other, and the end of it is, that neither of us can agree. However, it don't seem fair that Louisa Somerton should be made to suffer because her father don't happen to be liked among you; and as I see there's a good many here of my way of thinking, I shall make one to join them in protecting the poor girl from a parcel of people that act like so many savages."

"As you are so kind on one side of the question," sneered the shrew, "will you be equally so on the other, and go with us to help Harry Roden out of prison?"

"He'd be a fool if he did anything of the kind," exclaimed Joyce; "for all those that league together for that purpose will be very likely to get into the same trouble that he is in. So come along with me, friend Snizzle, for the sooner we get out of bad company like this, the better it will be for us."

"Why, what a precious coward you've turned all of a sudden," vociferated Josh Martin, who a

few moments before had joined the throng. "I used to think you was a chap that might be depended on in case of a rumpus; but it seems you begin to feel scruples of conscience, and when a fellow once gives way to that, I always fancy he is better suited for the company of the women folks than of men."

"You will let me act in the matter as I like, I suppose," said Joyce, by no means pleased with the tone of sarcasm with which this was uttered. "The truth is, I don't like to see a number of people against one; and as Louisa Somerton has never done anything to deserve the ill-feeling of these folks, I've told them that I will stand forward to protect her from their violence."

"Humph!" retorted Nell Dawson; "it's a pity the wench is engaged to the young officer chap, or you might have had a chance of marrying her yourself. Not that I could ever see that she was so very handsome as people make out; but then, you know, she is so good, that she must needs be coveted by all the young fellows for a wife."

"I had never any pretensions to that honour," replied Joyce; "though I might needs say I have always thought Lieutenant Granger a lucky fellow to be such a favourite of the girl's."

"He's such a favourite, that it seems she won't marry him," exclaimed Nell Dawson. "Maybe she thinks he isn't good enough for her, though, for my part, I've a notion that the poorest wretch in our island is her superior. A stuck-up, proud creature! I should like to have the serving of her as she deserves! I'd pull the house down about her ears, and then send her swimming in a pond of water, just to satisfy myself whether or no she is a witch."

"She is a *charming* girl, at any rate," said Snizzle, venturing upon an atrocious pun, which fortunately was not understood by the throng. "She has turned many a head in this island, and mine among the number! I have thought of popping the question, but that scarlet coat of Lieutenant Granger's don't leave me a chance, and so I've been thinking of bestowing my affections somewhere else."

"Fool!" exclaimed Nell Dawson, "you have had two wives already, and surely that ought to be enough, without looking to pick up a third."

"*One*, such as you, old woman, would have been a dose," retorted Snizzle, chuckling at having given her an answer that he well knew would rankle in her heart.

All the woman's fury was indeed excited, and for a moment or two it was doubtful whether poor Snizzle would not feel the weight of her arm. Upon reflection, however, she seemed to think he was beneath her notice, and thus the town crier escaped through his own utter insignificance. As the virago turned away from him, he was glad to make his way out of the crowd, and being followed by Dick Joyce, they proceeded in company towards the cottage of Louisa Somerton, resolving to watch from a short distance off to see if any of the mob made their way thither with a mischievous intention.

It was in vain that Nell Dawson endeavoured to persuade those about her to go in a body to the castle, and demand the instant liberation of the prisoner, Henry Roden. Self-preservation was the predominant feeling among them, and fearing lest their own liberties might be endangered by their endeavours to procure freedom for another, they wisely came to the conclusion that it would be better to separate, and return quietly to their homes.

At length, Nell stood alone upon the spot which had lately been so thickly thronged, and pronouncing her anathemas upon the cowards, as she called them, who had deserted her, she stood for some few moments to deliberate what steps she should next take.

Single handed, she had no hope of extricating Roden from the difficulty into which he had fallen, yet she resolved to present herself at the castle, and demand an audience of the governor, and represent to him the feeling of the islanders with respect to the course that had been pursued towards his prisoner. Courage and resolution she possessed enough of, and she had invective enough at her command to back the purpose she had in view. Turning, therefore, from the spot, she proceeded towards the castle, and, entering the lodge, desired the porter to inform his master that she wished to see him on important business.

"Tell me what the business is," said the man, "and I'll take your message to Sir Charles. At present, I know he is engaged, but I dare say he'll send word by me when it will be convenient for him to see you."

"Convenient, forsooth!" exclaimed Nell; "say I insist upon having an interview, and will not go away from the place till I have delivered my message."

"Indeed!" cried the porter. "If I was to take him such a message as that, he would order you to be turned away."

"He would find that more difficult than he imagines," replied the vixen. "People have a right to see him when they have business of importance to speak about, and you may tell him, if he refuses, that I will make my complaint to one that he is obliged to acknowledge as his mistress."

"You mean the queen, I suppose?"

"To be sure I do!" answered the woman. "Her majesty condescended to grant an audience very lately to Louisa Somerton, the daughter of a convicted murderer, and, as I consider myself fully equal to that girl, I have the same right to be heard. Ay, and I will be heard, too, even if they drag me to a prison for it."

"What is the occasion of these loud tones?" demanded Sir Charles Radcliffe, who was at that moment passing through the lodge. "Have you any complaint to make, my good woman, that you find it necessary to raise your voice to so high a pitch?"

"That will depend upon the kind of treatment I receive from you," replied Nell. "I came here to speak for a poor fellow that I believe has been hardly used, and it will only be acting with justice to give him his liberty."

"Of whom do you speak?"

"Harry Roden."

"And is it for him that you ask liberty?"

"It is," she replied; "greater criminals than he is have been got off lately, and I don't see why one man should be made to suffer, when another gets a free pardon by only asking for it."

"If you allude to Luke Somerton," exclaimed the governor, "you must be aware that the act which preserved him from an ignominious death was not mine, but that of a gracious sovereign, whom we are all bound to love and reverence. As for Roden, he has been guilty of no less than three offences: the first was being ringleader of the party that attacked and burned down the cottage of Luke Somerton—the second was prison-breaking, and the third an attempted assassination."

"But, mark me, Sir Charles," she exclaimed; "it was *only* an attempt, and the man still lives. With Luke Somerton the case was different, for he *killed* his victim, and yet is restored to liberty, as if he was free from crime."

"I know the circumstance is a sore subject to the people of this island," said the governor; "yet am I utterly at a loss to discover what reason there can be for so strong an expression of disapprobation at his escape, since the crime charged against him was not proved by direct evidence."

"Then why did the jury convict, and the judge sentence him to be hanged?" demanded Nell Dawson.

"The first," replied Sir Charles, "acted, no doubt, to the best of their judgment, and the latter only performed a necessary duty after the conviction had taken place. Mercy, however, is one of the queen's prerogatives, and, as there was reason shown for believing that Luke Somerton was the victim of circumstantial evidence, she gladly availed herself of the opportunity of granting the prayer of his heroic and most praiseworthy daughter."

"I'm sick of hearing people speak of her as if she had performed an act that no one had ever thought of before," exclaimed the woman. "I'll not find fault with the girl's trying to save her father's life, because it was only natural that she should do so; but I think the queen was in too great a hurry when she pardoned a murderer, and I think also, that the least she can now do is to give liberty to Harry Roden, whose crime is not half so heinous."

"That is a question which I am not called upon to decide," answered the governor. "If you think there are good grounds for it, let a petition in the prisoner's favour be drawn up and signed by all who think him worthy of royal clemency. I will myself undertake to convey it safely into the queen's hands, and you may be assured that it will receive from her all the attention and consideration that it merits."

"It would be thrown behind the fire, and no more thought of," answered Nell. "Luke Somerton might find favour, but it would not be so with a poor man who has no friends at court to back him with their interest."

"I am not aware that Luke Somerton had any friends to aid him," retorted Sir Charles. "On the contrary, he was out of favour, on account of his having joined the French, so that we may believe the act of the queen to have been one of spontaneous generosity and mercy."

"And who knows but he may fight against England again?" demanded the woman. "Such a man is not to be trusted; and as he has just left this place in his vessel, I suppose the next thing we hear of him will be that he has been taking some of our ships as he did before."

" There your bigotry and prejudice again show themselves," exclaimed Sir Charles Radcliffe. " You forget that there is such a thing as gratitude existing in the human breast, and look only on the darker side of the picture. Now I have formed a different opinion of Luke Somerton, for, having sacrificed his honour by fighting *with* the enemies of his queen, I believe he will now endeavour to retrieve it by waging fierce war *against* them. He will thus best show his estimation of the great favour he has received from the hands of Queen Anne, and will also regain that station in society which he has forfeited."

" I see I'm not able to argue the matter with you," replied Nell ; " but, for all that, you have not said anything yet to prove to me that Roden is not as deserving of mercy as Luke Somerton was."

" Why, Roden was detected in the very act of levelling a loaded pistol at a man against whom he is known to feel the most deadly hatred," answered the governor. " Besides, he has always proved himself to be one of the most discontented and factious fellows in the island, and has been regarded with suspicion and distrust."

" Ay ; give a dog an ill name and hang him," exclaimed Nell, tossing up her head with disdain ; " and so, because Harry Roden has been spoken ill of, he is not considered worthy of kindness or compassion ? But no matter, Sir Charles ; I'll follow your advice about having a petition drawn up, and when it has been signed by his friends, we shall see what sort of a reception the queen will give it. I know it will not be of any use, but it shall be tried for all that."

" And, according to my promise, I will take care that it shall reach its place of destination," said the governor. " You must be aware that I have no ill-feeling against the subject of our conversation, but he has offended the laws, and, having been committed to prison, I can take no further steps in his favour unless commanded to do so by her majesty, whose servant I am."

" I suppose I must be satisfied with that," said Nell. " The poor fellow, however, will be suffering imprisonment all the time ; and the most mortifying part of the affair is that Luke Somerton will be enjoying his liberty as much as if he had not the blood of Captain Aylmer to answer for."

" Why do you still persist in believing him guilty of that crime ?" demanded Sir Charles, anxious to remove an impression that was prevalent in the island. " We have reason to believe that the charge was a most unfounded one, and surely, for the sake of his daughter, the subject might be suffered to drop."

" For *her* sake !" repeated Nell, with a scornful curl of her lip, " I hate her, Sir Charles, and may, perhaps, prove how much before long."

" Take care what you are saying," exclaimed the governor ; " for it is dangerous to speak your mind too freely in the presence of one who is sworn to keep the queen's peace. I do not ask you if it was so, but it has been reported to me that you were among the foremost of the rabble concerned in the burning of Somerton's house, and, if that was brought forward, I should be compelled to award you the same fate that has befallen the man you are here to plead for. This I mention to you in the hope that you will henceforth see the madness of pursuing a course that must end in your own undoing."

" If I had cared for the consequences I should not have done as I have," replied Nell ; " and as for your knowing whether I was at the burning of Luke Somerton's cottage, I at once acknowledge ——"

" I will hear no more," interrupted Sir Charles. " It is unnecessary to make an avowal, because I am anxious that no further committals shall take place ; since it is to be hoped that the example already made of Roden will prove a sufficient warning to others that the laws are not to be broken with impunity. You will now leave me, and if you have an influence over those other misguided persons, I entreat you to exert yourself in bringing them to a sense of their imprudence. Say to them that I am willing to bury the past in oblivion, but that any further acts of violence will be punished with the utmost rigour and severity."

" Before I go," said the woman, hesitating, " I would ask you if there is no possible way to release Roden from prison ? He is not more to blame than any one else that attacked the house, and it seems hard that he should bear the punishment for all."

" I have no power beyond that which I have already stated," replied Sir Charles. " I will use whatever influence I may possess to obtain his freedom, and that is all I can undertake to do. But you seem strangely interested in the fate of this man. May I ask if there is any particular motive for such zeal ?"

" There is," she replied. " It was I that first persuaded him to make the attack, and I therefore feel that whatever sufferings he endures have been brought on by myself. Besides, we were about to be married ; and though I don't pretend to any very great share of feeling, I own that my thoughts are sorrowful when we reflect that we may never be allowed to see each other again "

" That will depend upon his behaviour, and the conduct he pursues in prison," answered the governor. " If he submits quietly to our rules and regulations, I shall be able to make a more favourable report of him, and it is probable that will not be without effect in mitigation of punishment. In the meanwhile, you must carefully avoid giving any annoyance to Louisa Somerton, whose only offence seems to consist in having exerted herself successfully in preserving her father from the ignominious death he was doomed to suffer."

" I shall not make any promise about it," exclaimed Nell Dawson ; " because I have not quite made up my mind what I shall do. It seems likely, however, that the people here will not trouble her any more, now that her father has left the island, and I shall not go single-handed to work till I know what is to be done with Roden. So you may make yourself easy about the girl, as far as I am concerned, though I won't undertake to say that everybody else will be of my way of thinking."

" You may, at all events, have influence enough to prevail on them not to interfere with a helpless girl."

" Not I," replied Nell. " Besides, if you feel so much interest in her behalf, why not take her into the castle, and have her under your own eye and protection ?"

"I have made her the offer," replied Sir Charles Radcliffe; "but she has hitherto resolutely declined it."

"At any rate," observed Nell, "I should think you could persuade her to marry Lieutenant Granger, who is always dangling after her. If she had him for a husband, there would be little chance of any harm befalling her."

"She knows my wishes upon that subject also," replied the governor; "but a high principle of honour impels her to let my suggestion pass unheeded. She believes the union would bring disgrace upon the young man, and, though loving him with all the sincerity of affection, she refuses to give him her hand till her father's name is cleared from the stain which at present attaches to it."

"I have heard something of this before," exclaimed Nell; "and in my opinion the girl is a great fool for her pains. She ought to know when a good offer is made her, and accept it without making a fuss about it, as if she was doing a great favour by marrying a man that's a great deal better off in the world than she is herself. Not that I care a dump about it; for, to speak the honest truth, I would rather see her unhappy than otherwise."

"And that, too, for no other reason than that she exhibited the most devoted love for her condemned parent."

"You may give what reason you like, Sir Charles," answered Nell; "but I never liked the girl, it must be confessed, and it is like gall and wormwood to me when I hear people praising her for an act which has no such great merit in it after all. To be sure her father would have died but for what she did to save him; yet, for all that, there's why few others, I believe, that would not have done the same thing, if they were placed in a like situation."

"And yet your animosity arises from the fact of her having performed that act of duty and affection."

"Ay, that's because I can't see why the favour should have been granted to her when it would have been denied to anybody else," replied Nell. "Besides, it's the opinion of more people than myself, that Luke Somerton ought to have met his fate on the gibbet; and it's enough to make people discontented when they see favours showed to a man that everybody feels certain is a murderer. Nay, as far as I and a great many more are concerned, Luke will ever be considered as a shedder of human blood."

"One would hardly think you could believe the crime of murder so great," observed the governor, "seeing that it is not very long since you acknowledged having been the chief instigator of an attack that was intended to have involved a father and his daughter in one doom."

"You must not judge of people's acts till you are acquainted with their motives," replied the woman. "We can all of us find excuses for our own deeds, let them be ever so bad, and, perhaps, if you knew mine, you would be inclined to think differently of me."

Having uttered these words in a mysterious manner, that left everything to doubt and imagination, she turned away, and instantly left the hall, without deigning to wait for any reply. Sir Charles, who had often heard of the woman, without having had an opportunity of seeing so much of her as he had on the present occasion, was lost in wonder at all he had heard and witnessed during the interview that had just passed. That Nell was in some degree deranged, he had no doubt, but there was a force and earnestness in some of her arguments that almost staggered him, and he was still lost in thought upon this all-absorbing subject, when the voice of Lieutenant Granger at length roused him to consciousness.

"I was about to speak to you on business, Sir Charles," said the young man, "but you seem to be so absorbed in reflections of your own, that I will defer my purpose till another opportunity."

"What is it you would say to me?" asked the governor, as the other was turning away to take his departure.

"Nothing but what will do another time," replied Granger; "it merely referred to the prisoner, Henry Roden, who, I hear from the turnkey, is so violent at times, that it is feared he intends doing mischief, unless great care is taken to prevent the execution of his design."

"Then let one of our people be set to keep a careful watch over him," said Sir Charles Radcliffe; "I was about to give orders to that effect, but this intelligence of yours renders the caution doubly needful. But what has given rise to the suspicion that he meditates violence?"

"He has declared that such is his intention," answered the lieutenant.

"In that case he had better be put in irons."

"That has already been done," replied Granger; "but he is possessed of such herculean strength that it is feared no bonds will be found strong enough to restrain him."

"We shall see about that," exclaimed the governor. "The fellow, I am aware, is desperate enough in all conscience, but it will be my fault if I suffer him to prove master when I have the means of quelling him in my own hands. He is resolute, I know, but he shall own himself conquered before I have done with him."

"Shall I order him to be placed in another cell, from which there will be less fear of escape?" asked Granger.

"We will not be in too great a hurry about that," replied Sir Charles Radcliffe. "We will first of all try whether milder means will not bring him to his senses; and, if that fail, it will be time enough to resort to more violent measures. I do not wish to punish him with unnecessary severity, yet, if need's must, I will show him that violence will do him less good than he imagines."

"I fancy you will find that a harder task than you seem to think for," returned the young officer. "The men here tell me they have tried every means they can think of to make him submit, but he is reckless of the consequences, and declares that he would rather perish in an attempt to regain his liberty, than exist any longer within the limits of a prison cell."

"That is mere bravado, depend upon it," said Sir Charles. "He thinks, I dare say, to intimidate us by excessive violence, but it remains for us to prove to him that the law possesses far greater strength than any he can pretend to. I'll have him bound neck and heels but what my authority shall be acknowledged in this place. I am not cruel or unmerciful, as you know, Lieutenant Granger, but if this ruffian urges me too far, he must take the consequences of his own madness. Why, it is scarcely a quarter of an hour since I was thinking how I could mitigate the rigour of his imprisonment, and yet now he compels me to adopt a course that will render the burthen more difficult to bear than ever."

"Upon my life, Sir Charles," said the young man, "I believe the fellow is not worth the trouble you would bestow upon him. He has always been at the head of every piece of mischief in the island, and, if ever he should happen to get loose, it will be a sorrowful day for some."

"I don't think there is much chance of his getting loose," said the governor. "I have just now been pestered almost out of my life to set him at liberty, but I refused to do more than intercede with the queen for a remission of the severer part

of the punishment he has rendered himself liable to."

"He deserves not the slightest mitigation," exclaimed Lieutenant Granger; "for it is to him that we owe all the violence that has kept the island in commotion for some time past. In this he has been ably assisted by a woman called Nell Dawson, who, by-the-bye, I saw leaving this place just as I was coming in."

"Aye," answered the governor, "she left me scarcely a minute before you made your appearance here. The woman pleaded hard enough for him; and, to tell you the truth, my heart almost bled for her, for, with all her other faults, she seems to feel an affection for the worthless scoundrel that he little merits."

"You must not believe one-half that she says," exclaimed Lieutenant Granger, "for she would say or do anything to get him out of prison, because

she cannot work the mischief she intends without his assistance and co-operation. Why, it is not above an hour since she was trying to excite a mob to go with her and assist in another attack upon Louisa; and when she failed in bringing them to her fiendish views, she came here with soft and plausible words to prevail upon you to have pity upon the only man she can depend upon to aid her in the project she has formed against an unoffending girl."

"Then I'm glad it was out of my power to grant her request," said the governor. "But, upon my word, she urged her entreaties with so much earnestness and apparent good feeling, that I quite regretted my inability to send her away happy with an assurance that Roden should have the liberty she supplicated."

"And what," asked the young man, "is she going to do next?"

"Why the next plan, I believe," answered Sir Charles, "will be to get a petition signed in his behalf by all her friends, and when that is done, I have promised to forward it without delay to Queen Anne."

"But I trust you will not do so now that I have told you the mischief she has in view?" said Granger.

"Why," replied the governor, "when once a promise has been given it canno tbe withdrawn unless some very special reason is given for it."

"And that special reason you may very well ground upon the information you have received from me."

"I am not quite sure of that," replied Sir Charles. "People are sometimes mistaken, in their over zeal to perform some notable feat in behalf of those they have a particular wish to serve. You have a notion that they intend some fresh outrage against Louisa Somerton, and a thousand dangers are at once pictured to your view. Now I am myself well aware of the animosity these people bear against the girl ; but the law is strong enough for her protection, and I will myself take care that no harm shall befal her whilst I have the honour to be entrusted by her majesty with the government of this place. You have heard me, Lieutenant Granger, and I would now ask if the assurance I have given you is sufficient to allay your fears respecting Miss Somerton ?"

" Of your own zeal I am perfectly well convinced," replied the young man, " but I am not quite so well assured that Louisa will be safe, if you let this ruffian loose upon society. We have already seen that no enormity is too great for him, and as he has once failed in perpetrating his fiendish revenge, there is but too much reason to fear that if another opportunity is given him, he will complete the task he has been thus endeavouring to accomplish."

" At all events, I will not do anything without giving it due consideration," said Sir Charles. " As for releasing him, that is altogether out of my power, for no one but the queen herself has the privilege of extending mercy towards those who have been tried and convicted. Nay more, if the prisoner proves restive under the restraint he has brought upon himself, it will but serve to tighten the bands with which he is already enthralled."

" Shall I visit him," asked Lieutenant Granger, " and endeavour to quell his violent spirit, by laying before him the consequences that must follow, if he pursues a course such as may render further restraint necessary ?"

" I think it would be better that you should not be the person who conveys that message from me," replied the governor. " Roden seems to have formed as strong an antipathy against you as he has against Luke Somerton and his daughter, and the sight of you might only serve to irritate still more the hatred that has engendered in his heart. It will be better, therefore, that Morley, our chief turnkey, should be the bearer of my message, as he knows how to manage a refractory spirit better than either you or I do."

" Shall I tell Morley what you wish him to do ?"

" Yes ; tell him to go and visit the prisoner without delay," answered Sir Charles Radcliffe. " You will briefly state to him what I want done, and, above all things, let there be no delay about it."

Acting upon this hint, Lieutenant Granger took his leave of the governor, and proceeding to the turnkey's room, told him in as few words as possible the conversation that had just passed respecting Harry Roden, and directed that steps should be instantly put in progress for checking the insubordination that had been manifested in the conduct of the prisoner. Immediately upon receiving these instructions, the turnkey hastened to that part of the castle in which the prisoner's cell was situated, and having unfastened the door he entered the narrow chamber in which Roden was confined. At first the gloom prevented his seeing the captive, but when his eyes became more accustomed to the obscurity, he saw that his charge was lying in one corner upon a heap of straw, either sound asleep, or else sulking, as he thought of the destiny which he had thus brought upon himself.

Morley spoke to him three or four times, but no answer was returned, till at length the turnkey, finding that every other means failed him, inquired if there was any person whom he wished to visit him.

" No," was the brief and sullen reply.

" What !" exclaimed the gaoler, " isn't there one friend in the world that you would like to see and converse with ?"

" You have had your answer," growled Roden; " leave me ; for it's a hard thing that a man can't be left to himself when he hasn't it in his power to get out of the way of his visitors."

" Well, you needn't growl so about it, when I came on a civil errand," returned the other. " I was sent by Sir Charles Radcliffe, because he heard that you had turned sulky, and I'm to tell you that if your conduct ain't a little more quiet than it has been, he will feel himself obliged to use other means to keep you under restraint."

" Then you may take him word back from me," answered the prisoner, " that I shall do as I please about it, and am ready to take the consequences whatever they may be. He'll put fetters upon my limbs, I suppose? Well, let him do so, for there's an old grudge against me, and he can't take a better opportunity of having his revenge than when I am in his power and unable to help myself."

" The governor owes you no grudge that I know of," answered Morley. " He's been sent here to do his duty to his queen and country, and if people will break the laws, they mustn't find fault with what follows. You would have murdered Luke Somerton and his daughter, and it's only fair that you should be made an example of."

The prisoner, who, till this moment, had continued lying upon the straw, now sprang up with a sudden bound, and glaring fiercely upon the turnkey, rushed forward, and seizing him in his herculean grasp, soon threw him prostrate upon the ground. This action had been so sudden and unexpected, that Morley had not an opportunity of defending himself, and he lay completely at the mercy of a man whose vindictive spirit would hurry him into any excess, even though it should be to dye his hands in the blood of his adversary. In this fearful situation he had no alternative but to call out for assistance, and fortunately this was not done in vain, for immediately afterwards another turnkey rushed into the cell, and dragged Roden away, just as he had got his hand upon the throat of his antagonist for the purpose of strangling him. In another moment Morley had sprung upon his feet, and after a short but stout resistance, the prisoner was secured to a strong chain, one end of which was fastened to the wall.

" So," exclaimed Morley, " you are not content with what you have already done, but you must needs want to wind up your crimes with murder! But I think you will not be able to do any more mischief now, so we'll leave you to the comfortable reflection, that whatever inconvenience you may suffer has been brought on by yourself."

" Had I killed you there would have been some consolation for me," exclaimed Roden, scowling vengefully upon the last speaker. "I have been brooding over my wrongs, and if Sir Charles Radcliffe had been here, instead of you, I would never have left go his throat whilst a spark of life remained within him."

"And pray what is the reason of your giving way to such bloodthirsty thoughts?" demanded the turnkey.

"To be rid of a life that is a burden to me," answered the prisoner. "I believe it is the governor's intention to transport me, and rather than drag on a life of misery and captivity, I made up my mind to commit an act that should send me to the gallows at once."

"And if it had not been for the arrival of assistance, you stood a very fair chance of having your whim gratified," exclaimed Morley. "Egad, you didn't give me much of an opportunity to defend myself, for it was a word and a blow with you, and the blow came first. But why you should have made an attempt upon my life I don't know, for I have never given you any cause of offence that I am aware of."

"It mattered not to me who I killed," answered Harry Roden. "My purpose would have been served as well by taking your life as that of anybody else; for they would have hanged me for it, and that was all I wanted."

"Well, it ain't everybody that's so anxious to fall under the hands of Jack Ketch," returned the other, "for I've known people that have tried all sorts of schemes to avoid the halter. And you yourself were not in such a hurry to be scragged a few days ago, or you would not have taken so much pains to escape from prison."

"Ay," answered Roden, "that was all very well to attempt once, but I know well enough a second chance won't be given to me. They'll consider me too dangerous a subject to remain in this country, and I would rather die at once than be sent away to end my days like a slave."

"You should have thought of that before you mixed yourself up in these riotous doings," observed Morley.

"Ay, it's all very easy to preach after the mischief is done," replied the prisoner. "I can now see, as well as you do, that I had no business to care whether Luke Somerton was hanged or not; but I didn't like to see favour shown to one that wouldn't be granted to another, and so, as there were others of my way of thinking, we agreed among ourselves that as the murderer of Captain Aylmer wasn't to die for his crimes, we resolved to take the affair into our own hands."

"And a very pretty affair you have made of it," exclaimed Morley. "You have got yourself into a prison, and after all that has taken place, you are never likely to leave it till they take you over the herring-pond."

"So it seems," answered Roden; "but I am prepared for the worst, and if they only give me a chance, I shall never live to see the place they have destined me for."

"What! you'd like to make away with yourself, I suppose, if the truth was known? But you may as well make up your mind that they won't give you an opportunity of doing that, for Sir Charles seems to have a notion that you have thoughts of that kind, and you may take my word for it that you will be so thoroughly well watched as not to give you the smallest chance for carrying your intentions into effect."

"We shall see," replied Roden, "for when once a man has made up his mind to do a thing, it ain't so easy to prevent him as you seem to think."

"Now, if you take my advice," said Morley, "you'll try to make friends with those that have got the care of you, and if things go on pretty smoothly, you may by-and-bye get a little more liberty than they allow you at present. But that will depend upon yourself, you know; so reflect upon what I've been telling you, and it will be all the better for yourself in the long run."

At this moment Sir Charles Radcliffe, who had been brought to the place by the news that had reached him of an attempt upon the life of the turnkey, entered the cell.

"What is this I hear?" he exclaimed, approaching the place upon which the prisoner had thrown himself. "Is kindness so utterly thrown away upon you, Roden, that you must seek the life of a man who performs no more than his duty in keeping a strict watch over you?"

"Kindness!" muttered the prisoner sullenly; "so you call it kindness to keep a human being chained up here like a dog? Why should I not have my liberty as well as Luke Somerton, who has done far worse than I have?"

"I am not here to answer your questions, but to inquire into the outrageous attack that has been made upon this man. What motive had you for seeking the life of a fellow-creature?"

"My only motive was that I might get hanged for it," answered the ruffian. "Transportation is a punishment that I dread more than anything else, for there the torture lasts a whole lifetime; but when once the hangman has finished his work, there's an end to a man's sufferings."

"Then you do not repent the cowardly act that was so providentially frustrated?" said the governor.

"Repent!" exclaimed Roden; "do you think I should have made the attempt if I was likely to repent directly afterwards? No, no, Sir Charles, I'm only sorry that a meddling fool came to prevent what I was doing, for if it had not been for him I should, by this time, have taken pretty well my last step up the gallows."

"Will any leniency shown to you under such circumstances prevail on you to become more calm and submissive to the restraint your own deeds have brought upon you?"

"What do you mean by leniency?" demanded the criminal.

"Suppose you were released from those bonds of which you complain," said Sir Charles, "would you, on that condition, give me your solemn promise never to make a similar attack to the one that has been so happily frustrated?"

"If I made a promise, it would only be to break it," answered Roden. "You have seen beforehand to what an extent of frenzy I have been driven, for even in your own presence I would have slain Lieutenant Granger, but for the arm that frustrated my blow. Then there was Luke Somerton, too,—he was within a hair's breadth of receiving a bullet through his head; but there, too,

I was foiled, and he yet lives on, while I am doomed to a punishment that to me is far worse than death."

"But it has been brought on by your own evil deeds," answered Sir Charles. "Passion seems to be your only impulse, and you now feel the dreadful penalty to which it leads. You have lost all your social rights, besides having forfeited the esteem of your friends."

"There you are wrong, Sir Charles," he exclaimed; "for I believe, as far as my friends are concerned, they are still as true to me as ever. They hate Luke Somerton as much as I do, and there isn't a man among 'em but knows that all I am suffering has been through his fault."

"Or rather through the unjustifiable hatred with which you regard him," returned the governor. "I have never heard of his having done an injury to any one in the island, and yet nearly all the people are up in arms, for no other reason, that I am aware of, than that they were disappointed on the morning when he was to have been executed."

"That's not the only cause, though it has a good deal to do with it," answered Roden. "The truth is, it is well known that he has been a traitor to his country, preferring to fight for her enemies, when he ought to have been on her side. And yet, after all that, he could obtain a pardon from the queen, though convicted of a cruel murder."

"How many times more am I to contradict that assertion?" exclaimed Sir Charles Radcliffe. "The royal mercy was not granted to him, without the whole affair having been carefully weighed and considered. Luke Somerton had no interest with the Queen of England, beyond that which was raised by the generous devotion of his daughter, who risked her own life in crossing a tempestuous ocean, for the purpose of preserving his. Queen Anne heard of her heroism, and as the proof against the parent was of a very equivocal nature, she wisely granted the petition which had been urged under such novel and peculiar circumstances."

"I know it's no use arguing the point with you, Sir Charles," said the prisoner; "but, on the other hand, nothing that you now say will convince me that a murderer can be a proper object for a sovereign's mercy."

"And yet," exclaimed the governor, "in no less than three instances you have attempted the same crime yourself."

"That was done, as I told you before, for the sake of being hanged, and put out of my misery," replied the prisoner. "I knew well enough that the same luck would not befal me that had come to the share of Luke Somerton; and, being tired of my life, I thought the best way was to be rid of it. But I have been foiled; and now that your people have bound me thus, I know there is nothing remaining for me but banishment and slavery."

"Even now that may depend upon yourself," said Sir Charles. "Give me reason to believe that you repent the past, and something may be done for the future to render your life less burdensome than you anticipate."

"I shall not humble myself now in the smallest degree," replied Harry Roden, sullenly. "What

I have done I am ready to answer for; but neither you nor any one else shall ever be able to make me show the white feather. No, no; if I must be sent away as a felon, there's no help for it, and I'll submit to my fate as quietly as I can. Something, however, may turn up in my favour, and if an opportunity should offer itself, I shall yet escape my doom."

"Do not anticipate an event so utterly improbable," said Sir Charles. "Henceforth a vigilant watch will be kept upon you, and any attempt to escape will certainly be punished with immediate death. I will now, however, leave you to reflect upon what I have said; and if any feeling of contrition should reach your heart, I will again visit you in this your gloomy place of confinement."

Sir Charles, followed by the two keepers, now left the cell; and the door being securely fastened, Henry Roden was left to the indulgence of his own wayward thoughts.

CHAPTER XLVII.

"A wild and reckless band,
Whose daring deeds have oft created fear,
Are now assembling.—Wilt thou assist
To scatter or destroy them?
The Emissary.

DURING the time that Sir Charles was with the prisoner, Lieutenant Granger was visited by Richard Emery, one of the revenue officers, who, having just learned some news of importance, came to confer with him upon the best means by which they should proceed.

"I have been informed," he began, "upon pretty good authority, that a large cargo of contraband spirits is to be brought on shore to-night, and so resolute are the fellows who are engaged in the affair, that I expect we shall have more than usual trouble and risk in thwarting their designs."

"And you wish, I suppose," said Granger, "to ask the governor for the assistance of a few soldiers?"

"That was the object that brought me here," replied Emery; "and I suppose there will be no objection on the part of Sir Charles to grant the assistance we require, since it is upon the queen's service the request is made."

"I have no doubt he will promptly yield to it," answered Lieutenant Granger. "But how happens it that you require on this occasion more than your usual force?"

"Why, the truth is," exclaimed the other, "these smugglers have grown bolder of late, in consequence of their having succeeded, on three or four occasions, in landing their cargoes without molestation. This has rendered them more confident; and their numbers having been considerably increased of late, they now seem to consider themselves quite strong enough to resist any force that we are able to bring against them."

"Then they must be made to find out their mistake," said Lieutenant Granger. "Have you ascertained, Mr. Emery, where they mean to attempt their landing?"

"Just under the East Cliff."

"A likely place enough for their purpose," said Granger; "but they will, by and bye, find out that we are aware of their plans, and prepared to thwart them. Do you know where those who are waiting their arrival mean to assemble?"

"Yes," replied the other. "They are to meet to-night in a cave close to the place where the goods are to be landed, and thither, if we go, we may fall in with them."

"Are they well armed?"

"They are."

"And are bold, resolute men, if we should come to a skirmish?"

"There is not a man among them but would rather die than yield himself a prisoner," answered Emery. "We may expect sharp work for it, lieutenant, I can assure you; but with resolution and courage on the part of our men, I think we are sure to capture them. At any rate, we have our duty to perform, and not one of the rascals shall escape, if I have the power to prevent it."

"And you may rely upon being well seconded, both by myself and those who are under my command," said Granger. "The service you require us upon is not much in our way, to be sure, for we aim at higher game than smugglers; but if there's likely to be a bit of a skirmish my men will be delighted, for, to tell the truth, they have grown tired of the quiet life they are leading here."

"And yet they might find active employment against these smugglers," answered Emery; "for the whole coast abounds with them; and as our force is not sufficiently strong to act as a check to them, they have now grown bold by success, and absolutely laugh our attempts at stopping them to scorn. It, therefore, becomes necessary to teach them that the queen's authority is still to be respected, and it is for that reason I came to ask your assistance."

"You shall have it, my dear fellow," exclaimed Lieutenant Granger. "I will join with you heart and soul, and these rascals shall get such a thorough routing that they shall not be likely to forget in a hurry."

"Then I may depend upon your meeting me?"

"Most assuredly you may," said Granger. "Where shall we meet on this momentous occasion?"

"In the Druid's Gap."

"At what time?"

"At ten o'clock to-night," answered Emery. "The boats are not expected to arrive till twelve; but I should like, first of all, to surprise the fellows in the cave, and after they are secured it will be easy to rout the others, and seize upon the goods they bring ashore."

"I will be faithful to my appointment," exclaimed Lieutenant Granger, "and will give directions for a dozen of my men to be there in waiting for me. Our combined numbers will then, I should imagine, be sufficient to effect the purpose we have in view; and if so, the island will be likely to be rid, for some time to come, of these free-trading scoundrels."

Upon this understanding they parted, and Lieutenant Granger, having given the necessary orders for his men to be at the place specified, proceeded across the fields in the direction of the cottage where dwelt the treasured idol whom he so fondly loved, but whom there was at present so little chance of his ever possessing. He found her at home, as he had anticipated; but, surprised at his unexpected appearance, she met him half way as he passed through the garden, and earnestly entreated him to defer his visit till some further opportunity.

"I fear," she proceeded to say, "you will think me ungrateful for the many acts of kindness you have shown me; but circumstanced as we at present are, your attendance here will draw upon us the observation I am so anxious to avoid. The prohibition may not last long; but till I am again under the protection of my father, it is hardly right that I should receive the visits of even so dear a friend as Lieutenant Granger."

"Nay," he exclaimed, "this is carrying your notions of female propriety rather too far. It is known throughout the island that I love you, Louisa, and were I to absent myself for any time, it would give rise to suspicions that all chance of our union was at an end."

"Let them think so," returned Louisa, with a sigh, "for I believe they will not judge wrong in the end."

"Why, you surely don't mean to tell me that I am never to have the happiness of calling you mine?" he exclaimed.

"Such seems to be the probability at present," answered Louisa. "You are aware already of the motives I have for coming to that determination, and at present I see no reason to believe that any alteration in your favour will take place. My father may never return, and ——"

"Why that, my dear Louisa, is the very reason why you ought to seek a protector in one who offers you an honourable love," he exclaimed, interrupting her.

"So you have told me on many occasions before," she replied, "and yet, obstinate though you may call it, I have not hitherto been convinced that I ought to bestow my hand where it could only convey dishonour. I feel myself degraded in society, and till that foul blot is removed I will remain even as I am at present."

"I will not urge the subject further, at present," exclaimed Lieutenant Granger, "because it is one that has been forbidden; you, however, know my feelings upon it, and will, perhaps, yield, when you reflect, that not only my happiness, but your own safety, depends upon the union. Sir Charles Radcliffe, too, is most anxious that our union should take place, for he sees but too plainly that, in your present unprotected state, you are exposed to dangers that he is unable to avert."

"Heaven, in its great mercy, has thus far aided me," replied Louisa, "and I am content to remain under its protection."

"Then even the wishes of your father are not to be complied with?"

"In the present instance," she replied, "I must be permitted to follow my own inclination. You may deem it a wilful and perverse one, but it is dictated by honour, and no argument—no persuasion—will ever effect the slightest change in the determination I have expressed."

"At any rate," said her lover, "you will not, I hope, forbid my visiting you as I have been used to do?"

"I cannot, nor do I wish, to refuse you that request," answered Louisa. "Your visits to me are, I know, kindly meant, but I would wish them not to be too frequently repeated; and you must not forget my previous injunction, to speak as little as possible upon the subject you have now entered upon. As for the danger you think I have to dread from these islanders, I myself apprehend none, though they have certainly shewn a feeling of hatred for which I cannot account."

"And their hatred, instead of diminishing, seems rather to increase," exclaimed Lieutenant Granger.

"Yet my worst enemy is in prison."

"It is that circumstance which has served still more to stir up the malevolence of these people," said her lover. "They regard you as the immediate cause of Harry Roden's misfortune, and that half-crazy woman, Nell Dawson, vows deadly vengeance against you for it."

"If she indeed bears malice against me, I must needs bear the brunt of it," replied Louisa. "I have witnessed much that confirms what you tell me, and yet I have never felt one moment's uneasiness upon the subject. She has the inclination to do me a mischief, but happily lacks the power to carry it into effect ; and, to tell you the truth, I care not if she kills me ; for though my years are not many, Lieutenant Granger, I have experienced so much adversity, that death would be a blessing to me, instead of a thing to be dreaded."

"So you think just at this moment," exclaimed the young man ; "but take my word for it, Louisa, in spite of the dark clouds that at present lour over you, a change will take place, ere long, that will amply compensate for the sufferings you have endured. You shake your head as if doubtful of my prophecy, and yet I hope, before many weeks have passed away, you will acknowledge that I saw farther into futurity than you were able to do yourself."

"Probably it may be so," replied our heroine ; "and it is scarcely needful for me to say how rejoiced I should be to confess myself mistaken. If my own anticipations have been gloomy, it has been the consequence of severe trials, such as few persons I hope and believe have undergone ; but that they are founded upon just grounds, I must still believe. Be that as it may, however, I have been much relieved by the kindness you have shewn throughout my trials, and, should circumstances take a more favourable turn ——"

"You will no longer withhold the consent for which I have so long and ardently prayed?" interrupted Granger.

"Nay, I said not that," she exclaimed ; "though I will go so far as to say, that I shall not refuse your offer when it appears that I can accept it without doing an injury to yourself. But, on the other hand, I would rather see you bestow your affections upon some other female, who would be more likely to render you happier than myself."

"I shall hold you to your promise, remember," exclaimed Lieutenant Granger. "You have said that, if your father should ever retrieve his honour, there shall be no further obstacle to our union. That event seems likely to be realised sooner than you expected, and, whenever the confirmation of it arrives, I shall never cease to urge my suit till you have promised to seal my happiness by a speedy marriage."

"You are now trespassing upon forbidden ground,

Lieutenant Granger," she exclaimed, as a faint smile passed over her countenance. "Let us change the conversation, or I shall regret having granted you this interview."

"We will speak, then, of your father," said her lover ; "he has been heard of, Louisa, and ——"

"Some evil has befallen him !" she exclaimed, in a voice trembling with apprehension and terror.

"Be not alarmed," replied Granger ; "at the time when the vessel which brought the news came away, he was well, and in high spirits at the prospect before him. I will not, however, disguise the fact, that he has been exposed to very considerable danger, but which was averted by the firmness and decision he manifested on the occasion."

"What was his danger?" demanded Louisa. "Has he been exposed to the peril of shipwreck?"

"No."

"He has been engaged in battle, then, and perhaps was wounded near unto death?"

"There your fears have again deceived you," exclaimed her lover. "The truth is, Louisa, a mutiny broke out among the men, and he would have fallen a sacrifice to their lawless fury, but for the resolution he exhibited, and the faithful zeal manifested in his behalf by Christopher Dalton."

"But he is still in peril," cried Louisa, her fears excited by the explanation thus afforded ; "the mutiny may have been allayed for the present, but men who have once forgotten the duty they owe their superior officer, are seldom to be appeased for any long time. They will appear to be contrite, but only to break out with redoubled fury on the first favourable opportunity that may offer."

"Let us hope that your prognostications will prove false," said the young officer. "It cannot be denied that men who have once broken out into open acts of insubordination are rarely to be trusted; but your father has already given them a convincing proof of the power he possesses over them, and they cannot but remember the lesson he has already taught them. The ringleader, I understand, fell at the moment he was about to assassinate his captain, and at his death the others were thrown into such consternation, that they were easily secured and put in irons."

"Were there many in the mutiny?" asked Louisa.

"Nearly the whole crew."

"Then how will he be able to work his vessel when deprived of the assistance of his men?"

"He will find less difficulty in doing that than you seem to imagine," answered Lieutenant Granger. "Some of the men repented of their rash conduct before the affray took place, and were of valuable assistance towards bringing about a favourable termination of the affair. Others among the refractory have been pardoned on a solemn promise being given to be more obedient in future ; and those who were not to be depended on, were to be taken to the nearest port and there dismissed ; others being taken in their place, to make up the number of the crew."

"And you have no reason to believe," said Louisa, "that any serious evil befel my father?"

"I am quite certain that he was safe at the time when word was sent over of what had taken place," answered Lieutenant Granger. "I should not have mentioned the circumstance to you at all, but that I feared you might hear it through some other channel, and in that case you might not have been convinced of your father's safety. And now, Louisa, I have news of a more cheering nature to tell you of. The war which has so long been carried on between this country and France is likely to be brought to a speedy termination; for overtures of peace have been already made, and it is the opinion of most people that an immediate ratification of it will take place."

" Heaven grant their prediction may prove correct!" exclaimed Louisa, her countenance beaming with mingled emotions of joy and gratitude. " I have scarcely ventured to hope for so favourable a result, but your words have excited new sensations, such as I little expected to feel. Should my father indeed return to England, I believe it will not be difficult to obtain for him a restoration of the queen's favour, and then, if no other obstacle should present itself, I will no longer reject the love you have proffered me."

" Thanks—a thousand thanks, dear girl, for that promise !" exclaimed the delighted lover. " I now feel assured that my happiness is not far distant, though I cannot see what other obstacle can stand in our way."

" Have you so soon forgot, then," she asked, " that my father is more than suspected of having been concerned with the smugglers who infest this island ?"

" I would fain forget it," answered Granger; " though I believe there is less criminality in the affair than has been imagined. The whole report has arisen from a mere suspicion, which no one has ever attempted to prove, and even should it have reached the ears of the queen, I do not believe she would take any heed of it. And as for the smugglers you speak of, Louisa, I rather think their game is nearly at an end; for I and the revenue officers are to meet to-night, and with a sufficiently strong body of men proceed to their retreat, when it is expected the whole of them will become our prisoners."

" The undertaking is a hazardous one," exclaimed Louisa, in a tone of alarm ; " and much I fear you will be marked by the reckless ruffians as one of their first victims."

" But they will not be prepared for the visit we are about to pay them," replied Lieutenant Granger. " Everything has been concocted with the greatest caution and secrecy, so that on our arrival they will be at our mercy before one effort can be made to defend themselves."

" Alas !" sighed our heroine. " I fear you represent the danger as being less than it really is. These men have long been the terror of the place —their deeds have ever been marked with violence and bloodshed, and when they find the peril in which they are placed, they will boldly risk their lives rather than yield themselves your prisoners."

" At all events, dear Louisa," exclaimed Lieutenant Granger, " there has been one good resulting from the latter part of our conversation : I have ascertained that my safety is of some value to you, and ——"

" Nay, I—I ——"

" It is in vain that you would deny it," he replied ; " my own vanity tells me that I am

right, and henceforth I shall feel relieved of half my anxiety. A new source of hope has been opened to me, and I shall now look forward with more anxiety than ever for the return of your father."

" But even when he does return," answered Louisa, " there will be as much uncertainty as ever. We know not that he will obtain the restitution of his forfeited title and estates, and unless he does that, my consent will never be given to the further prosecution of your suit."

" Do not make any rash determination of that kind," exclaimed Lieutenant Granger ; " for I have already told you that it is your hand alone I ask for, and that I should regard you none the less for being portionless. True, I have not much wealth of my own to boast of; but I have an honourable profession, and the commission I hold under her majesty will enable us to pass through the humble sphere that is best suited to us."

" But your station in society demands that you should not throw yourself away upon a portionless girl," replied our heroine. " Your friends will expect you to support the honour of your family, and that can scarely be done if your proposition was carried into effect. On the other hand, however, if my father should be restored to that of which he has been deprived, I should rejoice to make you the partaker of the brighter prospects that would then be opened to me."

" Then may Heaven grant a speedy realization of your hopes, dearest Louisa," exclaimed her lover. " I have myself little ambition to become wealthy by any other means than my own exertions ; but since our union seems to depend upon your father's restoration to his title and forfeited estates, I will henceforth look forward with hope to the hour when her majesty may be graciously pleased to grant your petition. For my own part, I believe there is little doubt that his former offences will be forgotten, and then, Louisa, I shall with confidence ask you to confirm the promise you have this day made me."

" And you shall not be disappointed," she replied. " Nay, the kindness and devotion you have ever manifested in my behalf, have won for you my highest esteem."

" *Esteem*, Louisa," he exclaimed, somewhat reproachfully, " is but a cold word for one who asks your love."

" Well then, *love* be it," she replied. " I will not deny that my heart is yours, and yours only ; and, if I have thus long refused to accept you as my suitor, it has only been because I deemed myself bound in honour not to involve you in the disgrace and shame that has fallen on my family."

" The motive was doubtless a good one," exclaimed Granger ; " and yet you little imagine the misery and anxiety it has occasioned."

" If I have caused you uneasiness," answered Louisa Somerton, " I have the consolation of knowing that it was not done with the intention of wounding your feeling. I knew myself to be worth scarcely a thought, and believed that long ere this you would have transferred your affections to one who would render you far happier than I can ever hope to do."

" But you are now convinced, I suppose," said her lover, " that when the heart is really and sincerely given, it is not so easy to tear it from the object of its choice? At least, I have myself experienced the utter impossibility of doing so, and should any hapless chance prevent our union, I should pass the remainder of my days in unceasing regret for the loss of that happiness which I once fondly believed was to be mine. Now, however, a brighter prospect opens before me, and in spite of your anticipations to the contrary, I will believe that your father's restoration to honour is near at hand. But, hark!" he exclaimed, as the distant report of a pistol met his ear, "that is the signal that my men have set off for the Druid's Gap, where they are to await my coming, previous to the attack we are about to make on these desperadoes."

"Again I caution you to be guarded as possible when you throw yourself among those fearful men," cried Louisa, yielding to the fears which she could no longer conceal from her lover. "You are about to hunt them to their den, and if report speaks truly of the ruffians, they are not likely to yield without committing fearful slaughter among those who molest them."

"Your warning, dearest Louisa, shall not be forgotten," exclaimed Lieutenant Granger. "This is the first open acknowldgement you have ever made upon which I could found my hopes of the future, and for your sake I will guard a life that, without your love, would be valueless to me."

He then left her, and proceeded on his way with a heart lightened of the cares and fears that had so long depressed it. He could now look forward almost with certainty to a happy termination of his suit, for love can see no obstacles, and those which had hitherto stood in his way now totally disappeared. He could no longer see any doubt that Luke Somerton would earn the pardon he was so desirous of obtaining, and when he returned to the esteem of his sovereign, the consent of Louisa would immediately follow. These thoughts were still passing through his mind when he reached the Druid's Gap, where he found the men impatiently awaiting his arrival. From the sergeant he learnt that they had met with no interruption during their progress to the place, and that consequently the persons against whom these proceedings were directed were unconscious, and therefore unprepared for the attack that was to be made upon them. So far then everything had gone on well, and being joined a few minutes afterward by Mr. Emery and the revenue men under his command, it was resolved to march silently and without further delay to the cave where it was well known the persons they were in quest of were to be found.

The distance they had to go was about half a mile, and keeping close under the shadow of the cliffs they reached it without being observed, though they occasionally saw some people strolling about the beach as if looking for the vessel which was expected to reach the shore about that time. Having reached the entrance of the cave, they heard the voices of several persons within, plainly denoting that the smugglers were enjoying themselves over their cups, and revelling in the thought of landing their cargo in perfect safety. After a short conference between Lieutenant Granger and Mr. Emery, the men were desired to follow them in

silence, and they proceeded in darkness through the first, or outer cave. They now perceived in the adjoining subterranean chamber, about a score of the smugglers seated round a table, listening to a man who appeared to be instructing them in the plans they were to pursue as soon as it was announced to them that the vessel they expected was in sight. Every now and then low murmurs of applause and approbation were uttered by his auditors, and the speech being finished, one of the men was desired to proceed to the beach in order to ascertain if their assistance was likely to be speedily required. This, then, was the moment of attack, and no sooner had the messenger approached the place where our party remained in ambush, than he was struck down by one of the soldiers, and at the same time a general rush was made into the inner cave.

So suddenly was all this done, that the smugglers had no time for preparation or defence, yet, impelled by the peril with which they were threatened, they rushed furiously upon their assailants, resolving to sell their lives dearly rather than yield themselves prisoners. For a few minutes, indeed, it seemed doubtful which way the conflict would end, but at length their leader having fallen severely wounded, a feeling of consternation and terror immediately prevailed among his lawless assailants, and with little more difficulty the smugglers were seized upon and disarmed. One of the ruffians, however, who had hitherto escaped notice, now rushed from his hiding-place, and snatching up a lighted torch, was in the act of applying it to a barrel of gunpowder, when Lieutenant Granger sprang forward and dashed him to the earth just in time prevent the perpetration of the fearful act of vengeance he meditated.

"Villain!" exclaimed the officer, "what is it you would have done? Know you not that the deed you were about to commit was one that would have carried destruction to your own people as well as ours?"

"I know all about that," replied the fellow, slowly rising, after his arms had been bound behind him. "I wasn't going to dash a lighted torch among the gunpowder without knowing what the consequences would be."

"Then you cared not for sacrificing your own life as well as those of your companions in iniquity."

"Better blow them to atoms than trust to the mercy that you, and such as you, are likely to show us," exclaimed the fellow. "Besides, you would have shared our fate, and I am only sorry that you were able to interrupt me in my act of vengeance."

"But having been happily frustrated in your murderous design, you have little to expect from any representations that we might otherwise have made in your favour," said Lieutenant Granger. "Those whom I have the honour to serve are not revengeful in their desire to deal out punishment to the guilty, but you have now put it out of my power to say anything in your favour."

"I don't want you to speak for me," retorted the fellow sullenly. "Whatever the punishment may be, I'm able enough to bear it without flinching, even though it may be to swing from the gallows."

"Which is very likely to be the case," observed

Mr. Emery; "for I now recognise you as the ruffian who shot one of my men in the execution of his duty. You are accused of murder, and will have to answer the charge which I shall soon be prepared to bring against you."

"You may make what charge you like," answered the fellow; "but I deny having had anything to do with shedding human blood. To be sure, if there's a determination to hang me, it's very little use my denying the business, so I suppose they'll send me to the gibbet, by way of making an example."

"Your villanous attempt just now," said Lieutenant Granger, "justifies us in believing you guilty of the crime that has been imputed to you. Mr. Emery, too, recognizes you as the party who murdered one of his men, and his evidence must bring you to that fate which is awarded to all who are found guilty of so atrocious an act. I would therefore have you prepare yourself for the worst, as, in the event of a conviction, your days are numbered."

"And the fewer they are in number, the better it will be for me," exclaimed the ruffian. "If they don't hang me, they'll send me abroad for life, and I'd rather die at once than drag on a miserable existence as a convict."

Finding that no impression could be made upon the hardened criminal, Lieutenant Granger now consulted as to the best course that could be pursued. After a brief conference it was resolved, that, as all the prisoners were well bound and secured, they might be left under the charge of a couple of soldiers, whilst the others, headed by their officers, proceeded to the beach, in order to prevent the landing of the smuggled goods, and to seize upon all parties whom they might find there engaged in the unlawful proceedings that were expected to take place. On their arrival, however, they found that the cargo had been already landed, and about a dozen people were busily engaged in removing the goods towards the cave where it had been intended to conceal them till an opportunity presented itself for conveying them to their final place of destination.

No sooner did the smugglers perceive that they were discovered, than the whole of them took to their heels; but their escape was frustrated by those who were immediately in pursuit, and having been secured, the others were brought from the cave, and the whole number marched to the castle, where they were to undergo an examination before the governor previous to being committed for trial. This being done, Lieutenant Granger went in search of Sir Charles Radcliffe, whom he found reading despatches which he had just received, and the perusal of which seemed to afford him no little surprise and gratification. He, however, listened patiently to the recital of his young friend, and then, having satisfied himself that the task entrusted to him had been executed in strict obedience to the orders that had been given, he burst forth with,—

"Well, my dear boy, I am delighted with the good account you have given of yourself, and I think you will be equally well pleased with the news I am going to tell you. I have received, as you see, letters and despatches from the Secretary of State, and, amongst other affairs of importance, I am informed that a treaty of peace has been agreed to between England and France, and in a few days the ratification is expected to take place."

"This is indeed joyful intelligence," exclaimed the young man, "for we may now expect the speedy return of Luke Somerton to this island."

No. 31.

"Ay, ay, that's sure enough; you will soon see him, my dear fellow, and then I suppose we may expect that the marriage of certain parties, whom I shall not mention, will take place without delay."

"I am, indeed, in hopes your anticipations in this instance are well founded," replied Lieutenant Granger.

"At all events you have my best wishes for your success," exclaimed the governor. "I believe the girl is likely enough to make you a good wife, though I could have wished she had not been quite so particular about matters that, to me, appear trifles. She has kept you in a constant state of suspense, when, in my opinion, she might as well have acknowledged that she loved you."

"Louisa Somerton has felt as much suspense upon the subject as I have myself," replied the lover.

"How do you know that?"

"Because she has confessed as much."

"Indeed! then it must have been very lately."

"Our last interview disclosed more than she has ever suffered herself to acknowledge before," replied Lieutenant Granger; "I am now satisfied that she loves me, and it only depends on certain circumstances—which I believe to be within probability—to render me one of the happiest fellows in her majesty's dominions."

"Humph! then she has quite got over that notion of hers about her father's name being allied with dishonour?"

"I will not go so far as to say that the feeling has been entirely removed," answered the young man; "but she herself entertains hopes that a happy change is about to take place in his prospects, and I have within the last three hours received an assurance from her own lips that she loves me, and will give me her hand immediately after her father has been restored to the honours of which he has been deprived."

"Oh, if that's all, I think I can lend a helping hand in the business," said Sir Charles Radcliffe. "I cannot boast of having much influence with my royal mistress, but with her secretary of state I am upon terms of intimacy and friendship, and I think my recommendation in this case will not be thrown away. At all events you may depend upon my using my utmost exertions; and, if they succeed, I shall be the happiest dog alive. By-the-by, my boy, you must positively invite me to your wedding, for I promise you there will not be a person present who will more rejoice at witnessing your happiness than myself."

"We must not make too certain that the affair will terminate so joyously as your kind wishes prompt you to imagine," answered Lieutenant Granger.

"What!" exclaimed Sir Charles, "are you going to be in the dumps after the girl has told you that she'll be yours?"

"On the contrary," answered the officer, "I am full of hope that all will turn out according to my wishes. The fact, however, cannot be concealed that my chance depends upon the accomplishment of certain events; and, till they have been decided, I must still remain in a state of painful doubt and uncertainty."

"Ah!" ejaculated the governor; "in other words, you don't believe that I shall be able to effect any good by urging the case of Luke Somerton to the secretary of state?"

"Indeed, my dear sir, I have every reliance in your zeal and kind feelings whenever you undertake a task that is to benefit a fellow creature," replied Lieutenant Granger. "I know you will use your utmost exertion to procure the restoration of Luke Somerton to the exalted state from which he has been driven; but I cannot help feeling a doubt as to the prayer being listened to by the queen."

"But she must listen to it."

"She will hear all we may have to urge," replied the young man; "but I am afraid she will not be inclined to pardon one who has so grievously offended her."

"The long and the short of it is this," said Sir Charles; "a great many stories have got abroad about Luke, who has the misfortune of having more enemies in the world than fall to the lot of most of us. These rumours have been magnified after passing through so many months, and it is likely her majesty has at length been induced to believe that he is as bad as has been represented."

"At all events," said Lieutenant Granger, "there is no doubt of his having fought against his country."

"Granted," replied the governor; "but though I am as much opposed to such an act of treachery, I can yet find an excuse for him, that I could not have discovered for any body else. The truth of the matter is this—Luke Somerton first of all fell into disgrace through the false representations of his secret foes—he was deprived of his honours, his property was confiscated to the crown, and he himself driven into banishment, that was rendered the more unbearable through the consciousness of not deserving the harshness with which he had been treated. His daughter was left to the care of a relative, and, perhaps, goaded by the sufferings he endured, he, in an evil moment, listened to the suggestions of those whose counsels he ought to have rejected with the indignation they deserved."

"In short," exclaimed the young man, "he took up arms and fought on the side of the enemies of his country."

"Well, there's no denying that," answered Sir Charles; "but he has since expressed the deepest sorrow for the error he committed, and has done all in his power to redeem the treachery he was guilty of. Nay, in these very letters which I have received, Luke Somerton is mentioned with considerable applause, as having done good service to his country in three or four engagements, in which he has taken vessels from the enemy of a size far superior to his own. Nay, these are facts that must operate favourably for him, and I do venture to hope that, on his return to England, he will be rewarded by an indemnity for the past, and a complete restoration of that which was wrongfully taken from him."

"Your news is indeed most encouraging," exclaimed Lieutenant Granger; "and I will now, with your permission, hasten to inform Louisa of the happy prospect which is about to gleam upon her, after years of suffering and anxiety such as few, I believe, have ever had the cruel misfortune to bear."

"There is no occasion whatever for you to put

yourself out of the way in the matter," returned Sir Charles, as he perceived his young friend was preparing to leave him. "The truth is, I thought Louisa Somerton ought not to be left in suspense a moment longer than was necessary, and I have, therefore, written to her, briefly stating all the contents of my letter that relate to her father, and by this time she is in possession of as many facts as you know yourself. So you see, my dear boy, I have anticipated you, though perhaps I have occasioned no little disappointment through not letting you be the messenger of these happy tidings."

"On the contrary, I am most grateful for the forethought you have displayed in the affair," exclaimed Lieutenant Granger. "It would have been rather late, I must confess, to go and break these joyful tidings to her; and the course you have adopted will ensure for her this night dreams of greater happiness than she has had for some time past."

"And I suppose your own pillow will be visited by equally brilliant visions?" retorted the governor, who sincerely rejoiced in the fortunate change that had taken place in the affairs of his young friend. "Egad, my boy, there's a wedding in perspective, at any rate, now, and if I have the honour of an invitation, I shall most certainly claim the privilege of dancing with the bride—that is, provided my old enemy, the gout, does not interfere to prevent the anticipated pleasure."

"We will not suffer such gloomy thoughts to mar the joy that at length dawns upon us," said Lieutenant Granger. "You will, I hope, be less happy than all your friends must wish to see you; and now, as there appears to be something like a certainty that my union with Louisa Somerton will take place, I care not how soon the long wished-for day arrives."

"Ah!" exclaimed the governor, "there is no restraining you impatient lovers when once matrimony is the point you wish to arrive at. And yet, I, perhaps, have no right to reproach you upon that subject, my dear boy; for I was once as ardent a lover as any of you, little thinking that the reality of marriage destroys the ideality of courtship, and brings us once more to the use of our right senses. But it's no use preaching to you on such matters at a time like this, so let us return to the subject we were just speaking about. The smugglers, you say, are all captured, and in safe custody?"

"They are, Sir Charles," replied Lieutenant Granger; "happily we lost none of our men in the affray, though three or four on the other side fell, I believe, mortally wounded. The prisoners are now in the cells beneath the castle, and await your examination into the case."

"Let them be brought before me the first thing in the morning," exclaimed the governor; "those whom you point out as being the worst among them shall be committed for trial, but the rest I will set at liberty, on their giving good security to refrain in future from their evil habits."

"There is one," replied the officer, "against whom Mr. Emery has a more serious charge to make. He is accused of having murdered one of the revenue men in a conflict that took place some since, and there seems to be little doubt of his identity."

"He must be kept separate from the rest; and his examination will not take place till after the other cases have been disposed of," said Sir Charles. "I well remember the murder you speak of, and that the assassin was supposed to have escaped from the island, as all attempts to discover him proved fruitless. I suppose he fancied the affair was forgotten, by his returning to the place which was the scene of his crime."

"I rather think he was never out of the island," replied Lieutenant Granger.

"Then our people must have been very careless in their search after him," exclaimed the governor, "and I will take care that a strict inquiry is made into the affair."

"The truth of it is," said the other, "I rather think there is less blame in the matter than you seem to imagine. We found him in the cave, where I dare say he has been ever since the night of the fatal affray in which the poor fellow lost his life. At all events, it is a place well calculated for concealment, and I can scarcely wonder at his having so long eluded the pursuit of our people."

"Be that as it may, the affair shall be strictly looked into," exclaimed Sir Charles; "this case has served to open my eyes a little, and, to prevent the cave being used for such bad purposes again, I shall order it to be so blocked up that it shall never serve as a resort for evil doers on a future occasion."

"It was by a miracle that you were saved the trouble of rendering the place useless," replied Lieutenant Granger; "for, had I been one instant later in rushing forward, the whole place, with every soul within it, must have been blown to atoms. The ruffian who is accused of the murder was in the act of applying a lighted torch to a barrel of gunpowder, and horror was in the countenance of every person present, when, impelled by the imminent danger I was in, I sprang upon the villain, and laid him at my feet."

"By Jove! you have had a narrow escape of it," exclaimed the governor. "You have done an act worthy of all praise, Lieutenant Granger, and I shall not fail to represent your intrepid conduct to the proper quarter. The scoundrel knew, I suppose, that his life was forfeited if he was taken, and cared not how many others he sacrificed in his fiend-like desire for revenge."

"There is little credit due to myself for what has taken place," answered the officer; "for, the truth is, the whole affair took place in so short a time, that I had no opportunity to consider what I was about to do."

"Ay, aye," exclaimed the governor, "it's all very well for you to deny yourself praise, but the truth is, you have saved the lives of a good many people, and if that deserves not reward, I know not what does. The queen shall learn of the intrepidity of conduct displayed by Lieutenant Granger, and if that don't obtain for him a captain's commission in her Majesty's service, I know not what will. If bravery like yours is not to be rewarded, I should like to know who will in future risk his life for the preservation of others—in fact, who will ——"

"You seem to forget," said Granger, "that in preserving the lives of others, I was also preserving my own."

"I don't forget anything of the kind," said the governor. "The facts are plain enough, I think—

you saw a ruffian about to blow you all up, and arrested his hand at the very moment when he was in the act of applying a lighted torch to a barrel of powder. You have done a meritorious act, Lieutenant Granger, and I am glad of the opportunity it gives me to recommend you to the Government, as an officer well worthy the promotion to which all men ought to aspire."

" For Louisa's sake, Sir Charles, I shall feel most grateful for such a reward as you have mentioned," said the young man. " The praise of my superiors will be most pleasing to her ; though it must needs be confessed I see little merit in having prevented the heinous crime that was meditated."

" Psha !" exclaimed the governor ; " why shouldn't you take credit to yourself for it ? In my opinion, saving the lives of our fellow creatures is more deserving of commendation than gallantry in the field of battle ; so, for once, my dear young friend, you must allow me to enjoy my own way of thinking. As for the girl, of course she'll be delighted to hear your good acts spoken of with approbation, and if it don't put an end to that foolish hesitation of hers, I shall be surprised and disappointed."

" It will not be without its good effects, I dare say," answered Lieutenant Granger ; " though, having pledged my word to abstain from the subject, I shall carefully avoid making any allusion to it. Her father, it seems, may be expected to return very shortly to England, and I hope the happiness which has been so long delayed will be within view."

" Upon my life, you have more patience than any other lover that I ever happened to be acquainted with," exclaimed Sir Charles Radcliffe. " I could never boast of so much, and perhaps that it is that makes me wonder the more at yours. I think, considering all things, she might have been less resolute in her determination, seeing the suspense and pain she has caused you."

" The trial has been a severe one, certainly," replied the other ; " but it has not been without its beneficial effects upon me ; for I know the refusal has caused as much pain to her as it has to myself, and may, therefore, fairly believe that her resolution has been caused by motives the most honourable and praiseworthy."

" No doubt of it—no doubt of it," returned the governor. " I believe all has been meant for the best, though I can't help feeling sorry for the pain it has caused two young people for whom I have a sincere regard. But never mind—matters begin to look better at last, and as her father will soon return, I hope the young lady's scruples will speedily be at an end."

" She no longer has any scruples," said Lieutenant Granger, " or at least they are such as I have very little to fear. She only waits the arrival of Luke Somerton with news that he has been restored to the favour of his royal mistress, and as that now seems to be pretty certain, I feel quite satisfied that my anxieties are nearly at an end."

" Upon my life it affords me sincere pleasure to hear you say so," exclaimed the governor, " for somehow or other, I at one time was almost as much in the dumps about it as you were yourself. The girl, I dare say, acted from a high principle of honour, but it was a sore trial for you, my boy, and

I only wonder you didn't give up your pursuit of her long enough ago."

" Had my passion been less ardent I might have done so," replied the young man ; " but my affection for Louisa Somerton was founded upon a long acquaintance with her many excellent qualities, such as I could never see in the possession of any other woman. I knew the motives that led her to reject my suit were such as did her the utmost honour, and my regard for her was increased, instead of being diminished, by her refusal to accept my hand till the character of her father had been cleared of the blot with which it had been defaced."

" Why, as for his character," exclaimed Sir Charles Radcliffe, " I believe few persons blamed him so much as you seem to imagine. It is, indeed, true that he fought against his queen and country during a portion of the late war, but it must be remembered that he did not do so till after his fame had been traduced by secret foes, and he was deprived of the title as well as the wealth which had descended to him from men whose names shone forth honourably in the annals of his country."

" I believe—if rumour may for once be relied on," said Lieutenant Granger, " her majesty has on several occasions expressed an opinion that Somerton had not deserved the hard treatment he has met with. There was, however, still a certain influence in direct opposition to him, and the consequence has been that even to the present time the queen has failed to do him that justice which he has a right to demand for the cruel persecution he has endured."

" Well, well," exclaimed the governor, " we must try to forget the past, and live in hopes that the future will render ample justice to all parties. For my own part, I see nothing but a life of happiness before you, and let that, my dear boy, afford you consolation for whatever wrongs may have occurred."

" The only wrongs I have to complain of," replied Lieutenant Granger, " are those which have been committed by private individuals. But for them, Luke Somerton would never have been driven to adopt the disloyal course which has brought disgrace upon him ; and consequently Louisa would have been spared those afflictions which for some time past have rendered her most unhappy."

" But her enemies already begin to acknowledge themselves powerless," answered Sir Charles Radcliffe. " Even the most virulent of them is now under safe custody, and ere many hours have past I expect an order will arrive for his being conveyed to a penal settlement."

" So far as Harry Roden goes, she is indeed safe," exclaimed the other ; " but he is not the only or most dangerous foe she had to fear. There is a woman named Nell Dawson, who has sworn to revenge the downfall of her friend, and it is from her that I apprehend more danger than from any one else."

" In that case Louisa Somerton had better come and take up her temporary abode in the castle," returned the governor. " She has refused the offer, it is true, on two or three former occasions, but I should think as her father is expected to arrive so soon, she will no longer object to an arrangement that she must see is quite disinterested on my part. Perhaps you will see her, Lieutenant Granger, and, if possible, prevail upon her to make this place her home till she goes to that which you are about to provide for her."

"I will do so," answered Granger, "but I fear the same objection will be raised as before. However, let that be as it may, I shall keep a strict watch over her, and should any attempt be made to injure her, the parties doing so will be frustrated in their evil designs. Night and day I will hover round her abode, and woe unto those who may be found near the place under circumstances that may appear conclusive of their guilty designs."

"Upon my life, Louisa Somerton ought to think herself a lucky girl to have found so valorous a champion," exclaimed the governor. "You have always shown an anxious desire to render good service in her cause, and if she is not grateful for it, I can only say that your kindness and zealous efforts have been thrown away."

"I have nothing to complain of in that respect," answered Lieutenant Granger, "for she has often acknowledged herself deeply indebted for the services I have performed, and regretted that circumstances should have interfered to prevent her rewarding me in the way I proposed."

"Patience, my dear fellow, they say is a virtue," exclaimed Sir Charles Radcliffe, "and if so, you certainly must be one of the best fellows in existence. For my own part, I am of a more fiery disposition, and had it been my fate to meet with as many disappointments as you have, there would have been at least half-a-dozen quarrels and reconciliations before this time. I should have told the lady that she ought to know her own mind at once, and not keep a poor fellow dangling at her heels, and sighing all the breath out of his body merely for the gratification of her own imperious whim."

"I have nothing to complain of in that respect," answered Lieutenant Granger. "She has been most candid with me from the first, and if I have been dangling at her heels, as you call it, the fault has been my own. The truth is, I fancied there was some little chance of ultimately succeeding, and, though almost hopeless at first, the result has proved that I was not altogether mistaken. She has consented, on certain conditions, to be mine, and I now have the cheering consolation of seeing that in a short time my fondest hopes will be realized."

"So much the better, my boy," exclaimed the governor. "I congratulate you upon the successful termination of your suit, though I must needs say the girl has been more self-willed in the affair than I could have wished. There was no reason, for instance, why she should have refused your offer on the grounds she did, though, I suppose, that must be overlooked, now that she seems inclined to yield to your entreaties."

"She has herself acknowledged her regret for the pain she inflicted upon me," said Lieutenant Granger; "and, for my own part, I cannot but confess that the motives which guided her conduct are such as deserve more of praise than censure. She loved me, Sir Charles, and for that reason refused to bring dishonour, as she thought, upon a man whose well doing in the world depended on the prudence that dictated his choice of a wife. Her father's misfortunes, she believed, would bring dishonour upon the husband of his child, and thus I have been compelled to endure all the agony of suspense through the mistaken kindness of Louisa Somerton."

"Well, my dear fellow," exclaimed the governor, "all I can say about it is, that you ought to have a double allowance of happiness to make amends for the gloominess of the days that are gone by. And I dare say you will not have to complain of your lot, for Louisa is a kind and affectionate daughter, and we may, therefore, feel pretty certain that she will make an excellent wife. So there's comfort for you, my boy, and I expect by-and-bye that you will be candid enough to acknowledge that I have been a good prophet on this occasion."

"I am already convinced of that," replied Lieutenant Granger, smiling, "or it is hardly likely that I should have been so anxious to secure her for my wife."

"Then it was not her beauty alone that first induced you to make an offer of your hand?" exclaimed Sir Charles Radcliffe. "Yours was no romantic affection, eh, Lieutenant Granger, but love founded upon good substantial grounds, and, therefore, expected to last for ever."

"Such as it was," answered the young man, "I can at least declare that it was sincere, and there is no doubt Louisa believed it to be so, or I should have been peremptorily dismissed when first my proposition was made to her."

"Well," said the governor, laughing, "if you want a good character you have only to send her to me, and I'll give you one. So, away with you, see your mistress without delay, and, if possible, prevail upon her to come here and make the castle her home till the return of her father. Surely she can't object to that, now that her prospects have begun to appear so much brighter."

"I'll try my best, at all events," answered Lieutenant Granger, "though I am rather inclined to think she is not likely to accept your well-intended offer. In about an hour I shall return hither to inform you of the result of my interview with her."

The young man took his departure, and Sir Charles Radcliffe, who felt pretty certain in his own mind that Louisa Somerton would not refuse his offer, gave directions for a couple of apartments to be prepared for her use. This done, he once more visited his prisoner, Harry Roden, to inform him that it was expected he would be removed from the island before the end of the week.

CHAPTER XLVIII.

Why this furious hate?
What fiend has prompted thee to seek the life
Of one who never harmed thee?

DON HERMAN.

WHEN Lieutenant Granger reached the cottage, he found that Louisa was not there, and, wondering what had become of her, he stood for some few minutes at the door, thinking she had gone out to take her usual stroll, and would return in a few minutes. Finding, however, that she did not make her appearance, he proceeded through the garden, with the intention of crossing the fields, and meeting her as she came back. Whilst he was passing along one of the walks, however, he was surprised at seeing Louisa in an arbour fast asleep. Undetermined whether to wake her or retreat without disturbing her slumbers, he stood gazing upon her for a few moments, when he was startled at seeing a figure stealthily approaching, and immediately recognised in the intruder no less a personage than Nell Dawson, the most relentless and implacable of all the enemies of our heroine. His first impulse was to step forward and demand the reason of her intrusion, but feeling anxious to satisfy himself as to the motive which had brought her there, he concealed himself from observation, where he could watch the motions of the woman without being seen, and prevent any mischief that might be contemplated.

Having looked cautiously round to see if she was observed, the woman proceeded to the entrance of the arbour, when, taking a phial from her pocket, she poured the contents of it into a glass of water that stood upon the table, and was then retiring with the same caution, when Lieutenant Granger, springing forward, seized her by the arm.

"Wretch!" he exclaimed, "what is it you would do? Would you poison an innocent girl, who never in her life has injured you even by a thought?"

"Poison!" cried Louisa Somerton, roused from her slumber by the loud exclamation of her lover. "But why do I see you here, Lieutenant Granger? What has this woman done that you have thought it necessary to hold her in restraint?"

"Let her answer for herself," exclaimed her lover. "She came hither to take your life, and, doubtless, her plot would have succeeded, but that chance brought me to your assistance."

"Is this accusation true?" demanded Louisa, reproachfully addressing the woman; "did you, indeed, come hither to destroy one who has never done you harm?"

"He has told you the truth," she replied, in a tone of indifference; "and my only regret is, that I have been thwarted when most I made sure of succeeding. I hate you, Louisa Somerton, and had I but slain you, I should not have cared for the punishment that would have followed; but it has ever been the same with me, for when most I made sure of carrying my design into execution, either Lieutenant Granger or some one else has interfered to prevent my doing so."

"What motive can you have," demanded the young man, "for seeking to destroy this unoffending girl?"

"I am not obliged to explain my motives to you," answered Nell, sullenly; "it is sufficient that I had reasons enough for the course I have adopted, and even now, if I only get my liberty again, I will pursue her in the same way that I have done before."

"But you will not have your liberty again," exclaimed Lieutenant Granger; "and therefore she will be henceforth safe from one of the most relentless of her persecutors. I shall myself be your accuser, before the governor, and when he hears the charge I have to make, he will take care to order such a punishment as will prevent all chance of your ever trying to injure Miss Somerton again."

"Humph!" ejaculated Nell Dawson, "he can't hang me, at any rate, for the attempt has not succeeded, nor can you prove that it was poison I just now poured into the glass."

Whilst she was uttering these latter words, she broke away from Lieutenant Granger, and attempted to dash off the fatal potion. In this, however, she was foiled, for again she was seized by the young man, who, to prevent any further violence, bound her arms with his handkerchief, and placed her at such a distance from Louisa that no further fear need be apprehended.

"Woman!" exclaimed our heroine, "notwithstanding your many acts of hostility towards me, I entertain no desire to be revenged upon you. I only ask your solemn promise never to molest me more, and when that is given I will plead to Lieutenant Granger to set you at liberty. So, do you accept or refuse the terms I have offered?"

"I refuse them," answered the woman—"scornfully refuse them; for if I gave such a promise I should have no intention of keeping it. I always regarded you with hatred, Louisa Somerton; but the feeling is now increased tenfold, since I see that you triumph in my defeat."

"I should not have taken your promise even if it had been given," observed Lieutenant Granger. "Your violence has been exhibited on too many previous occasions, and not even the most solemn oath would have been heeded under such circumstances as the present. As it is, you have thrown yourself into my power, and I shall now take care that in future Miss Somerton shall have one enemy the less to stand in fear of."

"But there are others in the island that like her no better than I do," replied the woman. "All those who are friendly to me are enemies of hers; and I would have her beware of them; for when it is known that I am a prisoner on her account, there's plenty that will be ready to revenge my cause."

"And if they do so," exclaimed Lieutenant Granger, "they must take the consequences of their own rashness; for those who are in authority here will show no mercy towards persons who wilfully break the laws of their country. So far, too much lenity has been shown them; but henceforth Sir Charles Radcliffe is determined to try what more rigorous measures will do. If a riot should take place, as you seem to threaten, the most prominent will be sent out of the island, and thus peace may, in the end, be restored."

"It is all very easy to say what is to be done," answered Nell Dawson; "but people are not to be frightened into submission by a few threats. My friends are no cowards, I can tell you, and as you will find out, after it is too late to see the folly of trying to govern people by terror."

"Woman," said Louisa, "it is through you, and such violent persons as yourself, that the island has been for some time past kept in a state of commotion. I have asked you to give a promise to abandon your malicious designs against my life, and you have rejected my proposal."

"Ay," she replied, "and will do so again as often as you make the same proposition. Besides, Lieutenant Granger has just now said that he would not listen to it, even if I was inclined to give such a promise."

"My reason for doing so," returned the young man, "is, that we have had ample experience of the malevolence of your feelings towards Louisa Somerton, and I do not believe your word is to be taken so long as your revenge remains unaccomplished. Even now I have detected you in a base attempt to poison her; and but for my fortunate presence here, you would have had to answer for, the heinous crime of murder with your own life."

"Oh," answered Nell, contemptuously, "as for the consequences, I knew them well enough before I came here; but it is not quite certain that you or anybody else would have been able to prove who it was that put the poison into yonder glass. Had the girl drank off the contents, she would have died long before assistance could have come, and there would have been no testimony that I was near the spot."

"Murder is rarely undiscovered," exclaimed Lieutenant Granger; "and, in such a case as this, my suspicions would have at once been directed towards yourself. On my own responsibility I should have directed you to be arrested, and no doubt proof would soon have been found to fix the perpetration of the crime upon you. Nay, so certain should I have been that yours was the hand which administered the fatal potion, that I would never have relaxed my efforts till I had brought you to the punishment with which crimes such as yours are always visited."

"Will you confess," said Louisa Somerton, "what motive induced you to seek my destruction by poison?"

"I will confess nothing," answered the woman. "You know well enough why I have taken so rooted a hatred to you, and let that be sufficient. I have tried to forget it, and perhaps should have done so, but this morning the first thing I heard was, that Harry Roden is to be sent out of the country, and I thought if he was to be punished for nothing, you should not come off scot free."

"And pray what has Miss Somerton to do with the banishment of Harry Roden?" inquired the officer.

"It has everything to do with it," replied Nell Dawson. "But for this girl's father there would never have been any disturbance in the island at all; and, as Luke Somerton was the beginning of the evil, it is only fair that he and his should be made to suffer for it. Aye, and they shall yet do so, you may take my word for it, unless the people I depend upon in this case have turned cowards all of a sudden."

"The islanders ought by this time to profit by experience," said Lieutenant Granger. "They have seen the madness of resisting the laws; and I am in hopes, from what has lately transpired, that they are at length inclined to be more peaceable than you give them the credit for."

"Aye, aye," she replied, "it is prudent of them not to blab their secrets to everybody. They know well enough the consequences that would follow the discovery of their designs; but I warn you not to make too sure that they have been cowed into quiet submission, merely because Harry Roden is punished with transportation, and that I am in a fair way of following him."

"Then the factious must be subdued as we have subdued others," replied the officer. "You have heard the fate that has befallen the smugglers; and, if necessity compels us, the mutinous subjects of her majesty will be quelled by the same means we used in that instance."

"I understand your threat," she exclaimed; "you would bring out the soldiers, and slaughter them by dozens."

"And if such should be the case," answered Lieutenant Granger, "the terrible alternative will have been urged upon us by themselves. I would myself gladly avoid the shedding of human blood, if it is possible, but order must be restored in the island, even though it be at the expense of a score of lives."

"Oh, let there be no violence, such as you speak of," cried Louisa Somerton, in alarm. "It is true that those who are guilty may deserve a severe punishment for their crimes, but think, I pray you, of the fearful consequences that must follow to those who have committed no wrong;—wives will be made widows—children will become fatherless, and thus ruin and despair will stalk hand-in-hand throughout this island."

"Such, my dear Miss Somerton, are ever the consequences of men's evil actions," replied Lieutenant Granger. "They know well enough the fruits of violating the laws they are bound to respect, and if they will reject the good advice of those who would persuade them against pursuing a destructive course, an example, such as I have spoken of, must be made."

"Aye, aye," exclaimed Nell Dawson, "but the laws you preach about are not applied equally to all persons alike, or there would be no grumbling. Why, I should like to know, was Luke Somerton pardoned for a murder, when Harry Roden is to be sent out of the country like a felon, for a mere trifling crime?"

"My father," replied Louisa, "as I solemnly believe, was never guilty of the crime he was accused of. There is every probability that Captain Aylmer fell by his own hand; and it was on that supposition that the queen was graciously pleased to grant her royal pardon."

"It's all very well for you to say that he was not a shedder of blood," said the woman; "but I and others are not so easily persuaded against our own senses. Wasn't there a mortal quarrel between them long before the murder was committed? and wasn't the pistol that was found near the dead man proved to have been in your father's possession a very few hours before the discovery of the crime took place?"

"It was a suspicious circumstance, certainly," interposed Lieutenant Granger, "and one that had very nearly proved fatal to the unfortunate accused. Upon cooler reflection, however, it appeared that the pistol might have come into the possession of Captain Aylmer, who used it against his own life. All, however, connected with the affair is dark and mysterious, and, in the absence of all direct proof, it is even surmised that the murder—if such it was—was committed by some other person, who hitherto has escaped suspicion."

"You must tell that to people that are not quite so hard of belief as I am," exclaimed the woman. "No one else had any quarrel with Captain Aylmer, so it's hardly likely that he should have fallen by any other hands than the person that was taken up and tried for it. I, for one, shall always consider Luke Somerton as the murderer of the poor fellow, and there's a good many more besides myself that believe him to have deserved hanging, though he was lucky enough to escape punishment."

"And, for that reason," said Lieutenant Granger, "you must needs prosecute his unoffending daughter!"

"That's because she was the means of getting him off," replied Nell. "If the man had been hanged, it would have been nothing more than justice, and, as he got off, we had a right to believe that it was a favour granted to his daughter without any just grounds being shown for it."

"And in your mad rage her life was to be sacrificed for filial affection that actuated her to encounter dangers that would have deterred stouter hearts than her own."

"If the sea had swallowed her it would have served her right," exclaimed the virago. "I remember the storm well, and everybody said it was impossible that her boat could reach the island in safety. I made sure she had gone to the bottom, and yet, just when the culprit was about to meet his doom, she reached the scaffold with the pardon she had obtained for her father."

"All that you have been saying," answered Lieutenant Granger, "only serves to prove the justice of the cause in which she was engaged. Heaven must have had her under its own especial protection, or she never could have escaped the fearful tempest that raged during the whole time that she was on the water. I had myself given her up for lost, and never shall I forget the transport that filled my heart when I saw her once more standing before me, safe and uninjured."

"Let me hear no more of this," exclaimed the woman, "for every word you utter goes to my heart like a poisoned barb. Release my arms, lieutenant, for these bonds hurt me—release me, I say, and I promise to follow you quietly and without resistance to the place where I am to be imprisoned."

"But will you promise, also, not to injure Miss Somerton, if I yield to your request?" he asked.

"I will," she replied; "not that I repent what I have done, but seeing that she is so well guarded, I will yield to the necessity of the case. For the present she has nothing to fear from me, but I do not promise as much if I should happen to be lucky enough to get my liberty again."

"I'll take you at your word," said the young man, setting her arms at liberty as he spoke. "You see, woman, that I am not disposed to deal harshly with you, but mind how you abuse the favour I have shown you. My eye will be constantly upon your actions, and should there be the least reason to believe that you intend to harm her, I shall immediately place you under the same restraint from which you have just been released."

"There is no fear that I shall break my word," answered Nell. "The girl is now under your protection, and as I cannot measure my strength against yours, I shall not be mad enough to attempt it. So lead on, and we will go to the castle, for I suppose that is where you intend to take me to?"

Taking his leave of Louisa, the young officer now set off with his prisoner, upon whom he kept a careful watch, lest she should make any attempt to elude his vigilance. Nell, however, showed no inclination to break the promise she had given, and they at length reached the place of their destination, where, the gates having been closed after them, Lieutenant Granger left his prisoner in the care of a guard, and proceeded to the governor in order to hear his commands as to what was to be done next. He remained absent about a quarter of an hour, and then returned to inform Nell that the governor had desired her to be immediately conveyed before him. This intimation she received in silence, and following him into the hall, she soon found herself face to face with the person in whose hands her destiny rested.

"So," exclaimed Sir Charles, "you have at length brought yourself into a dilemma that it will not be very easy to escape from. I warned you, Mrs. Dawson, not very long since, to desist from the violent course you were pursuing, and yet, scorning my advice, you have made a base attack upon a young female against whom you can allege no one case of injury."

"That is a matter best known to myself," she replied, sullenly. "I ought to know what motive I had for seeking her life, and you have no right to ask me a question that may afterwards be used against me."

"I don't ask you to criminate yourself," replied the governor; "but there can be no great harm in pointing out the mischief you have done by not taking my advice. Had you attended to your own business, and left the girl alone, you would now have been at liberty, instead of standing before me as a prisoner."

"You may as well keep your advice for those that ask for it," said Nell. "I have my own reasons for wishing the death of Louisa Somerton, and the thing would have been, too, by this time, if it had not been for the meddling interference of this young friend of yours. He happened to see me pouring the contents of a phial into a glass, and, suspecting my intention, he immediately rushed forward, and made me his prisoner. Had I but known what was going to take place, I should myself have swallowed the poisoned draught, and your excellency would have been spared the supreme pleasure of exulting in the downfall of Nell Dawson."

"Woman!" exclaimed Sir Charles, "you wrong me by supposing that I exult in your present unfortunate situation. I would gladly have saved you from it, had there been a possibility of prevailing on you to consider the certain consequences of the rash course you were pursuing. I told you that Louisa Somerton, during the absence of her father, was under my protection, and since you have turned a deaf ear to my solemn injunctions, I have no alternative but to proceed in this case as I should in any other. At present I shall not enter into an examination of the charge, but to-morrow you will be brought before me again, and it will then be my duty to commit you for trial for one of the worst crimes that a human being is capable of."

"What's the use of making such a fuss about it, when my doom is already determined on?" demanded the woman. "Louisa Somerton has received no injury from me, so I should like to know what charge this young gentleman has to make against me?"

"That of intending to poison Louisa Somerton."

"But the intent was prevented," answered Nell.

"Luckily for you, it was," replied the governor. "The design, however, is not denied—nay, you have even admitted the fact, and that being the case, you will henceforth be considered too dangerous a person to be entrusted with liberty. I am unwilling to consign you to a dungeon, but my duty is imperative, and I must either do so, or act against the oath I have taken to administer the laws fairly and impartially to all persons."

"Sir Charles Radcliffe, I have not asked you to show me any mercy," replied the prisoner, "and yet you preach to me as if you were really very sorry for the opportunity you have got of locking me up out of harm's way."

"The truth is,'" replied the governor, "I have just been told by Lieutenant Granger that you have boasted that, were you again at liberty, you would never desist till you had fulfilled your horrible design against the female whose life has been so providentially preserved. If there was no other

reason, therefore, I should consider it my duty to hold you in custody till means could be taken for placing Louisa Somerton beyond your reach."

"You would have had some little difficulty in doing that," answered Nell, "for, when once my mind is made up to a thing, I am not to be put off by merely removing a person to a distance from me. I could soon have found where she was taken to, and, let the trouble have been what it might, I should soon have been once more close upon her heels."

"I suspected as much," said Sir Charles Radcliffe; "and, therefore, the course I am about to pursue is the best I could have adopted. In the solitude of your cell you will have time to reflect and repent, and, should I by-and-by see any signs of real contrition exhibited, it will go towards obtaining a mitigation of the punishment you have brought upon yourself. This I state, in order that you may shape your conduct accordingly, and,

should you follow my advice, the consequences to yourself will be of incalculable advantage."

"There's no occasion to talk to me about that," exclaimed Nell, "because, all the advice in the world, whether it be good, bad, or indifferent, will be thrown away upon me. I know the consequences as well as you can tell me, and, if you have nothing better to offer me than a dry sermon, why the sooner you send me to my dungeon the better I shall like it."

"Let her be conveyed thither immediately," said Sir Charles, addressing himself to the sentinel, into whose custody she had been given. "I do not wish her to be treated with more harshness than is necessary for her safe keeping within this place, but you will see that no opportunity is afforded for her escape. To-morrow," he added to the prisoner, "you will again be brought before me to hear such evidence as your prosecutors are able to bring against you."

"They can have none to bring," answered Nell Dawson. "The girl has received no injury from me, and, as for putting poison into a glass of water, who is there that will dare to say I did not intend to drink it off myself?"

"That defence may be a very plausible one," replied the governor, "but when one circumstance is compared with another, I believe there are few persons that can entertain a doubt as to what your real intentions were. Your rancorous hatred towards the girl, and the deadly hostility with which you have for some time pursued her, all confirm the opinion that this was but another attempt to carry out your base intention. None will be deceived by your false asseverations, and, therefore, my advice to you is, to acknowledge the heinousness of your crime, and throw yourself upon the mercy of those who have the means in their power to mitigate the punishment which the law awards to such an offence as you have been clearly guilty of."

"I'm not going to whine and despair merely because I happen to have got into a little trouble," exclaimed Nell, undauntedly. "Whatever is to be my fate, I shall bear it without grumbling, and there's one consolation, that you can do no more than transport me. Poor Harry Roden and I shall be fellow sufferers, and I suppose we shall meet each other abroad."

"Don't make too sure about that," answered Sir Charles Radcliffe, "for each of you will be consigned to different masters, and it may be that hundreds of miles will separate you. Indeed, it is necessary that it should be so, for both are known to be dangerous characters, and those who are known to have been acquainted when in England, are never permitted to see each other when they arrive at the place to which they are banished."

"Well, then, I must console myself the best way I can," exclaimed Nell Dawson. "I dare say people can be as happy at Botany Bay as they can here, and, perhaps, I may take it into my head to mend my manners when I get there, in which case I suppose I may expect that they will not be quite so severe with me."

"That would indeed be a wise course to follow," said the governor, "and one that I should most earnestly advise you to think of seriously. You will find every disposition to encourage good conduct, and it may be that after two or three years you would have the remainder of your punishment remitted, when you might return to your own country and fulfil those duties of life which have, unfortunately for yourself, been but too much neglected."

"I ventured to promise her," interposed Lieutenant Granger, "that in the event of her promising to make no further attempts against Miss Somerton, that the case as it at present stands should be carried no further. This offer she, however, refused, and I was therefore compelled to bring her before your excellency."

"You were wrong, sir, in making such a proposition," exclaimed Sir Charles Radcliffe. "The crime, though not fully accomplished, was stayed only by your fortunate interposition, and it is, therefore, necessary that she should be made an example of to other evil doers. There is a restless spirit among these islanders that requires to be immediately checked, and I know of no better way to

do so than to punish such of them as happen to lay themselves under our power."

"And so I am to suffer for the faults of others, am I?" exclaimed Nell Dawson. "This may be justice, but I don't think it is exactly such as you would like, if my case happened to be yours. However, here I am in your hands, and so I suppose it would be so much time thrown away to argue it any farther."

"I have no alternative," replied Sir Charles, "but must administer the law exactly as I find it. If there is any hardship in the matter you have brought it on yourself, and must endure it with patience and resignation. The life of Miss Somerton must be protected, and I feel assured, after your own declaration, that she cannot be considered safe as long as you are at liberty. I counselled you as to the danger of the course you were pursuing, and as that was not listened to, I have nothing to reproach myself with."

"Perhaps you will tell me," said the prisoner, "how long it will be before my trial takes place?"

"In about three weeks' time," replied the governor. "That interval will be sufficiently long to enable you to prepare your defence, and, whatever may be the issue of it, I feel assured your fate will not be decided on without all the consideration it requires."

As Nell Dawson was about to reply to this, the governor gave a sign to the sentinel, and she was immediately led from the room, and conveyed to the gloomy chamber in which she was to pass the interval between that time and the period when the trial was to take place. From the moment that she left the presence of Sir Charles Radcliffe she became sullen and morose; she would make no reply to the questions of the man to whose custody she had been committed, but throwing herself upon a seat, she maintained a sullen and gloomy silence, from which nothing could rouse her. At length she was left alone, and then pacing up and down the narrow limits of her cell, she gave vent to the most furious invectives against all who had been opposed to her.

CHAPTER XLIX.

CONCLUSION.

TWO months passed away after the events just recorded, and in that interval both Roden and Nell Dawson were sent from the island to suffer that punishment which their crimes had brought upon them. No contrition was expressed by either of them, and both left the land of their birth with expressions of hatred towards their prosecutors, and of regret that their evil designs had been frustrated. The example which had been made of them, however, had the most beneficial effect upon those who had at one period been scarcely less criminal than themselves, and Sir Charles Radcliffe had the satisfaction of seeing that his conduct had had all the effect which he anticipated. The island which he governed became peaceful and tranquil, and those whose violence had so often disturbed the peace which he was empowered to maintain, returned to those industrious habits by which alone they could hope to maintain themselves in comfort and independence.

In the same interval Louisa Somerton had been

prevailed on by the governor to accept an asylum in the castle; but it was on the condition that she should not be further urged upon her marriage with Lieutenant Granger, till her father's return had entirely removed all doubts as to the anxiously looked for pardon. Day after day she looked for his arrival, yet nothing could be heard of him except that he had been in an engagement with an enemy's ship much larger than his own, and in which he had won high honour for himself, though it was at the expense of a severe wound, which some of the reports had asserted was likely to prove mortal. This had reached the ears of Louisa, and her grief at the intelligence was most intense, though it was in some degree mitigated by the kindness of the governor, who endeavoured to persuade her that the danger was not so great as she had been led to imagine.

At length intelligence was spread through the island that the vessel in which Luke Somerton left the place a few months before had cast anchor off the island. Sir Charles Radcliffe was the first to inform Louisa of this fact, but there was a hesitation in his manner that at once roused her suspicion, and dreading lest some evil had occurred, she eagerly inquired when he was coming ashore.

"Why, I believe, Miss Somerton, we may expect to see him almost immediately," replied the governor. "I have sent directions for him to be brought here, and ——"

"*Brought* here!" exclaimed Louisa, in accents of terror; "is he then ill?—dangerously ill?"

"I fear he is worse than I imagined," replied Sir Charles. "His wound, at first thought but little of, has assumed a more alarming appearance, and I regret to say that fears are entertained of its proving mortal."

Louisa Somerton listened to these words in silent anguish; her fears, it is true, had been for some time excited; yet now the certainty of her father's danger came upon her with an overwhelming feeling of despair that she could not control. For a few moments she stood fixed and immovable, and then sinking upon a couch, she buried her face in her hands, and gave way to the agony with which she was afflicted.

"Come, come, my dear girl," said the governor, in a tone of almost parental kindness; "this is more than I bargained for, or you should have heard these evil tidings from other lips than mine."

"When do you expect his arrival?" she asked.

"Immediately," replied Sir Charles. "I have sent my carriage down to the beach where he is to be brought ashore, and a chamber has been prepared for his reception, where you will see him as soon as he is able to bear the interview."

"I must see him as soon as he arrives," she eagerly exclaimed. "I will tend upon him, and, if Heaven grants my prayers, will yet restore him to health."

"I trust your filial solicitude will meet with its due reward," exclaimed the governor. "That you will do your best I am well assured, but, to confess the truth, Miss Somerton, I am afraid there is not much chance of saving his life. In short, it was hardly expected that he could have lived to return here."

"Why did I not know that before?" she demanded, wildly; "why was his danger kept from me when it seems to have been known to yourself and others?"

"Because we knew your regard for him," answered Sir Charles, "and feared to acquaint you with the melancholy fact till there was no possibility of concealing it from you any longer. You now know as much of the affair as I do myself, Miss Somerton, and I most earnestly entreat of you to endure it with that fortitude and resignation for which I have always considered you an example."

"But when was my fortitude or resignation taxed as it is at this moment?" demanded our heroine, in a tone of the most intense grief. "Have I not looked forward with hope to the period of my father's return, and now, alas! in what a fearful condition am I to find him! Would to Heaven that I had died ere this terrible affliction came to crush my lacerated heart."

A servant now entered the room and whispered to the governor, who, turning towards our heroine, exclaimed,—

"Your father, Miss Somerton, has just been brought here, and the first wish he has expressed is to see you without delay. Do not, however, let him see you in tears, for the pain of parting is sufficiently trying at all times, though more so when the grief of the survivor is excessive. Will you endeavour to put on an appearance of composure?"

"I will—I will," she eagerly exclaimed, and, taking the arm of Sir Charles Radcliffe, she proceeded to the room in which her father lay stretched upon a couch, apparently in the last agonies of death. Hearing her step, however, he seemed slightly to revive, and grasping the hand which she placed in his, he faintly said,—

"My child, this is not as I once fondly anticipated we should meet. And yet why should I regret a destiny that occurs to so many who follow the profession to which I have belonged?"

"Have you forgotten then," she asked, "that when you are gone away from me, I shall be left almost friendless and without a protector?"

"Nay, I must not stand by and hear you speak thus without remonstrating," exclaimed the governor. "I have been, and ever will be, a friend to you; and there is one other besides myself who will be a better protector to you than I can ever hope to be. Here is Lieutenant Granger," he added, as the young man entered the apartment, "who has waited long and patiently to obtain your favourable answer to his suit, and one better deserving your hand I know not in the whole list of my acquaintances."

"Believe me, young man," said Luke Somerton, taking the hand of the young officer, and placing in it that of his daughter, "you have ever been, as far as I am concerned, the chosen husband of my daughter. That she loves you, I am well assured, though, from motives which I will not now attempt to explain, she has hitherto withheld her consent to an union which I have myself wished for most ardently."

"But I trust she will do so no longer," said Lieutenant Granger, "for the only ground for her hesitation was the wish to see you restored to that station in society from which you had been temporarily banished. That period has at length arrived, and now that my own entreaties are backed by your approval, I trust that she will no longer leave me in all the misery of an unrequited affection."

"Do not call it an unrequited affection," answered Louisa, "because I have confessed to you, not long since, that no obstacle remains to our union after my father's restoration to the honours of which he has been deprived."

"Then, in my last hour," said Luke Somerton, "I have the consolation of knowing that the happiness of those I most love is secured. I have retrieved my lost honour, and, from what I have been told, her majesty is now willing to restore to me the estates which in an evil hour were forfeited. I shall not live to enjoy this change of fortune, but you, my dear Louisa, will become the object of the royal bounty, and that one thought alone is sufficient to render happy the last few moments of my existence."

"Nay, my dear sir," interposed Lieutenant Granger, "do not give utterance to fears that must yield such deep affliction to all your friends. You may yet recover, and render us happy by being once more among us."

"I tell you it is impossible," answered Somerton; "the doctor has declared that my case is hopeless, and I have ceased to entertain a hope that my life can be prolonged beyond a very brief period. I am content to see before me my daughter and the chosen of her affections, and my departure from this world will be cheered by the reflection that those whom I have most loved in the world will at length receive the reward of their long and faithful attachment."

"Is there no hope that your life will be spared?" cried our heroine, in vain endeavouring to conceal the tears which her father's sufferings had called forth.

"None," he replied, solemnly; "I feel, Louisa, that the hand of death is upon me, and even at this moment I can feel grateful that I have been permitted once more to see you. It was my wish to behold you again, that my latest blessing might be bestowed upon you, and to hear from your lips a promise that Lieutenant Granger shall possess the prize of which he is so worthy. That wish has now been gratified, and I can leave the world with the soothing confidence that my child will now enjoy that happiness which has been hitherto denied her."

"And in me," exclaimed the governor, "she shall ever find a friend to recompense her for the loss she is doomed to experience. Should her husband be called abroad in the fulfilment of his professional duties, she shall find a home beneath my roof, and I will be to her as a father and a friend."

"And I," added Lieutenant Granger, "will devote my whole life to render her's as happy as she deserves to be. She has consented to be mine, and in return for that inestimable favour I can never sufficiently show my gratitude."

"I well know your worth, my dear young friend," answered Luke Somerton, with increasing languor, "and the thought of her becoming your wife reconciles me to the separation that must now soon take place. I hoped to have lived some few years to witness the happiness of my child with the husband of her choice, but that anticipation has been frustrated, and I now bow with resignation to the will of Heaven. I have restored my name to honour, my dear Louisa, and henceforth the world will do me that justice which has long been denied me."

He seemed overpowered by the exertion he had made, and sank back upon the bed apparently lifeless. Suddenly he started up, and exclaimed, as the castle clock sent forth its solemn tone,

"Hark! what is the hour?"

"It strikes ten," answered the lieutenant.

"By Heaven, then, Aylmer calls me," murmured Luke, and sinking back upon the bed, he instantly expired. Who can describe the agony of Louisa, as she looked upon the lifeless remains of her father! She staggered back a few paces, and fell fainting into the arms of Sir Charles Radcliffe, who instantly bore her from the room.

*　　*　　*　　*　　*

In less than a month from the death of Luke Somerton, a packet was received from the minister of state, containing the intelligence that her majesty had ordered that all the possessions of her father should be restored without reservation to Louisa, and expressing a wish that she should be presented at court as soon after her bereavement as decorum would permit, as her majesty had further marks of her bounty to bestow.

All that remains for us now to say is, that as soon as the period of mourning had expired, Louisa, at the earnest entreaty of the governor, gave her hand to Lieutenant Granger, and the walls of the castle echoed to strains of music and the laughter of merry voices on the day of the marriage.

On the expiration of the honeymoon, our heroine and her husband repaired to London, where they received the greatest marks of favour from the queen, and the honour of knighthood was conferred upon Granger, with a promise of speedy promotion in the army. They then proceeded to Ireland, where, surrounded by a contented tenantry, they passed the remainder of their days in peace and tranquillity.